Jemima Montgomery Freifrau von Tautphoeus

The Initials

Jemima Montgomery Freifrau von Tautphoeus

The Initials

ISBN/EAN: 9783337049478

Printed in Europe, USA, Canada, Australia, Japan

Cover: Foto ©Andreas Hilbeck / pixelio.de

More available books at **www.hansebooks.com**

.

HAMILTON AND HILDEBOARDE

BY THE

BARONESS TAUTPHŒUS

AUTHOR OF 'QUITS!' 'AT ODDS' ETC.

Jemima (Montgomery) Freiherrin von Tautphœus

THE SLEDGING EXCURSION

LONDON

RICHARD BENTLEY & SON, NEW BURLINGTON STREET

Publishers in Ordinary to Her Majesty the Queen

1886

THE INITIALS

A NOVEL

BY THE

BARONESS TAUTPHŒUS

AUTHOR OF 'QUITS!' 'AT ODDS' ETC.

Jemima (Montgomery) Freiherrin von Tautpho

EIGHTEENTH THOUSAND

LONDON

RICHARD BENTLEY & SON, NEW BURLINGTON STREET

Publishers in Ordinary to Her Majesty the Queen

1886

PRINTED BY
SPOTTISWOODE AND CO., NEW-STREET SQUARE
LONDON

.

THE INITIALS.

CHAPTER I.

THE LETTER.

In the year 1836 (before the building of the Bayrischen Hof), the Golden Stag, kept by an old and very corpulent Frenchman, of the name of Havard, was considered the very best hotel in Munich. It was there that all crowned heads and royal personages took up their abode; and many and bitter were the complaints of English families obliged to turn out of their apartments to admit of the turning in of an emperor, king, or archduke! In the month of August, however, such guests were unusual; and, accordingly, a young English traveller had remained for a week in undisturbed possession of one of the most comfortable rooms of the house; he seemed, however, thoroughly dissatisfied with it, or with himself, walked impatiently up and down, looked long and listlessly out of the window, and then with evident effort and a stifled yawn, concluded a letter which he had previously been writing. A few lines of this letter I shall transcribe.

'I have continued to take notes most carefully of every thing I have seen or heard since I left you; but I fear, my dear sister, the Travels, or Wanderings, or Sketches with which I intended to astonish the world on my return home, must be given up; for in the present day one can travel from London to Jericho without a chance of seeing anything not already succinctly described in the guide-books! I thought I had discovered why my brother John never met with any amusing adventures when my father sent him abroad; he spoke wretched French and no German: poor fellow, I did him great injustice! For even I, who from not being the

B

first born, have a sort of natural claim to intellect,—even I, who have studied German for six years, and can speak French fluently,—even I, must write stupid commonplace letters, and acknowledge that composing a book is not so easy as I thought! I left home three weeks ago, and excepting that lucky explosion of the steam engine, after we left Cologne, nothing has occurred worthy of notice. I must endeavour to get among these Germans; for travelling through a country without becoming intimate with some of the inhabitants, though it may enable me to judge of the beauty of the scenery, will leave me perfectly unacquainted with the manners and habits of the people. The Erskines are not here at present, so all hopes from that quarter are at an end. I am told that the Munich world is in the country, and I believe it; for nothing can be more deserted-looking than the streets which represent the *west* end! After all, one cannot go on for ever looking at pictures and statues, &c.'

The young man folded up and sealed his letter, with a look of infinite vexation, and putting it in his pocket while he murmured something about 'taking it himself to the post-office for want of other occupation,' slowly left the room and sauntered down the staircase, drawing his cane along the iron stair-railing as he went.

On his return he sprang lightly up the stairs, followed by a waiter, who lit the candles and prepared to assist him in taking off his coat. The operation had proceeded about half way when his eyes fell on a letter which was placed conspicuously on the table. In a moment the coat was again on his shoulders and the letter in his hand.

'When did this come?'

'To-day, sir. Mr. Havard desired me to say, it was carried by mistake to a gentleman's room who left this morning early.'

He hastily opened the letter, and read as follows :—

'DEAR MR. HAMILTON,—I have this moment read your name among the arrivals in Munich, and write to tell you that we are for the present at Seon, a short journey distant from you. Our house is not at present habitable, and we have made this old monastery our head-quarters. It was some years ago a tolerably frequented bath, but, being no longer so, I shall have no difficulty whatever in procuring an apartment tor you. We shall be delighted to see you, and show you the beauties of our neighbourhood ;—perhaps, too, we can arrange a tour in the Tyrol together. John, I know, has joined his regiment, therefore I do not expect to see him, but probably Mrs. Hamilton is with you, in which case I am quite sure you will not leave Germany without having visited your sincere friend,   'A. Z.'

'How far is Seon from Munich? What sort of a place is it?' asked Hamilton.

'I am sorry I cannot give you any information, sir. Since I have been here no traveller has left for Seon.'

'Is there no mail or stage-coach to any place near it? There must be a post-town, or something of that sort.'

'I really do not know, sir.'

'Try and decipher the postmark,' said Hamilton impatiently, handing him the envelope.

'I think it is Altenmarkt, but I am not quite sure.'

'Give me my maps, if you please, and tell Mr. Havard I wish to speak to him for a few minutes.'

When he had left the room, Hamilton turned the letter in every possible direction, examined the seal, which was a small coronet with the initials 'A. Z.,' read it five or six times over, and in thought mustered his tolerably numerous acquaintance. Not an 'A. Z.' among them all! How very provoking! 'And yet the letter may be intended for me,' he murmured, twisting it round his fingers : 'It is not impossible that the writer may have thought that I was travelling with my aunt—why not? And John has actually joined his regiment very lately !—or—or—it may be some friend of my father's ; in which case, as I do not know the name, and cannot explain by letter, I consider it a sort of duty to go to Seon, and in his name thank the good-natured person for the invitation. But what if it were not intended either for me or for my father? No matter. The letter is addressed to A. Hamilton, Esq. ; if the writer intended it for an Abraham, an Achilles, or an Anthony, the fault is not mine. Alfred also begins with A. ; the address is to the Golden Stag ; my correspondent has seen my name or my father's in the newspapers; mentions my mother and my brother. What more can I require?'

And Hamilton required nothing more, for on this occasion

he was disposed to be easily satisfied. Besides, he was not
going to force himself upon any person or persons unknown—
he was merely going to Seon instead of Kissingen. Seon was
also a place of public resort, quite as desirable for him as any
other ; nor could he see anything wrong in making some inquiries about this A. Z. when he arrived there.

Mr. Havard entered his room just as he had resolved what
course he should pursue. 'Pray, Mr. Havard, can you tell me
how far Seon is from here ?'

'A day's journey, if you travel with a voiturier ; half a
day with post-horses.'

'If I engage a voiturier—are the carriages good ?'

'Generally, especially if you don't require much place for
luggage. I think I can procure a light carriage and tolerable
horses for you.'

'Thank you. To-morrow morning, at six o'clock, I should
like to be off, if possible.'

An unpleasant idea just then occurred to him, and it required an effort on his part to add, with affected indifference—

'By the by, Mr. Havard, perhaps you can tell me if there
have been any persons here lately whose names were the same
as mine ?'

Mr. Havard looked puzzled.

'My name is Hamilton.'

'Hameeltone — Hameeltone !' he repeated thoughtfully.
'We have a great many Hameeltone in our book. You
shall see directly. I will send it to you.'

'So,' muttered Hamilton, as he walked up and down the
room—'so, after all, the letter was not intended for me or my
father. This is in consequence of having such a common
name ! And yet the name in itself is good : but the Hamiltons
have multiplied so unconscionably of late that I have no doubt
we shall in time be quite as numerous as the Smiths ! Should,
however, no Hamilton have been here for the last week or ten
days, I conceive that I have a right to appropriate this letter,
for A. Z. says distinctly that he or she had that moment seen
my name among the arrivals in Munich, and with every allow-
ance for irregularity of post in an out-of-the-way place, chance
or unexpected delays, reference at least is made to some paper
of a tolerably recent date. Oh! thank you,' he exclaimed,
hurrying towards the waiter, who at that moment entered

the room with the strangers' book. 'Before you go, show me the name of the gentleman into whose room my letter was taken by mistake.'

He pointed to the name of 'Alex. Hambledon, from London.'

Hamilton turned back the leaves, six, eight, ten days, and no Hamilton before that time, as Mr. Havard had said, 'A great many Hamiltons.' He wished them, their families, and suites very agreeable journeys, closed the book, put A. Z.'s letter carefully into his writing-case, and after having desired the waiter to call him very early the next day, hurried to bed.

The next morning proved fine, and Hamilton felt in better spirits than he had done since he had left home, for he flattered himself that he was now about to diverge from the traveller's beaten path. and had a chance of seeing something new. The rather shabby carriage and sleepy-looking horses had not power to discompose him, and the voiturier, with his dark-blue linen blouse and short pipe, overshadowed by a bush of moustache, he thought absolutely picturesque. Most careful he seemed too of his horses, for they had scarcely left the suburbs of Munich when he descended from his box to walk up a small acclivity, and Hamilton then began to protest vehemently, but in vain, against the carriage being closed. The coachman continued to walk leisurely on, while he assured his impatient employer that he had purposely so arranged it, to prevent his being annoyed by the dust or sun, and that from the open sides he could see quite as much as would be agreeable of the flat country through which they were to travel.

'Is, then, the country so very ugly?' asked Hamilton, anticipating nothing less than an American prairie.

'Flat—very flat; but in the evening we shall have the mountains nearer.'

'You seem fond of the mountains?'

'I am a Tyrolean, and used to them. Life is not the same thing in these plains,' he answered, cracking his whip, but not touching his horses.

'A Tyrolean!' exclaimed Hamilton; 'oh, then, you can sing your national songs, of course. Do pray let me hear one of them.'

'What's the use,' he said, shrugging his shoulders; 'there's no echo for the jodel.'

'No matter, try it at all events, and you shall have an additional glass of beer at dinner-time.'

On the strength of this promise he 'lifted up his voice in song,' and shouted out a melody which there was no manner of doubt would have been 'by distance made more sweet,' but which, as he leaned on the door of the carriage, and poured the whole force of his stentorian lungs into Hamilton's face, almost made him vibrate on his seat.

'Thank you,' cried Hamilton, hastily—'thank you—that will do. I have long wished to hear a Tyrolean jodel, and am sure it must sound very well—in the mountains.'

'There's no music like it in the world,' said the man, as he seated himself again on the box, and laying aside his pipe, he continued singing for more than an hour, interrupted only by an occasional 'Ho—he—hot!' addressed to his horses.

The country was indeed flat but highly cultivated, and thickly wooded alternately,—the absence of all walls or fences giving to German scenery in general the appearance of a domain: they passed through, and saw in the distance, many pretty villages, while the mountains were becoming more distinct, and the scenery more interesting, every hour. Had not the day been intensely sultry, Hamilton would have insisted on the head of the carriage being thrown back, and the odious rattling windows opposite to him being removed; as it was, however, the shade was agreeable, and the almost imperceptible current of air, produced by the motion of the carriage, as it blew on his face, had the somniferous effect attributed to the Vampire's wing—he slept, and so soundly, that until the carriage stopped suddenly before a house on the roadside, not all the jolting and consequent thumping of his head against the hard side of the carriage could waken him; he then rubbed his eyes, stretched out his legs, and was endeavouring once more to compose himself to sleep, when the coachman informed him that they were to remain there two hours to rest and dine. He looked at his watch—it was twelve o'clock—then at the inn: it did not promise much; but near the door he caught a glimpse of a carriage in form and colour exactly resembling his own, containing, however, a number of packages which denoted female travellers. The blue band-boxes and embroidered bags decided his movements. He sprang from the carriage, and almost unconsciously ran his fingers through his hair as he entered the house. Passing through a

large room filled with peasants, he reached a smaller apartment containing some narrow tables, furnished at each side
with benches covered with black leather cushions. At one of
these tables sat three ladies, and an equal number of little
boys. Hamilton had learned to bow civilly, on entering a
room, to any persons who might be in it; after which, he
generally contrived to commence a conversation, and let
people know that he was an Englishman; having ascertained
that being one was a sort of recommendation, or, at least, an
excuse for all sorts of eccentricity. On the present occasion
his bow was returned, but no further notice taken; scarcely
even a look bestowed on him; this was, however, not at all
what he wished, for two of the party were young and remarkably pretty.

She who seemed to be the mother of the children, a tall gaunt
person, had her head and chin bound up with a large pocket-
handkerchief, and seemed to be suffering from toothache, which
rather puzzled Hamilton, when he had discovered that she had
apparently lost all her teeth, though by no means old, as appeared from her fresh-coloured features and hair untinged with
gray. The other two were very young and perfect personifi-
cations of German beauty—blue eyes, blooming cheeks, red lips,
and a profusion of brown hair most classically braided and
platted. That they were sisters scarcely admitted of a doubt,
so remarkable was their resemblance to each other—a nearer
inspection made it equally evident that one was much handsomer than the other. They were both tall and very slightly
formed, and their dark cotton dresses were made and put on
with an exactness that proved they were not indifferent to the
advantages bestowed on them by Nature.

Hamilton stood at the window, an object of interest, as it
seemed, to no one excepting the three little boys, who, with
their mouths full of roast chicken, turned round on their chairs
to stare at him, notwithstanding the repeated admonitions of
their mother, enforced by an occasional shake of the shoulder.
The young ladies, to Hamilton's infinite astonishment, took the
chicken bones in their fingers, and detached the meat from them
with their teeth! He felt at once convinced that they were
immeasurably vulgar, thereby forming an erroneous conclusion
very common on the part of his travelling countrymen, who are
not aware that the mode of eating is in Germany no such exact
criterion of manners as in England. His dinner was now ready,

and as he seated himself at the table one of his pretty neighbours glanced shyly towards him in a manner that proved he
had not been so unobserved as he imagined. With all the
vanity of youth he determined in his turn to play indifference,
traced diligently his route on the map which he had placed
beside him, and made inquiries about Seon. The lady with the
bound-up head tapped at the window, and asked her coachman
if he were ready to put-to the horses ; the answer was indis-
tinct; but the words ' late enough ' and ' Seon ' reached Hamilton's ears. Bonnets, gloves, and handkerchiefs were sought,
and the children given in charge to their maid to be packed
into the carriage.

'I think we had better get in with the boys and arrange
ourselves comfortably,' observed the elder lady, following them
out of the room.

' Comfort ! ' exclaimed one of the girls in a melancholy voice
as she tied on her bonnet ; ' comfort is quite out of the question.
I wish with all my heart we were at Seon !   On such a day as
this seven in a carriage is anything but agreeable ! '

' I should not mind,' answered the other, half-laughing, ' if
Peppy did not insist on sitting on my knee ; he kicks so incessantly that I suffered tortures on my way here.'

Hamilton advanced towards the speakers, and observed that
he was travelling to the same place, and his carriage was quite
at their service.   They blushed, and one of them seemed disposed to laugh, which encouraged him to add, that he would
promise to be perfectly quiet and on no pretence whatever to
kick ! Either his words or manner, or both, perhaps, displeased
them, for, having exchanged looks, they murmured something
unintelligible, and hastily left the room. He followed and saw
them get into their carriage, which was already more than
sufficiently filled with children and boxes; the maid endeavoured
to follow, but was obliged to remain long in the door-way while
a place was being prepared for her. Wishing to prove that he
had made his proposition with the intention of being civil, he
now approached the party and addressed the elder lady — told
her he was going to Seon, was travelling alone, had scarcely
any luggage, and had places for as many persons and parcels
as she chose to transfer to his carriage. She thanked him, and
hesitatingly regretted that her ' boys ' were so unmanageable—
perhaps he would be so kind as to give her maid a place. This
was not exactly what Hamilton had intended, nevertheless he

acceded with a good grace, and assisted the spruce-looking servant-girl to descend. One of the boys instantly commenced roaring, and declared he must and would go with her—he was lifted out of the carriage, and, with many apologies, Hamilton was asked to take charge of Peppy the kicker! But Peppy was not yet satisfied; he insisted so vociferously on his sister, 'Crescenz,' accompanying him, that his mother was at length obliged to consent, and when Hamilton looked at the pretty blushing face of this new addition to his party, he thought her mother's apologies not only tiresome but quite unnecessary. He had to wait some time before his coachman thought proper to depart, and made an attempt to express the pleasure he felt at having obtained so desirable a travelling companion, but the fair Crescenz seemed so overcome with *mauvaise honte,* that he thought it advisable for the present to avoid all conversation. When once fairly off, he rummaged out a couple of books, offered her one, and took the other himself. This proceeding seemed to surprise her, but had the effect he wished of making her feel less embarrassed. She turned over the leaves with a listlessness which at once convinced him that she was no reader, and he ventured to make a few remarks. The answers were at first merely monosyllables, but they required explanation, for he purposely misunderstood her. One subject of conversation led to another, and in about an hour they were talking as if they had been acquainted for months. She informed him that her father had a situation which scarcely ever admitted of his leaving Munich. That she and her sister had lost their mother when they were mere children, and they had been sent to school when their father had married again. They had returned home but a few weeks ago, and their stepmother having been ordered change of air, had chosen Seon, because the baths there had been of use to her on a former occasion. They had been very happy to leave school, and were equally happy to go to the country— especially to Seon.

'And why especially to Seon?' asked Hamilton.

'Oh, because I have heard so much of it from one of my school-friends.'

'Perhaps, then, you can give me some information. I have not the least idea what sort of a place it is.'

'I believe it is a great old monastery, with long corridors, where one might expect to meet the ghosts of the monks stalking about—and the windows look into dark courts—and on a moon-light night it is quite romantic walking in the cloisters ! '

'And did your friend wander about quite alone and by moonlight in such a place?'

'Oh, she was not *alone*,' said Crescenz, smiling and shaking her head slily.

'So I imagined—probably her mother or her sister walked with her.'

'Her mother was not there, and her brother-in-law would not allow her sister to walk by moonlight.'

'What a barbarian he must have been ! Who, then, could have been her companion ? It could hardly have been her father ? '

Crescenz laughed outright. ' Oh, no ; had it been her father, Lina would not have been sent back to school again. They said she had done all sorts of wild things at home ; that her head was full of nonsense, and she must be cured.'

'And was she cured ? '

'I suppose so, for some time after she left us again she married an ugly old doctor. Oh, he is so ugly ! His chin sticks out *so* !' In explanation she thrust out her full red underlip, forming thereby a better personification of a pretty, naughty child than an ugly old doctor. 'I was allowed to be her bridesmaid,' she continued, 'and as I knew all about Theodor, I asked her if she really were as happy as she seemed to be? And, can you believe it ?—she said that all the fine things she had told me of Seon and first love was stuff and nonsense—that she had invited Theodor to her wedding and intended to dance with him in the evening!'

'In fact the affair with Theodor was merely a flirtation,' observed Hamilton.

'I don't know what that means,' she answered, looking in-quiringly in his face ; 'it is an English word, I suppose?'

'Quite English,' said Hamilton, laughing, 'but your friend seems to have understood the meaning perfectly.'

'And yet she did not take any lessons in English,' said Crescenz, thoughtfully, 'but I remember her saying to me at school, that if she could not marry Theodor she would go into a nunnery ' And then to be satisfied with ugly old Doctor Berger !'

'You would not have acted so ? inquired Hamilton.

She was about to answer when her eye caught that of the servant opposite to them ; she coloured and remained silent. Hamilton had long thought this personage a bore, although she had been too much occupied with little master Peppy to have heard much of their conversation. It suddenly, however, occurred to him to repeat his question in French, and this removed all difficulties, for the young lady spoke so remarkably fluently that the conversation proceeded more flowingly than before. From the specimen given, it may be supposed that a sufficient quantity of nonsense was talked ; however, they contrived to amuse themselves so well that they actually drove up to the door of the *ci-devant* monastery, without having seen even a chimney to warn them that their journey was drawing to a close. Crescenz's stepmother was waiting to receive them, and overwhelmed Hamilton with thanks, while he, taken completely by surprise, had only time to whisper hurriedly to his travelling companion—'I shall certainly see you again, even if I should decide on leaving Seon to-morrow ;' and as he assisted her out of the carriage, he added, 'We positively must try the cloisters by moonlight.'

But no answering smile played round her coral lips Crescenz seemed metamorphosed. No sooner had her feet touched the ground than one glided gently behind the other, and a profound curtsey, such as very young ladies are taught to make by a dancing-master, was performed to his infinite astonishment ; a few neat and appropriate words of thanks were added, which, had they not been accompanied by a burning blush, he would have considered the most consummate piece of acting he had ever witnessed. Hamilton bit his lip and coloured deeply as he mechanically followed the landlady through a side-door into the monastery.

He was conducted up a back staircase to a long corridor, at the end of which was a small passage leading into a tolerably large cheerful room, to his great disappointment not bearing any perceptible marks of antiquity. On expressing some surprise he was told that the monastery had been twice almost burnt to the ground, and that only some parts of the original building remained. His room was the most modern of all, and had been the apartment of the Abbot, before the secularisation.

'Have you many people staying here at present?' asked Hamilton.

'Not many ; several left this morning, but we expect others next week.'

'And the names of those who are still here ?' asked Hamilton, in considerable alarm.

'Still here,' repeated the landlady, but at this instant the sounds of wheels and horses' hoofs made Hamilton rush to one of the windows. A small open carriage and its dust-covered occupant attracted his attention so completely, that, without waiting for an answer to his former question, he added, 'Who is that?'

'Ah, the Herr Baron !' cried the landlady, looking out of the window, and then quickly leaving the room.

The traveller started up in the carriage and looked round him. He was dressed in a sort of loose shooting-jacket of grey cloth, which completely concealed his figure, and his dark green felt hat was slouched over his face, leaving little visible excepting the moustache, surmounted by a well-formed aquiline nose. 'Is no one here?' he cried, exhibiting some very unequivocal signs of impatience, and a servant in plain livery came at full speed, followed by half-a-dozen men and women, who were soon all employed unpacking the carriage. Carpet-bag, meerschaum pipes of different forms and dimensions, newspapers, cigar-cases, boots, powder-horn, umbrella, double-barrelled gun, sketch-book, a very old pistol, a very new rifle, and some rolls of bread, followed each other in odd confusion. Some one at a window not distant from Hamilton laughed heartily; the traveller looked up, laughed also, and flourished his hat in the air. 'What a dusty figure!' exclaimed the invisible. 'Have you brought no trophy? No venison for our landlady ?'

'The chamois hunt was unsuccessful, although I remained out all night; but my new rifle performed wonders at the *Scheibenschiessen.*'

Another laugh from the window made him seize his rifle and jestingly point it upwards—it was, however, directly thrown aside, while he half-apologetically exclaimed, 'It cannot go off, I assure you. Look here—it is not even loaded,' and he grasped the ramrod to prove his assertion ; but some unexpected impediment in the barrel caused him to grow suddenly red. He raised the offending weapon as if with the intention of firing it off, but after a hasty glance towards the window, he gave it to one of the bystanders, requesting him to draw out the charge, and then ran quickly into the house.

In the mean time Hamilton's coachman had brought up his luggage, and a chambermaid waited to know whether or not he intended to sup below stairs. Supper would be in the little room through which he had passed on his entrance, as there were too few people for the saloon. Perhaps he wished to sup in his own room?

'By no means. I always prefer a *table-d'hôte*. Pray, can you tell me the names of some of the people here? I may, perhaps, have an acquaintance among them.'

'Major Stultz, from Munich. The family who have just arrived are the Rosenbergs, from—'

'I know—I know,' cried Hamilton, nodding his head.

'Then there is Mr. Schmierer, landscape-painter, and Count Zedwitz—his wife and daughter—'

'Who do you say?' asked Hamilton, suddenly recollecting A. Z.

'Count Zedwitz and the countess, and—

'Can they speak English?'

'Oh, no doubt; and French too, quite perfectly: they speak a great many languages.'

'They are not, however, invalids? That is, they are not here on account of the baths?'

'No; I believe they came to meet some friends whom they had intended to have visited. I heard the count's servant saying that their house, or the baron's, was full of masons and painters.'

'Ah! exactly—'

'But the old countess does take baths,' continued the chambermaid, 'and finds great benefit from them, too. The count is a favourer of Priessnitz and the Water Cure; and when he does not go to Graefenberg all places are alike to him where water is good and in abundance.'

'And his daughter?' asked Hamilton, now convinced that he had found A. Z.

'Oh, his daughter springs from her bed every morning into a tub of cold water with a great sponge in it, to please him, but I never heard of her having sweated, or—'

'Her having what?'

'Sweated! The count sent his bed and tubs here the day

before he came, and his servant Pepperl must tie him up every morning.'

Some one just then knocked gently at the door.

'Come in!' cried Hamilton. and to his no small surprise Crescenz appeared in the doorway. She blushed, and so did he, and then he blushed because he had blushed; and to conceal his annoyance he assumed a cold, haughty manner, and waited for her to speak. She stammered something about a reticule and pocket-handkerchief, as with the assistance of the chambermaid she moved his carpet-bag, and shook his cloak in every possible direction. Nothing was to be found, and she was just about to leave the room when Hamilton perceived the lost property under his dressing-case. As he restored it, and held the door open for her to pass, he took advantage of the opportunity, and returned her former curtsey with an obeisance so profound that it amounted to mockery, and as such she felt it, too, for the colour mounted through the roots of her hair, suffusing with deep red both neck and ears as she bent down her head, and hurried out of the room, followed by the chambermaid. Hamilton was so shocked at his rudeness, that he felt greatly inclined to run after her and apologise; and had she been alone he would certainly have done so, for it directly occurred to him that she had come herself to seek her handkerchief in order to have an opportunity of explaining to him the cause of her sudden and extraordinary change of manner. This made him still more repent his puerile conduct, and wish he had spoken to her. He looked out of the window to see if he were likely to meet her should he perambulate the much-talked-of cloister, but instead of the rising moon, angry thunder-clouds were rapidly converting the remaining twilight into darkest night. His hopes of a romantic interview and explanation were at an end: there was no chance of moonlight, and the acquaintance was much too new to think of a meeting in thunder and lightning! The supper-table seemed a more eligible place, and spurred both by contrition and hunger, he determined to repair to it with all possible expedition.

On leaving the small passage conducting to his room, he entered the long corridor which he had traversed with the landlady: on turning, however, as he thought to the staircase by which he had ascended, he suddenly found himself in a small but lofty chapel. It was too dark to see distinctly the decorations of the altar, but it seemed as if gilding had not been spared; two small adjoining apartments he next examined, and then completely forgetting whether he had entered from the right or left hand, he walked inquisitively forward until a broad, gloomy passage brought him to a corridor, which he instinctively felt to be the place where on moonlight nights one might perchance be disposed for romance. The doors opposite to him, placed close to each other, had probably belonged to cells; over each was a black-looking picture, portraits of the abbots, the faces and hands looking most ghastly in their indistinctness. A broad staircase was near, but fearing to lose his way completely, he contented himself for the present with reconnoitering the garden and a lake from a sort of lobby window. Woods and mountains were in the distance, but every moment becoming less distinct; the oppressive calm had been succeeded by a wild wind which bent the trees in all directions and ruffled the surface of the water. Interested in the approaching thunder-storm, he stood at the window until his reverie was interrupted by the sound of footsteps, voices, and the clapping of doors. He turned quickly from the window, walked to the end of the corridor, turned to the left, and entered a very narrow passage looking into a small quadrangular court, which seemed once to have been a garden; it still possessed a few trees, a fountain, and a luxuriant growth of rank grass. He mounted a flight of stone steps which brought him into the organ-loft, from whence he had a full view of the monastery church. The lamp which hung suspended before the altar threw fitful gleams of light on the objects in its immediate vicinity—all the rest was in shadow; behind the organ was a sort of vaulted, unfinished room, containing nothing but a most clumsy apparatus for filling the bellows. Just as he was about to leave this uninteresting place two persons entered the adjoining loft; recognising the voice of his travelling companion, and perceiving that she was accompanied by her sister, he commenced a precipitate retreat by another entrance than that next the organ; in his haste, however, he entangled his foot in the rope communicating with the belfry, so that his slightest movement might alarm the whole household. While endeavouring, as well as the darkness would permit, to extricate himself, he was compelled to become auditor of a conversation certainly not intended for his ears.

'And you don't think him at all good-looking?' asked Crescenz.

'I cannot say that his appearance particularly pleased me, but you know I only saw him eating his dinner; he seemed, however, to have an uncommonly good opinion of himself!'

'At all events,' said Crescenz, 'it was very obliging of him to take us in his carriage. I am sure if *you* had travelled with him instead of me, you would think quite differently.'

'Dear Crescenz! I have no doubt that he was agreeable, as you say so; and I agree with you in thinking him very civil, and all that sort of thing, but you cannot force me to think him handsome!'

'I did not say that I thought him handsome,' cried Crescenz, deprecatingly.

'No! Something very like it, then. Let me see; hum—a—most interesting person you ever saw; brilliant dark eyes with long eye-lashes; magnificent teeth, beautiful mouth, refined manners, and ever so much more! Now, I think him an effeminate-looking, supercilious boy, and—'

'Oh, I might have foreseen,' cried Crescenz, interrupting her sister, 'I might have foreseen that he would find no favour in your eyes, as he is not an officer with a long sword clattering at his side.'

'Sword or no sword,' answered the other, laughing, 'he would not look like anything but an overgrown school-boy, perhaps, a student, or—or an embryo *attaché* to an embassy.'

Hamilton's blush of annoyance was concealed by the darkness.

'I intended,' began Crescenz, hesitatingly, 'I intended to have told you something, but you seem to be so prejudiced against him that—'

'Prejudiced! Not in the least. I do not think him particularly handsome, that's all!'

'Well, you know I told you we talked a great deal during our journey, and—and a—in short, just as we reached Seon he said something about meeting me in the corridor by moonlight.'

'Just what I should have expected from him!' cried the other, angrily. 'How presuming on so short an acquaintance!'

'He is an Englishman,' said Crescenz, apologetically; 'and certainly did not mean anything wrong, for his manner did not change in the least when he saw mamma, while I was so dreadfully afraid she might observe—Oh! Hildegarde! What is that? Did you not hear something moving?'

'I think I did; let us listen.' A pause ensued. 'It's only the thunderstorm, and'—taking a long breath—'the ticking of the great clock.'

'How like some one breathing heavily!' exclaimed Crescenz, anxiously.

'And how dark it is! We can hardly find our way out,' said Hildegarde.

Hamilton did not venture to move; they were so near him that he heard the hands feeling the way on the wall close to where he stood. One reached the narrow passage in safety, the other stumbled on the stairs; and, as Hamilton unconsciously made a movement to assist her, the lightning, which had once or twice enabled him to distinguish their figures, now rendered him for a moment visible. It was in vain he again drew back into his hiding-place. With a cry of terror Crescenz raised herself from the ground and rushed into her sister's arms, exclaiming, 'I have seen him! I have seen him! He is here!'

'What! Who is here?'

'The Englishman! The Englishman!'

'Impossible! How can you be so foolish? Come, come! let us leave this place.'

'I saw him, and the lightning played upon his face, and he looked as if he were dead. I saw him, indeed I saw him!' cried Crescenz, sobbing frantically.

'Crescenz, dear Crescenz!' said her sister, vainly endeavouring to calm her.

Hamilton was inexpressibly shocked, and conceiving his actual presence would relieve her mind from the fear of having seen something supernatural, he came forward and explained, as well as he could, the cause of his being there. In the excess of his anxiety he seized her hand, called her Crescenz, and talked he knew not what nonsense. Her efforts to control her emotion were desperate. She forced a laugh, but the attempt ended in a scream, which echoed wildly through the building.

'Crescenz! Crescenz! have you lost your senses?' cried her sister. 'You will bring the whole house about us!'

Her words seemed likely to be verified, for lights began to glimmer in all directions.

C

'Mamma will come, and we may make up our minds to return to Munich to-morrow,' cried Hildegarde impatiently.

Hamilton's situation now became uncomfortable; it was, to say the least, not favourable for a first appearance among strangers, and the thought that 'A. Z.' might be among them was so overpowering that he stood perfectly petrified, and still unconsciously holding Crescenz's hand. 'As to you, the Englishman,' continued Hildegarde, angrily, 'your standing there can only increase our embarrassment. Begone! It is still possible for you to escape observation.'

He turned mechanically towards the organ-loft.

'Not there! Not there!' she cried vehemently. 'One would really think you a fool!'

Roused by this somewhat uncivil observation, Hamilton asked, in about as gentle a tone of voice as her own, 'Where the d—l shall I go, then, mademoiselle? You don't wish me to face all those lights, do you?'

'Go! go! go!' she cried with increased violence, and stamping the ground with her foot. 'You can cross the corridor before they reach the entrance to this passage.'

He ran, crossed the passage, stumbled up two or three steps to a door, which charitably yielded to his hand, and afforded him a retreat into—the church—for there he was again. Now completely confused, and feeling as if under the influence of nightmare, he threw himself into a seat and covered his face with his hands. Steps and inquiring voices came nearer and nearer. He heard scolding, wondering, expostulating; then all was quiet, and only Crescenz's subdued sobs reached his ear. All at once, to his no small dismay, the church became lighted; some persons with candles were in the organ-loft opposite to him; he could see them, however, in tolerable security, for his place of refuge proved to be the enclosed gallery formerly occupied by the monks. In the mean time the storm had increased, one flash of lightning was followed so immediately by thunder so loud that it seemed to shake the very foundations of the monastery. It served to disperse the assembly, for Hamilton heard soon after the retreating steps passing the door of the gallery, the opening and shutting of several doors, voices lost in the distance, and all was again still. He waited merely to assure himself that no one was in the way, and then cautiously commenced his retreat. A juvenile reminiscence made him smile as he now moved from his hiding-place; he remembered the time when he had hoped his 'new boots would creak,' and had even tampered with the bootmaker's apprentice when he had been so lucky as to have his measure taken without witnesses. And now, what would he not have given for a pair of slippers or anything but creaking boots! He had scarcely made six strides on tiptoe when a door opened and a head protruded itself. He trusted to the darkness for concealment, and leaned against the wall; the head had no sooner disappeared than, seizing the favourable moment, he rushed into a dark passage and ran, unconscious whether he turned right or left, until he reached a large open window. He looked out and saw the traveller's little green carriage being pushed towards the coach-house. Here was a sort of compass to steer by; his windows had the same aspect; *ergo*, that door must lead to his room. Before, however, he undertook another expedition, he thought it prudent to get a light. This caused a few minutes' delay; and when he again sallied forth he seemed destined to be more fortunate. Hildegarde and her stepmother walked before him, as if to point the way. They disappeared at the end of the passage, and he quickened his steps in order to overtake them on the stairs. The latter was speaking loudly, it seemed in continuation of a previous discourse. 'You may rest assured that your father shall have a full account of the whole affair. Such a disgraceful scene! Count Zedwitz sent his servant to inquire what was the matter, and recommended immersion in cold water. A good ducking would have most effectually quieted Crescenz's nerves, and I shall certainly try it next time. My health is not likely to be much benefited by a residence here, if I have to act duenna to you and your sister! Remember, I strictly forbid your walking in these passages after sunset in future. Do you hear?'

'Yes, Madame.'

'As to Crescenz being so afraid of lightning, that's all nonsense! I should like to know if all the young ladies at school scream in that manner whenever they see a flash of lightning!'

'The thunder was very loud,' began Hildegarde, 'and besides, you have not heard that she saw—'

'Well, well,' cried her mother, interrupting her, to Hamilton's great satisfaction, 'thunder or lightning—or both—there was no occasion for such a noise, and I give you warning that the very first time I have cause to be dissatisfied with you or your sister, back you shall go to school. Health is my object at

present, and every irritation of the nerves has been expressl.
forbidden by my medical adviser.'

To this speech no answer was made, and Hamilton followed
them at a distance into the supper-room.   He had lost so much
time in the organ-loft, that almost all the guests were already
gone.   The traveller, whose arrival he had witnessed, was in
the act of lighting a cigar, with which he immediately left the
room.   An elderly, red-faced, stout gentleman, with a tankard
of beer beside him, he soon discovered to be Major Stultz—
nor did it require much penetration to recognise Mr. Schmierer,
the painter, in the emaciated sentimental-looking young man
beside whom he seated himself.   Hildegarde and her stepmother were nearly opposite ; the former, after bestowing on
Hamilton a look which might appropriately have accompanied
a box on the ear, fixed her eyes on the table ; the latter bowed
most graciously, and commenced an interesting conversation
about the weather, the barometer, and her dislike to thunder-
storms in general.   When these topics had been completely
exhausted, Hamilton hoped something might be said of the
present inmates of Seon, but a long and tiresome discussion
on the merits of summer and winter beer followed.   Strauss's
beer was delicious—Bock had been particularly good this year.
'Bock!' cried Major Stultz, enthusiastically, 'Bock is better
than champagne!   Bock is—' Here he looked up with an
impassioned air to the ceiling, and kissed the two first fingers of
his right hand, flourishing them in the air afterwards.   Words,
it seems, were inadequate to express the merits of this
beverage.

'Did you see that picture at the Kunstverein * in Munich,
representing a glass of foaming bock, with the usual accessories
of bread and radishes ?' asked Mr. Schmierer.   'It was ex-
quisitely painted !   I believe his Majesty purchased it.'

'There is some sense in such a picture as that,' answered
Major Stultz.   'I went two or three times to see it; and
could scarcely avoid stretching out my hand to feel if it were
not some deception.'

'A judicious management of reflected lights produces extraordinary effect in the representation of fluids,' observed Mr.
Schmierer.

A pause ensued.   Major Stultz did not seem disposed to

* Society of Arts.

discuss reflected lights; the picture had evidently had no value
for him, excepting as a good representation of a glass of bock,
and his attention was now directed towards Hildegarde, whose
flushed cheeks and pouting lips rather heightened than de-
tracted from her beauty.

'Perhaps you would like to see the newspapers, madame?'
he asked, politely offering the latest arrived to her stepmother.

'Thank you; I never read newspapers, though I join some
acquaintances in taking the *Eilbote*, on condition that it comes
to us last of all, and then we can keep the paper for cleaning
the looking-glasses and windows.'

'There are, however, sometimes very pretty stories and
charades in the *Eilbote*. Young ladies like such things,' he
observed, glancing significantly towards Hildegarde.

'My daughters must read nothing but French, and I have
subscribed to a library for them. Their French has occupied
more than half their lives at school, and now I intend them to
teach the boys.'

'*I* should have no sort of objection to learn French from
such an instructress,' said the Major, gallantly.

'Indeed I don't think anyone will ever learn much from
her,' said Madame Rosenberg, severely; 'but her sister
Crescenz is a good girl, and the children are very fond of her.'

'You have two daughters!' exclaimed the Major.

'*Step-daughters*,' she replied, drily.

'That I took for granted,' he said, bowing as if he intended
to be very civil. 'The young ladies will be of great use to
you in the housekeeping.'

'That is exactly what has been neglected in their education;
if they could keep a house as well as they can speak French I
should be satisfied. When we return to Munich they must
both learn cookery. I intend afterwards to give the children
to one, and the housekeeping to the other alternately.'

'You will prepare the young ladies so well for their destination, that I suspect they will not remain long unmarried!'

'There's not much chance of that! Husbands are not
so easily found for portionless daughters!' replied Madame
Rosenberg, facetiously; 'however, I am quite ready to give
my consent should anything good offer.'

Hamilton looked at Hildegarde to see what impression this
conversation had made on her. She had turned away as much

as possible from the speakers, and with her head bent down, seemed to watch intently the bursting of the bubbles in a glass of beer. Had it been her sister he would have thought she had chosen the occupation to conceal her embarrassment— but embarrassment was not Hildegarde's predominant feeling; her compressed lips and quick breathing denoted suppressed anger which amounted to rage, as her stepmother in direct terms asked Major Stultz if he were married, and received for answer that he was a 'bachelor, at her service.' With a sudden jerk, the glass was prostrated on the table, and before Hamilton could raise his arm its contents were deposited in the sleeve of his coat.

'*Pardon mille fois!*' cried Hildegarde, looking really sorry for what had occurred.

'You irritable, awkward girl!'—commenced her mother; but for some undoubtedly excellent reason, she suddenly changed her manner, and added—'You had better go to bed, child ; I see you have not yet recovered from the recent alarm in the church.'

Hildegarde rose quickly from her chair, and with a slight and somewhat haughty obeisance to the company, left the room in silence. Madame Rosenberg continued volubly to excuse her to Hamilton, and, what he thought quite unnecessary, to Major Stultz also !

The Major listened with complacence, but Hamilton's wet shirt-sleeve induced him to finish his supper as quickly as possible, and wish the company good night.

CHAPTER II.

THE INITIALS.

HAMILTON thought there were few things so disagreeable as going to bed, excepting, perhaps, getting up again. He was incorrigibly indolent in this respect, and nothing but the most fresh and beautiful of mornings, aided perhaps by the transparent muslin curtains, which had admitted every ray of light from daybreak, could have induced him to get up and be dressed at six o'clock ; and that, too, without any immediate object in view, for three or four hours at least must elapse before he could venture to intrude on 'A. Z.' He was not a little surprised to find Crescenz and her sister already in the garden, but having no inclination for a renewal of the organloft scene, he turned towards a row of clumsy, flat-bottomed boats, sprang into one of them, and in a few minutes was far out in the lake, where he quietly leaned upon his oars and began to look about him.

Seon was originally built upon an island, and received its name from this circumstance, as is quaintly enough recorded in the *Introductio ad Annales Monasterii Seonentis*, of Benonne Feichtmaejr, Ejusdem Monasterii Professor :— 'When God saw that the wickedness of man was great in the earth, and that every imagination of the thoughts of his heart was only evil continually, he threatened the earth with destruction, and said unto Noah, "Make thee an ark," &c. So our blessed founder, *Aribo*, seeing in what unrighteousness mankind had again fallen, resolved also to build an ark, and to receive into it not only his own household, but all others who were willing to quit the wickedness of the world and save themselves from the deluge of sin. Accordingly he changed his castle called Buergel into a monastery, under the seal of the holy patriarch Benedictus, and recommended the same to the protection of the holy martyr Lambertus. The monastery was then named Seon, as the letters composing this word being reversed form the name of *Noes* (Noah) ; and the monastery representing the ark appeared to float in the midst of the lake, a place of refuge for all willing to seek it.'

Of the original building of 994 nothing remains but the church, now converted into a cellar, and the cloisters ; the other parts having been consumed by fire in the year 1561. In the course of time, however, and even before the secularisation of the monastery, it had been found convenient to connect Seon with the mainland by means of a road, over which Hamilton must have driven the evening before. And now, when viewed from the outside, Seon much more resembled a middle-aged German castle than a monastery. This impression it made on Hamilton, too, as he watched the numerous groups of people who had begun to enliven with their presence the pretty garden extending from it to the lake.

Crescenz and her sister continued to walk up and down, talking earnestly, and so often bestowing a look on the 'overgrown schoolboy,' that he felt convinced he was the subject of discourse. Their brothers soon after joined them, and a

very outrageous game of romps ensued between them and
Crescenz. Hildegarde still turned towards the lake, her eyes
fixed on him and his boat. 'Perhaps,' he thought, with the
vanity inherent to very young men—'perhaps she regrets her
rudeness to me last night. I like her all the better for not
playing with those unmannerly boys ; and at supper, too, I
observed that, although strongly resembling her sister, she is
infinitely handsomer !' He rowed to the landing-place, moored
the boat, and approached her quietly ; but it did not require
long to convince him that he had not been in the least degree
an object of interest to her, for she still gazed on the lake,
though his bark no longer floated on its surface, and not even
the sound of his voice when he spoke to her sister could induce her to turn round. He looked at his watch, and found
that by the time he had breakfasted he might prepare to visit
A. Z., that is, learn what chance he had of making a useful
or agreeable acquaintance. He inquired for the landlady, and
found her in the kitchen sending forth detachments of coffee
and rolls to the garden. To his great surprise and pleasure,
she ordered his breakfast to be carried to the arbour, where
the Countess Zedwitz and her daughter were breakfasting,
saying it was the only place unengaged in the whole garden.
With mixed feelings of anxiety and curiosity he followed.
While it was being deposited on the table, he observed that
a question was asked by a comfortable-looking dowager, and
the answer seemed satisfactory, for she nodded her head and
then looked towards him. He bowed, and was received with
a good-humoured smile. 'She knows me,' he thought, 'and
this is A. Z.' It did not, in fact, signify — but — he would
have preferred the daughter, who, although not in the least
pretty, had a merry expression of countenance, and looked so
fresh that he involuntarily thought of the tub of cold water
out of which she had probably sprung half an hour before.

'I fear, madame, you will think me an intruder,' he began,
with an affectation of diffidence which he was far from
feeling.

'Oh, by no mean,' cried the elder lady, in English, nodding
her head two or three times ; 'by no mean ! You are an
Englishman: I am ver glad to have an occasion to spick Eeng-
lish. Man lose all practice in baths ! I estimate me very
happy to make acquaintance with you.'

Hamilton assured her he felt extremely obliged — hoped,

however, to prove that he had a better claim to her notice than his being an Englishman. This she did not comprehend, for, like most Germans who are learning English, she seldom understood when spoken to, and preferred continuing to talk herself, to waiting or asking for an answer in a language which she knew by sight but not by sound. Accordingly, 'We have a very fine nature here!' was the reply he received to an observation which he had intended to have led to an interesting discovery of his being the son of her Munich correspondent. 'We have a very fine nature here!'

Hamilton looked puzzled, or she thought him a little deaf, for she spoke louder as she said, 'A very beautiful nature!'

He bowed and coloured slightly.

'Mamma will say, our prospects are very good,' said the younger lady, in explanation.

'Ha!—prospects!' he repeated.

'What you call lanskip—*paysage?* Is not good English? No?'

'Oh, very good English,' he answered, looking round him, prepared to admire anything or everything he could see. Now, they were in an arbour thickly covered with foliage; in order to render it impervious to the sun's rays, and the entrance being from the garden, there was no view whatever deserving the name of prospect. Hamilton knew not what to say, and was beginning to feel embarrassed, when the Rosenbergs luckily appeared and made a diversion in his favour. Crescenz and her sister advanced to meet their stepmother, who now entered the garden dressed in a most unbecoming dark-coloured cotton morning-gown, partly covered by an old shawl thrown negligently over her shoulders, and her hair still twisted round those odious leather things used for curling refractory ringlets.

'Who is that?' asked the Countess, to his great relief speaking German. 'Who is that person?'

'I believe her name is Rosenberg,' he answered; 'she came from Munich yesterday.'

'Ah, I know. That is the person who screamed in the gallery last night.'

'No, mamma, it was one of her daughters who screamed.'

'Oh, one of her daughters! They are very pretty,' said the Countess, raising her double *lorgnette* to her eyes—·really very pretty! and I think I have seen them somewhere before, but where I cannot recollect—'

'Oh, mamma, I know where you have seen them: they were in the same school with my cousin Thérèse, and we saw them at the examinations last year. Don't you remember the two sisters who were so like each other? And as we drove home with the Princess N——, she said that one of them was the handsomest creature she had ever seen! I think too she said she had known their mother!'

'Not that person in the odious dishabille! You are dreaming, child!'

'No, no—*their* mother was *noble*—she was a Raimond, had no fortune, and married a nobody, when she was old enough to have been wiser; her relations never forgave her, but after her death they offered to educate these two girls for governesses: their father would not part with them; but when he afterwards married a rich smith's daughter, she immediately insisted on his sending them to school.'

'I believe I do remember something of this—most probably a sister of our friend, Count Raimond, Agnes?'

'Mademoiselle's name is Agnes,' said Hamilton, quickly. 'Then, perhaps, you are the person who was so kind as to write me the letter which' . . . And he searched in his pocket for A. Z.'s letter.

'What!—what is that about a letter?' asked the old lady, hastily.

'Some mistake, mamma.'

'But he says you wrote to him, my dear.'

'No, mamma, I did not write to him; but I think it extremely probable that papa did. I know he wrote lately to an Englishman in Munich. He will be glad to see you, I am sure,' she added, turning to Hamilton; 'for although he speaks English very tolerably, he finds writing it extremely difficult; and the little note in question occupied him nearly an hour. When you have breakfasted, I can go with you to his room.'

Hamilton pushed away his coffee-cup, and stood up directly.

'Agnes! Agnes!' cried her mother, gravely, 'you know your father is sweating!'

'Yes, mamma, I know; but papa wishes very much to see his English correspondent. You have, probably, just returned from Graefenberg?' she said, addressing Hamilton. 'Have you no letter from Priessnitz?'

'Letters from Priessnitz! I have no letter excepting that which I received the day before yesterday from Count Zedwitz.'

'You wish, perhaps, to speak to papa before you decide on going to Graefenberg?'

'I—I have no intention whatever of going there, Mademoiselle,' said Hamilton, who did not exactly know who Priessnitz was, or where Graefenberg might be situated; for ten years ago Priessnitz's name was little known in Germany, and scarcely at all in England.

'Well, at all events, you had better speak to papa: I know he expects to see you.'

'If that be the case,' said Hamilton, 'I am sure I shall be very happy to make his acquaintance—I only feared the letter might have been intended for my father, as he has foreign acquaintances, and I have as yet none.'

'It is quite the same thing, I should think,' said the young Countess, as she led the way out of the garden. 'You can let your father know that you have seen us here. Papa was only sorry that he could not receive you at home; but our house is not at present habitable, and—'

'Ah!' cried Hamilton, springing up the stairs after her, 'that is exactly what he said in his letter.'

'Wait here until I have told him that you have arrived,' she said, tapping gently at one of the doors, which closed upon her immediately afterwards.

She did not return, but a tall gaunt servant appeared to conduct him to Count Zedwitz's apartment. On entering he perceived that a figure lay on a bed, but so wrapped in blankets and covered with down beds, that nothing was visible but the face, down which the perspiration rolled copiously. A reading-desk was placed on the breast, and a long quill, tightly pressed between the teeth, served to turn over the leaves of his book. Hamilton would have required some time to discover the use of the quill had it not been performing its office as he entered.

'I am rejoiced to see you—very glad you have become my letter, and seem to profit by it. You are good on the feet again.'

'Thank you,' said Hamilton, rather puzzled by this address, and half disposed to refuse the chair placed for him by the servant.

'You have been to Graefenberg ?—No !'

'No.'

'You have recover without Priessnitz ?'

'Recover !' repeated Hamilton ; 'I have never been seriously ill in my life : colds and all that sort of thing excepted—mere trifles, after all !'

'Trifles! well you Englishmen have odd idea !—Rheumatism is trifle !'

'Gout is more common with us,' observed Hamilton, somewhat amused.

'Well, gout, chiragra, podagra, rheumatismen, what you will, is no trifle at all ! You have had the gout?'

'No ; but I suppose I shall in time : it is hereditary in our family—my father has two or three attacks every year.'

'Your father! Is it your father who has had the gout ?'

'Yes, and I suspect my father is your correspondent, too. I really fear I am not the person you suppose me to be.'

'What! what do you mean?' he cried, endeavouring to raise himself in his bed, and looking precisely like a writhing cadisworm.

'I mean that I received a letter the day before yesterday, inviting me to come here ;—the seal was a coronet, and it was signed A. Z. I arrived ; made inquiries, and too hastily, it seems, concluded that Count Zedwitz, or one of his family, had written to me. Your daughter confirmed me in my error by saying that you had lately written to an Englishman in Munich, and wished very much to see him.'

'Hum, ha!—very odd !' murmured the Count, fixing his eyes sharply on Hamilton. 'May I ask your name ?'

'Hamilton,' replied the Englishman, with an ill-concealed attempt to repress an inclination to laugh.

'I have not the honour of knowing any one of that name,' said the Count, endeavouring, as well as his blankets would permit him, to look dignified. 'I am surprised, sir, you did not perceive the mistake sooner !'

'So am I,' replied Hamilton, his rising colour betraying the embarrassment he endeavoured to conceal ;—'but every moment some remark of yours made me doubt again ; besides,' he added, moving towards the door, 'I must confess, I wished to hear something of this water cure, which is quite new to me : I never heard of it until yesterday. However, I am extremely sorry for having thus forced myself upon your acquaintance, and can only regret that my correspondent has not written his name in full : from these initials, it seems, I have but a small chance of discovering the writer !'

' I don't know that,' cried Count Zedwitz, suddenly changing his manner : ' it is by no means improbable that the letter is from Baron Z. ; his wife is an English woman — I should recommend your seeing them before you give up your search. And—and—' he added, hesitatingly, ' as you seem interested on the subject of Hydropathy, I shall have great pleasure in lending you some books, and giving you every information in my power about Priessnitz and Graefenberg. In the mean time look over this little work—it is not necessary to be a physician to understand it. You will find here a description of Graefenberg, the establishment of Priessnitz, who dis-covered this most rational mode of curing all diseases ; and I doubt not you will soon be convinced of the uselessness of physicians and apothecaries, and place, as I do, all your reliance on cold water :—read what is said about perspirations, cold water drinking, and bathing : read and judge for yourself. I shall see you at dinner-time.'

Hamilton received the book with expressions of gratitude, which were really sincere. The happy termination of his interview made him feel that he had gained an acquaintance who might, perhaps, turn into a friend if he submitted to the ordeal by water.

CHAPTER III.

A. Z.

As Hamilton was on his way to his room to procure his credentials, viz., A. Z.'s letter, he chanced to meet one of the chambermaids, who offered to conduct him to Baron Z——'s apartment. To prevent the necessity of an explanation he sent her before with one of his cards, and she returned almost immediately, saying that Baron Z—— would be very happy to see him, and begged he would come to him as soon as possible. Hamilton immediately obeyed the summons, and found himself in the presence of the traveller with the long rifle. In the middle of a large room was a round table, com-pletely covered with shooting implements, beside which stood

Baron Z——, examining the identical rifle which he had pointed upwards the evening before. He advanced towards Hamilton with great cordiality, extended his hand, and exclaimed in English—

'Mr. Hamilton, I am very glad to see you ; my wife and I have been anxiously awaiting your arrival : for we are obliged to leave Seon after dinner to-day to go to Berchtesgaden. Now all is quite easy to arrange—you go with us—you admire the beautiful mountains—you see the salt mines, and then we arrange an alp party, or a chamois hunt together. Are you a good shot ? '

' No, I regret to say I am not,' answered Hamilton, not a little embarrassed, for his deficiency in this respect had furnished his brother John, greatly his inferior in other respects, with unceasing subject for ridicule; and he half expected some scoffing remark in answer.

' You like to fish, or hunt on horseback, better than chamois hunt, perhaps ?'

Hamilton acknowledged, much relieved, that he was very fond of a hunt on horseback; — he could ride, he said, much better than he could shoot.

'And I,' answered Baron Z——, good-humouredly, laughing, ' I can shoot better than I can ride. I thought it would be interesting for you to be acquainted with our sports, and—'

' It would interest me of all things to see anything of the kind, even as a mere spectator,' exclaimed Hamilton, eagerly. ' I accept your invitation with thanks.'

Baron Z—— now desired his servant to let his wife know that ' Mr. Hamilton, the Englishman she expected, had arrived,— and Joseph '—he called after him, ' take one of the carriage-boxes to Mr. Hamilton's room; he goes with us to Berchtesgaden.'

They were in the midst of a very animated discussion of what Hamilton knew very little about, viz., the latest improvements in fire-arms, when the real 'A. Z.' entered the room. How shall we describe her? Most easily, perhaps, by negatives. She was not tall, nor short, nor stout, nor thin, nor handsome, nor ugly, nor—nor—in fact, as well as Hamilton could define his ideas at such a critical moment, he thought the impression made on him was, that a pale, dark-haired person stood before him, whose countenance denoted sufficient intellect to make him conscious that he had better produce his letter and enter into an explanation at once. The absence of all recognition on her part made him at once conscious that he was not the person she had expected, and he stood before her, blushing so intensely that she seemed at length to feel a sort of commiseration for him. She bit her lip to conceal a smile, and, after a moment's pause, held out her hand, saying, 'I confess I expected to have seen your father, and am a little disappointed. You were such a mere child when I saw you last, John, that you have completely outgrown my recollection. You promised, indeed, to be " more than common tall," but I was not prepared for such a specimen of—. You seem to be an inveterate blusher, and very shy; perhaps that was the reason why your father wished to send you abroad before you joined your regiment? By the bye, I must have been misinformed, but I heard you had already joined! Now, pray don't waste another blush on me, but try to feel at home as soon as you can, and prepare to tell me directly everything about everybody !'

Hamilton moved mechanically towards the sofa, completely confused in every sense of the word, but at the same time greatly relieved in his mind. So, after all, the letter had been intended for his father, and she merely mistook him for his brother John—a common mistake, which he could easily explain. What a fool he would have been had he not come in person to inquire about this 'A. Z.,' who was evidently an old friend of his father! He began to breathe more freely, and overheard a few words which she addressed to her husband in a very low voice, in German: 'Did you ever see such a long-legged, bashful animal? He is, however, handsome, and would be decidedly gentlemanlike if he were less diffident. We must take him with us to Berchtesgaden, Herrmann.'

' I have already arranged everything,' he answered, nodding his head. 'He wishes to see a chamois hunt, and he shall, if I can manage it; at all events, he may stretch his long legs on one of our mountains.'

'Are you a sportsman?' she asked in English, turning towards Hamilton and seating herself on the sofa.

'Not the least in the world, as far as shooting is concerned,' he answered, stooping to arrange her footstool, and feeling once more unembarrassed, 'but I should like extremely to see a chamois hunt.'

'If you are not what is called a good shot,' said A. Z., 'I

should recommend the ascent of a mountain or alp instead of a chamois hunt, which is very fatiguing, and I should think must be uninteresting to a person who cannot shoot remarkably well.'

'Anything that is new or national will be acceptable to me,' answered Hamilton. 'I am anxious to profit by my residence in Germany, and see and hear as much as possible; most particularly I wish to become acquainted with some German families, in order to see the interior of their houses and learn their domestic habits.'

While he had been speaking, A. Z. had bent over a small work-box, with the contents of which she absently played. She now looked up, and repeated his last words: 'Domestic habits! Does that interest you?—But I had almost forgotten: your father wrote to me on that subject, and I had very nearly entered into an engagement for you with a family in Munich.'

'How very odd!' exclaimed Hamilton. 'My father never mentioned a word of anything of the kind to me; I do not think even my mother was acquainted with this plan.'

'You are mistaken. She referred to it in the only letter I have received from her for years. Indeed, I began to think, as my last letter had remained so long unanswered, that I was quite forgotten by you all, and the letter which you received in Munich was sent on chance. I purposely wrote in general terms, and signed with my initials, knowing that either your father or mother would recognise the handwriting, and you or one of your brothers would have no difficulty in filling the blank and be glad to have our address.'

'I assure you, however, I was extremely puzzled when I received your letter; nor can I conceive why my father made such a secret of an arrangement which naturally interests me so much. He seemed indifferent whether I passed next winter in Munich or Vienna, and left me perfectly free to choose which I preferred.'

'Perhaps because he knew that I had left Munich.'

'But he never spoke of any German friend or acquaintance in the least resembling you! He never, I am sure, mentioned your name!'

'It seems, then, I am quite forgotten; but, as I have expatriated myself, I have no right to complain, and it would be unreasonable to expect people to remember me now, or speak of me to their children. Nevertheless, I cannot forget

that I have experienced much kindness from your father and
mother in former times, and that I have spent months in
their house when you were at school. I shall be very glad if
I can in any way be of use to you.'

'Thank you. . . . . I *cannot* imagine what motive my
father could have had for secrecy and mystery on this occasion,' said Hamilton, musingly. 'The idea is excellent, if I
could only put it in practice. Perhaps you will be so kind
as to give me your advice and assistance?'

'Most willingly; and I shall begin by giving you my
advice to wait until you know something about your commission before you negotiate with any family whatever.'

'I am not going into the army—my uncle will not allow
me to go to India, so my father intends me to try my fortune
in the diplomatic line, and my principal object is to perfect
myself in speaking German. A respectable family, could one
be found willing to receive me, would answer all my purposes and fulfil all my wishes.'

'A diplomat! Then you must endeavour to conquer the
mauvaise honte with which you seem overpowered when speaking to strangers, or it will never do. You are now natural
and at your ease, and I tell you honestly, I can scarcely imagine
you to be the same person who, a quarter of an hour ago, stood
before me, blushing and squeezing his hat as if in an agony of
embarrassment!'

'And I was in an agony of embarrassment,' answered
Hamilton, laughing. 'I perceived when you entered the
room that you did not know me. I fancied that, perhaps, you
had not written this letter; or, that it was not intended for
me or for my father; and as I had already had one scene
about it this morning, I had no wish for another, fearing that
a *dénouement* with you might not prove so amusing as with
old Count Zedwitz.'

Hamilton now gave a short account of that little adventure,
which amused her so much, that she related it in German to
her husband before he left the room. There was something
in A. Z.'s manner towards him which peculiarly invited confidence—a sort of mixture of friend and relation. She appeared so interested in all his plans, understood so exactly
what he meant, without asking unnecessary questions, that
before half an hour had elapsed, he had confided to her
his intention of writing a book! She exhibited no sort of

astonishment at the monstrous idea ; he could not even detect a particle of ridicule in her smile as she approved of his intention ; hoped he had taken notes, and asked him what was to be the subject of his work.

'Germany, and the Domestic Manners of the Germans, or something of that sort.'

'I hope, however, you speak German well enough to understand and join in general conversation, and to ask questions and obtain information if necessary? It is unpardonable people writing about the inhabitants of a country when they are incapable of conversing with them.'

'I understand it perfectly when it is spoken, and I generally contrive to make myself intelligible.'

'A little more than that is necessary ; but perhaps you are too modest to boast of your proficiency.'

'I scarcely deserve to be called modest, although I am subject to occasional fits of diffidence. I believe I speak German with tolerable fluency, and only want opportunities of hearing and seeing. May I ask the name of the family with whom you were in treaty ? '

'I heard of two families, either of them would have answered; but—' she hesitated.

'But what?'

'After everything had been arranged, and I was on the point of writing to your father, I found that only one member of the family wished for you, and that was the person who on such an occasion was of the least importance. I mean the gentleman. He wished for your society to have an opportunity of speaking English, but as he spent the greater part of the day in his office, and went out every evening, you would naturally have fallen to the lot of his wife ; and although I praised you as much as I could without knowing how you had grown up, she told me plainly that she should consider you a bore, and that I could not oblige her more than by breaking off our negotiations. Under such circumstances I had no choice.'

' And the other?' asked Hamilton.

' The other was a professor at the university. I wrote to your father about him, but never received any answer.'

' A professor ! that does not promise much, nor would it answer my purpose. I should see little or nothing of domestic life.'

' You are mistaken ; I was half afraid you might see too much, for he had a wife and five sons. '

' Did his wife enter no protest ? '

' I did not see her ; but as they were not rich, and had already five young persons in their house, I concluded one more or less could make little difference.'

' But a—if another family could be found, I must say I should prefer it, and would rather not apply to the professor, excepting as a last resource.'

' We have no longer the option, for he has left Munich. I heard, indeed, of another family—but the objections were insurmountable.'

' On the part of husband or wife ? '

' This time the objections were on my side : there were unmarried daughters in the house.'

' Oh, that would be no objection at all—on the contrary—'

' I considered it a very serious objection,' said A. Z., quietly.

' I understand what you mean ; but surely you do not think me such a fool as to fall in love with every girl I happen to live in the house with ? I assure you I am by no means so inflammable.'

' Very possible ; but as I could not answer for your not being inflammatory, and am aware that German girls do not understand the word " flirtation," and are much too serious on such occasions, I thought it better to avoid leading you into temptation. Do not, however, be vexed ; I have many friends in Munich, and have no doubt of being able to find some family—'

' Where there are five unlicked cubs in the house,' cried Hamilton, petulantly interrupting her.

' Then, John, you will make the half-dozen complete,' she answered, laughing. ' But now listen to reason. A family who would consent to receive a young man as inmate in their house, and who, without any degree of relationship or connexion with his family, could enter into pecuniary arrangements with him about board and lodging, and all that sort of thing, must either be in straitened circumstances, or in a much lower rank of life than yours. I acknowledge that such arrangements are common here, and in some cases they are very judicious ; but when the proposal, as in this instance, came from a widow with three unmarried daughters, I found it very injudicious indeed, and refused at once. Without thinking you either a fool or disposed to fall in love with every girl you happen to reside with, I do think there is some danger of your forming an attachment which might cause you, and perhaps another person, great pain to break off, or which might hereafter prove embarrassing. Living in the house with three girls, who very probably would vie with each other in their endeavours to please you, would be a severe trial for the impenetrability of so very young a man as you are, and I doubt your standing the test.'

'But I assure you—'

' No doubt you will assure me that you have a heart of stone, and that at all events nothing could induce you to form a connexion with a person beneath you in rank, unworthy the name of Hamilton, or who would be displeasing to your father; but as you have had the good fortune to be the first-born, and consequently will inherit—'

'Pardon me for interrupting you, but I really must set you right on that point,—I am only number two.'

'What! are you not John ?' she asked, hastily.

'Had my name been John, I should not have opened your letter. It was directed to—'

' To Archibald Hamilton—'

'Excuse me, the address was to A. Hamilton, Esq., Goldenen Hirsch, and—'

'True, I ought to have thought of that before,' she said, mustering him from head to foot, while he began to feel some very uncomfortable misgivings. 'Is it—no, it is not possible that you are little Archy?'

'I am *not* little Archy,' cried Hamilton, starting from his seat and instinctively looking towards the door.

'Then, pray, may I ask what *is* your name?' she said, leaning her arm on the table and fixing her eyes on his face with a look of cool deliberation, which completely deprived him of all remaining self-possession.

'Alfred—Alfred Hamilton is my name!' he cried in a voice which he could scarcely recognise to be his own, and unable any longer to endure so unpleasant a situation, he seized his hat and a pair of gloves—which he afterwards found belonged to her —and rushed like a madman out of the room. He heard, or thought he heard, a stifled laugh—no matter—she might laugh if she pleased—he would laugh too ; and he attempted it on reaching his room, but the effort proved totally abortive ; and atter gasping once or twice for breath, he commenced striding up and down the room, talking angrily to himself. 'This is too much; I certainly did not deserve such annoyance! Could I do more to prevent mistakes than send my card and show the letter? The disappointment, too! I rather took a fancy to this A. Z.; had even persuaded myself that I remembered having seen her when I was a child! Pshaw! after all, she must be an artful person: that sort of motherly, good-natured manner, was all affectation to draw me out; and what a precious fool I have made of myself, telling her all my intentions! Of course she and her husband will laugh at me unmercifully, and tell every one in the house! I must leave Seon directly—I—but no, she was not artful! What on earth could be her motive? No, I was altogether to blame myself, or rather that letter!—the letter, the odious letter was the cause of all!' And he tore it angrily to atoms. At all events, this should be a lesson to him: he never would place himself in such a position again as long as he lived.

At twelve o'clock the great bell tolled, and Hamilton knew it was time to descend to dinner. He was busily employed writing, when some one knocked loudly at the door. 'Come in!' he cried, collecting the papers scattered about him; and Baron Z—— entered the room. He burst into a violent fit of laughter on seeing Hamilton's dolorous countenance, shook him heartily by the hand, and assured him he thought him a capital fellow, and had not the smallest doubt that he would make an excellent diplomat.

'But indeed, Baron Z——, I never meant . . . You must not think that I intentionally—'

'Don't explain—pray don't explain—I am so oblige to you! My wife think herself so clever! She write what she call "general terms;" ha! ha! ha! and when she explain to me what mean "general terms," I told to her that pass for one Mr. Hamilton so good as another—but she always think herself so clever!'

'I am extremely distressed—disappointed, I must say, at the frustration of all my hopes. I entreat of you to apologise for me—I leave Seon as soon as possible after dinner—'

'Yes; we leave Seon as soon as possible. I sent Joseph to pack for you while we go to dinner.'

'Am I to understand that you renew your invitation to me after what has occurred?' asked Hamilton, with a feeling of inexpressible pleasure.

'And why not? My wife write and I invite in general terms; and now, Mr. A. Hamilton, Esquire, let us go to dinner.'

'I should wish beforehand to explain—'

'To my wife? Oh, very well; we call for her on the way.'

'Here!' he cried, throwing wide open the door of her apartment, 'here I come to present my friend, Mr. A. Hamilton, Esquire; he wish in general terms to explain to you, and to kiss your hand.'

'The latter part of your speech is composed, Herrmann,' she answered, laughing. 'Mr. Hamilton does not yet know enough of the "Domestic Manners of the Germans," to be aware that kissing a lady's hand is a very common action; here is my hand—it is not, however, worth while blushing about it,' she added, drawing it back again, 'and Herrmann shall be your deputy; it would be difficult to bring a perceptible addition of colour to that sunburnt face.'

He took both her hands, and as he pressed them to his lips, declared he was very content to have such a clever wife!

CHAPTER IV.

A WALK OF NO COMMON DESCRIPTION.

'Do you smoke, Mr. Hamilton?' asked Baron Z——, as he assisted his wife into the carriage.

'I rather like a cigar sometimes.'

'I merely wish to explain to you, that if you wish to smoke now, you had better mount up here,' he said, seating himself on the front seat of the carriage. 'My wife is quite German in every respect, but she has not yet learned to like the smell of tobacco.'

'Nor ever will,' said A. Z.; 'nor shall I ever learn to like having guns so near me. Why are they not packed, as usual, into the long case?'

'You forget you have changed all arrangements since you find that Mr. Hamilton is called Alfred,' said Baron Z——, laughing.

'I only hope they are not loaded,' she said, carefully avoiding their contact. even with the hem of her garment, 'for I have no fancy whatever to have my death announced in the newspapers, after the words, "Dreadful accident!"'

'They are not loaded,' said her husband, puffing strongly from his newly-lighted cigar, as they drove off.

Hamilton was extremely amused at his comical situation, or rather at the events which had led to it, and after a few ineffectual efforts at suppression, he indulged in a fit of laughter, in which A. Z. joined, and it was some time before she could answer Baron Z——'s repeated inquiries as to the cause of their mirth.

' I really don't know, Herrmann, excepting that perhaps Mr. Hamilton is amused at finding himself in our company. By the bye, you do not perhaps know that he speaks very good German.'

' Like an Englishman, eh?'

' His German will prove a better medium of communication than your English, perhaps — but,' — she added quickly, changing the subject and speaking German,—'tell me, did you observe the new arrivals at the *table-d'hôte* to-day? Who are those two pretty girls?'

' Rosenthal, or Rosenberg, I believe, is their name.'

' A decided acquisition, as far as appearance is concerned. The one who sat beside Major Stultz at dinner is really beautiful. Don't you think so?'

' Yes, and Major Stultz thinks so too, I should think; he made prodigious efforts to be agreeable, but could neither obtain a smile nor look during dinner. Had I been in his place I should have tried the other, who is very nearly as pretty, and seems quite disposed to receive any attentions offered to her. I saw her looking towards our end of the table more than once, but could not ascertain whether she looked at me or your friend there.'

' My friend seems rather disposed to appropriate the looks, if I may judge from that rising blush.'

' By no means,' cried Hamilton; ' my acquaintance with the young lady is of very recent date.'

' I did not know there was any acquaintance whatever,' said A. Z.

' It scarcely deserves the name. We travelled part of the way from Munich together: their carriage was desperately crowded, and I proposed taking some of the travellers. Mademoiselle Crescenz, the nursery-maid, and a kicking-boy, called Peppy, were consigned to my care.'

' Such civility was very unusual on the part of an Englishman ; at least our countrymen are here generally supposed to
be selfish when travelling,' observed A. Z.

'Perhaps my motives were not quite free from an alloy of
selfishness : I rather dreaded the *ennui* of a long afternoon
alone in an uncomfortable carriage ; and besides, I was in search
of an adventure.'

' How did it turn out ?'

' Oh, we got on famously until we reached Seon ; but from
the moment Mademoiselle Crescenz saw her stepmother, her
manner totally changed ; so I concluded she intended to decline
my acquaintance, now that I could be of no further use to
her.'

'Your conclusion proved how very little you know of German girls in her rank of life.'

' Should one interpret these Germans by contraries ?'

' *Cela dépend.*'

'Perhaps, then, her sister intends to be very civil to me—
our acquaintance began by her calling me a fool ; and I overheard her saying to her sister, that I seemed to have an
uncommonly good opinion of myself, and looked like an
overgrown schoolboy.'

' There is no possibility of mistaking such demonstrations,'
said A. Z., smiling, and evidently controlling an inclination to
laugh, extremely displeasing to Hamilton.

'You seem,' he said, somewhat distrustfully, 'you seem
amused—perhaps at my expressing your thoughts in the words
of another person?'

' What I thought of you on your first appearance—'

'I already know. You thought me a long-legged bashful
animal : at least you said so to Baron Z——.'

'At that time I fancied I had a sort of right to criticise;
and had you really proved to be John or Archy, as I supposed,
you might have often been favoured with equally flattering
observations ; I should have considered you a sort of relation,
and you would, undoubtedly, have thought me a great bore.
Now the case is different, and I shall treat you with all possible respect ; but you must allow me to laugh, and promise
not to be offended at every idle word—'

'Offended!—oh, no! I should be extremely delighted if
you would act towards me as if I were John or Archy.'

'You are too young to appreciate such treatment—and – I

don't feel disposed unnecessarily to undertake the part of Mentor.'

' You fear the task would prove too troublesome?'

' Not exactly that—I rather like giving advice ; but—'

' You think I should do you no credit?'

' I really do not know, nor do I mean to try. Your search for adventures may bring you into some embarrassments which may not always turn out so well as on the present occasion.'

' My good fortune on the present occasion has been so extraordinary that I shall tempt fate no farther: my plan is formed. I shall spend the winter in Munich, studying German and the Germans. In the domestic circle of a private family—'

' Where there are no boys ?' asked A. Z.

' As a proof of my deference to your opinion, I shall make no objection even to five boys ; and also promise to avoid a widow with unmarried daughters.'

' I have some hope of you now !'

' Will you then be my Mentor during my sojourn in Germany ?'

' No.'

' But you said you liked giving advice.'

' And so I do : it is, you know, the only thing that everybody is disposed to give, and nobody likes to take. Ask my advice, and I shall give it ; although I know beforehand you will not make use of it.'

' Just as much as either John or Archy.'

' No such thing ! My advice to them would have been enforced by a little delegated parental authority, not to mention the probability of their having, from hearsay, very exalted ideas of my wisdom.'

' I doubt if their ideas on that subject could possibly be more exalted than mine.'

' Very appropriately answered—you really are an extremely promising young man !'

Hamilton bit his lip and blushed ; there was something in her manner so mocking, so unequivocally ironical, that he felt mortified ; his silent irritation betraying itself in spite of all his endeavours at concealment.

' You are offended,' she observed quietly, after a pause, ' and offended without any cause. I have, all my life, had a particular antipathy to very young men—it is quite impossible to talk to them without making remarks which they consider derogatory to their dignity. I did not mean to annoy you, and recall my words; instead of a *promising*, I now think you an *irritable*, young man. Does that please you better?'

'Infinitely better,' he answered, laughing;—'if not the words, certainly the manner is preferable. I can bear anything but being turned into ridicule.'

'What you now call ridicule will a few years hence take the name of badinage; but let us talk of something else, or still better—suppose we read. Here is the last "Allgemeine Zeitung," or "Blackwood's Magazine."'

'Do you take "Blackwood"?' inquired Hamilton.

'I get it and any books I wish for from the royal library. No one can be more magnificently liberal than the King of Bavaria, in this respect. When you go to Munich your banker can sign papers making himself answerable for any books which may be lost or injured while in your possession; and this is the only formality necessary to insure you the unlimited use of a library containing upwards of eight hundred thousand volumes.'

'But you do not mean to say that I, a foreigner, may take the books home with me?'

'Your ideas are too English to comprehend such liberality, and so were mine when I first came to Munich; but the fact is, you may take the books to your own apartment and read them at your leisure. Of course, you must be careful not to injure them in any way.'

'But if many people enjoy this privilege the books must be spoiled in time.'

'You think, perhaps, it would be wiser if the eight hundred thousand volumes were put into glass book-cases, and merely exhibited to strangers, instead of being placed at their disposition? As far as I can judge, however, from personal observation, the books are not either spoiled or even soiled; at least, none I have ever required; and you see,' she said, removing a paper cover from one of them, 'they are very nicely bound.'

'Do you read a great deal?' he asked.

'I once thought so, but on referring to the list of books actually read at the end of the year, it was so insignificant that I now make no pretension to being what is called a reader— a few memoirs, travels, an occasional novel, and the newspapers, fill up my time completely. But, now you really must take a

book, or admire the country in silence, for I cannot allow my
" Allgemeine Zeitung " to remain longer unread.   I have only
time for one each day, and I get into a fit of despair when they
accumulate.'

'I think if you won't talk to me I should like to smoke a
cigar.'

'A most excellent idea !   Take the coachman's place beside
Herrmann, who. I am sure, will willingly drive in order to have
the pleasure of your company.   You can talk over your intended expedition, and boast of the quantity of grouse you
would have shot had you been at home this August.'

The day had already closed as they drew near the little
village of Siegsdorf ; lights glanced gaily from the windows
of the houses, and from the small inn the sound of singing and
laughter was wafted far and wide.

'I don't think we could do better than stop here for the night,'
observed Baron Z——, turning abruptly to his wife.

'I expected some such proposition as soon as I heard the
sound of the zither,' she answered.

'May I ?' he asked, playing with the whip, while the horses,
apparently unwilling to pass by a stable, the comforts of which
they had probably experienced on a former occasion, turned of
their own accord into the roughly-paved yard, and stopped at
the door of the inn.

The landlady made her way with some difficulty through the
passage, which was crowded with peasants, to the door, where
she stood to receive the travellers, her rotundity of figure placed
in strong relief by the light behind her.   Baron Z—— merrily
returned the innumerable salutations made him, as, followed by
his wife and Hamilton, he led the way to a room reserved for
guests of the higher classes.   One table was still unoccupied,
and the landlady having with her apron swept away the crumbs
of bread, and removed some empty glasses which were upon
it, placed chairs, and asked what they chose for supper.

'I have part of a chamois in the house : perhaps the gentleman would like a ragout of it ?'

'Should you like some chamois for supper ?' asked A. Z.,
turning to Hamilton.

'Oh, of all things,' he answered, eagerly.

'It is rather a dry kind of meat,' she continued ; 'I have
eaten it but twice myself—once from curiosity, the second
time from—necessity.   You remember, Herrmann ?'

' Yes; when we came out of Tyrol and went to the Klamm. I think we ought to show, at least, one of the Klamms to Mr. Hamilton. An expedition of that kind will be something new to him, and a day more or less is of no consequence to us.'

'I am sure you are very kind,' said Hamilton, delighted at the word 'expedition,' but not in the least knowing what he was to see.

'We might have the carriage to meet us at Unken, and our landlady will get us the key of the woodman's house.'

The landlady nodded assent.

'And cold chickens and tongues, and coffee, and all those sort of things. I shall take guides from Ruhpolding.'

'Herr Baron!' cried a tall peasant who had been leaning against the half-open door and listening attentively to every word that had been said,—'Herr Baron! you promised to employ me the next time you went there; I could go to Traunstein for the key to-night, and meet you in Ruhpolding to-morrow.'

' Off with you, then!' cried Baron Z——, 'and be sure to be there at five o'clock to-morrow.'

' Or at half-past six,' said A. Z.; 'and don't forget to take the largest bags you can find.'

The man nodded his head, scraped one of his heavy shoes upon the floor, and disappeared.

Baron Z—— took up a guitar which was lying on the table, and commenced singing Tyrolean songs with such spirit and humour, that his audience unanimously joined in chorus, each taking the part suiting his voice with a precision so surprising to Hamilton, that he asked A. Z. if they had often sung together before.

' Never that I am aware of,' she answered, examining more attentively the singers; 'I do not think Herrmann is acquainted with even one of them.'

The music within seemed to inspire some musicians without, for no sooner had it ceased than the gay notes of a zither were heard; an instrument which Hamilton had never seen, and which A. Z. told him was well worth the trouble of an examination. He was about to leave the room for the purpose, when he met the landlady carrying in the soup for supper; he stopped embarrassed, but Baron Z——, without further ceremony, called in the peasant who was the best performer, and gave him a place beside him at the table. The man tuned his zither, and began to play what he called ' *Laendlers,*' perhaps from the word land or country—simple waltzes, to which the peasants dance, and which A. Z. assured Hamilton, when accompanied by a guitar, and the time beaten by the dancing of feet and snapping of fingers, at a target-shooting match, or a wedding, was the very gayest music she had ever heard.

They were all in high spirits the next morning when they met soon after sunrise, for the weather promised to be extremely fine, indeed sultry, if an unclouded sky at so early an hour might be depended upon. Hamilton was, therefore, not a little surprised at the number of cloaks and shawls with which the carriage was lumbered, and at Baron Z——'s dress. He had on the same grey shooting-jacket and green felt hat in which he had first seen him—but he had also black knee-breeches and worsted stockings drawn half way up his thighs, but which were so elastic that they could be pushed below the knees, where, clinging to the legs, they formed folds at a distance resembling top-boots. A large pouch hung at his side, and in his hand he carried a long pole with an iron point. Hamilton was also given one as he got into the carriage, and they drove off amidst the heartiest wishes for good weather and the enjoyment of it.

'Mr. Hamilton would have got on better without straps and with thicker boots,' observed Baron Z——.

'It is of no consequence, for to-day we have scarcely any ascent, if I remember right,' answered his wife.

'I ought to have equipped him,' cried Baron Z——, laughing. 'How do you think he would look?'

'As he is considerably taller than you are—there would be at least half a yard of leg uncovered.'

'The dress is certainly very becoming,' observed Hamilton, 'but I cannot imagine it particularly comfortable.'

'If you had to climb you would find it as comfortable as becoming,' answered Baron Z——, 'and that it is judicious admits of no doubt; all mountaineers have something similar, and you may be sure the dress was originally adopted for its convenience. It is unquestionably advantageous, having the knees uncovered in ascending and descending mountains.'

'And the monstrous shoes—' began Hamilton.

'Give a steadier footing, and preserve the feet from the pointed stones or rocks.'

'I remember,' said A. Z., 'the first time I ascended an alp I wore thin shoes and silk stockings; I came home nearly barefoot, of course, and with quite a new idea of an alp!'

'Oh, pray do give me some idea of one,' cried Hamilton; 'I —I must confess I have none whatever, for when people talk of alps, I cannot help thinking of *the* Alps.'

'I am not surprised at your question, for I doubt if the word be in the dictionary with the meaning attached to it here. People call the pasture lands on the hills, or lower parts of the mountains, "alps." Almost every farmer of any importance has one to which he sends the greater part of his cattle during the summer months, and there butter and cheese are made for the winter. Where the alps are extensive they are held by several persons, and instead of one little wooden residence, there are sometimes twenty or thirty.'

'A sort of an inhabited common, perhaps?'

'By no means. They are inherited or bought, or given in leases, and are sometimes very valuable.'

'The view from them is, of course, very extensive,' observed Hamilton.

'Generally, or I should not have been on so many.'

'And I,' said Baron Z——, 'always endeavour to pass the night on one of them when I am on a hunting expedition, for, besides the chance of a few hours' sleep in a hay-loft, one can warm oneself at a good fire, and breakfast before daybreak. You shall see an alp, and a chamois hunt also, if I can manage it, before you return to Seon.'

'I have no doubt of being able to mount any alp you please,' said Hamilton, 'but for a person who is not a good shot to undertake anything so dangerous as a chamois hunt——'

'Danger! There is no danger whatever.'

'No danger! Why, I have read frightful accounts of chamois hunts!'

'Read! Oh, so have I—and I don't deny that an accident may occur occasionally. In Switzerland, for instance, where the chase is free, the chamois have become so scarce and shy, that they have taken refuge in the highest parts of the mountains. There, and perhaps in those parts of Tyrol where they are only nominally protected, they are difficult to be got at—but in the neighbourhood of Berchtesgaden, Ischl, and Steyermark, a chamois is not much more difficult to shoot than a stag or a roebuck.'

'But,' said A. Z., 'you must confess that people always think more and talk more of a chamois hunt than any other. You would rather, I am sure, shoot a chamois than a deer!'

'That is true, but there is no use in making more of it than is necessary. Mr. Hamilton, with his present ideas, will be greatly disappointed, I fear.'

'No, for I was just going to tell him that I have been on mountains where the chamois have been seen springing from rock to rock in places to which I could easily have mounted if I had put on a pair of *steigeisen.*'

'What is that? What are they?'

'I scarcely know how to describe them; they look like pat-tens at a distance, and are buckled over the shoes in the same manner, but they are provided with four strong iron spikes, to enable you to plant your feet steadily in the ground or in the fissures of the rocks.'

'That's it!' cried Hamilton. '*They* were also in the description which I read.'

'Do not have too exalted an idea of the danger on that account,' answered A. Z., laughing; 'for I have heard that many people who inhabit the mountainous parts of this country use them when they walk on the snow in winter.'

'So, after all,' said Hamilton, 'a chamois hunt is quite a common sort of thing!'

'You are falling into the contrary extreme now,' said Baron Z——; 'for though it is no uncommon thing, strong sinews, good lungs, a quick eye, and a steady hand are always required in order to be successful.'

They arrived at Ruhpolding, and found their guides waiting for them—tall, strong-looking men, with sunburnt faces and bushy mustachios. Their dress was of coarser materials but in other respects quite resembling Baron Z——'s, excepting that their grey stockings, with a fanciful pattern in green, were short, and left their knees perfectly bare. On their shoulders were slung canvas bags, into which they imme-diately packed the cloaks, shawls, and provisions of every description.

A couple of miles beyond Ruhpolding the carriage was aban-doned, and the party commenced their expedition on a footway through the Fischbach Valley. The vegetation around them was of the richest colouring, the mossy grass under the trees of the deepest green, and wild berberry-trees, with their delicate leaves and pendant crimson berries, grew luxuriantly in every direction. A variety of beautifully delicate wild flowers pleased Hamilton's eye, but he looked on with some impatience, while A. Z. and her husband leisurely gathered and examined some, took others up by the roots, and placed all in a tin box, evidently brought for the purpose. Long and serious, too, were the discussions about them, which, as Hamilton did not understand, he was glad when, in contrast to this scene of fertility, their way brought them to the immediate base of the mountain, where it ran parallel with the dry bed of a torrent, almost deserving the name of river when, in spring, it rushes from its snowy source, sweeping away heaps of stones and trunks of torn-up trees, which, thrown high on either side, leave the valley between a scene of stony desolation. They continued for a considerable time between the almost perpendicular sides of the mountains, sometimes climbing over colossal masses of stone, at others enjoying the shade of the thick pine-trees or overhanging rocks, when, on passing an abrupt turn, a foaming waterfall seemed suddenly to prevent all further progress, for, after passing over the very path they were pursuing, it bounded from the rocks, which sometimes arrested, but could not impede, its progress, until having half exhausted itself in spray, it reached a solid bed of stone, and finally disappeared among the dark green fir-trees of the narrow valley below.

While Hamilton looked in silent admiration down the precipice, A. Z., her husband, and the two guides disappeared in the cavity of the rock behind the waterfall, and seemed greatly to enjoy his surprise when he discovered them sitting under the trees at the other side. While one of the guides unpacked his canvas bag, and laid the contents on the nearest rock, Hamilton joined them, and they remained beside the waterfall more than an hour, enjoying their frugal repast while resting in the shade, and tranquillised almost to laziness by the sound of the rushing waters. Baron Z—— was, of course, the first to move.

'Ah, there is a *châlet!*' exclaimed Hamilton, pointing towards some small wooden buildings on a green hill before them; below which a second waterfall, forming natural cisterns in the rocks, fell in cascades from one to the other. 'A *châlet* at last!'

'We call them *senner* huts here,' said A. Z. 'When men

have the charge of the cattle they are called *senners*; when women, *sennerins*. Let us go to where that girl is standing at the door of her hut; she seems an acquaintance of our guide's. These *sennerins*,' she continued, looking attentively at the one who was now about to supply them with cheese and butter,— 'these *sennerins* are the theme of almost all the national poetry and songs here in the mountains.'

'They would not inspire me,' said Hamilton, laughing. 'I see nothing very poetical about them, if this one may be taken as a specimen.'

'You do not understand their manners or mode of life,' said Baron Z——. 'Their isolated situation and primitive occupations are poetical—these mountains and endless forests are poetical—there is poetry in the sound of the bell, which answers to every movement of the grazing cow—in the tinkling of the little bells which, like castanets, denote the quicker motions of the goats!'

'True,' said A. Z., 'and you would find that round-faced, thick-legged girl picturesque, if not poetical, could we remain long enough for you to hear her singing to assemble her herd, and see her surrounded by her cows and goats this evening.'

'Shall we not pass the night in one of these sort of huts?' asked Hamilton.

'Not in a *senner* hut,' replied Baron Z——. 'It is the woodmen and foresters' *châlet* to which we are going; the ground is Austrian, but the woods are Bavarian; and it is through the Klamm that the wood is drifted for the salt-works at Reichenhall.'

'Through the Klamm,' repeated Hamilton, slowly and musingly.

'You look as if you did not know what the word Klamm meant,' observed A. Z.

'I must confess I do not, although I looked for it yesterday in my pocket-dictionary. The explanation was a spasm in the throat; or, close, solid, narrow—'

'Exactly,' said A. Z. 'The Klamm which we are now going to see is a long narrow passage made by a stream of water through a mountain of solid rock; but now let us move on, or we shall have to inspect it by torchlight.'

They all hurried forward towards the ascent before them and would probably have felt considerably fatigued had not the continual change in the scenery created unceasing interest.

E

Here and there a peasant's house, with its overhanging wooden roof, gave life to a picture that with all its sunshine would otherwise have been desolate in its loneliness, for no human being was visible. It seemed extraordinary that the ground was so highly cultivated, for road there was none; nor did there seem to be any communication with the world but by a narrow, and in some places rather dangerous, footway. Cattle were to be seen farther up the mountains, on those green spots of turf described by A. Z., and which are to be found sometimes even among the bare crags. These pastures can only be used for a short time in summer; and as the weather grows colder in autumn the cattle are driven down lower, until finally they are brought home for the winter, covered with garlands of wild flowers! While Baron Z—— was enthusiastically describing 'A return from the alp,' they had begun to descend into the valley, and already heard the sound of rushing water. Magnificent masses of rock prepared them for the cavern, into which they entered by a natural arch, over which, carved in the stone, are the words:

> ' Gutta cavat lapidem, non vi sed sæpe cadendo,
> 1833.'

'So the cave is altogether formed by the action of the water,' observed Hamilton, looking upwards.

'Altogether, as you will soon perceive,' replied Baron Z——. 'Some years ago this was a wild place, and frightful accidents often occurred, until our king had a way made through it for the convenience and safety of the persons employed in the drifting of the wood.'

The narrow bridge-like way of which he spoke was composed of strong beams and planks; and in the twilight which always reigns in the vaulted tunnel, it appears to hang suspended in the air, being supported by iron cramps driven into the solid rock. Underneath the water rages, and above the daylight enters sparingly by a few small isolated openings.

'One could fancy this the abode of the " Wild Huntsman,"' said A. Z.

'I know nothing of the wild huntsman,' said Hamilton, 'excepting from the scenery in "Der Freyschutz." Everything I have seen to-day, but most of all this wild cavern, reminds me of it. I should rather like to be here on a stormy night, to hear the wind whistling through these arches.

Although not very imaginative, I do think I could almost bring the wild huntsman to my view, just here where the sky begins to be visible.'

'Instead of the wild huntsman substitute the forester when he opens the sluices to let the wood drift through,' said Baron Z——. 'Fancy the rushing and roaring of the pent-up torrent, the dashing of the trunks of trees against these rocks, the terrific noise increased by the echo—'

'Oh, how I should like to see it!' exclaimed Hamilton, eagerly.

'I prefer a quiet sunset like the present,' said A. Z., beginning to ascend the steps which led out of the cavern. 'I can imagine what you have described, and acknowledge that wild weather heightens the effect of scenery such as this ; but still just in such places I particularly enjoy the repose of nature ; there is no tameness in it, for the possible change which may take place is ever unconsciously before the mind's eye.'

'That may be true,' said Hamilton, thoughtfully. 'I have seen but little wild scenery—never anything resembling this, excepting, as I said before, at the theatre, where I looked upon everything as very fine, but very impossible.'

'Few people in England are aware how very true to nature the "Freyschutz" is ; put the wild huntsman and the charmed bullets aside, and every target-shooting match in the mountains will bring the scenery and actors before you. Weber was in the habit of frequenting such places, and listening for hours to the untutored singers and zither players.'

'Who have we here?' cried Baron Z——, as they came within view of the woodmen's house, and he perceived several persons moving backwards and forwards.

They were strangers, and considered themselves such in a double sense—for they were Austrians! While A. Z. was explaining the extraordinary fact of Bavarians considering themselves foreigners in Austria, and *vice versâ*, Baron Z—— had entered into conversation with them, and a few minutes sufficed for him to guess the name of one who said he was there on business ; and from him he heard all he required about the others.

The supper, composed of the most heterogeneous materials, was eaten under the trees near the house, and it was not until late that they took refuge from the night air in the kitchen of the *châlet*, where a bright fire burned on the high open hearth which, like a long table, occupied the middle of the room, with wooden benches round it. A zither was found in the house and a young student, with long fair hair flowing over his black velvet coat, who had brought a guitar, slung troubadour-fashion over his shoulders, sang directly he was requested. A quartette was also soon arranged, and Hamilton, seated in a corner out of the glare of the fire, contemplated the party in silence.

At daybreak the next morning, long before the sun's ray could reach them, they were again in the Klamm, and passing through it, found another and much easier way than that of the previous day, which brought them to Unken. There they parted from their acquaintance of the evening before, who surrounded their carriage, bowing and shaking hands with a mixture of formality and friendliness which afforded A. Z and Hamilton subject of conversation for some time, the former observing, that had two English parties met in the same way they would never have joined so cordially, and instead of conducing to each other's amusement, would most probably have sat apart reciprocally watching to detect whatever was disagreeable or vulgar. 'I, for my part,' she continued, 'was exceedingly well satisfied with my companions, who were very communicative, and related a great many interesting particulars of their mode of life in Tyrol. I have promised to visit them should I ever be in their neighbourhood; their father is forester, and the eldest is engaged to be married to that silent shy man in the green shooting-jacket. However, he was not too shy to wait for her at the foot of the ladder, when he supposed we were all asleep.'

'So they really did take a walk by moonlight!'

'The moonlight did not last long; and I do not believe they went farther than the bench outside the door, where they found more company than they expected. Romantic feelings and sentimental contemplations are not confined to German women; there are few men here who would not sacrifice a few hours' rest on an occasion like yesterday to sit—and smoke in the moonbeams.'

'How ingeniously you always contrive to alloy your praise of us,' said her husband, laughing.

'And yet I am strict to truth; for the fumes of cigars ascended with the murmuring of voices last night to my window, and obliged me to close it.'

'Well, we shall have nothing of the kind to-night, as we are likely to be alone on the alp.'

'I have been thinking it would be as well if we were to go to Berchtesgaden, and sleep comfortably in beds; I do not feel quite equal to another night passed on the hay.'

CHAPTER V.

AN ALP.

To Berchtesgaden they went. We shall not follow Hamilton either when he inspected the saltworks, or visited the beautiful lakes in its immediate neighbourhood; nor would we accompany him to the alp, which he afterwards ascended, were it not to give our readers a slight idea of those excursions so common in the mountainous parts of Bavaria, and of the little importance attached to a chamois hunt. They were unceremoniously joined in their expedition by a number of hunters, foresters, and some officers who were on leave of absence. A. Z. went with them very willingly, as she heard that an acquaintance of hers was spending a few weeks on the alp for her health, enjoying what is called '*Sommerfrisch*;' and, in fact, on reaching the *châlet*, which was situated in the midst of the mountains, they found a very nice-looking, sunburnt person, sitting with her maid before the door. She was surprised to see the Z——'s, but not in the least to see the others, as she said scarcely a week passed that some one did not come to hunt; and on hearing that Hamilton spoke German, she pointed upwards towards the rocks before the house, and said that in the evening he would see the chamois leaping about there.

'She is destroying all the mystery of a chamois hunt,' said Hamilton, turning to A. Z. 'I could run up that mountain, I think.'

'I would not advise you to try it, nor, indeed, can I consent to your making any excursion on the mountains alone as long as you are travelling with us. Violent deaths are not at all uncommon here: it is not long since a girl gathering herbs fell over a precipice and was dashed to pieces; and a man was found nearly starved to death in a place to which he had climbed, but from which he found it impossible to extricate himself. That old man,' she added, lowering her voice, 'that old *Jäger*, who is now speaking to Hermann, had some dispute with his only son when they were on a chamois hunt together; people say, that a push from him in the heat of argument precipitated the young man thousands of feet below; his body was found in a dreadfully mutilated state, but there was no evidence against the old man, for they had been alone, and as such accidents are but too common, the exact state of the case has never been ascertained, and his confessor alone knows what happened.'

'Well, Hamilton, are you disposed to try a shot this evening?' asked Baron Z——; 'three or four chamois have been seen in the neighbourhood.'

'I shall go with you as a looker-on; but as I am a very bad shot, I think one of these poles will be of more use to me than a rifle.'

'We shall send some men up to beat them down to us,' said Baron Z——. 'There is no use in climbing more than is necessary.'

'Can you not use dogs?' asked Hamilton.

'They could never be properly trained, for although the chamois do not in the least mind the clattering of stones or gravel, any unusual sound immediately attracts their attention. A solitary hunter has only to avoid this, and to take care that the wind blows in his face, or, at least, not from him in the direction where he expects to find them. Their scent is something almost incredible, and only equalled by their shyness.'

'It is, after all, a very difficult shot,' said Hamilton.

'Only where they have been hunted until they have taken refuge in the most inaccessible places; for it has been proved that the chamois have no remarkable preference for very high or cold mountains—they only choose them in order to have a good retreat among the rocks when pursued.'

'That I observed too, last year,' said an officer who was of the party, 'at Prince Lamberg's, where there is the best chamois hunting in Germany, perhaps. They were there so well preserved that they were not more shy or difficult to shoot than other game: and instead of their only being to be found in the evening or at dawn, they rambled about all day, and when the weather was mild did not even seek the shade.'

'I have heard of Prince Lamberg's mountains,' said Baron Z——; 'he has fifteen or sixteen hundred chamois on them, I hear; but after all, when one can have them without much trouble one does not value them so highly; for instance I shot a chamois some years ago, in Bayrishzell, but was out nearly twenty-four hours before I got a shot—here is his beard, which I have preserved and worn ever since,' he added, taking off his hat and showing a little fan-like ornament which Hamilton had before observed without knowing its value.

' Then they have beards like goats ?' said Hamilton.

' No,' replied Baron Z——. ' This is called a beard, but it is the hair which grows along the back.'

' I see something very like a chamois up there,' said the officer, who held a small telescope to his eye.

Every one wished to look—some could not find the place—others imagined they saw *something*—one thought it was the stump of a tree—but some practised eyes having pronounced it to be the desired animals feeding, the party broke up and the chase began.

Hamilton climbed with an ease and lightness which surprised his companions, but he so often stopped to admire a handsome beech-tree, or to 'seek for fresh evening air in the opening glades,' that they by degrees went on, and he found himself at last alone on a spot where some convulsion of Nature had split the mountain partly asunder. He saw far, far beneath him the road into Tyrol : the heavy-laden waggons, which a few days before he had thought packed dangerously high, now wound, pigmy-like, along, the motion of the endless team of horses scarcely perceptible. Hill rose beyond hill, until the prospect was bounded by the grotesque masses of rocks which, rising from the wooded mountains, increase their gigantic appearance by their partial concealment behind those light wreaths of clouds which seldom entirely desert their summits. For the inhabitants of the valley, the sun had long disappeared, but around Hamilton everything was still in the glow of sunset : he seated himself on the mossy turf and deliberately resigned himself to contemplation. No place could have been better chosen, and he was therefore surprised and disappointed to find that the sublime thoughts which he had expected did not present themselves to his mind. He admired the surpassing luxuriance of the vegetation in the valleys, the different-coloured foliage of the trees ; the wild irregular course of the foaming river ;—he tried to think of the greatness of the Creator in His works, the insignificance of man and his endeavours—·in vain. An agreeable feeling of general satisfaction stole over him, while fancy conveyed him home to

his family, to his youthful friends. A handsome English residence rose before him, with well-kept lawns, gravelled walks,
and shrubberies; groups of people were visible among the
trees, and on the steps leading to the hall-door a large party
was assembled. Carriages and riding-horses were there;
laughing girls in their long habits, young men carelessly loitering near them. They were to visit a well-*preserved* ruin
in the neighbourhood — so often seen, it is true, that everything was thought of more than the nominal object. Camp-
stools, servants in livery, champagne and pineapples began
to chase each other in pleasing confusion before Hamilton's
mind's eye — when the distant report of a gun destroyed the
'baseless fabric' of his waking 'vision,' and he started up,
remembering with some amazement that he was engaged in a
chamois hunt ! 'It is of little consequence,' he thought, 'for
had I fired ten times, I should never have hit one.'

He plunged into the wood, and commenced a regular
and steady ascent, which he continued even after the
fir-tree had begun to dwindle into a dwarfy shrub, and
the beautiful wild rhododendron had disappeared altogether.
His path became steeper and more rocky, and at length
he was reduced to the necessity of creeping round the
intervening obstacles, and of supporting himself by the few
plants which vegetated among the fissures of the rocks. Not
a sound broke the silence around him; the moon slowly rose
above the darkening horizon, which was slightly streaked
with a faint crimson tinge, leaving on the dim grey of the
mountain tops the still perceptible reflection of the fading
sunlight. The valleys were in the deepest shade, and from
the dispersed peasant-houses lights began to twinkle. Hamilton
looked carefully round him to ascertain, if possible, his position, before he descended into the thick wood which lay beneath
him. The falling of some loose stones and a fragment of rock
in his vicinity made him start, but immediately supposing it to
be some of his former companions, he called out, that if any
one were there, he wished they would wait for him : a clattering of stones and scampering ensued, accompanied by a sharp
sound, perfectly incomprehensible to him, until, on a projecting
rock far above him, he perceived three chamois, standing in
strong relief between him and the cloudless sky, and gazing
irresolutely around them. They allowed him to examine them
for some time, as well as the distance and moonlight would

admit, but as he endeavoured to approach nearer they suddenly
sprang up the rocks, and sending a shower of stones and
sand over him, disappeared in a few seconds. By this time he
had lost all idea of where he might be, and although extremely
unwilling to increase his distance from the *châlet*, he saw
the absolute necessity of still climbing in order to see into
the Alpine valley in which it was situated. Perfectly unacquainted with the irregularities of the mountain, he kept as
much as possible in the light, following occasionally what he
supposed to be paths, but which were in fact the stony beds
of the mountain rivulets, formed by the thawing snow in
spring. He wandered on in this manner, sometimes ascending,
sometimes descending, for more than two hours, looking round
in every direction, but not a trace could he find of the *châlet*,
nor, indeed, at last, of any habitation whatever. On reaching
a part of the ridge of the mountain, he was somewhat startled
to find that the other side descended in a perpendicular precipice of rock, apparently so smooth and destitute of verdure
that it might be supposed a wall. He stopped,—and all A. Z.
had said to him recurred at once to his memory. The moon
was still too young to remain visible to him much longer, and
it would be totally dark by the time he reached the wood;
he saw no alternative but to stay where he was until morning,
and had actually chosen a place of repose, when the distant
sound of guns, fired at regular intervals, made him imagine
that he, and no longer the chamois, was the object of pursuit.
A faint echo of human voices, too, reached his ear, and he
shouted loudly in answer. A frightfully distinct echo from
the mountain opposite made him desist; he feared that his
deliverers might be misled, and he now hurried along in the
direction from whence the welcome sounds had first reached
him. Keeping on the top of the mountain, and avoiding any
place where the shadows of the rocks prevented him from
seeing his way distinctly, he walked and ran, and sprang and
vaulted with his long pole, until the moon disappearing behind
a mountain created a sort of half-night, which again forced
him to halt. Suspecting that the echo had misled him, and
fearing that he was farther than ever from his companions,
he perceived without regret the gradual cessation of the
treacherous sounds, and at length, with a sort of desperate
English calmness, he seated himself on the ground, and after
a few not very successful efforts to place himself comfortably

against a sandy bank, he took a cigar, lighted it, and crossing
his arms, resigned himself to his fate. The night proved
darker than he had expected, and he gazed on the starry
firmament until his thoughts became confused, and his eyes
closed in heavy slumber, which remained unbroken until the
cold breeze of breaking day caused a chill to pass through his
stiffening limbs. He rose, and looked about him with some
astonishment for some minutes, and then, with long strides,
began a rapid descent.

Great was afterwards his annoyance to find that instead of
arriving, as he had expected, at the *châlet*, he had quite reached
the base of the mountain, and that merely a narrow ravine
separated him from another of precisely the same description.
He stood for a moment irresolute, and felt—very hungry.
The sun had begun to colour vividly the eastern sky, and,
after a little consideration, he found that returning to the alp
would oblige him to mount again, and he was still very
uncertain in what direction it lay ; whereas, if he took another
course, he would probably in an hour or two find some opening
into one of the surrounding roads, where he could enter the
first peasant's house he should see, and procure something to
eat. In this conjecture he was perfectly right. Sooner than
he had dared to hope, a cheerful house, prettily situated on a
green hill, and surrounded by fruit-trees, rejoiced his eyes.
Some wild sunburnt little boys and girls announced his
approach, and when he came to the door he found a large
family assembled. His wants were soon made known ; and a
table, placed before the wooden bench which ran along the
front of the house, was soon covered with a rustic, but not
frugal, breakfast. An enormous loaf of dark-brown bread, a
basin of milk, covered with thick yellow cream, some pounds
of butter, honey, and cheese, fried eggs, and a sort of mashed-
up *omelette*, called *schmarn*. While Hamilton was eating,
the peasant's wife stood near, her youngest child on her arm,
and a couple of others leaning against her. She assured him,
if he had not been in such a hurry she could have made some
coffee for him ; she always bought coffee at the fair, and drank
it every Sunday ! She was so sorry her husband was not at
home, but she expected him every moment ; he had gone up
to the alp at daybreak with fresh rolls for the breakfast of the
gentlemen who had been out shooting.

As she spoke, a loud gay voice was heard in the distance

jodling, and the children all rushed down the hill and disappeared in the wood.

'That is probably your husband,' said Hamilton; 'I shall be glad to hear what sport they have had on the alp.'

'Oh! you were there, too—perhaps—I have been thinking and thinking where you could have spent the night; you did not look as if you had come from the town!'

'I dare say not,' said Hamilton, laughing; 'most probably I look as if I had spent the night among the rocks, and that is actually the case: I lost my way yesterday evening.'

The peasant soon after joined them, and to Hamilton's eager inquiries as to the result of the hunt, he replied that a chamois had been shot in the evening, but that the disappearance of a young Englishman who had gone out with them had spoiled everything; they had searched for him until dark, and that Baron Z—— had been out to look for him before daybreak; even the ladies had joined in searching, and one of them had been up nearly to the top of one of the mountains with the goatherd.

'Good heavens!' cried Hamilton, springing on his feet, 'they are searching for me. I must go to them directly.'

'It will do just as well if I send Peter to let them know you are here,' said the peasant, calling one of his sons and giving him the necessary directions: after which, murmuring the words, 'with your leave,' he seated himself at a little distance, and glancing towards Hamilton's outstretched feet, he observed with a smile, 'You would never have got up and down the alp again with those boots!'

'I believe you are right,' answered Hamilton, listlessly moving them so as to have a better view—'they certainly do look the worse for the wear. I never was so ill-shod in my life!'

'I dare say yesterday you might have danced at a wedding in them, but for the mountains they are not the right sort.'

'Most true,' said Hamilton, 'and if I ever make an excursion of this kind again, I shall not forget it. This is the first time in my life that I have been in a mountainous country.'

'And yet England is a fine country, they say?' observed the peasant, interrogatively.

Hamilton assented with a nod.

'I have heard it said at the Golden Lion in the town, that there is no end to the riches of the English!'

'Some are very rich, and some are very poor,' answered Hamilton; 'I believe the means of living—the necessaries of life—are more equally divided among the inhabitants of Germany.'

'Well, that I have heard too,' said the man: 'and now that you tell me there are no mountains—'

'Stay,' cried Hamilton, laughing, 'I did not say that there were no mountains; I only said that I had never seen them.'

'But all the Englishmen I have ever spoken to—'

'Are not very many,' said Hamilton, interrupting him.

'More than you think, perhaps. Before my father gave up the house and ground to me, I was for many years with a relation in Berchtesgaden, and used to row most of the strangers across the lake. Queer people they were, too, sometimes! One Englishman used to sit for hours under a tree near the back lake, and went there regularly every day for several summers; he looked half-dead, with his pale face and sunken cheeks, and it was dreadful to hear him cough: the people at the inn said he never was quiet at night, but wandered incessantly up and down his room. They said he must have been crossed in love—'

'Most probably he was dying of consumption,' said Hamilton.

'Very likely; that was what the doctor called it. He said it was a very common complaint in England—like the rheumatism here, I suppose. What my poor grandfather suffered from rheumatism the last forty years of his life is incredible; but he walked about and lived all the same to be past ninety years of age—and celebrated his golden wedding too!'

'His golden what?'

'Wedding. Perhaps you have no golden or silver wedding in England?'

'I confess I never heard of anything of the kind,' said Hamilton.

'Oh, the silver wedding is only on the twenty-fifth anniversary, and most people can celebrate that; but to be fifty years married, and to have a golden wedding, is a sort of event in a family. Though but a boy at the time, I shall never forget that day. This house was quite covered with garlands, and all the neighbours from far and near were assembled, and my grandfather and grandmother, dressed in their wedding-dresses, walked in procession with music to the church, and the priest married them over again, and preached such a sermon that every

one had tears in their eyes. We had a dinner, too, at the
" Lion," and such dancing and singing; and in the evening
there was no end to the noise and shouting when they drove off
together for the second time as bride and bridegroom !'

'How I should like to see such a wedding! Is there no
chance of one now in the neighbourhood?'

'Not that I know of. It is a rare thing; for generally
a year or two before the fifty years are at an end one or other
dies. The very wish to live it out carries the old people off, I
believe.'

'Do people marry early here?'

'Not often, for they must get the consent of the parish, and
prove that they can support a family. I was past forty before
my father resigned the house and land to me.'

'So he gave it to you during his life-time? Is that often
done?'

'Very often. I was to have paid him a pension, and he
intended to have removed to the town; but he could not leave
the place, and so we all lived together until his death. My
mother is still alive. You may have seen her on the alp: she
is always wandering about there.'

'Was your father obliged to ask the consent of your landlord
when he resigned?'

'He was obliged to get the consent of Government, and I
had to pay the usual fine of five per cent. of the value of my
house and ground.'

'Then you have no lease?'

'Lease! No, we have no lease.'

'And your land is hereditary in your family?'

'Yes; we have the usual taxes to pay, and we have fines in
cases of death, succession, or exchange of land.'

'Could you sell your property if you wished it?'

'No doubt—if I obtained the consent of Government; but
who would sell their land and be without a house or home?'

'I suppose it is always the eldest son who inherits?'

'No; we can make whichever child we please our heir; but
we generally choose the eldest son, who pays the other children
what is left them by will.'

The peasant's wife drew near, and afterwards the children
gathered round them; their mother, in the pride of her heart,
telling them to fetch their copy-books, and show the gentleman
how well they could write. He had not finished the inspec-

tion, or praised them half as much as they deserved, when the Z——'s and their companions advanced from the wood, and joyful recognition and long explanations completely changed the current of his thoughts.

CHAPTER VI.

SECULARISED CLOISTERS.

WHEN Hamilton returned to Seon, he found there an addition to the guests he had left, in the person of Count Zedwitz's son, a young officer who had come to spend part of his leave of absence with his family. His appearance was prepossessing, notwithstanding his very decided ugliness, his yellow hair impertinently degenerating into red in his bushy mustachios, and a forehead which would have delighted Gall, Spurtzheim, or Combe, but from which a painter's eye would turn away to seek some more pleasing object; his figure was tall and well-proportioned, but, notwithstanding his youth, it already denoted an inclination to stoutness.

Hamilton found him an agreeable companion; indeed, every one seemed to like him, especially Mademoiselle Hildegarde, who, Hamilton imagined, received his unobtrusive attentions with undisguised satisfaction; nor was it long before he discovered a sort of avoidance of his society on the part of both sisters. Crescenz, indeed, looked at him sometimes, but the moment her eye caught his it was averted, and a blush was sure to follow. Hildegarde never looked at him at all. They whispered together continually, took long walks alone, and became every day more melancholy. In short, there was something mysterious in their manner which excited Hamilton's curiosity, and he determined to see Crescenz if possible alone for half-an-hour, and question her on the subject; but this was not easily managed, for Hildegarde seldom left her side, and were she present there was no chance of hearing anything. He commenced a system of watching, which Crescenz unfortunately misinterpreted, while Hildegarde remained perfectly unconscious of it; he did not apparently interest her sufficiently to make her observe his movements; but Crescenz's blushes increased daily, and even her sister's presence could not prevent her from sometimes entering into conversation with him. He asked her once if Seon had disappointed her—if she were tired of it; and then, in a low voice, why she looked so sorrowful. A blush, and eyes suddenly full of tears, was the only reply he received. Hildegarde, who had partly heard the questions, drew her sister's arm within hers, and left him alone to think over all possible causes, but in vain; he then turned his observations towards her stepmother, but there he was completely at fault. She was very kind in her manner to Crescenz, while to Hildegarde she seemed to have increased in severity.

One day, Crescenz descended to dinner with eyelids so swelled from crying that her eyes were almost closed; her sister so pale, that Hamilton expected every moment she would faint; after a few ineffectual efforts to swallow, they rose suddenly and left the room together. Madame Rosenberg, who was sitting beside Major Stultz, made some hasty remark and followed them. She had not, however, been absent more than a few minutes when she returned with Hildegarde, and pointing angrily to her place at the table, desired her ' to sit down there, and leave her sister in peace.' She obeyed, but made no attempt whatever to eat. Young Zedwitz, who had established a sort of right to sit beside her, endeavoured to begin a conversation; without raising her eyes, she said a few words in a low voice, which at once made him desist, and he scarcely looked at her again during the time he remained at table.

It was a magnificent afternoon, and Hamilton was burning with curiosity, which he had determined to satisfy by some desperate effort during the course of it.

He ran along the corridor and bounded down the staircase into the garden. Zedwitz was not there, but his mother and sister were standing so near the door that Hamilton stumbled against them. He apologised, and then asked for Count Max, whom he said he hoped to have found in the garden.

'He was here a minute ago,' was the reply, ' but he is gone to look for somebody or something; I did not quite understand what he said.'

'It is very unkind of Max not to walk with us,' observed the young lady, with some irritation; ' he knows how dreadfully afraid I am of cows and dogs.'

Hamilton thought she looked at him, as if she expected that

he should offer to accompany her in the character of protector.
This, however, he resolved not to do, and was in the act of
retiring when the old Countess exclaimed, ' Oh, Mr. Hamilton,
if you are not otherwise engaged, perhaps you will accompany
us in our walk? My daughter is so easily frightened that
she cannot go any distance without some one to chase away
the cattle.'

Hamilton felt doomed. The request had not been made in
the most flattering terms, it is true ; but he could not do otherwise than acquiesce. The thought that young Zedwitz was
at that moment, perhaps, walking with the sisters, did not
make him feel amiably disposed, and he was considerably out
of temper when he commenced his walk. This could not,
however, continue, for both his companions were agreeable,
and though the old Countess suffered considerably from
asthma in ascending the hills, she contrived, nevertheless, to
commence a conversation, as it appeared to Hamilton at first,
in order to learn something of him or his family. Not, however, finding him disposed to be communicative, she desisted
from anything but indirect observations, which rather amused
him than otherwise, and then spoke unreservedly of her own
affairs.

They lived on one of their estates in the neighbourhood of
Munich, but they had spent the last two winters in the latter
place, on account of their daughter. It had not agreed with
the Count, and as her daughter was now *braut* (a bride), that
is, engaged to be married, they should in future live altogether
in the country. They had another residence in the mountains,
near Baron Z ——, which she would greatly prefer, but the
Count fancied the mountain air increased his rheumatism.
She supposed her son had told him all this, however.

' Our conversation has been principally about Munich, and
he has persuaded me to spend next winter there.'

' Were your movements so uncertain? Do your parents
leave you completely at liberty ?'

' Completely. I can spend the winter at Vienna, Berlin,
Dresden, or Munich.'

The conversation was changed, and Hamilton was so pleased
with both his companions, that he was actually sorry when
they reached Seon, though the walk had been long, and it was
so late that the guests were assembling for supper.

' Where are my girls? Are they not yet returned?' asked
Madame Rosenberg.

No one had seen them.

'They were with me the whole morning,' she continued, 'and only went out half-an-hour ago to the church at the other side of the water. Perhaps Mr. Hamilton will be so kind as to call them to supper.'

'Let me go with you!' cried young Zedwitz, starting from his chair.

'Thank you—I can find them without your assistance,' he replied, and then added, maliciously laughing, 'I know you have been lounging about this little lake all day, my good fellow, and must be as tired of it as a sentinel of his post.'

Zedwitz laughed too, but he was not so easily put off. He took Hamilton's arm, and they sallied forth together.

'You were long on guard to-day, Zedwitz—from dinner-time until now!'

'How did *you* like being caught to drive away the cows? I saw you being led off.'

'At first I did not like it at all—afterwards very much. I have taken a great fancy to your mother—still more to your sister.'

'My sister is the dearest little soul in the world. If you but knew her as well as I do! I am very sorry she is to be married so soon—her loss will to me be irreparable, and our house so intolerably dull without her, that I shall be under the necessity of choosing a wife with as little delay as possible.'

'Your mother told me she expects you will make a most desirable marriage.'

'With my ugly face? That is not very probable.'

'I understood from the Countess that you, as well as your sister, were already engaged.'

'By no means—certainly not!' cried Zedwitz, with a vehemence incomprehensible to Hamilton; 'joining hands for the purpose of joining estates is not at all to my taste.'

'I should suppose not,' observed Hamilton, carelessly, and a long pause ensued. At length Zedwitz observed abruptly, 'My parents are anxious for me to quit the army and marry; and yet I am quite convinced that when I propose doing so, they will object to the person I have chosen. In spite of my ugliness, or rather, perhaps, on account of it, personal beauty has a value in my eyes beyond what it deserves. I could not marry an ugly woman—could you?'

F

'I have never thought much on the subject,' replied Hamilton, laughing. 'My parents have strictly forbidden all such thoughts on my part for the next ten years at least.'

They now began to cross the shallow part of the Seon lake, on a long, narrow, wooden bridge—so narrow that it was inconvenient for more than two persons to walk abreast. When they had reached the slope leading up to the church on the other side, Hamilton suddenly stopped, and asked Count Zedwitz 'what Hildegarde had said to him at dinner, which had so effectually silenced him?'

'She told me not to speak to her, as she could not answer me.'

'Was that all?'

'Yes; but she gave me some hope that she would tell me why on some future occasion, and I was satisfied.'

'There is some mystery in the family! Don't you think so?' asked Hamilton.

'I am quite convinced of it. These poor girls seem very unhappily situated. I really pity them!'

'I both pity and admire them,' cried Hamilton; 'and, moreover, I am exceedingly anxious to find out this same mystery. Let us start fair, and see who will first obtain information.'

'Agreed.'

'My chances are but small,' observed Hamilton; 'with me both the young ladies are shy, and I myself am still more so!'

'You shy!' exclaimed Zedwitz, laughing.

'What! you don't believe me! You must have observed how I blush for the merest trifle!'

'Oh, yes—you blush, but it seems to be constitutional, however, for I never saw any one of your age so self-possessed.'

'My dear Count, you quite mistake my character, I assure you; it is a sort of anomaly—a mixture of modesty and assurance—'

'Assurance, perhaps—sometimes—the modesty I have never observed.' He stopped, and pointed to the two sisters, who were sitting on the trunk of a prostrate tree in a neighbouring field, their hands clasped firmly together, and each separately exhibiting a picture of grief which, independent of the youth and beauty of the mourners, was interesting from the difference of its expression. Crescenz seemed quite subdued by excessive sorrow; her whole form drooped, and she wept in silence, the tears coursing each other over her youthful cheeks unrestrainedly. Hildegarde held a letter tightly pressed in her hand and looked upwards. She might have been praying; but it seemed to Hamilton as if the eyes remained upturned to prevent the falling of the tears which had gathered in the underlids—an occasional almost imperceptible movement of the corners of the mouth, and an evident difficulty in swallowing, confirmed this idea.

'Hamilton, let us return towards the lake; it would be cruel to take them by surprise. We must talk loud, or in some way give them notice of our approach.' He turned away as he spoke, and so effectually did he put his intentions in practice, that when they again approached the sisters, they were walking apparently unconcernedly towards the church, and on hearing that they were expected to supper, quietly led the way to the wooden bridge. Zedwitz and Hamilton now commenced manœuvring; but as their intentions were similar, and the object not to engage the same person, they were almost immediately successful. Zedwitz seemed, indeed, at first determined that Hamilton should lead the way with Crescenz; but the latter soon gave him to understand that that would never answer, and after a few frowns, and shrugs, and shoves, he followed Hildegarde, who was already on the bridge.

Hamilton approached Crescenz, and whispered hurriedly, 'What is the matter? Why are you so unhappy? What on earth has occurred during my absence from Seon?'

'Nothing, nothing! Nothing has occurred which can in any way interest you,' she replied, walking quickly on.

'You are unkind, mademoiselle,' said Hamilton, slowly and reproachfully — 'unnecessarily unkind; from the commencement of our acquaintance, short as it has been, I have felt the greatest interest in all that concerns you. I see you unhappy —wish to offer any consolation in my power—and am treated with disdain.'

'I did not mean to treat you with disdain,' said Crescenz, softening, and walking more slowly.

'Your sister is not so cruel to Count Zedwitz.' In fact, they were just then speaking rather earnestly. This had great effect.

'What do you wish to know?' she asked, gently.

'I wish to know the cause of your unhappiness; I wish to know why you avoid me.'

F 2

'That I cannot tell you so easily! You will hear perhaps,
— but you will not understand what — that is—how — I
mean to say why I could not refuse. I — I cannot tell you,'
she cried, bursting into tears, and walking on so quickly, that
she had nearly reached her sister before Hamilton could say
in a whisper, 'To-night, at the foot of the broad staircase
leading to the cloisters — may I expect you?'

'No, no, no!'

'There will be moonlight; at nine o'clock I shall be there.'

'Oh, no! — not for the world!'

'The staircase is quite close to your room; grant me but five
minutes only.'

Her sister looked round, and, to prevent further discussion,
he added, urgently, but looking at the same time with affected
unconcern across the lake—

'You *must* come, or I shall spend the whole night in the
cloisters waiting for you.'

It was in vain she now endeavoured to refuse; he was deaf
to all excuses, and walked purposely so near her sister that
she was obliged to give up the attempt.

Before they entered the house, Zedwitz whispered triumphantly, 'I shall know *all* to-morrow morning.'

'And I to-night,' replied Hamilton.

'What? when? how? where?'

'That is my affair, not yours.'

'I shall find out, you may depend upon it.'

'I defy you!' cried Hamilton, laughing; but the next
moment, heartily regretting his foolish boast, he thought for a
moment of telling him his purpose, but the fear of compro-
mising Crescenz deterred him, and soon afterwards, perceiving
him earnestly engaged in conversation with Hildegarde, he
hoped he would forget all about the matter.

After supper, Madame Rosenberg, as usual, produced her
knitting, and Hamilton began a listless sort of conversation
with her, which lasted until her daughter had left the room;
it suddenly, however, took a turn, which rendered it to Hamilton interesting in the extreme. She had, according to her
own account, a most particular fancy for all Englishmen.
They were such agreeable companions; gave no trouble at
all; she had reason to know, for she had had Englishmen
lodging in her house for the last three years. She had two
furnished rooms, which she always let, and from experience

she now knew that Englishmen were in every respect desirable lodgers! Need it be said, that 'on this hint,' Hamilton had spoken, and that in a very short time an arrangement for board and lodging was concluded to their mutual satisfaction? It was then that she launched into praises of his nation, ending with the remark, that nothing would induce her, now that her stepdaughters were at home, to receive any but Englishmen under her roof. ' They were accustomed to domestic life, to female society, and did not think it necessary to talk nonsense to every girl with whom they happened to be five minutes alone. Did he know Mr. Smyth?'

Hamilton believed he knew two or three Smiths.

' I mean a Mr. Howard Seymour Smyth.'

' No.' Hamilton knew more Howards and Seymours than Smiths; he was happy in the consciousness.

' Perhaps you know Captain Black ?'

' I have not the pleasure of his acquaintance.'

' He was a most delightful person; lodged with us last year; dined, however, at Havard's *table-d'hôte*. You will be the first who has actually become a member of the family, as I may say. I wonder what Rosenberg will think of the arrangement.'

' May I beg of you to write to him to-morrow on the subject, as I have already given a sort of commission to the Baroness Z—— and—'

' Oh, dear! there's no necessity for writing; I always arrange these things alone; you have nothing whatever to do with him !'

' In that case, I may consider the affair as arranged,' said Hamilton, rising and going towards the side-table for his candle. She rose too, and they ascended the stairs together.

' I shall do everything in my power to make you feel comfortable and at home in our house,' she said, when wishing him good night.

As he entered his room, the great clock struck nine. He placed with some natural trepidation his candle behind the stove, and locked his door carefully, to prevent Zedwitz, should he come, from ascertaining whether he were there or not. ' He will think, perhaps, that I am in bed and asleep if he get no answer,' was his wise reflection as he dropped the key into his pocket and commenced walking on tiptoe towards the place of appointment. A few moments' thought convinced him that there was no necessity whatever for concealment, until he had reached the lower passages, where there were flower-stands, gardening tools, old doors, casks, and all sorts of lumber heaped up, as if on purpose to make places of retreat for gentlemen in his situation. He ensconced himself behind a capacious beer barrel, and waited patiently until he heard a step on the stairs: keeping carefully in the dark, he whispered, 'I am here; give me your hand.' But no hand was given; on the contrary, a scampering upstairs, three or four steps at a time, ensued, which was at first perfectly incomprehensible. Hamilton afterwards supposed that Crescenz had heard some noise in the corridor, and must wait for a better opportunity. Again he placed himself behind the friendly cask, and waited upwards of half-an-hour. At the end of that time, an odd rustling noise among the lumber made him start, but muttering the word 'rats,' he flung an old rake in the direction from whence it came, and all was still again. It had become so much darker, that he now took up his post near the staircase, and soon after, Crescenz appeared, looking timidly down into the obscurity. 'I am here; do not be afraid; there is no one near,' cried Hamilton, softly advancing towards her.

'I have only come—to say—that—that I cannot come.'

Hamilton in vain endeavoured to repress a smile. 'Well, come down the stairs and at least tell me why?'

She descended a few steps.

'Well, why?'

'Because I have not courage; I am always afraid in the dark.'

'But it is not dark in the cloisters; there is the most beautiful moonlight imaginable! Come!'

'Would not to-morrow at six o'clock, in the garden, do as well?'

'I cannot hear you,' answered Hamilton, becoming suddenly deaf; 'and you had better not speak too distinctly, as you may be heard by some one crossing the passage.'

'To-morrow morning in the garden,' she softly repeated, descending close to where he stood.

'I have been waiting nearly an hour!' was the answer which he gave, in order to change her thoughts.

'I could not help it: Hildegarde has only just fallen asleep.'

'We must not remain here, or we shall certainly be overheard. Come,' he whispered, drawing her arm within his,

'I cannot—I cannot—to-morrow before breakfast, or when you will; but not now. Let me go! Oh, let me go!'

And he would have let her go; but the thoughts of Zedwitz's raillery made him resolute. His first thought was to carry her off, but that appearing too strong a measure, he contented himself with holding her hand fast while pouring forth a volley of reproaches.

'And now,' he concluded, with an affectation of reasoning: 'now that you are so far, why retreat? Every one is in bed; no human being in the cloisters. I ask but five minutes; but I would speak with you alone—unrestrained.'

And while he was speaking he contrived to make her move along the passage. A moment after, they had reached the quadrangle, and stood in silent admiration of the calm seclusion of the spot. The echo of their footsteps was the only sound they heard, and the bright moonbeams not only lighted the monuments erected against the wall, but rendered almost legible the epitaphs of those whose tombstones composed the pavement.

He led Crescenz to a seat near the monument of the founder of the monastery, Count Aribo, and waited for her to speak; she had, however, no inclination to begin, but sat in a deep reverie, looking fixedly on the ground, and, as it seemed, more inclined to be sentimental than communicative.

Hamilton, more conscious than she was of the impropriety of her situation, and fearing that they might be seen by some of the servants, at length exclaimed with some impatience—

'Do not let us lose these precious moments, but tell me at once what has occurred.'

Crescenz became agitated, covered her face with her hands, but remained silent.

'For heaven's sake, tell me what is the matter?'

'I am very, very unhappy!' sobbed the poor girl.

'But why?—why are you unhappy?'

'Because I—I am going to me married!'

'Married! To whom are you going to be married?'

'To—to—Major Stultz.'

'Major Stultz! Why, this must be a very sudden business, indeed. Before I left Seon he seemed much more inclined to marry your sister than you!'

'Oh, of course he would rather have married Hildegarde, because she is so much cleverer and handsomer than I am; but she would not listen to him, and called him an old fool!'

'I admire her candour,' said Hamilton.

'And then she got into a passion when he persevered, and slapped him on the mouth.'

'Slapped him on the mouth!'

'Yes, when he attempted to kiss her hand; at least he says so; and Hildegarde thinks it may be true, as she was angry and struggled very hard to release her hand. He told mamma that he would not marry her now if she were ten times handsomer, and a princess into the bargain!'

'She seems of rather a passionate temperament.'

'Passionate! Yes, she sometimes gets into a passion, but it is soon over, and then she can be so kind to those she loves! No one knows her so well as I do, excepting, perhaps, papa, and he says if she were not passionate she would be faultless: with me she is never in a passion.'

'Perhaps because you yield implicit obedience to all her commands? But tell me why did not you follow her example, and refuse Major Stultz, if you did not like him?'

'He did not ask me; he spoke to mamma, and wrote to papa; and when all was arranged I had not courage to refuse; and he is forty-six years old, and I shall not be sixteen until next year!'

'That is a considerable disparity, certainly.'

'I should not mind the thirty years so much if his face were not so red and his figure so stout. I hate red-faced, stout men!'

'If he could change his appearance to please you, I have no doubt he would do so,' observed Hamilton, smiling.

'Hildegarde also dislikes red-faced men,' she added, pettishly.

'Whatever Hildegarde says must be right, of course,' said Hamilton, ironically; 'but I have not discovered that she dislikes Count Zedwitz, and he rather comes under the denomination red-faced.'

'Hildegarde says Count Zedwitz is very agreeable, and not in the least presuming.'

'And who does she say *is* presuming, if I may ask?'

'She says you are — or would be, if you were allowed.'

'I think she is wrong. And were she to meet Zedwitz here alone —'

'Hildegarde would never do such a thing — never! And

I ought not to have come, either,' she cried, starting from her seat and looking anxiously round. Then laying her hand heavily on his arm, and straining her eyes as if to see something more distinctly, she asked, in a scarcely audible voice, ' What is that?'

'What?—I see nothing.'

'There—there—in the corner! The moon is shining on it now—that figure!'

'Oh, that is a stone figure—a monument, or something of that sort. Let us go and look at it.'

'Not for the universe—I saw it move.'

'You fancied it moved; one can imagine all sorts of things by moonlight. Will you remain here, and let me examine it?'

'Oh, no—you must not leave me! I—I think it may be something unearthly. Oh, why did I come here?—why did I come here?'

'Don't be unnecessarily alarmed. I am convinced it is nothing but—'

'There, there—it moved again!' She grasped his arm and hid her face on his shoulder.

'Come,' said Hamilton encouragingly; 'let me take you to your room—to your sister!'

She trembled violently, but endeavoured to walk. The figure, however, seemed to possess the power of fascination—she would or could not remove her eyes from it; and though Hamilton assured her he remembered having seen it by daylight, and at first really thought so, he was soon unpleasantly convinced of his error. They saw the outline more and more distinctly every moment, and could even distinguish the large folds of the drapery in the moonlight. Hamilton tried to hurry her forward; but at that moment the figure, slowly and stiffly raising an arm, pointed threateningly towards them. This was the *acme*. Crescenz clung to him in an agony of terror; and while Hamilton whispered to her, 'For heaven's sake, not to scream—to think of the consequences were she to be discovered,' she writhed, as if in strong convulsions, gasped frightfully once or twice for breath, and then sank on his arm perfectly insensible.

Shocked beyond measure, but now convinced that some one had been amusing himself at their expense, Hamilton called out angrily, 'Cease your mummeries, whoever you are—and see what you have done!'

The moonlight fell on Crescenz's lifeless form while he spoke, and in a moment Count Zedwitz stood beside him. He endeavoured to exculpate himself by vowing that he had no idea of playing ghost when he had followed them.

'I don't care what you intended,' cried Hamilton, still more angrily; 'but I wish, at least, you had spared this poor girl such unnecessary terror.'

'I did not think of the consequences. It was very foolish— it was very wrong, if you will. But you must not think I was a listener: I declare most solemnly I did not hear one word of your conversation.'

'The whole world might have heard it!' cried Hamilton, impatiently shaking off the hand which Zedwitz had placed on his shoulder; 'the whole world might have heard it. But, what is to be done now? She shows no sign of life, and is as cold as a stone. Perhaps you have killed her!'

'Oh, no—she has only fainted. Let me go for a glass of water.'

'Are you mad?' cried Hamilton, detaining him forcibly; 'no one must ever know that she has been here with me—with us. Let us take her to her sister; she will never betray her, and will know best what means to employ for her recovery.'

And between them they carried Crescenz along the passage and up the stairs. Fortunately, the first door led to her room, and Hamilton desired Zedwitz to knock gently, lest other people in the neighbouring rooms might be awakened. But it was in vain he knocked; Hildegarde seemed to be enjoying what is called a 'wholesome sleep;' and at length, finding their efforts fruitless, Zedwitz volunteered to go in and waken her.

Hamilton heard the sleepy voice change into a tone of alarm, the anxious questions, and finally a request that he would leave the room. He did so, and in less than a minute Hildegarde opened the door in a state of great agitation. While Hamilton laid Crescenz on the bed, Zedwitz struck a light, and Hildegarde then asked him earnestly to tell her what had happened.

'My odious cloak has been the cause of all,' he answered, evasively: 'she saw me standing in the moonlight, and thought I was a ghost.'

'Saw you standing in the moonlight?—when?—where? Oh, go away, both of you!' she cried, vehemently, as the candle lighted her sister's pale features; 'go away, and leave me alone with Crescenz.'

They left the room and walked towards one of the windows looking into the quadrangle. After some delay Hildegarde appeared, and a dialogue ensued which Hamilton thought unnecessarily long, as he was not able to hear what was said; the moment, however, that he approached the speakers, the door was closed, and he was left to make his inquiries of Zedwitz.

'How is she?'

'Better, or quite well, I forget which; she fancied at first that she had been dreaming, but now she knows the contrary.'

'Hum! No doubt you exaggerated splendidly when explaining to Hildegarde just now!'

'Not I! I was thinking the whole time of that bewitching little nightcap, and how lovely she looked in it.'

'Pshaw! If you have any fancy for such caps, I recommend you to go to London. In any street you please and at any hour, you can see half-a-dozen such caps on as many Bavarian girls, whose employment is to scream "buy a broom," and who are just the most good-for-nothing creatures in the world!'

'And how do you know that they are Bavarians? I think it much more probable that they are Dutch girls.'

'In London people call them Bavarians; and I must confess they never interested me sufficiently to induce me to make inquiries.'

'Very likely; but when I tell you that Bavarians do not lightly forsake their country; that they are seldom so poor as not to have enough to live upon — our marriage laws provide against that; that London is a long way from Bavaria, and the steam-packets make it an easy matter for Dutch girls to transport themselves there; you will also think with me, that they are more probably Dutch than Bavarian!'

'How warmly you defend your countrywomen and their hideous caps!' cried Hamilton, laughing; 'but really,' he added, opening the door of his room, before which they stood, 'really the matter is not worth a dispute. The girls are Dutch, if you will have it so, but the caps are ugly, say what you will.'

'It depends so entirely on the wearer of the cap! For

instance, to-night I thought that cap the most becoming thing I ever saw!'

'Perhaps you also prefer one foot in a slipper and the other bare.'

'What do you mean?'

'I mean that the fair Hildegarde could only find one slipper in the dark, and patted about with her bare foot, as if it were the most comfortable thing possible!'

'I did not look at her feet; but even if I had, I should only have admired her forgetfulness of self in her anxiety about her sister.'

'You are right, Zedwitz,' cried Hamilton, with unusual warmth, 'quite right; and though I will not—cannot say that I think the nightcap pretty—I must acknowledge that I admired Hildegarde to-night more than anyone I ever saw. She is superlatively handsome, and it is the greater pity that she is such a devil!'

'A devil! Are you raving?'

'Not a bit of it. I advise you to take care how you make advances to her; she will slap you on the mouth for the slightest misdemeanour.'

'Slap me on the mouth!'

'Not the smallest doubt of it. She buffeted poor Major Stultz when he innocently made her a proposal of marriage, until his face from deep red turned to the richest purple.'

'Nay, now I know you are inventing—joking.'

'Not so much as you think, I assure you. Her sister is my authority. She softened the recital in some degree, it is true, by saying that Hildegarde was not often in a passion, and never with *her.*'

Zedwitz seated himself at the table, drummed on it with his fingers, and looked at Hamilton, as if he expected to hear more.

'Perhaps, after all,' said Hamilton, 'she is only a little hot-tempered. I have heard it asserted that passionate people were always good-hearted—in fact, most amiable, when not actually in a passion!'

'Who would have imagined that?' said Zedwitz, thoughtfully, 'and with such an angel's face!'

'Never trust an angel's face!' cried Hamilton, laughing. My brother John, who understands such things, says that angelic-looking women are very often devils, and if not, they are bores; and of the two I prefer a devil to a bore, any day —even for a wife!'

Zedwitz rubbed his hand across his forehead, and looked dissatisfied.

'So you think her ill-tempered?' he observed.

'I cannot exactly say ill-tempered, but I have already seen her in something very nearly approaching to a passion.'

'You!—where?'

'No matter; but she called me a fool, and stamped with her foot until I actually ran away from her.'

'I dare say you had provoked her past endurance; and I have now had an opportunity of judging how shy and modest you are. Not that I mean to blame you for supporting Crescenz as you did to-night in the cloisters. You saved her, no doubt, from a severe fall, but you took very remarkably good care of her.'

'It was very natural that Crescenz should cling to me when she was frightened,' said Hamilton, seriously, 'and equally natural that I should endeavour to protect her.'

'Oh, it was altogether extremely natural; only don't talk any more nonsense about being shy. You were anything but shy at the foot of the staircase—'

'Were you there, too?'

'Not very distant from you, disguised as a rat.'

'If I had managed to hit you with the rake, all this scene would have been avoided.'

'Perhaps; but do you know that you invited me yourself to come? I did not know where you were until you said, in the most insinuating manner, "I am here—give me your hand!"'

'So, you were the person who scampered up the stairs?'

'Yes, and scampered down at the other side, and found another way into the passage.'

'Well, I hope I shall not remain long in your debt, that's all.'

'Oh, your anger is over for this time, I hope. Rather let us now swéar an eternal friendship. The thing is possible, as we are not rivals.'

'Perhaps we may be, though—I rather took a fancy to Hildegarde to-night. Crescenz is almost too childish.'

'You are not serious, I hope,' cried Zedwitz, with what Hamilton imagined an affectation of alarm.

'I really don't know whether I am or not. I am only trying to get up a sort of flirtation to make the time pass agreeably while I am studying German ; for that purpose, in fact, one sister is as good as the other : indeed, Crescenz suits me, perhaps, better, because the affair will have a respectable termination when she marries Major Stultz.'

'Is she to marry Major Stultz ?'

'So Hildegarde has not even told you that ?'

'Not a word.'

'Well, let us open the window and smoke a couple of cigars in the moonlight, and you shall hear all about it, and have a full and true account of the boxing-match between Hildegarde and the gallant major.'

CHAPTER VII.

AN EXCURSION, AND RETURN TO THE SECULARISED CLOISTERS

MADAME ROSENBERG 'wondered' unceasingly the next morning, why Crescenz was not well enough to appear at breakfast. Zedwitz looked at Hamilton, and Hamilton looked at Zedwitz, and then they both looked at Hildegarde, whose eyes were fixed on the ground, leaving nothing but the long eyelashes, which rested on her cheek, visible. About the corners of her mouth played an expression which it. was impossible to define—but it seemed that Zedwitz was able to interpret it to his own advantage, for he seated himself beside her, and began a conversation in the very easiest manner possible. Major Stultz was fully occupied with a monstrous edition of a meerschaum pipe, and Hamilton turned to Madame Rosenberg, who showed every disposition to be friendly and confidential. From sundry winks and witticisms which she exchanged with Major Stultz, Hamilton perceived that she wished to excite his curiosity, and longed to tell him of Crescenz's engagement. But he pretended stupidity, and carefully avoided all leading questions. Suddenly it occurred to him to propose a party to the Chiem Lake the next day, and he was immediately warmly seconded by

Zedwitz. Major Stultz took his pipe from his mouth to say that the weather was so warm they might expect a thunder-storm, which on that lake would be dangerous. Madame Rosenberg, with a few wise nods, observed that 'under existing circumstances,' she thought that Crescenz might be allowed a little amusement, and the party was decided upon. Hamilton took Zedwitz aside, and asked him if he could not persuade his mother and sister to join them.

'My dear fellow,' was his answer, 'nothing in the world would induce my mother or sister to go with these people.'

'These people! Why, are they not respectable?'

'Respectable! oh, perfectly. Come, don't play innocence and force me to explain what you understand as well as I do. The two girls are treasures, and would be presentable anywhere if they had but a "*Von*" before their name, but their stepmother is vulgarity personified, and Major Stultz, you know, was a common soldier!'

'I know nothing at all about Major Stultz, excepting that he is a red-faced, jolly-looking, elderly man. He must have distinguished himself during the war, or he could not have obtained his present rank.'

'Yes, his personal bravery is undoubted; he was also an excellent officer — covered with wounds — made the campaign in Russia, and was one of the few Bavarians who returned home to relate the horrors of the retreat. I advise you, however, to avoid the subject when he is present, as he is rather diffuse upon it. His brother, a Nuremberger tradesman, died about six months ago, and left him a good deal of money; his wounds afforded him a good excuse for retiring from the service, and applying for a pension, and he told me, honestly, that he has been looking for a wife ever since, as he does not know what to do with himself.'

'The idea of taking Hildegarde to wife, in order to dispel *ennui*, was a proof of great discernment,' observed Hamilton, ironically.

'Rather say, most unpardonable effrontery,' replied Zedwitz, growing very red.

'A man of his discrimination,' continued Hamilton, provokingly, 'must be aware that Crescenz is but a bad substitute for her sister — Hildegarde, too, would have suited him much better; she would have kept him in order by—' Here he waved his hand significantly.

'How you harp on that subject, Hamilton!'

'I shall never mention it again if it distress you. I was really not aware—'

'Pshaw!' he exclaimed impatiently, turning away.

'As to Crescenz, poor girl,' continued Hamilton, 'I really pity her. Such a fearful difference of age and person makes it an odious sacrifice!'

'Not so much as you think, perhaps,' said Zedwitz, quietly; Stultz is a good-hearted man, and will let her do whatever she pleases. You will see how soon she will be satisfied with her lot in life!—perhaps even before her marriage!'

'It is at least to be hoped so,' observed Hamilton, drily.

'The *trousseau* will soon occupy her mind completely, and while exhibiting it to her friends and receiving their congratulations, she will learn to like the cause of all the preparations, and end, perhaps, by fancying herself a singularly fortunate person!'

, Crescenz entered the garden while they were speaking, and blushed deeply as she passed them. Hamilton felt the blood mount to his temples, and turned away that Zedwitz might not observe it.

'This is the. beginning of the comedy,' cried the latter, after a moment's pause, touching Hamilton's arm, to make him look round. He turned, and, through the foliage of the arbour, saw Major Stultz clasping a massive gold bracelet on Crescenz's arm. She appeared for a moment embarrassed and shy—then played with a padlock or heart, or some such thing which dangled from the bracelet, and finally she looked up at him, and—smiled.

'She is a thorough-bred coquette!' exclaimed Hamilton, indignantly. 'Zedwitz, I throw down the gauntlet and enter the list as your rival. I prefer running the chance of occasional chastisement from the fair hands of Hildegarde, to having anything more to do with such a silly, vain creature as this Crescenz seems to be.'

'Seems to be, Hamilton—and only *seems*. The circumstances must also be taken into consideration. She must marry this Stultz, whether she like him or not. That he is not the *idéal* of a girl of her age one can easily imagine. He suspects this, perhaps, and wisely commences by giving her a handsome present. That is probably the first gold bracelet she has ever had clasped on her arm. She is very young, childish, if you will, but neither silly nor very vain for feeling a little pleasure, and honestly showing what she feels. I see nothing reprehensible in her conduct.'

'Had you but heard her last night telling me how unhappy she was!'

Zedwitz shrugged his shoulders.

'How she talked of his forty-six years, and declared her hatred of red-faced men!'

Zedwitz laughed

'She mentioned also, that her sister had the same antipathy.'

'Sorry to hear it!' cried Zedwitz, picking up a handful of flat pebbles and pitching them one by one with considerable skill into the lake, watching them skimming along the surface with an interest that half provoked Hamilton.

'You seem to have a thorough contempt for my rivalship by daylight.'

'What do you mean? Did you not tell me last night that Crescenz suited you exactly, as you only wished to amuse yourself for a time.'

'Such *were* my intentions. May I ask what were yours? Or rather, what are yours?'

'Oh, certainly, you may ask, but you must forgive my not answering you, as I have not the most remote idea what I may be induced to do. I shall most probably be guided altogether by circumstances.'

He put an end to the conversation by walking towards the arbour where the arrangements for the next day's party were soon made. Major Stultz not venturing before Crescenz to say a word about storm or danger.

They left Seon at a very early hour the next morning, in two carriages. Madame Rosenberg, as usual, took her three boys with her, in order, as she said, to keep them out of mischief. Fritz, the eldest, on finding himself separated from her, immediately found amusement in climbing from the carriage to the box, and from the box into the carriage again, causing Hildegarde, who had charge of him, such anxiety lest he should fall on the wheel, that she could scarcely remain a moment quiet. Zedwitz assisted her so sedulously that he did not perceive an attack which Gustle directly commenced on the

G

buttons of his coat with a blunt penknife; and Hamilton alone, unoccupied, half listened to the desultory conversation of his companions, while admiring in silence the scenery, than which nothing could be more beautiful to an English eye. The fine old trees in the domain-like meadows which were bounded by extensive woods; the splendid lake appearing at intervals through openings which seemed made as if to show to advantage its extent, and the magnificent range of mountains beyond. The rippling of the water on the sandy shore brought at last such a crowd of home-recollections to his mind, that he leaned back, forgetful of all around him. Fritz's irritating gymnastics, Gustle's mischievous pertinacity, Hildegarde's angelic face, and Zedwitz's amusingly enamoured expression of countenance! The sudden stopping of the carriage made him once more alive to everything going on about him. The little manœuvres of Madame Rosenberg to place Major Stultz near Crescenz; the determination with which she insisted on Hildegarde's sitting between two of her brothers; the third she gave in charge to Zedwitz, and Hamilton had the honour of being reserved for herself.

Hildegarde and Crescenz were for the first time in their lives in a boat, and neither of them were quite at their ease. Crescenz exhibited her fear by various little half-suppressed screams, sometimes catching the side of the boat, sometimes the arm of Major Stultz. Hildegarde sat perfectly quiet, not venturing to look to the right or left, her colour varying with every movement of her unruly neighbours, who amused themselves by adding to the fears of their sisters by balancing the boat from side to side.

They landed first on the *Frauen Insel* (Woman's Island), hoping to be allowed to see the nunnery. While waiting for the necessary permission to enter, they wandered through the churchyard and into the church.

On the appearance of a tall, haggard, austere-looking man, in the long garment of a priest, Zedwitz advanced towards him, and begged admittance for the ladies; the scowling countenance convincing him at once that for him there was no chance whatever. He was volubly seconded by Madame Rosenberg, who with that want of tact not unusual on the part of uneducated women, actually attempted to be jocular with the awful-looking personage; but neither the polished address of Zedwitz, not the jocularity of Madame Rosenberg could prevail. He refused without ceremony, and in a very few words told them, that without bringing a permission from the '*ordinariat*' in Munich, they could not be admitted : the entrance of strangers disturbed the nuns, and was against the rules of the convent.

They turned away, Crescenz observing, timidly, that she would not like to be a nun where there was such a severe confessor.

'I hope you have no thoughts of being a nun anywhere,' observed the major.

'I should have no objection to such a confessor,' said Hildegarde: 'I rather prefer one who has something imposing in his appearance; it gives me the idea that he is above the weaknesses of human nature '

'What nonsense you talk, Hildegarde,' cried Madame Rosenberg, with evident irritation. 'It is only a spirit of contradiction which makes you pretend to admire a man who has been so disagreeable and uncivil to us all.'

Hildegarde walked more slowly, and Zedwitz, who had been lingering behind, immediately joined her.

'So you like stern-looking men?' he observed, in a low voice.

'I said I liked a confessor who had something imposing in his manner.'

'Oh! for a confessor merely? But for a friend, a lover, or a husband, you prefer something quite different? Don't you?'

'Perhaps I should,' she answered, carelessly.

'Or perhaps,' said Hamilton, 'you think of entering the nunnery here, out of pure admiration for that long gaunt man! There is no accounting for taste.'

'I do not intend to take the veil until you have become a monk.'

'When I become a monk, it will not be here; I shall choose a more hospitable place, and jolly companions, such as one generally reads of. The incivility of your friend with the austere countenance has greatly disgusted me.'

The buildings on the other island were very extensive. The church had been turned into a brew-house, and not long after its desecration, it was burnt. 'A very proper judgment,' as Madame Rosenberg observed, glancing meaningly towards her companions. Handsome broad marble stairs led to the upper apartments, of which a few have been lately modernised. The carved wood on the doors of the cells, and the picture-frames in the refectory were admirable.

'Altogether,' said Hamilton, looking out of one of the windows, across the lake—'altogether, a place where one could spend a fortnight very agreeably, with a gay party.'

'Or with Hildegarde and her sister,' said Zedwitz, in a low voice.

'If Crescenz were not so insipid with all her prettiness.'

They adjourned to the garden and dined under the trees. Hamilton studiously avoided Crescenz's vicinity, although he saw she was half disposed to be angry at his neglect. She endeavoured, in her simplicity, to pique him by listening with affected complaisance to Major Stultz's common-place remarks. She laughed, and encouraged him to give her brothers beer, when her mother was not watching them. This childish conduct, perhaps, Hamilton would have forgotten, had not the consequences been somewhat remarkable. The boys, unaccustomed to drink anything but water or milk, soon became almost intoxicated, and on their way to the boat, Fritz, a good-humoured, handsome boy, swaggered, sang, and shouted most boisterously; Gustle became quarrelsome, and pinched and pommelled him unmercifully. It was in vain Madame Rosenberg scolded and threatened punishment; they had not left the shore more than ten minutes when a regular scuffle took place; Gustle flung Fritz's cap into the water, and Fritz, merely taking time to knock down the offender, leaned over the side of the boat, snapped at his cap, and went heels over head into the lake! The screams of the ladies were beyond all conception piercing. Zedwitz, with an exclamation of horror, and regretting that he could not swim, leaned anxiously, and with outstretched arms, over the side of the boat. Madame Rosenberg started up and, with clasped hands, called for help in a voice of agony.

The danger was imminent. Hamilton sprang into the water and caught the boy as he rose, for the second time, at some distance from the boat; he was still conscious, and grasped his preserver's arm manfully. The scene which ensued it is impossible to describe. Gustle was boxed and Fritz was kissed, and Hamilton was thanked and blessed alternately. He declined entering the boat again; but partly held it and partly swam to the shore, where he heard with some surprise that the fishers who had rowed them, although they had spent half their lives on the lake, could not swim, so that had he not been there, Fritz would inevitably have been drowned.

From the commencement of his acquaintance with Madame Rosenberg, she had been disposed to like him, but from this event may be dated a sort of implicit reliance on her part, which afterwards caused him occasional qualms of conscience, as he felt that he was trusted sometimes beyond his deserts.

Fritz's clothes were dried at the inn. Hamilton's, however, not being composed of such light materials, he was obliged to leave them there, and borrow whatever he could get from an obliging old peasant, who was profuse in the offers of his wardrobe. It was amusing to see him in the brown trousers, a 'world too wide,' intended to be long, but which, after tugs innumerable, could only be persuaded to half conceal the calves of his legs, whose proportions were rendered somewhat doubtful by the capacious grey worsted stockings in which they were enveloped ; a long waistcoat of red cloth, and a remarkably short-waisted, long-tailed coat, in which a second edition of himself could have found place. These garments altogether formed a costume more original than becoming. Crescenz and Major Stultz laughed unrestrainedly ; Madame Rosenberg repeated her thanks with a suppressed smile, but Hildegarde, without speaking, made a place for him beside her in the carriage, of which he incontinently took possession. He imagined that she spoke more to him than to Zedwitz, on their way home.

Crescenz's efforts to bring Hamilton back to his allegiance were, for some days, as unremitting as they were various. She would never have succeeded had Hildegarde been one jot less quarrelsome ; but either from a naturally irritable temper, or some unaccountable antipathy on her part to Hamilton, they never spoke to each other without saying as many disagreeable things as possible. Hamilton felt that she disliked him and misinterpreted his every word and action, and this conviction and the fear that she might discover how much he had begun to admire her, made him, perhaps, ready to meet her more than half way when she was disposed for battle. Their conversations generally began civilly on his part, but something in her manner, or some unnecessary sharp answer, was sure to provoke an ironical remark or a slighting gesture, which invariably led to the commencement of hostilities.

It was after one of these engagements, in which she had exhibited more than usual vehemence, and he had excelled himself in the art of tormenting, that he found Crescenz alone in the garden. The contrast was irresistible for the moment —it was calm and sunshine after a storm. There she sat, busily employed knitting a stocking which, from its dimensions, might probably be intended for Major Stultz! Her fingers and elbows moved with a rapidity perfectly inconceivable; and as she had for the last four-and-twenty hours been enacting the sentimental and offended, he was allowed to admire her pretty face uninterruptedly as long as he chose; her heightened colour all the time convincing him that she knew he was looking at her. After a few significant coughs, which remained unnoticed, he turned to go away. She looked up and—sighed. This he imagined to be a sort of encouragement—perhaps it was intended for such, as the look which accompanied the sigh was reproachful. He seated himself beside her, while he admired the rapidity with which her work proceeded. The praises were unheeded.

'And who is the happy person destined to wear this?' he asked, playing with a huge piece of work.

'That cannot in any way interest you,' she answered stiffly, but she sighed again.

'Everything concerning you interests me; from the time I first saw you eating roast chicken even to the present moment—'

'You have an odd way of showing your interest, then. Hildegarde says you are always laughing at me!'

'What do you mean?' he exclaimed, though knowing perfectly what she meant, and prepared for the answer which he immediately received, and the implied reproaches for his neglect, which he had expected.

'But, Mademoiselle, you have told me yourself of your engagement—'

'Well, and what of that?'

'I could not think of interfering with Major Stultz. I dare not monopolise—'

'But, at least, you might speak to me sometimes.'

'There might be danger for me were I to do so.'

Crescenz looked immensely delighted and flattered, and her fingers moved faster than ever.

'Is it not customary here to consider an engagement almost as binding as a marriage?'

'I don't know,' she replied, innocently; 'I never was en
gaged until now ; but,' she added, hastily, 'but we are not yet
affianced—that will not be until the day after our arrival in
Munich.'

'Then you are still at liberty to amuse yourself with others?'

'Oh yes.'

'And I may talk to you without Major Stultz's having any
right to be jealous?'

'Jealous!' she repeated, blushing.

'I meant to say angry. Men at his time of life are difficult
to manage, but it seems you get on famously with him, and
have already forgotten all you said in the cloisters.'

'What did I say?' she asked, looking up.

'Merely something about being very unhappy, and so forth.'

'What's the use of being unhappy?' she asked, peevishly.
'Mamma says I must marry some time or other ; and such a
man as Major Stultz is not to be found every day.'

'I know not which is most to be admired, your astounding
resignation or her excellent reasoning.'

She looked at him for a moment, and then having satisfied
herself that he was not laughing, she said confidingly—

'Mamma has been very liberal, and promises me everything
in fifties and hundreds.'

'Fifties and hundreds!' repeated Hamilton.

'The smalls in hundreds—the large in fifties!'

'You will undoubtedly think me very stupid, but I have not
the most remote idea of what you mean.'

'I am to get a *trousseau*, such as mamma herself had ; all
the smaller things, such as pillow-cases, towels, and stockings,
a hundred of each! Table-cloths and such things in fifties!'

'Ha! That must naturally have made you think quite
differently of Major Stultz!'

Again she looked at him inquiringly.

'No ; it did not make me think differently of him—but what
can I do?'

'You cannot do better than try to like him as fast as
possible.'

'If he had only a *Von* before his name!' she observed, sorrowfully.

'Why, what difference would that make?'

'If he were *noble* I should not mind the difference of age.
My mamma was a countess!' she added, proudly.

'Then why not wish him to be count at once?'

'No ; that I could not expect, as I have no fortune, and papa is not a *Von.*'

'I should like to know the exact meaning of this *Von.*'

'It is the first grade of nobility; then comes ritter or chevalier ; then baron, count, prince, duke. I wonder how mamma could have married anyone who was not count or baron—but then, papa was so very handsome, and that makes a great difference !'

'Most undoubtedly ! A handsome face is a good letter of recommendation.'

'Are you noble ?' she asked, abruptly.

'I have no *Von* before my name,' answered Hamilton, laughing.

'Are you not count or baron?'

'Neither.'

'So you are only Mr. Ham*eeltone*?'

'Only Mr. *Alfred* Hamilton.'

He perceived that he had fallen deeply in her estimation, and—he fell in his own a few minutes afterwards, by a fruitless attempt which he made to explain to her the nature of the English peerage, and which he ended, by the assurance that had he been born in Germany, where every member of a family inherits the paternal title, he should, undoubtedly, have been a baron or count. She did not understand him, and he was glad of it, for he felt keenly the absurdity of his oration and the silly boast contained in the concluding remark. Where the *noblesse* is so extensive as in Germany, and where so many members of it are so extremely poor, one would naturally think it would fall in some degree into disrepute, or at least, that it would be regarded with indifference. This is, however, by no means the case, and there is no doubt that had her red-faced major been a count or baron, she would have willingly overlooked the other discrepancies. Even a *Von* before his name would have been a consolation, when combined with the happiness of having had a countess for her mother. These were Hamilton's thoughts during a pause in the conversation, and he partly continued to think aloud when he asked,

'Was she handsome ?'

'Who ?'

'Your mother.'

'I do n't know—I cannot remember her.'

'Are you—is your sister like her ?'

'Hildegarde is very like papa, and people say that I am very like Hildegarde.'

'You are extremely like each other, especially at first sight.'

'Oh, I know that Hildegarde is a great deal handsomer than I am !'

This was a fact, and Hamilton was puzzled for an answer, when she added, after a pause—

'But Major Stultz says I am much more loveable than she is !'

'Major Stultz is a man of discrimination,' said Hamilton, looking round him listlessly.

'He says, too, we shall be very happy when we are married!'

'I hope so, most sincerely.'

'He gave me a great deal of good advice the day we were at Chiem See.'

'Indeed ! On what subject ?'

'He said it was very foolish to trust very young men—that they were very faithless, and good for nothing.'

'All ! Did he say all ?' cried Hamilton, in a tone of mock deprecation.

'Yes, all,' she answered, petulantly. 'He advised me neither to trust them in words nor actions !'

'What extraordinary knowledge of the world he must have ! Altogether a remarkable person !'

'You are laughing at me—or—at him.'

'Laughing ! What an idea! Only look at me for a moment, and you will be convinced of the contrary.'

And she did look at him, and her eyes filled with tears as they met the calm unembarrassed gaze of his. A heavy step on the gravel-walk announced the approach of some one, and on turning round they perceived Major Stultz blowing the ashes out of his meerschaum pipe, as he leisurely walked towards a bank in the garden. Crescenz started as if she had been detected committing a crime, and with heightened colour, rose to join him.

'I thought you said you were at liberty to talk to me as much as you pleased,' observed Hamilton, ironically.

'And so I am ' she replied, seating herself again, whilst she glanced furtively towards her future husband. 'What have you got to say to me ?'

'Oh, a—what were we talking about? Major Stultz's excellent advice, was it not ? I should really like to hear all that

he said to you, for I can hardly think he spent his whole time
in railing at men who have the good fortune to be a score of
years younger than he is.'

'Oh, we spoke of other things also.'

'It would have been very odd if you had not.'

'We—spoke—of love !'

'Very naturally. I really should like to know the opinion
of such a man as Major Stultz on so important a subject.'

'He said,' she began, with a sigh,—'he said that people,
especially women, seldom had the good fortune to marry their
first love.'

'Rather a trite observation, and, on his part, unnecessary.
Surely if any man may hope to be the object of a first love, it
is Major Stultz ! You have only left school a few months—
are not yet sixteen years old. What could he mean by talking
to you about first love ?'

She was silent.

'Perhaps it was as a preliminary to his confessions. Did
he give you a history of his loves? Have they been very
numerous ?'

'No,' she exclaimed, almost angrily; 'he told me, on the
contrary, that I was the first person he had ever wished to
marry.'

'Did you remind him of his proposal to your sister ?'

This contradiction to his words seemed to have entirely
escaped her memory ; she coloured violently, and the ready
tears again prepared to flow. Hamilton felt that he was
amusing himself unpardonably at the poor girl's expense,
teazing her beyond what she could bear, and was preparing to
set all to rights again by playing a little sentiment, when she
rose precipitately, and with such ill-concealed annoyance, to
walk towards Major Stultz, that instead of picking up her
large ball of thread she drew it rashly after her. jerking it
over the flower-beds, and entangling it so effectually in a rose-
bush as she moved quickly on, that Hamilton ran to her assistance, and as he restored it to her said, in a low voice, in
French—

'This evening I shall be in the cloisters *before* sunset. Meet
me there, I entreat of you. I wish to ask your pardon, if I
have offended you.'

The shadows of evening had no sooner begun perceptibly to
lengthen, than Hamilton repaired to the cloisters, and amused

himself endeavouring to decipher the epitaphs on the various tombstones, until a light step close beside him made him look up, and he beheld—not Crescenz, but Hildegarde standing before him. He was about to pass her with a slight inclination, when she stopped suddenly, and said firmly—

'I am the bearer of a message from my sister.'

'The willing bearer of her excuses, no doubt.'

'I understood it was you who were to have made excuses,' she answered, coldly.

'Very true. I had to ask forgiveness for having offended her in the garden to-day ; as, however, the excuses are only intended for her ear, let us consider them made, and talk of something else.'

'I have neither time nor inclination to speak on any subject but the one which brought me here.'

'The communication must be important, if I may judge by the solemnity of your manner,' said Hamilton, looking calmly into the quadrangle.

'My sister desires me to say that she feels the impropriety of her former interview with you here, most deeply, and that nothing will induce her to consent to another. She has told you of her intended marriage : it is almost unnecessary to say, that under such circumstances a continuation of your present attentions will only serve to embarrass and annoy her.'

'Your sister never desired you to say that!' cried Hamilton, fixing his eyes steadily on her face.

'Of this you may be assured,' she continued, colouring deeply, 'that my sister will not again meet you alone, unless—unless—'

'Unless what ?'

'Unless you are more explicit, and give her the power of choosing between you and Major Stultz. It is not yet too late !'

This was what may be called coming to the point at once, and Hamilton was so taken by surprise that he could only stammer something about the shortness of his acquaintance, and believing that he did not quite understand what she meant.

'I believe Crescenz does not quite understand what you mean,' cried Hildegarde, indignantly. 'How I wish she could see with my eyes, and learn to despise you as you deserve!'

'You are really too flattering,' observed Hamilton, laughing.

' much too flattering ; but may I not be allowed to wish that
you would see me with your sister's eyes, and value me as I
deserve ?   However,' he continued, glad of an opportunity to
change the subject, ' although you have just deprived me of a
meeting with your sister, I shall not interfere with your
intended *tête-à-tête* with Count Zedwitz.'

The Count advanced towards them as he spoke.

' Your good opinion is of too little importance to induce me
to disclaim or enter into any explanation,' she replied, turning
quickly from him ; and bowing slightly to Zedwitz, she disappeared through one of the entrances to the cloisters.

' Hameeltone, that is not fair play!' cried the latter, laughing ; 'your presence here was not expected.'

' You do not mean to say you came here to meet Mademoiselle Rosenberg ?'

' And why not ?   You have met her sister here.   Why may
not I hope to be equally fortunate ?'

' Because—because—'

' Because you're handsome and I'm ugly, you think I have
no chance?'

' That was not what I meant.   The difference between the
sisters would rather form the obstacle—'

' Difference, indeed !' exclaimed Zedwitz.

' The difference is in intellect,' observed Hamilton ; ' in
person they are extremely alike.'

' You mean, perhaps, in figure ?' asked Zedwitz.

' In feature, too,' persisted Hamilton.

' Why, they have both brown hair, blue eyes, and red lips, if
that constitute likeness ; but while one has the mere beauty of
extreme youth, the other is the most perfect model of female
loveliness I ever beheld.'

' You are very far gone,' observed Hamilton, gravely.

' But tell me, honestly, did she promise to meet you
here ?'

' How can you ask such downright questions ?   There are
different kinds of beauty, and different kinds of dispositions.
I did not exactly judge it expedient to say, " Meet me this
evening in the cloisters ;" but I talked of the beauty of the
shadows here about sunset, and of my intention to finish a
little *aquarelle* drawing of the said cloisters, with a Benedic-
tine monk issuing from one of the adjoining passages—something just adapted for a lady's album.   I came.   Had you not

been here, I have no doubt I should have obtained a few minutes' attention in spite of my ugliness.'

'She came here, however, expressly to meet me,' observed Hamilton, maliciously.

The Count stopped suddenly, and looked inquiringly in his companion's face.

'She came with a message from her sister,' added Hamilton, quietly, and they again walked on together. 'In fact,' he continued, 'when you joined us, we were in the midst of a kind of altercation which made your presence, to me at least, a great relief.'

'An altercation! About what, may I ask?'

'About her sister. She asked me in pretty plain terms what my intentions were, proposed my entering the lists fairly and honourably with Major Stultz; and when I demurred, she talked angrily of despising me, and so forth. Depend upon it she will call you to account before long.'

'I am quite ready to be called to account.'

'You do not mean to say you think seriously of marrying?'

'I should be but too happy! There is no such luck in store for me!'

'You think she would refuse you?'

'I don't know; but I know my father would refuse his consent.'

'Run off with her, and ask his consent afterwards.'

'I wish I could, but that is impossible here. Marriage is with us a civil as well as a religious act. You have no idea of the formalities attending it, or the certificates necessary to make it valid; besides which, my being in the army increases the difficulty. That cursed caution money!'

'Caution money? What is that?'

'About nine hundred pounds of your money, without which no officer can obtain leave to marry. It is considered a sort of provision for his wife and children in case of his death, and is, probably, a very wise regulation, but is also sometimes a source of great vexation. I am by it completely placed in my father's power, for although I receive from him at present, in addition to my pay, ten times as much as the interest of the necessary sum, and though I know at his death I shall have more than a comfortable maintenance, yet as Hildegarde has no fortune, and I am not independent, our marriage is at present utterly impossible!'

' I advise you at all events to speak to your father.'

' I shall carefully avoid such a communication. Why, I cannot even hope for my mother's assistance, as the connexion would be in every respect disagreeable to her. I have but one hope. Through my sister's influence something may be done: she is a good child, and about to marry to please papa and mamma; first of all, however, I must speak to Hildegarde herself.'

' There you have everything to hope, for she is absolutely *civil* to you sometimes! You will probably enter into some interesting secret engagement?'

' That would be worse than folly. I could not be so ungenerous as to ask her to refuse, perhaps, an eligible establishment, should one offer, on the chance that I should marry her, should I live to become a second edition of Major Stultz! Suppose I wait ten years, Hildegarde's and my ideas would both be changed. I do not feel quite sure that at the end of that time I might not prefer some gentle, simple Crescenz, who would overlook my age and ugliness provided I made her handsome presents, and supplied her liberally with *bonbons.* I wish you had seen her face of delight just before I came here, when Major Stultz gave her a box of *bonbons,* which evidently had been ordered from Munich expressly for her, as it contained nothing but sugar hearts and darts, and kisses wrapt up in pink and blue papers, and doves billing, while almost bursting with the liqueur with which they had been ingeniously filled by the confectioner!'

' So! Now I know why the little coquette did not come to meet me! After having called me to account for my neglect so innocently, and talking such mysterious nonsense about her first love, she amuses herself eating sugar-plums, and sends her sister to me now. These German girls are inexplicable; one cannot talk to them without quarrelling, or being entangled in a labyrinth of sentimentality.'

' You must not judge of all from your slight acquaintance with two,' observed Zedwitz, laughing. ' Say what you please, but you cannot deny that they are fine specimens of the species.'

' Hildegarde is undoubtedly handsome, but then she is only amiable towards you,' said Hamilton, leaning against the side of one of the arches. ' I believe,' he continued, after a pause, ' I believe I am getting very tired of Seon, and, were I not engaged to these Rosenbergs, I should start at once for Vienna. Suppose we make a tour in the Tyrol together?'

Zedwitz looked embarrassed, and said, with some hesitation, 'I—a—am—half engaged to join the Rosenbergs in a party to an alp, and afterwards to Salzburg.'

'What! and I have never heard a word about it?'

'Oh, you will be invited as a matter of course. I had some trouble to manage it, as I do not enjoy the good graces of Madame Rosenberg. She expects her husband to-morrow, who comes here for one day to make the acquaintance of his future son-in-law. The day he leaves is fixed for our excursion.'

'How do we travel?—boys, of course, inclusive?'

'In whatever carriages we can get from here. In Traunstein we take a *char-à-banc*, which will accommodate us all.'

'For such parties it is a very agreeable vehicle, as we can all remain together; and when a division takes place, the chances that one gets a disagreeable companion are too great.'

'*Videlicet!*' cried Hamilton, laughing, 'Count Zedwitz wishes to be quite sure of enjoying the society of a certain young lady for three whole days.'

'You are right,' he answered, taking Hamilton's arm to leave the cloisters. 'Quite right. I trust you have given up all idea of being my rival?'

'I believe I must give up all such idea, if I ever had it, for Hildegarde told me just now that she despised me;—had she said she hated me, I might have some chance, but I am not equal to a struggle against indifference and scorn. I believe,' he added, laughing, 'I must make her hate me.'

'But you won't interfere with me, I hope?'

'Not at all. You will appear more amiable by the contrast.'

'What do you intend to do?'

'Were I to continue my present line of conduct,' answered Hamilton, with affected solemnity, 'it is possible that hate might be produced in time, but, in order to hurry matters, I shall be obliged to make desperate love to her sister. Hildegarde seems very vulnerable on that point. It will not also cost me much trouble, as Crescenz gave me a fair challenge to-day in the garden, and cannot reproach me hereafter.'

'Hamilton!' cried Zedwitz, stopping suddenly, and looking

at him attentively, 'you are certainly older than you acknowledge to be.'

'I understand the implied compliment,' replied Hamilton.
'You conceive my intellect beyond my years. My father
always said I was no fool; I am glad to find that others are
inclined to agree with him in this negative sort of commenda-
tion.'

'You are indeed anything but a fool; and if you fall into
good hands I have no doubt—'

'Good hands!' cried Hamilton, interrupting him; 'I have
no idea of falling into any hands, good or bad: I intend to
judge and act for myself.'

'Then you will pay dear for your experience, as others have
done before you.'

'We shall see,' replied Hamilton.

'You will feel,' said Zedwitz, seizing with both hands the
ends of his long mustachios, to give them a peculiar twirl
towards the corners of his eyes before he entered the room
where the company were assembled for supper.

CHAPTER VIII.

AN ALPINE PARTY.

THE next evening Madame Rosenberg invited Major Stultz
and Crescenz to join her in a walk to meet her husband. Hildegarde was desired to remain behind, and take care of the
children. Poor girl! she was not yet forgiven the atrocious
crime of having refused Major Stultz; and this punishment
she seemed to feel more than Hamilton could comprehend; for
as the trio walked off together, and left her alone, her eyes filled
with tears, and she seated herself on the stone steps of the entrance to the church with an air of such utter despondency,
that he turned towards the lake in order not to annoy her by
his presence, and even played with the two elder boys, to prevent them from tormenting her, until he heard the sound of
wheels and horses' feet, when, looking towards the road, he
saw, at no very great distance, a carriage, which stopped as it
reached the pedestrians, and out of which sprang a man, apparently much too young to be the father of either Hildegarde
or Crescenz. The children, however, cried 'Papa! Papa!'

and rushed towards him. Hildegarde—(pardon the horrible idea)—Hildegarde moved backwards and forwards like a chafed tigress in a menagerie, not daring to disobey her stepmother by quitting the place assigned her, and yet exhibiting anger and impatience in every limb.

As the party drew nearer, Hamilton observed that Mr. Rosenberg was indeed extremely youthful-looking, and must have been eminently handsome. That he was a kind father was evident at a glance, for the children clung to his knees so that he could scarcely walk, and Crescenz had taken complete possession of one of his arms. Just as he reached the place where Hamilton stood, and after being introduced to him as 'our English friend,' his eyes turned towards the spot where Hildegarde was so uneasily perambulating. Releasing himself at once from his companions, he advanced hastily a few steps, calling out, 'Why, how's this, Hildegarde? Why don't you come to meet me?' With a cry of joy she rushed into his arms, and whispered, in a voice almost suffocated by emotion, 'I dared not—I dared not!'

'You feel that you deserve to be scolded? Is it not so? Naughty girl!'

'But you have forgiven me—I know you have.'

Another embrace, and a look of evident forgiveness, not unmixed with pride and admiration, was the answer.

Madame Rosenberg bit her lip, and observed, angrily—

'You really encourage Hildegarde to give way to her violence of temper, instead of pointing out to her the impropriety of her conduct, as I expected.'

'What is past, is past,' he answered, 'and Major Stultz is satisfied.'

'Satisfied! I am the happiest man in the world!' exclaimed Major Stultz.

Crescenz smiled and blushed.

'Well, then, we are all happy. You take Crescenz, who is, if anything, too good and gentle, and I must for the present retain this passionate, good-for-nothing girl!'

He played with her hand as he spoke, and the dullest looker-on must have observed that she was his favourite child.

'You will very probably retain her all your life,' observed Madame Rosenberg.

'I don't think I shall. Somebody will be sure to find out

H

that she is as good-hearted as she is passionate—ill-tempered she is not—the darling !'

'Oh, she is very good-tempered when she has everything her own way—and papa to spoil her ! I don't envy the man who may get her.'

'I shall not pity him,' said her father, gently pressing her hand ; and then, turning to his wife and Major Stultz, seemed determined to change the conversation.

Hamilton left them, and when he found himself alone in the garden unconsciously began to consider—was, or was not, Hildegarde amiable ? or, was she merely a spoiled child, whose father, dazzled by her extreme beauty, thought faultless ? Her sister certainly loved her, and the children, although they preferred Crescenz, assuredly did not dislike her—in fact, her stepmother alone seemed to think her ill-tempered, and he felt strongly inclined to come to the conclusion that her father's evident partiality had provoked the jealousy of that apparently little-indulgent person.

On the ensuing day, Zedwitz and Hamilton had agreed that they would not give the Rosenbergs so much of their society as usual, but, knowing that they could make up for lost time afterwards, leave them to discuss their family affairs during the sojourn of Mr. Rosenberg. They prepared, with a very good grace, to spend the morning with Zedwitz's mother and sister in the garden, and, to the infinite surprise of both ladies, they seated themselves at the table in the arbour which they were in the habit of occupying. Agnes, who continued working with unnecessary assiduity, submitted for some minutes to be tormented, in a boyish manner, by her brother. He wrote upon the table with the point of her scissors, entangled her coloured wool and silk, upset her needle-case, and finally attempted to twitch her work out of her hand.

'You overpower me with your attentions to-day, Max,' she at length observed, with heightened colour ; 'I am no longer used to them.'

'You do not mean that you are annoyed at my playing with this trumpery ?' he cried, moving from her with affected anxiety.

She pushed aside her work with a contemptuous shake of the head, and then leaning her little fresh-coloured face in the palm of her hand, she gently but seriously reproached him for his long neglect of her, and his totally changed manner since he had come to Seon. He assured her, laughingly, that he had been only trying to wean himself from her society, as he was about so soon to lose her altogether. His mother said that moderation should be observed in all things, and though she did not require from him the attentions he had been in the habit of lavishing on his sister, yet she must say the contrast between his former and present manner was too striking not to be most painful to poor Agnes; and, for her part, she thought there must be some secret reason for such conduct. Here she moved uneasily on her chair, and coughed.

'Secret reason!' he exclaimed; 'what can you mean? I am utterly at a loss to—'

'Come, Max, you must greatly underrate my intellect or powers of observation if you imagine that I have not seen what has been going on for the last three weeks.'

'Going on?' he repeated.

'Yes; going on. You have been paying the most marked attentions to one of those Rosenbergs—'

'Which of them?' he asked, with an effort to look unconcerned.

His sister laughed, and said, 'Confess, honestly, Max, for if you really are in love, I think I must forgive your neglect.'

'Thank you, dear.. You know I once forgave you the same offence when proceeding from the same cause.'

'It is unnecessary,' she said, glancing towards Hamilton, and growing perceptibly paler; 'it is unkind to remind me so lightly of the most painful event of my life.'

She was about to leave them, when her brother seized her hand, saying, eagerly, 'Stay, you dear good creature! and forgive me. I quite forgot that Hamilton was present; but never mind him—pray stay! I confess that I am desperately in love with Hildegarde Rosenberg, and I want you to tell my mother, and ask her to give me her assistance and advice.'

His mother, of course, had heard what he had said, and now answered, quickly, 'Assistance, Max, you cannot expect from me; my advice is, that you return to Munich to-morrow.'

'I am engaged to ascend an alp with the Rosenbergs; indeed, I have promised to make an excursion with them which will last three days.'

'You will not find us here on your return,' said his mother, resolutely; 'I totally disapprove of your conduct in every respect, and will not afford you the excuse of passing your time with us, in order to continue it.'

'But, my dear mother—'

'I thought you were too honourable,' she continued, 'to pay attentions which could lead to nothing. You know your father will never consent to such a connexion!'

'I hoped—through your influence—in time, perhaps—'

'Hope nothing in this case from me; much as I desire to see you happily married, such a daughter-in-law—'

'I defy anyone to point out a single fault!' cried Zedwitz, eagerly; 'she is beautiful—Agnes, you who understand so well what beauty is, tell me—is she not beautiful?'

'She is the most beautiful person I ever saw,' answered Agnes, warmly; 'indeed, mamma, there is some excuse for Max's admiration.'

'I don't blame him or anyone for admiring her; but Max spoke just now of more than admiration. He must not forget that she is *not noble*, and that her family are odiously vulgar.'

'But she is not vulgar,' observed Agnes, kindly; 'I have spoken to her two or three times, and think her a very nice person.'

'Max knows that his father will never consent to such a match,' answered her mother; 'therefore, there is no use in talking more about the matter.' (She rose and prepared to leave them.) '·Want of fortune I could have overlooked, and you might have been sure of my assistance, although my hopes have long been fixed on another object; but—such a connexion as this—I never can, I never will sanction.'

Zedwitz waited until his mother was out of hearing, and then drawing nearer his sister, said—

'Well, Agnes, what is to be done now? Do you think she will tell my father?'

'I think not directly: she knows you can do nothing without his consent.'

'Agnes, I have a right to your assistance, and claim it: your reproaches led to this premature discovery—'

'Not at all; mamma has been watching you the last three weeks.'

'And pray why did you not tell me so?'

'I did not know it until a few days ago; and as you

never come near me, or even look at me now, I had no opportunity of speaking to you on that or indeed on any other subject.'

'How well you women know how to mix up reproach and excuse together! I acknowledge that I have neglected you unpardonably, Agnes; but you have promised to forgive me, and I now require your assistance—come, tell me what shall I do?'

'You really wish to marry this Hildegarde?'

'Most undoubtedly, if I can; but you know I am wholly in my father's power, and she has no fortune whatever.'

'The case seems rather hopeless at present,' said Agnes, seriously. 'Have you spoken to her? Would she wait a few years?'

'I have not spoken to her,' he answered, impatiently; 'and as to waiting two or three years, I would rather give up the idea at once.'

'That would indeed be the wisest thing you could do,' cried his sister, eagerly; 'for you may expect the strongest opposition from both papa and mamma. Do not join this alp party; you can easily find some excuse: and let us all go to Hohenfels together before these Rosenbergs return here.'

'How lightly you talk, Agnes!—just as if it only required a visit to the Z——s at Hohenfels to make me forget the last four weeks! I tell you I can never love another as I do Hildegarde; so you must propose something else.'

'Are you quite determined to go with them to-morrow?'

'Quite.'

'Suppose when you are gone I speak to papa; mamma will at all events tell him when she finds that you are actually off; but you know I can generally make papa do whatever I please —and if I explain to him that you are very unhappy—absolutely miserable—'

'Tell him that I am in the depths of despair, or in a state to commit any kind of excess! Say, that I talked of emigrating to America with Hildegarde;—tell him whatever you like, you dear little mediatrix! if you can only obtain his consent.'

'Suppose I succeed with papa, and mamma remains inexorable?'

'Oh, leave me to manage my mother; I have no fear of serious opposition from her.'

'There I fear you are quite mistaken,' said Agnes; 'but,' she added, gaily, 'let us hope the best.'

'Yes; and let us now take a walk, and you shall hear all my plans for the future.'

As they sauntered away together Hamilton heard Zedwitz say, 'I shall, of course, quit the army. My father will, probably, give me Castle Wolfstein, as he dislikes the mountains as much as I like them. We shall be near Hohenfels and the Z——s, which will be agreeable. As a married man, the father of a family, and all that sort of thing, I don't know any people I should like so much for neighbours.'

At a very early hour in the morning they all assembled to drink coffee. Mr. Rosenberg left at the same time for Munich; Hamilton concluding that he was satisfied with his wife's arrangement respecting him, as he shook his hand warmly at parting, and hoped to see him again in the course of the ensuing week. Madame Rosenberg gave various parting directions and commissions which Hamilton did not quite understand; neither did Mr. Rosenberg, he suspected, though he listened to his wife's orders with a patience which made it evident that he resembled Job in more respects than in having daughters than whom 'no women in all the land were found so fair.'

The *char-à-banc* which they were so fortunate as to obtain in Traunstein had five seats, and accommodated the whole party.

At the first respectably steep hill both young men sprang out of the carriage, and when it halted to take them up again, Hamilton had no difficulty in ceding his place beside Hildegarde to Zedwitz, who looked the personification of gratitude; and well he might, for poor Hamilton had got a most riotous companion, and was so placed that he could scarcely avoid overhearing the whispered plans of future happiness which were made, revised, and corrected behind him; while before, he could observe the tactics of Zedwitz, who, with no inconsiderable skill, was reconnoitring the ground previous to the grand attack which he was meditating.

The afternoon was far advanced before they reached the peasant's house where the coachman and his horses were to pass the night, while they pursued their way on foot. The ascent was steeper and longer than they had expected, and the heat intense. Hildegarde, Crescenz, and the two boys proved excellent pedestrians; Major Stultz toiled wearily after them; his efforts to appear vigorous deserved more success—but, alas! after having wiped the drops of perspiration from his crimson face at least twenty times, and even removed his stiff black stock, in order to breathe more freely —he sank exhausted on a fragment of rock, declaring that since his Russian campaign of 1812 he had never been able to recover the right use of his feet. Madame Rosenberg looked for a moment undecided what she should do; she wished to be civil, and offered, after some hesitation, to remain with him until he had rested, but on his declining she said at once that she would go on before and prepare the supper. Poor man! he looked wistfully towards Crescenz. Madame Rosenberg understood him, but shook her head disapprovingly, said she would leave him one of the guides, and begged he would not hurry himself in the least. Crescenz, who had been amusing herself with her two brothers, gathering flowers and picking wild raspberries, now turned to Hamilton, and, giving him a handful of the latter, told him she would show him where to get more. The invitation was irresistible, and, after telling her mother that they intended to overtake Hildegarde, who was still in sight, they hurried off together.

The conversation was at first desultory, interrupted by the scrambling through the bushes, and mutually offering the largest raspberries; by degrees, however, the fragrant fruit was neglected, and the flowers—even the beautiful pyrolas and sweet-scented cyclamen, gathered for and given to her by Major Stultz—were thoughtlessly picked to pieces and thrown away, while she listened to Hamilton's remarks or answered his numerous questions. She spoke without reserve of her mode of life at school—attached a girlish importance to her former companions' opinions and most trifling acts— complained of not having been allowed to speak during school-hours, and of being obliged to run and jump about at recreation time, when she would rather have sat in a corner to talk to her friend Lina; of having to listen to reading when at dinner; but most of all, of having had all her long hair cut off the day of her entrance.

'I was quite inconsolable about it,' she said, laughing, 'and cried for several days, but Hildegarde did not care in the least; perhaps,' she added, 'because she was a year older.'

Hamilton thought there might be another reason—the absence of personal vanity—but of course he did not say so. They had been ten years at school without ever having been allowed to spend a day at home.

'So,' she continued, 'we knew nothing at all of my step-mother, and very little of papa, though he used to come and see us often and talk to Mademoiselle Hortense about us. At the examinations they generally both came, and mamma used to bring us an iced tart; but Hildegarde would rather she had stayed away, as she was ashamed of her.'

' And why was she ashamed of her ?'

' Oh, because all the other girls had such nice mothers and aunts, and Hildegarde thinks mamma so very vulgar.'

' She seems, however, a good kind of person.'

' Oh, I dare say—but Hildegarde does not like good kind of persons.'

' Indeed ! Pray what kind of persons does she like, then ?'

' I don't know whether she would like me to tell you or not.'

' And I don't think you are obliged to ask her ?'

' That is true; and, besides, it is no harm to like counts and barons better than other people !'

' Not at all. You rather said that you had a fancy of the same kind yourself, a few days ago.'

' Yes—I confess I should like to be a *Von*, or a baroness, or a countess—but still there is a difference, for I am afraid of fine people, and Hildegarde likes them; I saw her getting books from the Baroness Z——, and speaking to those proud Zedwitzes the other day.'

' You think it, then, probable, that she rather likes the attentions of Count Zedwitz ?'

' I—don't—know. Hildegarde never speaks about such things when they concern herself, though she expects me to tell her everything ! I saw that old Countess Zedwitz talking to her in the garden yesterday—the Countess looked very red, and kept nodding her head continually, and Hildegarde was very pale and haughty. I asked her what they had been speaking about, but she did not choose to tell me. I dare say it was something disagreeable.'

' That is not impossible,' said Hamilton, musingly; ' in fact, rather probable. So, you don't know whether or not your sister likes Zedwitz ?'

'No. She only observed once, when we were speaking of beauty, that she did not think it necessary for a man to be handsome.'

'That was rather applicable to him; but he is so devoted that I should imagine him irresistible.'

'I don't think that is the way to please Hildegarde.'

'I should have thought devotion must have been pleasing to every woman.'

'But Hildegarde has such odd ideas! I remember hearing her say to Mademoiselle Hortense, just before we left school, that she rather thought she should like a man of whom she could be afraid!'

'Strange girl!' said Hamilton.

'Strange girl, indeed!' repeated Crescenz; 'and others think so differently! I should not like to be afraid of any-one I loved, and that is one of the reasons why I think that only people of nearly the same age should marry!'

Hamilton turned quickly to his companion, whose deep blush gave a special meaning to her last observation.

Hildegarde, Zedwitz, and Fritz, were far before them. Madame Rosenberg, with Gustle, and two guides loaded with provisions, equally far behind. They became sentimental, and often looked back to admire the view, which every moment increased in beauty and extent. She wished to be the inhabitant of one of the peaceful pretty peasants' houses which were scattered in the valley beneath them. Hamilton, of course, wished to bear her company. She sighed and murmured something about his understanding her, but fearing that Major Stultz never would. Hamilton declared, with unusual warmth, that it was dreadful to think of such a marriage!—such a sacrifice! And he was sincere, too, for the moment, for he thought of the Major as he had last seen him, while he looked on the blooming youthful face before him; and never had Crescenz looked so pretty! A few commonplace expressions of admiration were received with such evident pleasure, that Hamilton found the temptation more than he could withstand, and from admiration glided almost imperceptibly into a most absurd, but rather indefinite, declaration of love. The words, however, had scarcely passed his lips before he became conscious of his folly. His dismay is not to be described when Crescenz, covered with blushes, confessed that she had loved him from the commencement of their acquaintance, and added, that she was willing, for his sake, to brave both her father's and mother's anger by dismissing Major Stultz !

Hamilton was perfectly thunderstruck, and for some moments quite incapable of uttering a syllable; as soon, however, as he could collect his thoughts, he began in a constrained voice, and with a manner as agitated as her own, to explain that he was a younger son, totally dependent on his father, and that he could not by any possible chance think of marrying for at least ten or twelve years.

Crescenz looked at him for a moment reproachfully, and then, covering her face with her hands, burst into tears.

Hamilton never had been so angry with himself as at that moment; his fault was, indeed, unpardonable, and he felt that Crescenz was right when she pushed him from her and refused to listen to his excuses. The fact was, he had never thought she cared more for him than for any other person willing to pay her attention; and she had appeared so perfectly happy the day before—nay, that very day—that he had naturally imagined her now quite satisfied with her future prospects, and had expected her to understand what he had said more as a tribute to her youth and beauty, than as a serious proposal ; the more so, as he had not made the most distant allusion to marriage in all that he had said. He now walked sorrowfully after the weeping girl, whose secret he had learned by such unwarrantable thoughtlessness. It was in vain he tried to exculpate himself, by thinking she was an arrant flirt, and would soon forget him : he began seriously to doubt her being one ; everything in her manner that had led to that conclusion could now be interpreted otherwise ; her receiving Major Stultz's presents, and her apparent contentment, might have been affected to provoke his jealousy : her sister's words in the cloisters confirmed this idea. He did not give her credit for sufficient intellect to feel annoyed at having ' told her love,' but even that consolation was denied him ; for on distantly hinting that it was unnecessary any person should ever be made acquainted with their late conversation, she wrung her hands, and exclaimed bitterly—

' Oh, how could I be such a fool as to betray myself so !'

They walked on long in silence; but Crescenz was too good and gentle to be inexorable, and before the end of their walk he had obtained pardon and a promise of secrecy—the latter without difficulty, as she innocently confessed she was equally afraid of her mother's anger and her sister's contempt.

They reached the alp both totally out of spirits. Crescenz's melancholy face was a sort of reproach from which Hamilton would gladly have escaped; and he now heartily repented his having made an engagement with Madame Rosenberg. Until Crescenz's marriage had taken place he saw no chance of peace of mind or enjoyment of any kind, and many were the vows he internally made to be more circumspect in future.

'Come, Hamilton, you must look at the sunset,' cried Zedwitz, seizing his arm and leading him away. He was in oppressively high spirits, and talked on without waiting for an answer, or even perceiving that his companion paid no sort of attention to what he said. They stood on the top of the alp; behind, and on each side of them, forming a sort of crescent, were mountains of every possible form, from the gigantic rocky peaks on which the snow lay, to the richly-wooded mountain and green alp; with mountains, valleys, forests, rivers, lakes, towns, villages, in view; more than it was possible for the eye at once to enclose or the mind to comprehend.

Hildegarde and Crescenz joined them as the evening prayer bell tolled. At Seon this bell had generally been tolled while they had been at supper. The clatter of knives and forks and tongues had instantly ceased, and an awful stillness had taken place, which had not been broken by word or movement until the last sound of the bell had died away; when, as if a spell had been broken, each person had wished their neighbour a good evening, and renewed, with increased vigour, the interrupted occupation. It had always struck Hamilton as something very Mahometan-like, this sudden call to prayer, especially when it occurred in the midst of conversation, where the difficulty of commanding the thoughts must be tenfold increased. Not so did it appear to him this evening: as village after village, and every church spire far and near, sent their tranquil chimes over the plain, a feeling of enthusiastic devotion was irrepressible; it seemed as if the solemn tones, on reaching the mountains, paused to vibrate in the air while they recollected the prayers which they were about to bear to heaven on a thousand echoes. Zedwitz stood with his head uncovered and arms folded; Crescenz clasped her hands and moved her lips in prayer. Hildegarde's eyes were fixed so steadfastly on the golden clouds above her, that it was impossible not to think that at the moment she wished for the 'wings of a dove to flee away and be at rest :' a messenger from the *châlet* waited respectfully for the last sound to die away in the distance before he summoned them to supper. The interruption was unwelcome to them all ; but before they descended it was agreed that they should return again with the guides and make a bonfire.   They found Madame Rosenberg, as usual, bustling about, ordering and directing everybody and everything ; Fritz and Gustle stealing cake and sugar ; and Major Stultz, who seemed to have but lately arrived, was sitting in his shirt-sleeves wistfully eyeing a glass of beer which he was afraid to drink in his then state of heat, while, to hurry the operation of cooling, he was fanning himself with a red and yellow pocket-handkerchief! Hamilton glanced towards Crescenz, but as their eyes met, he regretted that he had done so, and determined that nothing should induce him to look either at her or Major Stultz for a long time again.   Something, however, he must seek to interest him, and he turned towards Hildegarde : a more dangerous study he could scarcely have found.   She was seated on the grass, outside the door of the wooden pavilion, beside her brothers, and, for the first time since he had known her, seemed occupied with them.   There was a quiet avoidance of Zedwitz on her part, which, in contrast to the coquetry of her sister, particularly interested Hamilton.   This scarcely perceptible avoidance was, however, unnoticed.   Zedwitz was too completely wrapt up in admiration, and had eyes and ears for her alone.   Weariness prolonged the meal, and twilight was deepening into night before they thought of moving.   Madame Rosenberg and Major Stultz said at length, that it was time to retire to rest ; the others remembered that they intended to make a fire on the top of the hill, and insisted on putting their plan into execution.   Major Stultz, afraid to oppose, followed Crescenz : the guides were put in requisition, and in a short time everyone was collecting wood and piling it in a heap.

The fire burned brightly, and coloured picturesquely the different members of the party, as they lay dispersed around, some seated on the stumps of trees, others extended on the grass—all weary, yet all interested in their novel situation. Hamilton, apart from the others, looked on without mixing in the careless conversation which was kept up—it was to him like a scene in a play ; he understood the double plot, and had

decided on making Hildegarde the heroine ; but was Zedwitz
the hero who, at the end, was to obtain her fair hand ?   No ;
unaccountably enough, he found that to suit his plan the old
Count must be perfectly obdurate.   Zedwitz was to give up
the affair as hopeless ; and Hildegarde ! Hildegarde was to—
to—remain at home ;—yes—that would do—an inmate still of
her father's house ; and now, unconsciously, Hamilton, from
supposing himself a spectator, became, in thought, an actor.
He was also in that house.—Hildegarde was to become insensibly aware of his good qualities and good looks—was, in fact,
to become desperately in love with him !—he, all the while,
stoically indifferent.   A feeling of honour was to make him
explain to her, in a most interesting scene, the impossibility
of a—she—Crescenz—Zedwitz—   Here the party round the
fire broke up.   The boys had fallen asleep, and were now being
carried by the guides to the *châlet.*   Madame Rosenberg, Hildegarde, and Crescenz, followed ; Major Stultz remained to
finish his pipe, and the two young men commenced fresh cigars ;
they did not exchange a word until their companion had left
them, when Zedwitz, pitching his cigar into the still glowing
embers, asked abruptly—

'Do you know where you are to sleep to-night?'

'Not I,' answered Hamilton ; 'but I do not expect the accommodation to be even tolerable.'

'We are to sleep together in a hay-loft.'

'I have done that before, and for one night it does not signify ; but Major Stultz?'

'Sleeps also in the hay-loft.

'And the boys ?'

'In the hay-loft.'

'And the ladies?'

'In the hay-loft.'

'Nonsense, Zedwitz!—you are joking.'

'I am perfectly serious ; there is but one bed in the house,
and it is so little inviting that no one has courage to make use
of it. We are all to sleep together in the hay-loft. I rather
enjoy the idea. Shall we go?'

'By all means.'

This, thought Hamilton, as they descended the hill together,
is something quite out of the common course of things. I
wonder what sort of a loft it is ?

The only light in the house proceeded from the kitchen fire,

which still burnt on the high open hearth : beside it were
seated one of the guides and a peasant girl, who had come from
one of the houses in the valley, and so wrapt up were they in
their evidently confidential discourse, that they were unconscious of the presence of strangers until Zedwitz laughingly
asked the way to the hay-loft.

'This way, if you please,' said the man, looking a little embarrassed, 'Take care you don't stumble, it is so dark.'

He was followed closely by Hamilton, and they both quietly
and cautiously mounted the somewhat ricketty ladder which
led to the loft, and entered it by a trap-door. It was very full
of hay, and, by the light which was sparingly admitted through
the solitary gable window, they could see several figures
stretched in different positions around them, but they could not
tell whether or not they were sleepers. Major Stultz was alone
communicative on that point—he lay with his mouth wide open,
and was snoring profoundly.

'I suppose, Hamilton, we ought to take the places near the
entrance ?' whispered Zedwitz.

'I cannot bear a draught,' replied the other, moving towards
the end of the loft, where Madame Rosenberg and the children
were lying. At his approach, two figures began slowly to roll
away from him—a stifled laugh and an angry hush betrayed
at once the sisters ; and no sooner had he and Zedwitz chosen
their places, than they perceived a partition wall of hay was
being built in their neighbourhood. Soon convinced that
Madame Rosenberg and the children slept, Hamilton felt
greatly inclined to commence a conversation with the two
girls ; but which of them should he address ? From Hildegarde
he had little hope of an answer—from Crescenz he felt that he
deserved none. It was in vain he urged Zedwitz to begin,
telling him that he could not sleep ; that the hay was too hot,
and the loft too cold, and too uncomfortable ; that he could not
remain quiet, &c., &c., &c. : his companion moved away from
him, saying, in a low voice, that he knew Hildegarde would not
speak, and that he had nothing to say to her sister. In a few
minutes he too was fast asleep, leaving Hamilton to compose
himself as he best could. After having tried all possible positions, he at length resigned himself to his fate, and determined
not to move again.

After half-an-hour's silence, Hildegarde and her sister began
to whisper to each other.

'Is not that man's snoring dreadful, Hildegarde? Confess, he looked odious this evening at supper, sitting in his shirt-sleeves like a shoemaker or tailor.'

'You see him to great disadvantage in a party of this kind, dear; at home I am sure he is quite different—and as to his snoring, you know even papa snores sometimes.'

'I know you are determined not to see anything that does not place him in an advantageous light, and I only regret you did not discover his perfections sooner—it would have saved me a world of misery!'

To this speech no answer was made, and a long pause ensued.

'Hildegarde, are you angry?' at length asked Crescenz, timidly.

'No; I am only tired of always hearing the same thing.'

'Forgive me, dearest, and I promise you have heard it for the last time; but now I expect that you will give me an answer to a plain question. You cannot pretend any longer to be blind to Count Zedwitz's attentions—what answer do you intend to—'

The whisperers had hitherto spoken inaudibly, but this question, from a change of position in the speaker, distinctly reached Hamilton's ears. Great was his curiosity to know the answer, but without a moment's delay he moved and coughed. Not a sound more was heard, not a whisper even attempted during the whole two long hours that he still lay awake and motionless, wishing for morning.

And when the morning came, Hamilton slept soundly; he saw not the sisters as they passed his couch on tiptoe; he heard not the proposal of Fritz to cover him with hay, or of Gustle to tickle him, or the admonitions of Madame Rosenberg, and her threats of leaving them always at home in future should they dare now to make a noise. When he awoke he found himself the sole occupant of the loft, and had at first some difficulty in recollecting how he had got there. It was still very early, and, in the hope of seeing the sun rise from the top of the alp, he hurried out into the fresh morning air. The sun was, however, beyond the horizon, and bright daybeams already tinted the mountain tops. A few minutes brought him to the spot where they had all sat round the fire the preceding evening; the charred wood marked the spot, and had Hamilton found there the society he expected, he would probably have taken time to have once more admired the prospect which had so delighted him a few hours before, and which was now even more beautiful in the distinctness of early morning; but he was a gregarious animal, and, finding himself unexpectedly alone, a hasty glance of admiration was all now bestowed on the diversified plain which lay beneath him, and then, with hasty steps, he retraced his way to the *châlet*. One of the guides met him at the door, and informed him that Madame Rosenberg and the others had been gone some time, and were to dress and breakfast at the farm-house where they had left the carriage. A short time sufficed to enable him to overtake the last detachment, consisting of Madame Rosenberg, Crescenz, and Major Stultz, and they pursued their way leisurely together. Hildegarde had been sent on before to order breakfast, and, on finding that Zedwitz intended to accompany her, had taken her two brothers. On reaching the farm-house, they found her busily occupied at a table placed under the trees, preparing bread and milk for the children—Zedwitz officiously assisting her.

'What! are you already dressed for Salzburg, Hildegarde?' cried Madame Rosenberg. 'You must have walked very quickly; I hope the boys are not overheated!'—and she carefully placed her hand on their foreheads to ascertain the fact.

'Oh, mamma,' cried Fritz, boastingly, 'we could have walked much faster! We could have been down the mountain in half the time! It was Zedwitz who was tired; he wanted us twice to rest on the way.'

'It would have been better than running the risk of giving the children colds,' observed Madame Rosenberg, glancing towards Hildegarde.

'Oh, we did not wish to rest, or Hildegarde either, though Zedwitz said he had ever so much to say to her.'

'Indeed!' cried his mother, looking inquisitively from one to the other; 'indeed!' She turned to Hamilton, who stood beside her, and whispered, 'I shall not be five minutes dressing; you will greatly oblige me by remaining here until I return.'

Hamilton made no answer; he waited, however, only until she was fairly out of sight, and then, nodding good-humouredly to Zedwitz, walked into the house. Madame Rosenberg's ideas of five minutes for dressing were not very defined. She was one of those persons who, at home the most incorrigible of slatterns, when they go out make it a point to be almost overdressed. Hamilton, Crescenz, and Major Stultz had long been waiting for her before she appeared, and to begin breakfast without her would have been an unpardonable offence. The delays seemed to have no end, for as she approached the table, Zedwitz, who had been standing apart, went towards her and requested to speak a few words to her alone. Major Stultz proposed waiting until after breakfast, but Zedwitz persisted in his request with a seriousness which scarcely admitted of a refusal, and the audience was accordingly granted. Hamilton wished to look at Hildegarde, but he refrained: had he done so his conjectures might have taken another turn, for surely had Hildegarde imagined herself the subject of conversation, she could not have leaned so calmly on her elbow without exhibiting the slightest particle of emotion! Crescenz did not seem to think her sister's imperturbability a conclusive argument—her eyes anxiously followed her stepmother's form, and nothing but the shortness of the conference, and ocular demonstration that they were simply arranging accounts, could have convinced her that she had been mistaken in her supposition that Zedwitz was formally asking permission to pay his addresses to her sister. She had dressed in a room at the front of the house, and from the window had seen them standing at the spring together. Zedwitz had spoken long and eagerly, and Hildegarde had apparently listened very calmly, but with evident interest, to what he had said. Her answer was short and decided, and she had left him abruptly, to interfere between her brothers, who were flinging the remains of their bread and milk at each other. It had cost both sisters considerable trouble to purify their garments before their mother saw them.

A small carriage was now drawn up to the front of the house, and a youthful peasant led out a young, strong-built grey horse, and began to arrange the harness. Zedwitz advanced quietly towards the party, and surprised them not a little by saying that he was about to take leave of them—he did not feel well, and would return to Seon.

'You are ill!' cried Hamilton, starting up from the bench where he had been lazily reclining; 'you are ill, and think of returning alone! That must not be allowed. I am quite ready to accompany you.'

I

'It is not necessary,' replied Zedwitz, laying his hand heavily on his arm, while he continued to take leave of the others, and hoped their tour might prove in every respect agreeable. 'The fact is,' he said, drawing Hamilton towards the little carriage, which it appeared had been got ready for him, 'the fact is, I am ill in mind, but not in body. Hildegarde has refused my suit so decidedly that I dare not renew it. The best thing I can now do is to return to Seon, and perhaps I may arrive in time to prevent my sister from speaking to my father. My rash haste may have injured my cause. How could I expect her to get accustomed to my ugliness and to care for me in so short a time?'

'I think,' said Hamilton, 'it is more than probable that her fear of the opposition of your family may have caused her refusal.'

'Not a bit of it! She never referred to my family, nor, indeed, had I time to mention them. She said she liked me very well as an acquaintance, but nothing more; she was sorry if her manner had led me to think otherwise. Now I was obliged, in justice, to exonerate her from even a shadow of coquetry, which in this case was disagreeable, as it was tantamount to charging myself with egregious vanity: but the most annoying and disheartening thing in the whole business was her coolness and decision of manner; it led me at once to form the conclusion that I was not the first person who had spoken to her on the same subject. Do you think it possible that her affections are already engaged?'

'I neither think it possible, nor even probable. Why, she has not left school more than two months.'

'Her sister left school at the same time, is a year younger, and yet has contrived to fall in love with you, and to promise to marry another in exactly half the time,' said Zedwitz, bitterly.

'Pray do not imagine anything of that kind,' said Hamilton, colouring deeply; 'she is merely one of those soft, yielding sort of beings who, with a more than sufficiency of vanity and coquetry in their nature, are ready to fancy themselves and others in love without rightly knowing what the feeling is. This Hildegarde is worth a hundred such. I like her decision of character, and she is certainly very handsome.'

'Handsome! She is perfectly beautiful!' cried Zedwitz; 'and I am convinced she is as amiable as beautiful!'

'If you are convinced of *that*, you are very wrong to give

her up as you are doing. Try what time and perseverance will do.'

'My dear Hamilton, if you had spoken to her, if you had even seen her when I pleaded my cause, you would think differently. When we meet again it will be as common acquaintances. But every moment is precious, and I must now be off. I shall take post-horses at the next town, and expect to reach Seon in the afternoon. I hope most sincerely that my sister has had no opportunity of speaking to my father. I shall scarcely be at Seon when you return; but you know my address in Munich, and I shall expect to see you directly you arrive there. Adieu !'

He sprang into the carriage, bowed to the occupants of the breakfast-table, and drove off, while Hamilton, leaning against the door of the house, looked after him. ' So,' he thought, ' this is the man I fancied full of German romance and enthusiasm! Why, my brother John could not have resigned himself to his fate more easily; but then he would have made a parade of his indifference. Englishmen are fond of doing so, while Germans, I suspect, are disposed to pretend to more feeling than they possess. Yet, after all, what could he have done? Shoot himself, like Werther? Absurd! What should I have done? I have not the most remote idea; but then, I have never got beyond temporary admiration for anyone. Very odd, too. Jack says he was in love before he was twelve years old. Precocious fellow! Zedwitz was right the other day when he said that my feelings and ideas were not those of a man of my time of life. However, I flatter myself that what I have lost in what he calls freshness of feeling, I have gained in other respects, and can now, in spite of my youth, calmly contemplate what is going on about me, while Zedwitz, so many years my senior, has been acting with all the rash impetuosity of a boy.'

In all the proud consciousness of premature knowledge of the world, Hamilton seated himself at the breakfast-table, and allowed Madame Rosenberg to pour out his coffee, and wonder without interruption what could be the matter with the Count, who, she insisted, had been quite well all the morning. His eyes glanced mischievously towards Hildegarde, but she apparently did not observe it. Madame Rosenberg now began deliberately to pack up the remaining sugar in her reticule. Half-an-hour later they were seated in the *char-à-banc* on their way to

Salzburg. A sort of discontent seemed to pervade the whole party for some time, but by degrees it yielded to the beauty of the scenery. Madame Rosenberg, having once spent some months at Salzburg, was now able to name each mountain as it appeared in the foreground, or made itself remarkable by its form in the distance. But the Untersberg interested her two sons more than anything else. This mountain, which here rises abruptly out of the Walser fields, and is of enormous extent, was, she told them, the prison and tomb of Frederick Barbarossa, or, as the peasants said, of Charlemagne. The questions and answers on this fruitful subject lasted until they reached Salzburg.

CHAPTER IX.

SALZBURG.

WHILE waiting for dinner at the hotel, Hamilton amused himself by turning over the leaves of the ' Strangers' book,' and saw among the latest arrivals the name of an uncle he had wished much to meet when he had been last in Salzburg ; he would then have been glad to have had an opportunity of presenting some respectable relations to Baron Z——, after the odd manner in which their acquaintance had commenced : he now wished to see his relations from more natural motives, without either the wish or intention of making them acquainted with his travelling companions. There is something peculiarly agreeable in hearing the voices of one's countrymen speaking one's own language in a foreign country ; even if they be merely common acquaintances, they rise at once to the rank of friends ; if friends, to relations ; if relations, we are astonished at the excess of our affection for them ! Something of this kind Hamilton experienced as he heard his uncle saying, ' A young gentleman inquiring for me ! What is his name ?' In a moment he had quitted the table, and was in the lobby before the question could be answered. The surprise, perhaps, heightened the pleasure felt by his two young and pretty cousins, and their reception of him was so unreservedly affectionate, that as they came near the door of the dining-room, Hildegarde and Crescenz exchanged glances, and then fixed their eyes on them with a slight expression of curiosity.

' What a pity you did not arrive earlier, Alfred ! We have

spent the whole morning sight-seeing, and now the horses are
being put-to, and we have scarcely ten minutes to ask each
other the thousand questions which—— But come to our rooms;
we cannot possibly talk before these people.'

'They would not understand us,' said Hamilton, following
them up the stairs, by no means displeased at the arrangement.

Madame Rosenberg soon became impatient at the duration
of his absence, and leaving word with the waiter that Mr.
Hamilton might follow them to St. Peter's Cellar, she proposed
herself as guide, and they set out on their excursion.

Hamilton accompanied his uncle and cousins to their very
handsome travelling-carriage, and as he bade them adieu for
the twentieth time, his uncle called out, 'God bless you,
Alfred ! I shall tell your father and uncle Jack that I found
you greatly improved. If they had kept you in London, your
brother John would have spoiled you, and made you just as
good-for-nothing as he is himself. Nothing like travelling for
enlarging the ideas. Good bye !'

The waiter informed Hamilton that the ladies were gone to
St. Peter's Cellar.

'Major Stultz, you mean ?' said Hamilton.

'No, sir — the ladies — perhaps they have gone to look at
the excavation in the rock. The cellar is in the mountain,
and is worth seeing.'

The monks of St. Peter are the actual proprietors of this
cellar, which adjoins, and in fact is still a part of the monastery ; it is the wine from their Hungarian vineyards which
is there sold, and the entrance to the drinking rooms is from
the principal quadrangle. Arrived there, Hamilton immediately accosted a man who, in a jacket and apron, and with a
green velvet cap on his head, stood before the entrance of the
excavation.

'Ladies ! Oh, ha — yes — they are within,' he answered,
leading the way through a small dark passage to two low
rooms filled with the fumes of tobacco. Hamilton entered,
and found his travelling companions actually seated at a table
drinking wine, in a room crowded with Hungarian officers,
who seemed equally surprised and amused at the unusual
appearance of such an addition to their society. Madame
Rosenberg was quietly sipping her wine, and talking earnestly
to Major Stultz near a window, quite unconscious of the
sensation which she and her party had created, and the by
no means whispered exclamations of admiration which were

echoed on all sides, and which produced most opposite effects on the objects of them. Crescenz looked half frightened, half pleased, and blushed incessantly. Hildegarde's countenance denoted annoyance bordering on anger as she sat biting her under lip, while every trace of colour had forsaken her face. Hamilton felt extremely irritated, and looked round the room with a portentous frown to see if any *one* had been more forward than the others, but in vain—broad, sallow, good-humoured faces and small sparkling black eyes met his angry glance wherever he turned ; and as the conversation was now principally carried on in their native language, he could only surmise, but no longer be certain of, the subject of discourse. The eyes of all were still turned on the two sisters ; and Hamilton, after a moment's hesitation, proposed escorting them to the Maximus Chapel, which was near, and where they could wait for their mother. Hildegarde started up without asking the permission, which, however, was accorded without difficulty; and the two boys, to their infinite annoyance, were also ordered off. On perceiving their mother engaged in confidential conversation with Major Stultz, they had freely helped themselves to wine, and were now in outrageous spirits. On entering the St. Peter's churchyard, they commenced springing over the graves in a most irreverent manner, declaring they had never before seen so jolly a churchyard! Crescenz looked infinitely shocked, entreated they would not make so much noise; and, finding her remonstrances useless, she turned towards the St. Margaret's Chapel, a small building in the middle of the burying ground, and leaning against the iron railing which formed at once its door and gable-end, she folded her hands reverently and prayed. The custom in Roman Catholic countries of leaving the church doors constantly open most certainly conduces to promote piety. Many a giddy girl, whose thoughts have wandered as unrestrained as her glances down the crowded aisle, has sought the same spot afterwards in solitude to offer up supplications and thanksgivings as fervent perhaps as ever were breathed. Much as has been said of the imposing ritual of the Church of Rome—of the almost irresistible effect of high mass when properly celebrated—it is nothing in comparison with the solemn silence of a weekday afternoon, when the stillness around makes the solitary foot-fall echo, and those who come to pray can bend the knee and clasp the hand without exciting the inquisitive gaze of a less piously disposed neighbour.

Hamilton had gone in search of the person who had the keys of the Maximus Chapel; on his return he found Hildegarde standing thoughtfully opposite a newly-made tomb, on which a placard was placed with the words : 'This tomb is to be sold.'

'I should like extremely to know your thoughts,' he said, quietly, placing himself beside her.

'Should you ?   They would scarcely repay you for the trouble of listening.'

'I am quite willing to make the trial.'

'But I am much too lazy to attempt collecting all the scattered thoughts of the last ten minutes.'

'The very last I can guess, perhaps,' said Hamilton ; 'your eyes were fixed on that placard, and you thought —'

'Well, what ?'

' " Where are now the future occupiers of that tomb ?" Am I not right ?'

'Quite right.   Wherever they are, and whoever they may be, they certainly have no wish to enter here : the buyers of *tombs* are seldom disposed to enter into actual possession.   But where is this Maximus Chapel ?   You said it was in the mountain, and I see nothing in the least like an entrance, although there are three windows and a wall up there.'

'The windows were formerly mere holes made in the rock, and ought never to have been glazed ; through the largest of them fifty monks, who had taken refuge with Maximus, were thrown headlong down the mountain by the barbarians who took possession of Salzburg in the fifth century.'

'And Maximus ?'

'He was hung.'

'That was a pity—I dare say he would have preferred being thrown over the precipice ?'

'Do you think so ?   As it all came to the same in the end, I should imagine it must rather have been a matter of indifference to him.'

'But I do not,' cried Hildegarde, stopping suddenly ; 'I think the manner in which one is put to death of great importance.   I am sure you would prefer being beheaded to being hung ?'

'The choice would be distressing ; but I believe you are right ; I should certainly choose being beheaded as the more gentlemanlike death of the two, though I remember reading in some book the horrible hypothesis—that the eye could see, the ear hear, and the brain think, for some moments after the head had been severed from the body !'

The guide jingled his keys. He probably thought the discussion of such subjects might be deferred until he had received his *Trinkgeld,* and he now threw open the gate and motioned to them to ascend. The tolerably numerous steps leading to the former abode and chapel of the anchorite were hewn in the mountain, the passage somewhat dark, and Hildegarde having declined any assistance, Hamilton, notwithstanding all his good resolutions to avoid Crescenz in future, turned towards her, was greeted with a soft smile, and his arm accepted as willingly as it was offered. He now took upon himself the office of guide, exhibited the chapel with its solitary Roman pillar, the sleeping-room of Maximus, and the place from which his companions had been precipitated. He was obliged to hold Crescenz, while she childishly stretched as far as possible over the mountain side, all the while declaring that she could not stand on the brink of a precipice without feeling an almost irresistible inclination to throw herself down it. No sooner had her two brothers heard this, than they rushed forward and thoughtlessly pushed her with a violence that might have had most fatal consequences, had not Hamilton at the moment thrown his arms quite round her and drawn her back. Crescenz screamed violently, Fritz and Gustle laughed immoderately, Hildegarde remonstrated angrily, and, in the midst of the clamour, Madame Rosenberg and Major Stultz joined them. Crescenz blushed deeply, and, with a voice trembling from agitation, related what had occurred, and complained bitterly of her brothers' rudeness. Madame Rosenberg scolded her for having looked down the precipice ; Hildegarde for not having watched her brothers, and prevented such a scene in such a place ; and concluded by seizing both the boys by the shoulders and shaking them violently, while she declared that she had a great mind to send them back to the inn, and not let them see either the Dom Church or the fountain. She turned to thank Hamilton for having taken charge of so riotous a party, but he had disappeared, annoyed at what had occurred, and internally vowing never to take charge of Crescenz or her brothers again.

Major Stultz had suddenly become jealous and out of temper—all the efforts of Madame Rosenberg to turn ' the

winter of his discontent' to 'glorious summer,' were vain ;
he followed her, half whistling, with his hands clasped behind
him, intending to look extremely unconcerned, while his
heightened colour, as they overtook Hamilton, betrayed to all
the cause of his annoyance. Crescenz seemed perfectly
indifferent, or rather half disposed to brave his anger ; for as
they stood by Haydn's monument, in the Peter's Church, she
placed herself beside Hamilton, and spoke to him in French.
It is true the conversation was about the skull of Haydn, and
the black marble urn which contained it ; but Major Stultz
could not be aware of this circumstance, and with increased
anger he strode down the aisle, seeming disposed to quit them,
had not Hamilton, weary of these misunderstandings, and
provoked by Crescenz's coquetry, said that he would meet
them at the hotel in an hour: he was going to the cavalry
stables to see the horses, which, of course, would not be
interesting to them, and, without waiting for an answer, he
walked away.

Hamilton's absence did not seem to have much improved
the state of affairs, for on his return to the inn no one but
Madame Rosenberg seemed disposed to be loquacious ; and
when they got into the *char-à-banc* which was to take them
to Berchtesgaden, Crescenz absolutely manœuvred to avoid
Major Stultz ; and on being ordered by her mother to sit
beside him, pouted in the most significant manner. Madame
Rosenberg chose this time to take charge of her two sons
herself; she thought their vicinity might interrupt the reconciliation between Major Stultz and Crescenz, which she
evidently wished to promote, but which seemed less likely
than ever to take place, as Crescenz chose now to appear or
to be excessively offended. This line of conduct had the
effect of making poor Major Stultz imagine that he had been,
perhaps, too hasty—unjust—uncivil—in short, he very soon
accused himself of being a savage! And as these thoughts
passed through his brain, his manners and words softened ;
he became humble, and even entreated forgiveness for the
unknown offence ; but all in vain. Crescenz scarcely answered him—in fact she had not heard him, for her whole
attention was absorbed in the conversation of her sister and
Hamilton, who were immediately before her—she fancied
that neither of them had disliked the arrangement which had
placed them together : the latter especially seemed determined

to amuse and be amused, and for more than an hour and a half the conversation never flagged. Madame Rosenberg occasionally joined in it, and Major Stultz also chimed in when he found all his efforts to obtain answers from Crescenz fruitless. They had nearly reached Berchtesgaden, and Hamilton had just begun to congratulate himself on having at length discovered the possibility of talking to Hildegarde without quarrelling, when Major Stultz abruptly asked him if he had been to see the Summer Riding-school.

'Can you doubt it? It is the prettiest thing of the kind I have ever seen—the *beau idéal* of an ancient theatre. That the tiers of seats are hewn out of the mountain, enhances its grandeur, and makes one forget that it is only a riding-school. What a place for a tournament, or for gladiators!—or what an arena for wild beasts!'

'Exactly what we all said when we were there to-day!' exclaimed Hildegarde.

'Yes,' said Crescenz, for the first time joining in the conversation; 'we all said that, but Hildegarde and I thought of Schiller's ballad of "The Glove;" didn't we, Hildegarde?'

Hildegarde nodded.

'It is odd enough, I thought of it too,' said Hamilton: 'the tiger attacked by the two leopards; the lion rising to join in the combat—I saw it all in imagination—fancied myself the Knight Delorges, and looked round to see if no Cunigunde were there to throw her glove amidst the combatants.'

'Did you think of any particular person as Cunigunde?' asked Crescenz, softly, and with a slight blush.

'Perhaps I did,' replied Hamilton, laughing.

'Oh, I should like so much to know who you thought of! Should not you, Hildegarde?'

'If Mr. Hamilton wish to tell—' began Hildegarde.

'I prefer walking up the hill into the town,' said Hamilton, springing out of the open side of the carriage.

'Let us all walk!' cried Madame Rosenberg, desiring the coachman to stop; 'my feet are quite cramped.'

Hamilton had hoped to escape further questioning, but Crescenz commenced again as they walked along together.

'Your avoidance of my question has raised my curiosity, and you positively must tell me of whom you thought in the riding-school to-day.'

'Pray, Crescenz,' said Hildegarde, 'do not force Mr. Hamilton to give an answer; it must be totally uninteresting to you. Remember the number of acquaintances he must have in England whose names are unknown to us.'

'If it had been anyone in England, or anyone unknown to us, he would have answered my question at once, and without hesitation,' replied Crescenz, with unusual decision of manner.

Hildegarde, struck with the reply, experienced herself a feeling of curiosity which greatly surprised her. She walked on in silence, and soon heard her sister continue, in a very low voice—

'I am sure you did not think of *me*!'

'Certainly not,' he replied, in the same tone; 'you are too kind and too gentle to place the life even of an enemy in such jeopardy.'

Crescenz seemed not quite to know whether she were satisfied or disappointed. She would have liked to have been his lady-love, would have wished to imagine that he would have picked up her glove at such imminent risk—yet his manner and words implied nothing flattering to the supposed Cunigunde; and although she did not quite understand his meaning, she knew that he had said that she was kind and gentle, and she felt that she ought to be satisfied. No so Hildegarde— she understood well the vanity and callousness of the character sketched in a few words by Schiller—she fancied that Hamilton disliked her, and an irresistible impulse made her turn to him, and say abruptly, 'You thought of *me*!'

The blood mounted to his temples and seemed to take refuge in his hair, as he returned Hildegarde's glance, yet hesitated in answering—but he could not deny it, and replied, after a moment's consideration, 'Thoughts are not subject to control; you have no right to make me answerable for them.'

'I have no intention of doing so,' she replied; 'I care too little about you to give myself the trouble of convincing you that you do not understand my character in the least. On the contrary, I confess that were you disposed to play the part of the knight, perhaps I might throw down my glove and be glad to get rid of you on any terms.'

'Even were I to be torn to pieces in your presence by the wild beasts'? I did not think you were so cruel!' said Hamilton, amused at her irritated manner.

'The danger for you would not be very great. You are the last person in the world to do anything of that kind.'

'Do you doubt my personal courage?'

'No; but I doubt your possessing knightly feelings.'

'I am, it is true, no Don Quixote, no knight of the sorrowful countenance—'

'No, indeed; you much more deserve the name of the knight of the scornful countenance — that is, if one could fancy you a knight at all.'

'I have no doubt, mademoiselle, that were your fancy to form one he would in no respect resemble me; however, we need not quarrel on the supposition of what we should have done had we been born a few hundred years sooner; it is evident you would not have chosen me for your knight—nor I—perhaps—you for my lady-love.'

'Oh, dear!' exclaimed Crescenz, 'if I had thought that you two would have quarrelled, I would not have asked any questions, though I do not understand why Hildegarde is so offended at being thought like Cunigunde, who, I dare say, was the handsomest lady present.'

'Your sister is not satisfied with being merely handsome; she wishes to be thought amiable also, and seems disposed to force people to say so, whatever they may think to the contrary.'

Hildegarde walked haughtily towards her stepmother, and reached her just in time to hear the concluding words of what appeared to be Major Stultz's remonstrances :—

'His being an Englishman does not in my opinion alter the case, or make him a less dangerous companion for your daughters. I do not presume to dictate. I merely offer advice, which you do not seem disposed to take; and nothing now remains for me but to beg of you to hurry as much as possible the preparations for Crescenz's marriage. A few scenes such as we have had to-day would soon cure me of all fancy for her. You told me she was good tempered, and I have found her so sullen since we left Salzburg, that it was impossible to obtain a word from her.'

'My dear Major, you may depend upon my reprimanding her severely for such conduct. You shall see—'

'By no means, madame—I don't wish her to be reprimanded. I shall speak to her myself, and tell her that I have a comfortable home to offer her; that I am disposed to be an indulgent husband, but that I am too old to play lover, and altogether decline entering into competition with such a rival as that tall Englishman, who, however, I can also tell her, has no more idea of marriage than the man in the moon!'

'But, my dear Major, I really must beg of you not to mention the Englishman to her. It will only put an idea into her head which I am convinced has never entered it. You forget what a mere child she is—not yet sixteen!'

Major Stultz turned round suddenly to look at his betrothed; the moment was unpropitious for removing jealous doubts. She was walking alone with Hamilton, and speaking with an earnestness totally foreign to her character, while the expression of her upturned eye denoted anything but childishness.

'This will never do!' exclaimed Major Stultz, angrily.

'You wrong her most assuredly,' cried Madame Rosenberg, with a sort of blind reliance on Crescenz's childishness, which this time, however, did not deceive her: 'you wrong her, and I will prove it by asking her what she is talking about. Crescenz, my love, we wish to know the subject of your discourse; it seems to be interesting.'

Crescenz answered without hesitation, 'I am defending Hildegarde; Mr. Hamilton and she have quarrelled about the ballad of "The Glove." He says she was rude; and I think he was rude; for he said if he had been a knight he would not have chosen her for his lady-love. I do not think of being angry, and he did not choose me either,' she added, glancing half reproachfully.

On another occasion Madame Rosenberg would have inquired further, and given, perhaps, an edifying lecture on politeness and propriety of language; she was now too well satisfied with Crescenz's answer to think of anything of the kind, and, turning triumphantly to Major Stultz, she whispered, 'You see I was right. I cannot answer for Hildegarde. Rosenberg says I do not understand her; but Crescenz *is* a good girl—almost too good and docile. You can make whatever you please of her.'

They all walked together to the inn, and 'The Glove' seemed to be quite forgotten.

CHAPTER X.

THE RETURN TO MUNICH.

HAMILTON's journey to Munich proved more agreeable than the commencement had promised. Hildegarde, the maid, Peppy, and Fritz were his companions : the others occupied the second carriage, and chose to be together, as Fritz sapiently observed, in order to talk secrets about Cressy's wedding. Hildegarde exhibited her dislike to Hamilton so artlessly that he could scarcely preserve a serious countenance, while he endeavoured to overcome it. The averted head—short, careless answers, and pertinacious discourse with brother Fritz—could not, however, long resist his efforts. He was possessed of no inconsiderable advantages, both of mind and manner, and of this he was, perhaps, but too well aware, sometimes unnecessarily undervaluing the intellect of others, while he indulged in a vein of satire most displeasing when it became evident. Hildegarde had noticed this in his intercourse with her sister, and was at first extremely guarded in her answers, but his manner was so unconstrained, his account of himself and his ideas so amusing and simple, that at length she also became communicative, and unconsciously displayed an extent of intellect for which Hamilton had not been prepared. Her acquirements were considerable for a girl of her age, and she spoke with enthusiasm of the continuance of her studies when she returned to Munich. Her father had quite an excellent library of his own, which he had promised to let her use, and her mother intended to subscribe to a circulating library, on condition that none but French books should be sent for or read. On Hamilton's inquiring further, she said, with a slight blush, that she was extremely fond of novels and poetry.

'Poetry!' he exclaimed, thrown off his guard; 'poetry! I should have imagined that more suited to your sister's taste than yours.'

No sooner had the word 'sister' passed his lips than he saw a sudden change in the expression of his companion's countenance ; he had, in fact, awakened a train of unpleasant reflections, rendered more disagreeable by a feeling of self-reproach for previous forgetfulness. Hildegarde retired from him as far as the limits of the carriage permitted, looking out of the window, without noticing his remark, and rendered all his attempts to renew the conversation abortive, by entering into a disquisition with her brother on the impropriety of bringing snowballs into the house in winter. With a smile, which Hildegarde would perhaps have denominated a sneer, had she seen it, Hamilton leaned back in the carriage, and was soon occupied in mental speculations on the change which one word had been able to produce, although the cause was by no means difficult to surmise. They did not speak again until they entered the inn where they were to dine. Madame Rosenberg was his companion in the afternoon, and so effectually did she contrive to beguile the time with a history of herself and her family, that he was actually sorry when, at a late hour in the evening, their journey ended, and both carriages began somewhat tumultuously to pour forth their contents.

The apartments were on the third story, and on bounding up the stairs to them, Hamilton was received by Mr. Rosenberg with almost as much cordiality as his future son-in-law, who had followed more slowly. A good deal of calling and running and dragging about of furniture ensued, but at the end of an hour or thereabouts they were all comfortably seated round a supper-table, which, although of the plainest description, and lit by a couple of tallow candles in brass candlesticks, more than satisfied Hamilton; and nothing could exceed the pleasure with which he looked around him. The novelty of his situation and the realisation of his wish to be domesticated in a private family, aided, no doubt, considerably to produce this frame of mind, for he was by nature and education fastidious; and had he not had an object in view, it is more than probable that the extreme homeliness of the house arrangements would have more disgusted than amused him. Madame Rosenberg stood with a napkin pinned over the front of her dress, while she carved a large loin of veal, and distributed to each, beginning with her husband, the portion which she judged sufficient for their supper :—a potato salad, which she had also prepared in their presence with oil and vinegar, was added; and Hildegarde and Crescenz carried round the plates, to Hamilton's great surprise, and indeed discomfort. It was in vain he jumped up and offered to assist them. Madame Rosenberg begged him to sit still; said that Hildegarde would bring him all he wanted; aud Crescenz, as in duty bound, would see that the Major had everything he required. With a coyness which would have been graceful had it not been slightly tinctured with affectation, Crescenz performed the required services; Major Stultz declaring that he had never in his life been so waited upon; that she was a perfect Hebe, and ending by catching her hand and kissing it passionately. Crescenz looked across the table, and, on finding Hamilton's large dark eyes fixed upon her, drew back, and behind the chair of her lover impatiently wiped the kiss, and with it some portion of gravy and potato which had probably adhered to his moustache, from her fair hand. On again looking towards Hamilton, half expecting some sign of approval, she found that he had turned to her father, and seemed altogether to have forgotten her presence. With some indignation she took her place at the table, and commenced her supper, internally vowing never to bestow either a word or look more on him; and, if possible, to convince him without delay of her extreme dislike to him. She listened with apparent interest, while her mother and Major Stultz settled the day but one after for their solemn betrothal, which was to give her the name of bride, a title only used in Germany during the term of engagement, and never after the ceremony of marriage has been performed.

Major Stultz rose to take leave, whispering a little while ostentatiously with Crescenz, and retired. Hamilton was accompanied by the whole family when he took possession of the two rooms appropriated to his use, at the back of the house. They looked into another street, and were accessible by a back staircase, which, Madame Rosenberg informed him, was considered a great convenience for single gentlemen, especially as she would give him a skeleton key which would open the house door, and admit him at all hours without the servants being obliged to sit up for him. Crescenz scarcely answered when he wished her good night, and he divined pretty accurately what was passing in her mind. He was heartily glad that she had adopted this line of conduct; was fully prepared to believe in her indifference : in fact, he gave her more credit for coquetry than she deserved, and determined in no way to interfere with her good resolutions, or Major Stultz, in future.

The next morning was wholly occupied by a visit to his bankers, the library, securing a place for six months at the theatre, and purchasing some toys for Fritz, Gustle, and Peppy. He reached home some time after twelve o'clock, and found that they had waited dinner for him, Madame Rosenberg delicately informing him of the fact by shouting from the nursery door—

'You may send in the soup now, Wally, for Mr. Hamilton is come.'

As far as Mr. Hamilton was concerned, the soup might have remained in the kitchen all day : he had not yet learned to eat ordinary German soup, which, when not thickened into a 'family broth,' very much resembled the weak beef-tea decocted by careful housekeepers for invalids ; he therefore played with his spoon until the boiled beef, which invariably succeeds, had made its appearance, and finished his repast with a piece of *zwetschgen* cake, which he found excellent, and much more easy to eat than to pronounce. The whole family rose from table at the same moment, and Hamilton was in the act of opening the door leading into the drawing-room, when he heard Madame Rosenberg call out—

'Hildegarde, pick up Mr. Hamilton's napkin; don't you see it lying on the floor?'

Hamilton sprang forward, raised, and threw it with a jerk across the back of his chair, not clearly understanding what possible difference it could make, and thinking Madame Rosenberg very unnecessarily particular. His surprise was therefore great when he saw Hildegarde take the crumpled towel, and, having endeavoured to lay it in the original folds, bind it with a piece of blue ribbon which had been placed on the table beside him for the purpose.

'Mr. Smith told me that people did not generally use napkins in England,' said Madame Rosenberg, sagaciously nodding her head.

'Not use napkins ! You surely must have misunderstood him : perhaps he said people did not use the same napkin twice.'

'Not use a napkin twice !' cried Madame Rosenberg. 'If that were the case, I should have a pretty washing at the end of the three months ! Rosenberg gets but two a week, and has moustaches. I expect that you will be able to manage like the girls, with one.'

'I shall certainly cultivate a moustache forthwith, if it were only for the purpose of getting the two napkins a week!' said Hamilton, good-humouredly laughing as he left the room.

K

CHAPTER XI.

THE BETROTHAL.

THE afternoon of the next day the betrothal took place. Hamilton had expected an imposing ceremony, but not one of the many persons assembled appeared to consider it as anything but an occasion for drinking wine or coffee and eating cake. Crescenz and her sister must be excepted : they both looked greatly alarmed; and when the certificates of birth, baptism, vaccination, and confirmation had been laid on the table, and the marriage contract read aloud and presented for signature, Crescenz fairly attempted to rush out of the room. She was brought back with some difficulty; and it was from Hamilton's hand that she received the pen with which she wrote her name. A present of a very handsome ring from Major Stultz seemed in some degree to restore her equanimity, and a glass of champagne, judiciously administered by her father, enabled her to receive the congratulations and enjoy the jokes of her bridesmaids. As evening drew on, the pianoforte was put in requisition, and dancing proposed. Hamilton immediately engaged Hildegarde; he was in England considered to dance well, and was, therefore, not a little surprised and mortified when, after a few turns, she sat down quietly, saying he was a most particularly disagreeable dancer.

'You are the first person who has told me so,' he observed, somewhat piqued ; for Englishmen are vulnerable on this point.

'Others have *thought* so, perhaps,' said Hildegarde, carelessly, and following with her eyes Crescenz and Major Stultz; the latter, forgetful of the hardships of his Russian campaign, and unmindful of the stoutness of his figure, was whirling round the room with a lightness which would have done credit to a man of one-and-twenty.

'How very well Major Stultz dances!' said Hamilton, when Crescenz and her partner soon after stopped near them.

'And you—why do not you dance?' asked Crescenz.

'Your sister says I dance badly.'

'I said you were a disagreeable dancer,' said Hildegarde ; 'other people may think differently, but I particularly dislike being held so close, and having—'

Hamilton's face became crimson, and she left her sentence unfinished.

'Perhaps people dance differently in England,' suggested Crescenz.

'Most probably they do not waltz at all there,' said Major Stultz.

Hamilton explained with extraordinary warmth.

'Well, at all events, it is, and will ever remain, a German national dance; and so, I suppose, without giving offence, I may say that we Germans dance it better than you English. I have no doubt that you dance country-dances and Scotch reels perfectly, but—'

'I have never danced either the one or the other,' said Hamilton, with a look of sovereign contempt.

'Well, Francaise's quadrilles, or whatever you call those complicated dances now coming into fashion here.'

Hamilton did not answer; he had turned to Crescenz, and was now insisting on her waltzing with him, that she might tell him the fault in his dancing. She murmured the words 'Extra tour,' which seemed to satisfy Major Stultz, and then complied with his request. It was singular that Crescenz did not complain of being held too closely; she was not disposed to find any fault whatever with his performance; and it was with some difficulty that he induced her to say that there was something a little foreign in his manner, and that she believed he did not dance *quite* so smoothly as a German.

'Your sister's personal dislike seems to influence her judgment on all occasions,' said Hamilton, glancing towards Hildegarde, who, still seated in the same place, was watching them with evident dissatisfaction.

'Hildegarde, come and help me to put candles in the candlesticks,' cried Madame Rosenberg : 'we cannot let our friends grope about in the dark any longer.'

Hildegarde rose ;—as she passed Hamilton she said, in a low voice :

'For personal dislike, you may say detestation when you refer to yourself in future.'

'Most willingly—most gladly,' cried Hamilton, laughing. 'I wish you to hate me with all your heart.'

'Then your wish is gratified ; I feel the greatest contempt—'

'Halt !' cried Hamilton, still laughing, for her anger

amused him. 'I did not give you leave to feel contempt :
I only said you might hate us—'

'Hildegarde ! Hildegarde !' cried Madame Rosenberg impatiently—'why, what on earth is the girl about?'

'Quarrelling, as usual,' muttered Major Stultz, shrugging
his shoulders.

'Oh, she is not quarrelsome !' exclaimed Crescenz; 'you
do n't understand her : she is right—quite right.'

'Right to hate me without, a cause !' cried Hamilton,
pretending great astonishment.

'I did not exactly mean—that is—I think—I believe—I
am sure Hildegarde does not hate you or anybody,' said
Crescenz, confusedly, and retiring hastily to that part of the
room which seemed by common consent appropriated to the
unmarried female part of the company. At this moment the
door opened, and Madame Rosenberg, followed by Hildegarde
and the cook, entered the room, carrying lighted candles. A
loud ringing of the house-bell was heard, and the cook, having
deposited her candles, rushed out of the room to open the door.

'I dare say it 's the Bergers,' said Madame Rosenberg, as
she walked towards the pianoforte with her candles.   'Better
late than never. I'm glad she 's come, for she plays waltzes
charmingly ; and as such days as this do not often occur in a
family, we may as well keep it up.'

Hamilton looked towards the door, and saw an elaborately
dressed and extremely pretty person, with very long and
profuse blonde ringlets, leaning on the arm of an elderly man
with a protruding chin. His recollection of having heard
something about her or her companion was brought more
distinctly to his mind when he saw Crescenz start forward
and embrace her, while she eagerly exclaimed:

'Oh, Lina ! I have *so* longed to see you !—*so* wished for
your advice !'

After she had spoken with great animation to the Rosenbergs
and her other acquaintances, she turned to Crescenz, who,
continuing to hold her hand, now reproached her for her
neglect of her.

'My dear creature ! I have been in Starnberg, or you
should have seen me long ago. The Doctor came for me
this afternoon, and I have not been more than an hour in
town. On such an occasion I was obliged to make myself
smart, and you have no idea how I hurried ! Is n't this dress

a love?—the Doctor's choice; he bought it at Schultz, and surprised me with it on my birthday! Conceive my being nineteen years old!' she continued in a whisper, leading Crescenz apart: 'I am really glad that I am married; I should have been obliged to wait an eternity for Theodore; he is now studying with the Doctor, visits the hospitals with him, and dines with us every Sunday!—Heigho!—'

'Is not the Doctor jealous?'

'Jealous! oh, dear no! Why should he be jealous? If Theodore had been rich, I should have preferred him, of course; but a poor student!—the thing was absurd! And yet I *did* love him—with all my heart, too!'

'I can easily imagine it,' said Crescenz, pensively; 'and in Seon, of all places in the world!'—and she sighed very expressively.

'Why, surely, dear, you did not find anyone at Seon with whom you could fall in love? I beg Major Stultz's pardon; but—a—the company at Seon is a—'

'Oh, there were some very nice people there this year! Count Zedwitz and his family; his son, I am almost sure, proposed to Hildegarde, though she won't acknowledge it.'

'Count Zedwitz! Why, surely, Hildegarde would not be such a fool as to refuse such a—'

'Hush! dearest,—it's the greatest possible secret; and Hildegarde would never forgive me if she knew—'

'I don't believe a word of it,' said the Doctor's wife, arranging a stray ringlet; 'I don't believe a word of it. Hildegarde would have talked enough if there had been even a shadow of probability of such a thing. As to her having refused him, that is out of the nature of things! I suppose, dear,' she added, shaking back her curls, 'I suppose, he turned to you when he was tired of Hildegarde? Did she frighten him with a fit of fury, as she did me the day I read the letter from her father, which she had mislaid in the school-room? Do you remember how she stormed, and called me dishonourable, and said that I was capable of any horrible act? I never forgave that Mademoiselle Hortense for not taking my part; but all the governesses were so proud of Hildegarde's beauty after her picture was painted, that she was allowed to do as she pleased.'

'Don't talk of her,' said Crescenz, in a low voice: 'I know you never liked her.'

'They called us the rival beauties at school, you know, which was quite enough to make us hate each other all our lives ; but now that I am married, all rivalry has ceased. I have got a position in society, especially since the Doctor has been called in to attend the Royal Family, and—'

'You don't say so !' exclaimed Crescenz, interrupting her.

'Yes, my dear. He is not exactly appointed ; but when the other physicians were out of town, he was sent for to attend one of the ladies of the court, who had been obliged to remain behind from illness, and she promised to use all her influence for him : indeed, his practice is so extensive that he does not require anything of the kind—but then, for appearance sake ; and it sounds well, you know—it sounds well !' And she played with her pocket handkerchief, which was trimmed with very broad cotton lace. 'But I forgot, you were going to tell me that you had fallen in love with somebody at Seon. If it were not this Count Zedwitz, who was it ?'

'Nobody,' said Crescenz, wiping her eyes with her little cotton handkerchief, ornamented with a few coarse indigo-dyed threads for a border,—'nobody !'

'I assure you, Cressy, as a married woman, I can give you much better advice now than in former days, when I was as silly as yourself. You had better confide in me.'

'I have nothing to confide,' replied Crescenz, diligently biting the before-mentioned blue thread border of her hand-kerchief.

'Well, if you don't choose to be confiding, perhaps you will be communicative, and tell me who is that very tall, very young, and singularly handsome man talking to your father, near the window ?'

'That's he,' said Crescenz, blushing.

'Who ?'

'The Englishman.'

'What Englishman ?'

'The Englishman that we met at Seon.'

'So !' whistled, rather than exclaimed, the Doctor's wife. 'So !—hem !—a—some excuse for a little sentiment, I must allow, Cressy. How does he happen to be here this evening ?'

'He is living with us ; he boards with mamma this winter.'

'So ! Can he speak German ?'

'Oh, yes, very well.

'Introduce him ; I should like to know him.'

'I *cannot.*'

'You cannot! Why, I could have introduced Theodore to all the world, and have ordered him about everywhere. Beckon, or call him over, like a dear.'

'Not for worlds!'

'I do believe you are afraid of him!'

'Afraid of him! What an idea!' said Crescenz, laughing faintly.

'Yes, afraid of him,' persisted her friend; 'and yet he is not at all a person to inspire terror.'

'Oh, no, not at all,' said Crescenz; 'I do n't think I am at all afraid of him. Why should I?'

'Why, indeed! See, Crescenz, he is looking this way now; just turn towards him and make some sign, or else I must apply to Hildegarde.'

'Oh, go to Hildegarde, if you like,' said Crescenz, half laughing; 'but most probably they have just been quarrelling; and in that case she will send you to papa or mamma.'

'For that matter, I might as well go to your father at once, as he is standing beside him; for a married woman it would be of no consequence, you know; but still I should prefer the introduction to appear accidental. Men are generally vain— especially Englishmen, they say.'

'Oh, he is not at all vain, though Hildegarde insists that he is; and says. too, that he ridicules everybody. She took an inveterate dislike to him at first sight.'

'Well, that does surprise me, for his appearance is certainly prepossessing; but I think also he *has* a tolerably good opinion of himself—in so far I must agree with her; but why should he not? He is certainly good-looking, probably clever, and no doubt rich!'

'Oh, he is very clever,' said Crescenz; 'even Hildegarde allows that.'

'Well, my dear, to return—will you introduce him or not?'

'Pray, do n't ask me.'

The Doctor's wife shrugged her shoulders, shook back her blonde ringlets, and walked, with an evident attempt at unconcern, across the room.

'Hildegarde,' she said, tapping the shoulder which had been purposely turned towards her, 'Hildegarde, will you introduce me to your Englishman? Crescenz says he is very clever; and. you know, I like clever people, and foreigners; but you must manœuvre a little, and not let him know that I particularly requested to make his acquaintance.'

'I never manœuvre,' replied Hildegarde, bluntly; 'you might have known that by this time.'

'I did not just mean to say manœuvre; I only wished you to understand that you were to manage it so that he should not think I cared about the matter; in short, it ought to be a sort of chance introduction.'

'Will you, by chance, walk across the room with me?'

'Impossible!'

Shall I call him over here by chance?'

'Call!—no, not call; but look as if you expected him to come. He will be sure to understand.'

'He will not; for I do not expect him in the least. Crescenz could have told you that we are not on particularly good terms. You had better ask mamma.'

'*Mein Gott!* What a fuss the people make about this Englishman! I think you are all afraid of him. Crescenz certainly is.'

'I dislike him; but I am not afraid of him, as you shall see. 'Mr. Hamilton!' she called out distinctly; and Hamilton, though surprised, immediately approached her. Madame Berger shook her hand and the pocket-handkerchief most playfully, and then took refuge on the sofa at some distance. Hildegarde followed, quietly explaining that Madame Berger wished to make his acquaintance because he was a foreigner, and supposed to be clever. Hamilton smiled as he seated himself beside his new acquaintance, and in a few minutes they were evidently amusing each other so much that Crescenz observed it, and said, in a low voice, to her sister, 'You were quite right, Hildegarde; Lina is a desperate flirt. Do look how she is laughing, and allowing Mr. Hamilton to admire her dress.'

'He is making a fool of her. Now, Crescenz, if you are not blind, you can see that expression of his face I have so often described to you.'

'I only see he is laughing, and pulling the lace of her handkerchief, which she has just shown him. I dare say he is admiring it, for it is real cambric and very fine.'

'He is not admiring it; his own is ten times finer.'

'Indeed! I have never remarked that: how very odd that you should!'

'Not at all odd,' said Hildegarde, quickly; 'everyone has some sort of fancy. You like bracelets and rings, and I like fine pocket-handkerchiefs.'

'Well, that is the oddest fancy,' said Crescenz, 'the very last thing I should have thought of. I do n't care at all for pocket-handkerchiefs.'

'Nor I for rings or bracelets,' replied Hildegarde.

'Come here, girls,' cried Madame Rosenberg; 'what are you doing with your two heads together there? Come and help me to make tea. Hildegarde, there is boiling water in the kitchen. Crescenz, you can cut bread-and-butter, or arrange the cakes.'

Tea was then a beverage only coming into fashion in Germany, and, in that class of society where it was still seldom made, the infusion caused considerable commotion. Hildegarde and her stepmother were unsuccessful in their attempt: the tea tasted strongly of smoke and boiled milk. Everybody sipped it, and wondered what was the matter, while Madame Rosenberg assured her guests that she had twice made 'a tea,' and that it had been excellent; the cook, Walburg, or, as she was called familiarly, Wally, must have spoiled it by hurrying the boiling of the water. Mr. Hamilton, as an Englishman, would, of course, know how to make tea; he really must be so good as to accompany her to the kitchen, and they would make it over again.

Hamilton agreed to the proposition with some reluctance, for he had found his companion amusing; but, as she proposed accompanying him, he was soon disposed to think that tea-making in a kitchen as amusing as it was new to him. Madame Rosenberg, Hildegarde, Crescenz, and Major Stultz followed, forming a sort of procession in the corridor, and greatly crowding the small but remarkably neat kitchen where they assembled. If it had not been for the stone floor, it was as comfortable a room as any in the house; the innumerable brightly-shining brass and copper pans and pots, pudding and pie models, forming the ornaments. Round the hearth, or rather what is in England called a hot-hearth—for the fire was invisible—they all stood to watch the boiling of a pan full of fresh water, which had been placed on one of the apertures made for that purpose. They looked at the water, and then at each other, and then again at the water; and then Wally shoved more wood underneath. Still the water boiled not; and Madame Rosen-

berg and Major Stultz returned to the drawing-room, Madame
Berger having undertaken, with Hamilton's assistance, to make
the most excellent tea possible.

'It is an odd thing,' she observed, seating herself on the
polished copper edge of the hearth, and carefully arranging
the folds of her dress, 'it is an odd thing, but nevertheless a
fact, that when one watches, and wishes water to boil, it won't
boil, and as soon as one turns away it begins to bubble and
sputter at once. Now, Mr. Hamilton, can you explain why
this is the case?'

'I don't know,' said Hamilton, laughing, 'excepting that,
perhaps, as the watching of a saucepan full of water is by no
means an amusing occupation, one easily gets tired, and finds
that the time passes unusually slowly.'

'All I can say is—that as long as I look at that water, it
will not boil.'

'Then pray look at me,' said Hamilton, who had seated
himself upon the dresser, one foot on the ground, the other
enacting the part of a pendulum, while in his hands he held a
plate of little maccaroni cakes, which Crescenz had just
arranged—'pray look at me. German cakes are decidedly
better than English—these are really delicious.'

'Oh, I am so fond of those cakes!' she cried, springing
towards him; 'so excessively fond of them! Surely,' she
added, endeavouring to reach the plate, which he laughingly
held just beyond her reach, 'surely you do not mean to devour
them alone!'

'You shall join me,' said Hamilton, 'on condition that
every cake with a visible piece of citron, or a whole almond,
on it belongs to me.'

'Agreed.'

Her share proved small, and a playful scuffle ensued.

Crescenz turned towards the window; Hildegarde looked on
contemptuously. At this moment Walburg exclaimed, 'The
water boils!'—and they all turned towards the hearth.

'How much tea shall I put into the teapot?' asked Madame
Berger, appealing to Hamilton.

'The more you put in the better it will be,' answered
Hamilton, without moving.

'Shall I put in all that is in this paper?'

Hamilton nodded, and the tea was made.

'Ought it not to boil a little now?'

By no means.'

'Perhaps,' said Walburg, 'a little piece of vanille would improve the taste.'

'On no account,' said Hamilton.

'The best thing to give it a flavour is rum,' observed Madame Berger.

'I forbid the rum, though I must say the idea is not bad,' said Hamilton, laughing.

Hildegarde put the teapot on a little tray, and left the kitchen just as her stepmother entered it.

'Well, the tea ought to be good! It has required long enough to make it, I am sure!' she observed, while setting down a lamp which she had brought with her. 'Crescenz, your father, it seems, has invited a whole lot of people without telling me, and he wishes to play a rubber of whist in the bedroom. I have no more handsome candlesticks, so you must light the lamp; the wick is in it, I know, for I cleaned it myself before I went to Seon, and you have only to put in the oil and light it.' She took Madame Berger's arm, saying, 'This is poor amusement for you, standing in the kitchen all the evening,' and walked away, without perceiving Hamilton, who was examining the construction of the hearth and chimney with an interest which greatly astonished the cook.

'Oh, Wally!—what shall I do?' cried Crescenz; 'I never touched a lamp in my life, and I am sure I cannot light it.'

'It's quite easy, Miss Crescenz; I'll pour in the oil, and you light these pieces of wood and hold' them to the wick.'

Crescenz did as she was desired.

'Stop till the oil is in, Miss, if you please,' said Wally.

The oil was put in, the wick lighted, the cylinder fixed, and Crescenz raised the globe towards its place; but either it was too heavy for her hand or she had not mentally measured the height, for it struck with considerable force against the upper part of the lamp, and broke to pieces with a loud crash.

'Oh, heavens! what *shall* I do?' she cried in her agitation, clasping the piece of glass which had remained in her hand. 'What *shall* I do? Mamma will be so angry! I dare not tell her—for my life I dare not. What on earth shall I do?'

'Send out and buy another as fast as you can,' said Hamilton; 'is there no glass or lamp shop near this?'

'I don't know,' said Crescenz, blushing deeply.

'Yes, there is,' said Walburg, 'in the next street, just round the corner, you know, Miss Crescenz . . . but a—' And she stopped and looked confused.

'I *must* tell mamma, or get Hildegarde to tell her. Oh, what a misfortune!—what a dreadful misfortune!'

'Go out and buy a globe, and do n't waste time looking at the fragments,' said Hamilton, impatiently, to Walburg. 'There is no necessity for saying anything about the matter.'

'But,' said Walburg, hesitatingly, and looking first at Crescenz, and then at Hamilton, 'but I have no money.'

'Stupid enough my not thinking of that,' said Hamilton, taking out his purse.

'That is at least a florin too much,' cried Walburg, enchanted at his generosity.

'Never mind! Run, run; keep what remains for yourself, but make haste.'

'Oh, indeed I cannot allow this,' said Crescenz, faintly; 'it would be very wrong—and—' But the door had already closed on the messenger.

'Suppose, now—mamma should come!' said Crescenz, uneasily.

'Not at all likely, as everyone is drinking tea.'

The drawing-room door opened, and the gay voices of the assembled company resounded in the passage.

'I knew it, I knew it; she is coming!' cried Crescenz; but it was only Hildegarde, who brought the empty teapot to refill it.

She looked very grave when she heard what had occurred, and proposed Hamilton's accompanying her to the drawing-room, as he might be missed and Major Stultz displeased: he felt that she was right, and followed silently. His tea was unanimously praised, but Madame Rosenberg exhibited some natural consternation on hearing that the whole contents of her paper cornet, with which she had expected to regale her friends at least half-a-dozen times, had been inconsiderately emptied at once into the teapot!

'It was no wonder the tea was good! English tea, indeed! Anyone could make tea after that fashion! But then, to be sure, English people never thought about what anything cost. For her part, she found the tea bitter, and recommended a spoonful or two of rum.' On her producing a little green bottle, the company assembled around her with their tea-cups, and she administered to each one, two, or three spoonfuls, as they desired it.

In the mean time, Mr. Rosenberg sat in the adjoining dark bedroom at the card-table—sometimes shuffling, sometimes drumming on the cards, and whistling indistinctly. Hildegarde had observed an expression of impatience on his face, and, to prevent inquiries about the lamp, she quietly brought candles from the drawing-room and placed them beside him.

'Thank you, Hildegarde,' said her father, more loudly than he generally spoke; 'thank you, my dear; you never forget my existence, and even obey my thoughts sometimes.'

'Why, where's the lamp?' cried Madame Rosenberg; 'where's the lamp? What on earth can Crescenz have done with the lamp?'

'Broken it, most probably,' said Mr. Rosenberg, drily. 'Hildegarde, place a chair for Major Stultz. She's a good girl after all, Major!—a very good girl, I can tell you.'

'No doubt, no doubt,' replied the Major, bowing over the proffered chair.

'Go and see why your sister does not bring the lamp!' cried Madame Rosenberg, impatiently.

As Hildegarde slowly and with evident reluctance walked to the door, she unconsciously looked towards Hamilton. He was listening very attentively to the rhapsody of sense and non-sense poured forth by the Doctor's wife, who only occasionally stopped to shake back, with a mixture of childishness and coquetry, the long fair locks which at times half concealed her face. Hamilton, however, saw the look, understood it, and gazed so fixedly at the door, even after she had closed it, that his companion observed it, and said abruptly, 'Why did you look so oddly at Hildegarde?—and why do you stare at the door after she has left the room?'

'If you prefer my staring at you, I am quite willing to do so.'

'You know very well I did not mean any such thing,' she cried, with affected pettishness; 'can you not be serious for a moment, and answer a plain question?'

'I dislike answering questions,' said Hamilton absently, and once more looking towards the door.

'Now, there you are again with your eyes fixed on that tiresome—'

He turned round, took a well-stuffed sofa-cushion, and, placing it before him, leaned his elbows upon it, while he quietly but steadily fixed his eyes on her face, and said—

'Now, madame, if it must be so, I am ready to be questioned.'

'You really are the most disagreeable person I ever met.'

'That is an observation, and not a question.'

'You are the vainest—'

Hamilton looked down, and seemed determined not to interrupt her again.

'Are you offended at my candour?' she added, abruptly.

'Not in the least.'

'Put away that cushion, and don't look as if you were getting tired.'

'But I thought you were going to question me?'

'No, I am afraid.'

'Well, then, I must question you,' said Hamilton, laughing. 'Why may I not look at Mademoiselle Rosenberg?—and why may I not look at the door, if it amuse me?'

'You may not look at the door, because in doing so you turn your back to me, which is not civil,' she replied, readily.

'Very well answered; but now tell me why I may not look at Mademoiselle Rosenberg?'

'Oh, you may look at her certainly; but—but—but—the expression of your face was not as if you disliked her.'

'And why should I dislike her?'

'I don't know, indeed—only Crescenz told me that you often quarrelled with her; and as Hildegarde knows no medium, she most probably hates you with all her soul. You have no idea of the intensity of her likings and dislikings!'

'Indeed!'

'At school she took a fancy to one of the governesses, the most severe, disagreeable person imaginable. Can you believe it? This Mademoiselle Hortense was able to do whatever she pleased with her; her slightest word was a command to Hildegarde. I have seen her, when in the greatest passion, grow pale and become perfectly quiet when Mademoiselle Hortense suddenly came into the room. It was, however, not from fear, for Hildegarde has no idea of fearing anybody: she is terribly courageous!'

'Altogether rather an interesting character,' observed Hamilton.

'Do you think so? I cannot agree with you. At school we all liked Crescenz much better.'

'Very possibly—I can imagine your liking the one and admiring the other.'

'As to the admiration,' said Madame Berger, looking down —'as to the admiration of the girls at school, that was very much divided; Hildegarde headed one party and I the other.'

'You were rivals, then?'

'We were, in everything—even in the affection of her sister. It was through Crescenz alone that I was able to teaze her when I chose to do so.'

'But you did not often choose it, I am sure.'

'Oh, I assure you, with all her love for Crescenz, she often tyrannised over the poor girl, and scarcely allowed her to have an opinion of her own on any subject. Cresoenz was a little afraid of her, too, at times. Cressy is the dearest creature in the world, but not at all brilliant : we all loved her, but we sometimes laughed at her too ; and you can form no conception of the fury of Hildegarde when she used to find it out. Crescenz has confessed to me, when we were alone, that her sister had often lectured her on her simplicity, and had told her what she was to do and say when we attempted to joke with her. Nothing more comical than seeing Crescenz playing Hildegarde.'

'Mademoiselle Rosenberg was considered clever?' asked Hamilton.

'Clever! why, yes—as far as learning was concerned she was the best in the school, and that was the reason that Madame and the governesses overlooked her violence of temper : she is very ill-tempered.'

'That is a pity,' said Hamilton, 'for she seems to have excellent dispositions.'

'I never could discover anything excellent about her,' said Madame Berger, biting her lip slightly.

'Perhaps,' observed Hamilton, 'she is more violent than ill-tempered ; and you say that she can control herself in the presence of anyone she likes.'

'But it is exactly these likings and dislikings that I find so abominable : for instance, she loves her father—well, he is a very good-looking quiet sort of insipid man—she however thinks him perfection, and is outrageous if people do not show an absurd respect for all his opinions. What he says must be law for all the world ! On the other hand, she dislikes her stepmother, who is nothing very extraordinary, I allow, rather vulgar too ; but still she has her good qualities. Hildegarde cannot see them, and will not allow Crescenz to become aware of them either ! Is not this detestable?'

'It is a proof that she has strong prejudices ; but—.'

The door just then was opened, and Crescenz entered the room, carrying the lamp and smiling brightly. It was heavy, and Hamilton rose to assist her in placing it on the table before the sofa where they sat.

'Thank you! oh, thank you!' cried Crescenz, with a fervency which Madame Berger thought so exaggerated that she found it necessary to explain.

'That dear girl is so grateful for the most trifling attention! It is generally the case with us all for a short time after we leave school.'

'There's the lamp!' exclaimed Madame Rosenberg, 'and not broken! What do you say now, Rosenberg? I declare it burns better than usual; the globe has been cleaned—eh, Crescenz?'

'Yes, Wally cleaned it a little; it was very dusty,' replied Crescenz, looking archly at Hamilton, and seeming to enjoy the equivocation.

Hildegarde blushed deeply, and walked into the next room.

Hamilton saw the blush, and looked after her, while Madame Berger whispered—

'Did you see that?—she is jealous of the praise bestowed on her sister.'

'Jealous! oh no,' said Hamilton, still following her with his eyes.

'I beg your pardon!' cried Madame Berger; 'I was not at all aware that I was speaking to an adorer: I really must go and tell her the conquest she has made.'

Perhaps she expected him to detain her, or she feared a rebuff from Hildegarde; for she waited a moment before she proceeded into the next room. Hamilton followed just in time to hear Hildegarde say—

'Pshaw! you are talking about what you do n't understand,' as she turned contemptuously away.

Madame Berger, to conceal her annoyance at Hildegarde's imperturbability, turned to Crescenz, who had been placed next Major Stultz, at his particular request, in order to bring him *luck.* Her presence, however, not having produced the desired effect, he was told by Madame Rosenberg that those who were fortunate in love were always sure to be unfortunate at cards, which seemed to afford him great consolation; while Crescenz smiled and played with his counters and purse.

'I am sure, Crescenz,' said Madame Berger, 'I am sure you are thinking what sort of purse you will make for Major Stultz this Christmas! You cannot allow him in future to use leather. I can teach you to make a new kind of purse, which is very strong and pretty.'

'Oh, pray do!' cried Crescenz, starting up; 'you know I like making purses, of all things. When will you begin it for me?'

'To-morrow, if you like. I say, Cressy,' continued Madame Berger, in a whisper, 'what makes Hildegarde so horribly savage this evening?'

'I did not observe it.'

'She is most particularly disagreeable, I can assure you. I attempted some most innocent *badinage* about Mr. Hamilton, and she—'

'Oh, about him you must not jest; she hates him so excessively—'

'Not a bit of it—and he does not hate her either.'

'You do n't say so!'

'I say so, and think so; and you will see that I am right. Why, he already makes as many excuses as your father for her ill-temper. If you had only heard him!'

'I did not think Hildegarde capable of playing double,' cried Crescenz, with emotion.

'She is capable of anything. Had you but seen the look of intelligence that passed between them when she left the room to inquire about you and the lamp, it would have convinced you at once. And then he watched the door, and—'

'Ah, yes!' exclaimed Crescenz, apparently greatly relieved; 'I understand. No, Lina, this time I am right, and you are wrong. I know why he looked at Hildegarde, and at the door.'

'You do!—do you? Then come and tell me all about it. By the bye, I should like to have a long talk with you, to learn how matters stand. This Mr. Hamilton is uncommonly good-looking and amusing; I should like to know what brought him to Seon, and how it happened that he came to live with your mother, and all that. If we have not time to-night, you can tell me to-morrow, while you are learning the purse-stitch.'

An appointment was made for the next day, and the party soon after broke up.

L

CHAPTER XII.

DOMESTIC DETAILS.

HAMILTON had gone out early to visit Zedwitz, and look at a horse recommended by Major Stultz. On his return, when walking towards his room, he heard some one singing so gaily in the kitchen, that as he passed the door he could not resist the temptation to look in. Crescenz was standing opposite the hearth, a long-handled wooden spoon in her hand, her sleeves tucked up, and her round white arms embellished with streaks of smut and flour; while a linen apron, of large dimensions, preserved the greater part of her dress from injury. Her face was flushed, partly from heat but more from pleasure. As soon as she perceived Hamilton in the doorway, she at once ceased singing, smiled merrily, and invited him to enter. Now to this kitchen Hamilton had taken rather a fancy; he thought it by many degrees the best furnished room in the house: in fact it was a pretty and cheerful apartment, and kept with a neatness common in Germany, where it is usual to see the female members of the burghers' families employed in culinary offices.

'I have got my first lesson in cookery to-day,' she exclaimed, joyfully; 'and I have assisted mamma to make a tart, and you see I am cooking these vegetables,' she added, plunging her wooden spoon into one of the pots.

'Oh, law, Miss!' cried the cook, 'that's the soup, and the noodles will be all squashed if you work them up after that fashion.'

'Well, this is the saur-kraut,' she said, eagerly drawing one of the saucepans towards her; 'this is the *saur-kraut.*'

'I could have told you that myself,' cried Hamilton, laughing; 'the smell is too odious to admit of a doubt.'

'But the taste is very good,' said Crescenz.

'I cannot agree with you; taste and smell are horrible in the extreme.'

'I never heard of anyone who did not like saur-kraut,' said Crescenz, with some surprise; 'do people never make it in England?'

'I never saw it, excepting at the house of a friend who had been long ambassador at one of the German courts, and then it was handed about as a sort of curiosity.'

'How odd! England seems to be altogether different from Germany?' she half asked, while shaking her head inquiringly.

'The difference is in many things besides the eating or not eating of saur-kraut,' answered Hamilton; 'but as you are such a famous cook I must beg of you to give me something else to-day, for I cannot eat your kraut.'

'Oh, yes,' cried Crescenz, delightedly; 'Wally, what shall we cook for Mr. Hamilton? I'm sure I never thought I should have liked this cooking so much!' As she spoke she with difficulty repressed an inclination to dance about the kitchen.

'Indeed, as you are learning it, Miss Crescenz,' said Walburg, 'it must be very agreeable. To think that you will so soon have a house of your own, and a rich husband who will let you have everything you like to cook! Tarts and creams every day. The Major knows what's good, or I'm greatly mistaken.'

This speech completely sobered Crescenz; had Hamilton not been present she might have been loquacious, but she now looked confused, and turned to leave the kitchen, saying it was time to wash her hands for dinner.

'But I thought you were going to find me a substitute for the saur-kraut?'

'Wally will send in something,' she answered, rubbing her arm with her apron to avoid looking up as she walked into the passage. Hamilton was so near her as she entered her room that a feeling of politeness prevented her from shutting the door, and he saw Hidegarde sitting at a small deal table between her brothers Fritz and Gustle—a few books and a slate were before her, and as the door opened she was returning a book to the former with the remark, 'This will never do, Fritz. You have not learned one word of your lesson!'

'*Kreuz! Himmel! Saperment!*' exclaimed Fritz, pitching the book up to the ceiling; this is exactiug too much!—when a fellow has been all the morning at school, and comes home for an hour or so to eat and amuse himself——to be set down in this way to learn French. I tell you what, Hildegarde, I shall begin to hate the sight of you if you plague me with these old grammars.'

'What shall I do with him?' asked Hildegarde, appealing to her sister.

'Fritz, learn your lesson—there's a love!' interposed Crescenz; 'see what a good boy Gustle is!' and she caressingly placed her hand on the shoulder of the latter, who was industriously rolling the leaf of his book into the form of a trumpet, and yawning tremendously.

'I will give up all idea of ever entering the *cadet corps*, or ever being an officer,' cried Fritz, kicking the book as it lay upon the ground, 'rather than write these odious exercises, and listen to Hildegarde's long explanations.'

'But think of the sword and the uniform, Fritz,' said Crescenz, coaxingly.

'*Donner und Doria!*—what is the use of a sword and uniform, when I must learn vocabulary, and write French exercises?'

'Come, Fritz,' cried Hildegarde, authoritatively, 'let me hear no more of this absurd swearing; it does not at all become a boy of your age. If you will not learn your lesson, I can, at least, correct your exercise.'

She stretched out her hand for the slate. Fritz anticipated her, seized, and flung it up in the air, as he had done the grammar; but it did not fall so harmlessly. Hamilton, who had been standing at the open door, rushed forward, but was too late to prevent its descending with considerable force upon her temple, where it made a wound, from which the blood instantly began to trickle in large dark drops. Hildegarde started up angrily, while Fritz, after the first moment of dismay had passed, ran towards her, and throwing his arms round her, exclaimed, 'Forgive me, forgive me!—indeed I did not intend to hurt you.'

'If papa has come home from his *bureau*,' said Crescenz, preparing to leave the room, 'I'll go this moment and tell him.'

'Stay!' cried Hildegarde, hastily; 'he says he did not do it on purpose: and, after all, I am not much hurt. You must not tell papa, or mamma either.'

'Well, you certainly are the best fellow in the world, Hildegarde,' cried Fritz. 'I declare I would rather be cuffed by you than kissed by Crescenz.'

'And cuffed you would have been, had you been near enough,' said Hildegarde, laughing, while she poured some water into a basin.

'Mamma will be sure to see the cut, and ask how it happened,' said Crescenz.

'I can easily hide it under my hair when it has stopped bleeding.'

'Now just for that, Hildegarde,' cried Fritz, 'I promise to learn as many lessons as you please for the next fortnight.'

Madame Rosenberg's step, and the jingling of her keys, alarmed them all. Hamilton turned to meet her in the passage, saying, 'Can I speak to you for five minutes?'

'To be sure you can, and longer, if you like,' she replied, hooking her keys into the string of her apron. 'Just let me look how things are going on in the kitchen, and I am at your service as long as you please. Put a cover on that pot, Walburg, and tell Miss Crescenz not to forget the powdered sugar for the tart, and the apples for the boys' luncheon. And now,' she said, turning to Hamilton, and leading the way to her room, 'what have you got to say? You look so serious that I suspect you are going to tell me that you dislike your rooms, as they look into a back street, and are near a coppersmith's.'

'I have slept too soundly to hear the coppersmiths,' said Hamilton, smiling; 'and during the day I have been too seldom in my room to be disturbed by them. In fact I find so much to amuse—I mean to say, so much to interest me as a foreigner in your house that I do not think half-a-dozen smiths could induce me to leave you at present.'

'I am glad to hear it, for I like you very much, and so does Rosenberg.'

'Then I may hope you will not be offended if I request to have wax candles in my room, and . . . . a—fresh napkin every day,' said Hamilton, with some embarrassment.

'This can easily be managed,' said Madame Rosenberg 'Neither Mr. Smith nor Captain Black ever asked for wax candles; but I suppose you have been brought up expensively. But you were going to say something else, I believe?'

'I was going to say that I have been looking at horses this morning which I feel greatly disposed to purchase, if I were sure of finding a stable near this, and a respectable groom.'

'Why, how lucky!' cried Madame Rosenberg. 'There is now actually a stable to let in this house; the new first-floors do n't keep horses, so you can have it all to yourself; and old Hans asked me only yesterday if I could not recommend his son to some one who wanted a groom or coachman! I will go down with you at once, and look at the stable, and you can speak to old Hans about his son.'

The arrangements were soon completed, and as they ascended the stairs together they met two very well-dressed women, who bowed civilly, but distantly, to Madame Rosenberg. When they had passed, she observed to Hamilton—

'The new lodgers for the first floor: they come on the 29th of this month, and have been looking at their apartments, which are being papered and painted. On the second floor we shall find our landlord, who has the warehouse below stairs, as he has six or eight children, and they make a tremendous noise; I am better pleased to live above than below them, though it is not so noble!'

After dinner, Hamilton, finding himself alone with Crescenz in the drawing-room, insisted on her giving him a lesson in German waltzing; she had just completed her instructions, and they were whirling round the room for the first time, when the door was opened, and Hildegarde, having looked in, closed it again without speaking.

'There, now!' cried Crescenz, walking with a look of great vexation towards the open window; 'was there ever anything so provoking! and after our explanation last night, too! but she really requires too much!'

'What does she require?' asked Hamilton, taking possession of the other half of the window, and leaning on one of the cushions which, as usual in Germany, were conveniently placed for the elbows of those who habitually gazed into the street. 'What does she require?'

'That I should never, for one moment, forget that I have promised to marry Major Stultz. I know quite well that she disapproves of my having danced with you.'

'And if you were to go to a ball now, would you not be at liberty to dance with whomsoever you pleased?'

'Oh, of course.'

'Then why not with me?'

'Oh, because—because—she knows that – I—that you—'

'In fact,' said Hamilton, 'you have told her of my inexcusable conduct the day we were on the alp?'

'No,' replied Crescenz, 'I have only told her that you cannot marry without your father's consent—that the younger sons of English people cannot marry—just what you told me yourself.'

'The recollection of that day will cause me regret as long as I live,' said Hamilton; 'thoughtless words on such a subject are quite unpardonable. I hope you have forgotten all I said!'

'I cannot forget, said Crescenz, looking intently into the street to hide her emotion; 'I cannot forget—it was the first time I had ever heard anything of that kind, and was so exactly what I had imagined in every respect.'

Hamilton bit his lip and replied gravely, 'It was the novelty alone which gave importance to my words; I am convinced, had you considered for a moment, you would have laughed at me as I deserved. Major Stultz must often have said—'

' Major Stultz,' said Crescenz, contemptuously, 'never speaks of anything but how comfortably we shall live together, and what we shall have for dinner, and how many servants we shall be able to keep, and all those sort of things which make it impossible to forget one year of his age, or one bit of his ugliness!'

'He is a very good-natured man,' said Hamilton, 'and, Zedwitz told me, has been a very distinguished officer.'

' You are just beginning to talk like Hildegarde,' cried Crescenz, impatiently, 'and from you, who are the cause of my unhappiness, I will not bear it.'

' The cause of your unhappiness!' repeated Hamilton, slowly; ' if I really could believe that possible, nothing would induce me to remain an hour longer in this house.'

' Oh, no!' cried Crescenz, hastily; 'no, I did not mean what I said. Oh no! you must have seen that I am not unhappy!—I —I am very happy!' and she burst into tears as she spoke.

' Well, this is a punishment for thoughtlessness!' exclaimed Hamilton, starting from his place at the window, and striding up and down the room. 'Surely, surely, such vague expressions as mine were, did not deserve such a serious construction!'

' Vague expressions!' repeated Crescenz, looking up through her tears; 'serious construction! Did you not mean what you said?'

' By heaven! I don't know what I said, or what I meant,' cried Hamilton, vehemently.

Crescenz's sobs became frightfully audible.

' Crescenz—forgive me,' he said, hastily; 'once more I ask your pardon, and entreat of you to forget my folly. Let this subject never again be mentioned, if you would not make me hate myself.'

' But,' sobbed Crescenz, ' but tell me, at least, that you were not, as Hildegarde said, making a fool of me. Tell me, oh, tell me, that you love me, and I am satisfied.'

' You—you do not know what you are saying,' cried Hamilton, involuntarily smiling at her extreme simplicity. ' You are asking me to repeat a transgression which I most heartily repent. Situated as you are, such a confession on my part now deliberately made would be little less than—a crime.'

' You mean because I am betrothed?'

He was spared an answer by Hildegarde's entrance with a small tray and coffee-cups. It was in vain that Crescenz turned to the window to conceal her tears—Hildegarde saw them, and turning angrily to Hamilton, exclaimed—

' This is most unjustifiable conduct—dishonourable—'

' Oh, stop, Hildegarde!' cried Crescenz, beseechingly. ' Pray stop. You are, as usual, doing him injustice, and misunderstand him altogether.'

' Do not attempt a justification,' cried Hamilton, impatiently: ' she will not believe you. And,' he added in a whisper, ' in fact, I do not deserve it.'

Walburg interrupted them by half opening the door and informing them mysteriously that an officer was without who had asked for Mr. Hamilton.

' Show him into my sitting-room, and say I shall be with him in a moment.'

' My visit is only partly intended for you, Hamilton,' said Zedwitz, entering the room. ' I wish also to pay my respects to Madame Rosenberg.'

He had scarcely time to glance towards Hildegarde before she left the room, followed by her sister.

' The young ladies are not particularly civil to you,' observed Hamilton, seating himself on the sofa.

' Why, you did not expect them to remain here with us, did you?'

' To be sure I did.'

' I did not, but I expect them to return with their mother.'

Crescenz did. Hildegarde did not. And, in consequence, Zedwitz's visit to Madame Rosenberg was very short, and he soon adjourned to Hamilton's room.

' Why, what's this?' cried Madame Rosenberg, peeping into

the coffee-pot. 'I do declare Mr. Hamilton has forgotten to drink his coffee!'

'Let me take it to him,' said Crescenz, advancing towards the table.

'You will do no such thing,' said her stepmother, waving her hastily back. 'No such thing—and I think—that is the Major—but it is no matter; it is not necessary to explain. Call Hildegarde.'

Hildegarde came, and was desired to carry the tray to Hamilton's room.

'May I not send Walburg?'

'You may not, because I have sent her on an errand, and the coffee is too cold to be kept waiting until her return, now that the fire is out in the kitchen.'

'But—but,' hesitated Hildegarde, 'Mr. Hamilton is not alone.'

'Count Zedwitz is in his room, but he won't bite you; so go at once, and don't be disobliging.'

Half-an-hour afterwards Hamilton was in the corridor, looking for his cane, which the children had mislaid. He turned into the nursery, and while rummaging there, Madame Rosenberg joined him, and hoped he had not found his coffee too cold.

'Coffee! no—yes! When, where did I drink it?'

'In your own room,' replied Madame Rosenberg, laughing. 'Your memory must be very short: I sent it to you by Hildegarde about half-an-hour ago.'

He looked inquiringly towards Hildegarde. She raised her eyes slowly from her work, and looking at him steadily and gravely, said, in French—

'I threw it out of the window rather than take it to you.'

'Next time I advise you to drink it,' said Hamilton, laughing, as he left the room with Zedwitz. While descending the stairs he observed—

'Well, that is the oddest girl I ever met, perfectly original. You have no idea how she amuses and interests me.'

'I can easily imagine it,' said Zedwitz, drily.

'But you can *not* imagine how intensely she hates me.'

'That was what you desired, if I remember rightly; and for your sake I hope you continue as indifferent as formerly,'

'Not exactly—I believe I rather feel inclined to like her unpolished sincerity and straightforward vehemence. She really would be charming sometimes, if she were a little less quarrelsome.'

' I never found her quarrelsome,' said Zedwitz.

' Of course not, when you were enacting the part of adorer. That makes all the difference in the world ! But what are you looking at ?' asked Hamilton, seeing his companion stop short at the street door. 'I see nothing but a couple of officers lounging about the windows of that brazier's shop opposite, which cannot contain anything particularly interesting, I should think.'

' Did you think they were admiring the coffee-pots and candlesticks ?' asked Zedwitz. 'That is only a feint ; I saw them looking up at the Rosenberg windows. It is a regular *window parade*, and they have been here nearly an hour, for I saw them in the street, as I entered the house. Let us cross over and see whether it be intended for Hildegarde or Crescenz.'

They crossed the street, looked up, and saw Madame Berger sitting at the window, teaching Crescenz the promised pretty and strong purse-stitch. Although the latter appeared extremely intent on her work, she was evidently aware of what was passing in the street ; for, as Zedwitz and Hamilton saluted, she bowed and blushed deeply.

' *She*, at least, has not yet learned to play unconscious,' observed Zedwitz, laughing ; 'Madame Berger can give her some instruction.'

' Do you know Madame Berger ?' asked Hamilton.

' Of course ; her husband is our physician. She is very pretty, and the greatest coquette in Christendom. I say, Raimund, what are you admiring in that shop ?' said Zedwitz, stopping suddenly opposite the brazier's, and addressing one of the officers.

' The kitchen utensils, Max ! I shall soon be obliged to purchase such things, and they have a kind of mysterious interest for me now.'

' You don't mean to say that you are going to keep a house—going to be married ?'

' My father says so, which is much more to the purpose, replied Raimund.

' And who is the happy woman destined to make you a respectable member of society ?'

' They tell me she lives in that house,' replied Raimund, pointing to the one they had just left.

' The third story ?' asked Zedwitz, quickly.

' No, Max ; for a *wife* I do not look so high,' replied the other, ironically.

' And when may I offer my congratulations ?'

' Not just now, if you please, for as I have never yet spoken to the lady, something might occur to prevent the thing ; but I have very nearly made up my mind.'

Zedwitz laughed, and walked on with Hamilton. ' I hope he has told the truth,' he said, musingly ; ' I hope he has told the truth, for I should be very sorry he made his way into the Rosenberg family. He is very clever, but a great reprobate ; has already seduced two girls of respectable connexions, and is not ashamed to boast of his success.'

' Were there no fathers, no brothers, no cousins, to compel him to make reparation ?' asked Hamilton.

' As it happened, there were none,' replied Zedwitz, 'but even if there had been, he has not the caution money, and could not marry. If he were serious just now, I suppose his father has discovered some rich *partie* for him, and that he will succeed, I do not for a moment doubt. He pretends to have a regular system of seduction, which consists in several gradations—it is disgusting to hear him descant on the subject.'

' But he will carefully avoid anything of that kind with his future wife,' said Hamilton.

' I was not thinking of his wife, for I do not know her ; I fear for the Rosenbergs—Hildegarde would be sure to attract him.'

' He would, however, have no chance of success in that quarter, I am sure,' said Hamilton.

' It is hard to say ; her nature is passionate, and I should be sorry to see her an object of attention to such a man. The fact is, I find it impossible to forget her, and as long as I know her to be free, I cannot cease to indulge hopes that she may eventually be mine. What I most apprehend is a sudden and violent passion on her part for some person as yet, perhaps, unknown ; for I believe her capable of loving desperately.'

' And you very naturally wish to be the object of this desperate love ? But how are you to obtain your father's consent to your union ?'

' Of that I have no hope whatever ; but as I am an only son,

I have every chance of pardon were I once married. My mother's opposition is much less violent, but quite as determined as my father's—and the astonishment of both indescribable when I confessed that I had been refused without explanation or chance of recall. All my hopes are now centered in my sister, who is a dear good little soul, and has promised to assist me when she can. By the bye, she made a remark which may, perhaps, interest you.' Zedwitz stopped and looked very hard at Hamilton.

'Pray let me hear it.'

'She said she was sure I should not have spoken in vain had not Hildegarde loved another—'

'Well, that was your own modest idea, was it not?' said Hamilton, interrupting him.

'Yes; but it was not my idea that *you* were the object of her preference.'

Hamilton laughed.

'Perhaps you are already aware of it?' asked Zedwitz, growing very red.

'No, indeed,' replied Hamilton, trying to look serious; 'I am only amused at your sister's strong imagination: were she, however, to see us together, and hear us speak, she would soon think differently.'

'You forget that my sister was at Seon, and had opportunities of making observations.'

'But she is not aware how desperately we quarrel: she does not know—'

'I have told her all that, and she insists that Hildegarde likes you without being herself conscious of it.'

'But I assure you she has told me more than once that she hates me.'

'I am glad to hear it,' said Zedwitz, drily, and immediately after he changed the subject.

This conversation, notwithstanding the little impression it had apparently made on Hamilton, took complete possession of his thoughts, as he walked home late in the evening. However incredulous he might at first have felt, the idea was too flattering to his vanity to be lightly abandoned; and no sooner had he admitted the possibility, than it became probability; nay, almost certainty. It is extraordinary what a revolution these reflections made in his feelings. Hildegarde was so remarkably handsome that he had been compelled to admire her person. Her odd, decided manners had always amused him ; but now that he imagined himself so much the object of her preference as to cause her to refuse the addresses of Zedwitz, his admiration began to verge towards love; and the manners which had before caused him amusement became the subject of deep interest, as affording a key to a mind which, with secret satisfaction, he felt he had always considered of no common stamp. Pleased with himself, and unconsciously prepared to be more than pleased with the subject of his thoughts, he bounded up the stairs, rang the bell, and was admitted by Hildegarde herself.

'Mr. Hamilton,' she said, with some embarrassment, 'I wish to speak to you alone for a few minutes, if you are at leisure.'

'I am quite at leisure,' replied Hamilton, following her towards the drawing-room. She walked directly to the window, and desired him so haughtily to 'shut the door,' that he felt half inclined to be angry. After waiting some time in vain expectation that she would begin the conversation, he observed, with some pique at her apparent imperturbability—

'To what extraordinary event, or to what singular good fortune, am I indebted for this interview, mademoiselle ?'

No sooner had he spoken than he perceived that her composure had been forced, that she was in fact struggling with contending emotions, and quite unable to utter a word. After some delay, she at last began in a constrained voice—

'Believe me, Mr. Hamilton, that nothing but my affection for my sister could have induced me to trespass on your time, or,' she added more naturally, 'subject myself to your sneers.'

Hamilton remained silent, and she again commenced with evident effort : 'You are aware that my sister's feelings towards you are more favourable than—'

'Than yours?' he asked, interrupting her.

'I have not requested this interview to speak of my own feelings,' she answered sternly, and turning very pale. 'I wish to point out to you how ungenerous, how cruel your conduct has been to my gentle, confiding sister. You know the influence you have acquired over her— you are aware that she is on the eve of marriage with another, and that other a person she has yet to learn to love ; instead of pointing out to her any estimable qualities he may possess, in order to reconcile her to her fate, you turn him on all occasions into ridicule, and—and—not content with changing her indifference for her future husband into positive dislike, you take every opportunity of paying her attentions, which, knowing the state of her feelings towards you, is a refinement of cruelty that you must acknowledge to be unpardonable.'

' You speak like a book, mademoiselle! Your affection for your sister makes you absolutely eloquent ! But would it not have been better had *you* consented to marry Major Stultz, and so saved your gentle, confiding sister from this unwished-for connection? You would, no doubt, easily have learned to love him, and estimate any amiable qualities he may possess !' He spoke calmly and ironically; but the idea of the beautiful creature before him as the wife of Major Stultz inflicted a pang of jealousy which sufficiently punished him for his impertinence. Hildegarde was perfectly unconscious of the feelings of her tormentor; he had intended to have irritated her ; for her self-possession wounded his vanity, while her too evident dislike cut him to the quick. He failed, however, for the first time, and most completely : either her affection for her sister, or the consciousness of right, prevented her from exhibiting even impatience when she again spoke :—

' You seem to have forgotten that Major Stultz's proposal to me was made after a two days' acquaintance. I refused him because I did not like him, and I knew it could give no pain to a man whose mere object was to have a wife to manage his household concerns. It never occurred to me that he would turn, half-an-hour afterwards, to my sister, and that my vehemence would only serve to make him more cautious, and her fate more certain. You know he applied to my stepmother, and wrote to my father. The answer was, a letter full of reproaches to me, and of entreaties and commendations to Crescenz, which, to her yielding nature, were irresistible : and I do believe, if given time, and were you not here, she might be reconciled to her lot. However little Major Stultz may have cared for Crescenz at first, it is impossible for him to remain long indifferent to so much goodness. I think he already begins to be sincerely attached to her ; in time gratitude and habit will enable her to return his affection, and they may, eventually, be very happy. At all events, my sister's fate is now irrevocable.'— She paused for a moment, and then added : ' Oh, Mr. Hamilton, be generous ! Spare her ! Leave Munich— or, at least, leave our house —'

' You require a great and most unnecessary sacrifice on my part, mademoiselle. Suppose I were able to convince you that my absence is unnecessary ?'

' You cannot do so,' replied Hildegarde, with a slightly impatient gesture.

' I have listened to you with patience, and expect in my turn to be heard,' said Hamilton, handing her a chair, which, however, she indignantly refused.

' Your sister has most probably told you—' he began.

My sister has told me nothing,' cried Hildegarde, interrupting him angrily, ' excepting that you said you could not marry, or even think of marriage ! The conversation which preceded such a declaration I can imagine!'

' Indeed ! It seems you have had experience in these matters.'

Hildegarde bit her lip and tapped with her foot on the floor, while Hamilton smiled provokingly and watched her varying colour.

' Ungenerous, unfeeling Englishman!' she cried at length ; ' I—I see you are trying to put me into a passion—but I am not angry, not in the least, I assure you,' she said, seating herself on the chair he had before placed for her. ' You said,' she added, in a constrained voice, ' you said you were able to convince me—'

' *You* have convinced me that you are a consummate actress!' cried Hamilton, contemptuously.

' I am no actress!' she exclaimed, starting from her chair with such violence that it fell to the ground with a loud crash. ' I am no actress! For Crescenz's sake, I have endeavoured to be calm, in the hope of making some impression on you, but you are even more thoroughly selfish than I imagined. This is the last time I shall ever speak to you !'

' Don't make rash vows,' said Hamilton, coolly. ' I dare say you will often speak to me, in time—perhaps condescend to like me !'

' Never ! I do not think there exists a more unamiable being in the world than you are ! I now see you are determined not to leave our house, and only wonder I

could have been such a fool as to expect you to act honourably!'

Hamilton turned to the window to hide his rising colour.

'You are vindictive too,' she continued, angrily, 'cruelly
vindictive. It is because you dislike me; it is in order to
make me unhappy that you trifle with my sister's feelings.
You do not, you cannot love her. She is not at all a person
likely to interest a man such as you are!'

'When did you discover that?' asked Hamilton, turning
suddenly round.

'No matter,' she replied, moving towards the door, somewhat surprised at the effect her words had produced on him.
'No matter; I see now that these conferences and quarrels are
worse than useless, and—'

'I quite agree with you,' said Hamilton, quickly, 'and am
most willing to sign a treaty of peace, on reasonable terms.
Suppose I promise never by word or deed to disparage Major
Stultz in future, and totally to abstain from all further attentions to your sister?'

'That—is—better—than—nothing,' said Hildegarde, slowly;
'and, as I am acting for the benefit of another, I ought not to
refuse a compromise. If you promise,' she added, hesitatingly,
'I—I think I may trust you.'

'And are you satisfied without my leaving the house?'

'I suppose I must be,' she replied, stooping to raise the
chair she had thrown down; Hamilton moved it from her, and,
leaning on the back of it, asked if he might not now hope, in
case he conscientiously performed his promises, that she would
in future be at least commonly civil to him.

'You have advised me to make no rash vows,' said Hildegarde. 'The wisest thing we could both do would be never
to look at or speak to each other again.'

'Perhaps you are right,' said Hamilton, gravely, 'but such
wisdom is too great for me—'

She left the room while he was speaking, without even
looking at him.

'Zedwitz and his sister were totally mistaken,' thought
Hamilton; 'but I am determined, since they have put it into
my head, to make her like me!'

CHAPTER XIII.

A TRUCE.

Does Mr. Rosenberg never spend the evening at home?' asked Hamilton, after having waited three weeks in expectation of becoming better acquainted with him.

'Oh, no; what could he do at home?' asked his wife, seemingly surprised at the question.

Hamilton was silent; he remembered that he had never seen Mr. Rosenberg converse with his wife.

'He never drinks his beer or reads the papers at home,' she continued; 'but you can go out with him whenever you like,—I wonder you do not, for it is very natural that you should find it dull here when you cannot go to the theatre.'

'I do not find it dull,' said Hamilton; 'and I should not go so often to the theatre if I had not heard that it was the best means to perfect oneself in a foreign language. By the bye, I received a letter from my father this morning, and he desires me forthwith to engage a German master; he expects me to write German as well as English when I return home, and says I should study German literature. I wished to have asked Mr. Rosenberg to recommend me some one, for, as I am not quite a beginner, I should like to have a person really capable of directing my studies during the winter. One can read a good deal in six months when the dictionary is no longer in requisition.'

'If you wish to study French, Hildegarde could give you instruction, for she understands it thoroughly; but German has been rather neglected in her education. I really think I must let her take lessons at the same time with you.'

'I shall be very much obliged to you,' said Hildegarde, bestowing, for the first time, a look of regard on her stepmother; 'very much obliged indeed.'

'That will be delightful!' said Hamilton, eagerly. 'I have always received my German lessons with my sister, and am particularly fond of learning in company.'

'May I not learn too, mamma?' asked Crescenz, timidly.

'What for?' asked her mother, with a laugh; 'have you not already secured a good husband, who is satisfied with you as you are? It would be time and money thrown away, and

M

you have enough to do preparing your *trousseau* at present. The workwoman comes to-morrow, and we must then begin in earnest. As to Hildegarde, she has thrown away an opportunity which I hope she may not hereafter regret. Husbands will not fall down from heaven to be picked up just when she is in the humour to marry: she must try in every way to improve herself now, as a time may come when she may be obliged to give instruction. Life is precarious; if anything should happen to your father—'

'My father!' exclaimed Hildegarde, anxiously. 'Has he been complaining lately? Do you fear a return of—'

'Your anxiety is unnecessary; he is at present perfectly well,' answered her mother, drily. 'I wish, when I am really suffering, you would sometimes show a little of the attention and anxiety which you bestow at times so unnecessarily on him; it would become you better, Hildegarde, than the cold heartlessness which you evince for everything that concerns me. Crescenz is quite different, and therefore I feel for her as if she were my own child.'

'But, mamma,' said Crescenz, in a very low voice, 'you are always kind to me!'

'And am I not kind to Hildegarde?'

Crescenz blushed, stammered, and looked anxiously towards her sister.

'No,' said Hildegarde courageously, 'you are not kind to me; perhaps I do not deserve it. I have no right to expect you to love me, but I have a right to expect you to be just.'

'I was disposed to be more than just to you at first, Hildegarde, if you had allowed me. Mr. Hamilton shall be judge between us.'

'Excuse me,' said Hamilton; 'I do not feel competent to give an opinion on such a subject.'

'Chance has, however, placed you exactly in a position to act as umpire; we must be satisfied with your decision, because we know you to be an unbiassed looker-on. My stepdaughters were with me but a few weeks before I met you at Seon—since that time you have been constantly with us. Hildegarde, shall I go on?'

Hildegarde murmured something about 'strangers' and 'family dissensions.'

'Mr. Hamilton is no longer a stranger; and as to the dissensions, such as they are, he has already been a witness to them. For my part, I should like to explain, but if you acknowledge that you have been unjustly and unnecessarily prejudiced against me, I shall be silent.'

'Mr. Hamilton is not so unbiassed an arbitrator as you suppose,' observed Hildegarde, looking up steadily while she leaned on the table.

Madame Rosenberg looked from one to the other with a puzzled air, until Hildegarde added, 'He will find it difficult not to lean to your side, and take your part, even if he wished to be just, because he dislikes me personally.'

'Another argument against you, Hildegarde!' cried Madame Rosenberg, triumphantly. 'Why should he dislike you more than another if you were not less amiable? Your own words condemn you!'

'Be it so,' said Hildegarde, with some emotion. 'No one loves me but—but—my father.'

'*I* love you, Hildegarde,' whispered Crescenz, gently taking her sister's hand, and at the same time looking timidly towards her stepmother—'I love you too.'

'I shall soon see *your* affection decline; it cannot be otherwise,' said Hildegarde, bending over her work to conceal the large tears which stood in her eyes, ready to fall when she could permit them to do so unperceived.

Madame Rosenberg was not a person of much observation, although possessed of a good deal of common sense. She heard the words, and answered to them : 'Of course, when Crescenz marries, you cannot expect any longer to be her first object; Major Stultz will, and ought to take your place in her affections—it is the way of the world, the law of nature!'

Hildegarde's work dropped from her hands. Hamilton, who was sitting beside her, picked it up; and as she stooped to take it from him, the tears which he had just been watching in stolen glances, now, to his infinite dismay, fell slowly on his hand. He started as if they had hurt him; and then, under pretence of seeking a book, left the room, hoping to find the discussion at an end on his return. He was mistaken; on again opening the door, Madame Rosenberg was speaking with even more than usual volubility : 'The fact is, Hildegarde, you cannot pardon my being a smith's daughter; although I was a much better match for your father than his first wife, with all her fine relations. What's the use of being a countess when one is penniless? Your mother had not even a respectable *trousseau*—there is scarcely anything remaining to be

M 2

given to Crescenz. And you know, yourself, your relations have been so unkind, that your father never intends to allow you to visit them ; and I am quite sure were you to meet them in the street they would look away to avoid bowing to you. Take my advice, Hildegarde, forget that your mother was a Countess Raimund, remember that your father is plain Franz Rosenberg; and though your stepmother *is* a smith's daughter, you ought not to forget that many of the comforts of your home come from her, and the produce of the much-despised iron-works. Cease to fancy yourself a martyr to a cruel stepmother. I might be a great deal worse than I am ; if you find me sometimes a little strict, it is only for your good, and necessary, too, at your age ! As to your refusal of the Major, I shall never mention it again—he has not gone out of the family, you know ; if he had not proposed to Crescenz, I could not have got over the loss, or forgiven you so easily. You must endeavour to correct your irritability of temper, and I am sure in time everyone will like you; even Mr. Hamilton will overcome his dislike to you.'

Hildegarde's varying colour showed how much she suffered during this speech ; and Hamilton was again on the point of leaving the room, when Madame Rosenberg called out, ' You need not run away again ; we have talked the matter out, and intend to be good friends in future—eh, Hildegarde ? Come here, and give me a kiss to prove that you bear no malice.'

Hildegarde put aside her work, approached her stepmother, and received her hearty kiss with an evident effort at cordiality.

' May I hope to be included in this reconciliation ?' asked Hamilton, holding out his hand with a smile.

Hildegarde pretended not to understand him ; and again took her place at the table.

' Hildegarde,' said her stepmother, ' you may give your hand to Mr. Hamilton ; he is an Englishman, and will put no wrong construction on the action. Captain Smith told me that shaking hands is a common English custom, and means nothing more than kissing a lady's hand here.'

' I should think it must mean a great deal less,' said Hamilton, laughing, while Hildegarde, after a moment's consideration, placed her hand in his, and unreservedly returned his firm pressure.

' Ah ! here comes the Major,' cried Madame Rosenberg, as a

slight knock was heard at the drawing-room door. 'Come in, Major, and tell us what you have been doing with yourself the whole afternoon ; we expected you to supper, and I should not be surprised if Crescenz were to scold you a little for your unusual absence.'

'I cannot imagine Crescenz scolding me, even if I deserved it, which, however, in this instance, is not the case,' said Major Stultz. 'I have spent the whole day lodging-hunting. The sooner I am established the better, as Crescenz must assist me to choose our furniture.'

'Why, what a hurry you are in!' said Madame Rosenberg, with evident satisfaction. 'Quite an ardent lover, I declare! However, I shall not be behindhand in performing my part. The workwoman comes to-morrow, and then we shall work our fingers to the bone—eh, Crescenz?'

Crescenz blushed, and smiled faintly.

'I should like very much to talk over the different lodgings with you, Crescenz,' said Major Stultz, growing very red. 'I have noted them for that purpose in my pocket-book. That is,' he added in a whisper, 'if we can go to another table.'

Madame Rosenberg heard the whisper, pushed a candle towards him, and pointed to a card-table at the other end of the room. No sooner were they established at it, than she jingled her keys once or twice as a sort of tacit excuse, and then left the room.

Hamilton, who was as usual sitting near the stove, pretended to be wholly occupied with a book; his eyes, nevertheless, wandered perpetually over it towards Hildegarde, who now began strangely to interest him. As the door closed on her mother, her hands fell listlessly on her lap, and by degrees became clasped round her knee, while she gazed steadfastly on the floor for several minutes. She then raised her head, and, having looked at her sister for some time, turned towards Hamilton, but so slowly, that he was able to fix his eyes on his book, although he coloured violently in doing so ; he thought she must perceive his confusion, and continued pertinaciously to read the words, although they conveyed no idea whatever to his mind. When he had reached the end of the page, he became curious to know whether or not she was still looking at him, and, after a moment's hesitation, he half turned over the leaf, and at the same time raised his eyes without moving his head : he had given himself unnecessary trouble to catch her glance—her eyes met his with the most unconcerned expression possible, and though he felt that he continued to blush, she either did not observe it, or attributed it to the heat of the room.

'I wonder you can sit so near the stove, and that you can read at such a distance from the candle,' she observed, quietly.

'I am rather surprised at it myself,' answered Hamilton, pushing his chair close to hers, so as to form a *tête-à-tête*.

'Perhaps if I snuff the candle you will be better able to read.' She snuffed the candle out.

'Thank you,' said Hamilton, vainly attempting to repress a laugh; 'I have no doubt I shall be better able to read now. Perhaps you have done this on purpose to make me feel that I ought to have snuffed the candle myself.'

'Oh, no, indeed,' said Hildegarde, joining half unwillingly in the laughter; 'I happened to overhear something which Crescenz said, and then I looked up and—'

Crescenz rose from her chair, looked at them both for a moment, and then, in a voice of ill-suppressed emotion, stammered out, 'They—they—are laughing at me—at us!'

'No, oh, no!' cried Hildegarde, eagerly taking up the extinguished candle to light it. 'No, indeed; Mr. Hamilton is laughing because I have snuffed out the candle, and I am laughing I do n't know why, for,' she added with a sigh, 'I am sure I never felt less inclined to be merry in my life.'

Crescenz sat down again, but followed her sister with her eyes as she returned to her place. Major Stultz in vain talked of his yellow sofa and six chairs, and asked her whether he should buy a long or a round table for her drawing-room; or proposed purchasing both if she wished it. She heard him not, for Hildegarde was again beside Hamilton, and he was leaning on the arm of his chair and looking at her as Crescenz had never seen him looking at anyone before.

'Crescenz! you do not hear a word I am saying,' exclaimed Major Stultz, at length. 'Not one word! If you wish it, we can return to the other table, and then you can watch your sister playing with the snuffers and the wick of the candle at your leisure.'

Crescenz did not answer.

'Perhaps,' he continued, yielding to an unconquerable feeling of jealousy, 'perhaps I have mistaken the object of your attention I do believe you are admiring the bold black eyes of that long-legged English boy!'

Crescenz blushed deeply, and turned away.

This was stronger confirmation than he had expected, and he now continued, in a low voice of suppressed anger, 'I have long suspected something of this kind, Crescenz; your mother desired me to say nothing to you about it, as she imagined you too innocent to be capable of such perfidy. I cannot, at my age, expect you to love me as I do you; but I did imagine that in time I should gain your affection. If this be not possible, tell me so at once, for I will not be made a fool of by you or anyone else!'

'I don't understand you!' cried Crescenz, terrified at his constrained manner and flushed face—'I don't in the least understand you!'

'Then I will speak to your mother,' he cried, rising hastily, and pushing back his chair with great violence. 'She will understand me quickly enough.'

'Oh, for heaven's sake, don't complain of me!' cried Crescenz, beseechingly, whilst the tears started to her eyes. 'I will do anything you please, and pay the greatest attention, if you will only promise not to tell mamma.'

'Then you did understand me?—and know what I was about to say to her?' he asked, frowning.

'Oh, yes—you were going to tell her that I would not talk about the furniture, and that I looked at Hildegarde playing with the snuffers, and—and—Mr. Hamilton with his foot on the stove, instead of listening to you!'

This speech was made with consummate cunning—a more common ingredient in the composition of weak characters than is generally supposed. Major Stultz's manner had frightened Crescenz—she feared the anger of her stepmother and the reproaches of her father, for she was essentially timid, and the want of moral courage made her affect a simplicity which, although in perfect keeping with her real character, was on the present occasion mere acting, as she had perfectly understood Major Stultz's meaning. She could not have answered better; he was deceived, and, while wiping the perspiration from his crimson face, he begged her to forgive his impatience; said that he had been guilty of entertaining odious suspicions; and though Crescenz continued to blush while he spoke, and would not raise her eyes from the table, he was too generous to distrust her again, and attributed her subsequent embarrassment altogether to timidity. Partly from a jealous recollection of the expression of Hamilton's eyes, partly from shame at her own duplicity, and annoyance at the unmerited praises now lavished on her by her lover, Crescenz began to weep bitterly: and poor Major Stultz was obliged to talk a deal of youthful nonsense in order to restore her equanimity, and induce her to continue the interrupted conversation.

In the mean time, the unconscious cause of all the disturbance had indulged in a long scrutiny of Hildegarde's beautiful profile. She put an end to it by turning to him, and saying, with a glance at his book, 'You must have been reading French or English—our German letters at such a distance from the light would have been illegible.'

'I have been reading Bulwer's last novel. It is extremely interesting.'

'Indeed! I wish you would lend it to me before you send it back to the library.'

'Is it possible you understand English and have never spoken one word to me!' exclaimed Hamilton.

'I do not see anything extraordinary in that,' replied Hildegarde, smiling.

'You speak French so remarkably well, that I know you have a talent for languages. I dare say you speak English perfectly!'

'I cannot speak a word.'

'You have not had enough practice, perhaps, but you understand it when it is spoken.'

'Not a syllable.'

'Then may I ask what you intend to do with this novel when I lend it to you?'

'Read it from daybreak until seven o'clock, and at night as long as my candle lasts,' replied Hildegarde, taking the book from him and looking at the title-page.

'If you can read that book and understand it, you must be able to speak a little,' observed Hamilton.

'I tell you, I can neither speak nor understand English when it is spoken, and yet I can read this novel, if you will lend it to me, quite as well as if it were French or German.'

'You have had an odd kind of master!'

'I have had no master at all—mamma thought English an unnecessary study, though I should have greatly preferred it to music. The master, too, was expensive, so I was obliged to give up all hope of instruction ; but I had heard of some person who had learnt to read and understand a language perfectly without being able to pronounce a word, and who found it very easy, when chance gave him an opportunity, to learn the pronunciation afterwards. I begged papa to buy me a grammar and dictionary, borrowed all the English books I could get from my schoolfellows, learned them almost by heart from having read them so often ; and when the Baroness Z——— lent me some English novels at Seon, I scarcely missed my dictionary, which I had left in Munich.'

'What extraordinary perseverance !' exclaimed Hamilton, with undisguised admiration.

'Mamma would call it obstinacy,' said Hildegarde, quickly. 'Nothing would induce me to tell her that I had dared to learn English after she had refused to let me take lessons !'

'There is a great difference between obstinacy and perseverance,' said Hamilton.

'The difference is sometimes difficult to define. My stepmother says I am obstinate—'

'I really do think your organ of firmness must be tolerably well developed,' said Hamilton, laughingly placing his hand on the top of her head.

Hildegarde coloured, and hastily pushed back her chair ; he saw she did not understand him, but he was too lazy to explain. The thought passed quickly through his mind, that it was odd his not having as yet met a single person who understood or was interested about phrenology, in Germany—the country of Gall and Spurzheim !—while in England most people had read Combe's works, attended lectures on, or had at least heard phrenology spoken of sufficiently to understand what he had just said. 'You can keep the book if you wish it,' he observed, in order to renew the conversation.

'But you have not quite read it,' said Hildegarde, 'and I can imagine nothing more disagreeable than resigning a novel before one knows how it ends. Perhaps other people do not feel the same degree of interest that I do, but—'

'I have often sat up until four o'clock in the morning to read an interesting novel,' said Hamilton.

'It must be very pleasant to have a light as long as one pleases at night ! Mamma is quite surprised when I ask for a candle oftener than every three days, and then she always observes that sitting up at night is very injurious to the health

and eyes, and I get nothing but little ends of candle for a fortnight afterwards.'

'I will give you as many candles as you can burn,' said
Hamilton, laughing.

'That was not what I meant,' said Hildegarde, in great confusion. 'I dare say mamma is right, for in summer, though I
only read in bed, from daylight until six o'clock, I have often
felt terribly fatigued during the day afterwards—I heard
mamma tell papa, that if you were *her* son, she would go
into your room every night at ten o'clock, and put out your
candles.'

'I do not exactly wish her to be my mother, for the sake of
having a living extinguisher, which I should consider rather a
bore than otherwise,' said Hamilton ; 'but if she were my
mother you would of course be my sister, and I should have
no objection to that relationship.'

'Have you a sister?' asked Hildegarde abruptly.

'Yes, an only sister, and I like her better than all my
brothers put together.'

'And you do not quarrel with her?'

'Never. She is my most intimate friend when I am at
home, my principal correspondent when I am abroad. She is
the most amiable, the most excellent of human beings !'

'Older ?—much older than you?' asked Hildegarde, with
some appearance of interest.

'Only a year or two,' replied Hamilton. 'We learned
French as children together, and afterwards Italian and German. You will take her place to-morrow or the day after,
when we begin our studies, and if you wish to learn to speak
English, I am quite willing to assist you.'

'Oh, delightful !' cried Hildegarde, unconsciously moving
her chair quite close to his, and leaning her hand confidentially
on the arm of it: 'delightful ! That is exactly what I long
wished for ; but,' she added hesitatingly, 'but I fear you will
expect me to—to—that is, not to—'

'What?' asked Hamilton, with a smile.

'Not to say what I think ; or—or quarrel in future.'

'I made the offer unconditionally ; we can fight our battles
all the same, whenever you feel disposed.'

'If that be the case,' said Hildegarde, apparently much
relieved, 'I accept your offer thankfully, and I hope I shall not
give you much trouble.'

'Suppose you take your first lesson now,' said Hamilton. 'As you merely require the pronunciation, let us begin with this book.' He laid it before her as he spoke, and they both turned towards the table. Hildegarde began at once to read, but with the most unintelligible foreign accent he had ever heard. He used his utmost effort to suppress his laughter, and did not venture to correct a single word. At the end of the page she looked up rather surprised, and encountered Hamilton's eyes brilliant with suppressed mirth, while every other feature of his face was drawn into a forced seriousness of expression, forming altogether so extraordinary a distortion of countenance, that she threw herself back in her chair, and burst into a fit of laughter.

'Why don't you laugh out if you feel inclined?' she asked, as Hamilton half covered his face with his pocket-handkerchief.

'I really was afraid of offending you,' he replied.

'Oh! you never can offend me by laughing openly; it is only by speaking ironically or sneering that you can annoy me, and make me feel almost inclined at times to give you a box on the ear.'

'I give you leave to do so whenever you please,' said Hamilton; 'but you will incur a penalty of which I shall most certainly take advantage.'

'And what may that be?'

'If my lips may not explain otherwise than by words, they decline the office.'

Hildegarde bent her face over her book, shaded her eyes, and remained silent.

'Go on,' said Hamilton; 'now that you have given me leave to laugh, I have lost all inclination.'

Hildegarde continued to read, looking up, however, at the end of every sentence, and asking for the necessary corrections.

When Major Stultz stood up to take leave, he put an end to the first of the English lessons, which were, however, continued with unfailing regularity every day from that time forward. A young medical student, recommended alike for his talent and poverty, was engaged to give German lessons, and, the drawing-room being found too subject to interruptions, Hamilton's sitting-room was converted into a study. The youthful preceptor seemed to enjoy his pupil's society, and often remained long after the conclusion of the lesson to discuss literary and philosophical subjects with Hamilton, and not unfrequently to smoke a cigar, Hildegarde having had the complaisance to profess to like the smell of tobacco when it was good.

CHAPTER XIV.

A NEW WAY TO LEARN GERMAN.

ONE day Madame Berger proposed spending the afternoon with the Rosenbergs, as her husband was to be absent until late in the evening; the offer was of course accepted, and she was received by Crescenz with delight, and conducted to her room. After removing her bonnet and carefully arranging her hair and dress, Madame Berger repaired to the drawing-room, seemed exceedingly surprised to find it unoccupied, and having opened the door of the adjoining bedroom and finding it equally deserted, she tapped Crescenz playfully on the arm, exclaiming, ' Well, my dear child, what have you done with your Englishman?'

'Nothing.' replied Crescenz, despondingly.

' I begin to think you were right, Lina; he certainly admires Hildegarde, and she now scarcely ever quarrels with him, and has even begun to ask his opinion on different subjects. They do nothing but read English and German together, and talk of their books until it is quite tiresome. Yesterday evening when they were discussing Faust and Mephistophiles, which I remember papa once said few people could altogether understand, I could not help reminding them of Schiller's ballad of " The Glove," about which they had once quarrelled so desperately : and can you believe it? they both began to laugh; but I saw that Hildegarde grew red, and I am sure she found it difficult not to fight the battle over again !'

' My dear Crescenz, you must take my advice, and put this Englishman quite out of your head. As to his studies, I know all about them, and I have heard that he is extremely clever and possessed of extraordinary information for his age ; he can talk of history, politics, commerce, and all those sort of things, like a professor ! I can set your mind quite at ease with respect to Hildegarde; her whole mind is bent upon profiting as much as possible by the instruction which she is receiving, and if your Englishman has any fancy for her, she is, as yet, quite unconscious of it. Heaven help him! when she finds it out, that's all—she will be a proper tyrant! For so far, however, nothing of the kind has become apparent on either side, and I have repeatedly made the most particular inquiries.'

'From whom? How did you hear all this? I don't understand—'

'Why, my dear creature, who of all persons in the world do you think has been engaged as teacher?—Theodore! Theodore Biedermann! *my* Theodore! He has told me that the hours he spends here are his greatest recreation, that Mr. Hamilton is the most noble, charming, intellectual person in the world, and that he already feels a friendship for him which can only end with his life.'

'And so Mr. Biedermann is Theodore,' said Crescenz. 'I should never have thought it.'

'Of course not, as I never spoke of him, excepting by his Christian name : you could not know him by inspiration!'

'No—but he is not at all what I fancied.'

'And pray what did you fancy him?'

'Indeed, I don't exactly know, but as you said he wrote beautiful verses and sang to the guitar, I thought he must look like a poet, a troubadour, or something of that sort.'

'Ha, ha, ha! what a child you are!' cried Madame Berger, superciliously, but at the same time colouring slightly. 'What a complete child! And pray, my dear, can you inform me how a poet or a troubadour ought to look?'

'Not in the least like Mr. Biedermann,' cried Crescenz, apparently roused to something like anger by her friend's manner. 'Not in the least like Mr. Biedermann, who is just the most commonplace of commonplace students, with his open shirt-collar and long Henri-quatre beard, and his light hair and eyes, and red face!—and—'

'Stop—stop—my dear! I understand you now. Theodore is not tall enough to please you—he ought to have dark hair, black eyes, long eyelashes, and a pale complexion, all very interesting, no doubt ; but people answering to this description cannot always write verses, or sing to the guitar, and I can tell you that Mr. Hamilton can neither do one nor the other. Your sentimental love and admiration are all thrown away on him, Cressy; he does not think of you, and the sooner you put him out of your little head the better.'

'You are unkind, Lina!'

'And you still more so, Crescenz—to disparage poor Theodore so unnecessarily.'

'But he is nothing to you now?'

'Oh, of course not—and still I must always have a very sincere regard for him—he, poor soul, is as desperate about me as ever! Heigho! I must confess, I half feared he would waver in his allegiance when I heard that he came here every day. Men are so fickle!'

'Why, surely, you did not think that I—'

'Oh! not at all, my dear—you are engaged, you know, so I never thought of *you*, but Hildegarde—'

'I can tell you, Hildegarde would never think of *him*,' cried Crescenz, triumphantly.

'Nor he of her, I assure you,' said Madame Berger; 'he will scarcely allow her to be handsome!'

'Well, to be sure!' said Crescenz. 'That does surprise me. I never heard of anyone who did not think Hildegarde handsome!'

'Beauty, my dear, is a matter of taste. Theodore does not deny her having regular features, but it is exactly that which he cannot admire: he says there is something statue-like in her whole appearance, a certain proud expression in the drawn-down corners of her mouth; in short, he said she was a person a man could admire, but never love. There is a great difference, as you will understand a few years hence.'

'I should like to know,' said Crescenz, somewhat impatiently, 'I should like to know if I shall be as much changed by marriage as you are, Lina. I am sure I hope not; for instead of springing about or talking good-humouredly as you used to, you are now always lecturing and calling me " child;" which, I must say, is very disagreeable. I shall soon be sixteen years old, and married too; and I won't be called " child" any longer.'

'I vow, Cressy, you have taken a lesson from your sister, and are working yourself into a passion. The Doctor says "child" to me very often, and I am not at all offended; but instead of quarrelling, you ought to try and amuse me, as I am your guest to-day. Where are Hildegarde and Mr. Hamilton?'

'They are studying German with Mr. Biedermann.'

'I know that already: but *where* are they?'

'In Mr. Hamilton's room.'

'Indeed! Oh, then, we may go there too, I suppose?'

'Better not—they left this room on account of the interruptions; and mamma has desired me not to go there.'

'Very proper, as a general rule; but when I am here to chaperone you, the case is different.'

'I do n't think I ought to go,' said Crescenz, drawing back.

'Pshaw! nonsense! When Hildegarde is there, there can be no impropriety for us!'—and as she spoke, she drew the only half-reluctant Crescenz after her down the passage.

'Are not the large rooms at the end his?' asked Madame Berger.

'Yes; but indeed it is not right to interrupt them—I am sure mamma will be angry.'

'Tell her I insisted on seeing Theodore,' replied Madame Berger, as she knocked loudly at the door, but received no permission to enter.

'I told you they were too busy to receive visitors,' said Crescenz.

'What an odd noise they make!' cried Madame Berger, listening at the door before she again knocked. 'What a very odd noise!' Her curiosity was excited; and, without waiting for an answer to her second summons, she opened the door, and discovered Hamilton and his German master completely equipped with foils and visors, fencing most energetically. Chairs and tables were heaped up in a corner, and so well matched and eager were the combatants that they long remained unconscious of the presence of spectators.'

'A new way to learn German!' said Madame Berger to Hildegarde, who was sitting at the window, reading.

'Our lesson is long ended,' she replied, closing her book.

'Then pray why did you not come to the drawing-room?' asked Madame Berger.

'Because it is quieter here,' replied Hildegarde.

'Quieter! Do you call this quiet? I could not read a word if I heard the clashing of swords.'

'They are only foils; and I have got used to the sound—boxing is quieter; but they are not well matched, I believe, as Mr. Bierdermann is only a beginner.'

'Why, Theodore, is it possible you are learning to box like an Englishman? I should like of all things to know what it is like. Pray do box a little for me.'

'No, thank you; I do not appear to advantage. In fencing we are well matched,' he said, playing with the foil as he looked towards Hamilton for confirmation; 'but you must not forget that you have promised to come to my room some day and try how you can manage a sabre.'

'Your horse is saddled, sir,' cried Hans, in a loud voice, at the door.

Well, come in,' cried Hamilton, 'and put the chairs and tables in their places: and, next time, when you see I have visitors, say nothing about the horse.'

'Beg pardon, sir; I thought only our young ladies were in the room.'

' Oh, promise to ride up and down the street to show your horse to us,' cried Madame Berger. ' I am so fond of seeing horses. Come, Crescenz, let us look out of the window—and you may come too, she added graciously to Theodore, as she left the room.

When Hamilton was about to mount, he looked up towards the house, but saw so many heads looking out of so many windows, that he desired Hans to parade the horse for him. It was in vain Madame Berger opened the window and called out to him—he stood with his arms folded, admiring the animal himself, while it was being put through all its paces, and then quietly mounting, rode very slowly from the door.

' Why, Theodore, you told me he was a famous rider,' cried Madame Berger, with evident disappointment.

' And so he is ; but he does not like to show off, it seems.'

' It would have been a vast deal civiler if he had stayed at home to amuse us to-day. It is going to rain, too, and I am sure he will be wet through and through—it is a comfort to think he deserves it.'

' He does not mind being wet,' said Crescenz, stretching her head as far as possible out of the window; 'he sometimes goes out when it is actually raining—Ah!' she exclaimed, faintly screaming, while she drew back and covered her eyes with her hand, 'his horse started frightfully at the corner of the street—if he had been thrown on the pavement !'

' Let me see,' cried Madame Berger, pushing past her to take her place. 'How provoking! He has turned the corner ! But, Cressy, I say, come here ;' and she whispered a few words, and pointed downwards towards the street, where the same officer who had been addressed by Zedwitz again stood near the brazier's shop, looking towards the window where they were assembled.

' I wonder who he is!' exclaimed Madame Berger, returning

his gaze with a steadiness almost amounting to effrontery. 'Do you know that officer, Theodore?'

'No ; but he will know you again,' he replied, laughing.

'I can pardon his looking towards this window,' said Madame Berger, intending to be ingenuous, while her manner betrayed considerable levity; 'I can pardon his looking towards this window, for I dare say he has not often seen three such pretty faces as ours together :' she attempted to draw Hildegarde towards her as she spoke.

'I don't choose to be exhibited,' cried Hildegarde, drawing back. The next moment she began to laugh, while she added, 'I can inform you, however, that you are quite mistaken, if you think this window parade be intended for you. I met that officer yesterday evening on the stairs when I was coming from the cellar with Walburg ; and she told me he is to be married in spring to the daughter of the new lodger—so you may be sure he is waiting to see Mademoiselle de Hoffmann, and not thinking of either you or Crescenz.'

'I am not quite so sure of that,' said Madame Berger ; 'for do you remember, Crescenz, we saw him standing there more than a fortnight ago, and before these Hoffmanns were in the house?'

'Very true,' said Crescenz, 'but he is certainly looking to the windows on the first floor now.'

'And he certainly *was* looking up here when I first observed him,' persisted Madame Berger. 'Pray, what sort of a person is this Mademoiselle de Hoffmann? Has anyone seen her ?'

'Walburg has seen her,' replied Crescenz, 'and she says she is not at all pretty, but the servants say she is very amiable, and an excellent housekeeper.'

'Probably not young,' observed Madame Berger, arranging her ringlets at the glass—'probably not young, if she be amiable and a good housekeeper ; these qualities belong to riper years.'

'She is not very young, I believe.'

'I thought as much,' cried Madame Berger, laughing, 'and he is certainly not thirty—do you think he is?'

'He seems to be young,' said Crescenz, peeping carefully from behind the muslin curtain.

'Crescenz, come away from the window,' said Hildegarde, authoritatively; 'it is not right to watch anybody in that way.'

'Well, Cressy, I can now congratulate you from my heart on

N

your approaching marriage,' said Madame Berger, maliciously, 'for I can assure you that Major Stultz will not require half so much obedience from you as Hildegarde—your marriage will be quite a relief from thraldom.'

'You are right,' said Crescenz, colouring; 'Hildegarde certainly does treat me as if I were a child;' and she walked reso·lutely towards the window as she spoke.

'You are now acting like a child, and a silly child into the bargain,' cried Hildegarde, with evident annoyance, as she left the room.

'Dreadful temper!' said Madame Berger, shrugging her shoulders. 'If she were my sister, I should soon teach her to pay me proper respect. But look here, Crescenz; the officer has bowed to the first floor, and is now crossing the street, as if he were coming into the house; I begin to think Hildegarde was right.'

'I am sure she was right, and I ought not to have looked out of the window—I will go at once and tell her so!'

'Before you go, let me give you a piece of advice. You have spoiled your sister, and taught her to make a slave of you —do n't give your husband such bad habits. Above all things —*never* confess that you have been in the wrong, and make him on all occasions beg *your* pardon.'

'But when I feel that I have done wrong I ought at least to confess it.'

'No such thing; you must always insist on being in the right—yield once, and you must yield ever after. I have had some desperate battles, I assure you, but the Doctor has been obliged to give way, and we now get on charmingly together. Whenever I have been giddy or extravagant, he must beg my pardon—ha, ha, ha!'

'But, Lina, how can that be?—for the Doctor is a very sensible man, and were he to act as you say, he must be a fool!'

'You do not understand me, child. You see, when I do anything he disapproves, he remonstrates or lectures, and then I sulk until he begs my pardon for having remonstrated or lectured. My offence in the mean time is forgotten. Do you understand?'

'Partly,' said Crescenz, thoughtfully.

'Do not listen to such advice, mademoiselle,' said Mr. Biedermann; 'I am sure Madame Berger is joking.'

'I am not joking,' said Madame Berger, tossing back her head.

'Then you have taught your husband to treat you as if you were either a simpleton or a spoiled child, to whom he yields for the sake of peace, while he loses all respect for your understanding.'

'Theodore,' said Madame Berger, with a slightly scornful laugh, 'I advise you to keep your opinions on such subjects in future until you are asked for them. You are talking of what you do not understand. Crescenz is about to marry a man thirty years older than herself—I have done the same, and speak from experience. Had I married a man of my own age, the case and my advice would have been different. For instance, had I married you, I should have been quite a different person.'

'I don't think you would, Caroline—nothing would have made you other than you are.'

'And am I not very charming as I am?'

'Charming? Yes, with all your levity—but too charming,' said Mr. Biedermann, preparing to leave the room.

'Well, for that acknowledgement I am inclined to pardon your former impertinence; but never while you live attempt a repetition of the offence.'

'I thought our former intimacy gave me a sort of right to—'

'Our former intimacy,' said Madame Berger, laughing, 'gives you no right excepting that of being my very obedient humble servant.'

CHAPTER XV.

THE OCTOBER FÊTE, AND A LESSON ON PROPRIETY OF CONDUCT.

IT was the first Sunday in October, and Major Stultz had just driven up to the door in a carriage, which he had hired to take his betrothed and her family to the October fête. In order to increase Crescenz's pleasure, he had promised to take the three boys also, and though Mr. Rosenberg had declared his intention to walk, their party was still uncomfortably large. Fritz, in his cadet uniform, mounted the box, fully convinced that the equipage had considerably gained in appearance by his presence, and the others were endeavouring to wedge in the children between them, when a servant came running to

the door, bearing a message from Madame de Hoffmann, who
offered a seat in her carriage to one of the young ladies, if they
did not mind going a little later.

'Oh dear!' cried Madame Rosenberg, 'now really that's very
civil—before I have returned her visit too ! Hildegarde, you
will accept the offer, of course, and, to tell you the truth, I am
glad you do not leave home so soon ; Mr. Hamilton has not returned from church, and I wish you to see that he gets his
dinner comfortably served. I know you don't mind being an
hour or so later, and the races don't begin until three o'clock.'

Hildegarde descended from the carriage, seemingly satisfied
with the arrangement, and the others drove off. She stopped
on her way up stairs at the first floor, and requested to see the
Hoffmanns in order to thank them, and ask when they intended
to leave. Mademoiselle de Hoffmann came to meet her, and
took her hand eagerly, while she exclaimed, 'Ah, I knew you
would be the one to go with us. Your sister of course could
not leave Major Stultz—but surely you will come in and stay
here until we are ready to go—in fact we are ready now, and
I am only waiting for my bridegroom, who is to accompany us
—I do not know if you are aware that I, like your sister, am a
bride.'

'I have heard so,' replied Hildegarde. 'Mamma intends to
offer her congratulations in form to-morrow.'

'I don't like being congratulated,' said Mademoiselle de Hoffmann, abruptly ; 'it would be better if people waited a year or
so, until they knew how a marriage turned out. It is after all
an awful sort of lottery for a woman, and if she draw a blank
. . . . But pray come into the drawing-room ; this is no place
to discuss such subjects.'

'I am sorry to say that I have some arrangements to make
at home, but I shall return as soon as possible.'

'Pray do,' said Mademoiselle de Hoffmann. 'I may as well tell
you that I have taken such a fancy to you, that I cannot help
hoping we are destined to be very good friends.'

'I hope so too,' replied Hildegarde, with unusual warmth of
manner, and laughing gaily. Hamilton passed the door at the
moment, on his return from church, and seemed not a little
surprised to find her bestowing so much friendliness on a person
he had supposed nearly a stranger. Hildegarde followed him
up the stairs, and, on entering their apartments, took off her
bonnet, and prepared to obey her mother's directions by bringing

m his dinner herself. Hamilton had already become accustomed to these attentions, and therefore her appearance—with a napkin pinned on her dress in the form of an apron, and carrying a little tureen of soup—by no means astonished him. Having placed it on the table, she walked to the window, took up a book, and began to read.

'Have you all dined?' asked Hamilton.

'Yes, and all are gone too,' replied Hildegarde.

'You don't mean to say that you must remain at home?' asked Hamilton, turning round quickly.

'Oh, no ; I am to go with the Hoffmanns.'

'How did you happen to make that arrangement?'

Hildegarde came towards him to explain, stood for a moment behind his chair, then seated herself at the table near him, and, while performing her office of waiter, entered into an unusually unrestrained conversation. They talked long and gaily, Hamilton at length beginning to think he would prefer staying at home with her to going to the *fête*, and was actually as much annoyed as she was surprised, when the Hoffmanns' servant announced the carriage, and said they were waiting for her.

The day was clear and warm, the sky cloudless, and of that deep blue almost unknown in England ; the sun shone brightly on the groups of merry pedestrians who still continued to pour out of the town and its environs towards the Thérèsian meadow. Notwithstanding the warm sunbeams, each peasant carried under his arm an enormous red or yellow umbrella, and many were furnished with cloaks, some were dressed in the mountain costume, with which Hamilton had become acquainted at Berchtesgaden ; but in strong contrast to their picturesque appearance, there were others from the plains, with their long coats reaching almost to their heels—two large buttons between their shoulders, as if to mark the waist, and broad-brimmed, low-crowned hats. The cloth of which these most ugly garments were made was good, and in many cases fine. The hats, too, were shining, and decorated with thick gold tassels, and even the most careless observer could not fail to remark the absence of any appearance of poverty.

Hamilton rode as fast as the crowd would permit, wishing considerably that all nurses and children had remained at home, and wondering what business they could have at an agricultural *fête* and races. Then he thought of Hildegarde—Hildegarde as he had last seen her, gay and unrestrained, laughingly giving her opinion of the Hoffmanns, and relating with what self-possession Mademoiselle de Hoffmann had spoken of her intended marriage, and then she had taken the half of his bunch of grapes with a sort of unconscious familiarity, flattering from its rarity. He had for some time been aware of a change in her manner, and he now began to hope that a feeling of good-will towards himself had been the cause ; in this he was, how-ever, partly mistaken—the reconciliation, or explanation—with her stepmother had mostly effected the change. She felt that she had been unjustly prejudiced against both, and, ever ready to act from impulse, she now went from one extreme to the other, and at once gave Madame Rosenberg credit for virtues which she scarcely possessed—blamed herself unnecessarily, and received any remains of severity on the part of her step-mother as a deserved punishment for her former unwarrantable dislike. Madame Rosenberg had not been insensible to the alteration which had taken place—she had more than once ob-served to her husband that 'Hildegarde was really a warm-hearted girl, and not nearly so often in a passion as she used to be. There was nothing like a mother's care to form a girl's character; she now understood how to manage her, and expected in time to like her quite as well as Crescenz.'

Hamilton, on reaching the Thérèsian meadow, looked round for the object of his thoughts—in a crowd of eight or ten thou-sand persons, the search was not immediately successful. The royal family had long been on the tribune, and the king was distributing the last prizes as Hamilton arrived. A movement in the crowd soon after commenced, which denoted preparations for the races ; Hamilton rode towards the place where the jockeys were assembled, but when there, his horse became sud-denly restive—he shied, reared, pranced, leaped forwards and sideways, and Hamilton, had he not been a practised rider, would have found it no easy matter to keep his seat. At length the animal seemed to become aware of the power of his rider, for his capers ceased by degrees, and he merely bent his head and tore up the ground with his fore foot. Hamilton was about to return to the interrupted inspection of the jockeys and their horses, when a voice close to him observed, ' You seem alarmed for the safety of your English friend, mademoiselle—ask him if he will not give his horse to our servant, and look at the races from the carriage.'

Hamilton turned quickly round, and found that these words had been addressed by Madame de Hoffmann to Hildegarde ; he rode close up to the latter, and said in a low voice, ' I have been looking for you in vain the last half-hour, and just as I had given up the search, I find myself beside you—pray present me to your friends; you have made me really wish to be acquainted with them.'

Hildegarde complied with his request, while an officer, who was sitting opposite to her, and who was instantly recognised by Hamilton as the admirer of the candlesticks and coffee-pots in the brazier's shop, waited for a moment, and then said, ' I hope you mean to include me; if you do not choose to allow me to come under the denomination of friend, you cannot refuse to admit my right to that of relation, and very near relation too.'

Hamilton looked astonished, and Hildegarde coloured slightly, as she laughingly added, ' My cousin, Count Raimund.'

Hamilton bowed with apparent indifference, but all that Zedwitz had said of Count Raimund flashed across his mind ; he now felt convinced that there was no doubt of his gaining admittance into the Rosenberg family, and on the most dangerous footing possible — as cousin ! He himself knew from experience all the advantages of this relationship, and the unreserved intimacy which it permitted, and though he tried to convince himself that Count Raimund, being already engaged to Mademoiselle de Hoffmann, would have neither time nor opportunity to pay Hildegarde extraordinary attention, a feeling of incipient jealousy, to which, however, he gave. in thought, the name of disinterested friendship, took possession of his mind, and he turned, with something more than curiosity, to examine this cousin, this Raimund, said to be so dangerous. He was a slight young man, with rather regular features, his mouth alone remarkably handsome, though his lips were, perhaps, too red and full for a man, his eyes light blue, hair and moustache remarkably fair ; his complexion, which varied with every passing emotion, sometimes almost pale, sometimes sanguine, gave an appearance of perpetual animation to a countenance which would otherwise have, perhaps, failed to interest at first sight. He immediately addressed Hamilton, spoke of England, hunting, horses, races—of English customs and sports, with such correctness that Hamilton could not help exclaiming, 'You must have been a long time in England, to understand these things so well !'

'My information is altogether acquired from reading, replied Raimund, smiling, and evidently flattered at Hamilton's remark ; either encouraged by it, or the approving smiles of his companions, he gave a description of races in different countries, from the most ancient to the present day, discovering considerable information, well applied, but brought it forward with such ill concealed arrogance, that Hamilton, already predisposed to dislike him, was soon disgusted, and taking advantage of the first pause, and some confusion among the bystanders, he suddenly and violently checked his horse, threw him on his haunches, and backing him out of the crowd, galloped across the field. The races began, and although the horses did not promise much, it was impossible not to feel in some degree interested; he crossed the field several times at full speed, and, in doing so, he passed and repassed the carriage in which Hildegarde sat, when, having met some Englishmen with whom he was slightly acquainted, he began to talk to them not very far distant from her.

'My fair cousin follows with her eyes, and rather seems to admire her English friend,' said Raimund, with a laugh. 'He certainly is handsome, but I never saw more haughty manners or prouder looks in my life. How does he contrive to get on with stepmamma ?'

'Exceedingly well,' answered Hildegarde. 'She gives him occasional lectures on his extravagant habits, which he receives with the most perfect good temper ; but they do not seem to have much effect. I rather think his parents must be very rich, although he never speaks on the subject, for they send him large sums of money, which he leaves at his banker's, as he says, with the best intentions possible—he can find no opportunity of spending it.'

'It seems the lectures on extravagance were scarcely necessary,' observed Raimund, with a slight sneer; 'from your account, he is more disposed to hoard than spend.'

'And yet he is really generous,' cried Hildegarde, warmly. 'Mr. Biedermann, who is giving him lessons in German, says that he has been munificent to him; and I know that he gave old Hans, only the other day, a complete suit of clothes for the winter to keep him warm when he is sawing the wood in the yard ; not to mention a great many occurrences in our house.

where, had he not been disposed to give, he would have acted quite differently.'

'You are eloquent in his praise,' said Mademoiselle de Hoff-mann, 'and will force me to think well of him ; though, to tell you the truth, I feel half inclined to agree with Oscar in thinking him proud. It is true I have only seen him for a few minutes, and on a very restive horse, but the glance which he bestowed upon us all was more scrutinising than agreeable, and he certainly did appear to have a tolerably good opinion of himself.'

'I cannot dispute that point,' replied Hildegarde, laughing; 'but I wish to do him justice when I can, as I am only by degrees getting over an inveterate dislike which I took to him at first sight without any reasonable cause.'

'So!' exclaimed Raimund; 'if that be the case, I am satis-fied. It must, however, be extremely disagreeable to have such a Don Magnifico forced into one's domestic circle. I wonder your father did not rebel ;— but, of course, he must do whatever your mother chooses.'

'Oh ! papa, mamma, and Crescenz liked him from the first,' said Hildegarde. 'I was the only person who quarrelled with him, because I imagined that he was laughing at us, or seek-ing amusement at our expense, while he considered himself far, far above us. On a nearer acquaintance, it is impossible not to think him agreeable, clever, and, I must say, perfectly un-affected.'

'My dear, if you continue in this strain,' said Mademoiselle de Hoffmann, laughing slily, 'you will force us to think you altogether in love with him !'

'By no means,' observed Raimund ; 'were that the case, she would be more reserved in her praise. I am rather disposed to think that this Englishman, by some unaccountable perversion of taste, must have given the preference to my other cousin. Come, confess, Hildegarde. As to his living in your house and not taking a fancy to one or the other, the thing is absolutely and totally impossible !'

'I believe,' replied Hildegarde, 'he—hé rather admired Crescenz until she was engaged to be married to Major Stultz.'

'Then he admires her still, you may depend upon it.'

'Perhaps he does ; it is difficult to know Crescenz and not both admire and love her,' replied Hildegarde; 'but, at all events, he has ceased to pay her any attention, and does not speak more to her than to me.'

'You may be sure he makes up for lost time when he sees her alone,' cried Raimund, laughing. 'By Jove, I envy him his present position; what capital fun to—to supplant that stout old major!'

'He never thought of such a thing.' cried Hildegarde, eagerly; 'he explained at once that he could not marry.'

'Better and better,' said Raimund, laughing oddly; 'he seems perfectly to know what he is about.'

'I don't understand you,' began Hildegarde; but Madame de Hoffmann called her attention to the races, and when they were over she had no time to think about the matter.

Hamilton could scarcely conceal his vexation on his return home, when he heard that Hildegarde was engaged to spend the evening with the Hoffmanns. Mr. Rosenberg left them, as usual, immediately after supper, Major Stultz altogether monopolised Crescenz, Madame Rosenberg busied herself with a pack of cards, which she shuffled, cut, and spread out on the table before her with extraordinary interest, whilst Hamilton, accustomed as he now was to talk or read with Hildegarde, and missing her more than he liked to perceive, held a newspaper in his hand, and employed his thoughts in forming uncomfortable surmises respecting her and her cousin.

'Very odd,' said Madame Rosenberg, thoughtfully, holding a card to her lips; 'very odd, indeed;—the marriage is not in the cards!'

'I thought you were playing patience,' said Hamilton, looking up.

'Oh, no; I have been cutting the cards for Crescenz,' she said in a low voice; 'and oddly enough her marriage is not in them. I must try it again,' she said. gathering up the pack and shuffling energetically.

Hamilton drew his chair to the table, and watched her as she slowly and thoughtfully placed the cards in regular rows before her, while murmuring, with evident dissatisfaction, 'This is Crescenz, and this is the Major, but ever so far asunder! And the marriage and love cards are all near him, while Crescenz's thoughts are occupied about a present. You are laughing at me, I see! Perhaps you don't believe that I can tell fortunes?'

'I am convinced you can do so quite as well as anyone else.'

'That is saying too much,' said Madame Rosenberg. 'Our washerwoman is very expert; but I know some who could astonish you!'

'I like being astonished,' said Hamilton, 'and promise to be so, if what you foretell come to pass.'

'But suppose Crescenz's marriage should be broken off—which Heaven forbid—what would you say then?'

'It will not be broken off, but it may be postponed. You said yourself, yesterday, that her *trousseau* could not be ready at the time expected; and as to her thoughts being occupied about a present, we all know that she is making a purse and cigar-case for Major Stultz.'

'Oh, if you explain everything in that way, I need not go on,' said Madame Rosenberg, laughing. 'Here, for instance, is a false person in our house—a very false person; he is followed, too, by a number of unlucky disagreeable cards!'

'And you can see all that in these cards?' cried Hamilton, laughing.

'Look here, and I will explain it easily,' said Madame Rosenberg. 'You see this ace is our house—'

'*Is* that an ace?' said Hamilton. 'The German cards are as difficult to learn as the handwriting. I do not know a single one of these cards.'

'They are easily learned. These are acorns, and these bells; these trefle, and these hearts.'

'But this ace of hearts is double; and what is the meaning of the basket of flowers and the blinded Cupid?'

'Only for ornament.'

'This, then, I suppose, is the king of hearts; but where is the queen?'

'This, I believe, answers to your queen.'

'What! the man leaning on his sword?'

'I see you do not want to learn—'

'And yet I should rather like to know what these acorns and bells are intended to represent,' said Hamilton.

'Crescenz, come here and explain in French,' cried Madame Rosenberg.

Crescenz came most willingly. In a few minutes, Hamilton imagined he knew the cards, and began to play some childish game which Crescenz taught him; they played for six-kreutzer pieces, and, as he continually mistook the cards, in the course of half-an-hour he had lost some florins. Crescenz's exclamation of delight and triumph caused Madame Rosenberg at last to look round, and no sooner did she perceive how matters stood, than she took the money which Crescenz had won, returned it to Hamilton, notwithstanding all his protestations, and, taking some red and white counters out of her work-table drawer, divided them equally between them, while she observed, that they might fancy them florins if they wished ; ' it would be much more proper for young people than really playing for money.'

' I hope,' Hamilton said to Madame Rosenberg, ' you will not treat me so like a child as to force me to take back what I have lost, but if you forbid our continuing to play, of course we must obey.'

' Well, play for kreutzers or pfennings, if you like, but it is a bad habit.'

The permission granted, Crescenz seemed to have lost all inclination to continue. She and Hamilton were soon after employed in building card houses, while they kept up a sort of murmured conversation in French, possibly very interesting to them, but unintelligible to Madame Rosenberg and Major Stultz—the former had commenced knitting, the latter sat watching the varying countenance of his betrothed, as she, sometimes lowering her voice to a whisper, seemed to speak pensively and quite forgot her occupation ; the next moment, however, with childish delight, slily blowing down the Chinese tower, which had apparently cost Hamilton a world of trouble to erect. How long this occupation might have continued to interest them, it is impossible to say, for Hildegarde's return caused Crescenz instantly to leave her place, and though Hamilton still continued to play with the cards, it was unconsciously. Crescenz's eager inquiries of how Hildegarde had amused herself, if the Hoffmanns had pleased her on a nearer acquaintance, and if she had seen the future husband of Mademoiselle Hoffmann, were answered quickly and decidedly.

' I have spent a delightful day ; the Hoffmanns are the most charming people I ever met, and the bridegroom is, without any exception, the most amusing and the cleverest person in the world !'

' Phew-w-w-w!' whistled Major Stultz.

' What is his name ?' asked Crescenz.

'Count Raimund. He is our very nearest relation—our first cousin!'

'Our cousin! But—but—I thought the Raimunds did not wish to know us.'

'We have no right to make him answerable for the unkindness of his parents, Crescenz, and all I can say is, that he spoke at once of our near relationship, and, as it was impossible to refuse to acknowledge it, we became intimate immediately. In fact, he gave me no choice, for he called me Hildegarde, and spoke of you as if he had known you all his life. He intends to call here to-morrow, to visit mamma!'

'Does he?' said Madame Rosenberg, drily.

'He says you are his aunt, as you have married papa.'

'It is singular he never discovered the relationship until to-day! During your mother's lifetime, I have heard, too, that the Raimunds pretended at times to forget your father's name. The fact is, my dear, he thought it would flatter me to fancy myself aunt to a Count, although there is actually no relationship whatever; and you thought so too, Hildegarde, or you would not have repeated so absurd a remark.'

Hildegarde's face became crimson. 'These were his words,' she said, with the quivering lips of half-subdued anger. 'You may, of course, put what construction you please upon them.'

'The words and their meaning are easily understood,' said Madame Rosenberg, laughing. 'But why he has so suddenly chosen to acknowledge a relationship with you and Crescenz, and force upon me the honour of being his aunt, is more difficult to comprehend.'

'Not at all, ma'am,' said Major Stultz, glancing from Hildegarde to Crescenz. 'Not at all. A young man is always glad to gain admittance to a house where there are young ladies.'

'But, my dear Major, the man is engaged to be married to Mademoiselle de Hoffmann in January, and all other young women must be indifferent to him now!'

'Some men never become indifferent to young women, ma'am, and, if I am not mistaken, this Count Raimund is one of these persons. I think I have heard that he has been very a—a—'

'Very what?' asked Madame Rosenberg, quickly.

'Very wild—if not very profligate,' replied Major Stultz, distinctly.

'Then I shall take good care that if he comes to-morrow, it shall be his last as well as his first visit. But you are quite sure of what you say? Otherwise, you know, Rosenberg might be dissatisfied, and think that I was uncivil from personal dislike, for I do dislike these Raimunds, and that's the truth. Fancy their pretending to think that I treated Hildegarde and Crescenz harshly after my marriage, and proposing to take them altogether from me!'

'I wonder why you did not resign us,' said Hildegarde, bitterly.

'For two reasons,' replied Madame Rosenberg. 'First, you were never to be allowed to see your father, and he did not like that part of the arrangement. Secondly, you were to be educated to become governesses, and were to remain at school until you were given a situation in some foreign family, as they only wanted to get you out of the way on account of the relationship. Now, I had a promise of one free place at the same school, and did not despair of working out the other, while by coming home for a time there was a chance of your marrying into the bargain. And I was right, for here is Crescenz well provided for, and if you continue to improve as you have done of late, I foresee that I shall not long have you on my hands either. But to return to this Count Raimund, Major—tell me all you know, or have heard about him.'

'I have heard more than I can tell you at present,' said Major Stultz, mysteriously; 'such things are not a proper subject of conversation before young ladies.' Hildegarde threw herself back in her chair and laughed contemptuously, as Madame Rosenberg adjourned to the next room with Major Stultz. 'This is the first time,' she said, looking after them, 'the first time that I have seen him attempt to act the part of son-in-law.'

'He is acting as a friend,' said Hamilton, gravely.

'How do you know that?'

'Perhaps I have heard more of Count Raimund than you imagine.'

'And suppose you have,' said Hildegarde, folding her hands together and looking Hamilton steadily in the face; 'suppose even you have heard all that can be said against him, what does it amount to? Failings, faults, if you will, which, as he himself said this evening, every young man has been guilty of—. Have you, yourself, been so immaculate that you feel authorised to judge him?'

Hamilton blushed deeply, but did not answer.

'I know,' continued Hildegarde, with increasing warmth, 'I know you think yourself superior to other people, but your present confusion proves that you have your weaknesses too, with this difference, that you the while pretend to be a pattern of perfection, and others honestly confess their faults!'

'Oh, Hildegarde!' cried Crescenz, deprecatingly.

Hamilton crushed the card which he held in his hand, looked vexed, but still did not attempt to speak.

'It is hard,' continued Hildegarde, more quietly, though her cheeks flushed deeply. 'It is hard to judge a young man like Oscar without knowing the temptations to which he has been subjected.'

Hamilton still remained silent; he began once more to build a tower with the cards.

'Do you not hear me?' she asked, impatiently.

'I am listening most attentively.'

'Then why do n't you say something?'

'Because a reply will only provoke another taunt on your part, and can answer no purpose whatever.'

'I see—you think I have been hasty—I did not mean it— I am sorry if I have offended you.'

Hamilton looked up and smiled, and Hildegarde continued : 'We have so few relations—so very few. Oscar is our *only* cousin. I cannot tell you how I felt to-day when he called me Hildegarde, and told me to consider him a brother. You will think me romantic when I assure you that I experienced an instantaneous prepossession in his favour, or rather a sort of affection which I thought it quite impossible to feel for a stranger! I suppose the recollection of my mother, faint though it be, partly caused this feeling. At all events, I have found it impossible not to think him the most amusing, clever —in short, the most fascinating person I ever met.'

'Oh dear! How I should like to know him!' exclaimed Crescenz.

'Then he is so very accomplished !—speaks French so perfectly—and plays the pianoforte as I have never heard it played. Fancy his being able to compose for hours together without ever being at a loss !—able to follow all his thoughts, and express them beautifully in music !—sometimes so sad, so melancholy, then gay or passionate, according to the impulse.'

'I was not in the least aware that you cared for music,' said Hamilton, interrupting her with a look of unfeigned surprise, 'you play the pianoforte so seldom, and—'

'And so badly,' said Hildegarde, interrupting him in her turn, ' so badly, that you concluded I must be incapable of appreciating good music when I heard it ?   On the contrary, I am so sensitively alive to its beauties that I cannot endure mediocrity, and beyond that I know I should never arrive, when I take into consideration my want of time and patience; but to appreciate Oscar's playing, only requires feeling—it is a sort of thing one never could get tired of—something like the conversation of a person who talks well.   I only hope you may soon have an opportunity of judging for yourself.   I wish, too, you could hear him read aloud.   I never imagined anything like it.   He read for Mademoiselle de Hoffmann and me, and we both felt cold and warm alternately—it was too delightful.'

'What did he read?' asked Crescenz.

'Heine's Poems,' answered Hildegarde, drawing from her pocket a small volume; 'this is called the Book of Songs; and he has given it to me.   Shall I read you " The Dream"?'

'By all means,' said Hamilton.

Hildegarde began, her voice trembling from eagerness.   She had, however, scarcely read a couple of verses, when her mother entered the room, and asked directly, 'What have you got there, Hildegarde ?'

'A book, mamma.'

'That is evident: but what book?   You know I do not wish you to read anything but French ; and this is German, and poetry into the bargain—and Count Raimund's too!' she said, taking it out of Hildegarde's unwilling hand.   'You see, Major, he has already begun with his books, just as you told me.   I dare say it is full of improprieties!'

'As well as I can recollect, you are mistaken,' said Hamilton.   'Some of the poems are beautiful, and all original, and full of talent.'

'If that be the case, I suppose I may let her read them—but the book must be returned as soon as possible.'

'But—' began Hildegarde.

Crescenz pulled her sleeve, and whispered,—'Don't say he gave it to you.'

Hildegarde shook off her sister's hand, while she said, 'The book is mine : he gave it to me ; and if I may read it, I may keep it, I suppose.'

'You may do no such thing,' cried her mother, with considerable irritation. 'Should Count Raimund come to-morrow, I shall return him his book, and request him to keep the remainder of his library for his own perusal. He would have done better had he given it to his betrothed instead of you ; and I shall tell him so.'

'I see you are determined to affront him,' said Hildegarde, angrily; 'and as you mean to return this book to-morrow, I may as well tell you that I shall not go to bed to-night until I have read every line of it.'

'Hildegarde! Hildegarde! I am afraid you are about to have one of your old fits of anger and obstinacy. It is unpardonable your being so childish now that you are nearly seventeen years old! However, since you act as a child, I must treat you as one ; and you shall not have more candle than will just light you to bed.'

Hildegarde put the book into her pocket, shoved her chair hastily back, and walked towards the stove ; Major Stultz, while wishing Crescenz good-night, observed in an audible whisper, 'What a lucky man am I that *you* have fallen to my lot!'

Madame Rosenberg accompanied him out of the room, first stopping at the door to say to Hildegarde and Crescenz, 'You must not think that I am actuated by personal dislike to Count Raimund if to-morrow I forbid him our house—he is a most dangerous person—has brought dishonour on two respectable families, and his last exploit was going off with the wife of one of his friends.'

Crescenz seemed utterly confounded by this speech, and turned to her sister, while she said, 'Oh, Hildegarde! if this be true?'

'It is true.'

'Why, you praised him just now, and—'

'Well, I am ready to praise him again; and yet it is true. He intends, however, henceforward, to lead a different life, and honestly confessed all his misdemeanors to Maria de Hoffmann and to me this evening. He did not spare himself, I can assure you.'

'His confession must have been very edifying,' observed Hamilton.

'It was very amusing,' replied Hildegarde, slightly laughing.

O

'He related with such spirit, described such comical situations, and begged Mademoiselle de Hoffmann to forgive his thoughtlessness with such fervour that she was not only obliged to pardon him, but also forced to confess that perhaps others would not have acted differently had they been subjected to the same temptations.'

'He seems to have proved himself a sort of victim,' said Hamilton, without looking up.

'Almost,' said Hildegarde. 'He was given all sorts of encouragement by the young ladies, who met him alone, and Madame de Sallenstein actually herself proposed going off with him.'

'He told you that, and the names also?'

'Certainly: he did not conceal the slightest circumstance, related all the conversations and adventures—no book could be more amusing! His first love was a daughter of a Captain Welden; there were four daughters, and they all took a fancy to him at the same time—the youngest was much the prettiest, and so—'

'Excuse my interrupting you,' cried Hamilton, 'but really I cannot endure to hear you talk in this light manner—Count Raimund must be a fiend incarnate, if he can change you so completely in one day!'

'Indeed I do think Hildegarde is changed,' chimed in Crescenz. 'I never heard her talk so oddly before — and, oh, Hildegarde, do you remember how hardly you judged Mr. Hamilton, when you only suspected that he—that I—I mean we—on account of Major Stultz, you know?—Oh, think of all you said in Berchtesgaden!'

Crescenz's eloquence did not seem to make much impression on Hildegarde,—she merely shook her head impatiently.

'I find I have altogether mistaken your character,' said Hamilton, approaching her, and leaning his elbow on the stove, 'altogether mistaken, it seems.'

'How do you mean?'

'I thought that, if from a false and romantic idea of generosity or liberality, you could be induced to overlook conduct like Count Raimund's, you would at least be shocked to find him boasting of his villany, and throwing the blame on his victims.'

Hildegarde blushed so deeply that it must have caused her actual pain; she threw herself into a chair, and turned away.

'Mr. Hamilton is quite right,' said Crescenz; 'it was not honourable of Count Raimund to throw the blame on Captain

Welden's daughter—and then to repeat everything and laugh! Oh, Hildegarde, he may be very amusing, but he cannot have a good heart!' She bent down towards her sister, and added in a whisper, 'Mr. Hamilton would never have acted so!'

'Mr. Hamilton is, most probably, in no respect better than other people,' replied Hildegarde, quickly, but without turning round.

'Why, Hildegarde, you seem to forget that you said only yesterday—that he was so superior to other people—so like somebody in a book you know, the hero who was too perfect to be natural, because he never was angry or—'

'Crescenz!' cried Hildegarde, literally bounding from her chair, 'are you purposely trying to irritate me? or are you really what Lina Berger has often called you, a simpleton— a fool? Anything so nonsensical or silly as your remarks, I never in my life heard!'

'Now, Hildegarde, do n't be angry; you know these were your own words.'

'I shall in future carefully avoid making any remark to you which I do not intend to be repeated to the whole world,' said Hildegarde, walking up and down the room, and speaking hurriedly. 'Everything that I say is misunderstood, and stupidly brought forward in the most provoking manner. Until to-night I had no idea of your excessive silliness!'

'You are right—I see—I understand now,' cried Crescenz, with tears in her eyes. 'I ought not to have repeated what you said before Mr. Hamilton, because he might think, perhaps, you liked him as I do—did, I mean to say—that is, he might fancy—'

'You tiresome girl, can you not at least be silent?' cried Hildegarde, stamping with her foot. 'Mr. Hamilton may fancy what he pleases, but he knows that I disliked him from the commencement of our acquaintance; and if I did begin to think better of him, I have again returned to my first opinion —he is in no respect better than others; and had he anything to boast of, I am sure he would do so quite as inconsiderately as Oscar, or anyone else.'

'I *hope* you are mistaken,' said Hamilton, quietly lighting his bed-chamber candle; 'but as I have never been put to the proof, I cannot answer for myself.'

Crescenz hung her head, looked uneasily towards her sister, who was about to reply, when Madame Rosenberg appeared at the door, and they all prepared to retire for the night. Hamilton did not, as was his usual custom, linger at their door to continue the interrupted conversation, or talk some nonsense not adapted for the rational ears of their mother; he walked quickly to his room, seated himself at the table, and, taking out his journal, was soon employed in writing the events of the day, with copious reflections. He was angry, very angry, with Hildegarde, and yet by some strange process of reasoning he firmly persuaded himself that not a particle of jealousy was mixed with his just indignation. He began to suspect that his admiration for her person had induced him to give her credit for virtues which she did not possess; he was even ready to allow that he had greatly overrated her in every respect; but still the idea of her becoming his first love had that day so completely taken possession of his mind, that it would not be banished, and, imagining himself, as a younger son, privileged to fall in and out of love as often as he pleased, with perfect impunity, he determined at once to enter the lists, and break a lance with Count Raimund. In England his position was known: Crescenz had already forced him to be explicit on the subject, and had, he supposed, informed her sister; he therefore conceived he had a right to pay Hildegarde all the attentions she would accept, while her opinion of Count Raimund's conduct that evening would, he thought, exonerate him from self-reproach, or future blame on her part. This was arguing most sophistically, and judging a few thoughtless words too harshly. He seemed to have forgotten that her mother had accused her of inordinate family pride, and it was this, perhaps, alone which had made her blind to her cousin's faults, and explained, if it could not excuse, the utterance of opinions so unlike any that Hamilton had ever heard her express. He recollected, however, with peculiar complacency, the words which Crescenz had repeated respecting himself, and which Hildegarde had not denied. She had found a resemblance between him and some hero in a novel; that is, she was beginning to make a sort of hero of him, and he had not read and studied with her for so many weeks without discovering that she had a warm imagination, romantic ideas, and passionate feelings. She did not, it is true, remind him of any particular heroine, nor, on consideration, did she seem adapted to form one at all, for who ever heard of a heroine whose passions 'oozed out,' like Bob Acres' courage, ' at the palms of her hands,' or found vent in the clapping of doors, and upsetting of chairs—not to mention considerable fluency of language when irritated? But then, her perfect face and figure covered a multitude of faults, her occasional violence of temper was rather amusing than otherwise, and, on taking into consideration her extreme youth, it merely proved an energy of character far more interesting than the gentle insipidity of her sister. He perceived that her cousin had made a deep impression on her, and imagined, in consequence, that his quiet and respectful manner had not been appreciated—he remembered having heard his brother say that very young or very elderly women prefer audacity to deference, and he wished with all his heart that it were morning, that he might begin a new line of operations. A knock at the door surprised him in the midst of these reflections, and made him hastily throw down his pen; scarcely waiting for permission to enter, Hildegarde had partly opened the door, and stood before him, her candle burnt down in the socket, and already emitting the fitful gleams of light which precede extinction.

'I dare say you are surprised to see me at this hour,' she began.

'Not at all,' cried Hamilton, pushing away his table, 'not at all, for I have just been thinking of you, and I suppose some sort of sympathy has made you think of me.'

'No, not exactly of you,' replied Hildegarde, with a smile, 'but I have thought of your candles! You have often offered me one when I wished to read at night, and I always feared it would be dishonourable to take advantage of your offer, as it would be deceiving mamma. To-night, however, I have given her fair warning, so, if you will permit me—'

Hamilton pushed a candle towards her, and was rather puzzled what to say next: she, in the mean time, very calmly extinguished her light and began to arrange the new one.

'I suppose you have half read your book by this time?' said Hamilton, at length.

'No,' said Hildegarde, while she rolled a piece of paper round the candle. 'No; I have been employed in making apologies to Crescenz. You must have thought me abominably rude to her this evening?'

'Rather,' replied Hamilton, greatly vexed to find that the determination to be audacious had made him more than usually restrained—almost timid in his manner.

'I thought you would have blamed me more,' continued Hildegarde, fastening the candle steadily, 'but even your judgment, with all its severity, cannot equal my own in rigour, when the moment of anger is past. Crescenz forgave me directly, and in her good nature tried soon to excuse my loss of temper, and to reconcile me to myself!'

'A fault must be forgiven when so acknowledged,' said Hamilton, lightly. 'But instead of talking of faults, which by the bye is not the most agreeable subject of conversation, suppose you read me this "Dream," which was so unpleasantly interrupted this evening.'

'Not now,' said Hildegarde, 'but I intend to write it out, and we can read it together to-morrow, when Mr. Biedermann is gone.'

'No time like the present,' said Hamilton, pointing to a place beside him on the sofa. 'Come, suppose we read the whole book?'

'If it were not so late, I should have no objection.'

'From your conversation this evening, I should not have expected you to make difficulties about such a trifle.'

'Conversation this evening?' repeated Hildegarde, thoughtfully.

'Have you then already forgotten all you said in defence of your cousin?' asked Hamilton, half laughing, while with his hand he gently induced her to take the unoccupied place beside him. 'I thought your memory was more retentive.'

'But my defence of Oscar has no sort of connection with my remaining here until two or three o'clock in the morning to read Heine's Poems!' said Hildegarde, quietly fixing her large blue eyes on Hamilton's face, with an expression of such perfect confidence, that his previous resolutions and his brother's opinions lost at once all influence over him, and not for any consideration would he have shaken the reliance on his integrity, legible in every feature of his companion's face. He blushed deeply, as he answered evasively—'Perhaps there is more connection than you are aware of, but you must wait until to-morrow, and then, if you wish it, I will tell you what I meant.'

'But why not now? I detest delay—besides, I shall forget to ask you to-morrow.'

'No, you will not forget,' said Hamilton, laughing.

'But why will you not tell me now?' asked Hildegarde.

'Because I fear to shock you unnecessarily.'

'But I am not easily shocked,' observed Hildegarde.

'So I perceived from what you said this evening.'

'It is really not generous of you to harp continually on my defence of Oscar ; I am willing to acknowledge that you were quite right in what you said about him—I know, too, I was wrong to be angry with mamma and Crescenz—but I do not like to be so perpetually reminded of my faults by you—you are not old enough—and—and—you bore me with your real or affected superiority.'

'Did I affect superiority, we should never have quarrelled,' replied Hamilton, with evident vexation. 'I only quarrel with my equals.'

'I quarrel with everybody,' said Hildegarde, with a sigh ; 'a passionate temper is a great misfortune—but I can and will learn to control it. Perhaps the fear of my losing my temper, and not the fear of shocking me, prevented you from telling your thoughts just now ? Do not wait until to-morrow, but speak freely and at once.'

'Excuse me,' said Hamilton, rising ; 'I have changed my mind, and will neither speak now nor to-morrow—I have no right to correct, and certainly no wish to bore you.'

'I might have guessed what your answer would have been, cried Hildegarde, petulantly. 'You store up every hasty word to bring forward just when I wish it forgotten ! If you will not tell me, I may as well wish you good-night.' She took up the candle, and walked to the door.

'Good-night,' said Hamilton, approaching as if to close it after her, and making no attempt whatever to detain her.

'As you feared to shock me,' said Hildegarde, stopping suddenly, 'I suppose I have done something very wrong!'—and she looked up inquiringly.

'I really do not know,' replied Hamilton, stiffly.

'You—you most disagreeable person —' she began, angrily, but, seeing that Hamilton was endeavouring to suppress a smile, she exclaimed,—'Well, if this is not affecting superiority, I do not understand you at all !—What must I say to you ? I was wrong to defend Oscar ; he is unfortunately a—a—great reprobate, I suppose, but he is my cousin, my only cousin, and I admire him more than anyone I have ever seen.'

'You had better tell him so,' said Hamilton, ironically.

'It is not necessary ; he is perfectly aware of his advantages,' she replied, in the same tone.

'So I perceived at the races to-day.'

'That he did not please you, I saw at once,' said Hildegarde, playing with the lock of the door; 'you looked so unfriendly and haughty, that the Hoffmanns could hardly believe all I said in your praise.'

'So you undertook my defence?' said Hamilton, quickly.

'Of course; I always defend the absent, especially when they are censured by people who do not know them. If Oscar had not been so attacked this evening, I should never have attempted to take his part—perhaps you do n't believe me?'

'I do believe you—but I cannot understand how Madame de Hoffmann could allow him to speak so very freely.'

'She is very deaf, and he was seated at the pianoforte; Marie at one side of him, and I at the other—he spoke very gently, and sometimes played a few chords, which gave the appearance of a sort of recitation—exactly what I imagined an improvisatore must be! I am sure he would make an excellent actor!'

'And I am sure he will prove a dangerous man,' said Hamilton.

'If he keep his promises, Marie will, nevertheless, be very happy with him—he is a person one must admire, and might easily love;—but I am keeping you from writing, and I dare say you would rather hear what I have to say to-morrow.'

'By no means—if you have anything more to say, I should like to hear it.'

'Oh, yes; I want to speak to you—about myself, not Oscar.'

'A much more interesting subject,' observed Hamilton.

'But then,' said Hildegarde, hesitating, 'you will probably give me some severe answer, and make me repent my humility.'

'I promise to give you no severe answer,' said Hamilton, exceedingly flattered.

'Then I must beg of you to forget what I said just now. I am quite aware that I have more faults than people generally have, and if you will take the trouble to correct them I shall be obliged to you. I have spent almost the whole of my life at school among girls of my own age; so, of course, I must know very little of the manners and customs of the world. I see Crescenz's simplicity quickly enough, and, to avoid falling into her errors, I try to act differently in every respect. Now, Crescenz, with all her weaknesses, makes herself beloved—not more than she deserves, for she is the most amiable creature in the world, while I am almost universally disliked. I think, therefore, something must be wrong ; I have no person whose advice I can ask. Papa overrates as much as mamma under-rates me, and neither of them understands me at all. Do you remember one evening mamma's saying that you, as an un-biassed looker-on, could judge between us? I refused you as arbitrator then, because I knew you liked mamma better than me ; but I am now willing to accept of you as judge, Mentor, or whatever you please, for I am convinced that you only dislike me just enough to see my faults without exaggerating them, so I promise to bear your corrections with as much patience as my natural impatience will allow.'

During this speech Hamilton had been leaning against the wall, endeavouring to look as sage as Hildegarde evidently thought him ; his eyes were bent on the ground, but a smile of ineffable satisfaction played round his mouth. Not for a moment did he hesitate to undertake the dangerous task. He would direct her studies, correct her faults, and make her mind as perfect as her form! What words he made use of to express this most magnanimous resolution he never himself could recollect ; that he had spoken intelligibly was evident, for Hildegarde held out her hand and smiled brilliantly as she once more turned to the door. ' I think,' she said, with some hesitation, ' I think I could sleep more soundly to-night if you would begin your office at once, and tell me what I have done to-day that is reprehensible.'

' I must of course, if you desire it.'

' Let me guess. It is not Oscar's defence?'

' No ; we have already discussed that subject,' replied Hamilton.

' My—my losing my temper this evening, when mamma made the remark about Oscar's saying she was his aunt?'

Hamilton shook his head.

' Well, then, my obstinacy about reading the book?'

' Humph !—obstinacy is certainly a fault, but that was not what I meant on the present occasion.'

' Ah ! now I know—because I asked you for a candle, and as I did not tell mamma I could get one from you, you think that I have acted dishonourably? Perhaps you are right, so I shall not take it, but go to bed in the dark as a punishment. Are you satisfied ?'

' I ought to be, for you have not only confessed your fault, but imposed penance on yourself; and yet I must still say that you have not discovered the error to which I alluded.'

' Then, now you must tell me, for I can think of nothing else.'

' Is it possible,' said Hamilton, the colour, as usual, mounting impetuously to his forehead: ' is it possible that you are not aware of the impropriety of coming to my room at this hour ? '

' I—I—came for—for the candle,' stammered Hildegarde, in painful confusion.

' I know you did; but you have remained here some time, and people—'

' Let me go—let me go !' she cried impatiently, pushing back the hand which he had placed on the lock of the door in order to have time to add a few words. ' Let me go: I desire— I insist.'

He drew back, and she rushed past him into the dark passage without turning round or stopping until she reached the door of her room. He merely waited until she had entered, and then once more sat down to write.

CHAPTER XVI.

THE AU FAIR, AND THE SUPPER AT THE BREWERY.

' WILL you go with us to Au fair?' said Madame Rosenberg to Hamilton the next day after dinner.

' Of course, but what is the Au ? I never heard of it.'

' One of the suburbs—at the other side of the Isar. There is a beautiful Gothic church there, which you can look at while I buy ticken to make Crescenz a mattress.'

' When do we set out ? '

' The sooner the better, for the Major has proposed a party to the Stubenrauch Brewery afterwards; we are to sup there.'

' At the brewery?'

' Yes ; the Major says the beer is excellent, and the roast geese delicious; Rosenberg enjoys the idea, of all things ;—he has a passion for roast goose ! '

' Oh, what fun !' cried Gustavus, jumping about the room. ' Mamma has promised to take me with her. It is a pity that Fritz has gone to grandpapa.'

' And may I go too ?' asked Peppy.

'You are too young,' replied his brother, demurely; 'you cannot walk so far.'

'I can, I can!' cried Peppy, commencing a roar.

'Hush!' said Madame Rosenberg; 'what is the child crying about?'

'Peppy wishes to go with us, mamma,' said Crescenz; 'I will take charge of him, if you have no objection.'

'You will, probably, have to carry him half the way home; but you may do as you please,' replied her mother, with a smile of satisfaction strangely in contradiction to her words. 'Off, and get ready, all of you!'

There was a joyous and noisy rush down the passage, while Madame Rosenberg, turning to Hamilton, observed, 'A very good girl is Crescenz. She shall not be a loser for liking my boys—that is certain.'

Madame Rosenberg was herself always the last to appear; she generally dressed her children, and had a long consultation with her cook before she went out. Hamilton found the rest of the party, with the exception of Hildegarde, assembled in the drawing-room, and was not long before he observed that Crescenz was making him the most unaccountable signs and grimaces. He approached her, apparently occupied in forcing his fingers into a tight glove, and said in French, 'Why are you making such horrible faces?'

Crescenz laughed good-humouredly, but, while pretending to look at his glove, answered hurriedly, 'Hildegarde is at the Hoffmanns', to return the book to Count Raimund. Go—go for her before mamma comes.'

He left the room, descended quickly the flight of stairs, stood before the Hoffmanns' apartments, and rang the bell. He now regretted not having as yet visited them, for though he would have particularly liked to see how Hildegarde and her cousin were occupied, he could not make his appearance for the first time so unceremoniously, and was, therefore, obliged to send in the servant with a request that Mademoiselle Rosenberg would return home immediately. He thought he heard Hildegarde speaking as the door opened, and perceived, from the sound of the moving of chairs, that she was taking leave at once. Not wishing to be seen, he left the passage where he had been standing, and retired to the landing-place on the stairs without. Hildegarde was accompanied by her cousin, who spoke French that the servant might not understand him. 'Adieu, dearest Hildegarde; your stepmother may forbid me her house, but she cannot change the course of nature and prevent our being cousins. I shall see you here, and often; promise me that at least.'

Hildegarde was about to answer, when she perceived Hamilton. The two young men bowed haughtily, mutual dislike legible in every feature.

'I suppose I may accompany you to your door, Hildegarde, even if it be closed against me ?'

'It is quite unnecessary,' she replied, moving up the stairs, evidently endeavouring to get rid of him.

'Raimund, however, followed, and, before he turned to descend, gently took her hand and kissed it, with a mingled expression of respect and admiration.

Hamilton scarcely waited for him to be out of hearing, before he observed, ' This, I suppose, is the most approved manner for cousins German.'

' It is less remarkable than the manners of cousins English,' replied Hildegarde. 'I have not forgotten your meeting with yours in Salzburg.'

'That was after a separation of several months, and—'

'Yes ; but it was something more than hand-kissing, which means nothing at all, you know, and, I hear, is rather going out of fashion.'

'And yet it is a pleasant fashion,' said Hamilton. 'I never kissed anyone's hand, but should have no objection to make a beginning now.'

Hildegarde held out her hand without a moment's hesitation.

'Not that one,' said Hamilton, hesitating ; 'your cousin's kiss is still upon it.'

The door opened suddenly, and she ran laughingly past him towards the drawing-room, just in time to enter it before her mother.

A few minutes after, they were in the street, Hildegarde, as usual, close to her father's elbow, but without taking his arm. Hamilton at first imagined Mr. Rosenberg's presence would be a restraint, but he found, on the contrary, that he encouraged Hildegarde to talk and give her opinion freely, enjoying even nonsense when it came from her lips, and laughing with a heartiness which Hamilton had imagined impossible for a person who had always appeared so calm and reserved. Everything and everybody who passed afforded her amusement; it was in vain Madame Rosenberg called to order; the laugh was partly stifled for a moment, to be renewed the next with double zest. Hamilton was extremely surprised, and began to think he should never be able to understand her character, and yet the simple fact was merely that, being naturally gay, she only required the certainty of being able to please to induce her to yield to her innate inclination. She was not herself aware of this, for, on Hamilton's making some remark to express his surprise, she said ' she believed she was only by degrees getting over the restraint of her school habits, all conversation being forbidden there, excepting during the recreation hours.

The crowd at the fair was immense. It was the first time Hamilton had seen anything of the kind, and he found it difficult to believe that in the paltry booths around him there could be anything for sale as good as might be had, with less trouble, in the town. The noise, the talking, and the bargaining amused him not a little, especially the latter; and he stood beside Madame Rosenberg for more than half-an-hour while she haggled about the price of some muslin. At the end of this time she was on the point of walking off (or, as she explained afterwards, pretending to do so), when the shopman called her back, and, with an assurance that he was giving her the 'article' for next to nothing, prepared to measure what she required. This was a bargain! She had gained twenty-one kreutzers, about seven pence, and had the annoyance of carrying a large packet home, for porters there were none. To anyone accustomed to English tradesmen, the almost positive. necessity of bargaining in the generality of German shops is extremely tiresome and disagreeable. It is more than probable that the tradesmen would gladly establish fixed prices were not the habits of bargaining as yet too strong in the middle and lower orders to be overcome.

The vociferous invitations of the Jews to inspect their wares were equally novel to Hamilton. 'Ladies, step here, if you please. Cheap gloves, elegant ribbons, scissors, bracelets, or soap. Have I nothing that I may show you, madame? Flannels, merinos, or cloth for the young gentlemen? Winter is coming, madame, and I promise you as great bargains as you will get anywhere!'

To all these speeches Madame Rosenberg gave an answer, generally of a facetious description; and while Hamilton thought her more than usually vulgar, he sometimes could not avoid laughing, the more so as everything she said was taken in good part, and a few words seemed to reconcile the vendors to her passing their booths without purchasing. The two little boys had become weary and hungry ; they leaned against the counters, occasionally upset the piles of goods ranged out-side the booths, cuffed each other when their mother was not watching them, and, when forced to stand quietly beside her, yawned until the tears ran down their cheeks. Hamilton took pity on them, and, finding a toyshop, soon filled their pockets and hands with playthings, making them by many degrees the happiest of the whole party.

'So!' cried Madame Rosenberg, as they returned to her, radiant with smiles, 'this is what you have been about; I thought Mr. Hamilton had gone to look at the church. We must all go together, it seems, and the less time we lose there the better, for the days are short and we have a long walk home after supper.'

They were not exactly the persons with whom Hamilton could enjoy seeing anything of the kind, and on entering the church he walked up the aisle alone. They all, however, fol-lowed him ; and Crescenz observed, in a dissatisfied tone of voice, 'And is this the church that every one admires so much ? It is not half so handsome as the *Allerheiligen*. I declare, if it were not for the painted windows, with the sun shining through them, I should say it was the most sombre church I had ever seen.'

'You have seen very few, my dear,' said her father, looking round him, and drawing nearer Hamilton.

'I have seen all the churches in Munich,' said Crescenz, 'and several of them are larger than this.'

'It would be difficult to form an opinion of the size of this building,' said Hamilton, thoughtfully, 'for the proportions are so admirably observed that nothing strikes the eye or distin-guishes itself above the rest. There is no point from which one can take a mental measure, and I am convinced it appears infinitely smaller than it really is.'

'But I expected to see a quantity of painted pillars and bright colours and gilding when I heard that it was Gothic,' ob-served Crescenz.

'I know nothing of architecture,' said Hamilton, turning to Mr. Rosenberg, 'but I form exactly a contrary idea when I hear of a Gothic church; the painted windows are the only colours which are admissible without destroying my ideal.'

'And yet,' said Mr. Rosenberg, 'Gothic buildings often combined colour with form. In northern countries, either from stricter simplicity of taste, or on account of the climate, the absence of colours is usual, and sculpture takes their place; but in the south, besides the painted ceilings, mosaics, and frescoes inside, the outsides of the churches were ornamented with coloured marble. It is a mistake to suppose that the Gothic and Byzantine architecture refused the assistance of colours; on the contrary, the most brilliant and strongly contrasted painting is common. To begin with the windows —'

'Rather let us dispense with them altogether,' said his wife, moving towards the door.

'I have no objection,' said Mr. Rosenberg, turning round to look back into the church, 'for they do not suit the gray monotony of the walls, and the gaudy colours playing so uncertainly on the cold surface have something, to me, altogether disharmonious. In almost all the old cathedrals,' he added, 'the walls and pillars were formerly gorgeously painted; and it is only in the later centuries that, either from want of taste or from poverty, they have been whitewashed'

'I was not aware of that,' said Hamilton. 'It cannot, however, make me change my ideas all at once. A Gothic church is always handsome, with its light pillars and pointed steeple and windows. I have never travelled in southern countries, and my taste for bright colours has not yet been made. Since I have been in Munich I have begun merely to tolerate them by degrees; and for this reason paintings of the middle ages do not please me, no matter how celebrated they may be. I cannot endure the bright red and blue draperies, or the terribly shining gold backgrounds which are so common in those pictures. I dare say it is great want of taste on my part, but the hard outlines appear to me unnatural, and the glaring colours offensive.'

'Very probably—when viewed deliberately in a picture gallery—but exactly these pictures were intended for churches, and churches with painted walls. You must allow that duller colours would have appeared weak or have been completely lost when submitted to the glowing stream of light which would have fallen on them from windows of blue, red, and amber-coloured glass!'

'All this never occurred to me,' said Hamilton; 'but I suspect, as you so warmly defend these bright colours, that you have seen and admired them in more southern climes. Have you been in Italy?'

'Many years,' he replied, while a sudden flush passed across his face.

'Papa has been in Spain and in Greece too,' said Hildegarde.

'And you never speak of your travels!' exclaimed Hamilton, surprised.

'Because I regret them,' said Mr. Rosenberg, sorrowfully. 'I did not travel expensively, and yet I wasted my whole patrimony, and the best years of my life, in foreign countries. I know not what I should have become at last, had I not by chance met Hildegarde's mother in Tyrol.'

'She—she was probably very beautiful,' said Hamilton, glancing unconsciously towards their companion.

'No,' replied Mr. Rosenberg, thoughtfully. 'She was interesting looking, but no longer young when we married. She was clever and warm-hearted—like Hildegarde here—and could love with a warmth perfectly irresistible to a man who had wandered for years, and was without a friend or near relation in the world. She gave me an object in life, but her affection, though of incalculable benefit to me, subjected her to trials and privations which only ended with her life. I was not worthy of such love!'

'Oh papa! I am sure you were,' cried Hildegarde, eagerly. 'And what are trials and privations when shared with those we love! It must be a compensation for everything when one is really loved! I should like some one to love me—not in a commonplace, rational, every-day sort of way—but passionately—desperately—'

'My dear girl—you don't know what you are saying! What will Mr. Hamilton think of you?'

'He will think I am talking nonsense,' replied Hildegarde, laughing, 'or perhaps he will not understand me. Mr. Hamilton is much too rational to love unwisely—and as to passion or desperation, I do not think it possible for him to form a tolerably correct idea even of the meaning of the words!'

'Hallo!' shouted Major Stultz, 'where are you three going? We are all waiting for you, and the roast goose is nearly ready!'

They turned back, and Hildegarde said in a low voice to

Hamilton, as they passed through the yard of the brewery, 'I am glad that there are not many people here, for though I like a garden party exceedingly, I think supping in a brewery must be vulgar. I wonder you came with us.'

'I like to see everything,' replied Hamilton, 'and besides, a man may go anywhere and everywhere.'

'Ah, how I should like to be a man!' she said, sighing.

'You are too young for such a wish,' said Hamilton; 'rather, like the Prince de Ligne, desire to be a woman until you are thirty, a soldier until you are fifty, and to spend the rest of your life as a monk.'

'I think,' said Madame Rosenberg, bustling past them, 'I think that, as the evening air is cool, we had better take possession of the little room at the end of the garden; there is a window in it which looks out on the road, and we can see everybody who goes by. Do you remember, Franz, we supped there with my father on pork chops and saur-kraut the evening before we were married?'

Mr. Rosenberg's previous conversation seemed to have made him somewhat oblivious—he confessed having forgotten the pork chops, but said that he had probably thought more of her than of them at such a time.

'I don't know that,' said his wife, 'for you scarcely spoke a word, and ate enormously. Now that I think of it, I dare say that was the reason you looked so miserably ill the next day—'

'I dare say it was,' replied Mr. Rosenberg, rubbing his forehead hastily, and then turning to little Peppy, who was dragging from his pockets the toys given him by Hamilton.

They supped, and Mr. Rosenberg and Hamilton had just lit their cigars, and Major Stultz drawn forth a pocket edition of a meerschaum pipe, which he prepared to smoke as an accompaniment to his third tankard of beer, when the sound of a number of gay loud voices, and approaching steps, made Madame Rosenberg hastily open the window which looked into the garden, and stretch her long thin neck to its utmost extent. She seemed half vexed as she drew back again, exclaiming, 'Well, to be sure! wherever we go—we are sure to see him. If he were alone I shouldn't care a straw, but he will, no doubt, bring all the others with him.'

'Who?' asked Mr. Rosenberg, very quietly continuing to puff at his newly-lighted cigar.

'Count Zedwitz, of course—he is always sure to find out

P

where we are going, and pursues us like a shadow!' replied his wife, glancing half suspiciously towards Hildegarde, who, however, sprang from her chair with even more than her usual vivacity, while she said to Hamilton, 'Can you not assist us to escape? This window is so close to the ground, that I think we could easily leap on the road. Pray persuade mamma to walk home with us, and leave papa to follow.'

Hamilton threw open the window, and in a moment was on the ground, holding up his arms towards her; she sprang down lightly without assistance; the two boys followed; but when it came to Crescenz's turn, she drew back, saying she was afraid.

'Oh, Crescenz! choose some other time, and some better occasion, for timidity,' cried Hildegarde, impatiently.

'If you cannot jump, make a long step,' said Madame Rosenberg, laughing, while she put her advice in practice by extending towards the ground nearly a yard of formless bone, and with Hamilton's assistance, and a slight totter, reached the road.

A tremendous clatter of swords in the garden seemed to alarm Crescenz. She threw herself completely upon Hamilton; and while he was endeavouring to place her steadily on her feet, the sound of wheels made him look round. A dark-green open carriage was at the moment turning round, and in the corner of it, vainly endeavouring to suppress a fit of laughter, sat A. Z.

Hamilton coloured violently as he approached her, and expressed his astonishment at seeing her at Munich.

'Hermann called on you a couple of hours ago,' she replied, but you were not at home; and, as we only remain a few days here, and I may not see you again, I must not forget to renew my invitation to Hohenfels. You must not, however, expect to see an English country-house, a park, or anything of that kind—prepare yourself for one of the simplest of German establishments, if you do not wish to be horribly disappointed. I should like you to see Hohenfels before the snow comes on, or after it is gone. When will you come to us?'

'In spring, if you please,' said Hamilton; 'I have at present so many engagements—'

'I need not ask you to drive back with me,' she said, looking after the Rosenbergs, 'but I can take those children and leave them at home—it is a great distance for them to walk.'

Hamilton was the bearer of a message to Madame Rosen-berg, who no sooner heard of the proposal than she turned back, approached the carriage, and commenced such a tor-rent of exaggerated thanks and apologies, accompanied by curtsies and bows, that Hamilton, who had lately begun to feel a sincere regard for her, was vexed, and looked at A. Z. as if to deprecate her mirth, while he silently lifted the two boys into the carriage.

It was unnecessary. A. Z. seemed to find nothing unusual in Madame Rosenberg's manner ; and when the latter raised her finger threateningly, and told the children, ' for their life to keep quiet, and not soil the Baroness's beautiful silk dress,' she replied, quietly, that ' she was too well accustomed to such youthful company to be in the least inconvenienced by a pair of dusty little shoes more or less.'

' An exceedingly civil person,' observed Madame Rosenberg, as the carriage drew off, ' an exceedingly civil person is your countrywoman. I am sorry we did not get better acquainted at Seon, for I liked her a great deal better than those Zedwitz, who were uncommonly grand, and seemed to think their son demeaned himself when he spoke to our girls. I did not court his company, I am sure, and I let him see it.'

' It is hardly just to make him suffer for his parents' faults of manner,' said Hamilton ; ' Zedwitz is extremely gentle-manly and good-humoured, and has not a particle of pride in his composition. Will you not assist me to defend the absent?' he added, turning somewhat maliciously to Hilde-garde.

' My defence would be as injudicious as useless,' she said, but in so low a voice that only Hamilton could hear her words ; ' he is indeed all you have said, and much more—excellent in every respect, I believe.'

' You do him but justice,' began Hamilton, though he would have preferred praise less warm in its expression; but at this moment they were overtaken by Mr. Rosenberg and Major Stultz, accompanied, to the surprise of all, by Count Zedwitz and Count Raimund.

' I have brought you two of the party from whom you ran away,' said Mr. Rosenberg, laughing, as he joined them. ' Count Zedwitz came into the room just in time to see Cres-cenz fly out of the window, and both he and Count Raimund prefer walking home with us to drinking the superlatively excellent Stubenrauch beer, although I praised it as it deserved.'

'It was truly delicious,' said Major Stultz ; 'I should have had no objection to another glass.'

'Hildegarde! Crescenz!' cried Mr. Rosenberg, 'this is your cousin, Count Raimund.'

Crescenz turned round instantly ; Hildegarde took her usual place beside her father, while she said, without hesitation, that she had already made her cousin's acquaintance at the Hoffmanns'. Hamilton saw a glance of such meaning pass between them as she spoke, that he indignantly walked forward towards Madame Rosenberg. Major Stultz and Crescenz soon joined them; and the former explained that Count Raimund had, in the free-and-easiest manner possible, claimed relationship with Mr. Rosenberg ; that he had spoken of his aunt—said that he recollected her perfectly—hoped he would present him to his cousins and his present wife, and allow him occasionally to visit his family.

'And Franz was, as usual, all civility,' said Madame Rosenberg, with considerable irritation.

'Why, to tell you the truth, it was not easy to be otherwise,' replied Major Stultz; 'his manner was so off-hand and sincere when he said that he trusted that Rosenberg would not make him a sufferer for family differences which had occurred when he was a mere child. They shook hands, and I was obliged to do the same, as he congratulated me on my approaching marriage, and said—'here Major Stultz diligently sought for his pocket-handkerchief, as he spoke—'said he was particularly happy at the prospect of being so nearly allied to an officer of whose personal bravery he had heard so much—or something to that purport.'

'It is too late to attempt opposition now,' said Madame Rosenberg. 'I intended to have refused his acquaintance, and forbidden him our house, without ever mentioning his name—it is now impossible. As to Franz, he has acted exactly as was to be expected; but after all you said yesterday evening I did not think you would cultivate his acquaintance on Crescenz's account.'

'Crescenz will, I hope, do me the favour not to speak much to him—' began Major Stultz. But Crescenz interrupted him by exclaiming, in a voice wavering between crying and laughing—

'I shall really be obliged to talk to myself at last! Every day a new prohibition!'

'What does the child mean?' said Madame Rosenberg, appealing to Major Stultz, whose colour visibly deepened. 'What on earth does she mean? Has she not her brothers, her sister, and you, and Mr. Hamilton, to talk to?'

'No!' cried Crescenz, while tears of vexation started to her eyes; 'he forbade my speaking to Mr. Hamilton before we came out to-day; and I am sure I don't know why!'

'Then I must tell you why,' said Major Stultz, restrained anger evident in the tone of his voice. 'It is because I have begun to discover that you give yourself a vast deal too much trouble to please this Mr. Hamilton—your—your vanity is insatiable; and, I must say, you are the greatest coquette I ever saw!'

Crescenz burst into tears.

Major Stultz seemed immediately to repent his speech. He attempted to draw Crescenz's arm within his, while he commenced an agitated apology: but she shrank from him, and between suppressed sobs stammered, 'If—if such be your opinion—of me—the—the sooner we break off our engagement the—the better—'

'Crescenz, are you mad!' cried her stepmother, catching her arm; but Crescenz broke from her, and hurried on alone.

'Oh, pray, Mr. Hamilton, do have the kindness to talk a little reason to that headstrong girl,' said Madame Rosenberg, turning to Hamilton, who had been walking close behind them.

'Excuse me,' he said, quietly. 'Now that I know Major Stultz's wishes on the subject from himself, he may be quite sure of my not speaking much to Mademoiselle Crescenz in future. I have no right whatever to interfere with his claims.'

'We know you never thought of such a thing. Don't we, Major?'

'Mr. Hamilton certainly admired Crescenz when at Seon,' observed Major Stultz, sullenly.

'A mere jealous fancy on your part,' said Madame Rosenberg, eagerly.

'Not quite,' said Hamilton. 'I plead guilty to the charge; in fact, I admire every pretty face I see, and both Mademoiselle Crescenz and her sister are remarkably handsome.'

'You see, Mr. Hamilton treats the whole affair as a joke.'

'It is no joke to me, however—I have been a precipitate fool, and ought never to have thought of marrying such a girl as Crescenz. Perhaps I do Mr. Hamilton injustice— but—'

'I am sure you do,' cried Madame Rosenberg, interrupting him, and then touching Hamilton's elbow, she whispered, 'Say something to him.'

'What can I say? Major Stultz can hardly expect that because he intends to marry a very pretty girl, everyone is to find her ugly and disagreeable, in order not to provoke his jealousy! I can avoid speaking to her, but I cannot think her one bit less pretty than she really is.'

'Come now, Mr. Hamilton,' said Madame Rosenberg, jocosely, 'I see you are trying to tease the Major; but you must not go too far, or he will not understand you. Crescenz is very good-looking, but I have no doubt you have seen many prettier girls in England.' She turned towards him once more, and said in a very low voice, 'I shall be greatly obliged if you will say that you admire Hildegarde still more than her sister.'

Hamilton found no difficulty in complying with her request, and was so eloquent on the theme given him that he not only convinced Major Stultz that he had been mistaken, but induced him even to banter him on his apparently hopeless love. Madame Rosenberg did not wait for this result; she no sooner perceived that Hamilton intended to comply with her request than she walked on beside Crescenz, and began a severe reprimand. Had she delayed a few minutes, she would have found the young lady more disposed to listen to her and profit by her advice.

Unfortunately, Crescenz had overheard what Hamilton had said before Hildegarde's name was mentioned; and her mind, buoyed up on a thousand vague hopes, would not now yield to the pressing reasonings of her mother: she said, sullenly, 'that Major Stultz was intolerably jealous—that his age rendered him unable to make allowances for younger people, and that he expected more than was reasonable if he thought she could marry him for any other cause than in order to obtain a home. She would tell him so the first convenient opportunity.'

'You will tell him no such thing,' cried Madame Rosenberg.

turning back, in order to try the effect of her eloquence on Major Stultz. She was a clumsy manœuvrer, but she generally gained her point, for she always meant well, and at times spoke with much worldly wisdom. On the present occasion, she took her future son-in-law's arm, and walked quickly on with him, leaving Hamilton, to his great annoyance, with Crescenz. He would willingly have joined the others, but they were too many to walk abreast, and neither Zedwitz nor Raimund seemed disposed to resign his place.

They walked together in silence for some time, Crescenz with an air of triumphant satisfaction, Hamilton with ill-concealed impatience. 'I hope,' she began at last, 'I hope that I have seriously offended Major Stultz this evening ; nothing would give me greater pleasure than the breaking off of this odious engagement.'

'It would have been more honourable had you done so before you left Seon.'

'Better late than never,' said Crescenz, gaily.

'To act dishonourably, do you mean ?' asked Hamilton, gravely.

'Ah, bah !' cried Crescenz, with imperturbable good-humour. 'You are talking exactly like Hildegarde now.'

'You are not acting as Hildegarde would,' said Hamilton, still more seriously.

'Don't praise her too much ; you are out of favour with her just now, I can tell you.'

'What do you mean?' asked Hamilton, quickly.

'I mean that I am sure you must have been very uncivil to her last night when you refused her the candle, for she cried a good half-hour before she went to bed ; and Hildegarde does not cry for nothing ! Perhaps, if I had gone for the candle you would have given it.'

'Perhaps,' answered Hamilton, absently.

'I am sure you would,' she persisted.

'Oh, of course, of course.'

'Well, I told her so, and wanted to get up and go to you—but she would not allow me.'

'She was right,' said Hamilton, endeavouring to overtake Madame Rosenberg, while she was speaking.

'Oh, for heaven's sake don't bring me again to mamma, I have been so lectured by her already—perhaps you heard what she said ?'

'No ; I was speaking to Major Stultz.'

'And *he* was so—so very rude to me—you have no idea.'

'He told you some unpleasant truths.'

'Truths !' exclaimed Crescenz.

'Yes, truths,' repeated Hamilton ; 'you are very pretty, and very good natured, but you certainly are a—a coquette—what we call in England a flirt.'

'Well, how odd !' exclaimed Crescenz. 'Do you know—I don't at all mind your telling me that—and I was so very angry with him. I declare now I should like to hear all my faults !'

'I dare say Major Stultz will enumerate them, if you desire it,' said Hamilton, now determinedly joining Madame Rosenberg, and remaining beside her the rest of the way home.

CHAPTER XVII.

LOVERS' QUARRELS.

THE moon was shining brightly on their house, as they lingered in the street to speak a few parting words. Mademoiselle de Hoffmann sat at an open window, and gazed pensively upwards.

'Should you not like to know the thoughts of your betrothed at this moment ?' asked Mr. Rosenberg, turning to Raimund.

'Not at all,' he replied, carelessly glancing towards the house ; 'I am sure they are commonplace, for a more matter-of-fact person does not exist than Marie de Hoffmann.'

'So,' cried Zedwitz, 'it is really true that you are going to be married ? I am glad to hear it, and congratulate you with all my heart.'

'Thank you,' said Raimund, musingly, while he turned from Zedwitz to Hamilton, and then to Hildegarde, as if they, and not Mademoiselle de Hoffmann, occupied his thoughts.

'When is it to take place ?' asked Zedwitz.

'What? ah ! my execution ? Some time in January, they say ; I wish it were sooner.'

'Of course you do,' said Zedwitz, laughing.

'That is,' said Raimund, the colour mounting to his forehead, 'I am afraid, if it be put off long, I shall get tired of the concern, and in the end prove refractory.'

Mademoiselle de Hoffmann had recognised and now addressed them from the window. Raimund was invited to supper, and entered the house with the Rosenbergs, while Mr. Rosenberg, who never spent an evening at home, walked off with Zedwitz.

The moonlight was so bright in the drawing-room, that on entering Madame Rosenberg declared that it would be folly to light the candles. She gave Crescenz a gentle push into the adjoining room, telling her to ' be a good girl, and make up her quarrel with the Major,' and then went to ' look after her boys.'

Hamilton looked out of the window, and hummed an air from Fra Diavolo.

' I am very tired,' said Hildegarde, taking off her bonnet ; ' our walk has been long and dusty ; and besides, I have talked a great deal, which is always fatiguing.' She stood beside and leaned out of the window with him.

Hamilton's humming degenerated into a half-suppressed whistle, accompanied by a drumming of his fingers on the window cushion, while his upturned eyes were fixed on the moon. They remained several minutes without speaking, until a murmuring of voices from the windows beneath them attracted their attention. Hamilton leaned farther out to see the speakers, but on recognising Count Raimund and Mademoiselle de Hoffmann, he drew back with a slightly contemptuous smile, while he said, ' Your cousin's observations this evening on his intended bride were by no means flattering.'

' He scarcely knows her yet,' said Hildegarde, seating herself on the window-stool.

' Scarcely knows the person to whom he is going to be married !' exclaimed Hamilton. ' You Germans have the oddest ideas on these subjects.'

' I see nothing odd in the matter ; it is an acknowledged *mariage de convenance.* Oscar proposes to marry Mademoiselle de Hoffmann because he has debts, and she has a large fortune ; and she accepts him because she is not very young, not at all pretty, and wishes for a good connection ; they are not, however, to be married until January, and are to endeavour in the meantime to like each other as much as possible. Can anything be more reasonable ?'

' Nothing, excepting, perhaps, their having delayed their engagement until the trial were over. I should like amazingly to know what the sensations of a man may be who sees for the first time a person to whom he is beforehand engaged to be married. A lady in such a situation is still more awkwardly placed.'

'There was no awkwardness whatever in this case. Marie was pointed out to Oscar in the theatre, he did not find that her appearance was disagreeable, heard that she was amiable, and consented to marry her. His father made the proposal for him, and Marie was given a whole week to consider before she was required to decide.'

'A *whole* week!' repeated Hamilton, laughing ironically.

Hildegarde rose abruptly, and was about to leave the window, when he exclaimed, 'Excuse my ignorance of German customs. I am really interested in what you have been telling me, and should like to know what finally induced Mademoiselle de Hoffmann to accept your cousin.'

'What induced her! They met at the house of a mutual friend, and though you do not know how agreeable Oscar can be when he chooses, you—you must have perceived that he is uncommonly good-looking.'

'Why, yes, he certainly is not ugly; but good looks on the part of a man is a matter of minor importance.'

'A handsome face is always an advantage. Don't you think so?' asked Hildegarde, laughing.

'An advantage? oh, certainly; but from what you have told me of Mademoiselle de Hoffmann, I thought her far too rational to attach much importance to personal advantages. I should have imagined her just the sort of person to appreciate a man like Zedwitz.'

'You do her but justice,' said Hildegarde; 'and I think that, were she given the choice, with time and opportunity to form an opinion, she would decide in favour of Count Zedwitz; but he has no debts, requires no fortune, and—is not likely to marry in this way; he certainly will not employ his father as suitor!'

'You seem to know him thoroughly; I was not aware that you had so exalted an opinion of him until to-day,' said Hamilton, biting his lip.

'If we had ever spoken of him when mamma was not present, I should not have hesitated to say that, with the exception of my father, I do not think there is a more amiable or generous-minded person in the world than he is.'

Hamilton attempted to smile in order to hide the jealousy which at the moment he keenly felt, and answered with affected eagerness, 'Will you allow me to tell Zedwitz what you have said? I know it will make him inexpressibly happy.'

'No, thank you,' replied Hildegarde, calmly — though even in the pale moonlight her deep blush was perceptible. 'It is equally unimportant now what he thinks of me or I of him.'

A pause ensued, which was broken by Hamilton saying, abruptly, 'If you really think Zedwitz so estimable, may I ask why you refused his proposal of marriage the day we were on the alp ? '

Hildegarde seemed utterly confounded, and remained silent.

'You may speak without reserve,' added Hamilton, ' for Zedwitz has told me everything.'

' I am not going to speak at all, unless,' she added, half laughing, 'unless you intend to begin your office of Mentor ; you seem altogether to have forgotten that you undertook last night to tell me my faults, and assist me to correct them. Have I done anything reprehensible to-day ? '

' Yes,' replied Hamilton ; ' I saw you bestow on your cousin this evening, when he joined us, a glance that gave me the idea of a previous understanding with him—'

' Go on,' said Hildegarde.

'Can you not explain or exculpate yourself ? ' asked Hamilton, with some embarrassment.

'Oh, of course—but I thought you would naturally say something about my having bestowed a glance of nearly the same kind on you when mamma talked of the pork chops, and my father's illness the day of his marriage ; that was in fact more reprehensible than the other, and shall not occur again.' She paused for a moment, and then continued, 'When you came for me to the Hoffmanns' to-day, I had just returned that unlucky book of poems to Oscar ; and, to prevent an unpleasant scene in our house, I partly told him what mamma had said—he, however, resolved immediately to try what he could do with papa, who he knew was too gentleman-like to be rude to him. I suppose he overheard me tell Marie where we were going this evening, and followed—his success was complete, it seems, and I could not resist the temptation to let him know that I perceived, and was glad of it. What else ? ' she asked, gaily.

' Your mother seemed to think it was odd that Zedwitz always knew where you were to spend the evening. Have you ever in any way let him know, or   ? '

'Really, this is too much,' cried Hildegarde, angrily.

' I will not be questioned in this manner—or on this subject—'

' You are right,' said Hamilton, quietly, ' and I resign my
most absurd office of corrector and improver.   You have,
however, no just cause for anger, for you not only proposed the
plan yourself, but reminded me of my promise.' He leaned
out of the window, and had recourse again to Fra Diavolo and
the moon.

' You are a horrible tyrant !' she exclaimed, after a pause,
' and I suppose if I leave your question unanswered, you will
think me capable of making Count Zedwitz acquainted with all
our walking parties !'

' What matters it what I think ?' said Hamilton, without
turning round.

' Your question is exceedingly offensive; and yet I must
answer it, and tell you that I am as much surprised as mamma
at meeting him so often—if I could avoid seeing him, I should
greatly prefer it.'

' Indeed !' cried Hamilton.   'Then you have no wish to
renew the—the—'

' None whatever,' replied Hildegarde, smiling.

' But if you think so highly of him,' persisted Hamilton,
' surely you must like him !'

' Like him,' she repeated; ' why, have I not told you that I
like him exceedingly ?'

' Something to that purport, certainly,' said Hamilton.   ' You
are altogether inexplicable, and I dare not ask an explanation.'

' You have no right,' said Hildegarde; ' what occurred
before yesterday does not come under your cognisance.'

' I am completely at fault,' said Hamilton, in a low voice, as
if reasoning with himself : ' Zedwitz told me that you had said
you liked him as an acquaintance, but nothing more.   This I
know is not the case ; therefore there must be some misunderstanding—he suspected a prior attachment, but that seemed to
me improbable.'

' Rather say impossible,' cried Hildegarde, laughing, ' for
the object of it must have been either Major Stultz—or you!
Ha, ha, ha !'

Hamilton did not laugh with her, and another long pause
ensued. His jealousy, or, as he to himself termed it, his curiosity,
prompted him to make another effort, and he again began : ' I

told Zedwitz he ought not to resign all hope, that probably the fear of opposition on the part of his family had influenced you —. He stopped, for Hildegarde bit her lip, and seemed agitated. She stood up—sat down—stood up again—and, after a moment's hesitation, said, 'I do not know whether I had better tell you all or nothing.'

'Tell me all!' cried Hamilton, eagerly; 'no one can feel more interested than I do in everything that concerns you.'

'The all is easily told,' she said, slowly—'I have no confession to make. You were right in your supposition—it would be dreadful to me to enter a family unwilling to receive me, for I am very proud, and his mother's unnecessary haughtiness—rudeness, I may say—to us all at Seon, showed me what I might expect. It was her evident avoidance of me that made me first aware of his attentions.'

'So,' Hamilton almost whistled, while an indefinable sensation of actual bodily pain passed through his frame, 'so, after all, you loved him!'

'No,' replied Hildegarde, turning away, 'but I believe I could in time have loved him.'

'No doubt,' said Hamilton, sarcastically, 'with his parents' consent, the match would be unexceptionable, and I only wonder you did not, on the chance, make a secret engagement with him. The old Count is killing himself as fast as he can, with cold water, and were he once out of the way, I suppose there would be little further difficulty. It is really a pity you were so taken by surprise that you had not time to think of all this!'

Hildegarde's eyes flashed, and, in a voice almost choked by contending emotions, she exclaimed, 'I deserve this insult for trusting you—these insidious expressions of contempt are more than I can bear, and, to prevent a repetition of them, I now release you most willingly from your promise of last night, and request you will in future altogether banish me and my faults from your thoughts.'

Hamilton would gladly have revoked his last speech, had it been possible—he felt that anger and jealousy had dictated every word—but it was too late. Hildegarde gave him no time for a recantation; she had left the room with even more than her usual impetuosity. He no longer attempted to deceive himself as to the nature of his feelings towards her: it only remained for him to consider how he should in future

act. That she did not care for him was evident, and the little
advance which he had made in her good opinion and confidence
he feared he had now lost. For a moment, he thought of a
retreat to Vienna, but then the idea of flying from an incidental
and perfectly harmless flirtation was too absurd!—besides—
could he hope that chance would be again so favourable, and
place him on the same terms of intimacy with another family?
It was not to be expected; so he resolved to remain where he
was—but to employ his time differently. He would study
more with Biedermann—attend lectures at the University,
ride, walk, call at the English Ambassador's, be presented at
Court, make acquaintance with the English in Munich, and
accept evening invitations. Hildegarde's indifference should
be met with at least apparent indifference on his part, and he
would take care she should never discover the interest which
he now knew he could not help attaching to her most trifling
actions. A low murmuring of suppressed voices from the adjoining room, which he had indistinctly heard, at length ceased
altogether, leaving nothing but the footsteps of an occasional
passenger through the solitary street to break the silence of
the night. He felt irritated and impatient, and, hoping that a
walk by moonlight might have a tranquillising effect, he turned
quickly from the window. Great was his astonishment on
discovering Crescenz standing beside him,—tears stood in her
eyes, as she laid her hand on his arm to detain him, and said, in
a scarcely audible voice, ' I must ask you a question—will you
answer me?'

' Certainly,' replied Hamilton, much surprised.

' Did you tell Major Stultz this evening that you had never
admired—never liked me?'

' No,—I rather think I said I admired both you and your
sister exceedingly.'

' I know you did,' cried Crescenz. ' I heard what you said,
and remember it perfectly—and now he—he wants to persuade
me that I am mistaken, and assures me you greatly prefer
Hildegarde, and that you said so to him most explicitly this
evening!'

' Must I then account for every idle word?' cried Hamilton,
impatiently. ' Surely it ought to be a matter of indifference to
you what I said!'

' Hush!—do not speak so loud—he is there.'

' Who?'

Major Stultz. He is waiting for me. I have such reliance on you, that I have told him I cannot believe what he has said —and now answer my question quickly. Have you ceased to care for me?—and do you prefer Hildegarde?'

'Pshaw!' cried Hamilton, taking up his hat and endeavouring to conceal his embarrassment. 'I like you both, and admire you both; but when Major Stultz was jealous this evening, I gave, of course, the preference to Hildegarde.'

'Is this the very truth?' asked Crescenz.

Her manner was unusually serious, but Hamilton was not in the habit of paying much attention to anything she said, and answered, with a careless laugh, 'What importance you attach to such a trifle!'

'If you can laugh, I have indeed mistaken you!'

'What *do* you mean?' asked Hamilton, exceedingly bored.

'At the beginning of our acquaintance,' said Crescenz, almost whispering, 'Hildegarde said you were amusing yourself at my expense; this I am sure was not the case; but Major Stultz not only says that you never cared for me, but insists that you have openly acknowledged a preference for Hildegarde.'

'And if this were true?' said Hamilton, twirling his hat on the end of his cane.

'If it be—I—can—never trust any man again!'

'A most excellent general rule, at all events; we are, in fact, not worthy of trust, and your sister says I am not better than others, you know!'

'Is this your answer?' asked Crescenz.

'If you will consider it one I shall be infinitely obliged to you, for I am really at a loss what to say—'

'It is enough,' she said, turning away.

'Stay!' cried Hamilton, perceiving at length that something unusual had occurred; 'stay—and tell me quickly what is the matter. What have you been saying to Major Stultz?'

'He accused me of liking some—other—better than I liked him—and I did not deny it; he named you—and—and—'

'I understand,' said Hamilton, quickly; 'and he told you that you were slighted. Come, I will explain everything to him satisfactorily.'

They entered the next room, but Major Stultz was no longer there.

'He has gone to—mamma!' cried Crescenz, clasping her

hands; and then sitting down, she added, with a sort of desperate resignation, 'I don't care what happens now!'

'But I do,' cried Hamilton; 'I will not be the cause, however innocent, of separating you and Major Stultz. I see I must go to him this moment and take the whole blame on myself; if you afterwards refuse to fulfil your engagement with him, that is your affair. This must, however, be the very last time we ever speak on this subject. It seems I must pay dearly for my thoughtlessness, but it will be a lesson which I am not likely to forget as long as I live.'

At one of the windows of the corridor Madame Rosenberg and Hildegarde were standing,—the former was speaking loudly and angrily: 'I never knew anything so absurd as Crescenz's conduct! To choose Mr. Hamilton, of all people in the world, for the object of a sentimental love! If she had not been a simpleton she might have easily perceived that he thinks of anything rather than of such nonsense. As to what the Major hinted about his having said that he liked you, that was said at my particular request; so don't you begin to have fancies like Crescenz!'

'There is not the slightest danger,' said Hildegarde, with a scornful smile.

'Where is Major Stultz?' said Hamilton, hastily opening the hall door.

'He is gone home, I am sorry to say. Oh, Mr. Hamilton, this is a most unpleasant business! If Crescenz's marriage should be broken off now, it will be an actual disgrace.'

'It will not be broken off. I can explain everything.'

'Let me give you a hint what to say,' cried Madame Rosenberg, detaining him, 'for he is exceedingly angry, and says we have all been deceiving him. Can you not, just to set matters right, say that you *have* paid Crescenz some attentions, and that you did admire her some time ago?'

'Of course I shall say that,' replied Hamilton, endeavouring to get away.

'Say, too, that she does not really care at all for you, and was only trying to make him jealous this evening because he called her a coquette. And then, to frighten him, you may as well add, that you will renew your addresses to-morrow if he do not at once make up his quarrel with her.'

'I shall tell him the truth, and blame myself—even more

than I deserve,' said Hamilton, closing the door and running downstairs.

'He certainly is an excellent young man!' exclaimed Madame Rosenberg, 'and, notwithstanding his youth, I see I may transfer the arrangement of this disagreeable affair to him. At all events, I can do nothing more to-night, and may as well go to bed. Tell Crescenz I do not wish to see her until to-morrow. What is said cannot be unsaid, and scolding now would be useless. What will your father say when he hears what she has done?'

Hamilton was longer absent than he had expected. He had overtaken Major Stultz just as he was about to enter his lodgings, had walked up and down the street with him more than an hour in earnest conversation, and had afterwards accompanied him to his rooms. It was past midnight as he quietly entered the house by means of the latch-key given him by Madame Rosenberg, whose voice he heard calling him the moment he had opened the door; and immediately after, her husband, in a long flowered cotton dressing-gown and slippers, appeared and invited him to enter their room. Hamilton hesitated; but on being again called by Madame Rosenberg he courageously advanced. A few oblique rays of moonlight and a dimly-burning night-lamp contended for the honour of lighting the apartment, and showing Hamilton a chair near Madame Rosenberg's bed, which she requested him to occupy while he related circumstantially where he had overtaken Major Stultz, what he had said to him, what Major Stultz had answered, and what chance there was of his forgiving and forgetting Crescenz's sentimental confession. Hamilton related as much as he thought necessary, and then said he was the bearer of a letter.

'A letter! Give it to me. That will explain all,' cried Madame Rosenberg.

'It is for—for Mademoiselle Crescenz,' said Hamilton, hesitating.

'No matter; on such an occasion parents have a right to make themselves acquainted with the true state of the case; besides, I don't quite trust Crescenz just now, although her father, for the first time in his life, has lectured her severely while you were absent. Franz, light the taper and let me see what the Major has written.'

Hamilton most unwillingly gave up the unsealed letter committed to his charge, and watched Madame Rosenberg with some irritation, as she, with evident pleasure, perused it. A more extraordinary night-dress he had never seen than that on which the light of the taper now fell ; he was, as may be remembered from his remarks at Seon, rather fastidious on the subject of nightcaps. Madame Rosenberg's was interesting from the peculiarity of its form, resembling a paper cornet, the open part next her face being ornamented by a sort of flounce of broad lace, and the whole kept on her head by a foulard kerchief tied under her chin. She wore a jacket of red printed calico, of what she would herself have called a Turkish pattern, the sleeves of which were enormously ample at the shoulders, proving that the fabrication was not of recent date. Her husband held the taper, looked over her shoulder, and seemed exceedingly pleased with the contents of the letter, which Madame Rosenberg returned to Hamilton, saying, ' I perceive you have very nearly said what I recommended ; and we are very much obliged to you. It really would have been a most unpleasant business had this marriage been broken off, and the Major more than hinted he would do so.'

'You are detaining Mr. Hamilton, my dear Babette,' observed Mr. Rosenberg, mildly.

She laughed—pulled and thumped her pillows, and again wished him good-night.

Hamilton found the door of Crescenz's room open ; she and her sister had evidently expected him—they were seated at the window, and, either for the purpose of enjoying the moonlight, or, as Hamilton afterwards supposed, to make their features less distinct, they had extinguished their candle. Hildegarde pushed back her chair, Crescenz hung her head at his approach. 'I have brought you a letter,' he said to the latter, ' which I hope will give you pleasure. Major Stultz will be here early to-morrow, and trusts in the meantime you will try to forget all that has passed between you this evening. He sees that his absurd jealousy was enough to provoke you to say all, and more too than you have said to him, and he is ready to believe that you spoke under the influence of extreme irritation. In short, he is sincerely attached to you, and it will be your fault if a perfect reconciliation do not take place to morrow.'

' I suppose he must have been very angry,' said Crescenz, in a low voice, while she twisted the letter round her fingers.

'I suppose he must have been very angry, as you remained out so long.'

'Yes, at first; but then I told him he had no right to be angry with you because you happened to be loved by others.'

'Indeed! Did you say that?' cried Crescenz.

'That is,' said Hildegarde, with a slight sneer, 'you have said exactly what mamma recommended!'

Hamilton felt extremely angry, but, resolved not to let Hildegarde perceive it, he answered calmly, though a slight frown contracted his eyebrows, 'No, mademoiselle—not exactly—for I said only what was the truth.' While he spoke, as if to brave her, he seated himself deliberately on a chair beside Crescenz, and took her hand, while he added, 'I told Major Stultz how much I admired you, how thoroughly gentle and forgiving you were, but I explained to him also, without reserve, my own position in the world, and all the miseries entailed on a younger ,on in England.' Hamilton here explained at some length the difference between the equal division of property among children so general in Germany, and the apparently unjust privileges of primogeniture in England—dwelt long and feelingly on the struggles and vexations of a younger son brought up in luxury, and then cast, with all his expensive habits, in comparative poverty on the world—the necessity of pushing himself forward by his talents—the impossibility of an early marriage! He spoke long and eloquently, and made an evident impression on both his hearers. Crescenz's tears fell fast on the letter, which she had unconsciously crumpled in her hand, without having thought it worthy of perusal. Hildegarde leant on a small work-table, her eyes fixed intently on Hamilton, her lips apart, and an expression of strong interest pervading her whole form; she followed him with her eyes, but remained immovable as he rose to leave them, and watched, with what Hamilton thought a look of subdued anger, while he pressed Crescenz's hands in both his, whispered his wishes for her happiness, and his hopes that she would not misunderstand him in future.

CHAPTER XVIII.

THE CHURCHYARD.

HAMILTON experienced a sort of satisfaction in avoiding both sisters for some time,—the idea that he was endeavouring to cure Crescenz of her too evident partiality, was almost sublime, and would probably have turned his youthful head, had not Hildegarde formed a counterpoise; her former dislike to him seemed to have returned with redoubled force. She scarcely looked at, never spoke to him, and seemed not in the least to observe that he no longer passed the evenings at home. He had found no difficulty in disposing of his time: introductions to a few German families had been followed by general invitations, of which he availed himself at first, with eager pleasure; but soon afterwards, with a feeling of indescribable ennui, he missed Hildegarde's society, and began to consider in what way he could imperceptibly renew their former intimacy—but this was more difficult than he had imagined, for the sisters seemed to have formed an alliance, offensive and defensive, against him. Crescenz no longer sang when learning to make pies and puddings in the kitchen, and if he looked in, she retreated behind the dresser. Hildegarde's door was now always shut, perhaps because the weather had become colder; but Hamilton imagined it was to prevent his leaning against the door-posts, to watch her giving her brothers instruction until dinner was announced. The rarity and shortness of his present intercourse served but to keep her in his memory, and perpetually renewed his regret for their last most unnecessary quarrel.

One cold fine morning, as he was leaving the house to keep an appointment with Zedwitz, he perceived her standing with Crescenz and her father at the passage window looking into the court. They were dressed in deep mourning, and held in their hands large wreaths of ivy, interspersed with clusters of red berries: they contemplated them with evident satisfaction, while their father spoke so earnestly, that Hamilton's approach was at first unperceived, and he heard Mr. Rosenberg say, 'You can easily imagine why I prefer going alone and at some other time. As long as you were at school, gratitude for my wife's attention forced me to accompany her to the churchyard—the task of placing the wreaths now devolves on you, and I wish you both to thank her as she deserves. You will not surely find it difficult to comply with my request?'

'I hope nothing unexpected has occurred,' began Hamilton, looking at the sable garments of the sisters.

'Nothing whatever,' replied Mr. Rosenberg, smiling. 'It is All Saints' Day, and my girls are going to place wreaths on their mother's grave. I suppose you too are on your way to the churchyard, like all the rest of the world?'

'No,' said Hamilton; 'why should I go there?'

'I don't know, indeed,' replied Mr. Rosenberg, 'excepting, as a stranger, it might perhaps interest you to see the decorated graves.'

'If there be anything to see, I shall certainly ride to the churchyard after I have kept my appointment with Zedwitz,' said Hamilton, stooping to examine the wreath which hung on Hildegarde's arm.

'My wife surprised Hildegarde with this wreath and a bouquet of superb dahlias this morning, and I have just been telling her that her mother's grave has been decorated every year in the same manner.'

'I am fully aware of my stepmother's kindness,' said Hildegarde, with some embarrassment, 'and am sorry I ever did her injustice.'

'That's right, Hildegarde,' cried her father. 'Now I know you will say all I wish—to-morrow we can go alone together, but to-day you must accompany your stepmother.'

Hamilton desired his servant to meet him at the churchyard, and rode off to the barracks; he had no difficulty in persuading Zedwitz to accompany him, after having told him that Hildegarde was there. 'I will go to meet the living,' he said, 'but not to pray for the dead, inasmuch as I not only doubt the efficacy of my prayers, but the existence of purgatory.'

'Hush!' said Hamilton, laughing; 'no good Catholics should entertain a doubt on that subject. I hope I shall not find you as unbelieving as my friend Biedermann, who has substituted philosophy for religion, and talks of the soul resolving itself into the eternal essence after its separation from the body.'

'No,' said Zedwitz; 'I am a good Catholic, and believe more than many professors of my religion. I go to mass every Sunday and holiday, and my mother takes care that I confess my sins once a year at least.'

'That same confession must be rather a bore,' observed Hamilton.

'Sometimes—rather,' replied Zedwitz, making his horse dance along the road.

'It seems as if all Munich had turned out in mourning,' said Hamilton; 'the crowd, too, reminds me of the October fête, but the faces do not exactly suit the garments. Is it not necessary to look a *little* sorrowful on such an occasion?'

'How can you be so unreasonable!' exclaimed Zedwitz. 'Many of these persons are about to visit the graves of relations who have been dead a dozen years! For my part, I find something respectable, almost praiseworthy, in the dedication of one day in the year to the memory of the dead, even though tearlessly spent.'

'I quite agree with you,' said Hamilton, 'and the idea of praying for their souls is poetical in the extreme. Had I been a Catholic, that is one of the tenets I should most tenaciously have believed. But,' he resumed, after a long pause, 'it seems odd that All Saints' Day, instead of All Souls' Day, should be chosen—can you tell me why?'

'No,' replied Zedwitz; 'you must ask some one better informed on these subjects than I am; all I know is, that the observance itself was instituted by one of the popes about twelve hundred years ago.'

'But I should have thought that, as none of the relatives of these people here have been saints, to-morrow, being All Souls, would be the proper day to choose.'

'Very likely,' answered Zedwitz, laughing. 'I have never thought about the matter; but I suppose the first of November is what you would in England call the most fashionable day. Ask my mother the first time you see her, and she will tell you everything about it. By the bye, when do you intend to visit us?'

'As soon as I have a second horse and a sledge. I enjoy the idea of sledging so much, that I wish with all my heart it would begin to snow to-morrow; but here we are, and I hope Hildegarde may prove a very loadstone to you; otherwise we shall scarcely find her among all these people.'

The crowd was immense, and they made their way slowly through it, but Hamilton was interested in the novelty of the scene; his companion's eyes wandered towards the different groups of dark moving figures, who occasionally stopped to sprinkle the graves of departed friends with water placed near for the purpose. Hamilton was occupied with the tombstones and crosses which were variously and tastefully decorated with wreaths, festoons, bouquets of flowers, and coloured lamps — even the graves of the poorest were strewn with charcoal, and ornamented with red berries and moss, while tearful groups surrounding those newly made, gave an additional shade of solemnity to a religious rite which Hamilton had been taught to consider superfluous.

The attempt to find the Rosenbergs, or rather Hildegarde, among the moving multitude, was long fruitless, and might have proved altogether so, had not they met the Hoffmanns and Raimund, who led them at once to the object of their search. Madame Rosenberg was preparing to depart, and held in her hand a brush dipped in water, which she shook over the grave. Hildegarde and Crescenz followed her example before they spoke to Zedwitz or Hamilton, but directly they laid it aside, the two boys, finding themselves unwatched, began a contest for it, which became so loud, that their mother, turning quickly towards them, and perceiving their irreverent conduct, seized the subject of dispute, and, bestowing a thump upon each, shoved them on before her, while she exclaimed, 'I ought to have left you at home, you tiresome children; you have never ceased plaguing me since we came out. Only imagine,' she said, addressing Hamilton; 'Gustle was twice nearly run over, and Peppy fell so often, that the Major was at last obliged to carry him!'

Zedwitz and Raimund had immediately joined Hildegarde. Raimund, whose mouth had been distended by a frightful yawn when they had met him, was now smiling radiantly, and evidently endeavouring to monopolise his cousin, who, however, seemed rather indisposed to listen to him, and bestowed her attention almost exclusively on Zedwitz. Raimund at length rejoined his betrothed, saying, loud enough for Hamilton to hear, 'Hildegarde knows what she is about, when Zedwitz is present; she has neither word nor look for her poor cousin!'

'You get words and looks enough from her every evening when she is with us,' observed Madame de Hoffmann, with some bitterness.

Hamilton turned round, and saw Mademoiselle de Hoffmann's

glance of reproach towards her mother, and Raimund's confusion. The words 'every evening' grated on his ear, and,
before he could arrange the unpleasant ideas which had once
entered his mind, they had reached the churchyard gate, and
Zedwitz, approaching him, whispered hurriedly, 'I would not
lose this walk home for any consideration. Your advice about
Hildegarde was excellent, and I am determined to follow it.
Pray let your groom take charge of my horse.'

'My advice!' repeated Hamilton, with a forced smile ; but
Zedwitz had left him, and the crowd had closed between them.
Murmuring some directions to his servant, Hamilton sprang
upon his horse—the animal, always restive, no sooner felt his
impetuous spring, than he plunged violently, and, on receiving
an angry check, reared, lost his balance, and fell backwards,
rolling over his rider, to the horror of all the bystanders

CHAPTER XIX.

GERMAN SOUP.

HAMILTON was taken up senseless. Zedwitz rushed to his
assistance. Madame Rosenberg could not leave her children,
but was obliged to hold them fast by their hands. Major Stultz
endeavoured, with a half-offended air, to tranquillise Crescenz,
whose screams had begun to subside into a flood of tears. Raimund coolly explained to Mademoiselle de Hoffmann that
Hamilton had been aware of the viciousness of the horse when
he purchased it, but had imagined himself too good a rider to
be thrown. Hildegarde, having obtained a flacon of eau de
Cologne from a stranger, was soon beside Zedwitz endeavouring
to restore Hamilton to consciousness ; he very soon opened his
eyes, looked round him, and on Zedwitz asking him where he
was hurt, began to speak incoherently in English.

'We must get a carriage, and take him home as soon as possible,' said Zedwitz : 'he seems more seriously injured than I
imagined from that slight wound on his temple.'

'Well, this is really dreadful!' exclaimed Madame Rosenberg ; 'and there is not a soul in our house, for I gave Walburg
leave to go out. Here is the key of the door – but what can
I do with the boys ?'

'Let me take charge of them,' said Madame de Hoffmann.

' I am as much obliged to you for the offer as if I could accept it,' replied Madame Rosenberg, ' but unfortunately they are so unruly that I cannot leave them with you more than with their sisters and the Major. There is no help for it. Hildegarde, you must go in the carriage and send old Hans directly for Doctor Berger.'

' May not I go too?' said Crescenz, timidly, ' I am so tired!'

' Oh, of course,' replied her mother, ironically; ' another fit of screaming would greatly benefit Mr. Hamilton. Here, Hildegarde, take the key and be off.'

On their way home, Hamilton alone was loquacious—he spoke English incessantly, sometimes murmuring, sometimes vehemently. Hildegarde blushed deeply, and appeared un-usually embarrassed, which Zedwitz interpreted to his own ad-vantage, totally unconscious that she understood the ravings of Hamilton, which had already revealed much that he was anxious to conceal from her; his last thought before his fall had been of her, his last feeling annoyance on her account, and he now unreservedly poured forth both with wild volubility.

' I think we had better bind a handkerchief over his forehead,' said Hildegarde at last. ' The motion of the carriage has made the blood flow.'

' I ought to have thought of that,' said Zedwitz, assisting her; ' he does not seem to know either of us, and evidently thinks you some other person. Who is this Helene of whom he is speaking now?'

' Some one in England, I suppose.'

' Poor fellow! most probably he fancies himself at home. I am very glad to perceive that he is beginning to be exhausted. There is something frightful in this sort of raving, even when one does not understand it.'

' Do you think there is any danger to be apprehended?' asked Hildegarde, calmly.

' I hope not; but his brain must be affected in some way, or he would not talk as he has done.'

Directly on reaching the house, they sent for Doctor Berger, who came, accompanied by Mr. Biedermann; the latter de-claring at once his intention of remaining to take care of his friend. Hamilton looked inquiringly from one to the other as they entered the room, and then said quickly in German, ' I know you.'

' I am glad to hear it!' said the Doctor, adjusting his

spectacles, and turning to Biedermann, he whispered, 'They have been unnecessarily alarmed, it seems.'

'Yes; I know you. You are the ugly old doctor with the protruding chin who married Crescenz, after she had walked by moonlight at Seon.'

The Doctor shook his head, and turned to Zedwitz for an explanation of the accident. This was quickly given, and he and Hildegarde waited with evident anxiety to hear the Doctor's opinion. It was not so favourable as they had expected; severe remedies were necessary, and a fortnight elapsed before Hamilton was pronounced quite out of danger. During this time, nothing could equal the attention bestowed on him by the Rosenberg family and his friend Biedermann, who passed every night on a sofa in his room. Zedwitz, too, spent daily several hours with him—perhaps the visits of the latter were not quite disinterested, for he often met Hildegarde, who was employed to amuse Hamilton, as he was neither allowed to hear reading, nor to attempt to read himself. As soon as he was pronounced convalescent, he had a constant succession of visitors every day; not only of his own acquaintance, but everyone who had seen him with the Rosenbergs; he felt at times perhaps quite as much bored as obliged, and remembered occasionally with regret that more dangerous part of his illness when Hildegarde had sat alone in his darkened chamber, and Crescenz gently opened the door every quarter of an hour to ask if he were better —her mother, at Major Stultz's instigation, having strictly forbidden her to enter the room. Even the fussy visits of Madame Rosenberg, who invariably insisted on half making his bed and thumping all his pillows, were recollected with pleasure, and he wondered at the impatience with which he had received these well-meant civilities, having once forgotten himself so far as to wish in very correct German that the devil would come *in ipsissima persona* and take her out of his presence!—which speech had so alarmed her for the state of his brain that she had immediately sent off for the Doctor.

The period of convalescence was not without its pleasures either, and Hamilton knew how to appreciate them. Hildegarde was obliged to read or talk to him whenever he chose, was forbidden to contradict or quarrel with him, and, when one day he complained of cold hands, she had been ordered to knit cuffs for him, and had done so with apparent pleasure— then she had learned to play chess in order to take Bieder-

mann's place when he could not come, and had to submit to be
checkmated as often as Hamilton pleased without losing her
temper. He had insensibly grown tyrannical, too—upbraided
her if she remained long out walking—refused to eat his dinner
if she did not bring it to him, and insisted on the whole family
spending the evenings in his room, thereby effectually preventing her from going to the Hoffmanns'.

Among Hamilton's most constant visitors was Madame
Berger, and she was always welcome, for she amused him.
' I should like to know,' she said one day, seating herself on
the sofa beside him, ' I should like to know how long you
intend to play invalid? It is astonishing how desponding,
almost pusillanimous, you men become when you are in the
least ill! I lose all patience when I see the Doctor feeling his
own pulse fifty times a day; and consulting half-a-dozen good
friends if his heart beat a little quicker than usual—while I
have palpitations every day of my life, and never think of complaining or fancying that I have a diseased heart! My father
was even worse than the Doctor: if he had but a cold in his
head, he immediately mounted a black silk nightcap with a
tassel pendant, wrapped himself up in his dressing-gown, and
wandered about the house discovering all sorts of things not
intended for his eyes or ears, and finding fault with everybody
and everything that came in his way, although at other times
the best-natured man imaginable. He had a habit, too, on such
occasions of eating a bowl of soup every half-hour, and then
imagining it was illness which prevented him from enjoying
his meals!'

Hamilton laughed, and at the same moment Hildegarde
entered the room, carrying a tray, on which was placed a
double-handled china basin, the contents of which, notwithstanding the cover, emitted a most savoury odour ; the little
slice of toasted bread on a plate beside it, seeming intended to
correct any doubts which might arise as to its being an invalid
soup. She placed it on the table before him, removed the cover,
and stood in waiting, as he first played with the spoon and
then fastidiously tasted it.

' You have not prepared this for me yourself,' he said, looking
up discontentedly.

' No,' she replied; ' I—I heard papa's voice, and begged
Walburg to—'

' I knew that,' cried Hamilton pettishly. ' Walburg always

forgets the salt.   Just taste it yourself, and you will be convinced that I cannot swallow it in its present state.'

'Let me try it,' cried Madame Berger.   'I am an excellent
judge of soup, have learned cookery and all that sort of thing.
Let me see,' she said, playing with the spoon exactly as Hamilton had done: 'let me see, the smell is excellent, but the taste?
—hum! might require a little more salt perhaps, but—but still
it is eatable; after a few spoonfuls one scarcely remarks the
defect—and,' she continued, raising the bowl to her mouth, 'and
when one swallows it quickly, it is really quite refreshing this
cold afternoon.'

Hamilton laughed; Hildegarde grew angry.   'You may consider this a good joke, Lina,' she exclaimed, 'but I find it very,
very impertinent.'

'Now don't get into a passion, my dear, about a miserable
bowl of soup,' said Madame Berger, laughing maliciously; 'it
is really not worth while.   Just go to the kitchen and bring
another, and I promise not even to look at it.'

'But there is no more.'

'Ah, bah! as if I did not know that there was soup put
aside for supper.'

'But not such soup as that,' cried Hildegarde ingenuously;
'mamma and Crescenz cooked it together, and I was not
allowed to touch it for fear of its being spoiled.'

'What an opinion they must have of her cookery!' remarked
Madame Berger, looking towards Hamilton.

'It is of no consequence,' he said, laughing; 'I do not deserve
any for having been so difficult to please.'

'I can bring you a cup of beef-tea; it is better than nothing,'
said Hildegarde, leaving the room.

'Most careful nurse,' cried Madame Berger, smiling ironically.

'Most indefatigable, most kind,' exclaimed Hamilton, warmly.

'And most domineering,' added Madame Berger.

'I have not found her so.'

'Because you have never contradicted her, perhaps.   For
instance, what would you take now to refuse this cup of beef-
tea when she brings it to you?'

'That would be ungrateful—almost rude,' said Hamilton.

'It will be bad enough to afford you an excuse, and I
promise to assist you to brave her anger,' said Madame Berger,
laughing.

Hamilton shook his head and looked a little embarrassed.

'Tell the truth, and say at once you *dare* not do it. She rules you, I perceive, as she does her sister Crescenz, all in the way of kindness; but no thraldom can be more complete. How I shall enjoy seeing you swallow the scalding water dignified with the name of beef-tea! I dare say this time there will be salt enough in it.'

'How mischievous you are!' cried Hamilton; 'I do believe you want us to quarrel merely for your amusement, after having remained for three weeks the best friends possible.'

'You are more than friends if you cannot take the liberty to refuse a cup of bad soup.'

Hamilton was about to reply, when the door was opened by Hans to admit Count Zedwitz.

'You have played truant to-day, Zedwitz,' said Hamilton, holding out his hand; 'I expected you an hour ago.'

'I have been skating on the lake in the English Garden; there was a famous frost last night, and—'

'Skating! Here, Hans, look for my skates directly; there is nothing I enjoy more than skating. We will go out together.'

'But,' said Zedwitz, hesitating, 'is it advisable to go out so late? Remember you have been more than three weeks confined to the house. What will the Doctor say?'

'Hang the Doctor!' cried Hamilton, rising.

'I am sure I am exceedingly obliged to you,' said his wife, pretending to look offended.

'By way of precaution, and not to lose time, we will drive to the lake in a hackney coach,' said Hamilton. 'Come with us,' he added, turning cavalierly to Madame Berger.

'I have no objection, provided you leave me at home on your way back.'

'Agreed,' cried Hamilton, entering his bedroom to make the necessary change in his dress.

Madame Berger was standing opposite a long glass arranging her bonnet, Zedwitz turning over the leaves of some new book, and Hamilton issuing from his room, when Hildegarde again appeared, carrying another bowl of soup; she was so surprised at the appearance of the latter, that she stopped in the middle of the room, and looked inquiringly from one to the other, without speaking.

'Mr. Hamilton is going out to take a drive,' began Madame

Berger, fearing Hildegarde might try to make him alter his intention.

'I am going with Zedwitz to skate in the English Garden,' said Hamilton.

'Perhaps, Hildegarde, you will go with us; I can play chaperone on the occasion,' said Madame Berger.

Hildegarde did not vouchsafe an answer, but turning to Zedwitz she said reproachfully, 'This is not an hour to tempt an invalid to leave the house for the first time.'

'I assure you I have not tempted him,' replied Zedwitz; 'I only mentioned having been skating to excuse my coming so late.'

'You surely will not think of going out this cold day,' she said, turning to Hamilton.

'The weather,' said Madame Berger, 'is not likely to grow warmer at this time of the year, and I suppose he must leave the house some time or other.'

'In fact, I am no longer an invalid,' said Hamilton, 'and the air, though cold, will do me good.'

'At least drink this beef-tea before you go,' said Hildegarde, approaching him.

'How on earth can you expect Mr. Hamilton to swallow such slop as this?' cried Madame Berger, raising the cover as she spoke.

Hildegarde angrily pushed away her hand.

'The carriage is at the door,' said Hans.

'Come,' cried Madame Berger, laughing, 'you have no time to drink this hot water at present, and if you do not make haste, I must decline going with you to admire your skating, for it will be too late for me. Have you courage?' she asked, giving Hamilton a look of intelligence.

Hildegarde had perceived that he wished to avoid drinking the beef-tea. She had placed it on the table, and was now standing near the stove, apparently tranquil, but a slight contraction of her brows, and the extraordinary brilliancy of her eyes as she followed the motions of each speaker, betrayed the anger with which she was struggling.

'I perceive you are annoyed,' said Zedwitz, when about to leave the room; 'but,' he added, quickly, while the colour mounted to his temples, 'you need not be uneasy about your patient. I will bring him back to you as soon as possible.'

'You are mistaken as to the cause of my annoyance,' said

Hildegarde, with a forced smile; 'I am angry with myself for having been such a fool as to prepare that soup.'

'You must excuse Hamilton this time. Madame Berger is such an impatient little person!' said Zedwitz, as he closed the door.

In the meantime Hamilton had nearly descended the stairs. 'I can tell you,' said Madame Berger, 'that Hildegarde is in a towering passion. Did you not see her eyes flashing, and her lips grow blue? I should not wonder if at this moment she were literally dancing in your room!'

'I should like to see her,' said Hamilton, stopping suddenly.

'But if you go back you will have to swallow the soup as a peace-offering,' said Madame Berger.

'Do you think so? Zedwitz, will you assist Madame Berger into the carriage—I must return to Hildegarde: but I promise not to detain you more than a minute.' He rushed up the stairs as he spoke, entered without noise by means of his skeleton key, and, passing through his bedroom, was able to ascertain the partial truth of Madame Berger's assertion. Hildegarde was walking up and down the room with flushed cheeks, talking angrily to herself, and pushing everything that came in her way. 'What a fool—what an egregious fool I was—to make a fire with my own hands to warm that soup!' She kicked the leg of the table as she spoke, making the plates and spoon clatter. 'If ever I warm soup for him again, I hope—yes, I *hope*, I may burn my arm as I have done this time.' She raised her sleeve and looked frowningly at the suffering limb, which in fact was extremely red and covered with blisters. While she endeavoured with her handkerchief to remove the long streaks of smut which still bore testimony to the origin of the mischief, Hamilton advanced, and, scarcely conscious of what he was doing, seized her hand, and held it firmly, while he gulped down the soup as fast as he was able. It was, as Madame Berger had said, very hot; and when he had deposited the bowl on the plate, tears actually stood in his eyes from the excess of his exertions.

'I feel quite warm now,' he said, turning to Hildegarde, who stood beside him in great confusion, fearing that she had been overheard, and, as usual, ashamed of her violence, now that it was over. She had covered her arm, and was endeavouring to release her hand, as he added, 'You were quite right when you said it was too late for skating to-day. I shall merely drive out for half-an-hour, by way of a beginning. This sacrifice I make to your better judgment.'

Hildegarde looked up ; her lips were no longer blue, and her eyes had regained their usual clear serenity. 'To-morrow,' she observed, with evident satisfaction, 'to-morrow you can go out directly after dinner, when the sun is shining.'

'Exactly ; pray don't forget to bespeak a little sunshine for me,' he cried, laughing, as he ran out of the room.

'Where is my little tormentor?' he asked, on perceiving that the carriage was unoccupied.

'How could you expect her to wait for you?' said Zedwitz, gravely; 'she has had the good sense to go home.'

'I am glad of it,' cried Hamilton, springing gaily into the carriage, ' very glad.'

'It is confoundedly cold,' said Zedwitz, impatiently throwing the folds of his cloak over his shoulder. 'I must say your minute was a long one !'

'Why, my dear fellow, considering that I had to drink all that hot water, and put Hildegarde in good humour again, I do not think I required much time.'

Zedwitz looked out of the window in silence. Hamilton leaned back and indulged in reflection of no disagreeable kind.

'Halt !' cried Zedwitz, suddenly. 'We are at the lake.'

'Let us drive on. I don't mean to skate to-day,' said Hamilton.

'You don't mean to skate?' exclaimed Zedwitz.

'No. I promised Hildegarde merely to take an airing.'

'Why did you not tell me that before?'

'Because I feared being deprived of your agreeable society.'

'Halt !' cried Zedwitz, vehemently : and the carriage stopped. 'I can tell you,' he said, kicking the door to assist Hans in opening it, 'I can tell you that you have just received an extremely great proof of my friendship, for if there be any one thing I particularly detest in this world, it is driving about in a machine of this kind. I have an inveterate antipathy to a hackney coach.'

'I understand and share your feelings on this subject generally speaking,' said Hamilton, amused at his violence ; 'but after being confined to one's room for three or four weeks, the air enjoyed even through the windows of a hackney coach is agreeable and refreshing. Come, you may as well drive back with me !'

'Sorry I have a most particular engagement,' began Zedwitz, who was now standing on the road, and stamping his feet on the frozen ground, as if they had been cramped.

'You forget you intended to skate with me,' cried Hamilton, laughing, while he jumped out of the carriage, took Zedwitz's arm, and walked off quickly with him, neither speaking for several minutes.

'Are you jealous?' asked Hamilton, at length.

'You know best whether or not I have cause to be so.'

'You have no cause—although I am sorry to be obliged to confess to you that I too begin to find Hildegarde altogether irresistible, but she does not care in the least for me; and even were it otherwise, my case is more hopeless than yours. Your parents will at least vouchsafe to make a flattering opposition, which, as you are an only son, *must* terminate in consent if you are firm—mine would overwhelm me with scornful ridicule were I to hint at anything so preposterous as an early marriage. It is I, in fact, who ought to be jealous, and desperately jealous too, if you knew but all.'

'But her anxiety about you just now—'

'Was more natural than flattering,' said Hamilton; 'she has got the habit of taking care of me during my illness, and even lately exacts a sort of obedience in trifles, which, however, I willingly pay, as she allows me to tyrannise in other respects.'

'But still, I consider you so very dangerous a rival—' began Zedwitz.

'By no means, for though I wish to gain some of Hildegarde's esteem, if not affection, I can never seriously speak to her on that subject, which alone could interfere with your wishes.'

'Do you advise me then to persevere?' asked Zedwitz.

'I must in future decline advising,' replied Hamilton; 'my confession just now was in fact tantamount to an acknowledgement of my incapacity to do so.'

'Ah, bah!' cried Zedwitz, 'your manner has convinced me that your love is not very deep-rooted—my fears are more for her than for you. If she once liked you, and confessed it, there is no saying how serious the affair might become.'

'Very true,' said Hamilton; 'you might in that case prepare for a voyage to the moon, where you would be sure to find my senses in a little phial, nicely corked and labelled.'

R

'Pshaw! Tell me seriously, what would you do in such a case?'

'Seriously—I believe I should act like a fool. Apply to my father with the certainty of being refused, and laughed at into the bargain—write to my Uncle Jack, that he might have time to make a new will and disinherit me—and then perhaps enter into a seven years' engagement!'

'Hildegarde would never consent to anything so absurd.'

'Not at present—but I thought you supposed her to return my—'

'Hang the supposition!' cried Zedwitz, impatiently, and they walked on in silence until Zedwitz again spoke. 'I wish, Hamilton, that at least you would promise to tell me if ever you do enter into any kind of engagement with Hildegarde.'

'No,' said Hamilton, firmly, 'I will make no such promise. Let us start fair: we both love her, each after his own manner. I will be honourable and tell you that you stand high in her estimation, and that the fear of the opposition of your family, and not indifference on her part, caused her former refusal. I have had to combat with her personal dislike, and if I have overcome it, a very lukewarm kind of regard has taken its place. To counterbalance your advantages, I live in the same house, and see her daily—hourly—often alone.'

'Let us start fair in good earnest,' cried Zedwitz, eagerly, 'but, in order to do so, you must establish yourself in my quarters. The rooms which belong to my father when he is in town are at your service; neither he nor my mother comes to Munich this year, as Agnes' marriage takes place before the Carnival. We will live together, visit the Rosenbergs together, and at the end of two or three months write a letter to Hildegarde, and—'

Hamilton began to laugh. 'Had you proposed this plan at Seon, I might have agreed to it, but now it would be absurd to think of such a thing. Putting all other feelings out of the question, Hildegarde has become absolutely necessary to me. When I am ill she tends me; when I am well she reads with me, or for me, and amuses me; and when I am out of temper she quarrels with me!'

'In the last particular I could supply her place,' said Zedwitz, 'for I could quarrel with you easily enough. If I thought you really loved her, I should not so much mind, but you are deliberately seeking a few months' amusement at her expense, and endeavouring to gain her affection, without any object whatever, for as to your seven years' engagement I cannot for a moment believe you serious. Perhaps Englishwomen may consider this pardonable, but my countrywomen—'

'Your countrywomen unfortunately do not understand the meaning of the word flirtation,' said Hamilton, interrupting him. 'I wish I had time and opportunity to explain it to them.'

'Explain to me what flirtation is,' said Zedwitz, gravely.

'No,' said Hamilton, 'I shall do no such thing, for I see by your face that you are ready to preach a sermon upon the crime of endeavouring to please any of your fair countrywomen, without having both the intention and power to marry with all possible despatch; and now, will you come upstairs with me?'

Zedwitz shook his head.

'I do not mean to press you,' said Hamilton, 'for I must say I never found you less amusing than to-day. I wish you would make an agreement never to mention Hildegarde's name to me.'

'It is an excellent idea,' said Zedwitz, 'but, as I am sincerely attached to her, I hope you will consider it no breach of confidence, should I warn her against this flirtation love of yours.'

'None whatever,' replied Hamilton, laughing. 'You cannot say more and will not probably say half as much in your warning as I have already said, when she was present, to her sister Crescenz.'

'You are incomprehensible,' cried Zedwitz, shrugging his shoulders, and walking off with a slight frown on his usually good-humoured countenance.

CHAPTER XX.

THE WARNING.

HAMILTON prided himself upon being an excellent skater: it was, therefore, with no little satisfaction that he perceived the next day that he had been followed to the lake by the Rosenberg and Hoffmann families. No sooner, however, had Zedwitz seen the former, than his skates were thrown aside—a place beside Hildegarde secured, and he accompanied them home. This occurred several days successively, and Zedwitz at length, on finding that he had regained his former intimacy, ventured to give the proposed warning.   Hamilton was at the moment sweeping before them, 'on sounding skates, a thousand different ways,' and exhibiting more than usual grace and animation. He began judiciously by praising his rival—commended his person, his varied information and talents, the more extraordinary from his extreme youth, and then regretted that he had lost almost all the freshness belonging to his time of life, that his ideas were altogether those of a man of the world, that the society of an elder brother, an accomplished *vaurien*, had evidently been of great disadvantage to him, and had given him opinions, especially with respect to women, which were dangerous in the extreme. Hildegarde had listened with a composure so nearly verging on indifference, that Zedwitz, almost reassured, regretted having said so much, and, had she continued silent, would have, perhaps, softened his last remark, but she looked up suddenly, and said with her usual energy, 'Mr. Hamilton has never spoken of his brother to me; therefore I know nothing about him. You are, however, mistaken as to his opinion of women—he thinks much more highly of them than men generally do, and that he likes their society is evident by his remaining so much at home with us. Mamma says she never knew any young man so perfectly well educated, and so excellent in every respect.'

Zedwitz was not aware of the peculiarity in Hildegarde's disposition which led her invariably to defend the absent: he was therefore greatly vexed, and with difficulty stammered, 'And you—you—perhaps—think equally high of him?'

'Perhaps I do—the more I know him, the better I like him,' replied Hildegarde, bluntly.

'I am answered,' murmured Zedwitz, biting his lip; 'my warning comes too late—he knew it when he gave me leave to speak.'

'Who gave you leave? What warning?' asked Hildegarde, quickly.

Zedwitz had gone too far to recede, and he now became perfectly explicit. Hildegarde again listened calmly, and when he ceased, observed, half reproachfully, 'When Mr. Hamilton speaks of you it is not to warn me—but let us pass over that. I must, however, tell you that you have not in your warning said anything which I have not already heard from himself.'

'That's it!' cried Zedwitz, with ill-concealed impatience; 'he acted honourably in putting you on your guard, but he now considers himself at liberty to win your affection if he can!'

Hildegarde seemed struck by this remark, and walked on in silence. Zedwitz excused himself for having spoken against his friend, on the plea of jealousy, and then urged his own cause with great fervour. While thus speaking, they had taken a wrong turn, and were loudly recalled by Madame Rosenberg, who 'wondered what on earth they could have been thinking about!' Zedwitz had no opportunity of renewing the conversation, but he was apparently satisfied on finding that she was not displeased.

When Hamilton returned home that evening, Hildegarde was at the Hoffmanns'. She had not visited them for a long time, and on her return, he inquired with extreme affability after each member of the family, Cousin Oscar included. She seated herself as far distant from him as possible, and, while answering his questions, seemed to think more of the coloured wool, which she was arranging in the basket, than of what she was saying.

'Did your cousin read for you this evening?' asked Hamilton, moving his chair towards her.

'No; he tried a quantity of new music which Marie had just received. Crescenz, do tell me how you distinguish your greens at night? They all appear blue to me!'

'The names and numbers are pinned on each colour,' replied Crescenz, pushing forward her neatly-arranged basket for inspection.

Major Stultz said something about young women of orderly habits making good wives, which she did not seem to hear, but when Hamilton, in returning the basket, observed, that the colours were so judiciously arranged that they reminded him of a rainbow, a smile of childish delight brightened her youthful features, and made her look so pretty that he playfully held back the basket, and began a series of questions on the different colours, exhibiting an excess of ignorance on the subject, which seemed to amuse *her* infinitely more than Major Stultz, who first drummed on the table, then pushed back his chair, and finally told her, somewhat testily, that 'she was preventing Mr. Hamilton from reading his newspaper.'

Hamilton understood the hint, and resigned the basket with a slight laugh; Crescenz blushed, and, with evident displeasure, followed Major Stultz to another table, where he proposed reading her the letters which he had that day received from Nuremberg.

Hamilton drew his chair close to Hildegarde's, while he observed, 'I am very glad that you have no one who has a right to forbid your speaking to me.'

Hildegarde bent over her work for a minute, and then looking up, asked abruptly, 'What sort of a person is your eldest brother?'

'The best-natured fellow in the world, good-looking, and amusing. You would be sure to like him, if you could pardon his speaking the most execrable French imaginable.'

'Is he amiable?'

'Amiable? Oh, very amiable!'

'And not a *vaurien*?'

'*Tant soit peu*,' said Hamilton, laughing; 'but not half so bad as your cousin Raimund.'

'Is he much older than you?'

'Several years; but may I ask why my brother has so suddenly become an object of interest to you?'

'He does not interest me in the least,' began Hildegarde; but at that moment Hamilton, whose hand had been wandering through the entangled skeins of wool in her basket, suddenly drew forth a small book which had been concealed beneath them; her first impulse was to prevent his opening it, but she changed her mind, and, though blushing deeply, continued to work without uttering a syllable.

Hamilton turned over the leaves for some minutes in silence. 'Who recommended you to read the works of Georges Sand? he asked, as he placed the book beside her on the table.

'Oscar: he told me they were interesting, and extremely well written.'

'They are both the one and the other, and yet nothing would have induced me to advise you to read them—especially this volume. I am surprised you did not yourself perceive that it was not suited for a person of your age or—'

'Pshaw!' cried Hildegarde, impatiently; 'mamma wishes me to read French that I may not forget the language; the best writers of the day are, of course, the best for that purpose, and Oscar says all French novels are more or less of this description. He told me that I need not have any scruples, for that these works were written by a woman, and might, therefore, be read by one.'

'So, then, you had scruples ?'

'I have none at present,' said Hildegarde, taking up the volume; 'besides,' she added, drawing her chair close to the table, 'I positively must know whether or not the heroine marries the young poet.'

'Marry!' cried Hamilton, laughing ironically; 'there is not one word of marriage in the whole book—that would be much too unpoetical. I can hardly, however, imagine that *this* heroine really interests you—a heroine whose thoughts and reasonings are those of a woman who has plunged into the whirlpool of earthly pleasures, and from satiety learned to despise them. I wish it were any of the other works of Sand, or—or that, for your sake, Madame Dudevant had been less glowingly graphical in some parts of her work. If,' he added, half inquiringly, 'if you merely read to know the end of the story, it is easily told; the events are few, and I am ready to relate them to you.'

'Oscar has a much higher opinion of my intellect than you have,' observed Hildegarde, slowly turning over the leaves; 'he says my character is so decidedly formed, that I may read, without danger, whatever I please.'

'That was gross flattery,' said Hamilton, 'for no girl of seventeen can read a work of this description without danger. The religious speculations alone make it unfit for you—but stay, I can prove it; read half-a-dozen pages aloud for me— where you please; the chances are in my favour that I prove myself right.'

'It is not exactly adapted for reading aloud,' said Hildegarde, with some embarrassment.

'That is an infallible criterion by which you may know what to read for the next ten years,' said Hamilton.

'But I dare say I could find many parts which I should have no objection to read aloud.'

'Read, then,' said Hamilton, with a provoking smile.

Hildegarde began. 'The style at least is faultless,' she observed, at the end of a few minutes.

'Perfect,' said Hamilton; 'but go on.'

She continued; by degrees her voice became less firm, a deep blush overspread her face, she turned away her head from him, and his eyes rested on her small and now perfectly crimson ear, and yet she persevered until the words almost seemed to suffocate her, when, throwing down the book, she exclaimed, 'You were right; I will not read any more of it, nor any of the others recommended by Oscar.'

'May I write you a list?' asked Hamilton, eagerly.

'Pray do,' cried Hildegarde, turning round; 'I promise to read them all.'

A leaf was hastily torn out of his pocket-book, a pencil carefully pointed, and two hours scarcely sufficed to bring this most simple business to a satisfactory conclusion, so various were the observations and discussions to which it gave rise.

CHAPTER XXI.

THE STRUGGLE.

THE following Sunday, Hamilton saw the whole Rosenberg family, with the exception of Hildegarde, walking in the English Gardens. It appeared odd that she should have remained at home when her father was present, and he for a moment thought of asking the reason; on consideration, the hope of finding her alone made him turn his horse's head directly homeward, and, on riding into the yard, he looked up to her window, expecting as usual to find her there ready to greet him and admire his horse—but not a human being was visible; even his servant, not expecting his return so early, had disappeared, and he was obliged to lead his horse into the stable himself. He entered the house by the back staircase, visited all the rooms, and even the kitchen, but found all deserted. Madame Rosenberg's room was also unoccupied, but through the partly open door of it he saw Hildegarde sitting on the sofa in the drawing-room, reading so intently that she was perfectly unconscious of his presence. The deep folds of her dark-blue merino dress, with its closely-fitting body, gave a more than usual elegance to her tall, slight figure, as she bent in profile over her book, and Hamilton stood in silent admiration unconsciously twisting his riding-whip round his wrist, until his eyes rested for the second time on the book which she held in her hand. He started, hesitated, then hastily strode forward and stood before her; doubt and uncertainty were still depicted on his countenance as Hildegarde looked up, but her dismay, her deep blush, and the childish action of placing the hand containing the volume behind her, were a confirmation of his fears that she was reading the forbidden work. 'Excuse me for interrupting you,' he said, with a forced smile, 'but I really cannot believe the evidence of my own eyes, and must request you to let me look at that book for a moment.'

'No, you shall not,' she answered, leaning back on the sofa, and becoming very pale while she added, 'It is very disagreeable being startled and interrupted in this manner. I thought you told mamma you would meet her at Neuberghausen.'

'Very true; perhaps I may meet her there; but, before I go, I must and will see that book. On it depends my future opinion of you.'

'You shall not see it,' cried Hildegarde, the colour again returning to her face.

'The book!' said Hamilton, seizing firmly her disengaged hand. 'The book, or the name of it!'

'Neither; let me go!' cried Hildegarde, struggling to disengage her hand.

Like most usually quiet-tempered persons, Hamilton, when once actually roused, lost all command of himself; he held one of her hands as in a vice, and, when she brought forward the other to accelerate its release, he bent down to read the title of the book, which was immediately thrown on the ground, and the then free hand descended with such violence on his cheek and ear that for a moment he was perfectly stunned; and, even after he stood upright, he looked at her for a few seconds in unfeigned astonishment. 'Do you think,' at length he exclaimed, vehemently—'do you think that I will allow you to treat me as you did Major Stultz, with impunity?' And then, catching her in his arms, he kissed her repeatedly and with a violence which seemed to terrify her beyond measure. 'I gave you fair warning more than once,' he added, when at length he had released her. 'I gave you fair warning, and you knew what you had to expect.' She covered her face with her hands, and burst into a passion of tears.

'I cannot imagine,' he continued, impetuously walking up and down the room—'I cannot imagine why you did not, with your usual courage, tell me at once the name of the book and prevent this scene.'

Hildegarde shook her head, and wept still more bitterly.

'After all,' he said, seating himself with affected calmness opposite to her, leaning his arms on the table, and drumming upon the book, which now lay undisputed between them, 'after all, you are not better than other people! Not more to be trusted than other girls, and I fancied you such perfection! I could have forgiven anything but the—the untruth!' he exclaimed, starting up. 'Anything but that! Pshaw! Yesterday, when you told me that the books had been sent back to the library, I believed you without a moment's hesitation— I thanked you for your deference to my opinion—ha, ha, ha! What a fool you must have thought me!'

Hildegarde looked up. All expression of humility had left her features, her tears ceased to flow, and, as she rose to leave the room, she turned almost haughtily towards him, while saying—'I really do not know what right you have to speak to me in this manner. I consider it very great presumption on your part, and desire it may never occur again.'

'You may be quite sure I shall never offend you in this way again,' he said, holding the book towards her. 'What a mere farce the writing of that list of books was!'

'No; for I had intended to have read all you recommended.'

'And all I recommended you to avoid, too! This—this, which you tacitly promised not to finish——' He stopped; for, while she took the book in silence, she blushed so deeply, and seemed so embarrassed, that he added, sorrowfully, 'Oh, how I regret having come home! How I wish I had not discovered that you could deceive me!'

'I have *not* deceived you.' said Hildegarde.

Hamilton shook his head and glanced towards the subject of dispute.

'Appearances are against me, and yet I repeat I have not deceived you. The books *were* sent to the library yesterday evening—but too late to be changed. Old Hans brought them back again, and I found them in my room when I went to bed. I did not read them last night.'

'But you stayed at home for the purpose to-day,' observed Hamilton, reproachfully.

'No; my mother gave the servants leave to go out for the whole day, and, as she did not like to leave the house quite unoccupied, she asked me to remain at home. I, of course, agreed to do so; without, I assure you, thinking of those hateful books. I do not mean to—I cannot justify what I have done. I can only say in extenuation that the temptation was great. I have been alone for more than two hours—my father's books are locked up. I never enter your room when you are absent, and I wished to know the end of the story, which still interests and haunts me in spite of all my endeavours to forget it. The book lay before me; I resisted long, but at last I opened it ; and so—and so—'

'And so, I suppose, I must acknowledge that I have judged you too harshly,' said Hamilton.

'I do not care about your judgment. I have fallen in my own esteem since I find that I cannot resist temptation.'

'And is my good opinion of no value to you?'

'It was, perhaps; but it has lost all worth within the last half-hour.'

'How do you mean?'

'I have seen you in the course of that time suspicious, rough, and what you would yourself call ungentlemanlike.'

'A pretty catalogue of faults for one short half-hour!' exclaimed Hamilton, biting his lips.

'You were the last person from whom I should have expected such treatment,' continued Hildegarde, while the tears started to her eyes, and her voice faltered, 'the very last; and though I did get into a passion, and give you a blow, it was not until you had hurt my wrist and provoked me beyond endurance.' She left the room, and walked quickly down the passage.

'Stay!' cried Hamilton, following her, 'stay and hear my excuses.'

'Excuses!—you have not even one to offer,' said Hildegarde, laying her hand on the lock of her door.

'Hear me at least,' he said, eagerly. 'I could not endure the thought of your being one jot less perfect than I had imagined you—that made me suspicious; the wish for proof made me rough ; and though I cannot exactly justify my subsequent conduct, I plead in extenuation your own words, " The temptation was great."'

Hildegarde's dimples showed that a smile was with difficulty repressed, and Hamilton, taking courage, whispered hurriedly, 'But one word more—hear my last and best excuse; it is that I love you, deeply, passionately ; but I need not tell you this, for you must have known it long, long ago. Hildegarde, say only that our perpetual quarrels have not made you absolutely hate me!'

Hildegarde, without uttering a word, impetuously drew back her hand, sprang into her room, and locked the door. He waited for a minute or two, and then knocked, but received no answer. 'Hildegarde!' he cried, reproachfully, 'is this right—is this kind? Even if you dislike me, I have a right to expect an answer.'

'Go!' she said in a very low voice, 'go away! You ought not to be here when I am alone.'

'Why did you not think of that before?'

'I don't know. I had not time. I—'

'Nonsense! Open the door, and let me speak to you for a moment.'

No answer; but he thought he heard her walking up and down the room.

'Only one moment,' he repeated.

'I cannot, indeed I cannot. Pray go away.'

He retired slowly to his room; even before he reached it he had become conscious of the absurdity of his conduct, and the prudence of hers. That she no longer disliked him, he was pretty certain; that she had so discreetly avoided a confession of other feelings was better for both, as it enabled them to continue their intercourse on the same terms, while the acknowledgment of a participation in his affection would have subjected her to great annoyances, and placed him in a most embarrassing situation. He was angry with himself—recollected with shame that he had repeated the error which he had so much cause to regret on a former occasion, and mentally repenting his own loquaciousness, and rejoicing at Hildegarde's taciturnity, he resolved never to refer to the subject again. A ring of the bell at the entrance-door induced him to stop and await her appearance. She did not answer the summons, and it was repeated, accompanied by a few familiar taps on the door. Still she did not move. Again the bell was rung; the knocks became louder, as if administered by some hard instrument, and finally her name was loudly and distinctly pronounced.

'I am coming, papa,' she cried, at last, running forward, and opening the door precipitately.

Count Raimund sprang into the passage, closed the door

with his shoulder, leaned upon it, and burst into a fit of laughter at the dismay legible on the features of his cousin.

'Oscar,' she began, seriously, 'you must come some other day. Mamma is not at home now, and I have been left to—'

'I know, I know,' he cried, interrupting her. 'I saw them all in the English gardens—your chevalier Hamilton, too, galloping about like a madman; and for this reason, my most dear and beautiful cousin, I have come here now, hoping for once to see you alone. Do not look so alarmed; I am only come to claim the advice which you promised to give me on the most important event of my life.'

'Not now, not now,' said Hildegarde, glancing furtively towards the end of the passage, where, in the shadow of his door, she distinguished Hamilton's figure leaning with folded arms against the wall; 'some other time, Oscar.'

'What other time? I never see you for a moment alone— even at the Hoffmanns'; although my good Marie is too rational to bore me with useless jealousy, does not her deaf old mother watch every movement and intercept every glance with her cold, grey, suspicious eyes? I sometimes wish the old lady were blind instead of deaf; she would be infinitely less troublesome.'

'Oh, Oscar!'

'Conceive my being doomed to live in the vicinity of such eyes, dearest creature, and you will pity me, at least!'

'You are not in the least to be pitied—for the Hoffmanns are most amiable,' said Hildegarde, hurriedly. 'But now I expect you will leave me.'

'Expect no such thing! On the contrary, I expect that you will invite me to enter this room,' he replied, advancing boldly towards her.

'If you enter that room,' said Hildegarde, sternly, 'I shall leave you there, and take refuge with Madame de Hoffmann, who, I know, is now at home.'

'Don't be angry, dearest; all places are alike to me where you are. All places are alike to me where I may tell you without reserve that I love you more than ever one cousin loved another.'

'The time is ill chosen for jesting, Oscar; I never felt less disposed to enjoy anything of the kind than at this moment.'

'Indeed! Then let me tell you seriously that I love you to distraction.'

'Oscar, even in jest, I do not choose to hear such nonsense.'

'By heaven, I am not jesting!'

'Then, betrothed as you now are, your words are a crime.

'Be it so; there is, however, no crime I should hesitate to commit were you to be obtained by it. As to breaking my engagement with Marie, that is a trifle not worth considering; but what am I likely to obtain by doing so?'

'Dishonour,' said Hildegarde, firmly and calmly.

'Hildegarde,' he exclaimed fiercely, 'do not affect a coldness which you cannot feel; do not drive me to madness. My love must not be trifled with; it is of no rational, every-day kind, but violent as my nature, and desperate as my fortunes.'

'That is,' thought Hamilton, 'exactly what she wished. If he continue in this strain, she will not shut the door in his face. But I have had enough of such raving, and will no longer constrain her by my presence.' He entered his room and closed the door.

For more than half an hour he impatiently paced backwards and forwards, stopping only when he heard Raimund's voice suddenly raised. At length he thought he heard a stifled scream, and rushed to the door, scarcely knowing what he feared or expected. Hildegarde was holding her cousin's arms with both hands, while she exclaimed, 'For heaven's sake, Oscar, do not frighten me so horribly!'

A loud ringing of the house bell, and the sound of many voices on the stairs, seemed to be a relief to her, while Raimund appeared considerably agitated. 'Hide me in your room, Hildegarde; I am lost if the Hoffmanns find me here.'

'And what is to become of me should you be found there?' she asked, while a deadly paleness overspread her features, and she irresolutely placed her hand on the lock of the door; then glancing down the passage and beckoning Raimund to follow, she led the way to Hamilton's room. 'Mr. Hamilton,' she said, with a trembling voice, 'will you allow Oscar to remain a few minutes in your room, and when no one is in the passage, have the goodness to open the door leading to the back staircase for him?'

'The part which you have assigned me in this comedy, mademoiselle, is by no means agreeable, but I will not be the means of causing you embarrassment; Count Raimund may easily be supposed to have voluntarily visited me, and there is no necessity for a retreat by the back staircase, unless we have some motive for wishing to give his visit an air of mystery.'

'Ah, very true,' said Hildegarde, in a hurried, confused manner, while she moved aside to let her cousin pass.

Hamilton's speech made more impression on Raimund; he looked furious, and seemed to hesitate whether or not to enter the room. Again the bell rang, and Hildegarde was in the act of springing forward, when Raimund caught her arm, and while a fearful frown contracted his brows, with closed teeth, and in the low voice of suppressed rage, he whispered, 'One word; is it Zedwitz? or—or—' He looked towards Hamilton.

Hildegarde's face became crimson; she flung off his detaining hand, and ran to the hall door, which she threw wide open, leaving him to retreat precipitately into Hamilton's room, where, with folded arms, he strode towards the window, after having murmured the words, 'Sorry to intrude in this manner.' Hamilton moved a chair towards him; he sat down for a moment, but the next jumped up, and going to the door, partly opened it and looked into the passage.

'I saw Count Raimund enter the house more than half an hour ago,' observed a very loud voice, which Hamilton recognised as Madame de Hoffmann's, 'and as I knew you were all out walking, and only Mademoiselle Hildegarde at home, I expected to see him leave it again immediately.'

'I think, mamma, you must have been mistaken,' said Mademoiselle de Hoffmann, putting her mouth close to her mother's ear.

'I have the misfortune to be somewhat deaf, Marie, but my eyes are as good as yours, and with these eyes I saw him enter this house.'

'You are quite right,' said Raimund, advancing with the easiest manner and most unconcerned smile imaginable. 'I knew that Marie had gone out with Madame Rosenberg, and, not imagining that my future mother-in-law could be so much interested in my movements, I ventured, without informing her of my intentions, to visit my friend Hamilton.'

'But Mr. Hamilton is out riding,' cried Madame de Hoffmann.

'Perhaps he *was* out riding, but I have had the good fortune to find him at home nevertheless.'

' Then he must have come up the other staircase, or I should have seen him through the slit in our door, where I watched you walking upstairs.'

' Very possibly,' said Raimund, contemptuously.

' Marie,' said Madame de Hoffmann, in what she intended for a whisper, but which was audible to all, ' Marie, my child, I do n't believe a word of all this. The Englishman is no more in the house than the man in the moon.'

' Confound your suspicions !' muttered Raimund, angrily. ' I suppose, then,' he added, with a frown, ' I shall be obliged, in order to satisfy you, to ask Mr. Hamilton to show himself to the assembled household.'

He seemed, however, so very unwilling to make the request, that Madame de Hoffmann's suspicions received confirmation; she turned from him, saying, with a laugh of derision, ' Perhaps Hildegarde can assist you in making him appear !'

Her words acted like a charm. Hamilton, who had been an immoveable listener of all that had passed, no sooner heard her name mentioned than he mechanically rose, and, taking his hat and whip, issued forth. He forced a smile as he passed the Hoffmanns and Madame Rosenberg, which, on approaching Hildegarde, changed into an expression of contempt that neither her swelled and tearful eyelids nor her excessive paleness could mitigate.

After his return home he remained in his room until supper was announced, and even then delayed some minutes to insure Madame Rosenberg's being in the drawing-room when he reached it. She was endeavouring to persuade Hildegarde to leave the stove, near which she was sitting with closed eyes, leaning her head in her hand.

' If you would only eat your supper, Hildegarde, it would quite cure your headache, which is probably caused by your having spent the day in a heated room. Next time I shall leave old Hans in charge of the house; for, had you been out walking with us as usual, you would have had no headache, I am sure. Do n't you think so too, Mr. Hamilton ?'

' I think it very probable,' he answered, seating himself beside Madame Rosenberg.

' And do n't you think if she took some soup she would be better ?'

' Perhaps.'

' Hildegarde, I insist on your trying it—or go to bed at

once. You make your head worse by sitting so close to the stove.'

Hildegarde, without speaking, moved to the vacant chair at the other side of Hamilton, and slowly and reluctantly sipped a few mouthfuls of soup.

By some singular anomaly, Hamilton found himself suddenly in remarkably high spirits—he looked at Hildegarde, and, congratulating himself on being free from thraldom, gazed with a gay smile on her pale features until they were suffused with red, and great was his triumph to feel and know that there was no sympathetic blush on his own countenance. He told Madame Rosenberg of an engagement he had made with Zedwitz, to accompany him to Edelhof on the following morning, to attend the marriage of his sister, and requested to have his breakfast at an early hour the next day.

'And you intend to remain away a whole fortnight! How we shall miss you!' cried Madame Rosenberg.

'You are very kind to say so,' replied Hamilton, laughing.

'And I think so too, though you seem to doubt me. You know I like you better than any of the Englishmen I have had in my house. Captain Black was not to be compared to you, nor Mr. Smith either, although he used to tell me so often that he was noble even without a *Von* before his name, and that he could be made a chamberlain here if he wished it, as he was related to the Duke of Buckel,* which always appeared to me such an odd name for a duke, that I was half inclined to doubt there being any such person.'

'We have a Duke of Buccleuch—' began Hamilton.

'Very likely he pronounced it that way; I am sure I heard it often enough to know; but I never can learn an English word until I see it written, and never should have learned his names if he had not constantly left his cards lying about on the tables; I dare say I shall find some of them in the card-basket still.' She commenced a diligent search while speaking, and soon held up a card, on which was printed in large German letters the name of Mr. Howard Seymour Scott Smith.

'He used sometimes to say that the last word ought to be left out, for that his real name was Scott.'

---

* Buckel means, in German, back, or more generally humpback. It seems that Madame Rosenberg took it in the latter sense.

'Perhaps he inherited property with the name of Smith?'

'No; he said something about a marriage certificate having been lost; that before he was born there was great irregularity in such things in England.'

Hamilton laughed.

'Is it not true?' asked Madame Rosenberg.

'Oh, very possibly.'

'He told us, too, that in Scotland people could be married without any certificate of birth, baptism, or confirmation — without even the consent of their friends. Franz says this is a fact, and that the existence of such a law is a great temptation to thoughtless young people.'

'I have no doubt it is,' replied Hamilton; 'I would not answer for myself were I led into temptation. A great-uncle of mine made a marriage of this kind, and it proved a very happy one; his friends, to provide for him quickly, used all their interest to send him out to India, where he made an enormous fortune, and, as he has no children, has been, ever since his return, a sort of lawgiver in our family. I should not have been here now if old Uncle Jack had not said that travelling was necessary to make me a man of the world, and that in Germany alone I could learn to speak German well.'

'But,' said Madame Rosenberg, 'this marriage was a fortunate exception; for,' she added, with sundry winks and blinks towards Hildegarde, 'for marriages against the consent of relations seldom or never turn out well. Let me give you some more salad, and then, as you are to leave so early to-morrow, I may as well pack up your things to-night.'

'By no means,' cried Hamilton. 'I must beg of you to send for Hans.'

'Oh, young Hans is much too awkward, and the old man is gone to bed hours ago. I have been thinking, if you intend to keep Hans, that I will begin to teach him to be handy, and instead of Hildegarde's arranging your linen, he must learn to do it from this time forward.'

'That would be very kind of you,' said Hamilton.

'For the sewing on of buttons and all that,' continued Madame Rosenberg, delighted at the idea of giving instruction, 'he must, of course, apply to you, Hildegarde.'

Hildegarde, who had been leaning back in her chair, diligently puckering and plaiting her pocket-handkerchief, looked up for a moment and replied, 'Yes, mamma.'

'I shall send for Hans and give him the first lesson to-night,' said Madame Rosenberg, moving towards the door.

'Wait a moment and I can accompany you,' cried Hamilton, quickly; 'I shall be ready directly.'

'Don't hurry yourself,' said Madame Rosenberg; 'you will have time enough before Hans comes up; and I must first see if Peppy have fallen asleep, and if he be properly covered. Don't hurry yourself.'

Why did Hamilton bend over his plate? and why did the colour mount to his temples as the door closed? Did he begin to entertain doubts of his indifference? or did he dread an explanation with Hildegarde? He scarcely knew himself, but he felt uncomfortable, and gave himself a quantity of trouble to prevent his companion from observing it.

The distant roll of carriages had already informed them that the opera was over; but it was not until the sound of voices in the usually quiet street had made the immediate return of her father, sister, and Major Stultz probable, that Hildegarde summoned courage to say, in a very low voice, and without looking up, 'What must you think of me—'

'Do you wish to know what I think of you?' asked Hamilton, with affected negligence.

'Yes; but do not again judge too harshly.'

'I think,' he said, facing her deliberately, 'I think you are very beautiful.'

'Pshaw!' cried Hildegarde, pushing back her chair angrily. 'I expected a very different answer.'

'Something different,' said Hamilton, in the same tone. 'Something about distraction and committing crimes, perhaps?'

'What occurred to-day is no subject for a jest,' she said, seriously.

'So I thought a few hours ago, also,' said Hamilton: 'but, now, the whole affair appears to me rather amusing than otherwise. Perhaps, however, your cousin alone is privileged to speak to you in this manner, in which case, you must pardon me for endeavouring to recollect what he said; but it was so well received that—'

'It was not well received!' cried Hildegarde, interrupting

s 2

him. 'You know it was not; and I am ready,' she added, after a pause, 'ready to repeat you every word of our conversation.'

'Thank you,' said Hamilton, coldly; 'but I have already heard enough to enable me to imagine the remainder.'

'Perhaps,' said Hildegarde, hurriedly, 'perhaps you heard —and saw—'

'I heard a declaration of love after the most approved form, a proposal to commit any crime or crimes likely to render him interesting and acceptable to you. I remember to have once heard you tell your father that you wished to be the object of a love of this kind; but I did not wait to hear your answers; it was your half-suppressed scream which made me foolishly imagine you wished for my presence. When I saw you, I perceived at once my mistake, and returned to my room.'

'Then you did not see the—the dagger—'

'What dagger?' asked Hamilton, his curiosity excited in spite of himself.

'Oscar's dagger—he threatened to stab himself!'

'Ha, ha, ha!' laughed Hamilton. 'I really did not think him capable of acting so absurdly. I gave him credit for too much knowledge of the world to treat you to such an insipid scene.'

'Then you do not think he was serious?'

'I am sure he was not. The dagger was purposely brought for effect. He has proved himself an excellent actor to-day —tragic as well as comic, it seems.'

'It was cruel of him deliberately to frighten me,' said Hildegarde, thoughtfully.

'It was unpardonable—inexcusable his doing so,' cried Hamilton, 'for he thought you were alone, and took advantage of finding you unprotected.'

'Most men take advantage of finding us unprotected. After the events of to-day, I may say all men do so,' replied Hildegarde, with so much reproachful meaning in her glance that Hamilton rose from his seat, and began to perambulate the room, occasionally stopping to lean on the stove, until her father's voice and approaching steps made him suddenly move forwards towards her, as if he expected her to speak again. She remained, however, silent and motionless; and, at length, overcome by a mixture of anxiety and curiosity, and with an ineffectual effort to appear indifferent, he said, quickly, 'I thought you were going to tell me what you said that could have given your cousin an excuse for producing a dagger?'

'You did not choose to hear when I was willing to tell you; and now—'

Here Madame Rosenberg entered the room, and Hildegarde rose, saying that 'her head ached intolerably, and she would now go to bed.'

'Good night!' said Hamilton. 'I hope your headache will be cured by a long sleep, and that you will be quite well when we meet again.'

'Thank you; before that time I shall most probably have altogether forgotten it,' said Hildegarde.

That means, thought Hamilton, she will not pour out my coffee to-morrow at breakfast.

CHAPTER XXII.

THE DEPARTURE.

HILDEGARDE did not appear the next morning, and Hamilton breakfasted with Madame Rosenberg sitting opposite to him in a striped red and white dressing-gown; her hair, as usual, twisted up to the very roots with hair pins, to prepare curls which, however, seldom made their appearance at home, excepting on the evenings which the Hoffmanns spent with her. She sat opposite to him, and watched while he vainly endeavoured to improve his coffee by adding alternately cream and sugar. 'One never enjoys a breakfast at this early hour,' she observed, at length; 'the coffee is, however, quite as good as usual; I made it myself.'

'I have no doubt of it,' said Hamilton, 'but the fact is, I am so accustomed to your daughter Hildegarde's preparing it for me, that I do not know the quantity of cream and sugar necessary—by the bye, I hope her headache is better this morning?'

'She said so,' replied Madame Rosenberg, 'but I found her so feverish, and looking so wretchedly ill, that I have forbidden her getting up until Doctor Berger sees her.'

'You do not apprehend any serious illness, I hope?'

'Oh, no; but Crescenz tells me she slept very uneasily, had frightful dreams, and at one time during the night fancied

some one intended to stab her! Such an idea! I suppose,'
she added, after a pause, 'you expect Count Zedwitz to call
for you?'

'I believe so,' said Hamilton, absently.

'I am beginning rather to like him,' observed Madame
Rosenberg.

Hamilton did not appear to hear her.

'You are going to a gay house,' she added; 'at least it will
be gay on such an occasion.'

'What occasion?' asked Hamilton, looking up.

'Why, did not you tell me that the only daughter was
going to be married? And is not a wedding a very gay
thing?'

'Not always,' said Hamilton, 'for brides generally shed tears
and infect the bridesmaids, and the mamma half faints, and the
papa is agitated, and when the bridal party leave, the house is
immensely dull, until it fill with new people again. Altogether,
a wedding is a very deadly-lively festivity, excepting to the
two principal actors.'

'I will prove the contrary,' said Madame Rosenberg; 'you
shall see how gay our wedding will be—that is, Crescenz's!
Did I tell you that it must be deferred until the Carnival?'

'Not a word; I thought it was to take place before
Christmas.'

'Marriages are seldom or never celebrated during Advent,'
said Madame Rosenberg; 'but, at all events, Major Stultz's
sister has died suddenly, and he must leave for Nuremberg
to-morrow.'

'I am sorry he has lost his sister,' said Hamilton, compassionately.

'Why, in fact, the loss is rather a gain,' said Madame
Rosenberg. 'He knew very little about her—she was unmarried, rich, and stingy—always on the point of making a fool of
herself, by marrying some young student or officer. Now the
Major quietly inherits all her property—a very pretty addition
to what he already has. I told Crescenz yesterday evening
that she had drawn a greater prize than she expected.'

'And what did she say?'

'Why, not much—but she looked exceedingly pleased; her
father has told me since that he thinks she is glad that her
marriage is put off, and does not care in the least about
the money, of which she has not yet learned the value. This

may be partly true—Crescenz may have no objection to a delay, but she is now quite satisfied with the Major, and has no wish whatever to break off her engagement. Count Raimund has been of great use to her!'

'How do you mean?' asked Hamilton, surprised.

'Why, his unpardonable negligence towards Marie de Hoffmann forms a fine contrast to the Major's attentions and handsome presents. Crescenz is very childish, but she has perceived the difference, nevertheless, and I have not neglected the opportunity to tell her that all young men are careless lovers, and still more careless husbands, and that I am sure she will be much happier when she is married than Marie!'

'The carriage is come! The carriage is come for Hamilton!' cried Peppy, rushing into the room; 'and Count Zedwitz is coming up the stairs! and Crescenz is hiding behind the kitchen door! and Walburg is gone with Gustle to school! and Dr. Berger is in Hildegarde's room! and papa is putting on his coat! and he wants you to come to him!'

'Well, have you any more news to tell me before I go?' said his mother, taking up her bunch of keys from the breakfast table. 'Good morning, Count Zedwitz—you must excuse me —Dr. Berger is here, and—'

'No one ill, I hope?' said Zedwitz.

'Hildegarde is ill,' replied Hamilton; 'have you any objection to waiting until we hear what the Doctor says?'

'Quite the contrary,' said Zedwitz, sitting down, evidently alarmed.

'In the meantime, I can tell Hans to carry down my luggage,' said Hamilton.

Hans was despatched with the portmanteau, carpet-bag, and dressing-case; but Hamilton, instead of returning to his friend, watched till Madame Rosenberg and the Doctor had left Hildegarde's room, and walked up the passage together. A moment after he was at her door, and had knocked.

'Come in,' said Hildegarde, almost gaily; 'I am not so ill as you suppose!'

'I am very glad to hear it,' said Hamilton, entering as he spoke.

'I—I—expected papa,' said Hildegarde, blushing deeply.

'I more than half suspected the permission to enter was not intended for me,' said Hamilton, 'but I really cannot leave you without having obtained pardon for having offended you last night. I cannot quit you for so long a time without the certainty of your forgiveness.'

'It is granted—or rather I have nothing to forgive,' replied Hildegarde, 'for you were quite right not to listen to my confession, though I remained up on purpose to favour you with it.'

She had become very pale while speaking, and Hamilton was forcibly reminded of all her long and unwearied attentions to him during his illness. He wondered how he could ever, even for a moment, have forgotten them, and remained lost in thought, until, slightly pointing towards the door, she wished him a pleasant journey and much amusement. Instead of obeying the sign, he walked directly forward, saying, 'You mu~t not expect me to believe that I am forgiven until you have told me all I refused to hear yesterday evening.'

'How very unconscionable you are!' she said, with a faint smile. 'When, however, I tell you that I wish you to leave my room, that I am too ill to talk, I am sure you—'

'Oh, of course, of course,' said Hamilton, quite aware of the reasonableness of her demand.

'Only one thing you must tell me, and that is, what you said to Raimund which could induce him to threaten to kill himself.'

'Do not ask me,' said Hildegarde, uneasily.

'But that is exactly what I insist upon knowing,' persisted Hamilton.

'You said you came to ask forgiveness, but it seems you have fallen into your usual habit of commanding, and—'

'I do not command,' cried Hamilton, interrupting her; 'I do not command; but,' he added in a very low voice, and approaching still nearer, 'I entreat—I entreat you to tell me what you said to him.'

'I reminded him that he was betrothed to my friend,' began Hildegarde, slowly and unwillingly.

'Well, well; and then—'

'And then—I said—I could not like him otherwise than a —a cousin.'

'But surely, situated as he is, he must have expected just such an answer from you. Were he free and independent, you would probably have spoken differently. Did you not console him by telling him so?'

Hildegarde remained silent, her eyes almost closed.

'And if you told him that,' continued Hamilton, 'there was no possible excuse for the dagger scene : he might have been despairing, but not desperate, on such an occasion. Tell me, Hildegarde, did you say that?'

'No,' she replied, almost in a whisper; 'no! for though I admire Oscar, I do not love him at all.'

'Then you must have said something else !'

'You are worrying me,' she murmured, with an expression of pain.

'I see I am,' cried Hamilton. 'Forgive me, but I must ask one question more. Did he not ask you if you loved another ?'

'Yes,' said Hildegarde, turning away her face, which was once more covered with blushes.

'And you acknowledged ?'

'I acknowledged. I confessed my folly to put an end to the wildest ravings and most impracticable schemes imaginable.'

'And you named the object of your preference ?'

'Oh, no, no, no !'

'Hildegarde,' cried Hamilton, hurriedly, 'tell me at once— answer me quickly—have you chosen Zedwitz ?'

Hildegarde turned still more away, but did not answer.

'I understand your silence. You have chosen well—and,' he added, after a slight struggle, 'wisely.'

Hildegarde made an impatient gesture with her hand.

'Do not mistake me,' he continued, eagerly. 'I am convinced your choice has not in the least been influenced by interested motives. Zedwitz is in every respect worthy of your regard.'

Hildegarde raised herself quickly on her elbow, and seemed about to speak, but the words died on her lips when she perceived Crescenz, who had, as usual, entered the room noiselessly, standing between them. She shrank back, her colour changed several times with frightful rapidity, but her voice, though faint, was perfectly calm as she requested her sister to close the window-shutters, and every trace of emotion disappeared as her father, entering, seated himself beside her bed, and observed that she looked more like a marble statue than a living person.

Hamilton was at the moment unable to articulate : he shook Mr. Rosenberg's hand, and left the room precipitately. In the drawing-room he found the Doctor assuring Madame Rosenberg that Mademoiselle Hildegarde would be perfectly

well in a day or two.   Hamilton, nevertheless, requested her
to write to him, and, having obtained a promise, he began to
hurry Zedwitz's departure.

'Does your servant not go with us, Hamilton?' asked Zedwitz.

' He is to follow with Madame Rosenberg's letter to-morrow.
Be sure to bring the letter, Hans!' said Hamilton, as he
wrapped himself in his cloak, and sank back in the corner of
the carriage.

CHAPTER XXIII

THE LONG DAY.

HAMILTON could not help feeling flattered at the evident pleasure which his return caused to every member of the Rosenberg
family.   The two little boys began immediately to tell him
that the Christmas-tree was expected the next day.   Gustle
said that he had written a list of all the toys he wished for,
had placed it under his pillow, and that the little child Christ
had come for it and carried it off.   'So, you see, I must have
been very good, or he would not have taken the list, and I
shall get all the things I wrote for.'

' And,' said Peppy, ' mamma met the infant Christ in the
Ludwig Street, and he asked if I had been a good child, and
when mamma said yes, he promised to fly into the nursery to-
morrow evening, and light the candles, and bring me a gun,
and a cart, and bonbons, and ginger-bread.'

' To-morrow is Christmas-eve,' said Madame Rosenberg, ' a
great day with us.   Captain Smith told me that you do not
celebrate it in the same manner as we do.   As to Gustle,' she
added in a whisper, ' he is a cunning little fellow, and only
half believes what he says, but Peppy has still all the innocent
faith of childhood.   I, for my own part, firmly believed that
Jesus gave me all my Christmas presents until I was nearly
ten years old; but children now are not so easily made to
believe what we say.'

' I don't quite like this idea,' said Hamilton.   ' Speaking in
this way seems to me to be irreverent, and must oblige you to
tell the children a number of untruths.'

' Ah, bah!' cried Madame Rosenberg, laughing; ' you are
all too particular in this respect.'

'I think,' said her husband, 'that as long as they *can* believe it they may, and when they cease to do so, they naturally think that it is God who has given us the means of gratifying their wishes, and so the gifts after all come from Him.'

'Oh, how I enjoy the idea of my Christmas-tree this year!' exclaimed Crescenz.

'Of course you do,' said Madame Rosenberg, 'as you know that you will get so many presents. The Major returns to-morrow in order to give you the gold chain and topaz orna·ments he promised, and perhaps he may bring something of his sister's for you from Nuremberg.'

'And what do you expect to get?' said Hamilton, turning to Hildegarde.

'I don't know,' she replied, looking with a smile towards her father, 'but I have a sort of idea that I shall get my first ball-dress and some books. Mamma has promised me a tree for myself, so perhaps I shall give you some of my bon-bons.'

'How I wish to-morrow were come!' cried Gustle.

'I wish dinner were on the table,' said Mr. Rosenberg, 'although we get nothing now but veal to eat, which my wife considers a sort of preservative against cholera.'

'You are just as much afraid of cholera as I am, Franz,' she said, and then added in a whisper to Hamilton, 'He laughs at me, but he takes drops and pills every night. While you were at Edelhof, we had some scenes which would perhaps have alarmed you. First, I thought I had got the cholera. Then the cook made herself ill by eating the apples which I had given her that the children might not ask for them. Then Peppy—'

'Dinner is on the table,' cried old Hans, merely putting his gray head into the room.

'That's right,' cried Mr. Rosenberg, 'and now I request that the cholera be no more named among us. A fine of six kreutzers for every time the word is said.'

'Oh, as to not saying the word cholera,' began his wife.

'A fine, a fine!' cried Mr. Rosenberg; 'the money shall be put into a box and given to the poor.'

'Oh dear!' exclaimed Crescenz, 'I must take great care, or all my pocket-money will be spent on the cho—'

Hildegarde's hand was on her mouth before the word was

pronounced.   The little boys clapped their hands, Hamilton
laughed, and Mr. Rosenberg said that he was sure that his
wife and Crescenz would prove themselves the most charitable
by their contributions.

The next morning Hamilton spent in choosing his presents;
he was for some time exceedingly puzzled, and wavered long
between books and bronze, glass and gold. At length he recollected having heard Hildegarde once say that she wished for
nothing in this world so much as a little watch, but that she
feared she never would be in possession of one.   This decided
at once his doubts, and, as the others interested him less, he
had soon completed his purchases with a large box of toys for
the children.

On his return, he found Fritz at home for the holidays ; he
was sitting at the drawing-room window with his brothers, all
three yawning and looking most melancholy. 'What o'clock is
it?' was the exclamation as he entered.

'Four o'clock,' said Hamilton; 'but why do you look so
sorrowful?'

'Two whole hours to wait,' sighed Fritz.

'Two long hours,' yawned Gustle.

'Two hours before the angel comes to light the candles and
ring the bell,' said Peppy.

'Pshaw! Mamma might light the candles at five o'clock ;
it will be dark enough, I am sure,' said Fritz in a whisper to
Hamilton.

'Where are your sisters?'

'They are with mamma, hanging the bonbons and fastening
the wax tapers on the trees, I suppose ; but when the presents
are being brought in, they will be sent off too, though
Crescenz thinks herself old enough to light the candles and do
everything.'

'In what room are they?'

'In the school-room, but you need not expect to get in; both
doors are locked.'

'What do you think the little child Jesus will send you?'
asked Peppy, approaching Hamilton confidentially. 'Did you,
too, put a list under your pillow, like Gustle?   Next year, if I
can write, I shall ask for so many things.   Trumpets, and
drums, and harlequins.   What do you think you will get?'

'Bonbons, probably.'

'And something else, too,' said Gustle, nodding his head.

'You promised not to tell,' cried Fritz, threateningly approaching his brother.

'Do n't you think,' cried Gustle boldly, 'that because you wear a uniform I am afraid of you. I 'll tell what I like—'

Fritz caught him by the collar, Gustle threw off his arms and a considerable scuffle ensued.

'Hildegarde has not finished the travelling bag,' shouted Gustle, angrily, ' and papa says it is just as well, as it was not a civil sort of present.'

At this moment Hildegarde and Crescenz entered the room.

'Turned out! turned out!' cried Fritz and Gustle, unanimously joining in the attack on their sisters.

Hildegarde smiled; Crescenz grew red, and observed, that everything was ready; there was nothing more to be done.

'Turned out all the same,' said Fritz, 'though you are nearly sixteen, and going to be married. Ha! ha! ha!'

'You are very ill-natured, Fritz, always talking of my going to be married, though you know I dislike its being spoken of.'

'Not you! Did n't I see you playing grand with Lina Berger, when I was at home last Sunday? You both seemed to consider Hildegarde beneath your notice, and she is worth a dozen such as you, and a hundred such as Lina Berger.'

'I was learning to make a new kind of purse.'

'As if I did not know that the purses were all made! No; you were talking of old Count Zedwitz, who was so ill that the Doctor had to visit him at his castle. I heard all you said, and understood you too, though you spoke French.'

Hildegarde became very pale, turned suddenly to her sister, and said, in a scarcely audible voice, 'Crescenz, you surely have not had the cruelty to explain to Lina Berger, or gratify her curiosity?'

'Lina suspected almost everything, and asked me so many questions that I did not know what to say. You forget that the Doctor was sent for, and that the old Count was ill from mental agitation : I dare say he told him everything.'

'What he left untold you have supplied. It is the last time I shall ever confide in you.'

'Do n't be angry, Hildegarde,' cried Crescenz, with tears in her eyes; 'surely it is no disgrace to you that such a man as Count Zedwitz wished to—'

'Silence!' cried Hildegarde, sternly, 'and never mention his name again.'

'Whew!' whistled Fritz; 'Hildegarde is in a passion. Look at her eyes! Fight it out, Cressy, and then make it up again!'

But Crescenz, seizing her sister's hands, faltered, 'Oh, Hildegarde, forgive me; I have done wrong, but you know that Lina always makes me do as she pleases. Forgive me—only say that you forgive me this time!'

'I forgive you,' said Hildegarde, 'but I never can trust you again.'

The sound of Madame Rosenberg's voice speaking to Major Stultz, in the adjoining room, made Crescenz spring up and follow the children, who ran to meet him.

Hamilton looked at Hildegarde, but did not utter a word. Every feature of her face expressed intense annoyance, as she slowly turned to the window, and leaned her head against it. The greetings in the next room were cordial; the children boisterously reminding Major Stultz of the presents which he had promised to bring from Nuremberg.

'They are come or coming,' he answered; 'I had them all packed up; and only think, the infant Christ met me on my way here, took them all from me, and promised to place them under the Christmas-tree this evening himself.'

'Well,' cried Fritz, 'I must say that this 24th of December is the very longest day in the whole year.'

'And yet it is generally supposed to be one of the shortest,' said Major Stultz, laughing; he advanced towards Hamilton and shook his hand.

'You are a new arrival as well as myself, I hear. All my people in Nuremberg tried to persuade me to stay there in order to be out of the way of the cholera, and they would perhaps have succeeded, had not my impatience to see Crescenz again been so great; besides, I hope to hurry matters by my presence, and that, in about a fortnight at furthest, Madame Rosenberg—'

'I have no objection, my dear Major; but Franz has taken it into his head that Crescenz ought to wait until after her birthday, and go to one ball with her sister before her marriage. We do not yet know when the first museum ball will take place.'

'Pooh, nonsense! She can go to the ball after our marriage just as well as before it;—eh, Crescenz?'

Crescenz smiled unmeaningly, and Hildegarde turned the conversation by telling her mother that the Hoffmanns had requested permission to come to the Christmas-tree in the evening, to see the presents.

'You have invited them, of course. The Bergers are coming too, and old Madame Lustig; I invited her because I intend to ask her to take charge of you all some day next month, as I have promised to visit my father at the iron-works; besides, she has taken a deal of trouble about work-women for Crescenz, and all that sort of thing; I expect her to offer to stay here to-night, and take care of the children until we return from the midnight mass. I hope, Major, you can remain awake until twelve o'clock.'

'In Crescenz's society I can answer for myself; otherwise I must say I consider nine o'clock as the most rational hour for retiring to rest.'

'But you will go with us to hear the high-mass at midnight, won't you?'

'Oh, of course.'

'Come, girls, assist me to arrange the tea-things; we will not, however, employ Mr. Hamilton to make tea this time, but he may help to carry the long table out of the next room for us.'

Hamilton and Major Stultz carried in the table, and every-thing was soon arranged for the expected guests.

CHAPTER XXIV.

THE CHRISTMAS-TREE AND MIDNIGHT MASS.

THE Hoffmanns arrived, and with them Count Raimund. Hamilton watched Hildegarde's reception of the latter, and, forgetting the three weeks which he had passed at Edelhof, was surprised to find that she met her cousin without the slightest embarrassment; he perceived, too, that Raimund had con-trived to ingratiate himself with Madame Rosenberg; she greeted him with a familiar nod as he entered, and the children's manner (no bad test of intimacy) convinced him that Raimund's visits must have been numerous during his absence.

Fritz smiled saucily, and raised his hand to his forehead in military salute ; Gustle, with his usual rudeness, seized his coat, and began to swing himself backwards and forwards by it ; while .Peppy took possession of the unbuckled sword, and rode round the room upon it, until his mother, irritated by the noise, forcibly took it from him, and, shoving him with his brother Gustle into the next room, declared that if they were so ill-behaved, the infant Christ would pass by their house, and they would get neither Christmas-boxes nor bonbons. ' Do you know,' she said, turning to Count Raimund, ' that Mr. Hamilton is quite shocked at my telling the children such stories ? he says—' But the entrance of the Bergers and Madame Lustig gave her thoughts another direction. The latter was a red-faced, stout, jolly-looking widow, of at least fifty years of age ; her nose was extremely thick, and her forehead extremely low ; she seemed very glad to see everybody, and made tremendously low curtseys in all directions. Madame Berger immediately took possession of Hamilton, saying that she had a lot of messages to deliver from Theodore Biedermann.

' I hope he intends to come here to-morrow ; I shall be glad to see him, and commence my studies again.'

' If we may believe him,' said Madame Berger, laughing, ' Hildegarde has made great progress during your absence : he says she writes German as well as French now, and that is saying a good deal : but he complained bitterly of the noise which the children made while he was giving his lessons, and regretted the tranquillity of your room.   Of course, I reminded him of the day I found you fencing !'

' Our lesson was over when you arrived; I assure you we were always exceedingly attentive and well behaved.'

' And Hildegarde sitting there reading, as if she were quite alone.   By the bye, have you begun your English studies with her again?'

' Not yet ; but I am quite ready, if she feel disposed.'

' You intend, perhaps, to enter the ranks of her adorers ?'

' I only aspire to being among her friends at present.'

' But I can tell you she will not be satisfied with anything less than the most unlimited devotion.'

' I dare say she will find people enough willing to comply with her demands.'

' Do you think so? If everything ends like the Zedwitz

affair, it would be better if she turned her mind to something rational. You know,' she added, lowering her voice confidentially, 'you know that at Seon, and also here, she encouraged Count Max Zedwitz in every possible manner; met him in the cloisters, and sat beside him at table every day at Seon, and here let him know every time she went on a walking party—'

'I think,' said Hamilton, 'you are rather mistaken in supposing that she—'

'Oh, I am not at all mistaken. She made him, in the most artful, deliberate manner, so in love, that he actually took it into his head to marry her. Such an idea, you know! and his father a Knight of St. George, and all that!'

'I was not aware that his father being a Knight of St. George could make any difference.'

'What! When they can prove sixteen noble generations on both sides! When Count Max can become a Knight of St. George whenever he pleases! When marrying a person who was not noble would deprive his children and children's children of the right of claiming an Order which can be obtained on no other terms!'

'Ah! I understand.'

'Hildegarde,' continued Madame Berger, 'was always desperately proud, and her greatest ambition is to marry some one of rank. A man must be a count or baron at least, before she thinks him worthy of her notice. Now, such a man as Count Zedwitz was just what she wished, and she persuaded him to write a letter making her a formal offer of his hand; this she exhibited in triumph to her father, who, however, had received about the same time from the old Count a most furious epistle, telling him that his son's fortune and rank entitled him to look for a wife among the first families in Germany—that a marriage with Mademoiselle Rosenberg now, or at any future period, was totally out of the question. He supposed that Mr. Rosenberg would not desire any other sort of connection for his daughter, and therefore had better join him in putting an end to any further intimacy. This, with a few other impertinences of the same description, made even good quiet Mr. Rosenberg outrageous, and he insisted on Hildegarde's refusing Count Max—if that may be called a refusal where marriage was a chimera!'

'Not so much a chimera as you imagine,' said Hamilton,

T

'for Zedwitz had procured the necessary security—as I happen to know, for he himself told me so at Edelhof—and his father cannot disinherit him.'

'So! Well, if that be the case, Mr. Rosenberg might as well have pocketed the affront—namely, the letter—and let his daughter marry him. Perhaps, after his anger has cooled, he may wish he had acted differently; or at least wish that he had left an opening for a renewal of the affair.'

'Hildegarde has made a great sacrifice to please her father,' observed Hamilton.

'Not so great as you suppose; for Crescenz told me she was quite as angry as her father about the letter.'

'Of that I have no doubt; but, nevertheless, the sacrifice was great.'

'You mean on account of his rank, or the fortune which his miserly old father is always increasing? Hildegarde has such an exalted idea of her beauty that she imagines she can find a Count Zedwitz whenever she pleases. Crescenz says she took the whole business very coolly, after the first burst of anger was over. When Count Zedwitz had left, her father as usual praised her conduct extravagantly, and, with tears in his eyes, thanked her for her compliance with his wishes. What do you think she did? Told him in her customary ungracious manner that she did not deserve either his praises or thanks, for that it cost her no great effort to dismiss Count Zedwitz!'

'Extraordinary—inexplicable girl!' murmured Hamilton.

'Not at all,' cried Madame Berger, colouring. 'Not at all; for, added to her pride, she is naturally violent and has strong passions. I am convinced she will never marry anyone who is not of rank, but it is both possible and probable that she may take it into her head to fall desperately in love with some one whom she considers beneath her. I have strong suspicion that she has done so, and that Theodore Biedermann is the favoured individual.'

'Biedermann!' repeated Hamilton, amazed.

'Yes, Theodore Biedermann; but with him she will find all her arts and vehemence useless. He scarcely even allows her to be good-looking.'

'I think you are altogether mistaken about her,' began Hamilton. 'I never perceived the slightest—'

'You have been absent more than three weeks,' said Madame Berger, interrupting him. 'If I have made a right guess,

Hildegarde will receive a severe lesson, which I hope may be of use to her!'

'How do you mean?'

'I mean that Theodore will treat her love with the scorn which it deserves.'

Hamilton shook his head, and laughed—rather ironically.

'How long are we to continue in the dark?' asked Mr. Rosenberg from the other end of the room. 'Pray, Babette, let us have at least a pair of candles, that we may not be blinded when your tree dazzles our astonished eyes!'

The candles were unwillingly granted, and Madame Rosenberg left the room mysteriously with Madame Lustig.

'Come here, boys!' cried Mr. Rosenberg. 'Let us take our station near the door, that we may enter the first.'

Doctor Berger came towards Hamilton, and began a conversation about the different ways of celebrating Christmas in different countries, and the habit of giving presents at that time or on New Year's Day, while Hamilton's eyes involuntarily strayed towards Hildegarde, who, sitting at the other end of the room with Count Raimund and Mademoiselle de Hoffmann, was speaking eagerly with the latter, all unconscious that her cousin was gazing at her with an emotion which his sanguine temperament betrayed in rapid changes of colour, although he did not seem to take any part in the conversation.

At length a bell was rung, and the door thrown open which led to the schoolroom. The children rushed forward with shouts of joy, followed somewhat tumultuously by their father and his guests. Hamilton was the last, and had more time to prepare his eyes for the blaze of light which they had to encounter. In the middle of the room was a large round table, on which was placed a tall fir-tree, hung with a profusion of bonbons, of the most varied colours, and sparkling like gems as they reflected the light of the hundreds of wax-tapers which were fastened on the dark green branches in their vicinity. On the top of the tree was a diminutive angel, dressed in gold and silver; in the moss which covered the root was a wax infant, surrounded by lambs. The table itself was heaped with toys of every description, from drawing-books and boxes for Fritz, to drums and trumpets for Peppy. There were two other tables with smaller trees, to which Madame Rosenberg conducted Hildegarde and Crescenz. The noise

T 2

was excessive; everyone spoke and nobody listened; old Hans and the cook were not forgotten; they stood with their Christmas-boxes and packets of gingerbread, laughing spectators, near the door.

Hamilton received a cigar-case from Madame Rosenberg, which she had worked most elaborately for him during his absence, and from Crescenz a scarlet purse, glittering with steel heads; this he particularly admired, while Major Stultz told him he was half inclined to be jealous, it was so much prettier than the one which she had made for him. The presents which Hamilton offered in return were accepted with the best grace imaginable, and he now amused himself watching Crescenz's face as she opened the various parcels and inspected the contents of the numerous boxes and caskets on her table. Some natural disappointment was at times legible, when instead of the expected jewels, respectable rows of forks and spoons met her eager eyes; but at length a case of red morocco disclosed such treasures, that Hamilton, after having listened to her expressions of rapture for a few minutes, moved towards Hildegarde, who stood before her table, turning over the leaves of some books which had been placed beside the expected ball-dress and wreath of roses.

'I have nothing to offer you,' she said, as he approached, 'nothing but some bonbons;' and she began to untie some from her tree as she spoke.

Hamilton took them, and, with unusual diffidence, presented the case containing the watch. She had no sooner opened it than she blushed excessively, and endeavoured to replace it in his hands;—failing in her endeavour, she put it on the table, saying, 'Mr. Hamilton, I cannot possibly accept anything of such value.'

'Your mother and sister have not pained me by making any difficulties,' he said, reproachfully.

'Then you must have given them something very different.'

This was undeniable, and Hamilton was silent. Mr. Rosenberg came to his daughter's assistance, to Hamilton's annoyance agreed with her, and 'hoped the watch was not definitively purchased.'

'Of course it is,' said Hamilton; 'I never dreamed of such a trifling thing being refused.'

'It is only trifling in size,' said Mr. Rosenberg, holding it towards his wife, who had joined them. 'Fortunately, howevei, a watch will be quite as useful to you as to Hildegarde, and you can use it yourself.'

'But, unfortunately, I have already two—one which I received from my uncle, and one from my mother,' said Hamilton, in a tone of great vexation.

'If that be the case,' said Madame Rosenberg, in a low voice, to her husband, 'perhaps—'

'Babette!' he exclaimed, 'you don't know the value of such a watch as this! Englishmen do not consider value as we do—I only thought if Mr. Hamilton had really bought it for Hildegarde, and cannot use it himself, it will be ungracious if she refuse it!'

'Very ungracious, indeed!' cried Hamilton, eagerly.

Madame Rosenberg drew her husband aside, and began a whispered discussion. Hildegarde leaned against her table in painful embarrassment, while Hamilton quietly drew from his pocket a long gold chain which he had not before ventured to produce, and attached it to the watch.

'I shall not be allowed to accept it.' said Hildegarde, shaking her head.

'You will,' said Hamilton.

He was right; her father, in a reluctant, half-annoyed manner, gave his consent. 'Thank you! Oh, thank you!' cried Hamilton, with such warmth that Madame Berger came skipping from the other side of the room, exclaiming, 'I positively must know what Hildegarde has given you; you seem so uncommonly pleased!'

'That is a secret,' said Hamilton, laughingly turning away, while she pursued him with guesses.

'It is not the half-finished travelling-bag, at all events, for you could not put that into your pocket. Nor is it a purse, or a cigar case. Oh, I know – a pair of slippers, or a portfolio worked on silk canvas? You may as well tell me, for I shall hear at all events from Crescenz! Have you seen what splendid ornaments the Major has given her? And the three bracelets? And then such loves of coffee-spoons as her godmother has sent her from Augsburg—and Cressy is so childish that she does not care in the least for spoons!'

Madame Rosenberg went round the room distributing bonbons and trifling presents, which sometimes caused great amusement when they contained an allusion to well-known foibles or peculiarities. The tapers on the tree were nearly burnt out. Mr. Rosenberg desired old Hans to extinguish them, and, having placed candles on the table, the children were left to play with their newly-acquired treasures, and the rest of the party adjourned to the drawing-room.

Everyone seemed happy excepting Raimund, who, with a flushed face and contracted brow, took the place assigned him beside his betrothed, and poured into her ear at intervals his discontented observations, her good-humoured, laughing answers appearing to act like fuel on the malevolent fire burning within him. At length he suddenly started from his chair, and, pleading business of importance at the barracks, he left the room with little ceremony, and negligently trailed his sword after him along the corridor.

'Well,' said Madame Rosenberg, as she carved a prettily-decorated cake into neat slices; 'well, we can do without him now that the Major is here to take his place at whist or taroc, but I cannot conceive what has put him out of temper!'

'Who is out of temper?' asked Madame de Hoffmann, who, as usual, had only heard the last words.

'Nobody, mamma,' answered her daughter, quickly. 'Poor Oscar!' she added, turning to Hildegarde; 'I believe he is annoyed at not being able to give me such presents as your sister has received from Major Stultz. It would have been better had we not come to your Christmas fête; I had no idea it would be so splendid.'

'That is a fancy which papa and mamma have in common,' answered Hildegarde; 'but Crescenz being a bride has made our Christmas unusually brilliant, I suppose. I dare say, however, your tree was very handsome. Why did you not invite us to see it?'

'Oscar did not wish it—and he forbid my saying that this bracelet was from him, when Crescenz showed me hers. I hope he does not think I expected or wished for such presents as she has received! By the bye, dear, do tell your mother not to make any remarks when he is a little odd at times, for mamma, who you know at first so wished and promoted our marriage, has lately been endeavouring, under all sorts of pretences, to break it off. If it were not for Oscar's father's extraordinary patience with her, I do believe our engagement would be at an end at once. I dare not tell her how sombre and dissatisfied he has become of late; she would attribute it to the supposed preference for you, which I cannot persuade her is an absurdity, although she begins to see that it is not returned on your part. Madame Berger has been endeavouring to enlighten her—'

'By telling her something very ill-natured of me, most probably,' said Hildegarde.

'She told us a long story about that good-natured Count Zedwitz this morning, of which I do not believe anything, excepting that he wished to marry you, and that his family perhaps were opposed to the match; and she ended by saying that you had taken a fancy to that young student, Biedermann, who is giving you lessons in German.'

'Just like her!' exclaimed Hildegarde, indignantly.

'Oscar, who was present, laughed excessively; indeed he was so amused at her chattering, that he became quite gay, and was more amiable than I have known him for a long time, until he came here and saw Crescenz's bracelets and that watch which Mr. Hamilton gave you.'

Hildegarde bent down her head to hide a blush of which she was but too conscious. 'I have no intention of keeping the watch longer than this evening,' she said, after a thoughtful pause; 'it is a much too valuable present to accept from a —a stranger—but that is of no consequence to Oscar, who might easily have found some better employment than laughing at me with Lina Berger!'

'My dear creature, he was laughing at her! He says she was jealous about that little Biedermann!'

'Pshaw!' cried Hildegarde, impatiently.

'Will you not at least tell me the true state of the case about Count Zedwitz?'

'Not now—not now, Marie—in fact I never wish to mention the subject again,' said Hildegarde, rising abruptly and going towards the door, which, however, she had no sooner reached, than she was recalled by her mother, and desired to carry round the cake to the expectant company, who had been already supplied with weak tea strongly perfumed with vanilla.

Hamilton was so occupied by Madame Berger, that he did not observe Hildegarde as she passed him; his companion's eyes followed her for some time furtively, and then turning to him, she observed with a laugh, 'Did you not see how Hildegarde's hand trembled as she offered us the cake? I am sure she has been in a passion, though I cannot imagine about what, as she has only been speaking with her friend Mademoiselle de Hoffmann!

Berger has become physician to the Hoffmanns ever since
your illness; they took such a fancy to him, and are so
civil to me, that I often visit them now. By the bye, that
Count Raimund is charming, but he does not seem to care in
the least for his betrothed, who certainly is not at all pretty.
She did not look half pleased at his talking so much to me
this morning! A little pug-faced person such as she is, has
no sort of right to be jealous, you know, and the sooner she
learns to bear his paying attentions to other women the better!'

'How kind of you to give her such a lesson!'

'I see, by your manner, that you think me ill-natured,' said
Madame Berger.

'Or malicious!' said Hamilton.

'Perhaps I was a little,' said Madame Berger, with an
affectation of repentive pensiveness. 'After all, Mademoiselle
de Hoffmann is a good-natured, a most inoffensive person!'

'She is sensible and well-informed too,' said Hamilton,
warmly.

'You take your opinion from Hildegarde, who you know
has no medium. Pray do n't ask her what she thinks of me,
that's all. See! she will not offer us any cake this time,
because we took no notice of her when she passed before.'

'I did not see her,' said Hamilton; 'I believe I was
admiring the ring which you told me had been given you by
one of the Doctor's patients.'

'But the ring was still on my finger, and perhaps she
thought—'

'What?' asked Hamilton, laughing, as he followed Hildegarde, and obtained the piece of cake which he requested.
Madame Lustig, who did not perceive his vicinity, observed to
Doctor Berger, 'Your wife is getting on at a great rate with
that young Englishman to-night!'

'It's a way she has,' he replied, shrugging his shoulders;
'opposition only makes her worse, so I generally pretend not
to see her. At all events, I have discovered long ago that
the Englishman's heart and thoughts are elsewhere, even
when he is apparently completely engrossed by my Lina.'

Hamilton looked at Hildegarde, and thought he perceived
something like a smile playing round the corners of her
mouth as she turned away—he walked slowly to his seat,
and began to eat his cake with an earnestness which soon
became offensive to his lively neighbour.

'I suppose she forbade your talking any more to me?' she observed, after some time.

'Do you mean Madame Lustig?'

'Madame Fiddlestick!—you know I mean Hildegarde.'

'She did not speak to me.'

'Perhaps a look was sufficient?'

'She did not look at me.'

'But you looked at her?'

'Undoubtedly—I like looking at her—and at you too, if you have no objection.'

'I see I shall be obliged to complain of you to the Doctor— and I can tell you he is horribly jealous at times!'

'How very considerate of him, to stand with his back to us all this time,' said Hamilton, laughing; 'one would almost think he did it on purpose! But see, the children are coming to say good-night, and the Hoffmanns seem to be going—'

'I suppose the Doctor will insist on my going too!' said Madame Berger. 'He has no sort of consideration for me, and the idea will never enter his old head that I should like to go to the midnight mass with you—all.'

The Doctor did insist, and the company departed together. Mr. Rosenberg at once declared his intention to go to bed; his wife said she would doze on the sofa until it was time to go to church; Major Stultz placed himself, as usual, beside Crescenz and her work-basket, and began a whispered conversation, which, however, in time perceptibly flagged, for Crescenz's fingers moved more quickly than her tongue—the monotony of his own voice on the otherwise unbroken stillness in the room naturally produced drowsiness, with which the Major long and valiantly combated—but it was in vain he endeavoured to sit bolt upright in his chair, occasionally staring wildly round him. After having made a succession of sleepy obeisances, of such profundity that Crescenz's demure smile almost verged into laughter, his arms sank at length heavily on his outspread legs, his head sought support on the uncomfortably low back of his chair, his jaw fell, and the long-drawn breathing degenerated into snores both loud and long.

Such influence had Hildegarde acquired over Hamilton, that the fear of incurring her displeasure prevented him from laughing aloud, or at first even looking up; after some time, however, pressing his lips firmly against his book, his eyes glanced over it with a mixed expression of mirth and curiosity, from one sister to the other. Crescenz seemed embarrassed, but there was not a particle of either dislike or impatience in the look which she bestowed on the sleeper. She bent towards her sister, and said in a whisper, 'If I could manage to put a sofa cushion on the back of the chair?'

'An excellent idea,' said Hildegarde, taking up one, and preparing to assist her.

'Give me the cushion, and do you move his head,' said Crescenz, timidly.

'No, dear; that is your office,' replied her sister, half laughing.

'But if he should wake?' cried Crescenz, drawing back.

'He will scarcely be angry,' said Hildegarde, approaching with the cushion.

Crescenz took it from her, and began to insinuate it between his head and the chair—her movements were so gentle, that she succeeded without awakening him—his mouth closed with a slight jerk, while uttering a grunt of sleepy satisfaction, as his chin dropped on his breast.

Nothing could be less attractive than Major Stultz's face at this moment, with his puffed-out crimson cheeks, and wrinkled double chin—but Crescenz saw him not; with a good-humoured smile she tried to arrange still better the supporting cushion, and then stood behind him with all the immoveable serenity of a Caryatide. Hildegarde walked to the window, and, holding her hands at each side of her temples, endeavoured to look out into the darkness. 'We shall have rain, I fear,' she observed to Hamilton, who had followed her.

He opened the window—it was a cold, cheerless night; the flickering lamps throwing unsteady gleams of light across the street.

'The weather is not very inviting,' said Hildegarde, drawing back into the warm room, with a slight shudder.

Hamilton leaned out for some time in silence, and then whispered, 'Who is that?' He pointed to the opposite side of the street, where a figure, muffled in a cloak, had been standing opposite the house, and now began to walk quickly away. 'Do you know who that was?'

'I think it was Count Zedwitz,' answered Hildegarde.

'You knew he was there? You came to the window to see him?'

' No,' said Hildegarde, quietly.

' Then how could you know him so directly?'

' I recognised the cloak he used to wear at Seon.'

' Ah—yes—true—poor fellow!' said Hamilton.

' How inclined you are to suspect me!' said Hildegarde, reproachfully.

' One might suspect, without blaming you, for giving Zedwitz a gleam of hope to lighten his despair!'

' I should blame myself—for it would be unpardonable coquetry.'

' Coquetry! when you really love him!'

' Love him!' repeated Hildegarde, hastily.—' No—yes—that is, I like him—I like him very much.'

At this moment all the church bells in Munich began simultaneously to send forth loud peals. Madame Rosenberg raised herself on her elbow, and exclaimed, ' What are you about, Hildegarde? Shut the window, and do n't let the cold night air into the room.'

Hamilton closed the window. When he looked round, he perceived Major Stultz with the sofa cushion on his knees, offering a profusion of thanks to Crescenz, who stood smiling beside him.

In a few minutes they were on their way to the Frauen Church. It was crowded to excess, and brilliantly lighted, chiefly by the number of wax tapers which had been brought with the prayer-books, and now burned brightly before each kneeling or sitting figure.

The music was excellent: and as Hamilton soon observed that extraordinary devotion was chiefly practised by the female part of the congregation who occupied the pews, and that those in his vicinity who stood in the aisle amused themselves by looking around them in all directions, he by degrees followed their example, and, his tall figure enabling him to overlook the sea of heads about him, he gratified his curiosity to the fullest extent. He observed that Crescenz's eyes stole not unfrequently over her prayer-book to bestow a furtive glance on him or on Major Stultz, who stood near her, but Hildegarde was immoveable—her profound devotion surprised him. She spoke so much less of religion than her sister, that he had come to the erroneous conclusion that she was less religious. The burning taper threw a strong light on her bent head and clasped hands; and as he suddenly recollected some remark of Zedwitz's about the Madonna-like expression of her regular features, he unconsciously turned to seek his friend, to ask him when and where he had so spoken. His astonishment was lost in emotion on perceiving that Zedwitz was actually not far distant from him, his whole appearance wild and disordered, his haggard eyes fixed on Hildegarde's motionless figure.   The service ended, she closed her book, and rose calmly, while Madame Rosenberg extinguished their three tapers and deposited them in her reticule. As the lights one after another disappeared there was a universal move towards the nearest doors.   Hamilton was about to follow the Rosenbergs, when he felt himself drawn in a contrary direction by a powerful arm, and Zedwitz whispered, ' One word before you go home ; ' and they were soon brought outside the church with the crowd.   It was raining torrents, and several persons attempted to return again into the aisle, while they despatched messengers or servants for umbrellas. The carriages rolled rapidly away in all directions, and Hamilton, in a few minutes, was walking with his friend under the leafless trees in the Promenade Platz.

'I am ill,' said Zedwitz, ' really ill—this sort of life is not to be endured—I shall get a fever, or go mad, if I remain here.'

'You do look ill,' said Hamilton, 'and change of air and scene might be of use to you—but is it advisable to remain out in this rain, if you are feverish ? '

' Certainly not advisable—but I cannot set out on my travels without taking leave of you.'

' Travels ! Where do you mean to go ? '

' To Paris—or Rome—or Athens—or Jerusalem.'

' Will your father consent ? '

' I think so.   To-morrow I intend to go to Lengheim and commence negotiations—I have determined on quitting the army, at all events ; for I have no fancy for country quarters, and as to remaining in Munich, the thing is impossible.   What are all my resolutions when I see her?—and see her I do—continually—although unseen by her, or any of her family.'

' You were in the street this evening, I know. She recognised your cloak immediately.'

' My cloak! Ah ! very true— I must have another.   Adieu, Hamilton ; I will not detain you longer in the rain—we shall scarcely meet again before I leave—'

'Write to me, then,' said Hamilton; 'I should like to know where you are to be found. Perhaps I may join you in spring.'

'You shall hear from me,' cried Zedwitz, seizing his hand, and holding it firmly. 'One word more—promise me to act honourably by Hildegarde, and not to take advantage of her isolated situation when her sister has left the house.'

'I have never thought of acting otherwise,' replied Hamilton, calmly.

'I suppose I must be satisfied with this answer,' said Zedwitz, wringing his friend's hand as he hurried away.

It was too late to overtake the Rosenbergs; nevertheless Hamilton walked quickly home. He was surprised to find the house-door open, the staircase perfectly dark, and several persons speaking at different distances upon it. On the third story, Walburg, who was endeavouring to open the door of the Rosenbergs' apartment, was loudly assuring her mistress that when she left the house with the umbrellas, the lamp had been burning—she had trimmed it on her way downstairs. Major Stultz and Crescenz were not far distant, for they occasionally laughed, and joined in the conversation. Hamilton began to grope his way along the passage; as he gained the foot of the stairs, Hildegarde, who had probably only reached the first landing-place, exclaimed—'Is that you, Mr. Hamilton? You had better wait until we have a light.'

Before he had time to speak, a voice quite close to her answered for him.

'You have startled me,' cried Hildegarde; 'I thought you were at the foot of the stairs.'

Not a little surprised to find himself in the presence of a second self, he stood still to hear what would follow.

'How did you happen to be separated from us?' asked Hildegarde.

'Met some friends at the church-door, and stopped to speak to them,' replied the voice in French.

'You must be completely wet!'

'Not at all.'

Hildegarde laughed.

'You do not believe me! Feel my arm—not even damp!'

A pause ensued—perhaps the arm was felt—the midnight representative lowered his voice and spoke eagerly. Hamilton advanced a few steps and heard the concluding words—

'Surely, surely, if you consider me a friend, you will let me know the true state of the case. Is it friendship for Mademoiselle de Hoffmann that makes you of late avoid your cousin with, I may say, such exaggerated care ?'

'Exaggerated care!' repeated Hildegarde, with evident surprise.

'Well, well—never mind that—we have no time to weigh words just now; but, tell me quickly, was it to please your father —or in anger—or indifference—that you refused Zedwitz?'

'Have you any right to question me in this imperious manner?' cried Hildegarde, moving quickly on.

'No,' replied the stranger, striding after her. 'No; and it is a great relief to my mind to find that I have not. I was beginning to fear you had a—misunderstood me - would think perhaps I had trifled with your feelings : in short, I thought you were unkind to your cousin and had refused Zedwitz from having formed expectations which can never be realised. Painful as it is to me to say so, I must nevertheless tell you that nothing was farther from my thoughts than—'

'Villain!' cried Hamilton, springing forward. 'How dare you take advantage of the darkness to traduce me in this manner! Who are you?'

A violent and silent struggle ensued, but the darkness was so complete, that the stranger contrived to free himself from Hamilton's grasp, bounded down the stairs, and closed the hall-door with such violence that the whole house shook. Hamilton would have followed, but Hildegarde's hand had grasped his arm, and she entreated him, almost breathlessly, to remain quiet.'

'Do not go after him ; it will serve no purpose whatever. I ought to have known,' she added, walking up the now lighted staircase, 'I ought to have felt at once that it was not you.'

'It would have shown extraordinary discernment on your part,' said Hamilton, 'for not only did he whisper, and choose a foreign language which he probably knows we often use, and in which you could not easily detect the difference of expression—but he also asked the very questions which I should have asked long ago, had I dared.'

Hildegarde hurried forward, while Madame Rosenberg called from the top of the stairs, 'You were determined to let us know that you had shut the house-door after you, Mr. Hamilton, but I was glad to hear that you were at home, for it is raining torrents ; and, as you have neither cloak nor umbrella, you must be wet to the skin.'

'I believe I am rather wet,' said Hamilton, composedly allowing himself to be felt by his attentive hostess.

'Take off these clothes directly, or you will get one of your English colds.'

'A cold never lasts more than a day or two here ; I am no longer afraid,' said Hamilton, following her into the drawing-room in the hope of speaking a few words more with Hildegarde, but Madame Rosenberg insisted on his going to bed, and, as a bribe, promised herself to bring him a piece of cake and a glass of wine.

The whole family were in the deepest sleep, and not a sound was heard in the house, when suddenly, about three o'clock in the morning the Rosenberg bell was rung long and violently. A great commotion ensued, and the cook, having been sent downstairs to open the house-door, returned in a minute or two, preceded by Count Zedwitz's servant, who, running towards Hamilton's room, seemed only able to pronounce the word Cholera !

'Who is that ?' cried Madame Rosenberg, drawing a little black shawl tightly over her shoulders and following him with hasty steps. 'What does the man mean ?'

She found him standing in Hamilton's room, explaining that his master had returned home ill about one o'clock ; that he had gradually become worse, and had now the cholera ; he had refused to send for Mr. Hamilton, but the doctor had said some one ought to be with him who could write to Edelhof directly.

'I must say I think it very unnecessary that Mr. Hamilton should be exposed to any danger of the kind,' interposed Madame Rosenberg. 'I dare say Count Zedwitz has other friends or relatives to whom he can apply.'

The man said he had not been long with Count Zedwitz— he had seen him more with Mr. Hamilton than anyone else— and then he looked inquiringly towards Hamilton, who, having sprung out of bed the moment the bell rang, had finished his hasty toilet undisturbed by the presence of Madame Rosenberg. His answer was throwing his cloak over his shoulders, and advancing towards the door.

'Surely you will not run the danger of getting the cholera for a mere acquaintance of yesterday !' she cried, anxiously placing herself before him.

'The danger is by no means so great as you suppose,' said Hamilton. 'I doubt the cholera being contagious.'

'But I do n't in the least doubt it,' cried Madame Rosenberg, 'and I feel quite sure you will bring it into our house. Have some consideration for us, if you have none for yourself!'

'The best plan will be not to return for a week or so,' said Hamilton. 'In fact, not until you let me know that you no longer fear infection. Hans must bring me whatever I require, as soon as it is daylight.'

'But he must not go backwards and forwards,' began Madame Rosenberg.

'Oh mamma!' exclaimed Hildegarde, who was standing in the passage; 'will you not speak to papa about it? I am sure—'

'Go to your bed!' cried her mother, interrupting her testily, 'and do n't stand shivering there until you get the cholera too: go to your bed. I assure you,' she said, turning apologetically to Hamilton, 'I assure you I do n't mean to be unkind; but I have a family, and it would be awful were the cholera to come amongst us. Suppose I were to lose Franz, or one of my boys, or even Hildegarde—'

'Do not speak of anything so dreadful,' cried Hamilton, instantly seizing the last idea. 'Nothing will induce me to return until even the shadow of danger be past.'

'And you do not think me ill-natured?'

'Not in the least.'

Hildegarde was at the door of her room as he was about to pass. He stopped to take leave.

'Use whatever precautions you can against infection,' she said, warmly returning the pressure of his hand; 'and,' she added, hurriedly, 'and do n't be angry when I send you the watch you gave me last night. Papa agrees with me in thinking such a present too valuable to be accepted from a—an acquaintance. Do n't forget to let me know, as often as you can, by old Hans, how Count Zedwitz is!'

Hamilton dropped her hand with an impatient jerk, and hurried from the house, without speaking another word.

CHAPTER XXV.

THE GARRET.

'Stop, sir! stop, if you please!' cried Zedwitz's servant to Hamilton, who was beginning to run down the street; 'Count Max is not in his own house—he is here, just opposite—at the brazier's.'

'At the brazier's!' exclaimed Hamilton. 'What induced him to go there?'

'Do n't know, sir,' replied the man; 'he has been lodging there the last week or two.'

'Lodging there!' repeated Hamilton, as he crossed the street—'that is an odd idea.'

The man opened the house-door with a latch-key, took up a candle which was burning on the staircase, and walked up to the very top of the house. They passed through two or three empty garrets before they reached the one which Zedwitz had chosen for his sleeping apartment. The furniture contrasted strangely with the whitewashed walls, sloping ceilings, and windows protruding from the roof. A handsome bedstead, wardrobe, sofa—several large arm-chairs—and tables covered with writing and drawing materials, found, with difficulty, place in the ill-shaped room. A stranger was sitting by the bed—he rose as Hamilton approached.

'So they have brought you here after all!' said Zedwitz. 'I hope at least you have been told the true state of the case that you know that I have the worst description of cholera?'

'You know I do not consider it infectious,' replied Hamilton, 'and if I can be of any use, I am prepared to remain with you.'

Zedwitz pressed his friend's hand.

'If I am not better in a few hours,' he said, slowly, 'that is, when there is no hope of my recovery, you may write to Edelhof. I do not wish to see any of my family—not even Agnes; coming from the country, they would be too liable to infection.'

'But,' said Hamilton, 'I do not see Doctor Berger—why have you not sent for him?'

'Because I am here, and not in my own house, and he tells

U

everything to his chattering wife, who relates with interest all she hears to whoever will listen to her.'

'But why *are* you here?' asked Hamilton.

A violent spasm put an end to the conversation; nor was it possible to renew it. Zedwitz hourly became worse, Hamilton proportionably anxious. At length he sent not only for Doctor Berger but also for his friend Biedermann, and when they had declared Zedwitz's case almost hopeless, he wrote, as he had been desired, to Edelhof, and employed his servant Hans as courier.

Late in the evening Zedwitz lay motionless from exhaustion. Biedermann had more than once held a feather under his nostrils to ascertain if he still breathed. Hamilton rose slowly from his station by the bed, and walked cautiously to one of the small windows. On reaching it, he stumbled over a large telescope which was pointed against a round hole, evidently cut in the window curtain;—he was about to remove the telescope to avoid a recurrence of the noise which he had just made, but, on second thoughts, he seated himself on a chair conveniently placed beside it, and applied his eye to the glass.

In a moment he was in Madame Rosenberg's drawing-room; the muslin curtains were not closed, and he saw the preparations for the rubber of whist—the candles and counters arranged, the entrance of the Hoffmanns, accompanied as usual by Raimund. The latter soon seated himself at the pianoforte, and, from the different movements of his person and hands, Hamilton tried to imagine the music to which the others (not the card-players) listened apparently with the most profound attention. He had heard so much from Hildegarde of her cousin's extraordinary talent for music, that he expected to see her immediately move towards him. Great was therefore his surprise, when she walked to the window most distant from him, and, drawing still farther aside the small transparent curtains, turned her face upwards, exactly in the direction of the window from which he was looking out. He could not any longer see her features, but he imagined her looking at him, and he involuntarily pushed back his chair. Did she know where he was? Or had she already known that Zedwitz was in her neighbourhood? He tried to remember if she had been in the habit of going to the window—he believed not—but he recollected her immediate recognition of Zedwitz in the street the evening before. The scene on the stairs recurred to his memory with extraordinary exactness, and a sudden suspicion, like a flash of lightning, made him see Zedwitz as his midnight traducer. He strode towards him; but the angry question died on his lips when he beheld the livid features convulsed with pain. Zedwitz was not only perfectly conscious of his dangerous state, but of everything passing around him; he glanced towards the window, and asked in a low, hoarse voice, ' Have you seen her?'

' Yes; she is looking at the windows of this room.'

A long silence ensued; and then Hamilton was called out of the room to speak to old Hans, who had been sent by Hildegarde to make inquiries about Zedwitz.

' How does Mademoiselle Hildegarde know that we are here?' asked Hamilton.

' She inquired of my son this morning when he was packing your clothes. She hopes that you will take care of yourself, and says you must be sure to smell this little silk thing, as it will save you from infection.'

Hamilton smiled as he received from the old man a *sachet* containing camphor.

'Perhaps you will give me a line for mademoiselle; she is very uneasy.'

Hamilton wrote a few lines with his pencil.

' She said,' remarked old Hans, ' you must hang it on your neck, and that she would pray for the wearer every morning in the Frauen Church.'

'Did she say that?' cried Hamilton, hastily. ' At what hour will she be there?'

' Between six and seven o'clock, I should think,' answered the man, with a look of intelligence by no means agreeable to Hamilton.

'You need not say that I asked you this question, Hans; it might prevent her from going to church, you know.'

'If you please, I can say you don't think of going to the Frauen Church to-morrow morning.'

' Say nothing at all, excepting that I am obliged to her, and shall wear the amulet,' replied Hamilton, abruptly turning away.

The Countess Zedwitz, her daughter, and son-in-law arrived before daybreak the next morning. They were at first so agitated that they could not speak a word; Zedwitz, on the contrary, was perfectly calm. 'I expected you, mother,' he said, kissing her hand; 'I knew you would come to me. but I wish that dear Agnes and Lengheim had remained at home. You must send them back in the course of the day.'

The Countess spoke long and earnestly with Doctor Berger, and then returned to her son's bedside. She told him that his father continued ill and confined to his room; that he wished to see him again; was ready to forget all cause of difference between them, and she hoped, as soon as he could be removed, he would return with her to Edelhof.

Zedwitz was too weak to discuss his plans for the future, although immediately after the arrival of his relations he had a change for the better. At five o'clock Doctor Berger gave hopes of his recovery, and an hour afterwards, Hamilton was on his way to the Frauen Church.

The rain had turned to sleet, and the sleet to snow since he had last been out. Large flakes now fell noiselessly around him: he saw them not—Hildegarde alone, and alternate fears that he should not, and hopes that he should, see her, occupied his thoughts.

There were not many people assembled; but the church is large, the altars numerous, and it was some time before he discovered the kneeling figure of her he sought. Walburg, with her shining braided hair, silver head-dress, and large market-basket on her arm, was standing in the aisle; *her* prayers seemed ended, for she gazed cheerfully around her, and even nodded occasionally to her basketed acquaintance as they passed. She immediately recognised Hamilton, and stooped down to whisper to Hildegarde, who instantly rose, and Hamilton saw her face suffused with blushes as she walked towards him. They left the church together, and Hildegarde's first words were, 'How pale and tired you look! I hope you are not ill.'

'Not in the least,' said Hamilton; and it did not escape his observation that her principal anxiety seemed about himself.

'You will be glad to hear that Zedwitz is better at last; we had no hope of his recovery until about an hour ago.'

'So I have already heard from Mr. Biedermann, who was so kind as to call just before I left home.'

'Ah! you have seen Biedermann?'

'Yes,' and then she added, after a pause, 'now that Count

Zedwitz's family have arrived, you ought to think of yourself, for even if you do not fear infection, you must remember that unusual fatigue is dangerous at present. You have been two nights without rest—you who require so much more sleep than anyone else, as I heard you tell mamma more than once.'

'That was only an excuse for my unpardonable laziness,' replied Hamilton, smiling; 'I intend to go to Havard's to dress and breakfast before I return to Zedwitz. Have you any message for him? I shall deliver it faithfully.'

'None, excepting my good wishes,' said Hildegarde, turning away. 'Walburg, you may now go to the grocer's—I can walk home alone. Good morning, Mr. Hamilton.'

Hamilton bowed gravely, waited with due propriety until Walburg was quite out of sight, and then ran after Hildegarde, and endeavoured, while still panting for breath, to thank her for the amulet, and her kind anxiety on his account.

'My father more than shares my anxiety about you,' she said, calmly; 'he was greatly distressed at hearing that mamma had in a manner banished you from our house. Should you get the cholera now, and not be properly taken care of, how could we write to your family? What could we say to them?'

'You mean in case of my death. By the bye, I never thought of that. Do not walk so fast—I want to speak to you, and I know you must dismiss me at the next turn. Should I die of cholera—'

'It is time enough to talk of death when you are ill,' said Hildegarde, hastily.

'No; it will be too late then. Twenty-four hours are more than enough to finish a man's life now. Will you undertake to write to my sister, and arrange my effects?'

'Are you joking?'

'Not in the least. You will find in a rosewood case a number of papers—a journal, in fact. These papers must be carefully sealed, and addressed to my sister. There is also a miniature—'

'I know—' said Hildegarde.

'How do you know?' cried Hamilton, stooping forwards to catch a glimpse of her features; 'how do you know anything about that?'

'Lina Berger examined your dressing-case one evening when she was in your room. Crescenz was present, and naturally told me of the miniature—I often reminded her of it.'

'Indeed!   And for what purpose?'

'To prevent her forgetting that you had not even a heart to bestow on her.'

'You were right.   But to return to the miniature: the original possesses, indeed, a large portion of my affection—' Hamilton stopped; he had flattered himself that his companion would, in some way, betray feelings either of jealousy or curiosity, but she walked on steadily without looking at him, and when he paused, she observed, 'You must make haste: we are just at the corner; you need not tell me about the original, but say what you wish me to do with the picture.'

'Should we never meet again, unfeeling girl,' said Hamilton, half laughing, 'you must send the picture to my father, for it is my sister Helen's portrait.'

As he spoke, they had reached the place where he knew he must leave her. She stopped, and said quickly, 'Mr. Hamilton, I have in this instance done you great injustice; I thought your heart was bestowed on the original of the miniature. Without this explanation, I should certainly have regarded your conduct towards us as unpardonably heart—less!'

'Not quite,' said Hamilton lightly; 'I really had a heart at my disposal some time ago; younger sons are allowed to have hearts in England, and to give them away as they please; few people there think it worth while to accept so worthless a thing as a heart alone.   In Germany the same rational idea seems to prevail—'

'Not so,' cried Hildegarde, warmly; 'a heart is always of value—must be of value to everyone, especially to every woman.'

'You are making a collection of such valuables, I think,' said Hamilton. 'Your cousin's has been forced upon you; Zedwitz's, to say the least, you tacitly accepted; what you intend to do with mine—'

'I must go home now,' said Hildegarde, glancing uneasily down the street: 'it may he remarked if I stand here so long with you—'

'Do not be alarmed,' said Hamilton, smiling; 'I have no intention of ever again favouring you with avowals of affection as absurd as useless.   You were quite right not to listen to me, but you must have the kindness not to listen to my midnight representatives either. Such men must not speak for me.'

'Do not think about that any more,' said Hildegarde. 'I dislike the recollection of my stupidity.'

'If I only knew who it was,' said Hamilton, contracting his brows.

'You possibly suspect Oscar; but when I referred to the subject yesterday evening, he did not in the least understand what I meant, and afterwards denied having seen me from the time I had received my Christmas presents.'

'So, then, it was Zedwitz,' said Hamilton, musingly. 'I am sorry for it; our friendship is at an end.'

'Oh, no,' cried Hildegarde: 'perhaps it was not Count Zedwitz; it is not like him to act so; besides, he never speaks French with me, and—and his manners are always so respectful. Oh, no, I do not think—I am quite sure it could not have been Count Zedwitz.'

'How can you, who are always so rational and candid, talk so? You know it must have been one or the other; no one else could have any motive for asking those questions; I only wish—'

'And I wish,' said Hildegarde, interrupting him, 'I wish you would not either think or speak again about this disagreeable affair. Oscar has denied knowing anything about it; therefore you have no pretence to seek a quarrel with him. You have scarcely a right on suspicion to withdraw your friendship from Count Zedwitz.'

'On suspicion! No: but I shall certainly ask him if he were on the stairs of your house on Christmas-eve.'

'He will say that he was not.'

'If he do, I shall believe him.'

'And I also,' said Hildegarde, moving onwards.

'You think highly of Zedwitz?'

'Most highly. I have already told you so.'

'And of your cousin?'

Hildegarde was silent.

'And yet you continue intimate with him, and tolerate his rhapsodies!'

'He is my cousin—he loves me—and—if you must know all, I—I fear him now!'

'You!—you fear him?'

'Yes; I fear his love and his jealousy—his frightful bursts

of passion—his horrible threats. But, look, there is Walburg just now coming home; I must enter the house before
her. Adieu!'

The Zedwitzes were profuse in their thanks to Hamilton, and
used all their eloquence to induce him to return with them to
Edelhof. No argument, however, could prevail on him to quit
Munich. Before Zedwitz left, he gave Hamilton the assurance
that he had not been in the Rosenbergs' house on Christmas-
eve. 'If you require proof,' he added, 'I can give it. You
may remember I told you that I felt very ill. Could a man in
the state I was then, think of such mummeries? Besides, when
we parted, I went home, that is, to our house in —— Street,
changed my clothes, which were wet, and drank some wine.
You can inquire of our old housekeeper.'

'It is quite unnecessary,' said Hamilton. 'I should rather
apologise for having thought you capable of such conduct,
even in joke. Hildegarde did not for a moment suspect you,
although she had heard her cousin's denial.'

'Excellent girl!—she did me but justice. Much as I
should like to know her feelings towards me, I never, even if
I had an opportunity, would resort to such means of obtaining
information.'

The carriage rolled to the door. Hamilton assisted his
friend down the narrow staircase. 'What do you mean to do
with yourself until you are allowed to return to the Rosenbergs?' asked the latter, as he pressed heavily on his arm.

'I shall buy another horse, and a sledge. If the snow last,
I rather expect some amusement.'

Arrived in the street, Zedwitz was obliged to lean exhausted
against the house. He was with great difficulty lifted into the
carriage, and, as he sank back in the corner, his languid eyes
turned slowly to the windows of the opposite house. Crescenz
and her brothers were looking out, Hildegarde was not visible;
he slightly touched his cap, and turned away. His mother
and sister were making a final effort to induce Hamilton to remove to Edelhof or Lengheim. Zedwitz saw the uselessness
of their endeavours, and calling Hamilton to his side, whispered,
'If you should be ill, remember your promise to send for me
directly.' He then placed his hands on his shoulders, and
kissed him on both sides of his face. Completely abashed by
this proceeding, Hamilton blushed excessively, and stammered
a few incoherent words as the carriage drove off.

CHAPTER XXVI.

THE DISCUSSION.

'Oh, Hildegarde!' cried Crescenz, pushing back her work-table in order to be able to see better from the window; 'Oh, Hildegarde—look, look! There is Mr. Hamilton driving such a beautiful sledge up our street; and the horses are prancing and dancing, and shaking their red tassels and silver bells! Oh, how pretty! How I wish he would take me out with him!'

'Babette!' cried Mr. Rosenberg from the next room, 'Mr. Hamilton is just passing our house, and seems in perfect health. How long do you mean his quarantine to last?'

'I have no objection to his returning to-morrow,' answered Madame Rosenberg, who was arranging one of the chests of drawers in the drawing-room. 'You may tell him so, if you like, this afternoon.'

'Not I!' said her husband. 'You banished him, and you may recall him too. If, however, you really wish him to return, you had better make haste, for he seems to be amusing himself very well at Havard's, and is always surrounded by a number of acquaintance. I must confess I miss him more than I expected.'

'I wish him to return, of course,' said Madame Rosenberg, pushing in the drawers with some violence; 'but for another week or so, I must say I have no objection to his remaining where he is. I can hardly believe that he will escape the cholera—he is so careless! Always going out without a cloak, and being wet through—wearing thin boots and no flannel waistcoat! Heating his stove and opening his windows. Running out in the middle of the night every time that there is an alarm about a house on fire. What can one expect from such doings?'

'As you please, my dear,' said Mr. Rosenberg, contentedly, 'You know I never had any fancy for lodgers in our house; he is the first I have been able to tolerate. I think, however, you should not allow him to pay for his apartments here and at Havard's too!'

'Oh, of course not,' said his wife; 'though I am sure that is the very last thing he would think about—he is excessively careless about money.'

'So it seems—and I suspect he is spending more than is necessary at present.   He gives suppers every night.'

'I do n't believe that!'

'You may believe it—or rather believe me, for I supped with him after the theatre yesterday.'

'You!'

'Yes.   There were also three young Englishmen, and that little Lieutenant Mayer, who goes everywhere, playing cards and making himself agreeable.'

'Lieutenant Mayer!   How did Mr. Hamilton become acquainted with him?'

'Oddly enough : he met him in the English Gardens one evening before he went to Seon, and either knocked him down or was knocked down by him—I really forget which ; but a fact it is that Hamilton invited him to supper without remembering his name, and they insisted on my introducing them formally to each other.'

'Well to be sure!' exclaimed Madame Rosenberg.   'If ever I heard of such a thing!'

'He wishes exceedingly to return to us,' continued her husband ; 'he said so when I was leaving—indeed, he gave me to understand that his guests were merely invited to prevent him from thinking too much of our quiet household!'

'Oh, if that be the case, I consider it a sort of duty to bring him back here, and out of the way of temptation,' said Madame Rosenberg, joining her husband, and leaving Hildegarde and Crescenz alone.

They had been interested auditors of this conversation as they sat together working.   'How I like him for inviting that Lieutenant Mayer to supper without knowing his name! Do n't you?   It is so English!   I am very glad he is coming back to us!'

'His return ought to be a matter of indifference to you,' said Hildegarde, without looking up.

'But I cannot be so indifferent as you are!' cried Crescenz, petulantly.   'And though I am going to be married to Major Stultz, Lina Berger says that Mr. Hamilton may still be "*mein Schatz*" just the same, and no harm!'

'Lina Berger talks great nonsense,' said Hildegarde, with heightened colour.   'This is, however, worse than nonsense!'

'And yet she could give you some good advice, if you

chose to listen to her,' observed Crescenz, nodding her head sagaciously.

'I do not require any advice from a person I so thoroughly dislike and despise.'

'Oh, that's just the same with her; she says she always disliked you, but she despises you now that you have fallen in love with Theodore Biedermann!'

'What an absurd idea!' said Hildegarde, contemptuously. 'Marie de Hoffmann has already told me something of that kind.'

'Lina told me long ago that Mr. Biedermann did not think you at all handsome!'

'That I think very probable,' said Hildegarde.

'And she says now, he is just the person to teach you not to fall in love without provocation!'

'I think he is more likely to teach me to write German grammatically!' answered Hildegarde, with a careless laugh.

'And do you really not care for anybody, and you a whole year older than I am!' exclaimed Crescenz, with unfeigned astonishment. 'Lina first thought you liked Mr. Hamilton, until I assured her you hated him. Then she said you had taken a wild kind of fancy to our cousin Oscar. Then she thought you were pretending to like Count Zedwitz on account of his rank and—'

'I am sure I ought to be obliged to you, Crescenz, for discussing my affairs in this manner with my greatest enemy,' said Hildegarde indignantly; 'but,' she added, pushing back her chair, 'there is no use talking to you!'

'I am quite prepared for remarks of this kind,' said Crescenz, with a ludicrous imitation of Hildegarde's natural dignity of manner; 'Lina says there is no bearing you since I have been engaged to be married!'

'So,' said Hildegarde, throwing down her work—'but I do not quite understand the—'

'Oh, it is easily understood—you are older, and think you ought to have been the first.'

'This is really too absurd,' cried Hildegarde, laughing good-humouredly.

'Oh, laugh as much as you please—but since we have returned from Seon, you have become quite a different person!'

'Did Lina put that into your head also?' asked Hildegarde, quickly.

'Oh, no,' cried Crescenz, while her eyes filled with tears, 'I did not require Lina to point that out to me. Silly as you think me—I can feel—you are quite changed.'

Hildegarde bit her lip—walked to the window—came hastily back again, and throwing her arms round her sister, kissed her cheek, while she whispered, 'Dear girl, I am not in the least changed in my affection for you; but you know yourself that every word I speak to you is repeated to Lina Berger; and how can you expect me to trust you?'

'But,' said Crescenz, looking up, 'but you know I often repeated what you said when we were at school, and you only scolded a little sometimes. Now, you scarcely ever get into a passion, and are so cold, and so careful what you say—just like Mademoiselle Hortense!'

'Like Mademoiselle Hortense?'

'Oh, I don't mean that you have her thick nose, and high shoulders,' said Crescenz, smiling through her tears, 'but you scarcely take any notice of me, and are always talking of books with Mr. Hamilton!'

Hildegarde was silent.

'And then you speak English now more than French, and Lina says—'

'Don't tell me what she says; don't name her to me again,' cried Hildegarde, impatiently.

'No—no, I won't,' said Crescenz, alarmed.

'Odious person!' continued Hildegarde, turning away, 'I can never forgive her for having embittered the last weeks we shall probably ever spend together.'

'Well,' said Crescenz, drying her eyes, 'at all events we shall get on better after my marriage. You know you must have a sort of respect for me then.'

Hildegarde turned round to see if her sister were joking; but Crescenz looked perfectly serious.

'Respect is due to married persons,' she continued, neatly folding up the work which her sister had thrown on the chair. 'Mamma says so—and then, you know, I shall be quite another sort of person when I am the mother of a family—'

Hildegarde laughed unrestrainedly.

'Madame Lustig says I may have a dozen children!—They shall all have pretty names—not one of them shall be called Blazius, that I am determined—they shall be Albert, Maximilian, Ferdinand, Adolph, Philibert.'

'Philibert is not a pretty name,' said Hildegarde, interrupting her merrily.

'Do n't you think so? Well, we can choose another—Conrad,
for instance?'

'Or Oscar?'

'Oh, no, because I should imagine a sort of resemblance to
Cousin Oscar, and I don't—quite—like him—that is, not very
much, though he is my cousin. He is very cross sometimes,
indeed, almost always to your friend Marie—but oh! Hildegarde, one very pretty name we have forgotten, and of a very
handsome person too—Alfred! Mr. Hamilton, you know—is
not Alfred a pretty name?'

'Yes.'

'And he is certainly handsome? Even you must allow that?'

Hildegarde was spared the answer, for Madame Rosenberg
entered the room, and having discovered that the tip of
Crescenz's little nose was red, immediately declared it was
from want of exercise, and sent both sisters to play at battle-
dore and shuttlecock in the nursery with their brothers.

She then despatched a message to Hamilton, which caused
his immediate return to her house.

CHAPTER XXVII.

THE SLEDGE.

HAMILTON's sledge was the subject of discussion the very first
evening of his return—he, of course, proposed their making
use of it, and assured Madame Rosenberg she might trust
herself and her daughters to his care without fear.

'Oh dear—I'm sure I should not be in the least afraid,'
cried Crescenz.

'And yet you are the greatest coward in the house,' said her
mother. 'I am sure you will scream so often that Mr. Hamilton will refuse to take you a second time.'

'Allow me to observe,' said Major Stultz, his face increasing
in redness as he spoke—'and I conceive I have some right to
give an opinion on the subject—that I totally disapprove of
Crescenz going out in Mr. Hamilton's sledge.'

'Are you afraid to trust her to my care?' asked Hamilton,
laughing.

Major Stultz rapped on the table with his fingers, and looked significantly towards Madame Rosenberg.

'You surely do not think I shall be so awkward as to upset the sledge?' continued Hamilton.

'I have the highest opinion of you, Mr. Hamilton, the highest opinion —where horses are concerned,' began Major Stultz, with some embarrassment, while Hamilton rubbed his upper lip to hide a smile. 'Had you a carriage instead of a sledge, the case would be different, and I—but I see you understand me.'

'Not in the least,' said Hamilton, looking up in unfeigned astonishment.

'Crescenz does, however,' said Major Stultz, turning to his betrothed, whose face was suffused with blushes.

Madame Rosenberg had been occupied with little Peppy— she was arranging the broken harness of a wooden cart-horse, which had been dragged somewhat roughly round the room. She now looked up, and observed in a low voice, and with a sort of expressive wink at Major Stultz, 'Mr. Hamilton, being an Englishman, knows nothing about sledging rights. Keep your own counsel, and he will never think of claiming it.'

'He may claim it from whoever he pleases,' cried Major Stultz, blun'ly; 'but not from my Crescenz, that's all!'

'What is it—what is my right? What may I claim?' asked Hamilton, quickly.

No one seemed disposed to explain, until at length Madame Rosenberg replied, laughing, 'Neither more nor less than a kiss, which is a sort of old privilege allowed a gentleman if he drive a lady in a sledge! Now, I know that from me you will not claim it, because I am neither young nor pretty—nor from Hildegarde, because you don't like her well enough—nor from Crescenz because she is betrothed. So really, Major, I see no reason for making such a serious face.'

'I intend to drive Crescenz myself in a sledge,' said Major Stultz; 'I take it for granted she will enjoy it quite as much with me as with Mr. Hamilton.'

Crescenz bent her head over her work, and said not a word.

A heavy fall of snow during the night, and a clear blue sky the next day, proved most propitious : and after dinner, the sledge was brought to the door. Madame Rosenberg and her son Gustle were carefully assisted by Hamilton into the light, fantastic vehicle, while Hans, not unnecessarily, held the horses' heads. No sooner were the spirited animals released, than they bounded forward with a vehemence which caused Madame Rosenberg to utter an only half-suppressed scream, while the child, participating in his mother's alarm, seized Hamilton's arm, and clung to it with all his strength. One of the horses reared dangerously. 'Gustle, you must not touch my arm, or the reins!' cried Hamilton, shaking him off. 'They will be quiet in a moment,' he added to Madame Rosenberg, who had closed her eyes and compressed her lips as if prepared for the worst; but notwithstanding all his endeavours, the horses pranced and danced and bounded, to the great admiration of the passers-by, while poor Madame Rosenberg sat in a sort of agony. She did not speak a word until they had reached the Nymphenburg road, but there every sledge they met increased her terrors, and at length she spoke,—'Oh, dear, good, excellent Mr. Hamilton—turn back and take me home again—I know you are too good-natured to enjoy my anxiety —if it were only for Gustle's sake, see—Oh!—Ah! The child is frightened to death almost, and no wonder! I declare if I had not come out in my slippers, I would walk home—Oh, pray stop—turn—before we meet that sledge coming towards us. When your horses hear the bells of the other sledges, they get quite wild! Dear, kind Mr. Hamilton, I shall love you all my life if you will only take us home again.'

Gustle, shocked by his mother's unwonted humility of manner, and imagining himself in the most imminent danger, commenced roaring with all his might, and Hamilton turned his horses, while assuring Madame Rosenberg they were the gentlest animals in the world, and it was only the fine weather that had put them in spirits.

On their return they found a respectable-looking hackney coach placed on a sledge waiting at the door. Crescenz, her little brother Peppy, and Major Stultz, were preparing to enter it.

'I will go with you,' cried Madame Rosenberg, joining them. 'Gustle must not lose his drive—Mr. Hamilton's horses are much too wild for me!'

'I thought as much,' said Major Stultz, with evident satisfaction.

'Am I permitted to ask Mademoiselle Hildegarde to go with me?' asked Hamilton.

'Yes: but you must tell her how your horses have frightened

me, and you must promise to drive on the Nymphenburg road, where we can see you, and you must not go farther than the palace and back again.'

'Agreed,' said Hamilton.

'And you must on no account quit the sledge or enter the inn.'

'Of course not.'

Hildegarde was surprised to see him so soon again. He explained, and asked her if she were afraid to trust herself to his care.

'No; I believe you drive well.'

'Rather—but I have never had a sledge until now—and they seem slippery concerns.'

'I have heard that being thrown out of one is more uncomfortable than dangerous,' said Hildegarde, laughing, as she entered her room to dress herself.

The horses pawed the half-frozen snow, and were even more impatient than before—but this time no hand was laid on his arm, no stifled scream vexed his ear. Hildegarde admired the silver serpents which ornamented the front of the sledge—the silver bells which glittered on the harness, and the gay scarlet tassels which the horses flung in the air with every movement—the blue sky—the dazzling snow; and Hamilton, perfectly reassured, was soon able to prove to his horses that he no longer feared to correct them.

In a few minutes, they had overtaken and passed the hackney sledge containing the rest of the party, nor was it long before they reached Nymphenburg.

'What shall we do now?' said Hamilton; 'I promised your mother not to go farther than the palace. I am sure the others are not yet half way here. Must we go home so soon?'

'Drive round and round this inclosure until they come; it will amuse us, and exercise the horses,' replied Hildegarde.

They drove round several times, each time quicker than the preceding, while Hans, with extraordinary energy, cracked the pliant leather whip peculiar to sledges. Several people collected to look on, among others a carter, with an empty waggon. One of his horses was young and unbroken; as the sledge passed, it plunged, and rattled its heavy harness; Hamilton's horses shied, dashed into the deep snow heaped up beside the road, upset the sledge, and then struggled violently to make themselves free. Hamilton still contrived to hold the reins until his servant came to his assistance, and then rushed to Hildegarde, who had been thrown to some distance. A crowd had gathered round her.

'Hildegarde, dearest, are you hurt?' he asked, anxiously.

'Not in the least,' she answered, laughing, while she shook the snow from her cloak; 'not in the least! I was thrown at the first jerk into the fresh snow, and every time I attempted to get up, I fell back again, until I received assistance, for which I thank you,' she said, turning to some strangers; and then she added hurriedly to Hamilton, 'Let us go home.'

The sledge had been easily set to rights, and they once more drove off at a furious pace.

'As wild a young pair as ever I saw,' observed an officer to his wife, as they turned towards the inn to rest, and refresh themselves with a cup of coffee.

'We have disobeyed your mother,' began Hamilton, 'unintentionally indeed, but—'

'How do you mean?'

'Why, she forbade our leaving the sledge on any account whatever,' said Hamilton, laughing. 'Now, I don't in the least mind being lectured by her, but I confess I do not enjoy the idea of Major Stultz's triumph. How unmercifully I shall be laughed at!'

'I don't see any necessity for saying anything about the matter,' said Hildegarde; 'if you choose to be silent, I shall never refer to the subject. In fact, I was altogether to blame; it was my proposition driving round that inclosure, and it was I who encouraged you to worry the horses, in order to show you that I was not afraid of them.'

'The carter and his young horse were to blame,' said Hamilton; 'he ought not to have come so close to us. But I should be very glad to escape Major Stultz's heavy raillery. Do you hear, Hans?—you fell out of the sledge in your sleep; not even to your father must you say otherwise than that my horses are as steady as oxen. Do you understand?'

'Yes, sir.'

Perhaps the fear of being questioned induced Hamilton, when returning, to pass the others so quickly that he did not hear their cries to him to stop, and return to Nymphenburg. Perhaps the wish to be once more alone with his companion for half an hour, made him urge his horses to their hardest

x

trot ; if the latter had been his object, his annoyance may be conceived, when on reaching home, just as they had begun to ascend the stairs together, gaily laughing, he perceived Count Raimund standing above them. He had seen their arrival from the Hoffmanns' window, and rushed out under pretence of a joke, but in reality to waylay them. Hamilton could not conceal his vexation ; he frowned, and muttered the words, 'everlasting bore !' which made Hildegarde's countenance change in a manner that irritated her cousin. 'Hildegarde, I must speak to you,' he began, abruptly.

'Speak on,' she said, continuing to ascend the stairs.

'I must ask you a question—and—we must be alone.'

'You are peremptory—ask differently, and per—haps I may comply with your request.'

Count Raimund grasped—not gently—his cousin's arm— she turned round—became very pale—and requested Hamilton in a low voice to go up stairs—she would follow him directly.

'Do you really wish me to go ?' he asked, hesitatingly. 'Do you remain willingly with your cousin ? Remember,' he added, indignantly, 'the nearest relationship cannot authorise such—'

Count Raimund made a violent gesture—Hildegarde placed herself between them, and said, hurriedly, 'I—I do wish to speak to Oscar,' and Hamilton instantly left them.

Directly he was gone, her manner totally changed. 'Your question, Oscar, and quickly !' she said, haughtily. 'I have no intention of remaining on the cold staircase more than a few minutes.'

'Gently, gently, Hildegarde. You think the danger is over now your treasure is out of sight—but you see how ready he is to quarrel, with all his coolness—be careful, or—'

'Your question,' said Hildegarde, leaning against the wall with a sigh of resignation.

'Did this a—this Englishman condescend to claim his sledg-ing right from you ?'

'No.'

'Did not think it worth while !' said Raimund, sneeringly.

'Very probably. Have you anything else to observe ?'

'Yes, false girl !' cried Raimund, vehemently ;' 'you know this is not the case—you know he loves you—his every look betrays him—but by Heaven, if you grant him what I, your nearest relative, have so long implored in vain—his life shall be the forfeit—'

'Always threatening !' exclaimed Hildegarde, indignantly.

'It is my only means to obtain a moment's attention from you. He little knows that to his influence alone I am indebted for every favour—for every common civility, I receive from you !'

'He little knows that, indeed !' said Hildegarde, bitterly ; ' were he aware of it, he would soon release me from my thraldom.'

'Tell him—tell him. I desire nothing more than that matters should come to extremities! You look incredulous, Hildegarde. Hear me and judge for yourself. Pecuniary difficulties have often made men put an end to their existence —and you know what mine are! Add to this, a violent and hopeless love, and the certainty of being obliged in a week or ten days to marry a person for whom I never can feel a particle of either affection or admiration !'

'But who is worthy of both !' cried Hildegarde.

'Perhaps so — I wish Marie every happiness with another. For myself,' he added, folding his arms and looking musingly down the stairs, 'I wish to die, to die soon—and quickly—but not by my own hand. They say it is a fearful crime to commit suicide ! Were I certain of being shot by Hamilton, I should not hesitate—he must then leave Bavaria, and you, for ever—but the chances are, I should shoot him—I hate him so intensely, that the temptation would be more than I could resist—'

'Horrible!' cried Hildegarde, covering her face with her hands. 'How can you deliberately think of committing murder?'

'That's it—that's what I mean ; you see, Hildegarde, death is my only resource, but I shudder at the thought of staining my hands with other blood than my own. The double crime is more than I can resolve upon.'

'Ah, I see now,' she said, forcing a smile ; ' you àre only trying to frighten me, as you have often done before.'

He shook his head, and continued: 'As long as I had the faintest hope of obtaining your affection, I was a different being ; you might have made of me what you pleased—and I should have gained your love but for this supercilious Englishman, for you were disposed to like me at first.'

' As a relation—yes—'

More than that—much more, Hildegarde,' cried Raimund, vehemently.

' And had I loved you more than as a cousin, what purpose would it have served? Our relationship is too near to permit of a marriage.'

' Nothing easier than obtaining a dispensation,' cried Raimund, eagerly, and in a moment losing all violence of manner and voice.

' But we are both without fortune,' said Hildegarde.

' I could quit the army. There are many situations which I could obtain. We should be poor, indeed, very poor; but what is poverty when—— Oh, Hildegarde! has this consideration caused your coldness? or are you—— What a fool I am!' he exclaimed, passionately. ' She treats me like a madman from whom she would escape without witnessing a paroxysm! Go! You have tortured me—deliberately—most horribly. Go! I would hate you if I could!'

Hildegarde began slowly to ascend the stairs; as she turned to the next flight an unusual sound made her look downwards, and she perceived her cousin vainly endeavouring to suppress the fearful emotion which agitated his whole frame. A man's tears are a phenomenon too rare to be seen unmoved. Hildegarde stopped and held out her hand. ' Oscar, dear Oscar, what I said was not in heartlessness, but in the hope of convincing you of the utter impossibility of our ever being more to each other than cousins. Think of your solemn engagement to Marie—of your promises to your father. Remember that no situation you could ever obtain would enable you to pay your debts!'

· True—most true. I was dreaming just now,' said Raimund, with forced composure. ' I am sorry to have kept you so long here—in the cold. Go! Mr. Hamilton is waiting for you!'

' He is not. I shall most probably not see him until evening.'

Raimund looked up, smiled mournfully, and then rushed down the stairs.

A minute later Hildegarde was in her room; her cloak and boa almost suffocated her, and she shook them off impatiently, sunk on a chair, and murmured, ' What shall I do? What ought I to do? Oscar will quarrel with him—kill him, and I shall be the cause. He must leave Munich—leave us, and return to England.' Here she sprang from her chair, and walked up and down the room for a few minutes. ' Is there, then, no other way of keeping him out of danger? Suppose he could be induced to go to the Z——s' ? He said he intended to visit them. If he could only go until after Oscar's marriage? A fortnight—only two weeks, and all danger will be over ! I must speak to him, even if he insists on knowing everything. I wonder is he in the drawing-room ? '

He was not, nor in the schoolroom, and she had not courage to seek him in his apartment. She hoped to find an opportunity in the course of the next day, although with female quickness she had already observed that he no longer sought to be alone with her, or in any way to occupy her attention. Hamilton's motives were honourable, but he could scarcely have chosen a more judicious mode of conduct in order to facilitate their intercourse; it had already convinced Mr. Rosenberg of his indifference to his daughter, just when he had begun to entertain suspicions to the contrary, and confirmed Madame Rosenberg in the idea that Hamilton actually disliked her.

After wandering about the house for some time, Hildegarde returned to her room, and endeavoured to arrange her thoughts, and her balls of coloured worsted and silks, until the return of her family. They came late, and talked loudly and gaily on their arrival. When Crescenz entered the room, she immediately exclaimed, ' Oh, Hildegarde, we have had such a pleasant party—such a number of people, and such good coffee!—and the Bergers—Oh, dear, I was so sorry that you and——but I had almost forgotten, mamma says you must make tea directly for Mr. Hamilton; he is going to the theatre; there is an opera, and he wishes to hear the overture.'

Hildegarde pushed back her work-frame, and left the room to seek the breakfast-service of highly-gilt china, which Madame Rosenberg had received as a wedding present, and which, though certainly intended by the donor to have been ' kept for show,' she had latterly appropriated to Hamilton's use, whenever he drank tea alone, and this was generally the case the evenings he went to the theatre. When she carried it to the drawing-room, she found her father, mother, and Major Stultz with him, and as she poured out the weak beverage, and arranged the plate of bread and butter, her

mother continued speaking: 'We thought you did not choose
to hear us—but then what motive could you have?'

'What indeed?' said Hamilton.

'The Major shouted the words "Nymphenburg" and "coffee"
as loud as he could; he thought they might give you an idea
what he meant.'

'We heard nothing. The confounded bells made such a
noise.'

'The bells are very useful when it grows foggy, or dark, as
we found this evening,' observed Major Stultz.

'Hildegarde, you may light the candles—Mr. Hamilton
cannot find the way to his mouth.'

Hildegarde brought them, while Crescenz, who had joined
the others. continued repeating, 'So pleasant, so gay! So
many people! And then about the upset—did you relate
about that?'

'No,' cried Hamilton, looking up; 'pray tell me about it.
You do n't mean to say you were upset?'

'Oh, no! But a young Englishman and his wife were
thrown out of their sledge to-day when they were driving
round the palings at Nymphenburg. Captain What's-his-
name told us all about it, and they were so young and so
handsome, he said.'

'Your countrymen can drive mail-coaches better than
sledges,' said Major Stultz, laughing.

'It is not proved that they were English,' said Hamilton,
with a smile only perceptible to Hildegarde. 'They may
have been Germans.'

'Zimmermann said they were certainly English, and he
understands the language. The lady thanked him in French
for extricating her out of the snow; he said she was quite
English looking, and uncommonly handsome.'

'I have no doubt of his judgment on that subject,' said
Hamilton.

'And,' said Crescenz, 'her husband seemed so fond of her,
and said all sorts of things to her when he assisted her into
the sledge again!'

'All sorts of things!' cried Hamilton, laughing. 'Such as,
for instance—?'

'Oh, I cannot say the English words—I have never heard
you say anything that sounded like them.'

'Of course not—I must wait until I have a wife, I suppose.'

Hildegarde's face had flushed during this conversation. Hamilton seemed so much amused with it, that he forgot the overture he had been so anxious to hear. 'Your friend did not know at all who they were?' he asked, bending over his teacup.

'Not in the least,' answered Major Stultz; 'but the lady made a great impression on Zimmermann; he seemed altogether to have fallen in love with her!'

'Oh, ho!' exclaimed Mr. Rosenberg; 'what did his wife say to that?'

'She said she had no cause for jealousy, the Englishwoman did not look at anyone—she only seemed anxious to assure her husband that she was not in the least hurt, though she must have been considerably bruised, and she appeared to wish everyone else at the bottom of the sea! A good example for you, Crescenz, next month, eh?'

Crescenz looked silly, and turned away.

'Half-past six!' cried Mr. Rosenberg, looking at his watch; 'I must be off. Mr. Hamilton seems to forget that he intended to go with me to the theatre. The overture will be over.'

'But not the ballet,' said Hamilton, 'and the ballet in "Robert" is what I like best; 'if I be in time for that and the Princess's aria, I am satisfied.'

Mr. Rosenberg, who went regularly four times a week to the theatre, and particularly disliked arriving late, partly from the fear of being obliged to walk over his neighbours' feet in order to reach his chair, partly from long habits of punctuality, after a few minutes' indulgence of civilly expressive impatience, quitted the room, bowing over his watch, which he still held in his hand, as a sort of excuse to Hamilton.

'I thought you intended to go too?' said Crescenz to Major Stultz.

'Yes; Zimmermann has given me his place to-night, but I believe I shall wait for Mr. Hamilton.'

'I shall be delighted,' said Hamilton, 'but you must not expect me to leave this warm room for an hour at least.'

'An hour!' exclaimed Major Stultz; 'why, half the opera will be over.'

'Very likely, but I have heard it so often.'

'Do you forget the ballet?'

'Very likely I shall,' said Hamilton.

'I knew,' cried Crescenz, 'I knew he did not really care for the ballet.'

'Excuse me, but I do care for the ballet, and I should care more for it if the dancers were prettier, and had not such thick ankles!'

'Smooth water runs deep,' said Major Stultz. 'It is a pity, Crescenz, your mother did not hear that speech; she would hardly have believed her own ears!'

'Why not?' said Hamilton; 'do you mean to say that you do not, or did not formerly, like seeing a ballet, and pretty women too?'

'We will not discuss this subject in the presence of the young ladies,' said Major Stultz.

'There is nothing to discuss,' said Hamilton, carelessly; 'I like seeing pretty faces, and pretty ankles, and graceful figures, and I believe I am not singular in my taste; perhaps, however, you prefer the flowing hair which will be exhibited to-night. By-the-bye, one girl has the very longest and thickest hair I ever saw. Have you not observed it?'

'Yes; Crescenz's, however, is nearly as long, I should think,' replied Major Stultz, touching the thick plaits which were wound round the back of her head.

'She would make a charming ballet dancer in every respect,' murmured Hamilton in French, while he laughingly glanced towards her.

'What does he say?' asked Major Stultz, who observed that Crescenz blushed and smiled alternately. 'What does he say?'

'To think of his caring so much for a ballet!' answered Crescenz evasively, while she still blushed and then laughed as she added, 'And you know all mamma said about his being so religious, and not going out in the evenings, or on Sunday to the theatre.'

'I suspect your mother has a better opinion of him than he deserves,' whispered Major Stultz. Crescenz, however, shook her head so incredulously, or so coquettishly, that he added. 'Do not think me jealous; it is impossible now that I know who is the real object of his devotion.'

'Ah, you mean Hildegarde,' said Crescenz, carelessly.

'Oh, no!'

'Who then?' asked Crescenz, turning towards him quickly, curiosity depicted in every feature.

Who?'

'I can scarcely tell you—as he has chosen a married woman—'

Crescenz looked aghast. Major Stultz's jealousy conquered his usual circumspection—the moment was too favourable for making an impression—he bent towards her and whispered, 'No other than your friend Madame Berger.'

'Impossible!'

'Certain, nevertheless. When your mother forbade his returning here, he was invited to spend his disengaged evenings at her house. He knows the Doctor well; besides, Berger is Zedwitz's physician, and they have often met lately. Had the thing been feasible, Hamilton would, I have no doubt, have taken up his quarters in their house!'

Crescenz, for once in her life, seemed to think, and think deeply. All Major Stultz's efforts to continue the conversation were fruitless; she bent her head over her work, and scarcely heard his excuses and regrets that he was going to the theatre without her. After he had left the room there was a long pause. Hildegarde had been leaning her head on her hand for the last half hour, apparently unconscious of what was going on about her. Crescenz moved softly towards her, and, on pretence of consulting her about her work, contrived to relate what she had just heard.

Hildegarde became so suddenly and remarkably pale, that Hamilton, who was in the habit of watching her, immediately perceived it, and exclaimed, 'What is the matter? Are you ill?'

'Not in the least,' she answered, hastily rising, and walking to the other end of the room.

'But is it not odious?' cried Crescenz, indignantly; 'she is the very last person I should have thought of!'

'And the very first I should have suspected,' said Hildegarde.

The house-bell rang, and a slight noise in the passage was followed by the entrance of the person who had been the subject of conversation. 'How very odd!' exclaimed Crescenz, while Madame Berger, advancing towards Hamilton, held out her hand, saying, 'A l'Anglaise, how I like your English custom of shaking hands—it is so friendly! Bon soir, Hildegarde. Give me a kiss, Cressy. Here I am, come all in the snow on foot to talk over our first ball, eh? and to arrange the party of which we spoke,' she added, turning to Hamilton.

'How provoking—and I am just preparing to go to the theatre!'

'You most uncivil person! Can you not bestow half an hour on me?'

'An hour—two hours if you in the slightest degree wish it. My regrets were for myself'

Hildegarde and Crescenz looked at each other.

'I have not,' he continued gaily, 'forgotten the pleasant evenings which I spent in your house during my banishment; they will ever remain among my most agreeable recollections.'

'Perhaps I may give them a place among mine too,' said Madame Berger, seating herself on the sofa, and taking her knitting apparatus out of her pocket. Her fingers were soon in such quick motion, that it was impossible to follow them, but so expert was she in this kind of work, that her head turned in every direction, and her eyes wandered round the room as if she had been totally unoccupied. 'Why, girls, what is the matter with you both this evening? I never saw you so dull. We can fancy ourselves *tête-à-tête*,' she said, laughingly, to Hamilton, 'if you would only cease playing with your tea-spoon, and sit down beside me here.'

Hamilton immediately took the offered place, and Madame Berger, half playfully, half maliciously, turned quite away from the sisters. 'Well,' she continued, glancing covertly towards them, 'to-morrow is our first ball; of course you have heard of our muslin dresses and wreaths of roses!'

'No,' said Hamilton; 'I only returned here yesterday evening, and have heard nothing about it. Where is the ball?'

'At the Museum. You are a member of the club, I believe —it is there you read the foreign newspapers, you know. I shall keep a waltz, or galoppe for you.'

'To-morrow, did you say? and I am invited to a private ball at Court! If it were only the day after!'

'This all comes from the cholera!' cried Madame Berger, in a tone of vexation. 'Everything heaped together at the end of the carnival! There is to be a masquerade at the theatre on Monday; you said you wished to go to one; let us, at least, arrange something about that!'

'Can you not promise to be of the party?' said Hamilton, turning to Hildegarde.

'It will altogether depend upon papa,' she answered coldly, and then left the room without looking towards the speakers.

'Come here, Crescenz,' said Madame Berger, 'come here, and I will tell you how we can manage it; your mother intends to go some day or other to see her father. Why not on Monday, if Mr. Hamilton offers his sledge?'

'Oh, she is so afraid of his horses, that nothing would tempt her to take them.'

'Well then—the Doctor must lend his old greys, for on Monday both she and your father must be out of the way. Do n't be so stupid as to say this to Hildegarde, however.'

'Oh, mamma would never trust us with you alone,' said Crescenz.

'I suspected as much, and have engaged old Lustig to go with us; she will do whatever we please, and I have promised to arrange a "Bat" for her like my own; we will all go as bats. Shall we be black or white?'

'Which is the most becoming?' asked Crescenz.

'Becoming! Why, child, I do believe you do n't know what I mean? A bat, as mask, means a domino so arranged that one cannot see even the form of the head, the smallest lock of hair, or even quite know whether the person be a man or a woman!'

'I thought we should have had something pretty,' said Crescenz, disappointed, 'such as Grecian costumes!'

'You may dress yourself as a Grecian, or a Turk, if you like, but you may be recognised and tormented. For my part, I go to worry others, and have decided on a black domino—a complete capuchin, Mr. Hamilton and Madame Lustig, the same —you and Hildegarde may of course arrange as you please.'

'Oh dear! I am afraid Hildegarde will not go without asking papa's leave.'

'Do n't say a word more about the matter to her; she will think we have forgotten it, and when papa and mamma are gone, I will come and arrange everything!'

'Oh dear, how nice!' cried Crescenz, seating herself confidentially beside her friend, but a moment after she sprang up, assumed a dignified air, and walked towards the door.

'You do n't mean to leave us, Cressy?' exclaimed Madame Berger, surprised.

'I am going to tell mamma that you are here,' she replied, stiffly.

'Oh, my dear creature, she has heard from Walburg long ago. She is engaged with the children, or counting linen, or something of that sort. Stay here, like a love, and play propriety.'

'But I don't choose to play propriety,' said Crescenz, angrily, as she left the room.

Madame Berger looked amazed for a moment, and then burst into a fit of laughter. 'I do believe the child is jealous!' she exclaimed. 'How ridiculous! how amusing! I wish it were Hildegarde—I would give—what would I *not* give to make *her* jealous for half an hour! It would be sublime! Theodore could assist me if he chose.'

'You think she likes him?' said Hamilton.

'He says not, but I can discover no other person. Can you believe that she cares for no one?'

'She cares a great deal for her father,' answered Hamilton.

'Ah, bah—a person of her violent temperament must have a *grande passion* before this time!'

'I have not lately seen anything like violence,' said Hamilton.

'A certain proof that she is desirous of pleasing some one.'

'I should have no objection to be the person *she* is desirous of pleasing,' said Hamilton. 'She is perfectly amiable with her father—should she bestow one of the looks intended for him upon me, I confess, I should be—'

'And has she really never tried to make you say civil things to her?' asked Madame Berger, quickly.

'On the contrary, she has provoked me to say very *un*civil things sometimes.'

'And so you have been obliged to amuse yourself with poor simple Crescenz?'

'Who,' said Hamilton, 'is the most innocent being in the world—a pretty child—'

'A pretty fool,' cried Madame Berger; 'but let us talk of our masquerade—you will go at all events?'

'Certainly.'

'And dressed in black—and masked?'

'Agreed.'

'You have no idea how amusing it is! One can say all sorts of impertinent things—even to the royal family when they are present. Masks are allowed perfect impunity.'

'But should you be discovered afterwards?'

'I shall deny knowing anything about the matter, of course.'

Hamilton had not time to reply by word or look, for at this moment supper was announced.

CHAPTER XXVIII.

A BALL AT THE MUSEUM CLUB.

'I HOPE we shall have no visitors,' said Crescenz, the next day, after having examined herself for some time attentively in the glass which was between the windows in the drawing-room. 'I hope we shall have no visitors, for these curl-papers are certainly not becoming. If mamma had allowed, I should have passed the day in my own room, that nobody might see them. Don't you think me very ugly to-day?' she added, turning to Hamilton, who, as usual, was close to the stove.

'You are not ugly, but the curl-papers are,' he answered, looking at her over his book.

'But we shall look so well with long curls in the evening,' she said, half appealing to her sister, who was standing at the window with some intricate piece of work. 'What a pity one cannot have curls without curl-papers !'

'They are dearly bought if you are obliged to have your hair twisted up in that manner all day,' said Hamilton.

'I thought Englishwomen very often had long curls.'

'So they have, but they never appear in a drawing-room with curl-papers.'

'They certainly are very unbecoming,' said Crescenz, again inspecting herself in the glass. 'I have a great mind to arrange my braids again. After all, my hair will perhaps fall out of curl during the first waltz. You know, Hildegarde, at the examinations I was obliged to fasten up the curls with a comb?'

'Yes, but I remember the curls became you extremely—'

'Hildegarde,' whispered Crescenz, coming close to her sister, 'you know Mr. Hamilton cannot go to the ball, and if he thinks the curl-papers so very ugly—'

'I should think Major Stultz's opinion of more consequence to you,' answered Hildegarde; 'and,' she added loud enough to be heard, 'you know if Mr. Hamilton dislike so much seeing curl-papers, he has only to avoid looking at us for the remainder of the day.'

Hamilton closed his book, looked out of the window at the thickly-falling snow, and then left the room. Crescenz immediately exclaimed, 'Oh, Hildegarde, you have offended him ! How can you be so unkind ?'

'Is it unkind to tell him not to look at us for a few hours?' Hildegarde asked, laughing.

'You are so unnecessarily rude to him sometimes—yesterday evening, for instance, you scarcely answered him when he spoke to you.'

'Because I was occupied with my father. I hope you have no objection to my preferring his conversation to Mr. Hamilton's!'

'But you were only talking about the opera to papa, who would have been very glad if you had allowed him to hear what Mr. Hamilton was telling Lina Berger about a pic-nic party on the Thames. Lina says he is the most fascinating young man she ever met, not even excepting Theodore Biedermann.'

'And Mr. Hamilton will tell you, if you ask him, that Madame Berger is the most fascinating young woman he ever met, not even excepting Crescenz Rosenberg.'

'Oh, dear! I forgot to tell you that Major Stultz was quite mistaken. Lina explained everything before she left yesterday evening. Mr. Hamilton only went to hear her play waltzes!'

Hildegarde shook her head incredulously.

'You do not believe her?'

'No.'

'Well, I do; and I will manage to find out from Mr. Hamilton the whole truth.'

'Don't attempt anything of the kind, Crescenz; you will only make yourself ridiculous.'

'We shall see,' said Crescenz, nodding her head as she left the room.

When she returned to the drawing-room, her hair was braided in the usual manner; and she rather unwillingly confessed that she had seen Hamilton, who had said that he thought braids infinitely more becoming than curls for young and pretty persons!'

'I greatly fear Mr. Hamilton is beginning to amuse himself again at your expense,' observed Hildegarde, with some irritation.

'He did not seem to be amusing himself; he spoke quite gravely, and papa, who was present, agreed with him.'

Hildegarde's hands rose to her head, and her fingers impatiently contracted themselves round the offending curl-papers. 'If I had known that papa thought so, I should never have curled my hair, but now it is too late; Mr. Hamilton will think I have tried to please him, and—'

'Oh dear, no,' cried Crescenz; 'he did not seem in the least to think I had braided my hair to please him. He was talking to papa about religion and philosophy, and some acquaintances of the name of Hegel and Schelling.'

Hildegarde smiled. 'If they were talking of Hegel and Schelling, I dare say he has forgotten us and our curls. I could not possibly think of sacrificing my ringlets to please *him*, and papa I shall probably not see until evening.'

Hamilton took her advice more literally than she just then wished: he remained in his room the rest of the day, and thus avoided seeing her again. She felt that a few words spoken in a moment of irritation had deprived her of all chance of seeing him alone for a few minutes in order to induce him to avoid her cousin, and go the ensuing week to the Z——s'; but she consoled herself by thinking, that at least they were not likely to meet during that evening, as Raimund had not been invited to the ball at Court, and was to accompany his betrothed to the Museum.

As soon as it was dusk, the sisters disappeared. Madame Rosenberg in vain sent to request they would come to supper. They were not hungry. They could not eat. 'Quite natural!' observed their father, helping himself to some salmi and cold turkey. 'Quite natural! Who ever heard of a girl eating before she went to her first ball? I suppose, however, they will soon be dressed; so I think, Babette, you might now put on your brown silk dress and pink turban; it would be a pity if they were to lose a dance! Mr. Hamilton has offered to leave us at the Museum on his way to the palace.'

Madame Rosenberg poured out a glass of beer, drank it quickly, and left the room. A few minutes afterwards, Hildegarde and her sister entered, in all the charms of youth and white muslin. 'Is she not beautiful?' exclaimed Crescenz, for a moment forgetting herself in her admiration of her sister. 'Is she not beautiful? Ah, I knew you would admire curls,' she added as a sort of reply to Hamilton's look of most genuine admiration. 'Curls are prettier than braids after all.' She drew her hand, as she spoke, over her smooth shining hair, and glanced regretfully towards the looking-glass.

Hildegarde turned from Hamilton with a slightly conscious blush. Never had he seen or imagined anyone so lovely as

she appeared to him at that moment. The long waving ringlets
of her rich brown hair relieved the slightly severe expression
of her almost too regular features, while her beautifully formed
figure, seen to advantage in her light ball-dress, attracted
equally by its roundness and delicacy. Had Hamilton seen
her for the first time that evening he would have been captivated. When we, however, remember that she had been for
months the object of his first love—that he had resided in the
same house, and had had opportunities of knowing and judging
her by no means commonplace ideas, as they had studied
together, and that he was at a time of life when the feelings
are most impetuous—we may form some idea of the emotion
which, for some minutes, deprived him of the power of utterance. Hildegarde was so perfectly independent in thought
and action, she required so little of that protection which her
sex usually seek, that, had she not been eminently handsome,
she would probably have found more people disposed to admire
her character than love her person. Men especially do not
often bestow affection on such women; but, when they do, it
is with a degree of passion which they seldom or never feel
for the more gentle and weaker of the sex. And so, irresistibly attracted by her beauty, and perhaps hoping to find
feelings as strong as her mind, three men now loved her with
characteristic fervour—her cousin, with an intensity bordering
on insanity; Zedwitz, with the glowing steadiness of his
disposition and years; and Hamilton, with all the ardour of
extreme youth.

'I thought Hildegarde would have worn one of my bracelets
this evening,' said Crescenz; 'I offered her the choice of them
all.'

'That was very kind of you, Crescenz,' said her father;
'but Hildegarde does not care for ornaments of that kind.'

'But look at that ugly little hair bracelet, which she insists
upon wearing,' said Crescenz, laughing. 'If she had bracelets
of her own, she would wear them, I am sure. Everyone must
like bracelets!'

Mr. Rosenberg took Hildegarde's hand, and raised her
passive arm towards his eyes, in order to inspect the bracelet.
'It is not ugly, nor ill-chosen either,' he observed, smiling.
'A black bracelet makes an arm look fairer still; but I own I
did not think my treasure studied such things!'

Hildegarde, with a look of annoyance, hastily unclasped the bracelet, and threw it into her work-basket.

'Don't be offended, Hildegarde. Every woman should endeavour to improve her appearance as much as possible. Your arm is round and white, and the bracelet pretty; it ought, perhaps, to have been a little broader, but the horsehair was scarce, it seems! However, you can wear it very creditably: at a little distance, people will think it the hair of some very dear friend.'

Madame Rosenberg made her appearance at this moment, in a state of ludicrous distress. She had tried to force her large hands into a pair of small French gloves. One, from its elasticity, had been drawn somewhat over the half of one hand, leaving the other half and the wrist quite bare; but the other had burst asunder across the palm, and she now held it towards her husband with a look of mock despair.

Hamilton had in the meantime been playing with the discarded bracelet; Hildegarde attempted to take it out of his hand, but he held it nearer the light, observing in a low voice, 'This is not *horse*-hair. It cannot be your father's or your sister's, for they have brown hair; nor your cousin's; nor—'

'Give me my bracelet,' said Hildegarde, impatiently. He held it towards her with both hands, and a look of pretended alarm. She half smiled, and extended her arm, while, with a degree of trepidation which he in vain endeavoured to overcome, he placed the tongue in the serpent's head which formed the clasp. When he looked up, her head was averted, and she was jesting with her father about her chance of finding partners or being left sitting.

'Pray keep one waltz or galoppe in reserve for me,' said Hamilton. 'I shall be at the Museum between ten and eleven o'clock.'

Hildegarde murmured a sort of assent, but the expression of her countenance denoted anything but satisfaction. She became grave and thoughtful. It was impossible not to perceive the change, and, with ill-concealed mortification, Hamilton turned to her father: 'Your daughter does not know, perhaps, that I have learned to waltz since I came here. I am no longer a bad dancer.'

'Oh, dear! I always thought you danced extremely well,' said Crescenz.

'I may depend upon your keeping a waltz free for me, if Major Stultz will permit it?'

'Oh, yes; that is,' said Crescenz, correcting herself, 'if you can remember your engagement with me when Lina Berger is present.'

'Madame Berger has no influence whatever upon my memory.'

'No; but upon your heart.'

'None whatever. She is very pretty, very amusing, very flattering — everything you please but loveable.'

'Well, if she only heard you say that,' began Crescenz.

'The carriage has been at the door this long time,' cried Madame Rosenberg, tying a large handkerchief over her ears and pink turban. 'Let us be off.'

Crescenz touched her sister's hand, and whispered, 'You see, dear, I was right.'

Hildegarde bent her head, but did not speak.

Hamilton heard, saw, but only partly understood. Had Hildegarde been jealous?

The ball at Court was not in the least less brilliant than any of the preceding; but Hamilton was not disposed to admire the rooms, or the fresco paintings, or the candelabra, or even his own form in the long glass, placed so conveniently at the door of one of the reception-rooms. Figures in blue and pink crape passed and repassed him scarcely observed, so completely had a form in white, with a wreath of roses in her hair, taken possession of his imagination. His abstraction attracted even the notice of royalty, and it was with a deep blush that Hamilton stammered some excuse when asked why he did not dance as usual.

At ten o'clock he withdrew, bounded down the stairs which he had thought so tiresome to mount a couple of hours before, found his carriage waiting, and drove to the Museum. The contrast was great, but he heeded it not; Hildegarde was everything to him. He glanced quickly round the room, and immediately discovered the object of his search walking composedly towards the dancers with a tall officer in the guards; he was about to leave the room again in a fit of uncontrollable irritation, when he remembered his engagement with Crescenz. The moment she saw him, she spoke a few words eagerly to Major Stultz, smiled, and then walked a step or two towards him.

'I knew you would come,' she said, with evident pleasure, and showing her little ball-book; 'see, you were written for two dances, that I might be quite sure of being disengaged.'

'Thank you,' said Hamilton; 'you are very kind. I can remain but one hour, and as your sister seems to have forgotten her engagement with me, perhaps you will give me the second waltz also?'

'Oh, I dare not; Major Stultz will never consent. I am sure I wish he would go home, he is so sleepy already. But,' she added, after a pause, 'I am quite sure that Hildegarde will dance with you.'

In the course of the dance, Hildegarde and her partner came close beside them. Hamilton at first pretended not to observe it, but Crescenz naturally spoke to her sister.

'Mr. Hamilton fancies you will not dance with him, but I am sure he is mistaken; he says he cannot remain more than an hour, so you must promise him the next waltz or galoppe, whichever it may be.'

'If he really wish it,' said Hildegarde; 'but he looks so very seriously English to-night, that if I were to propose dancing with him, I am sure he would say no!'

'Try me,' said Hamilton; 'or rather write my name in your book, that I may be sure you are in earnest.'

'You must trust to my memory, for I have neither ball-book nor tablets. I have no one,' she added, looking archly towards her sister, 'I have no one to supply me with ball-books and bouquets;' and she bent her head over her sister's hand, which could scarcely clasp the geraniums, heliotropes, and China roses with which it was filled.

A moment after she had joined the dancers, and Hamilton stood thoughtfully beside his partner.

'Do you not admire my bouquet?' she asked, holding it coquettishly towards him.

'Exceedingly; for the time of year it is beautiful.'

'Major Stultz waited at the door to give it to me. It was an attention I never expected from him.'

'Why not?' asked Hamilton, absently.

'Oh, because he was so many years a soldier, and in the wars, and in Russia, and all that. I thought it was only young—a—a—persons with whom one danced, who gave bouquets.'

'Very true,' said Hamilton, laughing, 'and it is disgrace-

Y 2

fully negligent of young—a—persons to forget such things sometimes.'

'I assure you,' stammered Crescenz, 'I did not mean—I did not think—'

'I know you did not,' said Hamilton.

'He knows you *never* think, my dear,' said Madame Berger, who had overheard the last words when taking the place behind them.

'She never thinks or says anything unkind,' said Hamilton, warmly.

Madame Berger looked up saucily, and then turned to her partner, a gay student, to listen to some nonsense about her long blonde ringlets.

'Lina is angry that you have not asked her to dance,' said Crescenz, as she returned to join her mother. 'Suppose you were to waltz with her next time; I know Hildegarde will not be in the least offended.'

Hamilton shook his head. 'I am not so much afraid of giving offence as you are; besides, you may be mistaken.'

'No,' said Crescenz; 'I am sure I am right, for I remember her saying she would keep a waltz for you, and you said you could not come at all. Oh, I remember it, for I was so sorry when you said so, that I did not care at all for the ball, or my new dress, or—'

Hamilton unconsciously pressed Crescenz's hand; her heightened colour immediately reprimanded him for his imprudence, and he turned to Madame Rosenberg, and asked her how she liked playing chaperone?

'Better a great deal than I expected,' she answered, laughing; and then, lowering her voice, she added, 'Our girls are certainly very pretty; you have no idea how civil all the men are to me on their account. Franz is enjoying a sort of triumph to-night, but the Major is not quite satisfied; he says the young officers have been talking nonsense to Crescenz, for she has been blushing every moment. Now I have told him a hundred times it is from the heat of the room and the exertion of dancing. It would be better if he would go down to the club-room and smoke his pipe; he cannot expect the child to sit beside him all the evening as she does at home. She has very properly done her duty, and already danced twice with him, and more he cannot require. He has no sort of tact, the Major. Fancy his wanting her to fix her wedding-day

just now, when she is thinking of anything in the world but
her marriage. I never knew anything so injudicious!'

Poor Crescenz had been condemned to a place between her
mother and Major Stultz. Hildegarde had emancipated her
self completely; she hung on her proud father's arm, walked
about the rooms, and talked unrestrainedly. Hamilton had to
seek her when the music again commenced; she left her
father directly, and walked towards the dancing-room, but
scarcely had she entered it when Count Raimund approached,
exclaiming, 'Where are you going, Hildegarde? Do not forget that this galoppe is mine.'

'No, Oscar; it was the second that I promised you.'

'That cannot be, Hildegarde, for I am engaged to dance it
with a—Marie. I believe—I am quite certain—you promised
me this one.'

'And I am *quite sure*, Oscar, that you are mistaken. *Quite
sure!*' began Hildegarde, with her usual decision of manner;
but the angry expression of her cousin's countenance made
her hesitate. 'Perhaps, however,' she added, looking from
one to the other, 'perhaps, as Mr. Hamilton is an Englishman,
and does not care about dancing, he will be rather pleased
than otherwise in being released from what he probably considered a duty dance.'

'By no means,' said Hamilton, firmly holding the hand
which she endeavoured to withdraw; ' I am not so indifferent
as you seem to imagine. You have promised to dance with
me, and I am not disposed to release you from your engagement.'

'Nor I either,' said Count Raimund, while the blood
mounted to his temples, and was even visible under the roots
of his fair hair.

'You think perhaps I ought to feel flattered,' said Hildegarde, scornfully, ' but I do not—on the contrary, I think you
both, I mean to say—Oscar extremely disagreeable. I shall
not dance with either of you,' she added, seating herself on
a bench, and beginning to tap her foot impatiently on the
floor. The two young men placed themselves on either side
of her.

'I hope,' she said, turning to Count Raimund, ' I hope you
are satisfied, now that you have deprived me of the pleasure
of dancing a galoppe, to which I have been looking forward
for the last half-hour?'

'My satisfaction depends entirely on who the person may be with whom you anticipated so much pleasure in dancing.'

'You know perfectly well that I was not engaged to you and did not think of you.'

Count Raimund played with the hilt of his sword, which he had laid on the form beside him.

'Oscar,' continued Hildegarde, after a pause, in a low voice, 'don't be so unjust, so tyrannical as to deprive me of my galoppe. Choose somebody else. See, there is Marie still disengaged—go quickly, before any one else can—'

'Thank you,' said Raimund, interrupting her; 'you are very kind, but I have no inclination whatever that way. Marie may be very good for household purposes, but I must say I rejoice in the idea that our marriage will free me from these ball-room duties towards a person I have scarcely learned to tolerate. In fact, I believe I detest her, so has she been forced upon me!'

'Oscar, Oscar—take care. Do not speak so loud. What would people think of you, were you to be heard? Some one may tell Marie, and make her repent her disinterested conduct towards you—she does not deserve to be made unhappy, especially by you!'

'What did you say, sir?' cried Raimund, speaking angrily, across Hildegarde, to Hamilton.

'I have not had time to say anything,' he replied, laughing.

'But you looked as if you agreed with my cousin?'

'My looks are expressive, it seems,' said Hamilton, coolly.

'Perhaps you intend to inform my betrothed of what I have just now said,' cried Raimund, still more angrily.

'My acquaintance with her is of too recent date to admit of my doing so.'

'Do you mean deliberately to insult me?' asked Raimund. in a voice of suppressed rage.

'No, Oscar,' cried Hildegarde, laying her hand hastily on his arm; 'it is you who are endeavouring to commence a quarrel with Mr. Hamilton. You feel that you are in the wrong, and that you ought not to have made such a remark in public of a person to whom you are to be married in less than a week.'

'*You* may say what you please to me, Hildegarde, but neither Mr. Hamilton nor any one else shall dare by word or look to imply—'

Hamilton turned away with a smile of unequivocal contempt.

'What do you mean, sir?' cried Raimund, starting from his seat, and facing him while he folded his arms.

'I mean that this is no place for such words—still less for such gestures,' replied Hamilton, glancing round him. The loudness of the music, however, had prevented them from being heard.

'Oscar,' cried Hildegarde, vehemently, 'sit down beside me. Listen to me—you *must* listen to me. You are altogether in the wrong—you are rude and irritating, and ought to be ashamed of yourself. Do not try Mr. Hamilton's patience further.'

'I have no intention of doing so,' said Raimund, biting his lip and frowning fearfully.

Hildegarde looked anxiously, first at her cousin and then at Hamilton, to whom she said in a low voice, 'I do not know which is most to be feared—your coolness, or Oscar's ungovernable temper? But this I have determined, that neither shall stir from this place until a reconciliation has taken place. You, Oscar, are bound to apologise for your unprovoked rudeness and—'

'Ha, ha!' laughed Raimund. 'You are a most excellent mediatrix, my charming cousin, but believe me, explanations are better avoided. See, we have already forgotten the whole affair.'

Hildegarde looked uneasily towards Hamilton; he appeared to be intently watching the dancers as they flew past him.

'It is useless your trying to deceive me,' she began, once more turning to Raimund, but he immediately interrupted her by saying, 'Pray, is all this unnecessary anxiety on my account, or—on his?'

'My anxiety is divided. Surely,' she continued, almost in a whisper, 'you will not be so foolish as to commence a quarrel in this unreasonable manner? What will Marie and her mother think, should they hear of it? What right had you to ask for an explanation of Mr. Hamilton's looks? You are seeking a quarrel; and do you think by acting in this manner you are likely to increase my regard for you! Oh, Oscar! have you forgotten what you said about a double crime?' The music played loudly, and Hildegarde bent towards her cousin, and continued to speak for some time. Raimunds countenance cleared by degrees; he raised his eyes to her face with an expression of undisguised admiration and love, and then whispered an answer which made her blush and turn away.

' You know your influence with me is unbounded. On this condition I will do or say whatever you please,' he added, endeavouring to catch her eye.

' It is ungenerous of you to take advantage of my fears,' said Hildegarde, rising.

Hamilton asked her if she wished to return to her father; she seemed scarcely to hear him, appearing lost in thought for some moments. She again consulted the countenances of her two companions, again became anxious, and finally turning to Raimund, said, with some embarrassment, ' After all, it is not worth talking so much about—I accept the condition—perform your promise.'

' Time and place to be chosen by me?' said Raimund, loudly and eagerly.

' Do not make any more conditions,' cried Hildegarde, impatiently, ' but perform your promise at once.'

' This must be understood,' said Raimund, ' or else—'

Hamilton felt himself growing very angry; he turned to leave them, when Count Raimund called him back: ' Mr. Hamilton, a moment if you please. Hildegarde has convinced me that I have been altogether in the wrong just now. If I have offended you, I am sorry for it; I hope you do not expect me to say more !'

' I did not expect you to say so much,' replied Hamilton, coldly.

A sudden flush once more overspread Raimund's face, an internal struggle seemed to take place; but after a glance towards Hildegarde, he said calmly, ' If I did not feel that I had been the aggressor, not even the offered bribe could have induced me to apologise.'

' Bribe—offered !' exclaimed Hildegarde, almost indignantly.

' No, not offered. Favour conceded, if you like it better— we will not dispute about words. Mr. Hamilton, my cousin is free, and can dance when she pleases.'

' I imagine she could have done so before, had she wished it,' said Hamilton, haughtily.

Raimund walked away as if he had not heard him, and buckled on his sword with an air of perfect satisfaction.

Hamilton stood by Hildegarde as if he were turned to stone. The words, which had been so mysteriously spoken, seemed to have completely petrified him. Hildegarde, too, stood immovable for a minute, and then turned as if to leave him.

'Do you not wish to dance?' asked Hamilton in a constrained voice.

'No—I mean yes—yes, of course,' she replied, moving mechanically towards the dancers.

Hamilton's feelings at this moment would be difficult to define. As he put his arm round her slight figure, intense hatred was perhaps for the instant predominant—he was in such a state of angry excitement, that he had gone quite round the room before he perceived that he was actually carrying Hildegarde, who was entreating him to stop.

'Get me a glass of water,' she said, moving unsteadily towards the refreshment-room, and sinking on a chair behind the door. She had become deadly pale, and was evidently suffering, but seemed determined to conquer the unusual weakness which threatened to overcome her.

When Hamilton again stood beside her he no longer felt angry; bending towards her, he whispered, 'If you repent any hasty promise which you may have made to your cousin, I shall be happy to be the bearer of any message or explanation.'

'Repent!' murmured Hildegarde. 'No; I have promised, and I do n't repent: but you—you must not speak any more this evening to Oscar; he has apologised for his rudeness, and I know you are too generous ever to refer to the subject again.'

'But he spoke of some bribe—some favour,' began Hamilton.

'That is my affair, and not yours,' replied Hildegarde, rising as the dancers began to pour into the room. 'And now take me to my father. After all,' she added, forcing a smile, 'I believe I have wasted a great deal of genuine alarm on a pair of very worthless young men!'

'So it was not repentance about this promised favour, but anxiety about us, which has nearly caused you to faint?'

'Just so; my fears perhaps magnified the danger, but there was danger—more than you were aware of. Avoid my cousin,' she added, earnestly; 'he is reckless now, but I trust better times are in store for him.' Though still fearfully pale, she walked steadily towards the end of the room, where her father and mother were standing.

Raimund saw Hamilton leaving the room a few minutes afterwards, with hasty steps and a disturbed countenance. He looked after him, and observed with a sarcastic smile to an acquaintance who was near him, 'I have spoiled that English-man's supper; he is not likely to enjoy his *pâté de foie gras* or champagne under the orange-trees at court to-night!'

CHAPTER XXIX.

A DAY OF FREEDOM.

SOME days passed over remarkably tranquilly. Crescenz's marriage was to take place in a fortnight, and she and Hilde-garde had promised to be bridesmaids to Marie de Hoffmann, the beginning of the ensuing week. Hildegarde made no further effort to warn Hamilton about her cousin; perhaps she now deemed it unnecessary, as the young men openly showed their mutual antipathy, and avoided even the most formal intercourse.

One fine afternoon, when Hamilton was about to drive out in his sledge, he perceived Crescenz hovering about him mysteriously. Major Stultz, who was in the room, seemed to embarrass her, but at length she murmured in French, 'I have something to say to you.'

'I have been aware of it for the last half-hour, and have remained here on purpose to hear it,' said Hamilton.

'You always forget that Mr. Hamilton speaks German perfectly well, Crescenz,' observed Major Stultz. 'I take it for granted you have no secret from me!'

'Oh, dear, no,' said Crescenz, with a slight laugh; 'I always speak French when I am not thinking of anything particular. You know for many years I never spoke any other language;' and while she spoke, she carelessly upset her work-basket, the contents of which rolled in all directions on the painted floor.

'Dear me! how awkward I am!' she exclaimed, half laugh-ing, while Major Stultz, with evident difficulty, began to pick np the dispersed articles. 'My scarlet wool is behind the sofa; Mr. Hamilton, will you be so kind—'

Hamilton moved the sofa; there was no scarlet wool, but a slip of paper dropped from Crescenz's hand; he immediately took possession of it, and her eyes sparkled with pleasure. 'Thank you, thank you; I believe I have everything now. Oh, by the bye, Mr. Hamilton, if you have time, I wish you would call on Lina Berger, and ask her why she has not been here since the ball?'

Hamilton hesitated.

'Tell her my wedding-day is fixed, and I want to consult her about my veil. You will go to her, I hope?'

'If—you—wish it—but—'

'No buts; I hate buts,' said Crescenz, laughing, and then making an inexplicable grimace to him apart.

When out of the room, he inspected the slip of paper, on which was written in French—

'You have offended Lina Berger by not dancing with her. Make up your quarrel as fast as you can, or we shall lose all chance of going to the masquerade.'

'I had forgotten all about the masquerade,' thought Hamilton, 'and must make my peace directly with the little person. She shall drive out with me this very day to arrange matters. Fortunately she has said at least half a dozen times that she likes sledging; I ought to have taken the hint long ago—'

What his excuses were is not recorded—they did not seem to interest him particularly, as only the result is known. Madame Berger drove out in his sledge, the party was arranged, and the next morning, at breakfast, a note was brought to Madame Rosenberg, offering Doctor Berger's carriage and horses for the day of the masquerade.

'How good-natured of Lina to remember that I wished to see my father and introduce the Major to him!' she exclaimed, handing the neatly-written note to her husband; 'I would rather it had been any other day than Monday, as you know Mademoiselle de Hoffmann's marriage is to take place on Tuesday, and it will be disagreeable returning home so early the next day; however, that cannot be avoided.'

'Easily enough, I should think,' observed Mr. Rosenberg, quietly; 'Mr. Hamilton has often proposed lending us his horses, and all days are alike to him, I know.'

Before Hamilton could answer Madame Rosenberg exclaimed, 'His horses! Not for any consideration in the world! Besides, his sledge is only for two persons and a servant, and I wish to take the boys and the Major with us.'

'In that case I think we had better take a job-carriage for a day and a half.'

'No use in paying for what we can have for nothing,' said

Madame Rosenberg; 'so, if you have no objection, I shall accept the offer.'

'As you please,' said her husband; 'a visit to the Iron Works is not exactly what I enjoy most in the world.'

'Crescenz,' said Madame Rosenberg, taking no notice of this remark, 'Crescenz, just put on your bonnet, and slip over to old Madame Lustig's; ask her if she can take charge of you and Hildegarde on Monday; but she must spend the whole day here, and promise to sleep in the nursery.'

Crescenz left the room, not without slightly glancing towards Hamilton, and primly pressing her lips together to repress a smile.

'I don't like Madame Lustig,' said Hildegarde, abruptly.

'Why?' asked Hamilton.

'Because she so evidently tries to please everybody.'

'Better than evidently trying to please no one,' said her mother sharply. 'However, whether you like her or not, if she take charge of you and Crescenz on Monday, I expect you will do whatever she desires, and consider her as in my place.'

Hildegarde looked up as if about to remonstrate—caught her father's eyes—and then bent over her coffee-cup, without speaking.

Madame Lustig made no difficulties and many promises. She arrived the next morning, when they were all breakfasting together at an unusually early hour, listened patiently to Madame Rosenberg's directions about locking the house-door, and fastening the windows, and examining the stoves, and then accompanied them to the carriage with Hamilton, Hildegarde, and Crescenz. Major Stultz seemed very much inclined to remain behind, but Crescenz whispered rather loudly, 'that mamma had been so kind about her *trousseau*, that he ought to visit grand-papa!'

'What an artful little animal it is after all!' thought Hamilton, 'and how different from—' He looked towards Hildegarde, who, all unconscious of their plans, after having twisted a black silk scarf round her father's neck, stood rubbing her hands, and slightly shivering in the cold morning air.

'Adieu, adieu,' was repeated in every possible tone, while the carriage drove off. A moment afterwards, Crescenz was scampering up the stairs, dragging Madame Lustig after her, and when Hamilton and Hildegarde, who followed more leisurely, reached the door, they were obliged to remain there, for Crescenz, dancing a galoppe with Madame Lustig, was now forcing her backwards the whole length of the passage at a tremendous pace, the jolly old woman keeping the step, and springing with all her might, for fear of falling. Hamilton and Hildegarde looked on laughing.

At length they stopped for want of breath. 'Well—what—shall we—do first?' said Crescenz, twisting up her hair, which had fallen on her shoulders.

'Do—!' panted Madame Lustig, as she leaned against the wall. 'You have nearly—killed me—this is not the way to make me able to go to the masqu—'

In a moment, Crescenz's apron was over her head, and a new struggle began.

'I asked you what we should do first?' cried Crescenz, laughing. 'Suppose—suppose we make ice-cream? You have a good receipt, I am sure; let us make the cream, and Mr. Hamilton and Hildegarde can turn it round in the ice-pail!'

'Shall we not first arrange with Walburg about dinner?'

'Oh, dinner! How very disagreeable to be obliged to eat dinner! Cannot we (for once, just, by way of a joke),' she said, coaxingly, 'have something instead of dinner?'

'But,' said Madame Lustig, 'on Mr. Hamilton's account, you ought—'

'Oh, I have no objection to dining on ice-cream,' said Hamilton, laughing.

'You see!' cried Crescenz, 'Mr. Hamilton is so—so——. You see he will do whatever we wish.'

Hamilton amused himself singing aloud the cookery book in recitative, until, in the course of time, he was duly established with Hildegarde, near a window in the corridor, a large bucket of ice between them, in which was placed the pail containing the cream. They turned it round alternately, and Crescenz occasionally inspected the process, dancing with delight as it began to freeze.

The arrival of Madame Berger seemed to increase the commotion in the kitchen. She closed the door, but Hildegarde distinctly heard the words 'congratulate—freedom for one day at least — make good use — amusement — Hildegarde — hush.' A short whispering ensued, and at length Madame Lustig made her appearance, inspected the ice-cream, and proposed putting it outside the window. 'There is no use in your tormenting yourself longer, my dear,' she said, smiling; 'we have something else to interest us. Come, we must hold a consultation.'

'About what?' asked Hildegarde.

'About a masquerade; were you ever at one?'

'Oh, yes; at school we had one almost every year; I was always ordered to be a Greek or Circassian.'

'Ah, that was children's play among yourselves; but I mean a real masquerade!'

'You mean the public masquerades at the theatre, perhaps?'

'Just so; should you like to go to one?'

'To be sure I should, of all things!' cried Hildegarde eagerly. 'When is it?'

'To-night.'

Her countenance fell. 'Oh, if we had only known it sooner! If we had only been able to ask papa!'

'There! I told you,' cried Madame Berger, coming out of the kitchen, followed by the others. 'I knew she would make all sorts of difficulties, and spoil Crescenz's pleasure!'

'I am sure,' said Madame Lustig, 'neither your father nor mother would have any objection, when I go with you, and Madame Berger, and Mr. Hamilton.'

'It is true mamma said I was to do whatever you desired me—' began Hildegarde, with some hesitation.

'Oh, I will *command* your attendance, if that will be any relief to your conscience,' cried Madame Lustig, with a loud laugh.

Hildegarde coloured deeply, and looked towards Hamilton; he was eating almonds and raisins from a plate which Madame Berger held towards him. 'Let us talk about our masks, and not about our consciences,' cried the latter. 'I must go home to dinner, or the Doctor will be impatient. We are to be black bats; black silk dresses; black dominoes, with hanging sleeves and hoods; masks half black, and a knot of white ribbon under the chin, that we may know each other. How many dominoes shall I order?'

'For us all, Lina, for us all!' cried Crescenz, eagerly.

'We may as well dress at your house,' cried Madame Lustig; 'it is not necessary that Walburg should know anything about the matter. The Doctor will have gone out before seven?'

'Oh, yes; you may come at half-past six. I must have time

to dress Mr. Hamilton, as well as myself, you know! Adieu, —*au revoir!*'

Immediately after dinner, Hildegarde put on a black dress, and came to the drawing-room, where Hamilton was sitting, or rather reclining, on the sofa, reading; she leaned slightly over him, and, almost in a whisper, asked if he were disposed to give her advice, should she request it.

'I don't know,' answered Hamilton, looking up with a smile. 'I have been so long dismissed from the office of preceptor, that I have quite got out of the habit of giving advice.'

'Forget that you have been preceptor, and take the name of friend,' said Hildegarde—'we shall get on better, I think.'

'I like the proposition,' cried Hamilton, quickly rising from his recumbent position. 'Our ages are suitable. Let us,' he added, laughing, 'let us swear an eternal friendship.'

'Agreed,' said Hildegarde, accepting his offered hand. 'And now, tell me, shall I go to this masquerade or not?'

'I thought you had already decided.'

'Not quite. I wish very much to go, that is the simple truth. but I fear that, under the name of obedience to Madame Lustig, I am trying to persuade myself that I am following my mother's injunctions, while, in fact, I am only seeking an excuse to do what I wish. Do you understand me?'

'Perfectly.'

'And you think, perhaps, I ought not to go?'

'I think, indeed I am sure, that I can give you no advice on the subject. I am too much interested in your decision to be a "righteous judge."'

'How are you interested?'

'Simply thus: if you do not go, the whole party is spoiled for me.'

Hildegarde was silent for more than a minute. She did not disclaim; she knew he had spoken his thoughts. 'If,' she said at length, 'if I had only known it in time to have asked my father's leave, I really do think he would have had no objection.'

'If you think that, you may decide on going with a clear conscience.'

'Is this your opinion—advice?'

'I give no advice,' said Hamilton, laughing; 'I only wish you to go.'

'Then I will go,' said Hildegarde, thoughtfully; 'go—notwithstanding a kind of misgiving which I cannot overcome, a sort of warning—a presentiment—'

'I should rather have suspected your sister of having misgivings and warnings than you,' said Hamilton; 'yet she seems to have none.'

'She is governed by her wishes, and Lina Berger; besides, it is not likely that anything unpleasant should occur to her!'

'And to you?' asked Hamilton, surprised.

'Not likely either,' said Hildegarde, gaily; 'for, thank goodness, Oscar must spend the evening with Marie when they are to be married to-morrow.'

Raimund had been but once at the Rosenbergs' since the ball, and had played cards the whole evening. Hamilton knew that she had not since spoken to him. Yet, no sooner had she pronounced her cousin's name than all his feelings changed; he bit his lip, and walked to the window.

'I wish—' began Hildegarde; but she suddenly stopped, for she recognised Raimund's voice speaking to her sister in the passage. Hamilton strode across the room.

'Oh, stay, stay, I entreat of you!' she cried, anxiously.

'Do you not wish to be alone with your cousin?'

'No, no, no—that is,' she added, hurriedly, 'yes—perhaps it is better—'

'As you please,' said Hamilton, moving again towards the door.

Hildegarde seemed greatly embarrassed.

'If you would only promise not to say anything to make—'

'I really do not understand you,' cried Hamilton, impatiently.

'When he has been here for a minute or two,' she said, quickly, 'go for Crescenz and Madame Lustig; say they must come here—must remain—' Her cousin entered the room while she was speaking.

'I am sorry to interrupt you, my dear Hildegarde,' he said, with a stiff and evidently forced smile, 'but I come to take leave—'

'Take leave! What do you mean?'

'I am to be executed to-morrow, you know.'

'Ah! so—'

'It is particularly kind of you and Crescenz to put on mourning for me beforehand,' he continued, glancing gravely at her black dress.

'Oscar, how can you talk so?' said Hildegarde, reproach-fully; 'such jesting is to-day particularly ill-timed.'

'By heaven, I am not jesting. I never was less disposed to mirth than at this moment,' he answered, falling heavily into a chair, and drawing his handkerchief across his forehead.

'Have you been with Marie?'

'Yes.'

'And you will return to her?'

'I suppose I must.'

Here Hamilton precipitately left the room to summon Madame Lustig and Crescenz; but they were much too busily engaged in the manufacture of a complicated cake to follow him, so he hurried back alone to the drawing-room, and found Hildegarde—in her cousin's arms. She was not struggling, she did not even move as he entered, while Raimund, not in the least disconcerted by his presence, passionately kissed her two or three times. At length she suddenly and vehemently pushed him from her, exclaiming, 'Go: I hate you!'

'You hate me! Hate me, did you say? Let me hear that once more, Hildegarde,' he said, losing every trace of colour as he spoke.

'No, no – I do n't hate you—but you have acted very—very ungenerously,' said Hildegarde, with ill-suppressed emotion.

'I understand you: but you will forgive me this last offence, I hope?'

'Yes, I forgive you, and will try to forgive you all you have done to worry and alarm me since our acquaintance began,' said Hildegarde, bitterly; 'but this must indeed be the last offence.'

'It will be, most certainly,' said Raimund; and taking both her hands, he looked at her long and earnestly, and then left the room without in any manner noticing Hamilton.

A long pause ensued. Hamilton's eyes were riveted on his book, which he had again taken up; but he never turned over the leaf, nor did he move when he became conscious that Hildegarde was standing beside him.

'That was the fulfilment of the promise made at the ball on Saturday,' she at length said, in a very low voice. 'I knew that his mind was in a state of unusual irritation, and his claiming a dance, which I had not promised him, proved his wish to quarrel with you. My fears alone made me con-sent.'

z

Hamilton turned round. A light seemed suddenly to break upon him; and Hildegarde's motives for many inexplicable actions became at once apparent. His first impulse was to tell her so, and to assure her of his increased admiration and affection; but he recollected, just at the right moment, that all such explanations from him were a waste of words and time; that he had told her so more than once himself. So, after a short but violent internal struggle, he said, with forced serenity, 'My reliance on you will henceforth be unbounded.'

She seemed perfectly satisfied with this answer. Notwithstanding its *laconicism*, she fully understood the extent of confidence which would in future be placed in her, and she left the room with a light heart.

CHAPTER XXX.

THE MASQUERADE.

FOUR muffled figures quitted the Rosenbergs' apartments about six o'clock in the evening, and, not long after, a light figure bounded up the stairs, and knocked with closed hand on the door. Walburg cautiously looked through the grated aperture, but, on recognising Count Raimund, she immediately opened it.

'Where are your young ladies gone? I saw them leaving the house a few minutes ago.'

'They are gone to spend the evening with Madame Berger, I believe.'

'Did you hear them say anything about going to the masquerade?'

'No; but Miss Crescenz did nothing but run about and whisper the last half-hour, and Madame Lustig took the house keys with her, and said I might go to bed if they were not home before ten o'clock. I am almost sure they intend to go to the masquerade; and Miss Crescenz might have trusted me, as I should never have said anything about it.'

'Perhaps you are mistaken,' said Raimund, absently. 'At all events, it is better to say nothing about it to Madame Rosenberg;' and he slowly descended the stairs, and walked towards Doctor Berger's house, remaining in the street near it until he saw the five black masked figures enter a carriage.

Though all studiously dressed alike, he easily recognised Madame Berger's small and Madame Lustig's stout figures, while Hildegarde and Crescenz were sufficiently above the usual height to make the group remarkable.

It was early when they entered the theatre, but the house was already crowded; the tiers of boxes were filled with spectators, who, later in the evening, joined the masks in the large ball-room formed by the junction of the pit and stage. Crescenz became alarmed when surrounded by a number of squeaking masks, and clung to Hamilton's arm. Madame Berger and Madame Lustig, on the contrary, laughed and talked with a freedom which rather shocked Hamilton. Hildegarde at first answered gaily all who addressed her; for she felt that she was perfectly unknown: but after some time, she perceived that two masks had joined their party, and seemed determined to remain with them. A slight young Turk had attached himself to Madame Berger, while a mysterious black domino followed her like a shadow.

'How much pleasanter it must be to look on from above!' she observed, at length. 'One has all the amusement without the press and anxiety of the crowd.'

'Oh dear! I have got quite used to it now,' said Crescenz, 'and am not at all afraid.'

'If there are places in the boxes to be had,' said Hamilton, 'and you are willing to leave this turmoil, I am quite sure I can procure them for you.'

'Oh, thank you! Let us ask Madame Lustig.'

But Madame Lustig protested against the plan. She could not allow them to leave her—it would be quite improper if they were to be seen alone with Mr. Hamilton—indeed, she would rather they were not seen at all, and she positively could not leave Madame Berger with that troublesome Turk, not having the least idea who he might be.

'There is no use in asking Lina,' said Crescenz to Hamilton, who had moved towards Madame Berger. And indeed, all his arguments proved vain. 'People should not go to masquerades who did not know how to enjoy themselves! She had no idea of coming to the theatre to mope away the evening in a box— she could do that four times every week; besides, the presence of Mr. Hamilton was necessary for propriety's sake, and she could not, and would not, dispense with his attendance.' All this was poured forth with a volubility in French that attracted

z 2

the attention of the bystanders. 'No ; the gay little devil of a mask must not think of going, nor her corpulent friend either !' And they were again drawn on with the crowd. Hamilton followed with the sisters, who now ceased altogether to speak. Crescenz had also become aware that they were followed by a black, taciturn figure, which, as she whispered to Hamilton, put her in mind of the Inquisition, and all sorts of horrors.

'But,' said Hildegarde, who had heard her remark, 'we are also quite black, and probably make the same disagreeable impression on other people.'

'He seems quite unknown ! I have not seen him speak to any human being—' said Crescenz.

'Nor have we either for the last half-hour,' answered her sister.

'Oh, my dear, if *you* have no objection to having him at your elbow all the evening, I have nothing more to say,' cried Crescenz : 'that is quite a matter of taste.'

'Is he annoying you in any way?' asked Hamilton.

'Not in the least,' answered Hildegarde. 'The crowd is so great that he could not easily leave us, even if he wished it.'

In the meantime, Madame Berger and Madame Lustig, encouraged by the masks around them, had begun to follow the unmasked groups who had descended from the boxes. They knew the private histories of most persons, and were so unmerciful in their remarks—so mischievous in the distribution of their bon-bons and devices—that they at length found it expedient to plan a retreat, which was no longer easy, as they were followed by several persons who wished to find out who they were. A dance which was to be performed by the *corps de ballet*, in costume, seemed to favour them. They had only time to whisper to each other, 'Home, as fast as possible by the front door of the theatre,' when they were pushed about and separated in all directions. Several coaches were in attendance ; Hamilton immediately procured one, and they were soon in it, laughing merrily over their adventures.

'How well we all managed to come together after all !' cried Madame Berger. 'I really had begun to fear we should not get rid of my Turk—who could he have been?'

'I don't know,' said Madame Lustig, yawning, 'but I am glad that we five are safely together again, and not running about looking for each other, which might easily have happened.'

'It often does happen,' said Madame Berger, counting her

companions, 'One, two, three, four, five—There was a black familiar of the Inquisition following Hildegarde all night—I really was afraid he might have been among us !'

To her house, according to agreement, they all repaired to change their dresses. Hamilton assisted them to descend from the carriage; the last person sprang unaided to the ground, threw the black domino back with a quick wave of the hand, and discovered the figure of the Turk. 'Good night, Madame Berger !' he cried, in a feigned voice, 'good night—good night!' and with a gay laugh he darted down the street.

'Was there ever anything so provoking !' exclaimed Madame Berger, in a voice denoting great annoyance. 'What have I said to him to-night? Or rather, what have I not said to him ? How vexatious ! He must have borrowed a domino from a friend in order to get among us !'

'But,' cried Madame Lustig, in a voice of alarm, 'one of us must have been left behind.'

'It must be Crescenz,' cried Hamilton. 'I will return to the theatre directly for her.'

'It must be Hildegarde,' cried Crescenz, who stood beside him.

Without uttering a word, he sprang into the carriage, and the coachman drove off. His anxiety was indescribable; in the crowd he had felt the absolute necessity of releasing the arm of one of the sisters, and, deceived by the extreme likeness in their figures, he had almost forcibly retained Crescenz, who chanced to be at the moment followed by the silent mask, and whom he consequently mistook for her sister.

At the theatre he dismissed the coachman and began making inquiries. 'A black domino alone, separated from a party of friends ?' 'Numbers of black dominoes had been seen—many had been separated from their friends!' was the usual answer; at length a footman, who had been lounging at a distance, observed, that 'about half-an-hour before, a black domino, a lady, had been stunned by a blow from the pole of a carriage, and had been carried off by another black domino.'

'That may have been Hildegarde!' cried Hamilton, in a state of fearful anxiety.

'I think that *was* the name he called her,' said the man, preparing to walk away.

'He! Who is he ?' asked Hamilton.

'I do n't know; he said he lived close by, and that he was a near relation.'

'Raimund!' almost groaned Hamilton, as he rushed out of the theatre towards the lodgings, which he knew were in one of the adjoining streets.

The door at one side of the entrance-gate was slightly ajar; it had probably been left so by some servants who had stolen off to the masquerade, and did not wish to announce their return by ringing the bell. Raimund's rooms were on the ground floor; a couple of steps led to them. Hamilton ascended; the door was open; he entered a narrow passage, and stood opposite the entrance to one of the chambers; knocked first gently, then loudly; shook the door, no sound reached him; at length he moved towards another door, and called out, 'Hildegarde, for heaven's sake, if you are here, answer me!'

He thought now he heard some one moving in the room.

'Let me in! Open the door!' he cried, pushing with all his strength against it.

'Wait a moment,' said a voice, which he with difficulty recognised as Hildegarde's; 'wait—I—must—take the key from—'

'Heaven and earth, Hildegarde! how can you be so calm, when you know how anxious we must be about you! Are you alone?'

'No—yes!' she answered, quite close to the door.

'Count Raimund, you have no right to make a prisoner of your cousin. Open the door directly!' cried Hamilton, shaking it until the hinges rattled.

He heard at length the key placed with a trembling hand in the lock—it turned, and Hildegarde stood before him. The hood of her capuchin was thrown back, and her features, deadly pale and rigid in an expression of horror, met his view. She pointed silently towards a figure lying on the ground, which, when Hamilton approached, he found to be the corpse of her cousin! He must have shot himself through the mouth, for the upper part of his head, hair, and brain, were scattered in frightful bloody masses around. A more hideous object could hardly be imagined; he turned away, and, seizing Hildegarde's hand, drew her out of the room, while he whispered, 'What a dreadful scene for you to have witnessed!'

Scarcely were they in the street when, putting her hand to

her head, she exclaimed, 'My gloves—mask—handkerchief are
in his room. Is it of any consequence?'

'Of the greatest,' cried Hamilton. 'If your name be on the
handkerchief, it may lead to most unpleasant inquiries. Wait
here—I must return to the room.'

As he entered the room for the second time, he observed an
appearance of confusion in it, which, in his haste and anxiety
about Hildegarde, had before escaped his observation. Her
gloves and handkerchief he found near the stove, and not far
from them, to his great surprise, a dagger! On the table,
beside the small shaded lamp, stood a wine bottle and tumblers;
writing materials and several letters were heaped together;
and, on glancing towards them, he found one addressed to
Hildegarde, which he immediately put in his pocket, and then
prepared to leave; but, to his dismay, he heard the sound of
approaching voices, and at once his unpleasant, perhaps
dangerous, situation occurred to him. His known enmity to
Raimund made it absolutely necessary for him to endeavour
to leave the house without being recognised, and, having tied
on Hildegarde's mask, he took refuge in a small wood-room,
ready to escape the first opportunity that should offer. The
persons whose voices he had heard were servants; one of them,
a French girl, was speaking while he gained his hiding-place,
and he heard her say, 'The old lady desired me to call her son;
I would not go into his room for all the world at this time of
night.'

'What does she want with him?'

'Oh, she says she heard the report of a gun or pistol a short
time ago, and is alarmed. She asked me if I had not heard
it too?'

'And did you hear it?'

'How could I, when I was not in the house? The best
thing I can do is to say that Count Oscar has not yet returned
home. I am afraid she won't believe me, as he never remains
late at those Hoffmanns'.'

'But you may tell her that I saw him going to the
masquerade at nine o'clock, in a black domino. We can
knock at the door, and, if we get no answer, he is not there.'

'And if he should answer?'

'Why, then, we can speak to him all together.'

'While they knocked at the door, Hamilton glided out; but
not, as he had hoped, unseen, for they turned and ran after him

into the street, calling out, 'Count Oscar! Count Oscar! Madame la Comtesse wishes to speak to you.'

Hamilton shook his hand impatiently towards them, which made them desist, and then breathlessly joined Hildegarde, who was standing motionless on the spot where he had left her.

'I ought not to have allowed you to return,' she said, clasping her hands convulsively round his arm. 'It was thoughtless, selfish of me. Had you been seen!'

'I have been seen, but not recognised,' said Hamilton. 'I put on your mask, and some servants mistook me for Count Raimund.'

'Can that lead to any discovery?' asked Hildegarde, stopping in the middle of the cold, cheerless street.

'On the contrary, I rather think it will prevent any discovery being made until to-morrow morning.'

'His wedding-day!' said Hildegarde, with a stifled groan. 'Oh! what will Marie de Hoffmann think of him?'

'She will perhaps guess the truth,' said Hamilton. 'I believe this marriage was the immediate cause of the rash act.'

'Perhaps I am also to blame,' said Hildegarde, in a scarcely audible voice.

'It may be : but most innocently, I am sure. It was not your fault that your cousin loved you so madly.'

'I—I—did not exactly mean that,' said Hildegarde, with a shudder.

'Then, what did you mean? Tell me all that occurred. That is,' added Hamilton, for the first time since he had joined her recurring to his former fears, 'that is, if you can.'

'I can, and will, though the recollection is most painful,' said Hildegarde, in an agitated manner ; and, after a moment's pause, she began : 'Having been separated from you all, I naturally endeavoured to reach the front door of the theatre, where we had agreed to assemble as soon as possible ; always, to my great annoyance, followed by the black domino, who, in the end, proved to be Oscar. Had I known it sooner, it would have saved me a world of horrors. I was excessively alarmed, as you may imagine, and, forgetting my character as mask, inquired in my natural voice, of every one I met, if they had seen four black dominoes together? Every one had seen dominoes such as I had described ; and after hearing that some had left in carriages and some on foot, I at length determined to walk home alone. Taking advantage of the confusion caused by several parties endeavouring to drive off together, and hoping by that means to escape from the domino who had become an object of terror to me—like a thing in a dream—I ran at full speed out of the theatre. In order to reach the quieter streets, I unfortunately turned towards the advancing line of carriages—the crowd was enormous, and I was buffeted about in all directions, until at length the pole of a carriage threw me down and completely stunned me—'

'So it was you! And were you hurt?' asked Hamilton anxiously, and stopping to look at his companion. Strange to say he had, until that moment, forgotten what he had heard at the theatre!

'No—not much—my shoulder is bruised, I believe—but my head fell on the ground, and I was insensible for some minutes. Some one, probably Oscar, must have seized the horses' heads and forced them backwards. When I recovered, I felt myself supported by him, and recognised his voice immediately. There was a terrible stamping of horses, and noise, and swearing about us, and I made a violent effort to walk. With Oscar's assistance, I reached the next street; he proposed my going into his lodgings for a few minutes until I felt stronger, which I at first refused, but, becoming so faint when we were passing his house that I could scarcely stand, I thought it better to go willingly than perhaps be carried there in a state of insensibility. A lamp was burning in the room when we entered, and wine was on the table; he poured me out a glass without speaking, which I immediately drank, and then sat down on the sofa to rest. In the mean time, he walked silently up and down the room, and then returned to the table, where he quickly swallowed several tumblers of wine. Alarmed by his manner, I immediately stood up, and declared that I was quite able to return home. If he were not disposed to accompany me, I would go alone. His answer was, locking the door and putting the key in his pocket.'

'And you?' asked Hamilton, quickly, 'what did you do?'

'I cannot describe the undefined terror which this proceeding caused me: but on seeing the dagger, with which he had once so frightened me, lying on the table. I suddenly seized it, and retreated towards the stove. He asked me what I meant: but I only answered by repeating the words "Open the door—let me go—let me go." He, however, then informed me that he had no intention of doing either one or the other—he was determined for once that I should hear him, and answer him ; and he ordered me peremptorily to give him the dagger. I, of course, refused ; and—and—'

'Well?'—said Hamilton, breathlessly.

'A violent struggle ensued: he wrested it forcibly out of my hand, and, I believe in trying not to hurt me, was wounded himself, for I saw blood trickling down the blade, as he held it triumphantly up in the air. In springing to the other side of the stove, I found a bell-rope. Perhaps I wrong Oscar, but I believe the fear of that bell alone preserved me from further insult.'

'He must have been perfectly desperate,' observed Hamilton, taking a long breath.

'He appeared so to me,' continued Hildegarde, shuddering. 'I saw him change colour as I grasped the rope : but, with wonderful coolness, he advised me to refrain from summoning witnesses to my being in his room at such an hour of the night : that I had entered willingly, and no human being would believe my assertion of innocence, as unfortunately his reputation was such that mine would be lost should I be seen and recognised. Though trembling with anger, I perceived the justice of his remark, and carefully avoided ringing, though I held the cord tighter than ever. He came nearer and nearer, and talked long about his love, and despair, and hatred of you. I was too much agitated to understand much of what he said ; and I believe he perceived it at last, for he threw himself at my feet, and declared he would die there. I pushed back his hands with disgust, and told him that he need not hope again to terrify me—I knew he had no thought of dying, but I once more requested him to open the door and give me my liberty. He started up frantically, and, taking a small pistol from the table, again approached me. I asked him if he intended to murder me. He looked capable of that, or anything else, at the moment, and when he pointed it towards his own head, I—' Hildegarde paused, and covered her face with her hands. Hamilton did not speak, and she again continued : 'I did not—indeed I did not for a moment think him serious, he was such a consummate actor ! I had seen him in less than half an hour change from calm to furious so often, that I thought this was only a new effort to work upon my feelings. I never could—had I dreamed of the consequences—at all events, I shall never, never be able to forgive myself!'

'You have not told me what you did,' said Hamilton, in a low voice.

'I—laughed—and no sooner had he heard the horrid mocking sound of my forced laughter than he pulled the trigger, and fell, so horribly mangled, to the ground!' She leaned against the corner of a house, and gasped for breath. 'Do you think,' she asked at length, 'do you think that I was the immediate cause of his death?'

'No,' said Hamilton: 'I can give you nearly the assurance that he had intended to commit suicide—this very night, perhaps—his table was covered with letters, and one addressed to you I brought away with me.'

'Now Heaven be praised, that this sin is not on my soul!' she cried, fervently, and then added, 'I have nothing more to tell you—I don't know how the time passed until you came— it appeared very long, but I never thought of going away. You will understand why I was so dilatory in opening the door, when you recollect that the key was in the pocket of his waistcoat.'

'And now,' said Hamilton, hurrying towards Madame Berger's house, 'let me recommend secrecy. I do not think anyone will imagine that we know of this melancholy affair. Should we speak of it, we might be suspected of knowing more than we may be disposed to relate.'

'I quite agree with you,' said Hildegarde, 'and have not the slightest wish to speak of it to anyone—not even to my father —for, never having spoken to him about Oscar, my confidence, coming too late, might offend him, as it did about Count Zedwitz.'

'You will have to make a great effort, and conceal every appearance of agitation from your sister and Madame Lustig,' said Hamilton. 'I think we had better avoid the proposed supper at Madame Berger's. Give me your capuchin, and I will bring you your bonnet and cloak.'

Hildegarde seated herself on the stairs, and leaned her face on her hands.

Hamilton's appearance without her caused instantaneous and great alarm; but when he said she was waiting for them on the stairs, they became almost angry.

'So she won't come to supper!' cried Madame Berger. 'Just like her—an eternal spoil-sport.'

'I fear she has caught cold,' said Hamilton, looking around for the cloak. 'You forget how long she has been in the streets in her light dress.'

'But,' said Madame Lustig, 'she must say she caught cold making the ice-cream at the passage window. I shall never have courage to confess that we have been at this masquerade, and that she has been running about the streets at this hour of the night! Was she far from the theatre when you met her?'

'I found her in —— Street,' replied Hamilton, evasively, and beginning to heap up cloaks and boas on his arm.

'Not so fast, if you please,' cried Madame Lustig. 'Give me my cloak—I have no fancy for catching cold.'

'This is too provoking,' exclaimed Madame Berger; 'I thought we should have had such a merry supper—the Doctor in bed, and everything so nice. Take a glass of wine, at least, before you go, Mr. Hamilton.'

He quickly drank the wine, and then ran downstairs. Hildegarde stood up, and allowed him to put the cloak on her shoulders, fasten it, sling her boa round her throat, and even place her bonnet on her head; she merely asked, 'Are they coming?'

'Hildegarde,' cried Madame Berger, who accompanied the others with a candle in her hand, 'I take it very ill of you to spoil my supper in this manner; you might have come up if only for half an hour.'

'You have caught cold—you are ill,' whispered Hamilton, in English.

'I am sorry to spoil your supper-party, Lina, but I am really ill, and must go home,' said Hildegarde, in so constrained and husky a voice that Madame Lustig, mistaking it for hoarseness, hurried down the stairs, exclaiming, 'Good gracious, the child can hardly speak! What will her father say to me?'

About an hour after, while Hamilton was still walking uneasily up and down his room, he heard some one knock at the door; on opening it, he was scarcely surprised to see Hildegarde. No trace of colour had returned to her face, but her features had regained their usual calm, statue-like expression.

'I knew I should still find you in this room,' she said, with a faint smile. 'You may give me my letter; I can read it now.'

It was on the table, and Hamilton pushed it towards her. She sat down, drew a candle near her, and, shading her eyes with one hand, held the letter steadily with the other. When she had finished reading it, she gave it to Hamilton, saying, 'That is a wild composition—how fortunate that it fell into your hands! Had it been sent to me, I should have been placed in a most unpleasant position. My father, my mother, would have read it—I must have explained, and Marie de Hoffmann would perhaps have heard of Oscar's dislike to her, and have blamed me more than I deserve.'

Hamilton read the letter, and when she took it out of his hand, she tore it to pieces. 'I wish I could burn these remnants,' she said, crushing them together in her hand.

'Nothing more easy,' said Hamilton, pointing towards the stove. They walked to it, and deliberately burned the pieces one by one: the incoherent sentences becoming once more legible in a charred state before they crumbled into ashes.

'Thank you,' said Hildegarde, turning away; 'and now, good night.'

'Will you not take a candle? or, shall I light you?' asked Hamilton.

'Neither: I do not wish to wake Walburg.'

As Hamilton held the door open, he recollected vividly the last time she had been in his room at night. She was too much preoccupied to think of it; but, stopping suddenly, she turned to him, and said, 'Do you remember my warning, my presentiment of evil?'

'Perfectly,' he answered: 'but I think the idea was caused by your imagining you were about to do something which your father perhaps might not quite approve.'

'You account for everything rationally, and will of course not believe me when I tell you that I knew and *felt* beforehand that Oscar would come to our house yesterday, and act precisely as he did.'

'I do believe you: but it was your natural understanding which made you think he would take advantage of your parents' absence to claim your promise. Then the almost certainty of my presence, to give the performance a zest. Perhaps, however, the strongest motive of all, but which you could not have known, was to take leave of you. I must do him the justice to say, I believe he thought he saw you for the last time then.'

'Would that it had been!' said Hildegarde. 'I could at least have regretted him as a near relation, and felt pity for his untimely end.'

'And do you not feel this?' asked Hamilton.

'No,' answered Hildegarde, sternly. 'In recalling calmly his words and actions this night, I find him wholly unworthy of esteem. My recollection of him now, stained with blood, is hideous, most horrible.' She shuddered while she spoke, and then walked down the dark passage without looking at Hamilton, who held his door open until she had entered her room.

CHAPTER XXXI.

WHERE IS THE BRIDEGROOM?

HAMILTON's slumbers were disturbed by confused dreams of Hildegarde and Raimund: but towards morning he fell into a heavy sleep, from which he was awakened by the return of Mr. Rosenberg, his wife, and children; the latter, probably, to indemnify themselves for their forced good behaviour during their absence, now scampered riotously up and down the corridor, blowing little wooden trumpets, which had been given them by their grandfather just before they had left him.

When Hamilton was dressed, he found the whole family assembled at breakfast, all in high spirits. Crescenz sprang to meet him in her bridesmaid's dress, looking so pretty that Major Stultz's laboured compliments were for once not only pardonable, but even allowable.

'Only think!' she exclaimed, 'Hildegarde does not like being bridesmaid, though Marie is much more her friend than mine! She says she has got a headache and a cold.'

'I knew,' observed Madame Lustig, 'I knew she would catch cold when I saw her turning the ice-cream yesterday. I ought not to have permitted it.'

'The cold is not of much importance,' observed Madame Rosenberg. 'I rather think she dislikes putting on a thin white muslin dress in the morning.'

'A very natural dislike at this time of year,' said her husband. 'It makes me freeze only to look at Crescenz.'

'Oh, I do n't feel at all cold,' cried Crescenz; 'I was down at the Hoffmanns, too, and there is such a splendid *déjeûner* laid out!—and Marie really looks quite lovely in her white silk dress and orange-flowers!'

'You must excuse my doubting your last assertion, Crescenz,' observed her father, smiling. 'Mademoiselle de Hoffmann is a most amiable, excellent person, but as to looking quite lovely in any dress, the thing is impossible.'

'This day week,' said Major Stultz, pompously, 'we shall see a bride who looks lovely in every dress!'

At this moment Hildegarde entered the room : her paleness was still more apparent than the night before, and her drooping eyelids showed plainly that she had not slept. She wished Hamilton good morning without looking at him, and then turned to her father.

'My dear child,' said the latter, taking her hand compassionately, you seem really ill. Shall I send for Dr. Berger?'

'Oh, no!' she answered; 'I—I—am only cold,' and she walked shivering to the stove.

'It will soon be time to go downstairs,' said Madame Rosenberg. 'I think we had better dress ourselves for the occasion. This *hint*,' she added, 'is intended for the Major too — he seems to forget the present in anticipation of the future.'

Major Stultz laughed, bowed to Crescenz, who was not looking at him, and left the room with his future father-in-law.

The moment the door closed, Crescenz bounded towards her sister. 'Oh, Hildegarde, you have no idea how beautifully arranged everything is downstairs! What a pity there are to be so few people! It was very stupid of Oscar to prefer driving off into the country at this time of year, to having a gay dance in the evening! However, Marie is quite satisfied. Do you know, the old Countess Raimund was below, looking so red and apoplectic. She did not take the least notice of me, though I heard her ask who I was. I dare say her husband would not acknowledge us either : but he was not there. They said he was to come with Oscar. Another carriage has just driven up to the door. Perhaps that may be Oscar. I wonder, will he be married in uniform? No—these are some acquaintances of the Hoffmanns—we do n't know them—'

As she continued at the window, her sister approached

Hamilton. 'Is not this a melancholy mummery?' she said, glancing at her bridal dress. 'I feel as if I were under the influence of a frightful dream, forced to act against my inclinations, and in momentary expectation of some dreadful catastrophe. Am I then really awake?' she added, extending her cold hand to him.

'I hope at least that I am not dreaming,' he said, holding it firmly, and looking at her until a transient flush passed across her pale features.

'It will be impossible for me to appear surprised when I hear what I already know but too well,' she said.

'No one will observe you in such a moment, and I will endeavour to remain near you.'

Here Madame Rosenberg summoned them, and they all descended the stairs together. There were about twenty persons assembled, to whom Madame de Hoffmann was talking in her usual loud, sharp manner, while she paid particular attention to a grand, stiff-looking, elderly woman, in whom Hamilton immediately recognised the mother of Raimund. Hildegarde and Crescenz went into the adjoining room, where the bride was loitering until the arrival of the bridegroom. Hamilton walked to the window, and awaited in anxious silence the expected scene; a minute after Count Raimund's carriage drove to the door. Without waiting to see who descended from it, Madame de Hoffmann conducted her daughter into the drawing-room, and, while occupied in receiving the congratulations of her assembled friends, the poor girl did not perceive that her mother had been somewhat mysteriously called out of the room; soon after the Countess Raimund was summoned, and she returned no more: Hamilton saw her assisted into her carriage and driven off. Then a couple of elderly gentlemen and Mr. Rosenberg were sent for; the latter alone returned, deprived of his usual serenity, and evidently at a loss what to say. He approached Mademoiselle de Hoffmann, looked around the room, and then said, 'I am sorry to be the bearer of unpleasant tidings—but—Count Raimund has become so suddenly and alarmingly ill that his mother has been obliged to return home—and —the marriage—cannot possibly take place—to-day.'

'Ill!' exclaimed Marie, growing very pale. 'Where is my mother?'

She entered at the moment, and Hamilton saw from her extreme agitation that she knew all. She spoke hurriedly and confusedly with her guests, unconsciously showing her impatience to get rid of them.   The Rosenbergs were the last, and were about to retire, when Marie laid her hand on Hildegarde's arm, and begged her to remain with her.

'Mademoiselle Hildegarde will not be able to offer you much consolation, Marie,' said her mother bitterly; 'there is little or no chance of Count Raimund's recovery.'

'While there is life, there is hope,' said the poor girl, bursting into tears. 'I suppose he has got the cholera; but many people have recovered from it, and why should not he?'

Madame Rosenberg left the room, followed by her husband, Crescenz, and Hamilton.

About an hour afterwards, Hildegarde returned home and changed her dress. She found her father, mother, and Major Stultz talking eagerly in the drawing-room; the moment she appeared, her father exclaimed, 'See! there is Hildegarde already in mourning!   I am sure a natural feeling of propriety induced her to put on a black dress.'

'A natural feeling of pride,' cried Madame Rosenberg; 'she wishes people to know that a Count Raimund was her cousin; her aunt, however, the Countess, examined her superciliously enough through her *lorgnette* to-day, without in the least appearing to remember the relationship.'

'What is the matter?' said Hildegarde, appealing to her father.

'The matter!' cried Madame Rosenberg; 'your father most absurdly wishes you and your sister to put on mourning for your worthless cousin, and proposes Crescenz's marriage being deferred until after Easter.   Heaven knows, in these cholera times, where we may all be in six or seven weeks.'

'Babette,' said her husband, reproachfully, 'this is going too far.'

'Well, I did not quite mean to say so much, but I am against any further delays; let the girls wear mourning if you wish it, and I promise to arrange the wedding so quietly that no one will know anything about the matter.'

'This is a reasonable proposal,' said Major Stultz. 'Crescenz can put on her mourning after her marriage, and wear it for six months, if you wish it.'

'A few weeks, for decency's sake,' said Mr. Rosenberg, 'I certainly do desire.   Count Oscar at least acknowledged the relationship, and his parents' neglect cannot alter the position

A A

of my daughters, or prevent them from mourning the unhappy end of their mother's nephew.'

In the meantime, Hamilton had approached Hildegarde, and asked her how her friend had borne the intelligence.

'We did not venture to tell her. She still thinks and talks of cholera; but,' she added, in a low voice, 'imagine Madame de Hoffmann taking me aside, and in the most abrupt and unfeeling manner informing me of the real facts, fixing her small inquisitive eyes on my face the whole time. She little knew how well prepared I was for her intelligence.'

'What did you say?'

'Very little. That it was a melancholy affair altogether. That Oscar had possessed some good, and many brilliant qualities, but that had he lived, I feared he was not calculated to have made Marie happy.'

'Did she agree with you?'

'More than I wished. She said, that after the first month she had endeavoured to draw back, but that the Raimunds had not allowed her. She had long perceived that Oscar did not care for her daughter, and had suspected that I was the object of his love, and that I returned it too, but she said she was now convinced of her error, and begged my pardon for her unjust suspicion.'

'And you?'

'I pardoned her without difficulty, as you may suppose. Indeed, Oscar's conduct must have alarmed and irritated any reasonable mother. Marie's blindness has been incomprehensible to me.'

'You forget that love is blind.'

'Yes, to faults, but not to flagrant neglect.

'To weaknesses, faults, ill-usage, to everything,' said Hamilton.

'I suppose it is so,' said Hildegarde, thoughtfully; 'Marie certainly was blind to all his errors, and will probably ever remain so. I was dazzled myself at first, as you may remember.'

'Perfectly,' said Hamilton, drily.

'I know I have a sad habit of taking likings and dislikings,' she continued, listlessly.

'Yes, and on such occasions you are not exactly blind; you can even mistake faults for perfections.'

'I am afraid that it is true,' said Hildegarde, leaning back

in her chair, with half-closed eyes, and speaking very slowly.
'I remember for some time thinking Madame de Hoffmann
agreeable and entertaining ; her severe remarks I mistook for
wit, until they were directed against myself.'

'And what an antipathy you took to me at first sight,'
observed Hamilton.

'You have no idea how she disliked you,' cried Crescenz,
who had, unperceived, approached them. They both started,
and then blushed as she continued ; 'if you had only heard her
in Berchtesgaden, railing at the cold, proud Englishman.'

'Crescenz,' said Hildegarde, with evident effort, 'don't let
us talk of that now ; I cannot defend myself against you both
to-day ; I am too tired.'

'Perhaps you begin to think differently of him,' said Crescenz,
archly ; 'Lina Berger may, after all, be right. When we were
waiting for you last night at her house, she said she thought
your hatred might in the end turn into—'

'Oh, Crescenz,' gasped Hildegarde, in so unnatural a tone,
that her father called out, 'Why, what's the matter there ?'

'Hildegarde is getting into a passion,' said Madame Rosenberg ; 'do you not see how she is changing colour ?'

And changing colour she was with frightful rapidity ; no
one but Hamilton knew that she had been twenty-four hours
without eating, for in the hurry of preparing for the wedding,
her not breakfasting had passed unobserved. None but he
knew the shock which her nerves had received the night
before, the constraint under which she had since been labour-
ing ; he alone understood that Crescenz's last remark was the
drop which made the cup of bitterness to overflow, and yet he
was quite as much shocked as the others, when, stretching out
her arm, and vainly grasping the air for support, she fell
senseless on the floor.

'Crescenz, what have you said to your sister ?' cried her
father rushing forward.

'I don't know—I don't remember. What did I say ?' she
cried, appealing with a look of alarm to Hamilton.

Mr. Rosenberg raised Hildegarde, who, however, gave no
sign of returning life ; he was so alarmed, and trembled so
violently, that Hamilton was obliged to assist him to lay her
on the sofa, while Crescenz opened the window, and Madame
Rosenberg went for water. Their united efforts at length
brought her to consciousness ; she opened her eyes, perceived

her father's look of terror as he hung over her, and while assuring him that she was quite well again, relapsed into a state of insensibility, which lasted until she had been removed to her room, and placed on her bed.

Doctor Berger was sent for. He hoped her illness might prove of no consequence, but she must be kept very quiet; there were symptoms which might lead to typhus or brain fever. Crescenz repeated this opinion to her sister, who, on hearing it, immediately desired to see Hamilton.

'But not now; not here,' said Crescenz.

'No, I believe I must write a few lines, and you can give my note to him as he passes on his way to his room.'

Crescenz brought a pencil and paper, and Hildegarde wrote in English:

'You have heard the doctor's opinion of my illness; I think myself it will only prove a severe cold. Should it, however, end in fever, and should I become *delirious*, you must go to Mademoiselle Hortense, one of the governesses in our school, tell her my situation, and say I request her to come and take charge of me. My stepmother will be satisfied with the arrangement, and you have no refusal to fear; my motives you will easily guess.'

'May I read it?' asked Crescenz, as she received the paper from her sister. 'Ah! it is English; how fond you are of everything English!'

'It is a commission to Mademoiselle Hortense: you may see her name,' said Hildegarde. 'Mr. Hamilton can more easily go to her than you can.'

'Oh, if that be all, I am glad you have chosen him, for you know I am horribly afraid of her.'

'I know,' said Hildegarde, pressing her hand on her forehead, and turning away.

The next two days were passed over in uncertainty, and Hamilton wandered about disconsolately enough, but on the third, Hildegarde appeared to relieve his mind, and so great was her father's joy at her recovery, that he actually spent the whole evening at home, without even requiring a rubber of whist.

CHAPTER XXXII.

THE WEDDING AU TROISIÈME.

SEVERAL days passed over. Count Raimund's death had been much discussed among his acquaintance, who almost unanimously agreed in thinking he had committed the rash act to avoid a connexion so much beneath him. He was more regretted than he deserved; his various talents having made him unusually popular, and, in the society in which he had moved, people were not generally in the habit of studying character, or seeking motives of action. His circle was, however, so completely unknown to the Rosenbergs, they were so totally without any sort of communication with any member of it, now that Count Zedwitz had ceased to frequent their house, that they heard none of the remarks — not one of the particulars. It spared Hildegarde much anxiety, for his wounded hand, the blood-stained dagger, and open door, had caused many inquiries; and, had it not been for a letter which he had written to his father (in the vain endeavour to exculpate himself), might have led to suspicions of murder.

The Rosenbergs heard nothing, and the preparations for Crescenz's marriage began; they were conducted with ostentatious secresy to please Mr. Rosenberg, who had consented to its taking place sooner than had been expected, as the Hoffmanns had left the house, and removed altogether to Augsburg. Madame Berger had promised to play waltzes if the company should prove numerous enough to enable them to dance, and Madame Lustig had spent two or three afternoons cooking for the supper. On the wedding-day, Hamilton was not a little surprised to find Crescenz sitting composedly at breakfast in her gingham morning wrapper, while her father left the room to go to his office as usual.

'I believe I have dressed too early,' he said, glancing at his studied toilet; 'may I ask at what hour —'

'At five in the afternoon,' answered Hildegarde. 'Mamma has determined to keep her promise, and has desired our friends to meet us at the Frauen church. On our return it will be almost dark, and no one will know that we have a wedding in the house.'

'But we shall dance,' cried Crescenz, 'and Major Stultz said I might waltz as often as I pleased with you this evening!'

'How very kind!' said Hamilton, smiling; 'and how often do you intend to make use of the permission?'

'That depends upon you, I should think,' she answered, blushing.

'You had better not trust to my discretion. I shall be tempted to make up for lost time, and dance with you the whole evening. You have put no sugar in my coffee,' he added, turning with a look of mock distress to Hildegarde. 'Did you forget it on purpose to punish me for being so late?'

'No. I — I was thinking of something —'

'And that something?'

'Is not of much importance. I was thinking that had you made that speech to Crescenz, a few months ago, I should have been angry, for I should have imagined you were amusing yourself at her expense — whereas I now know that you mean nothing, but that you will dance two or three times with her this evening.'

'And,' said Hamilton, warmly, 'and that I like to dance with her, and am obliged to her for wishing to dance with me. I meant that too.'

'I knew you did,' cried Crescenz, triumphantly. 'I am sure I always understood you better than Hildegarde, notwithstanding all her cleverness; but from the time that Count Zedwitz told her that you were already quite a man of the world, a—a —what was the word, Hildegarde?'

'I do n't remember the word,' she answered calmly.

'It meant, I remember,' said Crescenz, 'a person who was too cold and calculating for his years—who was too worldly to have much feeling.'

'That was unjust—that was saying too much,' cried Hamilton, colouring.

'So Hildegarde thought also, but she has always insisted that you are proud and calculating, and that you seek to amuse yourself with other people's feelings and weaknesses.'

'Is this your opinion of me?' said Hamilton, turning to Hildegarde.

'It *was*,' she replied steadily.

'Oh, Hildegarde is not afraid to say what she thinks; her

opinion of you must have greatly changed, if it be what you would like to hear.'

Hildegarde moved behind her sister to hide the intense blush which now spread over her features, and, placing her hand on her shoulder, perhaps to prevent her from turning round, she said, in a low voice, and with an embarrassed manner, 'Crescenz, you have no idea, I am sure, how you are paining me at this moment. You are forcing me to confess that I have not in this instance acted towards you with my usual candour. I have the very highest opinion of Mr. Hamilton.'

'Well, to be sure!' exclaimed Crescenz, while she endeavoured to catch a glimpse of her sister's face, but Hildegarde moved still further back, and continued—'That I disliked him at first is most true, more on your acount, however, than on mine; for his open hostility to me was excusable—his covert attentions to you unpardonable.'

'But,' said Crescenz, who seemed altogether to have forgotten Hamilton's presence; 'but when did you begin to think differently of him?'

'From the time that he has ceased to be the subject of altercation between us,' answered Hildegarde, bending over her sister, and kissing her forehead.

'But, Hildegarde,' cried Crescenz, turning round with unexpected energy, 'before we went to the ball, do you remember, when I told you that Lina Berger had said that Mr. Hamilton might still be my *scha*—'

Hildegarde's two hands closed over her mouth, and the word was stifled in utterance. 'Good gracious! I quite forgot he was still here,' she cried, making a slight effort to laugh, and then running out of the room.

A long pause ensued. Hildegarde began to arrange the cups and saucers on a tray, until Hamilton, without looking up, asked her if she could remember the very time when her opinion of him had changed.

'Perfectly; it was the night of Crescenz's quarrel with Major Stultz. Your explanations by moonlight in our room were upright and honourable.'

'And you forgave my having flirted with her at Seon?'

'Yes; and I forgive your having tried to do the same with me here.'

'The case is totally different,' began Hamilton.

'There is some difference, I allow,' said Hildegarde : 'you warned me so well, that it would have been inexcusable my not understanding you—besides, I had the advantage of hearing from Count Zedwitz, that you considered yourself at liberty to act as you pleased, after having so fairly warned me.'

'Zedwitz's love for you made him forget his friendship for me altogether,' said Hamilton, with some irritation.

'I do not blame your conduct to me,' said Hildegarde, 'you wanted to improve yourself in German, and found quarrelling or flirting with me the most exciting method. I have profited by your society also, for I have not only learned to pronounce English, but,' she added, with an arch smile, 'I begin to understand something of the art of flirting too, of which, I do assure you, I knew nothing when our acquaintance began.'

'Oh, do not say that,' cried Hamilton, 'you are only joking, I am sure, for you have no inclination that way, but your sister Crescenz—'

'My sister Crescenz knew nothing of your propensities that way at Seon, and, therefore, I blame your conduct towards her. Your love, if you ever felt any, was pardonable ; people cannot help that, I believe—but your endeavours to make her dislike Major Stultz were quite unpardonable.'

'I acknowledge it,' said Hamilton, gravely, 'and regret it.'

'That fault you were able in some measure to repair,' continued Hildegarde, 'but perhaps you are not aware that you have been the cause of frequent altercations between me and my sister—and that almost total estrangement has taken place between us in consequence.'

'And is that my fault too ?' asked Hamilton.

'I don't know,' she replied, sorrowfully. 'Before we became acquainted with you, we never had the most trifling difference of opinion—and now we never think alike, and all confidence is at an end !'

'You take the matter too seriously,' said Hamilton; 'I am convinced your sister is not aware of any estrangement.'

'I am afraid you are mistaken—' began Hildegarde, but at this moment Crescenz entered the room ; she was dressed to go out, and asked her sister to accompany her.

'May I go with you ?' asked Hamilton.

'N——o, I rather think not,' replied Hildegarde.

'But he may come for us in an hour or so,' said Crescenz, nodding to him with a smile.

' Tell me where I shall find you.'

Crescenz coloured and hesitated. ' In—in my—in the—in Major Stultz's apartments—'

' We are going to arrange the furniture,' said Hildegarde, closing the door.

The hour had scarcely half elapsed, when Hamilton found himself again with the two sisters : he was without ceremony desired to make himself useful, and immediately employed in assisting to arrange a press which was to be filled with linen—afterwards the chairs and tables were moved about in all directions, the *étagère* admired, and finally they adjourned to the kitchen, where Crescenz, with amusing exultation, exhibited one by one her culinary utensils to Hamilton, explaining their uses, and assuring him that though her mother intended to give her Walburg as servant, she was determined to cook everything herself. While she was yet speaking, old Hans came to say, she was expected home — they were to dine earlier than usual, and the hairdresser was expected before two o'clock. She became very pale, and after having dismissed him, sat down on a little wooden stool, and began to cry. Hildegarde silently made a sign to Hamilton to leave them, and greatly wondering at the sudden change, he walked back to the drawing-room.

On glancing round at the furniture which Crescenz considered so splendid, he could not help smiling at the frugality of her taste. Was he to be envied for his more lavish ideas? Assuredly not. Everything in this world, from the diamond to the first thing beyond the absolute necessaries of life, is valued fictitiously. The actual worth depends on the mind of the possessor, and is regulated in civilised countries by unconsciously-made comparisons—the mental effort losing itself in the result. To Crescenz, the thin white muslin curtains were quite as desirable, even on a cold day in February, as to Hamilton the richest silk—the yellow sofa, with its hard stuffed cushions and perpendicular sides, was intended to be a seat of honour for a guest, and was not adapted for reclining—even Hamilton must have failed in discovering a posture of repose upon it, and he had a most decided talent for making himself comfortable. The six chairs had long thin legs, but the wood which had been spared on the legs had been conscientiously bestowed on the backs, which were tastefully formed to represent hearts. A table, two chests of drawers, and the *étagère* completed the furniture of the room. As Hamilton stood before the latter, trying to admire the cups, saucers, glasses, and bronze candlesticks, arranged upon it and reflected in the looking-glasses, which for that purpose formed the back, Hildegarde and her sister entered; Crescenz, with the traces of recent tears on her face, nevertheless, looked complacently around her, for the twentieth time arranged the folds of the curtains, dusted the table with her handkerchief, and then led the way downstairs.

At five o'clock a party of about sixteen or eighteen persons assembled in the private chapel of the Frauen church to witness the marriage of Major Stultz and Crescenz Rosenberg. The bride shed no tears; she looked very pretty and very shy—the bridegroom rather stouter and redder than usual. Madame Rosenberg openly expressed her satisfaction, and hoped the day was not far distant when she should be in the same place, and for the same purpose, on Hildegarde's account. Hildegarde was pale and silent, and Mr. Rosenberg alone showed that he was endeavouring to control his emotion.

On their return home, they found the rooms lighted, and supper prepared under the superintendence of Madame Lustig. They spent three hours at table, and then they danced, and then they ate, and then they danced again until past midnight, when, to conclude the festivity, punch was made. Let it not be supposed that this was, as in England, a simple mixture of water, sugar, and cognac, or rum. In Germany it is a complicated business, and, notwithstanding the previous preparations of Madame Lustig, Madame Rosenberg and three or four matrons accompanied her to the kitchen to assist in the brewing. Each had a different receipt—and a separation of the parties became absolutely necessary, as one proposed using black, another green tea, for the mixture, while the others were for rice-water or wine. Hamilton, who had become a sort of authority in the house on all subjects, was consulted; but on his venturing to suggest pure water, Madame Rosenberg, laughingly, pushed him towards the drawing-room, saying, it was evident he knew nothing about the matter,—he might dance until the punch was ready!

Most excellent it proved to be, however concocted, when at length Madame Rosenberg appeared with a soup-tureen full and dispensed it ladlewise to the surrounding company, who then crowded around Major Stultz and Crescenz in order to clink their glasses, and partake of a colossal sponge-cake, which the latter distributed in ample portions.

A short time afterwards old Hans announced 'the carriage for Miss Crescenz,' and she retired with evident reluctance to put on her shawl. The whole company prepared to leave at the same time, and were soon altogether in the corridor. Crescenz embraced her stepmother, and somewhat formally thanked her for her kindness and generosity. She held out her hand to Hamilton, and then threw herself into her sister's arms, and burst into tears. 'Come, come, Crescenz,' cried her father, with an attempt at gaiety he was far from feeling; 'this will never do—you are taking leave as if seas, and not streets, were to separate us. Come,' and he drew her arm within his, and led her down stairs. The others followed, all but Hildegarde, and, after a moment's hesitation, Hamilton. They returned to the deserted drawing-room, where Hildegarde threw open the window, and leaned out.

They soon heard Crescenz's voice saying cheerfully, 'Good night, Lina—good night, papa—good night, Hildegarde.'

'Good night,' answered her sister from the window, and the carriage drove off.

'Well, have we not spent a merry evening?' cried Madame Rosenberg, triumphantly, as she almost breathlessly entered the room a few minutes afterwards. 'This has been a gay wedding after all, you see, Franz.'

'It has,' he answered, sinking dejectedly on the sofa; 'I am quite provoked with myself for feeling so low-spirited. I believe I am not well.'

'Ah, bah!' cried his wife, laughing, 'if you had been ill, you could not have supped as you have done. Perhaps, how-ever, you have eaten too much fish, or turkey, or ham. At all events, I am sure you are tired and sleepy, so you may go to bed, while we put everything in order again.'

Mr. Rosenberg, as usual, followed his wife's advice without contradiction. He held Hamilton's hand for a moment, as if he intended to say something more than the good night, which was scarcely audible.

CHAPTER XXXIII.

A CHANGE.

HAMILTON was awakened about three o'clock in the morning by Hildegarde rushing to the door of his room, and exclaiming, 'For Heaven's sake get up—get up and come to my father—I am afraid he has got the cholera. You have seen people ill, and know the symptoms. Oh, come—we do not know what to do !'

'Send for the doctor,' cried Hamilton, 'I shall be with you in a moment.'

On entering Mr. Rosenberg's room, Hamilton found Hildegarde standing beside his bed, while Madame Rosenberg was walking up and down the room, gesticulating like a person in a state of mental derangement.

'Oh, Mr. Hamilton,' she exclaimed, the moment she perceived him ; 'tell me, only tell me that Franz has not got the cholera, and I shall be grateful as long as I live ! It would be too hard were he to have it now, when people say there is nothing more to fear. Last week, only one man—quite a decrepit old man, died of it ! I am sure Franz has only eaten too much supper yesterday evening. Do n't you think so ? Say that he has not got the cholera, and I shall believe you implicitly.'

But Hamilton could not say so, nor unfortunately Doctor Berger either ; the case was at once pronounced a bad one, and, in a fearfully short time, quite hopeless. Consternation and dismay pervaded the whole household, when on the morning of the third day, poor Mr. Rosenberg was no more. Completely overpowered by the suddenness of her own bereavement, Madame Rosenberg retired to her room, unable to speak to anyone.

Major Stultz immediately undertook the necessary arrangements for the funeral, and gave directions for the printing of circular letters to announce the death to distant relations and friends—a custom which saves the mourning family the performance of a most painful duty. Hamilton took the two little boys to their sister Crescenz. Her married life had begun in anxiety and sorrow, and Hamilton felt some natural trepidation at seeing her again, under such painful circumstances ; but her grief was of the most tranquil description ;

the tears flowed unrestrainedly over her round rosy cheeks, and when they ceased, left not a trace behind. Although but a few days had elapsed since she had left her family, a not quite willing bride, she had already begun to repeat her husband's words as oracles. Hamilton half smiled as he heard her 'Thank goodness, that she at least was provided for, and had a home!' She hoped poor dear Hildegarde would not now begin to repent having refused such a man as Major Stultz, the more so as that refusal precluded the possibility of her ever residing with them!'

Poor Hildegarde! She had not bestowed one thought, much less a regret, on Major Stultz. Hamilton, on his return, found her sitting in her room, perfectly motionless, with parched lips, and eyes devoid of tears. He hoped she had at length begun to think of herself, recommended her to try to eat something and to go to bed. She looked at him as if his words had not conveyed the slightest sense to her mind— walked uneasily up and down the room for a few minutes, and then said with a shudder, 'I am so afraid of his being buried alive! Do you think he was quite—quite dead? If I could only see him once more!'

'And who would be so cruel as to prevent you?' exclaimed Hamilton. 'If it be any relief to your mind, I will remain in his room to-night!'

'In his room!' she cried, clasping her hands convulsively; 'he is no longer there—they have taken him away to the dead-house—'

'The dead-house! Where is that?'

'In the burying-ground. They have watchers there, I believe, but still he is among all the frightful corpses, and should he come to himself—imagine how horrible! You will go with me—you will let me see him once more! I cannot else believe that he is really dead!'

'I will go with you there, or anywhere you please,' said Hamilton, completely overcome by her evident wretchedness.

The weather was unusually inclement; a storm of falling sleet almost blinded them as they waded through the half-melted snow which lay on the road outside the town: but Hildegarde seemed unconscious of all these impediments, and hurried on silently until she reached the churchyard, where she turned to a building which had escaped Hamilton's observation on a former occasion, and walked directly up to a row of glass doors, and stood as if transfixed with horror. Hamilton was in a moment at her side, and it must be confessed that to those who were not inured to the various aspects of death, the scene which presented itself was shocking in the extreme. On tables in the interior a long row of open coffins were arranged, their ghastly tenants dressed with a care that seemed to mock the solemnity of death and interment. A young officer was in his uniform, as if about to appear on parade ;—an elderly gentleman dressed for a ball ;—a young girl, whose half-opened mouth and eyes showed the struggle with which soul and body had parted, was crowned with flowers, and a long white veil lay in light folds over her bare arms and white dress, reaching almost to the satin shoes which covered the stiff cold feet as they protruded beyond the coffin in hideous rigidity. Mr. Rosenberg was now scarcely recognisable—his livid features were contracted, and not a trace remained of that beauty for which he had been so remarkable. Hamilton turned away, but again his eyes encountered death. Another and lighter room was filled with the corpses of poorer persons and children : the latter indeed seemed to sleep, and on them the wreaths of flowers did not appear misplaced.

Hildegarde seemed unable to tear herself from the spot, nor did Hamilton feel disposed to disturb her, until he perceived a number of persons hurrying to and fro, and torches glimmering in the churchyard ; he then asked a woman who appeared with a bunch of keys in her hand, if there was to be a funeral.

'I believe the Countess Raimund is to be buried this evening,' she answered.

'Not one of these ?' cried Hamilton, pointing to the place where Hildegarde stood.

'Yes ; just there beside the gentleman who died of cholera —that old lady in black satin with her mouth wide open—it was shameful negligence of those about her not to close it before the jaw stiffened !'

'Hildegarde,' said Hamilton, drawing her arm within his ; you must now leave this place. There is to be a funeral.'

'I know—I heard,' she said, allowing herself to be led away, with her head still turned towards the chamber of death. 'The only precedence which the Countess Raimund can now claim of my father,' she added, bitterly, 'is that of first descending into the grave ! How absurd all pride appears when standing at the threshold of a charnel-house !'

'Very true,' said Hamilton, 'but how seldom the proud—how seldom anyone thinks of such a place ! Where are you going now ?'

'To my mother's grave.'

He made no opposition, for he hoped that some sudden recollection would put an end to the unnatural calmness of her manner, and was for this reason not sorry to perceive that the gravedigger had already been at work ; the place was measured, and some shovels full of earth had been thrown over the grave she came to visit.

She seemed for a few minutes to pray, and then sat down beside the stone cross, and began assiduously to arrange the leaves of the still green, though withered, ivy wreaths which she had placed on it in November.

'I am trying your patience unpardonably,' she observed at length, rising from her cheerless occupation; 'and it is all to no purpose.'

'What do you mean ?' asked Hamilton.

'I expected to feel something like sorrow for my father's loss. You will be shocked when I tell you that I cannot feel anything resembling it. Before I came here I thought my odious apathy was caused by doubts of the reality of his death ; those doubts are all removed—I know that he is dead —that in a few hours he will be in the grave, and moulder beside my mother's skeleton ; and I do not, cannot feel anything like grief !'

'You are too much stunned by the suddenness,' began Hamilton.

'Not so,' said Hildegarde, quietly, 'I assure you I never felt more perfectly contented than at this moment: were it not that I shudder at my total want of sensibility.'

'If it be insensibility,' said Hamilton; 'but you have so much decision, so much firmness of character, that——'

'No, no,' she cried, hastily interrupting him; 'this is not firmness. Do not imagine that I feel emotion which I am endeavouring to conceal, or suppressing tears ready to flow; I only feel an almost irresistible inclination to walk or run without stopping !'

'I am surprised that you do not find yourself completely exhausted,' said Hamilton. 'It would certainly be more natural, when one takes into consideration that you have not slept for three nights, or eaten anything for nearly two days!'

'And you also have passed three sleepless nights,' said Hildegarde, 'and without the hopes and fears which made the want of rest imperceptible to me. I ought to have remembered that sooner.'

'I was not thinking of myself,' cried Hamilton. 'And your hopes and fears,' he added, in a lower voice, 'I have most truly participated. Will you never believe that your joys are my joys, your sorrows my sorrows?'

He waited in vain for an answer, Hildegarde leaned heavily on his arm and breathed quickly; he at length caught a glimpse of her face, and was so shocked at the convulsive workings of her features, that he beckoned to one of the numerous hackney coachmen returning from the churchyard, and silently placed his unresisting companion in the carriage. She sighed so deeply, and then gasped so fearfully for breath, that he let down all the windows, and experienced the most heartfelt pleasure, when at length she burst into a passion of tears.

She wept unrestrainedly until they reached home, but, even on the stairs as they ascended, Hamilton perceived a return of her former unnaturally composed manner.

During the next day, Madame Rosenberg was almost constantly surrounded by her friends and acquaintance. Towards evening, Crescenz drew her sister aside, and whispered, 'Oh, my dear Hildegarde, this is an irreparable loss for you!'

'Irreparable indeed!' said Hildegarde, moving her head dejectedly; 'I wish it had pleased God to let me die instead of my father—few would have mourned for me!'

'I 'm sure, dear, I do n't know what is to become of you now! I can't bear to think of it, but I suppose you will have to apply to Mademoiselle Hortense to get you a situation as governess; you know she promised to do so whenever you wished it——'

'I know,' said Hildegarde, rubbing her forehead with her hand, and biting her underlip with an expression of great distress. 'Let us talk about that some other time—I cannot *think* yet.'

'It was Lina Berger who talked about it; she said she was sure that mamma would not propose your remaining with her, and Major Stultz says that——'

'Crescenz,' said Hildegarde, with some impatience, 'say what you please to me from yourself, I am ready to hear you, but do not torture me now with the opinions of either Lina Berger or Major Stultz.'

'Well, to be sure! And how often have you said that you considered him a sensible man!'

'I have not changed my opinion, but as I know he can feel no sort of interest in anything that concerns me, I do not wish to hear what he has said.'

'Ah, I see, Mr. Hamilton has been telling you—he smiled so strangely when I was speaking to him yesterday, that I was sure he would tell you everything—I indeed wished to have had you with me directly; it was my first thought, but Blasius said that what occurred at—at Seon—you know, made it quite impossible!'

'Mr. Hamilton told me nothing of all this,' said Hildegarde. 'I thank you for your kind intentions, dear Crescenz. I can imagine that Major Stultz's refusal to comply with your wishes has pained you; but you may set your mind at rest, for I feel, even more intensely than he can, the impossibility of my ever becoming an inmate of his house.'

'Well,' said Crescenz, apparently greatly relieved; 'I'm sure I am glad to hear you say so: for though he talked very sensibly, and all that, this morning, I could not help crying, and was quite uncomfortable at the idea of speaking to you about it; I was afraid you might think that, now I am married, I love you less.'

'Four days is too short a time to work such a change, I hope,' said Hildegarde, with a melancholy smile; then suddenly seizing her sister's hands, she exclaimed, 'O Crescenz, love me! Love me still—as much as you can. Think how I shall miss my father's affection!'

'Very true, indeed! As Blasius says, my father bestowed his whole affection on you, and quite overlooked me!'

Hildegarde gazed at her sister for a moment in silence, and then turned away with tearful eyes. She saw that Crescenz would soon be lost to her for ever. Major Stultz already directed her thoughts and words as completely as she herself had done when they were at school together. She watched her returning to their stepmother's room, and then walked slowly towards the door leading to the passage. Hamilton was standing at the stove—had heard the sisters' conversation,

B B

and filled with compassion for her deserted position, he seized her hand as she passed, and passionately pressed it to his lips without speaking. When she raised her heavy eyelids to look at him, she saw that his eyes were suffused with tears.

' I—thank you—for your sympathy,' she murmured, with trembling lips, as she withdrew her hand, and hurried out of the room.

CHAPTER XXXIV.

THE ARRANGEMENT.

AFTER the interment of Mr. Rosenberg, some time passed over in melancholy monotony. Madame Rosenberg employed herself principally with the inspection and arrangement of papers; Hildegarde wandered about the house, endeavouring, in an absent manner, to make herself useful. She even tried to assist the new cook, but her efforts were so completely unsuccessful, that her mother begged she would desist, as she had no sort of talent in that line.

Mr. Rosenberg had been a kind husband and an affectionate father; Hamilton had invariably found him an agreeable companion, but his constant occupation in his office, and an inveterate habit of going out every evening, had made his society an occurrence of such rarity, that Hamilton in a short time became quite resigned to his loss; in fact, but for the mourning dresses, Hildegarde's unconquerable dejection, and the never-failing tears of Madame Rosenberg, as she circumstantially related to every visitor the history of her husband's illness and death, he would soon have forgotten that he had ever existed. He attended the College lectures, studied German with his friend Biedermann, rode, walked—in short, continued all his former occupations, with the exception of his quarrels with Hildegarde—these had now entirely ceased; he obeyed her slightest directions, anticipated her wishes with a sort of quiet devotion so completely directed to her alone, but so unobtrusive, that Madame Rosenberg failed to observe more than that they had learned to live peaceably in the same house together, and praised them both more than once for having ceased their silly and useless quarrels.

One day, about the beginning of April, Hildegarde recalled him just as he was about to leave the house, saying that her mother wished to speak to him; he laughingly demanded if the probably not very important communication could not be deferred to another day, as he had promised to meet some friends at Tambosi's in the Hofgarten. Hildegarde gravely shook her head, and said she believed her mother was waiting for him.

'What a bore!' he exclaimed, striding along the passage; 'I suppose I shall be detained half-an-hour to hear a lecture about having forgotten to extinguish the candles last night, or having burnt my boots on the stove! I really wish, Hildegarde, you would give your new cook instructions about my room— it is not at all necessary that your mother should be informed every time an accident occurs there.'

Madame Rosenberg was sitting at an old-fashioned scrutoire, furnished with innumerable diminutive, secret, and apparent drawers; she had a small packet of bills beside her, and various heaps of money before her. When Hamilton entered, she immediately moved back her chair, and pointed to another, beside her, which she wished him to occupy. Now Hamilton had already become a little spoiled by Madame Rosenberg's indulgence, praises, and deference to his opinion; he had learned to like her, and even overlook her vulgarity; but in proportion as his affection had increased, his respect had decreased, and, like the spoiled son of a weak mother, he now stood leaning against the door, refusing, with an impatient gesture, the offered chair, and murmuring some unintelligible words about business and appointments.

'I shall not detain you long.' said Madame Rosenberg, drawing out of her pocket an enormous linen handkerchief, and wiping away two large tears, which were obtrusively rolling down her cheeks, 'I ought to have spoken to you long ago, but I have been thinking over and over the means of rendering my communication less disagreeable.'

'So,' cried Hamilton, closing the door and advancing towards her, 'so it is not about the boots you are going to lecture me.

'No,' she replied, half laughing, 'though I must say—'

'I know all you are going to say,' cried Hamilton, laughing 'extravagant habits, horrible smell, danger of burning the house, and all that! Suppose it said—I am very contrite indeed, and promise not to burn either shirt or boots for three weeks to come, and not at all when the weather is warmer, and the stove is not heated.'

BB 2

'In three weeks, and when the weather is warmer, we shall be too far apart for me either to lecture or detain you in my room against your will.'

'My dear Madame Rosenberg,' exclaimed Hamilton, springing towards her, and not only seating himself on the previously disdained chair, but drawing it so close to hers, that she involuntarily drew back: 'my dear Madame Rosenberg, you surely do not mean that I must leave you ?'

'I do, indeed,' she answered, nodding her head slowly and despondingly, and again the monstrous handkerchief was put in requisition. 'I'm sure,' she added, somewhat surprised at the varying emotions depicted on his countenance; 'I'm sure its very kind of you to be so sorry to leave us—I thought the loss was wholly on our side.'

'I have spent seven of the happiest months of my life in your house,' began Hamilton.

'Six months and one week,' said Madame Rosenberg, interrupting him. 'You were three weeks at Havard's, you know, and when we are settling our account, the three weeks must be deducted, for, as poor dear Franz said—'

'I should like to know your intentions with respect to Hildegarde,' said Hamilton, who had not heard one word of the explanation.

'Hildegarde goes with me to the Iron Works, as people now call them; poor Franz was so uneasy about her on his deathbed, that I promised him she should never leave my house, excepting with her own free will, and always have the power of returning to it when she chose, and that she should receive on her marriage a trousseau in every respect like her sister's.'

'This promise must have been a great relief to his mind,' observed Hamilton.

'It was,' said Madame Rosenberg, and the tears flowed fast, as she added, 'I would have given him everything I have in the world, to have made him contented in his last moments. We lived so happily together during the twelve years which we passed in this house. I cannot remain here any longer—the house—the furniture—Munich itself has become odious to me. I intend to return to my father. Fritz will be made a gentleman, as his father wished it, at the military school. Gustle must be his grandfather's successor at the Iron Works; he has, at all events, no great love of learning, and Peppy is too young to be taken into consideration at present.'

'Take *me* with you to the Iron Works,' said Hamilton, abruptly.

Madame Rosenberg looked at him as if she did not quite comprehend.

'Take me with you to the Iron Works,' he repeated.

She shook her head. 'It is no place for you,' she said, steadily, 'nor is my father, though an excellent man, a companion for you. Your parents would be dissatisfied, and with reason, were you to bury yourself in an insignificant village, just so many miles from Munich as to prevent your being able to avail yourself of the advantages, which you told me you had found here, for the completion of your education.'

Hamilton felt the justness of her remark, and did not attempt to contradict it ; he had, however, no intention of quitting a family of which Hildegarde was still to be a member ; nor did he much concern himself about the satisfaction or dissatisfaction of his parents, just at that moment. He understood Madame Rosenberg perfectly, and changed his tactics. Throwing himself back in his chair, he said, with apparent resignation, 'Well, I suppose I must spend the ensuing five months at Havard's, that's all !'

'At Havard's ! What an idea !' exclaimed Madame Rosenberg, 'to be giving suppers and drinking champagne every night ! I never heard of anything so absurd.'

'Why, where else can I go ? I cannot well take a lodging and engage a cook and housemaid for myself, can I ?'

'No,' replied Madame Rosenberg, half laughing ; 'not exactly that—but a lodging, or a family might be found. Suppose, for instance, that Madame Berger should have proposed taking you, in case the Doctor have no objection, eh ?'

'I am sure I have none,' said Hamilton, vainly endeavouring to suppress a smile as he added, ' She is one of the prettiest little women I ever saw, and with time and opportunity I have no doubt I shall fall desperately in love with her. You will not be there to sustain me with your good advice—and—a—but at least you will be answerable for the consequences, as you will have led me into temptation.'

'Good heavens ! Not for the world would I take such a responsibility on me !' cried Madame Rosenberg, with a look of amazement ; 'Lina, too, so giddy and thoughtless, and the Doctor never at home ! It would never do, I see. But who would have imagined that you would think of such a thing at your age !'

'I am just at the age to act more from impulse than reason, and I consider you too much my friend, not to speak candidly to you. If Major Stultz were not so insufferably jealous, you could make me over to Crescenz—my regard for her is really of the most blameless description, and will never be otherwise.'

'Oh, the Major would never listen to such a proposal.'

'Then I have no alternative but Havard's—Havard's or your house,' he continued, taking her large hard hand and pressing it fervently; 'dear Madame Rosenberg, let me go with you; I have a sort of presentiment that it is the only means of keeping me out of mischief; besides, I can ride or drive into Munich two or three times a week.'

'But I have no room for you,' she cried, with a look of distress; for the earnestness of his manner had begun to move her.

'You must make room for me,' urged Hamilton.

'And as to your horses and Hans—'

'Oh, I can easily find quarters for them in the neighbourhood.'

'You will have to sleep in a room without a stove—'

'I don't want a stove in summer.'

'Well then,' she said, hesitatingly, 'if you think that you can be satisfied with the accommodation which I have at my disposal, you may accompany us to the country. Should our manner of living, or what I fear more, my father, not suit you, you can leave us, you know; we will part friends, at all events.'

'Don't talk or think of parting,' cried Hamilton, gaily. 'I am sure I shall find your father a most worthy person—we shall get on famously together. When do you leave? It will be quite delightful to breathe the country air. I assure you I feel already impatient to be off.'

'On the 24th I purpose leaving Munich,' said Madame Rosenberg, once more drawing her chair towards her scrutoire, and beginning to count her little heaps of money.

'Are these Iron Works romantically situated?' asked Hamilton.

'N—o. They are on the high road at the end of the village; but there is a fine old oak wood quite close to us.'

'Ah! an oak wood,' repeated Hamilton, thoughtfully.

'We have also a garden and orchard behind the house; the

smoke from the forge indeed spoils the flowers greatly, but there is an arbour under the trees where we can breakfast, and drink coffee after dinner in summer — the arbour is quite covered with roses and honeysuckles.'

'Ah, that is delightful!' cried Hamilton, in vision imagining himself sitting with Hildegarde in the rose and honeysuckle arbour.

'But you are forgetting your appointment,' observed Madame Rosenberg, who had been in vain endeavouring to correct a fault in her reckoning.

'A civil way of telling me to leave you in peace,' said Hamilton, laughing.

'Not at all, I assure you. If you have really no appointment, I shall be glad to talk over my plans with you.'

'I *had* an appointment,' he said, looking at his watch, 'for which I am too late. I have another, for which I am a few minutes too early.'

'A few minutes,' repeated Madame Rosenberg, 'that will never do for me. In your "few minutes" I can only inform you that you must go for a few days at least to Havard's, until I have got everything in order. Hildegarde and the children I intend to pack off the day after to-morrow.'

'Oh, pack me off, too, with Hil—— with the children,' cried Hamilton, eagerly. 'I wish you would consider me really as one of them.'

'Well, I am sure I have always done so since you have been with me. Poor Franz often said I took great liberties with you.'

Hamilton smiled. 'I suppose,' he said, turning towards the door, 'Hans may pack up my chattels; you will send me to the country with the children.'

'No, no, no,' cried Madame Rosenberg, hastily, 'that will never do; I must write to my father and explain. If he knew the sort of person you are—he would never consent to your becoming an inmate of his house!'

'Am I, then, so very disagreeable?' asked Hamilton.

'Quite the contrary—but you do not understand my father. In short, it is better to tell you at once—why should I be ashamed to say it? He was a common journeyman smith—so extremely industrious, of such enormous strength, and with so much talent for mechanics, that he made himself not only useful, but altogether indispensable to my grandfather, who, rather than lose him, gave him his daughter in marriage. Our forge became in time an Iron Work, and he is now the richest man far and wide. To see him, you would not suppose so ; he is neither changed in manner nor dress—' Madame Rosenberg paused.

'Well?' said Hamilton.

'Well!' she repeated, a little impatiently. 'It is plain enough, I think, that such a man will not suit you—or you suit him.'

'I do n't know that,' said Hamilton. 'A man who has turned a forge into an Iron Work, and who from having nothing has become rich by honest means, must be possessed of good sense and good talents too. As to his appearance or dress—a man's coat—'

That's just what I am afraid of,' cried Madame Rosenberg.

'Do you think I attach such importance to a coat? I assure you that I am determined to like your father with and without a coat.'

'I will write him *that*, and it will at once put an end to our difficulties, for if I may say *that*, he will never imagine you are so fastidious—'

'I do n't quite understand—' said Hamilton, with a puzzled air.

'It would never do—you see—were we to inconvenience him,' said Madame Rosenberg, 'or force him to change his mode of life. He likes to work and dine in his shirt sleeves, and is not over particular how his meals are served—this I can change, perhaps, but against the shirt sleeves I can do nothing, and I know it is very vulgar ; Franz told me so often enough.'

'I have no sort of objection to his shirt sleeves,' said Hamilton, 'provided he allow me to wear a coat. What matter ! If this be the only reason why I should not go with Hildegarde and the children the day after to-morrow, I think you may waive all ceremony and tell your father that I belong to the family. You have made an agreement to keep me for six months longer.'

'That is a good idea,' said Madame Rosenberg, laughing. 'I will write to him to-morrow, and I dare say I shall have an answer in a day or two.'

Hamilton perceived he had gained every concession he could reasonably demand, and left the room quietly and thoughtfully.

Hildegarde had prepared her brothers for their afternoon

walk, and was waiting with some indications of impatience for his appearance. He had been forbidden to walk with her, but had established a sort of right to be informed where she intended to go—that he should ride near her, or at least become visible during her walk, was a sort of tacit agreement.

'The Nymphenburg road,' cried Gustle, springing towards him. 'May I have one of your canes?'

'And may I, too, have one to ride upon?' asked Peppy.

'Yes,' said Hamilton. 'Hildegarde will show you those you may take.'

'Oh come, Hildegarde,' cried Gustle, pulling her rather roughly; 'come and choose the canes for us. I must have the little black one with the horse's head on it.'

But Hildegarde showed no inclination to move. 'You were a long time in my mother's room,' she said at length, with some embarrassment.

'Not longer than was necessary to make her consent to take me with her to the country. Oh, Hildegarde, what pleasant walks we shall have in the oak wood, and how much happier we shall be there than here! Were you ever at these Iron Works?'

'Not since I was a child,' answered Hildegarde, smiling as she had not smiled since her father's death; 'I remember the noise of the hammers was incessant, and the house shook a good deal, and the white window curtains were very soon soiled.'

'We shall get used to the hammers, I dare say,' said Hamilton, laughing. 'As to the house shaking, that must be imagination, and the window curtains can be easily changed, you know.'

'But mamma said nothing in the world would induce her to take you with us. How did you persuade her?'

'I can tell you all that when I return home. Excuse me as well as you can, should I be late for supper. Good-bye!'

'Where are you going?' asked Hildegarde.

He whispered a few words, and then hurried down-stairs.

CHAPTER XXXV.

THE DIFFICULTY REMOVED.

IT was late in the evening, and Hamilton had not yet returned. Madame Rosenberg began to get a little uneasy, and very impatient, when fortunately Madame Berger arrived to complain bitterly of her husband, who had declined receiving Mr. Hamilton as an inmate of his house on any terms. 'He says I am too young—and he is too often absent—and people might talk ! Did you ever hear anything so absurd ? '

' I believe he is right,' said Madame Rosenberg, 'you are too young——'

' I wonder it never occurred to you that your step-daughters were still younger ! ' cried Madame Berger, glancing towards Hildegarde, who was sitting at the window, looking into the street.

' The case is quite different,' said Madame Rosenberg, 'we are a large family; and where a father and mother are in a house——'

' Pshaw ! ' cried Madame Berger, impatiently ; ' Cressy liked him for all that, better than she will ever like her husband, I suspect.'

' Who told you that ?' cried Madame Rosenberg, with a look of amazement.

' My own eyes,' replied Madame Berger, with a slight laugh ; ' and not Hildegarde,' she added in answer to a look of suspicion, which Madame Rosenberg had cast on her step-daughter. ' Believe me, neither the presence of father nor mother can prevent these things.'

' Crescenz is most happily married,' began Madame Rosenberg.

' So am I—but I preferred Theodore Biedermann to the Doctor, as you well know. You need not look so astonished at hearing me speak the truth, Hildegarde. I vow one would almost imagine you heard this for the first time ! As if Cressy had not betrayed me long ago, not to mention Mademoiselle Hortense, who of course used me as a scarecrow for the whole school ! Excepting, perhaps, the dear, good old Doctor,' she continued, ' there is not one of my friends or acquaintance who does not know that I nearly cried my eyes out about Theodore.'

'And is it possible you have not told Dr. Berger?' cried Hildegarde, turning quickly round. 'Did you not feel bound in honour——'

'No, mademoiselle,' replied Madame Berger, sharply; 'I did not feel myself bound in honour deliberately to destroy my domestic peace—I leave it to you to make such a confession when you are going to be married, if you think it necessary!'

'I am afraid Hildegarde is not likely to be married at all, now that we are going to live at the Iron Works,' sighed Madame Rosenberg. 'The only neighbour we have is the *Förster*, and he——'

'Lord bless you!' cried Madame Berger, 'Hildegarde would never look at a *Förster* if he were not by chance a count or baron. Had Mr. Hamilton been a *Milor*, she would never have thought of quarrelling with him, I can tell you!'

'Caroline!—Madame!' exclaimed Hildegarde, with a vehemence that made Madame Berger retreat a few steps from the window, while she cried, with affected fear, 'Good heavens! I had no idea that you could get into a passion about *him!* And here he is,' she added, springing again to the window, as she heard the sound of a horse's hoofs on the pavement; 'here he is, and I suspect there are few *Milors* to be compared to him; he certainly is the handsomest creature I ever saw! An ideal of an Englishman! *Un amour!*'

'Lina,' said Madame Rosenberg, reproachfully, 'you must forgive my observing that this language is not proper for a young married woman.'

'Ah bah, as if I were serious! Have you forgotten that you used to say I always spoke without thinking? Now Hildegarde there, thinks without speaking, perhaps!'

'Not of Mr. Hamilton,' said Madame Rosenberg. 'for she did not even look out of the window at your *amour*, or whatever you called him. Hildegarde, go and tell him we have waited nearly two hours for him, that supper is ready, and that I beg he will come just as he is, and not make an evening toilette, for once in a way.'

She had not time to deliver her message, for Hamilton entered the room with unusual precipitation, and handed Madame Rosenberg an enormous, ill-folded, large-wafered letter.

'From my father!' she exclaimed, with surprise.

'Yes; he has no sort of objection to my accompanying you to the Iron Works; he says you may take me instead of Fritz'

'A good idea,' cried Madame Berger, as she came from behind the window-curtain; 'it is, however, Mr. Hamilton's, and not your father's.'

'It is in the letter, however,' said Madame Rosenberg, eagerly perusing the inelegant specimen of penmanship; 'but I do not see anything about Hans or the horses.'

'Oh, I said nothing about them: they can go to the inn.'

'But we have a stable——' began Madame Rosenberg.

'I know you have, and a pair of stout greys in it. Your father has promised me a lift into Munich every Saturday, when he sends in his iron.'

'On the cart?' asked Madame Berger.

'Yes,' said Hamilton, 'there are places for two on the seat in front. The offer was very civil, considering the shortness of our acquaintance.'

'It is a proof at all events that he has taken a great fancy to you,' said Madame Rosenberg, with an air of great satisfaction; 'and as you wish to go with the children, Hildegarde must arrange your room for you. Do you hear, Hildegarde?'

'Yes, mamma.'

'Your grandfather made most particular inquiries about you,' observed Hamilton, turning to Hildegarde.

'He is not *my* grandfather, he is no relation whatever of mine,' she answered in French, while her colour heightened rapidly, and seemed to be reflected in Hamilton's face, which became crimson.

'I don't understand French,' said Madame Rosenberg, looking at them alternately; 'but I think I can guess; however, it is no matter—read this letter, Hildegarde; in it you will find everything, and more than you could have heard from Mr. Hamilton. My father is willing to act towards you as a relation—do not, by an ill-timed exhibition of pride, turn his kindly feelings towards you into dislike.'

She received the letter, and the not undeserved rebuke in silence; while Hamilton, to divert Madame Berger's attention, began a description of his meeting with Mr. Eisenmann, of their discourse and supper.

'It must have been delicious, the whole scene,' cried Madame Berger; 'I shall pay you a visit at the Iron Works, the very first day the Doctor can let me have the horses.'

'Pray bring the Doctor with you when you come,' said Madame Rosenberg, unconsciously glancing towards Hamilton.

Madame Berger saw the glance, observed that Hamilton laughed, and immediately inquired the cause. Madame Rosenberg refused to tell her, and she appealed to Hamilton, who, immediately, with the most perfect composure, and without the slightest reserve, repeated all the part of their morning conversation which related to her. She seemed to enjoy the recital, and Madame Rosenberg's face of horror, equally. 'One thing is certain,' she said, when he had ended, 'had you been so many months in the same house with me, as you have been with Hildegarde, we should have —'

'You seem altogether to forget the Doctor,' said Madame Rosenberg, interrupting her, almost angrily.

'To tell the truth, I sometimes do forget that I am married, —but Mr. Hamilton understands *badinage* perfectly, so you need not look so shocked at my *bavardage.*'

'I wish you would speak German,' said Madame Rosenberg, fidgeting on her chair; 'you use so many French words, that I cannot understand the half of what you say.'

'I believe I had better go home,' cried Madame Berger, good-humouredly; 'allow me to hope you will be civiller to me when I visit you in the country! *Bon soir.*'

'Good night,' said Madame Rosenberg, drily, without making the slightest effort to detain her.

CHAPTER XXXVI.

THE IRON WORKS.

In a few days, Hildegarde, the children, and Hamilton were established at the Iron Works; her recollections proved tolerably correct; the noise of the hammers was almost incessant, not even ceasing during the night, and as the house adjoined the Iron Works, it shook at times until the windows rattled. Hamilton did not much notice the white curtains, but, from pure sympathy with Hildegarde, he regretted the smuts which fell flake-like in the garden, and seemed destined to rob the coming flowers of half their beauty. Old Mr. Eisenmann was not a little proud of his garden, and great was his satisfaction when he found Hildegarde willing to assist him in cultivating it. The plants which most interested Hamilton were the numerous cactuses which filled all the windows in the front of the house, and whose brilliant flowers already made every passer-by stop to gaze at them. Nothing could equal the old man's delight on such occasions; if the weather were warm enough, he generally opened the window, and related how he had managed his plants during the winter, in order to make them blow so early; and it had been Hamilton's un-affected admiration of these cactuses, as he had walked up to the house, which had formed the commencement of their acquaintance.

During the fortnight which preceded Madame Rosenberg's arrival, Hamilton enjoyed the most unrestrained intercourse with Hildegarde; he watched her making the coffee in the morning—sat beside her at the open window looking into the garden, and accompanied her in her walks with her brothers in the oak wood; here there was a small chapel in which she daily prayed, while Hamilton, leaning against the entrance, stared absently at the votive offerings hung around, or endea-voured to decipher the old German prayers and texts of Scripture, which, with their inhuman illustrations, were pasted on the walls. The two boys generally scampered about, but joined them when they sat down on one of the numerous benches under the trees. Hamilton usually held a book in his hand, out of which he sometimes read a few lines, especially when any obtrusive wanderers made their appearance, though on week-days, pilgrims to the little chapel, who afterwards came to beg a few kreutzers, were the only interrupters of their studies, meditations, or conversation, as the case may have been.

'I wish,' he said, as they loitered through the fields on their way home, the evening before Madame Rosenberg's arrival, 'I wish I were certain of spending the next six months as I have done the last fortnight. I cannot tell you how I have enjoyed myself: much as I like your stepmother, and not-withstanding all her kindness and indulgence to me, I dread her coming more than I can express—everything will be changed—and any change must diminish my happiness.'

'You have nothing to apprehend but a removal of the furniture in your room,' replied Hildegarde, with a quiet smile; 'but I cannot expect any longer to eat the bread of idleness—I must learn to cook, and wash, and iron!'

'You will never be able to endure such work,' exclaimed Hamilton.

'I shall try it for a few months, at all events. And as long as you are here,' she added frankly, 'I think I can bear it, as your society and friendship will be an indemnity for most annoyances.'

Hamilton's expressions of gratitude she interrupted by continuing—'After all, what shall I do more than girls in my rank of life must always do? Even Crescenz, since her marriage, has learned to iron. Did you not see her ironing Major Stultz's shirts when we went to take leave of her?'

'Yes, but he is her husband; and it was a mere ostentation of usefulness on her part, for your mother told me she need not do anything of the kind, if she did not wish it. Crescenz, however, does not appear misplaced when so employed—but you—'

'Strictly speaking, I am not more misplaced than she is. We have both received an education beyond our station in the world. I have, perhaps, profited more by the instruction bestowed on me than she has; but you must allow that *she* has shown infinitely more capacity for the necessary duties of life.'

'If it be her duty to iron her husband's shirts,' answered Hamilton, laughing, 'I must say she performs it in the most charming manner possible. Nothing could be more coquettish than the black silk handkerchief twisted round her head to prevent her from feeling the draught of air, or the sleeves tucked up just enough to exhibit the dimples in her white arms! I must say, Crescenz is perfectly aware of all her personal advantages.'

'And who is not aware of them?' said Hildegarde, 'or rather, who does not overrate them?'

'You do not, most certainly!' cried Hamilton. 'I am convinced you do not think—'

'That I am handsome?' said Hildegarde, interrupting him quietly; 'I know it perfectly well. You are shocked at my candour,' she added, after a pause, on observing that he continued silent; 'it would have been more proper to have disclaimed—but after all, what worth have regular features, when they are inanimate? And mine are so, I know.'

'You are mistaken,' said Hamilton, 'I have never known anyone whose features have expressed so many various emotions as yours have during the few months of our acquaintance.'

'That I have felt more than during the whole of my previous life is most certain,' she said, thoughtfully; 'it seems, then, I have not been able to acquire that composure of mind and feature which Mademoiselle Hortense so often told me would be essentially necessary for my happiness.'

'I am rather inclined to hate that Mademoiselle Hortense without ever having seen her,' cried Hamilton. 'I think she wished to make an actress of you!'

'No; she wished to make a good governess of me, as my stepmother desired her, and she saw that my pride and violence of temper would prove serious obstacles. My gratitude to her is unbounded for all her care and attention during so many years. She is my only hope for the future, too; on her I depend to find me some respectable situation, should my residence here become uncomfortable.'

'Have you ever seriously thought of taking such a step?'

'I believe I have talked more than thought on the subject. One thing I have resolved upon, and that is, to go as far as possible from home.'

'Should you like to go to a foreign country?'

'Foreign, as you understand the word—no, but I am not likely to have the power of choosing. Mademoiselle Hortense's connexions are all in Alsace, and my destination will probably be Strasburg.'

They walked on in silence, each absorbed in thoughts of no very agreeable description. As they drew near the house, Mr. Eisenmann came to meet them, accompanied by the *Förster*, who had begun to drop in regularly every evening, to drink a glass of beer with the old man. Hamilton greatly approved of the arrangement, as it left him at liberty to talk unreservedly in English to Hildegarde, who, however, would have preferred his absence, from the time that Hamilton had made her observe that his eyes were fixed upon her incessantly, and followed her wherever she went.

'This is the last evening you will be my housekeeper, Hildegarde,' said Mr. Eisenmann, as she pushed his arm-chair to the table, and placed his newspaper, which seemed to contain nothing but advertisements, beside the small brass lamp. 'I can give you a good character, girl; you have a way with you that has made the people here obey you at once. She will make a good wife one of these days—eh, Mr. Hamilton? Eh, Förster Weidmann?'

Hildegarde smiled, and continued to perform her different evening duties. She gave her brothers their bread and milk, assisted the awkward maid-servant to arrange the supper-table, made the salad, carved the fowl, and presented each their plate, with such quiet unobtrusiveness, that her motions were only apparent by the rustling of the large bunch of keys she was to resign to her mother the next day, but which now hung glittering in steel chains at her girdle *à la châtelaine.*

Hamilton had been agreeably surprised at finding Mr. Eisenmann by no means so illiterate as he had expected. On every subject relating to his trade he was perfectly well informed, and in other respects his opinions were those of a shrewd, intelligent man. He spent the greater part of each day at the Iron Works, his hands thrust into his pockets, a short and very brown meerschaum pipe between his teeth, and his eyes following the movements of his workmen; and sometimes, when provoked by their want of skill, or too dilatory movements, after a few impatient ejaculations, throwing aside his coat and working with them. In his house, too, Hamilton had now frequently seen him in his shirt-sleeves, without feeling any of the horror expected by Madame Rosenberg; in the evening, he generally mounted a black silk nightcap, and when he had finished smoking his pipe and drinking his tankard of beer, and the Förster had taken leave, overcome by the fatigue of early rising and his daily exertions, he usually fell fast asleep, leaving his two companions to whisper, until the Schwarzwald clock struck nine, when, wakening without any apparent effort, he sent them to bed, and retired for the night himself.

This evening—this last evening, as they chose to call it—the Förster showed no inclination to move, and his eyes now seemed to follow the motions of Hildegarde's lips, as she murmured an occasional sentence to Hamilton. He tried in vain to join in their conversation; spoke of bringing his zither, proposed teaching them to play it, if they desired; and, not finding either of them disposed to appreciate either his conversational or musical talents, he turned to the now drowsy old man, whom he contrived to waken completely by some reference to the eternal 'good old times.'

'Pray, Hildegarde, turn away from that man,' said Hamilton, bending down to her, as she sat on one of the children's low chairs beside him; 'as long as he can look at you, he finds it impossible to tear himself away. It is absolute cruelty. He is depriving Mr. Eisenmann of his sleep this evening. Unpardonably inconsiderate!' he added, almost angrily.

Hildegarde, without an attempt at deprecation, lit a taper, and retiring to the other end of the room, where there was a thin-legged rickety table, she took from a cupboard the large house account-book, a hideous leaden ink-bottle, and a well-worn pen, and began to add and subtract with a diligence which would have put Hamilton's temper to the proof, had not the Förster almost directly stood up to take leave; but the old man was now quite roused, and, moreover, disposed to be loquacious; he let his visitor stand before him in the awkward posture of a shy man, wishing to get away, and not knowing how to manage it, while he observed, 'When people say the old times were good, and the present times are bad, I always feel obliged to contradict them. No offence, good Mr. Weidmann, but in my youth I have often heard just the same thing said; and in those times, as in these, the greater part of mankind had to earn their bread in "the sweat of their face."'

'I suppose so, sir. I wish you a good night.'

'I allow,' resumed Mr. Eisenmann, addressing Hamilton, 'that some nations are much happier than others. Of England I know nothing, excepting the manufacturing towns—'

'When were you there?' asked Hamilton.

'Soon after the Peace. I went there on business.'

'And what did you think of England? I should like to know what impression was made on you by our great manufacturing districts.'

'I saw much to admire, but nothing to make me think the English a *happier* people than the Bavarians,' replied Mr. Eisenmann, with a low, satisfied laugh. 'I would rather have been born a smith here than there, for, besides the instruction which I received for nothing in my childhood, I had during my youth my Sunday and holiday pleasures, my merry dances, and my pot of beer in good company, and with good music, too, of an evening, and a lot of other things of which your English workmen had not an idea when I was among them. It may be different now—'

'I am afraid it is not,' said Hamilton; 'but surely our manufactories must have astonished you?'

'I should have understood very little of my business if they had not,' replied Mr. Eisenmann. 'In this respect, England is a giantess, but, like a giantess, ought to be admired at a distance, and not examined in detail.'

'I perceive,' said Hamilton, 'that the people with whom you associated have made an unpleasant impression on you.'

'Perhaps so; but I am inclined to think it was a correct one. I mixed with people whose habits and mode of life are, and will ever remain, totally unknown to you—it was probably before you were born, too, and may, as I said before, be quite different now—at all events, it is too late to talk more about it to-night; I must look after my workmen, and then it will be time to go to bed.' He lit his candle, and walked towards an office which communicated with the Iron Works.

'What a different person Mr. Eisenmann is from what I expected!' observed Hildegarde.

'He is different from what I expected, too,' answered Hamilton.

'I am beginning to have quite a respect for him,' she continued; 'in short, to think him a remarkably clever man.'

'You are always in extremes, Hildegarde; first you unnecessarily underrated, and now you overrate him!'

'I suspect,' said Hildegarde, laughing, 'you are annoyed at his not thinking the English workmen happier than the Bavarian; his remarks, however, appeared to me very intelligent; he is quite willing to allow England her superiority in manufactures, though not in the felicity of her lower orders. For a person in his station in life you must allow—'

'Yes,' said Hamilton; 'for a person in his station in life, I do think him unusually well-informed and rational; but what I find most to admire about him is, that he has not stood still between his thirtieth and fortieth year, as most men who are not actually moving in the world do, and which I verily believe is the cause of those never-ending praises of the good old times.'

'He is the first person,' said Hildegarde, 'that I have heard actually give the present times the preference to those of his youth!'

'He has followed the changes of the world,' said Hamilton; 'and that is a proof of intellect less often given than people

c c 2

imagine. Everybody's youth must be, I should think, more agreeable than their old age. The world is full of pleasures for youth, which by degrees slowly but surely, even under the most fortunate circumstances, cease for the aged. Happy those who, like Mr. Eisenmann, can understand and appreciate the improvement in the world; still more happy those who, when old, can find enjoyment in witnessing pleasures they can no longer participate in.'

'I am waiting to bid you good night,' said Mr. Eisenmann at the door; 'this is the last time I shall go the rounds, for I mean to resign my office to my daughter to-morrow. She locked all the doors and bolted all the windows for many a year before she was married !'

'He has come just in time,' said Hamilton, rising; 'I believe I was getting very prosy.'

'And I very melancholy,' said Hildegarde.

The old man bade them good night, and watched them gravely as they ascended the stairs and separated on the lobby.

CHAPTER XXXVII.

AN UNEXPECTED MEETING, AND ITS CONSEQUENCES.

MADAME ROSENBERG took possession of her father's house more quietly than had been expected; he resigned his keys and authority with a solemnity which quite subdued her, and a whole week elapsed before any extraordinary bustle was perceptible; at the end of that time a scrubbing, and washing, and painting began, which drove the old man to the neighbouring inn, and Hamilton into Munich for some days. It was very disagreeable, but certainly the house appeared metamorphosed when it was at an end, and no complaints were heard, excepting a few faint murmurs from Mr. Eisenmann about the vine which was trained against the front of the house being covered with whitewash.

Hildegarde, to her infinite satisfaction, was not obliged to learn cookery; she had shown a too decided distaste and want of talent; she became, however, a tolerably expert ironer, and it was amusing to see Hamilton sitting, day after day, beside the table covered with heaps of linen, a volume of Schiller or the Philosophy of Herder in his hand, reading aloud, in order (as he explained to Madame Rosenberg) to improve his German accent, about which his family had become very anxious of late, and from which he concluded they had some hopes of placing him at one of the German courts. However, he did not feel particularly interested on that subject, nor indeed on anything that had reference to the future; he lived from day to day, reckoning the time profitably or unprofitably spent according to its having been, or not having been, spent in Hildegarde's society. He might truly say with Proteus of Verona—

> I leave myself, my friends, and all for love
> Thou, Julia, thou hast metamorphosed me ;
> Made me neglect my studies, lose my time,
> War with good counsel, set the world at nought.

And three months passed like so many days, and three more would have followed them in blissful monotony, had not a circumstance trivial in itself led, in its consequences, to an abrupt termination of this mode of life, or waste of life—whichever the reader may consider it.

The Munich Midsummer Fair had commenced, and Madame Rosenberg, not having found time in one day to make her usual purchases, decided upon going a second; she put it off, however, until the very last, and, when the morning came, was suffering so much from headache that she was obliged to remain as home. As they had promised to dine at twelve o'clock with Major Stultz, she thought it better to send Hildegarde and Gustle; and though at first she insisted that they were to go in their grandfather's little old carriage, she at length yielded to Hamilton's remonstrances and entreaties, and after he had passed a good half-hour at her bed-room door, making promises of the most varied description, allowed them to drive with him and be under his care during the day.

Crescenz received them as usual with childish delight ; her greatest pleasure on such occasions was to astonish them with a variety of tarts and sweetmeats, and they always found it difficult to get away. On this day it was easier, for she intended to accompany them to the fair. Blasius had insisted on her buying some new muslin dresses, he was so thoughtful and so generous! In fact, they were a very merry party, for Major Stultz had ceased to be jealous; his wife now really liked him, and was more obedient than a child: the thought of disputing his will had never entered her mind, and she appealed to him in the most infantine manner on every occasion; while, captivated by her beauty and innocence, he was invariably indulgent and generous almost to prodigality. She assured her sister, therefore, with the most perfect sincerity, as they walked together through the fair, that she considered herself the most fortunate woman in the world; that she could never have been so happy with anyone as with Major Stultz—no, not even with Mr. Hamilton—Blasius had quite convinced her of that.

They loitered about nearly two hours, and Hamilton, unutterably wearied, was slowly following Hildegarde, carrying her various little parcels of ribbons and pins, until the arrival of Hans with the carriage should relieve him, when he was suddenly seized by both arms, and familiarly addressed by some persons behind him. They were two of his nearest relations, passing through Munich on their way home from Italy, and were evidently more glad to see him than he to see them.

'Where have you been hiding yourself, Alfred? We were at your supposed lodgings, and no one could tell us anything about you! Any letters left would be called for, they said, which sounded very mysterious, as, had you left for Vienna or Berlin, your letters would have been forwarded *sans façon*, I suppose. Come, give an account of yourself. I shall be asked a thousand questions, you know, when I go home—that is, if you do n't accompany us, which you might as well do, all things considered—and—Uncle Jack.'

No; Hamilton had no intention of returning home until the very last day of his leave of absence had expired.

'Well, as we start in a day or two, you will spend the evening with us at least?'

At this moment Hans appeared, and said 'the carriage was ready.' Hamilton desired him to wait at the termination of the booths; and then turning to his companions, said, with some embarrassment, 'Spend the evening with you! Oh, of course—but I have promised to drive home a lady who lives a little out of the town.'

'Oh, there's a lady, is there—?'

'Yes; she is at present with her sister, making some purchases.'

'Ah, perhaps these are also some of them?' cried one of his cousins, peeping with an affectation of extreme care into one of the parcels. 'Ribbons, I declare, and hairpins!—ergo, young. Where is she?'

'I do n't—know,' replied Hamilton, looking down the row of booths, at one of which Hildegarde was standing.

'It's that tall girl with the small waist—I'm certain!'

'Well, it is that tall girl,' said Hamilton, half laughing; 'the sooner you let me go to take her home, the sooner I shall be back with you.'

'Let him go! Let him go!' cried his other cousin; and Hamilton, with an impatient gesture, walked quickly on, followed at a little distance by both. He took a hasty leave of Major Stultz and Crescenz, and hurried Hildegarde to the end of the fair. Just as she and her brother were seated in the phaeton, and Hamilton was taking the reins in his hand, his cousin called out, 'Hollo, Alfred! you never asked where we were stopping. I think you are going to give us the slip!'

'You are at Havard's, I suppose,' said Hamilton, not in the least endeavouring to correct the impatient movements of his horses.

'Yes. Wait a moment! I want to ask you a question.'

Hamilton bent down; his face, by degrees, became crimson, and he glanced furtively at Hildegarde, as if he feared she might have overheard the whisper; but she, quite unconscious that so many eyes were fixed upon her, was leaning back, and absently twisting her purse round her fingers.

Hamilton drove off at a furious rate, but scarcely were they out of the town, when, throwing the reins to Hans, he stepped over the seat, and placed himself beside Hildegarde.

'I am surprised,' she observed, with a smile, 'that you did not remain with your friends, and send us home with Hans.'

'It would have been the wisest thing I could have done: it was confoundedly stupid my not thinking of doing so. Stop!' he cried to Hans; but directly after, sinking back on his seat, he added, 'No—go on,' and then murmured, 'It is too late now. The best plan will be not to return. The less he knows, the less he can talk about.'

Hildegarde bent forward. 'Talk about what?' she asked.

'You cannot understand,' he answered, quickly.

'No; I perceive I cannot. I have not the most remote idea whether or not you were glad to see these friends.'

'They are my relations, my cousins; and that one who last spoke to me—did you observe him?'

' Not particularly.'

' That is Harry Waldcott, a great friend of my brother John's, the most amusing, worthless, extravagant fellow in the world. Were he to find out where I am, he would come to the Iron Works to-morrow, establish himself at the inn, use my horses, abuse myself, laugh at your stepmother, bully Mr. Eisenmann, and, for all I know, fall in love with you !'

' Dreadful person !' cried Hildegarde, laughing.

' As it is, he has seen enough—too much, unfortunately; I think,' he continued, with increasing irritation of manner, ' I think I hear his exaggerations to my father, his insinuations when talking to my uncle ! No ; he shall never know where I am—nothing shall tempt me into Munich for a fortnight at least !'

' You think, perhaps, that your father and uncle would disapprove of your being at the Iron Works ?'

' Think !' cried Hamilton, ' I am sure of it. My father would say I was losing my time; my uncle, that I was making a fool of myself !'

Neither of them spoke a word until they reached home, and Hamilton was remarkably thoughtful during the remainder of the evening.

The next day he was as cheerful as ever ; and having from his window seen Hildegarde walking towards the arbour with some paper and an inkstand in her hand, he took up the book they were reading together, and followed her. She had just finished making a pen when he entered, and throwing it on the table, she leaned forward and began, rather formally, ' Mr. Hamilton—'

' Pray call me Alfred—I have long wished it, and we are quite intimate enough to admit of your doing so. I called you Hildegarde the first month I was in your house.'

' It is, perhaps, an English custom,' she said, half inquiringly.

Hamilton did not answer. The fact was, at the commencement of their acquaintance, he had considered both Hildegarde and her sister so infinitely beneath him in rank, that he had almost immediately called them by their Christian names.

' I suppose,' she continued, ' if I know you well enough to call you Alfred, I may venture to say—'

' You may venture to say anything you please.'

'Well then—Alfred—I think the sooner you leave us—leave the Iron Works—the better.'

'Do you?' he said, with a tolerably successful effort to appear unconcerned. 'I suppose what I said yesterday, when I was vexed, has made you come to this conclusion.'

'Yes : and though I cannot perceive that you have exactly been making a fool of yourself, I think it is very evident that you have been losing your time here.'

'I wish I could lose the remainder of my life in the same way. I have been immeasurably happy lately.'

'You said your cousin would exaggerate—would insinuate—'

'Did you understand what I meant, when I said that?' cried Hamilton, quickly.

'I believe I did ; and I half wished you had allowed him to come here, and see that he was mistaken ; he would soon have perceived that your friends have no cause for anxiety—that friendship alone exists between us.'

'He would have seen no such thing, Hildegarde, at least as far as I am concerned ; and that you know as well as I do. That you have limited your measure of regard for me is a proof of—of—no matter what; I am most happy that it is so.' And Hamilton felt at that moment as unhappy and indignant as he had ever done in his life.

'Do you not think,' said Hildegarde, bending over the table, as she played with the pen, 'do you not think it would be better to leave us before you are ordered to do so?'

'No,' answered Hamilton, almost harshly.

'But,' she continued, bending still lower, to conceal her heightened colour, 'but suppose I were not here, would you still remain?'

'Can you doubt it?' cried Hamilton, ironically. 'How could I ever willingly quit this tranquil retreat? The pastoral beauties of these grounds! The society in every way so suited to my tastes and habits! The—'

'Enough, enough!' cried Hildegarde, seizing her pen; and with burning cheeks, but steady hand, she rapidly wrote a letter, while Hamilton, standing at the entrance, watched her with an odd mixture of anger and admiration. He waited until she had signed her name, and then, placing his hand on the paper, asked if the letter concerned him.

'I might easily equivocate, and say no, as you are neither

directly nor indirectly mentioned in it; but that would not be the truth. The letter is to Mademoiselle Hortense. I am now quite resolved to leave—this place.'

'May I read it?'

'If you insist—'

He took the letter; it was in French, short and forcibly written, as most letters are when composed under the influence of excited feelings. Hamilton's anger increased as he read; her proud determination of manner irritated him beyond measure, and, ashamed of the agitation which his trembling hands betrayed, he first crushed, and then tore it to pieces.

'My letter!' cried Hildegarde, starting up with all her former vehemence of manner. 'How dare you—' She stopped, and sat down, breathing quickly and audibly.

'You are in a passion,' said Hamilton.

'I was,' she replied, taking a long breath: 'it is over.'

'Oh, no; be angry, I entreat; say—do something outrageous, or I can have no hope of forgiveness. We have changed characters; you have learned to control your anger, and have me now in your power: be merciful!'

'Rather tell me to be candid,' she replied, rising; 'writing that letter in your presence was an unnecessary display of self-control; I—was not as calm as I wished you to suppose me.'

'Well, you certainly are the most honourable—'

'Don't praise me,' she said, hastily; 'I cannot listen to you when I am so dissatisfied with myself. I fancied my temper was corrected; I find it has merely not been tried.'

'Your temper is a very good one,' said Hamilton. 'That you doubt yourself, and are on your guard, is rather an advantage than otherwise. I always have been considered so good-tempered, that when I feel angry, it never occurs to me to conceal it; and the consequence is, that you have seen me forget myself more than once.'

Just then Madame Rosenberg entered the garden, holding a very diminutive note in her hand. 'I am come,' she said, 'to remind you of a promise which you made to a lady, I hope with the consent of her husband.'

'I don't know any lady likely to remind me of a promise, excepting, perhaps, Madame Berger.'

'Exactly; the Doctor will not be at home to-morrow, and, as the weather is so fine, she proposes spending the day here.'

' Well?' said Hamilton.

' Well—and Crescenz and the Major write to know if you will take them also in your phaeton, when you drive into Munich for Lina?'

' Oh, certainly,' said Hamilton, laughing; 'it was to Crescenz I made the offer, and it was Madame Berger who accepted it. You may remember, Hildegarde, the beginning of the month, when we all went to drink coffee at the Stultzes', and had such excellent ices afterwards. I wonder they did not say anything yesterday, when we were with them.'

' I suppose,' observed Madame Rosenberg, 'that they saw Lina after you left; but, at all events, you will go for them?'

' Yes, and at a very early hour.'

' Oh, of course,' she cried, nodding her head, jokingly; ' that means at ten o'clock, most probably.'

' It means at five o'clock.'

' Ah, bah! as if you could get up at four!'

' I can, and will. Crescenz must give me breakfast, and I hope to be out of Munich before seven for various reasons.'

' The dust, perhaps?'

' Dust or dirt,' said Hamilton, carelessly. ' If Madame Berger cannot leave so early, we can send Hans with the carriage at a later hour; though I would rather she would stay at home, as far as I am concerned.'

' I cannot believe that,' said Madame Rosenberg, ' for I never saw you get on with anyone as you do with her; if I were the Doctor, I would not allow it.'

' Nor I either, if I were the Doctor,' said Hamilton, laughing; ' but he is not, perhaps, aware that her usual vivacity degenerates into romping when she is here, and she is much too young and much too pretty for anyone to expect that I—'

' Oh, after all, there is no great harm; you only scamper about like a pair of children, but I should not like to see either Crescenz or Hildegarde doing the same.'

Hamilton looked at Hildegarde: there was something in the expression of her face which made him imagine that she, perhaps, had not quite approved of the scampering about of which her mother spoke.

' Am I to write an answer to this note?' she asked, as she took it out of Madame Rosenberg's hand.

Her mother nodded her head, and left the garden. Hildegarde wrote, and Hamilton again leaned against the entrance of the arbour, and looked in.

'Are you waiting for this letter, too?' she asked, smiling.

'I was not thinking of it,' he replied. 'I want to know if you, at least, believe that I would rather Madame Berger did *not* come here to-morrow?'

Hildegarde began to scribble on the blotting-paper with great diligence.

'I see you do not believe me.'

'I do, partly, especially if you think you must be quieter than on former occasions, now that mamma has remarked it. The fact is, I think Lina altogether to blame, and I have often admired your forbearance.'

'Thank you,' cried Hamilton; 'I am quite satisfied now.'

'Do not be quite satisfied with yourself,' said Hildegarde, 'for I must tell you honestly, that I am quite disposed to be unjust to Lina—more than ready to put an unkind construction on all she does or says.'

'Why?' asked Hamilton, with a blush of pleasure, as a faint vision of the 'green-eyed monster' approaching Hildegarde floated before his imagination. 'Why?'

'Because I dislike her. We waged war with each other for nearly ten years.'

'Ah! I remember; she told me you were rival beauties at school.'

'There was no rivalry on my part,' said Hildegarde, quietly. 'I never hesitated to acknowledge her beauty; it is of the most captivating description, and, even when she is most disagreeable to me, I admire her person.'

'You dislike her mind — her disposition, which is so different from yours,' said Hamilton.

'I cannot tolerate her want of truth and honour; her, to me, unfathomable cunning. In one word, I despise her.'

'You have been at no pains to conceal it,' observed Hamilton.

'There was no necessity,' said Hildegarde, beginning to fold up her note; 'but,' she added, 'you must not let my opinion weigh with you; you know I have strong, and often unreasonable, prejudices. At all events, Lina's faults are not of a description to prevent one from passing a long summer's day very agreeably in her society.'

'She is, certainly, an amusing person,' said Hamilton.

'She is clever,' said Hildegarde, gathering up her writing materials to carry into the house; 'no one can deny that she has intellect; at school there were few to be compared to her.'

CHAPTER XXXVIII.

THE EXPERIMENT.

THE morning was bright and still cool, though promising a sultry day, as Hamilton prepared to leave the Iron Works. To the astonishment of Madame Rosenberg, it was still so early that she was obliged to wish him good morning from one of the windows, her night-cap still on her head. Hildegarde was standing before the horses, giving them lumps of sugar which they had learned to expect from her, and looking so fresh and beautiful that Hamilton began to grudge the few hours which civility required him to absent himself from her. Kneeling on the seat of the phaeton, he looked up towards Madame Rosenberg, and asked if it would not do just as well if he sent the carriage with Hans?

'Lina Berger will never forgive you,' she answered, or rathei shouted from the window.

'Dear Crescenz will expect you to breakfast,' said Hildegarde, pushing away the head of one of the horses which had been resting on her arm : 'I am sure she has already arranged all her prettiest cups and saucers for you—do n't forget to admire them.'

Hamilton drove off. He found Crescenz not only waiting for him, but, with her head stretched far out of the window, watching for his arrival. She ran to meet him, exclaiming, 'How good-natured of you to come on so short a notice, and so early too !' and then, between the history of her cups, and a discussion about her new half-mourning, the time passed until her husband made his appearance to eat a hasty breakfast, for he was quite as anxious as Hamilton to leave Munich early, he so very much disliked both heat and dust. They called for Madame Berger ; she was dressed in the very extreme of the fashion, and bounded lightly up to the seat beside Hamilton.

'Let me see how your horses can step out ! ' she cried, while leaning back to offer Crescenz her little tightly-gloved hand.

Hamilton was quite willing to gratify her, his horses ready to second him—at that early hour the road was but little encumbered by carts or carriages, and passed the few they met. The phaeton rolled with a velocity that made Madame Berger laugh so heartily, that poor Crescenz's stifled screams were for some time inaudible. At length Major Stultz spoke : ' Mr.

Hamilton, may I beg of you to drive a little slower; Crescenz's nerves are not in a state to bear—'

'Why, good gracious, Crescenz!' exclaimed Madame Berger, 'you don't mean to say you are frightened? Mr. Hamilton drives so well that there is not the slightest danger.'

'Oh, no! I dare say not,' said Crescenz.

'I should not be afraid,' continued Madame Berger, 'if it were night, and pitch dark into the bargain!'

'How very courageous!' observed Crescenz, timidly.

In the mean time, Hamilton endeavoured to 'draw in his flowing reins,' but

—— a generous horse
Shows most true courage when you check his course.

His horses were no longer to be restrained, and their impatient springing and dancing alarmed Crescenz more than ever. At length, she could endure it no longer, and, when little more than half way, insisted on getting out of the phaeton; and Hamilton had the mortification of seeing her take her husband's arm, and, with a look of infinite relief, begin to walk off as fast as she could.

'You always lead me into mischief of some kind or other!' cried Hamilton, provoked at Madame Berger's laugh of derision. 'I shall keep out of your way as much as I can the rest of this day!'

'You will do no such thing,' she answered, saucily. 'Those two fools trudging along the road there only live for each other at present. Hildegarde will not talk to me, and I have not the slightest intention of spending the day with either Madame Rosenberg, who lectures me about my duties towards the Doctor, or old Mr. Eisenmann, who talks of nothing but cactuses and iron! If you don't mean to be civil to me, turn back and leave me at home again.'

'Civil! Oh, I have every intention of being civil, but I would rather avoid such scenes as we had the last day you were with us. I was obliged to explain and excuse—'

'And who has a right to demand an explanation, I should like to know?—Hildegarde, perhaps?'

'No,' answered Hamilton; 'it was Madame Rosenberg who seemed to think—'

'Never mind what she thinks! We mean no harm, and I do

not see why we should not amuse ourselves. But I must tell you something which I observed the last time I was with you —Hildegarde certainly does not like our being such good friends!'

'I do n't think she cares.

'You do n't know her as well as I do. Without particularly caring for you, she may—in fact, she must have become accustomed to your attentions—for who else have you to talk to? Now any lessening of the homage one has been used to is sure to irritate. Should you like to make her jealous?'

'Jealous!' repeated Hamilton—and he thought of what had occurred the day before in the garden. Could he in any way provoke her jealousy, he should be able perhaps to judge of the state of her feelings towards him; if, as she professed, but which he could not quite believe, friendship was really all she felt for him, why then, the magnanimous plans, the colossal sacrifices he had lately so often meditated, would be thrown away, and he might after all share the fate of Zedwitz. Here was an opportunity of making the trial, without committing either Hildegarde or himself. The temptation was strong to make the experiment; and he again repeated, very thoughtfully, the word 'Jealous!'

'Yes, jealous; jealous of your allegiance. She will at first think I am to blame, but you must show her the contrary. You—'

'Stay!' cried Hamilton. 'What will Madame Rosenberg say?'

'No matter what; I shall give her no opportunity of lecturing me. She is too good-natured to tell the Doctor, and Biedermann will never hear anything about the matter.'

'Biedermann?'

'Yes, Theodore; he would be much more angry than the Doctor, I suspect.'

'But what right has he—'

'Oh, none in the world; but you see I have got accustomed to his attentions, and cannot do without them. He is enormously prosy sometimes; but then he loves me—even when he is scolding I can observe it, and attribute half his lectures to jealousy. One likes a little *sentiment* sometimes, you know, and, once accustomed to these sort of *petits soins*, it is impossible to resign them without an effort, of which I confess I am incapable. I should die of *ennui*.'

'But,' said Hamilton, 'do you not think there is danger in a —a connection of this kind?'

'Danger! Not the least. He knows that I loved him for-merly in a foolish, girlish sort of way, and, had we been in England, I have no doubt we should have gone off together, and been miserable for life. The Doctor is a very kind, indulgent husband, but he has not time to be attentive, and, as I have no family to occupy my time, I require some one to talk to and amuse me. Theodore is well educated, clever, honourable, and all the sermons of all my relations and friends together will not make me give him up. The world may talk, and perhaps condemn me—I care not, for I know that I never have done, and never mean to do, anything wrong.'

'And,' said Hamilton, 'if Biedermann were to marry?'

'Not very probable for many years; but if he were, I should find some one else. You, for instance, would suit me very well, if you were likely to remain here; though I am afraid I should find you troublesome.'

'I am afraid you would,' said Hamilton, as he drew up his horses before the Iron Works.

Hildegarde ran out, expecting to see her sister; her disap-pointment changed into surprise when she heard what had occurred, and she said at once that she would go to meet her. Perhaps she expected Hamilton to accompany her, but he either was, or pretended to be, too much occupied with Madame Berger to hear what she said, and she set out alone.

More than an hour elapsed before Crescenz, Major Stultz, and Hildegarde appeared, all a good deal overheated, for the day had already become warm. They joined the others in the garden, and began to saunter up and down the narrow gravel walks, or to seek the shade under the apple-trees in the orchard. Mr. Eisenmann immediately gathered a bunch of fresh roses for Crescenz, and Madame Berger, turning to Hamilton, desired him to bring her some also.

'I do n't know whether or not I can obey you,' he answered, laughing. 'I have been forbidden to pull flowers without leave, ever since the day I beheaded some scores of roses with my riding-whip.'

'Your punishment is at an end,' said Hildegarde, smiling; 'I am glad to perceive you have not forgotten it;' and, as she spoke, she pulled a half-blown rose and gave it to him.

'Ah! that is just the one I was wishing to have,' cried Madame Berger, holding out her hand.

'You shall have another, but not this one,' said Hamilton.

'*That*, and no other,' cried Madame Berger; and, after some laughing and whispering, he gave her the flower.

Hildegarde was surprised, although, by a sort of tacit agreement, she and Hamilton usually avoided any exhibition of their intimacy or friendship when Madame Berger was present: the latter continued, 'I have an odd taste, perhaps, but my favourite flower is the common scarlet geranium. I do not see one here.'

'The only plant I had,' said Mr. Eisenmann, 'I gave to Hildegarde, and she gave it to Mr. Hamilton to put on his flower-stand.'

'Oh, if it belongs to you,' said Madame Berger, with a light laugh, 'I must have a branch of it directly;' and she bounded into the house as she spoke.

'This is too much,' cried Hamilton, running after her. A minute or two afterwards a violent scream was heard from his room, of which both windows were open.

'Shall we go and see what has happened?' whispered Crescenz to her sister.

'No; it is better to leave them alone.'

'Lina is growing worse and worse every day,' said Crescenz. 'Blasius does not at all like my being with her, since people have begun to talk so much about her.'

'What do people talk about?'

'They say that Mr. Biedermann is now constantly with her; never out of the house. In fact—'

At this moment Hans ran past them towards a shed, at the end of the orchard, where garden utensils and flower-pots were kept, and, having taken one of the latter, was returning to the house, when Crescenz asked what had happened.

'I don't exactly know, ma'am; I believe Mr. Hamilton put a geranium on the top of the wardrobe, and Madame Berger, in trying to take it down, let it fall, and it is broken to pieces.'

'The pot or the plant?' asked Hildegarde.

'Both, I believe, mademoiselle,' answered Hans, hurrying into the house.

'How long is she likely to remain with him upstairs?' asked Crescenz.

'Until dinner-time, perhaps,' answered Hildegarde, care

D D

lessly; 'he has got a number of paintings on china and new books to amuse her. But now you must come and see what a quantity of work I have done lately; you have no idea how useful I can be ; even mamma praises me sometimes !'

The afternoon amusement was, as usual, a walk in the oak wood. Hamilton and Madame Berger soon wandered away from the sisters, and, after waiting for their return more than an hour near the little chapel, Hildegarde and Crescenz began to walk home. 'Well, Hildegarde, what do you think of this ?' asked the latter, looking inquiringly at her sister's grave countenance.

'Nothing,' she replied, quietly.

'So Blasius was quite mistaken, it seems ; he said that Mr. Hamilton had long liked you, and that you were beginning to like him.'

'He was quite right,' said Hildegarde; 'we do like each other very much, especially since my father's death ; he was so very kind at that time.'

'Blasius said it was more than mere liking. Now, if you cared for him as Blasius supposed, his conduct to-day must vex you; you could not help feeling jealous.'

'I have no right.'

'Oh, one never thinks of right on such occasions,' said Crescenz, smiling. 'I remember the time I used to suffer tortures whenever he whispered and laughed with Lina. There was a time, too, when I could not have endured his preferring you to me, but now —'

'Now?' repeated Hildegarde, inquiringly.

'Now, I do n't think about him, and I like Blasius so much that I never think of comparing them. Mr. Hamilton is certainly very handsome, but, as Blasius says, one gets so accustomed to good looks that at last it makes no impression at all. By the bye, how improved Peppy is since he has been in the country!' she added, as the child ran to meet her. 'I declare he will be quite as handsome as Fritz ; it is impossible not to like such noble-looking creatures. I must say they are both a thousand times more loveable than Gustle, who promises to be extremely plain, and not in the least like either of us.'

Hildegarde smiled at the discrepancy between the commencement and end of her sister's speech, but took no notice of it, and they spent the rest of the day in the arbour, talking over their school adventures, Crescenz's house affairs, and Hildegarde's plans for the future.

Hamilton and Madame Berger did not return until just before supper-time; they entered into no explanation, and made no excuses; the latter merely observed, when arranging her hair in Hildegarde's room, 'I really never spent a pleasanter day. Mr. Hamilton is positively charming—quite a love. I must not forget to wear the wreath of ivy he took such trouble to choose for me;' and, while speaking, she twisted a long light branch with its deep-green leaves among the tresses of her fair hair, and, pushing back with both hands the mass of ringlets which covered her face, bestowed a glance of satisfied vanity on the looking-glass, and flourishing her pocket-handkerchief left the room.

'I never saw Lina look so pretty as she does to-day,' observed Hildegarde.

'And do you really not feel angry with her?' asked Crescenz, as she put her arm round her sister's waist, and they began to descend the stairs together.

'Angry with her for having taken a long walk with Mr. Hamilton?'

'Ah, bah! you know very well what I mean.'

'No, dear Crescenz; I am not in the least angry,' whispered Hildegarde, with a gay laugh, as she entered the room where the others were just placing themselves at table. Hamilton looked up, and beheld her clear brow and cheerful smile with painful uncertainty; Madame Berger bent towards him and whispered, 'You were right.'

'How? When?'

'She does not care a straw for you. I never believed it until to-day.'

Hamilton bit his lip and slightly frowned.

'Oh, don't be annoyed about it; you cannot expect to succeed with all the world, you know. I suppose, having nothing else to do here, you have given yourself some trouble to please her, and it is disagreeable to find oneself mistaken; but you may remember I told you long ago that she would exact a kind of love which few men are capable of feeling—a sort of immaculate devotion, not to be expected from your sex now that the times of knighthood are passed. She will never, in these degenerate days, find anyone to love her as she imagines she deserves.'

D D 2

'And yet,' said Hamilton, 'she has so little personal vanity.'

'That I consider one of her greatest defects. What is a woman without personal vanity? Avoid during the rest of your life all who have not, at least, a moderate quantity of it; without it we are abnormous, unnatural, and it is impossible to know how to manage us.'

'You have really given me a great deal of information to-day,' said Hamilton, laughing; 'a few walks with you, and I should become a perfect tactician.'

'If you choose, however, to try Hildegarde further,' said Madame Berger, 'you must manage it yourself. She may think you now, for all I know, a victim to my arts and wiles, and more worthy of pity than anger.'

Partly from pique, partly because he was amused, Hamilton devoted himself altogether to Madame Berger for the rest of the evening. He drew his chair behind hers after supper, and they continued together in the little dark parlour, even after all the family had withdrawn to enjoy the long warm July evening in the garden.

It was almost night when Crescenz came timidly into the room, and in an embarrassed manner said, 'that she was too much afraid of Mr. Hamilton's horses to drive home with him, and that Mr. Eisenmann had offered his carriage—'

'His cart, my dear, you mean,' said Madame Berger, interrupting her, without moving a feature of her face. 'I recommend you to have a few bars of iron laid at the back; the horses will be all the quieter; they are accustomed to the sound, you know.'

'I—I thought,' said Crescenz, 'that you would, perhaps, prefer going home with me, instead—'

'Oh, not at all, my dear! I would not separate you and Major Stultz for the world; besides, I am not in the least afraid of either Mr. Hamilton or his horses. You see,' she added, turning to Hamilton, 'I take it for granted that you will leave me at home.'

'Of course. I am only sorry,' said Hamilton to Crescenz, 'that you will not go with us; I can almost promise that the horses will be quieter than in the morning.'

'Thank you,' said Crescenz, rather stiffly; 'but even if they were I should now decline your offer, as Lina has shown so plainly that she does not wish for my company, or, indeed, for anyone's excepting yours.'

'I am overpowered at the severity of your remarks,' cried Madame Berger, catching her arm, with a light laugh. 'How fortunate that the darkness hides my blushes! I say, Cressy,' she added, in a lower voice, 'is it for yourself or for Hildegarde that you have entered the lists?'

'I—I—do n't understand you,' said Crescenz, releasing her arm, and hurrying out of the room.

'Order your carriage,' said Madame Berger, turning back for a moment to Hamilton; 'order your carriage as soon as possible, or I shall get a lecture from Madame Rosenberg, and I am not in a humour for anything of the kind just now.'

The carriages were at the door together. 'Hans may drive,' cried Hamilton, springing into the phaeton after Madame Berger; and as long as they were in sight he seemed to be wholly occupied with the arrangement of her shawl.

'Hildegarde! Hildegarde! where have you hidden yourself?' cried Madame Rosenberg, about an hour afterwards, and a voice from the very end of the orchard answered, 'Here, mamma; I am coming directly.' But even while speaking, Hildegarde turned again, and with folded arms and lingering steps continued her sentinel-like walk.

The next day Hamilton felt very uncertain whether or not he had acted wisely. Hildegarde was so upright and free from coquetry herself, that he feared she would not easily understand his motives, were he, in exculpation, to explain them; and even if he made them evident, she would condemn them. He met Madame Rosenberg on his way to breakfast; heard the half-joking, half-serious expostulations he had expected, and replied to them, as usual, with a mixture of petulance and impertinence.

He approached Hildegarde, hoping sincerely that he should find her angry, or at least offended, but all his efforts to discover anything of the kind failed; she was perhaps a little less cheerful than usual, but not enough to admit of his questioning her. Before dinner she received a letter; the handwriting was unknown to him, but, though burning with curiosity to know from whom it came, when he saw her unusual trepidation on receiving it, he dared not ask her, though he would not have hesitated to have done so the day before. In the afternoon, when he expected her to walk, she sent Gustle to tell him that she had a long letter to write and could not go out. The next few days she chose to assist her mother in preserving fruit, and then appeared an interminable quantity of needlework to be done. Hamilton felt the change which had taken place in their intercourse without being able to cavil at it. He felt that he was to blame, but he nevertheless got out of patience, and began to drive into Munich every day. No one seemed to think he could be better employed, and many and various were the commissions given him by the different members of the family.

One day, just as he was telling Hildegarde that he should not return until late at night, as he intended to go to the opera, Madame Rosenberg entered the room; she held in her hand a silver hair-pin of curious filagree-work, and exclaimed, rather triumphantly, 'Well. here is Lina Berger's silver pin, after all; not found in the garden, where she said she lost it, but in your room, under the wardrobe. Monica saw it when she was scouring the floor.'

'Very likely,' said Hamilton; 'Madame Berger mounted a chair to get at my scarlet geranium, which I hoped to have placed out of her reach on the top of the wardrobe. By making a spring she caught the flower-pot, but descended on the edge of the chair, which fell with her to the ground. I was greatly alarmed, as after the first scream of fright she became unusually quiet; and although she said she was not hurt, she lay on the sofa without moving or opening her eyes long after I had transplanted my poor geranium—and mourned over it,' he added, looking towards Hildegarde.

Madame Rosenberg laughed. 'That was a trick to prevent you from scolding her about the plant, which she saw you rather valued.'

'Perhaps it was,' said Hamilton, colouring, 'and I never suspected it.'

'Well, you can tell her your present suspicions to-day, when you give her the hair-pin, you know;' and she held it towards him as she spoke.

'I never go to Madame Berger's,' said Hamilton, and he was glad to be able to say so; 'but if you choose to give it to Hans, he can leave it at her house when I go to the theatre.'

'Hildegarde, make a little parcel of it and write her a line,' said Madame Rosenberg.

Hildegarde took her brother Gustle's pen, and on a leaf of his copy-book wrote a few severe words, which not even the usual 'dear Lina,' or the schoolfellow *tutoiment*, could soften.

Hamilton smiled, and unconsciously pulled his glove towards his wrist until he tore it. 'These are the worst gloves I have ever had,' he cried, impatiently throwing them on the table; 'that is the second pair I have spoiled to-day.'

'The gloves seem to be very good,' observed Madame Rosenberg, taking them up, 'and, as they are a very pretty colour, Hildegarde may as well mend them for you; but while she is doing so, you must seal and direct this parcel to Lina.' And leaving them thus employed she walked out of the room.

'Permit me,' said Hamilton, half jestingly, a few minutes afterwards, as Hildegarde returned him the gloves, 'permit me to kiss your hand;' and then he added, 'This seals our reconciliation, I hope?'

'We have had no quarrel, and require none,' answered Hildegarde.

'Yet you have been displeased—angry with me—have you not?' asked Hamilton.

'I have had no cause—I have no right—'

'But you know what I mean?'

'I think I do,' replied Hildegarde, half smiling, and quite blushing.

'And what did you suppose were my motives? What did you think of me?'

'I thought, after all your professions of regard for me, you might have waited until you reached England before you began a new—flirtation.'

'Then you were a little—a very little jealous, perhaps?'

'I think not—I hope not,' said Hildegarde, quickly, 'for it would be very absurd, most ridiculous. In fact,' she added, frankly, 'I did not care how much you devoted yourself to Lina, until I perceived that you wished me to observe it.'

'I did wish you to observe it. I hoped to have elicited some spark of feeling from you in that way, after having failed in all others.'

'And Lina Berger was the person chosen as assistant—as confidant, perhaps?'

'I had nothing to confide. I have never made any secret of my feelings towards you.'

'So you wished to show Lina Berger and everyone else what you supposed were my feelings towards you? It was an ungenerous intention, Mr. Hamilton, all things considered, as any weakness on my part would have merely served to give you a useless triumph; but,' she added, with heightened colour, 'I am not offended, not in the least angry with you—or jealous—and, for the short time we are likely to be now together, I hope we may be as good friends as we have been for the last few months. The whole affair is really not worth talking about.'

'I hope, however, you do me the justice to believe me perfectly indifferent to Madame Berger?'

'About as indifferent as she is towards you. You flatter each other, and vanity draws you together.'

'And you do not mind our being drawn together?'

'Not in the least,' said Hildegarde, composedly.

'I believe you—I believe you. I am thoroughly convinced of your indifference, and require no other proof. I am sorry for it, but—perhaps it is all for the best.' At the door he turned back, and added, 'We have not quarrelled, Hildegarde? We are friends, at least?'

'Friends! oh, certainly, though ever so far apart,' answered Hildegarde, with a forced smile. 'One so poor in friends as I am, grasps even at the name.'

Hamilton noiselessly closed the door, and she bent over her work until some large tears began to drop on it, and a choking feeling in her throat induced her to go to the open window, where she leaned out as far as the numerous plants would permit, and gazed long into the orchard without distinguishing a single object that lay before her.

CHAPTER XXXIX.

THE RECALL.

ABOUT a fortnight after the foregoing events, as Hamilton was one morning sitting listlessly in the arbour at the end of the garden, Hildegarde came towards him carrying a large packet of letters, which Hans had just brought from Munich. As she placed herself beside him he looked at the different handwritings, and murmured, 'My sister Helen—my father—John, and—from Uncle Jack, too! With what different feelings should I have received these letters a short time ago! Don't go away, Hildegarde. I have no intention of making you any reproaches or speeches, and I may, perhaps, want your advice about fixing the day of my departure.'

She sat down on the steps leading into the arbour, leaned her elbow on her knee and her head in her hands, and remained perfectly immoveable for more than half an hour. She was not musing on the past, or thinking of the future; she heard her heart beat distinctly, and would, perhaps, have endeavoured to count its throbs, had she not felt irresistibly compelled to listen to a most inharmonious and lamentable ditty sung by the cook, as she scoured her kitchen furniture near an open window. Some vague ideas of the happiness of those whose thoughts never soared beyond the polishing of pots and pans, or the concocting of meats within them, floated through her mind; and then appeared a vision of a nunnery garden, with very green grass and long gravel walks; and then Hamilton rustled the paper of his letters, and she expected him to speak, and when he did not she again listened to the monotonous song, and wondered if it had no end.

The song continued, but she ceased to hear it, for Hamilton spoke at length, and she turned round to answer him.

'These letters contain the recall I have been expecting,' he said, folding them up, 'and also a large sum of money for my journey—more, much more than I shall require; my uncle measures my expenses by my brother's. In short, neither he nor any of my family have in the least degree comprehended my position here—their ignorance would shock you——' He stopped, evidently embarrassed. His uncle's letter would, indeed, have shocked her; he had offered to send Hamilton any sum of money necessary to buy off the claims which Hildegarde or her family might have upon him.

'I suppose,' said Hildegarde, 'they expect you home directly.'

'They rather wish me to visit the Z——s, as they have become acquainted lately with some of their connections.'

'And you intend to do so?'

'Yes; I have no particular wish to return home directly, though I see they expect me in about a fortnight or three weeks.'

'In that case you will have to leave us soon—very soon.'

'How soon?' asked Hamilton, endeavouring to catch a glimpse of her face, which was, perhaps, purposely averted.

'You are the best judge of that,' she answered, rising from her lowly seat; 'if leaving us be disagreeable to you, the sooner you get over it the better.'

'It is more than disagreeable—it is painful to me.' He paused, and then added, hastily, 'I shall take your advice and leave to-morrow.' More than a minute he waited for her to speak again : one word or one look might at that moment have changed all his plans ; but, finding that she remained silent, he slowly gathered up his letters, and walked thoughtfully into the house.

Madame Rosenberg talked more than enough ; she thought it necessary to put the whole house in commotion, and was so anxious to prove to him that all his clothes were in order, that she followed him to his room, and actually herself packed all his portmanteaux and cases ; she then seated herself on one of the former, and began to question him about what he intended to do with Hans, the horses, and phaeton.

'I shall take Hans to England with me, and leave the horses at Munich to be sold. I dare say Stultz will take the trouble of looking after them for me.'

'Dear me, how surprised he will be—and Crescenz and Lina Berger ! Really, the whole thing is so unexpected, that one has not time to think, or feel, or understand—'

'That is just what I wished,' said Hamilton ; 'I hope not to have time to think or feel, for I leave your house most unwillingly ; but leave it I must, as my father and uncle expect me home in a week or two, and I am going first to the Z——s'.'

'Pray give the Baroness my compliments,' said Madame Rosenberg ; 'it was very civil of her taking the children home— that evening, you know.'

Hamilton remembered the evening, but he thought it was very probable he should forget the compliments.

'Sorry as I am to lose you,' continued Madame Rosenberg, 'I must say I think your relations are right to insist on your return. As my father said yesterday, a young man with your capabilities being allowed to waste your time as you have been doing, is perfectly incomprehensible.'

'My object was to learn German, and I have learned it,' said Hamilton.

'It would have been better for you if Hildegarde and Crescenz had not spoken French so well. My father says, too, you speak English now with Hildegarde ; I'm sure I don't know how she learned it. I never could learn French, though I have often tried, and I am not a stupid person in other things. I'm very glad, however, that she has learned English,

though I formerly thought it unnecessary. Four languages
for a girl not yet eighteen is pretty well, as poor dear Franz
used to say, and—'

'Four languages,' repeated Hamilton; 'what is the fourth?'

'Why, do you not know that she speaks and writes Italian
quite as well as French? Mademoiselle Hortense is a half
Italian, and she spared no pains in teaching her, most fortunately as it has turned out, for the lady with whom she is likely
to be placed particularly requires Italian, as she is going to
Italy next year.'

'So Hildegarde is to leave you also?'

'Yes. I was at first very unwilling, and, indeed, should not
have consented were I still in Munich; but, you see, here she
is never likely to marry, and after her sister has made such an
excellent match, she would not be satisfied with our Förster.
Mr. Weidmann, I am afraid.'

'I should think not,' said Hamilton.

'Now, as she is certainly remarkably handsome,' continued
Madame Rosenberg, 'and within the last year greatly improved,
too, I should not at all wonder if at Frankfort or Florence she
were to pick up some one—'

'Not at all unlikely,' observed Hamilton.

'Or if old Count Zedwitz were to die, perhaps his son might
again—'

Hamilton began to stride up and down the room with
unequivocal signs of irritation.

'I see all this is uninteresting to you,' said Madame Rosenberg, placing her hands on her knees to assist her in rising
from her low, unsteady seat. 'How can I expect you to care
whom she marries, or where she goes, or, indeed, what becomes
of any of us now? In a few weeks you will have forgotten
us altogether?'

'How little you know me!' cried Hamilton, taking her hand
as she was passing him. 'I shall never forget you or the happy
days passed in your house, and am so sincerely attached to you
and all your family, that nothing will give me greater pleasure
than hearing of or from you. I shall leave you my address in
London, and hope that you, and your father, and the children
will often write to me. When Fritz comes home for the holidays
I shall expect a long letter, not written from a copy, and in
his best handwriting, but unrestrained, and telling me everything about you all.'

'Well, I really believe you do like us,' cried Madame Rosenberg, the tears starting to her eyes, 'but, after all, not as well as we like you; and now I think I had better leave you, or else I shall make an old fool of myself.'

Hamilton's hours that day were winged; they flew past uneasily, like birds before an approaching storm. The afternoon, evening, and night came; Mr. Eisenmann dozed, Madame Rosenberg inspected her sleeping children, and Hildegarde and Hamilton for the first time sat gravely and silently beside each other; neither of them had courage to attempt the mockery of unconcerned conversation; each equally feared a betrayal of weakness, and it was a relief to both when the time for moving arrived. Mr. Eisenmann retired quietly to his room on the ground floor; Madame Rosenberg, after wishing Hamilton good night, took the house keys out of the cupboard and commenced her usual nightly examination of all the windows and doors. Hamilton sprang up the stairs, and watched at the door of his chamber until he heard Hildegarde separate from her mother and begin to ascend; he waited until she had deposited her candle and work-basket on the table in her room, and as she afterwards advanced to close the door, he called her out on the lobby, and said, hurriedly, 'Hildegarde, I shall have no opportunity of speaking to you alone to-morrow, and must take advantage of this to ask you to forgive and forget all my faults and failings.'

'I cannot remember any,' said Hildegarde.

'You say so, but I know you think that I endeavoured to gain your affections without any fixed purpose. That is true— I mean, this *was* true until lately—but that is of no importance now. Then I must confess I—I was not sorry for the unpleasant termination of the affair with Zedwitz. I now, too, see that I ought not to have come here with you; still less should I have endeavoured to make you jealous, or—'

'Oh, I give you absolution for all,' cried Hildegarde, interrupting him, 'and hope you will endeavour to forget how often you have seen me impatient or in a passion.'

'I have already forgotten it, and wish I could forget everything else besides that has occurred during the last eleven months. We have been eleven months together, have we not?'

'I believe so,' answered Hildegarde, thoughtfully. 'It appears to me much longer; my life has been so different from what it was before that time, I feel almost as if I had known you eleven years.'

The sound of closing doors no longer distant made Hamilton whisper anxiously, 'I shall not find it easy to part from you with becoming firmness before so many witnesses to-morrow, Hildegarde; still less should I have courage to entreat you once more to accept the little watch which you so unkindly returned to me last Christmas. Will you again refuse it?'

'No,' she replied; 'although I should have greatly preferred something of less value. I only wish I had anything to bestow in return; but I have nothing, absolutely nothing.'

'Stay!' said Hamilton, with some hesitation. 'You have something which you value highly, though I do not know why—a little mysterious bauble, which I should like to possess.'

'Name it, and it is yours,' said Hildegarde, eagerly.

He placed his finger on the hair bracelet which she constantly wore.

'Ah, my bracelet!' cried Hildegarde, with a look of surprise. 'If you wish for it, certainly; in fact it is better.' She held her arm towards the door of her room, that the light from the candle might fall on it, and Hamilton thought he saw tears in her eyes as she endeavoured to unclasp it.

'I only value it because you appear so attached to it,' he said, half apologetically. 'Before it comes into my possession, however, you must tell me whose hair I am about to guard so carefully for the rest of my life; not Mademoiselle Hortense's, I hope?'

'No,' said Hildegarde, holding it towards him.

'Tell me whose hair it is,' he cried eagerly, for Madame Rosenberg's heavy step, and the jingling of her large keys, became every moment more audible, and as she approached the staircase, he again repeated, 'Whose hair?' but Hildegarde, instead of answering, sprang into her room just as a long ray of light from her mother's candle reached the spot where they stood. Madame Rosenberg found Hamilton's door shut, and Hildegarde on her knees beside her bed, with her head buried in her hands.

And Hamilton never suspected that the bracelet he examined so long and earnestly that night was made of his own hair, obtained at the time he had been wounded in the head, by the fall from, or rather with, his horse.

The whole family were assembled at an early hour the next morning to witness his departure. Madame Rosenberg unreservedly applied her handkerchief to her eyes; her father looked grave; the two little boys, half frightened at the unusual solemnity of the breakfast-table, whispered and nudged each other, while Hildegarde, pale as the wife of Seneca, was apparently the only unmoved person present.

Hamilton took leave of all the workmen and servants, shook hands with Mr. Eisenmann, was kissed in the most maternal manner on both cheeks by Madame Rosenberg, embraced the little boys, and held Hildegarde's hand in his just long enough to cause a transient blush to pass over her features and make her look like herself.

After he had driven off, he turned round in the carriage to take a last look, and it seemed to him as if her beautiful features had turned to marble, so cold and statue-like were they. Madame Rosenberg was returning into the house, talking to her cook; the old man was gaily playing with the children; Hildegarde stood alone, motionless on the spot where he had left her. 'Is that indifference?' thought Hamilton.

CHAPTER XL.

HOHENFELS.

It was late on the evening of the ensuing day when Hamilton reached Hohenfels, a moderate-sized, high-roofed dwelling-house, having two dark-coloured massive square towers as wings. It was beautifully situated on the side of a rocky mountain, from which circumstance it probably derived its name. Avenue there was none; the narrow private road which conducted to it (though passing through woods with opening glades which, even without their splendid mountain back-ground, would have successfully rivalled any avenue Hamilton had ever seen in England) was evidently intended to serve equally as an approach to several comfortable peasants' houses, which, apparently, more than the genius of an engineer, had originally directed its course.

The buildings at a little distance from Hohenfels Hamilton now instinctively knew to be a brewery and its appendages, and he examined them with curiosity and interest. Though he did not quite consider beer (as some one has not inaptly pronounced it) a fifth element in Bavaria, he had at least so frequently heard its merits, demerits, and price canvassed, that he began to attach considerable importance to the subject, and rather prided himself on being able to talk about it.

On driving into the court, he looked up along the range of windows, and discovered with great pleasure A. Z. standing at one of them. He had not had time to write, or in any way to announce his visit ; therefore her first look of surprise rather amused him when they met, and she regretted that her husband was on a hunting expedition, and would not be at home until the next day; he was glad that no letter from him had interfered with the arrangement. They supped together under a large chestnut-tree, commanding an extensive view of woods, mountains, and a large part of the Chiem Lake, now glittering in all the radiance of a magnificent sunset.

'I had no idea,' said Hamilton, 'that you were so near home when I met you at Seon last summer. I understand now why you were always on the move, and we saw so little of you. By the bye, I should like to hear something of the Zedwitzes ; they are relations or intimate friends of yours, I believe ?'

'Distant relations, but very near and dear friends,' answered A. Z. 'I am sorry I have nothing satisfactory to tell you. the old Count is killing himself as fast as he can with cold water ; his wife had a fit of apoplexy this summer, from which she is, however, nearly recovered ; and Maximilian has, you know, been constantly from home since that unpleasant business with the Rosenberg family. He was with us for a few weeks, and I never in my life saw a man in such a state of desperation; his only consolation was talking to me about this " cunningest pattern of excelling nature," this Hildegarde, and as I had a great deal to do in my house, and could not always find time to listen to him, he used to wander about, writing sonnets I should imagine, from the poetical expression of his dear ugly face.'

'So he told you all about it ?' said Hamilton.

'Yes ; and all about you too — that is, all he knew about you. He seemed to have dreaded you excessively as a rival ; indeed, he does so still, for, were his father to die, I have not the smallest doubt he would renew his proposal, and perhaps be accepted.'

'I admire his patience and perseverance,' said Hamilton,

ironically; 'one downright refusal such as he received would
have satisfied me.'

'Circumstances might materially alter the state of the case,'
said A. Z. 'Suppose this flirtation with you quite over—you
have left, most probably, without any sort of serious explanation ; now I have no doubt you are very charming, but, you
know, people do get over hopeless affairs of this kind in the
course of time ; and in the course of time, too, Maximilian
will be at liberty to marry whoever he pleases. I cannot
imagine his being refused again, he is so exactly the sort of
man most women like.'

'He does not think so himself,' observed Hamilton.

'That is his great charm,' said A. Z.   'Diffident, enthusiastic men are almost always popular.   I have a decided
predilection for them.'

'I think, however, you are singular in your taste,' said
Hamilton.

'Not at all,' rejoined A. Z. ; 'the secret may be, that such
men think less of themselves and more of the person they wish
to please, but, in nine cases out of ten, you will find that it is
an ugly man who inspires real affection.   It is very creditable
to our sex, you must allow; one so very seldom hears of a
man who loves a really ugly woman.'

'Perhaps you are right,' said Hamilton ; 'my experience has
not been great.   I only know that I am now very seriously,
and, I fear, hopelessly in love with a very young and very
beautiful woman.'

'You will get over it,' observed A. Z., laughing.   'A few
months in London, if it were not so late in the year—'

'You are mistaken,' said Hamilton, gravely; 'neither a
few months nor a few years either are likely to change my
feelings.'

'I am sorry to hear it,' said A. Z., thoughtfully; 'never will
I sign a letter with my initials again.'

'I had quite forgotten that your note was the cause of all
this evil,' said Hamilton, smiling ; 'but there would be no evil
at all if Hildegarde liked me.'

'So it is all on your side,' observed A. Z., with some surprise.

'I don't know, but I am afraid so.   If it will not bore you, I
should like to explain, and ask your advice—'

'Stay!' cried A. Z.   'I don't at all know this Hildegarde,
and I' now do know something of you and your family, and

shall therefore certainly recommend you to break off the affair, if you can do so with honour; and that you can do so is scarcely to be doubted, if you imagine her indifferent to you.'

'But suppose she had been indifferent only because I said I could not marry?'

'It would prove that she is as prudent as she is pretty, and that is saying a great deal,' answered A. Z., gaily; 'and as you can *not* marry, the least said about the matter the better.'

'You do not quite understand the state of the case,' began Hamilton. 'You see I have a granduncle—'

'Called Jack,' observed A. Z.

'Exactly,' said Hamilton; 'and this Uncle Jack made a fortune in India, in those times when fortunes were to be made there, and added to this fortune by speculations in the funds at the end of the last war; we have consequently a great respect for him.'

'Of course,' said A. Z.; 'people always have a respect for rich uncles, both in books and real life. I never had one, but I can imagine the thing.'

'As he had no children,' continued Hamilton, 'my father prudently chose him as godfather to his eldest son, who was accordingly afflicted with the name of John; but even in his earliest youth it was found that the name would not cover the multitude of his sins, poor fellow, and while I was still a mere child my uncle declared that John would inherit from his father more than he would ever deserve, and that I, and I alone, should be his heir. He defrayed all the expenses of my education, gave me ponies and pocket-money, and would have paid my debts, I do believe, without hesitation, if I had had any, at Cambridge. Since I have been here, too, he has sent me large remittances through my father, and has latterly, I suspect, forbidden the words of wisdom which usually accompanied them. The first letter I ever received from him was the day before yesterday; he had heard—more than was necessary, more than was true—of Hildegarde; and can you imagine his proposing to send me money to buy off—to pay—to satisfy— pshaw!—where is the letter? You must read it, or you will never understand—'

'*He* does not understand—that is very evident,' observed A. Z.; 'you need not show me the letter, but go on.'

'When I told Hildegarde that I must return home, she

E E

recommended my leaving directly; she had, indeed, advised me to do so before the letter arrived.'

'And did she give you this advice without any apparent effort?'

'Without apparent effort? Yes; but she is not to be judged from appearances. She has been educated by a Mademoiselle Hortense, who has given her the idea that, besides controlling her temper, which is naturally hasty, she should endeavour to conceal all her feelings, and, if possible, stifle them altogether. If Hildegarde had not been naturally warm-hearted, hot-tempered, and intellectual, such an education would have completely spoiled her.'

'But,' said A. Z, 'after having lived nearly a year in the same house, if you can have any doubts about her caring for you—'

'Stay!' cried Hamilton, interrupting her. 'You are not, perhaps, aware that I proclaimed myself a younger son, and said I could not marry, even before I entered the Rosenbergs' house: and as, until very lately, I never *seriously* thought of sacrificing my really brilliant prospects, Hildegarde is still unconscious that, even with the best intentions, I could have acted otherwise than as I have done. I have been more calculating and worldly-minded than befits such an attachment; but latterly, as the time drew near when I knew we must part, I was ready to brave all my family, and be disinherited by my uncle, if she had only said one word, given me one look, from which I could have felt certain that she loved me.'

'I suppose,' said A. Z., rising, and walking towards the house, 'I suppose, from what you have just said, that you have some fortune independent of your family—enough at least to buy bread and butter?'

'I have five thousand pounds, a legacy left me by a distant relation, but it is not at my disposal for two years. This would not be enough for England; but I think here, as you say, it would, perhaps, buy bread and butter—'

'Oh, yes!' said A. Z., laughing, 'and roast veal and pudding into the bargain; but that is not all that is to be considered. You ought not to make so great a sacrifice without considering long and carefully both sides of the question.'

'Oh, I have considered only too long,' answered Hamilton; 'but I see you cannot understand me, or know Hildegarde, without reading my journal. I had some intention of leaving it under your care, at all events, and I shall only beg of you never to refer to that part of it which relates to Count Oscar Raimund.'

'I think I already know,' said A. Z. 'His father showed me the letter he had written the day he shot himself : does Mademoiselle Rosenberg know that she was the cause?'

'But too well, as you will perceive from my journal,' answered Hamilton ; 'you really seem to know everybody and everything, which, however, no longer surprises me, as I am myself willing on so short an acquaintance to confide in you. I suppose other people have done the same.'

'Not exactly,' answered A. Z. ; 'but as I know the Zedwitzes, the Raimunds, the Bergers, and even Mr. Biedermann, and as you, from the peculiarity of the commencement of our acquaintance, rather interested me, I have thought it worth while to listen, and remember all I have heard about you.'

'How very kind !' said Hamilton.

'You say that thoughtlessly,' observed A. Z., laughing ; 'but it really was kind of me, for I greatly prefer talking to listening on most occasions.'

'Will reading my journal bore you ?'

'Not in the least. I shall be curious to know the impression made on you by all you must have seen of the domestic manners you were so anxious to become acquainted with last year. Have you given up all idea of writing a book on the subject ?'

'I have been a much too greatly interested actor to have thought of anything of the kind, as you will see.'

'Before I read your journal,' said A. Z., 'that is, before I feel any interest in this Hildegarde, you must allow me to point out to you all the disadvantages of the step you propose taking, and remind you that the sacrifice of parents, relations, the friends of your youth, your country, and your native language, ought not to be lightly made. I speak from experience.'

'But you told me,' said Hamilton, 'that you felt quite naturalised—that you had become a very Bavarian ! I know too you are more than contented ; you are happy. The Countess Zedwitz told me so.'

'Very true,' answered A. Z. ; 'but I am a woman, and that alters the case materially. Both our nature and education induce us to conform to the habits of those about us. We have no profession, no career in life to give up ; we have only to learn to enlarge or contract our sphere of action, according to the circumstances in which we may be placed. For instance, Mademoiselle Rosenberg would most probably without hesitation go with you to England, were your uncle to consent to your marriage.'

' I cannot help thinking that—perhaps—she would,' answered Hamilton.

' And if she did, she would never have any cause to regret having done so ; for, besides being united to the person she loved, she would only have to learn to live luxuriously; and habits of that kind are easily acquired ; but after having so lived, frugality is more difficult of acquirement—and that would be your task.'

' But I have tried it,' cried Hamilton, eagerly ; ' I have made the trial this last year. I see that riches are not necessary to my happiness—I am convinced that with Hildegarde and a cottage—'

' So you would live in the country ?'

' Of course.'

' And in the mountains ? '

' Here, in your neighbourhood, if possible.'

' You are bribing me,' cried A. Z., ' more than you know. I am in want of such neighbours, and although it is getting cool,' she added, drawing her shawl round her, ' still, as it is not yet dark, we may as well return to the chestnut-tree, and perhaps walk to the beech-wood, which you saw from it.'

On ascending a slight acclivity, a more extensive view of the Chiem Lake became visible, and a peasant's house, with its overhanging roof and long balcony, stood before them—it was built almost in the mountain, at least it appeared so at a little distance ; a noisy stream rushed out of the rocks beside it, and formed a series of cascades, while endeavouring to reach the green fields and dark wood beneath. Under the numerous fruit-trees which surrounded the house, with their overloaded branches bending to the ground, were several wooden benches ; on one of these A. Z. seated herself, while Hamilton, attracted by the light from some windows on the ground-floor, seemed disposed to inspect the premises more closely. A loud chorus of voices made him hesitate.

' They are at their evening prayers,' observed A. Z. ; ' it is better not to disturb them. Come here, and listen to me — You have not often seen a house more beautifully situated than this, most probably?'

' Never.'

' The mountain peasants know how to choose a site ! You have no idea how highly they value a view of this kind, or how they feel the beauty of their scenery; their eyes and minds are from infancy accustomed to grand and striking forms — the want of them causes the ennui and listlessness called *maladie du pays, nostalgie,* or *Heimweh,* from which all mountaineers suffer, more or less, when in a town or distant from their mountains. I can understand it, as I have actually felt this *maladie,* for which, by the bye, we have no English name, when I was obliged to remain in Munich for some time about two years ago. The peasant to whom that house and all those fruitful fields below us belong, is about deliberately to die of this most lingering and melancholy disease ; he intends to emigrate to America !'

' Oh, what a fool ! ' cried Hamilton.

' I have said as much to him, but in rather more civil terms,' answered A. Z., ' but all to no purpose ; perhaps when you know his motives you may think differently, though I cannot. The extreme cheapness of education in Bavaria is a great temptation to the peasants, when their sons distinguish themselves at the German schools, to let them continue their education, learn Latin, and afterwards study at the University. It is a common thing for them to rise to eminence in the learned professions, and the eldest son of my friend Felsenbauer here would most probably have done so, had it not chanced that when he had nearly completed his studies, that revolutionary attempt of the Students took place in the year 1830, of which you may perhaps have heard. Whether or not he were implicated is unknown : but after having concealed himself for some time, and found that all his most intimate friends had been imprisoned, he wrote to his father for money and went off to America. He has married an American, and is so advantageously placed at Cincinnati, that he is most desirous to have his family near him, and his letters are from year to year more pressing. The old man is now only waiting to find a purchaser for his house and grounds —'

' I understand,' said Hamilton, laughing. ' You think that house, with a few alterations, might be made as comfortable as it is pretty. What price does he demand ?'

' About twelve hundred pounds : but he will not get more than a thousand for it, and is therefore likely to have to wait for

a year or two before he finds a purchaser ; so you have plenty
of time either to buy it or change your mind, which I suspect
you will do after your return home.   At all events I recommend your inspecting it some day with Herrmann, who understands such things perfectly—it will not be uninteresting to
you to know the financial position of a peasant of this kind,
and if he have the smallest hopes of your ever being a purchaser, he will unreservedly show you all his accounts.'

   While they were speaking, the peasant and his wife, followed
by their second son and a daughter, came out of the house, and
a long conversation ensued.   It was so dark when A. Z. proposed leaving, that the old man insisted on accompanying her
home with a lantern.

CHAPTER XLI.

THE SCHEIBEN-SCHIESSEN (TARGET-SHOOTING MATCH).

BARON Z—— returned the next day, was delighted to see
Hamilton, and went about with him everywhere, showing and
explaining whatever he thought likely to interest him.   One
of their excursions was to the marriage of a wood-ranger with
the daughter of an inn-keeper who lived deep in the mountains.   There was to be a dance and target-shooting match as
wedding festivities ; and it was with no small satisfaction that
Hamilton, at an unmentionably early hour in the morning,
followed Baron Z—— to his room, to choose one of his rifles for
the latter.   Hamilton did not, as on a former occasion, listen
with indifference while he descanted on their merits, but
examined them carefully, poised them on his hand, and pointed
them out of one of the windows at the little belfry of the
house he had visited with A. Z., and which he now chose as a
target.

   'You really look as if you understood what you were about,'
observed A. Z., who was pouring out their coffee.   'If you
have gained nothing else by your residence in Bavaria, you
have at least learned to get up in the morning, and to use a
rifle!'

   'Both decidedly German accomplishments,' replied Hamilton,
laughing ; 'and how I have acquired them you will learn when
you look over my journal.'

'Which I intend to do to-day, when I am alone and quiet,' said A. Z., 'and then we can talk about it whenever you are disposed.'

'Time to be off!' cried Baron Z——; and Hamilton found himself soon after driving through the wildest passes of the mountains at an hour which he formerly had considered ought to be devoted to sleep in a darkened chamber.

The road was still in shadow, though the sun shone brightly on the rocks above them, and it was only through an occasional cleft in them, or a widening of the pass through which the road lay, that the warm rays occasionally tempered the bracing morning air. For the first time since Hamilton had left the Rosenbergs, he felt exhilarated—disposed to enjoy life as he had formerly done. It must not be supposed that he was beginning to forget Hildegarde—quite the contrary. His mental struggles were over—absence, that surest test of affection, had proved to him that without her the best years of his life would be clouded: so completely had the world, and all relating to it, been changed to him during the last year, so different were all his ideas from what they had been, that his recollections of home were becoming ruins, and it was with difficulty that his imagination supplied the broken walls and crumbling window-sills of his former splendid visions of pomp and riches. His only fears now were of Hildegarde herself. He half dreaded a repulse; but he had resolved to brave even that; and since his resolutions had been formed, he had again begun to feel pleasure in everything surrounding him. When Baron Z—— stepped out of the little low carriage, which he called a 'sausage,' to gather bunches of the beautiful wild rhododendron, commonly called *Alpenrosen*, Hamilton sprang joyously up the side of the mountain with him, and experienced a boyish satisfaction in scrambling higher and higher still, to obtain a branch with deeper-coloured flowers, or a few sweetly-scented cyclamens.

Their destination was a village, which as nearly resembled a nest as could well be imagined, so completely was it surrounded by mountains, all wooded nearly to the summit; there were about thirty houses and two large inns. Baron Z——'s brewery supplied the place with beer, and it was, as he informed Hamilton, in the characters of a brewer and his friend that they that day appeared. They were, however, persons of considerable importance, as Hamilton soon discovered, for the marriage had been delayed until their arrival, and the gay procession was then first formed, with which, preceded by loud music, in which a flageolet contended in vain with a couple of horns for predominance, they marched to the church. Hamilton, on perceiving that all the men had large bouquets of flowers, and streaming ribbons in their hats, immediately decorated his with *Alpenrosen*. As to Baron Z——, neither he nor any of the other numerous gentlemen who came in the course of the day to shoot could be distinguished at a little distance from the peasants. The strong shoes, worsted stockings, black breeches, leather belts with their curiously-worked initials, loose gray shooting jackets, and slouched hats with black cock feathers, were common to all. A nice observer might perhaps have discovered a difference in the materials; but even that was generally avoided. If ever a German nobleman feels that those who are not in his class are equal or superior to him, it is at a *Scheiben-schiessen*. There the best shot is the best man. The consciousness of strength and power, which the free use of arms, and the habit of seeking pleasure and fame in their dexterous use, imparts, is not without its national importance; such men can scarcely fail to make good soldiers, or defend their mountain homes in time of war.

Excepting while they dined, Baron Z—— never ceased shooting. Hamilton, contented with having acquitted himself creditably, began at the end of a couple of hours to wander about; he first looked into the room where the wedding banquet was being slowly served: it had already lasted more than three hours, which is scarcely to be wondered at. as, between the courses, the more youthful part of the company made their way up the crowded staircase to a large room under the roof, where they danced; the measured sound of the waltz step forming a sort of metronome to the musicians, who, at times, seemed more attentive to the movements of those about them than their occupation, thereby occasionally producing such extraordinary and wild sounds that Hamilton allowed himself to be pushed up the stairs into their immediate vicinity. Finding a quiet corner, he tranquilly smoked his cigar and looked on, an amused spectator of a scene which formed for him a picture of the most interesting description, from its novelty and thoroughly national character.

The room, spacious and well floored, was immediately under the roof, of which the rafters, and, on close inspection, the tiles, were visible. The musicians, placed in a corner and well supplied with beer, blew, whistled, and scraped with all their might; the violoncello, with its eternal tonic, dominant, and subdominant, acting as whipper-in to the other instruments. The trumpet, occasionally raised to one of the windows in the roof, informed the absent of the opportunity they were losing, or served as an invitation to the lazy. Diminutive beer-barrels connected with strong planks formed seats along the walls, and on them the half-breathless dancers, in their picturesque costumes, occasionally sat and rested. A few elderly peasants were established round a table behind the door, and near them stood a fine specimen of a rustic exclusive, with his arms folded, and bright blue eyes audaciously following each dancing pair as they passed. He lounged against the wall until, seeing some known, or loved, or pretty girl, he was moved to touch her partner on the shoulder, and, however unwilling the latter might be, he was obliged in courtesy to resign her until she had taken some turns round the room with the interloper, who, on returning her to her partner, thanked *him*, and the flushed and panting girl invariably looked delighted at this most approved mode of publicly doing her homage. Hamilton observed about half a dozen beauties who never were allowed to rest for one moment.

Light and shade were disposed as the most fastidious painter could desire; the rays of the afternoon sun, as they entered by the open windows, rendered even the tremulous motion of the air and the usually imperceptible particles of dust apparent, while the gradually dispersing light made the silver-laced bodices of the women glitter, and the beaming faces of the men to glow more deeply. Here for the first time Hamilton saw the real *Ländler* danced, the waltz in all its nationality —as unlike anything he had ever heard so denominated as could well be imagined. It was a German fandango with nailed shoes instead of castanets, but there was life, energy, and enjoyment in every movement. The origin of the name of waltz for this dance is from *walzen*, 'to turn round,' and this the dancers did regularly, though not quickly when together, but they often separated, and then the movements were as uncertain as various, accompanied on the part of the men by the snapping of fingers, clapping their knees with both hands, and springing in the air, while ever and anon they uttered a piercing peculiar cry, something between shouting and singing. During the time the men performed these wild gesticulations, their partners waltzed on demurely before them, and when they joined each other again it was usually with a few decided foot-stampings that they recommenced their rotatory motions.

It was long before Hamilton felt disposed to leave this scene of rustic festivity; when he did so, it was but to witness another of a different kind, for, as the evening approached, and the noise of the rifles began by degrees to cease, all the singers and zither-players in the neighbourhood assembled in the garden. It was in the midst of them that Hamilton was found by Baron Z——, and though he soon after joined the latter and his friends at another table, he still turned round and endeavoured to hear the words or hum the chorus of their songs.

'Our national music seems to interest you,' observed an elderly gentleman in a green shooting jacket, drawing his chair close to Hamilton's.

'Very much; but I find it rather difficult to understand the words, though I hear them very distinctly.'

'Of course you do; a foreigner must always find it difficult to understand our different dialects, and we have many.'

Baron Z—— took a little book of songs out of his pocket, and handed it to Hamilton, who, after a few unsuccessful attempts, at length was able to read and understand one of them. 'Are these songs ancient or modern?' he asked, after a pause.

'These,' answered Baron Z——, 'are of an uncertain age, and are common in the Bavarian highlands; but we have some national songs of the same description which are extremely ancient.'

'We know,' observed the elderly gentleman, 'we know from the poems of Walter von der Vogelweide, that even at the end of the twelfth century the peasants had their own songs, which, to the great annoyance of the celebrated poet, were gladly heard and highly valued by the princes and knights of his time. The highest nobles then danced to their own songs, as you may sometimes see the Austrian peasant do to this day. The rhymes of the *Niebelungenlied** and other old German epic poems are precisely of the same description as these songs, which is also a proof of their antiquity.

* The Niebelungenlied is a very ancient poem, greatly valued, but little read—like the works of Chaucer and Spenser in England.

'And is the music as old as the poetry?' asked Hamilton.

'I believe so,' replied Baron Z——; 'it was intended for dancing as well as singing, as the universal name of *Schnader-hüpfel* denotes ; the word *schnaden* means to talk or chat, and *hüpfen* to jump or dance about.'

'And is all your old national music of this gay *Schnader-hüpfel* description?' asked Hamilton.

'Oh, no ! We have melancholy and sentimental too ; but our mountaineers are too gay and happy a people to allow the mournful to predominate, or even to have its due share in their music ; the sorrowful thought of one verse is sure to find consolation in a jesting contradiction in the next. The Alpine songs are generally of this description, and the girls who have the charge of the cows on the Alps sing them together, and continue to do so after they have left the mountains, which has caused them to become familiar to the inhabitants of the valleys. Then there is the jodel, the song without words, which has so much resemblance to the *ranz des vaches* of the Swiss, and which requires both practice and compass of voice.'

'Oh, I remember,' said Hamilton, 'what you and some of the others sang when we were on the chamois-hunt last year; sometimes it sounded like water bubbling, and then came some queer high notes and a sort of shout—it was quite adapted to the mountains—quite beautiful when there was an echo. I should like to learn it.'

'You will find it more difficult than you imagine,' said Baron Z——; 'that is, if you have ever learned to sing; my wife has never been able to manage it, and she has often tried.'

'I shall learn to jodel and play the zither, too,' said Hamilton ; 'that is, if I ever come to reside in Germany.'

'*If*,' said Baron Z——, and then he joined in the chorus of the song which was being sung at the table nearest them.

* * * * *

'How different the same scene looks in the gradually increasing light of early morning and the deepening shades of approaching evening !' observed Baron Z——, as he leaned back in the carriage on their way home, and looked along the valley through which the road lay : it had become so narrow, that it seemed about to close altogether, while a towering mountain, facing them as they advanced, appeared to prevent all further progress; 'and yet I scarcely know which is to be preferred in a country of this description.'

'The evening, certainly, the evening;' said Hamilton, looking round; 'but a little earlier. The sun should still be on those rocks above us, and make them successively yellow, red, copper-coloured, and violet, as I have seen them every evening from the garden at Hohenfels.'

'I wish,' said Baron Z——, 'I wish that we could see them from the top of our alp to-night; we cannot expect this unclouded weather to last much longer.'

'Have you an alp of your own?' asked Hamilton.

'No; but I have rented one for the last two years, and find it answers very well; the greater part of my cattle are there now. It was not, however, of my cows and calves that I was thinking, but of the chamois on the mountain near the alp, of which the Förster from G—— told me this morning. Now, as you acquitted yourself so well to-day at the *Scheiben-schiessen*, I do not see why you should not become a sportsman at once.'

'Do you think I should have any chance?'

'Why not? You must make a beginning some time or other.'

'I suppose game is very plentiful here?' said Hamilton.

'Not what you would call plenty; at least, we have not grouse or black cocks as my wife tells me you have in Scotland.'

'But I have heard of splendid *battues* in the neighbourhood of Munich.'

'I dare say, in the royal chase, where eight or nine hundred hares, and other game in proportion, have been shot in one afternoon—but that is not my idea of sport. I prefer a chamois-hunt to all others; next to that, black cock; and I am quite satisfied if I shoot three or four during the season.'

'Are the black cock so difficult to be got at?'

'More troublesome than difficult, though I have occasionally found them almost as high on the mountains as the chamois! It is the waiting and watching—the being up before sunrise—that gives me an interest, though it generally disgusts others whose actual profession it does not happen to be.'

'I suppose,' said Hamilton, 'it is the actual profession of these Försters? There was one near the Iron Works, and he always supplied Madame Rosenberg with game: she paid him for it, however.'

'Of course she did,' replied Baron Z——, laughing; 'and if you shoot a chamois, you must pay for it too; that is, if you wish to keep it. I have myself no game whatever, but, as the Förster rents the whole chase in my neighbourhood from Government, I have as much sport as I please, and, in fact, as much game too : I pay for whatever I retain, and so do all the others to whom he has given the permission to shoot; but I suspect his profits are not great, for we have a number of *Wildschützen* — wild hunters — poachers you call them, I believe, in England.'

'Yes; one hears of them continually in the country. I begin to have a faint idea that they may be great nuisances.'

'I have no intention of exactly undertaking their defence,' said Baron Z——; 'but here in the mountains, where almost every man is a good shot, and the ideas of some are rather confused as to the better right which one man may have more than another to shoot an animal roaming about among the rocks, the crime is, to say the least, venial. I, for my part, could never pursue a Wildschütz with the wish to catch him; but between them and the Försters there is the most implacable hatred and deadly war. When they meet without witnesses, it not unfrequently happens that they fire at each other! If the Förster fall, he is immediately missed—if the Wildschütz, it often remains long undiscovered. Last winter the body of a young man was found on one of the mountains here, several weeks after his friends had, first privately and then publicly, sought him. There is little doubt that he was shot by one of our wood-rangers, and the man was immediately arrested, but no sort of proof could be obtained; the day of the young man's death was unknown; the wood-ranger had been on that mountain, but also on others, about the supposed time; shots had been heard by some wood-cutters, but not more than could be accounted for by the game brought home; in short, he was set at liberty, but the fate of the Wildschütz, who was a handsome, good-humoured fellow, created much interest and pity : so you see there is so much danger, and so little profit, so much romance, and so little vulgarity about them altogether, that they are not unfrequently the subject of a song, or the hero of a legend. I am not even quite sure that the suspicion of a young man being at times a wild hunter would injure him in the opinion of any girl born and bred among the mountains !'

'I dare say not,' said Hamilton. 'Women higher born and better bred have not unfrequently similar feelings, and the very word is in itself the essence of romance! You must allow that it sounds a vast deal better than Förster, or Forstmeister, or Forstcommissär, or Forstinspector. Everybody seems to be Forst-something in this part of the world.'

'And are we not surrounded by forests? Are not all our mountains covered with wood?' asked Baron Z——, laughing. 'Can you wonder that in a country where wood is used as fuel the care and culture of it should be of the greatest importance?'

'Then these Försters are not a—exactly gamekeepers?'

'No; the preserving of the game is, however, always in connection with the woods and forests. The Forstmeister, Forstactuar, Försters, and Forstpracticants are appointed by Government; the under Förster, or wood-ranger, is the only thing at all answering to your idea of game-keeper.'

'And what have they all to do?' asked Hamilton.

'Can you not imagine the care of all these woods giving a number of people employment?' asked Baron Z——, looking round him. 'The never-ending felling and drifting, and selling and planting; the corrections of the rivers used for drifting; the care of the game, and a hundred other things, which I do not just now remember. The *Forstwesen*, as we call it here, requires as much, and as peculiar study, at the University, as theology, philosophy, law, physic, or any other branch of learning. Had I been given my choice, I should have preferred it to all others.'

'And what did you study? I mean especially.'

'Law,' answered Baron Z——; and while he spoke, the carriage rolled into the paved court of Hohenfels.

CHAPTER XLII.

A DISCOURSE.

THERE had been a thunder-storm during the night, and the rain descended the next morning in torrents. 'I fear, Hamilton, our party must be put off for a short time,' observed Baron Z——, as he walked from one window to the other, in a disconsolate manner, after breakfast. 'How I detest a hopeless day of this kind !'

'I remember,' said A. Z., 'that when I was an accomplished young lady, I rather liked a day of rain when I had a drawing to finish, or a new song to study—I do not dislike it to-day either, but for a very different reason. Had it been fine, I must have gone to the alp, to do the honours of my dairy to Mr. Hamilton, and now, without any incivility on my part, I can stay at home and quietly inspect the making of a hundred-weight of soap, which cannot be any longer delayed ; and I expect,' she added, turning to Hamilton, 'or rather I hope, on your way from the brewery, where of course you will go to smoke with Herrmann, you vill visit me—in the washhouse !'

'And can you really make soap ?' asked Hamilton, rather surprised.

'I really can, and really do, as you shall see—but, perhaps, you do n't care about soap-boiling ?'

'I—rather hoped—that, perhaps, to-day you would have had time to talk to me about—'

'Oh, I always find time to talk,' said A. Z. 'My soap will be ready before dinner ; it was begun yesterday evening, and has been boiling all the morning ; so you see, after our coffee, we shall have the whole afternoon, and no chance of visitors!'

Just as all the bells in the neighbourhood were chiming noon. Hamilton walked into the washhouse, and there found A. Z., standing beside an immense boiler, filled with a substance very much resembling porridge ; she was examining some of it as it trickled down a piece of flat wood, which she held in her hand, and having dipped her finger into it, and found that it formed what she called a thimble, she appeared satisfied. Some few directions she gave to a little old woman, who seemed very learned on the subject of soap-boiling, and then she wound her way through the surrounding tubs and buckets and pails to Hamilton, and with him went unceremoniously to dinner.

When Hamilton, a couple of hours afterwards, joined A. Z. in the drawing-room, he found her turning over the last leaves of his journal, as she sat in a large arm-chair, beside the slightly-heated stove ; she turned round immediately, and observed, 'Well, Mr. Hamilton, you—"rather—hoped I should find time to talk." I have time now, and only wait to hear what is to be the subject of conversation.'

He drew a chair close to her, and said, 'First of all—your opinion of Hildegarde.   Does she care for me ?'

'I am afraid she does,' answered A. Z.

'How can you say "afraid," when you know it is what I most wish—my only chance of happiness?   I fear nothing but a refusal now.   Have you not observed that she has never said a word which could make me for a moment imagine she cared in the least for me ?'

'Judge her actions, and not her words,' answered A. Z.

'And if her actions should denote more friendship than love ?'

'The friendship of a girl of eighteen, for a man of one or two and twenty, is very apt to degenerate into love.'

'And you call that degenerating ?'

A. Z. nodded her head, and said, 'We have no time to discuss that matter now, nor is it necessary ; but there is something I should like to say to you, if you will allow me.'

'I allow you—wish you to say anything—everything you please.'

'Before I read your journal,' she continued, turning quite round to him, 'I was disposed only to think of you and your interests, and recommended you to return home, without again seeing Mademoiselle Rosenberg, or entering into any engagement with her.   I give you the same advice now—but—for her sake—on her account !'

'And this you say, supposing her attached to me, and knowing that I am willing to sacrifice everything I most value for her !' said Hamilton.

'Yes ; I consider the whole affair as the purest specimen of first love that it is possible to imagine—so sincere on both sides that, were there no impediments to your marriage, I think you might pass your lives very happily together.   But the sacrifices you are about to make, she will not, I fear, be able properly to estimate; and you must be very different from most young men of your age and position in the world, if you have steadiness enough, after two whole years' absence, to return here, change all your habits, and bury yourself in these mountains for the rest of your life !'

'I think—I am almost sure—that for Hildegarde I can do so.'

'If you do, I shall have a colossal respect for your character; but in the mean time forgive my doubting it.   Your uncle will send you to Paris, give you unlimited command of money ; the temptations are great there, and, with your brother John and your cousin Harry as companions, I fear that at the end of the first year you will write Mademoiselle Rosenberg a letter to say, "that finding it impossible to obtain the consent of your family to your union, you will not *drag the woman you love into poverty* !" I believe this is the usual phrase used on such occasions ? And you can do this without even incurring the censure of the world; for who knows anything of Hildegarde? No one will ever hear that for your sake she has refused Max Zedwitz; and that she will again do so, if engaged to you, is a matter of course; and no one will know that your desertion will condemn her either to being a governess, or to a nunnery for the rest of her life, for she will never marry a Major Stultz, or a Förster Weidmann!' A. Z. paused, but, as Hamilton did not speak, she continued, 'I see my doubts rather offend you, but such conduct is, I am sorry to say, common, and I know you too little to estimate your character as it, perhaps, deserves. And now let us consider the other side of the question—I mean Hildegarde's : she has never, you say, betrayed herself to you, still less, I am sure, to anyone else. To most women, the feeling of wounded pride, the sense of shame at being publicly slighted and forsaken, is quite as painful to bear as the real loss of the love on which all their visions of future happiness are built—all this may still be spared Hildegarde. You have left her without explanation; she thinks highly of you, for she does not know that you could have acted otherwise than as you have done—none of her family have the least idea that she cares for you—she even flatters herself that you are not aware of it— she will long remember you after you have ceased to think of her, but the remembrance will be unmixed with pain. When Maximilian again meets her, she will tell him that she never can return his affection, that she never can feel anything but friendship for him—but—she will marry him, make an excellent wife too—and may some fine day, in this room, beside this very stove, quietly talk of you, and wonder that she could ever have preferred anyone to her excellent husband, whom we may suppose sitting just where you are now!'

'Really a most agreeable picture,' cried Hamilton, with ill-concealed irritation of manner. 'And pray what is to become of me ?'

'I have already said, you will forget more quickly than she

F F

can; and so, after enjoying the world and its pomps and vani-
ties for a few years, you will marry a Lady Jane or a Lady
Mary Somebody, who will be quite as amiable—if not as
beautiful as Hildegarde.'

'You are considering this affair much too lightly,' cried
Hamilton, starting from his chair almost angrily; 'you talk as
if it were a mere flirtation.'

'No: I have ceased to consider it such,' rejoined A. Z.,
gravely. 'I wish to save you from self-reproach, and Hildegarde from real unhappiness hereafter. The bitterness of
parting is now over on both sides. With the best intentions
in the world, circumstances might induce you to write the
letter I spoke of—Hildegarde's feelings now are very different
from what they will be when she has accustomed herself to
think of you as her companion for life. I would willingly save
her youth from a blight which, however her pride and strength
of mind may enable her to conceal it, will prevent the develop-
ment of all her good qualities, and perhaps turn her generous
confidence into suspicious distrust, her warmth of heart into
callousness for ever—but I have now said enough—too
much, perhaps;' and she walked to the window, which she
opened, to ask Baron Z——, who was in the courtyard, what
he thought of the weather.

'No chance of a change,' he answered; 'the barometer is still
falling, and it will not clear up until there is snow on the
mountain-tops, most probably.'

'That is the only disagreeable thing in a mountainous
country,' observed A. Z., turning to Hamilton. 'When it
begins to rain, it never knows how or when to stop. I am
sorry, on your account, that the fine weather has not lasted a
little longer; but to-morrow we shall have a box of new books,
and perhaps you may find something to interest you among
them.'

'I am sure,' said Hamilton, 'that you will agree with me in
thinking that I ought not to delay my return to Munich even
a day longer, now that I have quite decided on my future plans.
I wish, if possible, to prevent Hildegarde from going to
Frankfort, where that Mademoiselle Hortense intended to
send her.'

'I scarcely know what I ought to say,' replied A. Z. 'It is
not to be expected that you will remain here listening to my

long stories, and the rain pattering against the windows, when you have a good excuse for leaving.'

'A reason—not an excuse,' said Hamilton.

'Well then,' said A. Z., as she closed the window, 'though I do not ask you to give me a lock of your hair, I feel so much interested in your affairs, that I hope you will "Trust me, and let me know your love's success," in a few lines which you may find time to write to me after you have reached home.'

CHAPTER XLIII.

ANOTHER KIND OF DISCOURSE.

TWENTY-FOUR hours afterwards Hamilton was in Munich, on his way to Major Stultz's. He had not yet taken leave of Crescenz, and hoped, when ostensibly doing so, to obtain from her some information about her sister's plans and prospects. His old acquaintance, Walburg, was delighted to see him, informed him that 'her mistress was at home, quite alone—the Major had gone to sup with some officers who had been in Russia with him;' and, while speaking, she threw open the drawing-room door. Crescenz turned round, and then, with a blush of pleasure, rose quickly and advanced towards Hamilton, exclaiming, 'I knew you would not leave Bavaria without coming to see me! I said so to Blasius, and to Hildegarde too!'

'So you have spent another day at the Iron Works, and can tell me how they all are?'

'No,' replied Crescenz; and the smile faded from her features as she added, 'Hildegarde was here, on her way to Frankfort.'

'So she is gone—actually gone!' cried Hamilton.

'She left us the day before yesterday. Blasius says he is glad our parting is over, for I could do nothing but cry all the time she was here.'

'And Hildegarde?' asked Hamilton.

'She appeared quite contented with her future prospects, and tried to make me so too.'

'Quite contented?' repeated Hamilton.

'Yes. Blasius says she has not much feeling, and that I

am a fool to waste so much affection on her; but he does not know how kind she was to me for so many years at school, helping me out of all my difficulties, and taking my part on all occasions — he has no idea what Hildegarde can be to those she loves.'

'Nor I either,' said Hamilton.

'Of course not,' said Crescenz, smiling, 'as she only latterly began to like you; but for ten years she was everything to me. After we left school, indeed, or rather from the time we were at Seon, she changed a good deal, certainly. You know the time that—'

'I know,' said Hamilton.

'But when she was here last week, she was just what she used to be. I could have fancied we had gone back two or three years of our lives.'

'So she was quite cheerful!' said Hamilton, with a con-strained smile. 'It seems she felt no regret at quitting the Iron Works?'

'Not much, I should think, when you were no longer there,' answered Crescenz.

'What! What do you mean?' asked Hamilton, eagerly.

'Why, as you were the only person who could talk to her, she must have found it very dull after you were gone, I suppose.'

'Oh!' said Hamilton, 'is that all? Perhaps she did not even say as much—did not speak of me at all?'

'Oh, yes; we often spoke of you,' said Crescenz, nodding her head.

'I flattered myself, at one time, that Hildegarde liked me—' began Hamilton.

'She does like you; she said so repeatedly, and quite agreed with me in everything about you; but she does not like you as Blasius thought she would when you first went to the Iron Works. He said then it was very inconsiderate of mamma to take you there—that she ought to have insisted on your leaving her house when papa died.'

'She did propose my leaving,' said Hamilton.

'Yes, I know—that was after Blasius had spoken to her— and he was so angry, when he heard you were going to the country, after all. He said—he said—'

'What?' asked Hamilton.

'That, with such opportunities, he should not be at all

surprised if you and Hildegarde went to—the—devil ! He sometimes does use such very improper words.'

Hamilton could not help smiling.

'You think I am joking,' she continued, 'but I assure you he said such dreadful things that I cannot repeat them ; and I was so glad when I went to the Iron Works to perceive that Hildegarde did not like you—in that way—'

'In what way?' asked Hamilton, irresistibly impelled to talk to her as he had done in former times. She blushed so deeply, however, and became so painfully confused, that he added gravely, 'You mean that you saw she only liked me as an acquaintance, or friend, and I believe you are right.'

'Yes, that is exactly what I meant,' said Crescenz, apparently greatly relieved; 'for that last day, when you seemed to like Lina Berger more than you had ever done either of us, she did not in the least mind it—quite laughed at the idea !'

'Did she?' said Hamilton, with a look of annoyance which Crescenz alone could have failed to observe.

'Hildegarde never will tell me anything,' she continued, 'but I have made a discovery all the same.'

'Have you?' cried Hamilton, with a look of interest which her observations were seldom calculated to produce. 'What is it?

'I have found out at last who it is that she really loves.'

'Indeed! Are you quite sure?'

'You shall hear how I found it out. Lina Berger came here, not to take leave of Hildegarde, for you know they dislike each other, but because she wished to hear something about you. Now Hildegarde answered all her questions with the greatest composure, and when Lina found that she could not embarrass or annoy her about you, she suddenly turned the conversation and spoke of Count Zedwitz ; the moment she pronounced his name Hildegarde's whole countenance changed, and then Lina went on, and told her that the old Count was dying, that Doctor Berger had been several times to see him, and said he could not live more than a week or ten days ; and that, as his son had been written for, and was probably on his way home, she now seriously advised Hildegarde not to leave Munich, or at least Bavaria, until all chance was over of his renewing his proposal of marriage to her—that is, if she had still the slightest hope that such unheard-of good fortune was in store for her ; above all things, she ought to avoid going to Frankfort, as, notwithstanding all

Count Zedwitz's professions of liberality, the idea of her having been a governess *might* be revolting to him !'

'Poor dear Hildegarde !' cried Hamilton, compassionately. ' Was she very angry ?'

'She became so pale and agitated that I expected some terrible scene, such as we used to have at school ; but, to my great surprise, she thanked Lina for her good advice, though she did not mean to follow it, said she considered being a governess no sort of a disgrace ; rather the contrary, as it led to the supposition, at least, that her acquirements were more than common, and that what Count Zedwitz might think on the subject was at present a matter of indifference to her—and then she went out of the room, and did not return until Lina was gone.'

'But surely you do not infer from this that she loves Zedwitz !' cried Hamilton, cheerfully. ' It seems to me as if almost the contrary conclusion might be drawn.'

'You have not heard all,' said Crescenz. 'After Lina was gone—though I knew she had only been trying to vex Hildegarde—I thought the advice might be good, as Blasius had said several times that it would be such an excellent thing if that cross, proud old Count would die at once, and leave his son at liberty to marry Hildegarde. It is very wrong to wish anybody to die, but Blasius does not mind saying things of that kind. I do n't think he means all he says, though, about the devil, or people being damned—it would be very terrible if he did ; and I am sure he learned all those odious expressions in that frightful Russian campaign—'

'Well, a—and so—,' said Hamilton, ' when Hildegarde again came into the room, you probably recommended her remaining here ?'

'Yes—but you know I never could expect Hildegarde to follow my advice—and when she refused, I only just ventured, in a whisper, to ask her if she thought that Count Zedwitz still loved her—and she said, "Yes, better than anyone ever loved, or will love me—better than I deserve," and then she went to the window and pretended to look out, but I saw that she was crying. I am quite sure she has made up her mind to marry him, but I do n't understand why she is so unhappy about it, especially as he is a Count, and Hildegarde is so fond of rank !'

'Is she ?' said Hamilton, absently.

'Oh, yes; rank, riches, station, and somebody to love her exclusively—and Count Zedwitz can give her all these things, you know!'

'Very true—your arguments are conclusive,' said Hamilton; and now it is time for me to go—'

'But you will come again?' said Crescenz; 'you will come to take leave of Blasius?'

Hamilton shook his head.

'And are you really going away for ever?' asked Crescenz; and her eyes filled with tears as she added, in a slightly tremulous voice, 'Hildegarde said we should never hear of, never see you again!'

'And she said it, I am sure, with less regret than you do!' exclaimed Hamilton, bitterly.

'I dare say you think me very foolish,' said Crescenz, trying to smile, while large tears coursed each other down her cheeks.

'I think you very kind,' said Hamilton.

'If Blasius were at home, you would have stayed a little longer, perhaps—I wish Blasius were here.'

Hamilton thought it was quite as well he was not, but he did not say so; and after taking leave of her, much more affectionately than he had dared to do of her sister, he left the house considerably more thoughtful than he had entered it.

CHAPTER XLIV.

THE JOURNEY HOME COMMENCES.

HAMILTON left Munich the next day in the mail for Frankfort; he had secured the place beside the conductor in the front part of the coach, which formed a kind of open carriage, and where he intended to smoke, and think, and sleep undisturbed. His late conversation with Crescenz had made a deep impression on him; it had again filled his mind with doubts and fears, which deprived him of his habitual cheerfulness, while his usual source of amusement when travelling—studying the characters or foibles of his companions—had lost all interest for him. He did not ask the name or condition of any one of the persons with whom he moved under the same roof a whole night and two days, and no one contradicted the young student, who, on leaving at Wurtzburg, observed, with a glance towards Hamilton, 'As unsociable a fellow as ever I met! A thorough Englishman!'

He wandered about the streets until the coach was again ready to start, and then, although the weather had completely cleared up, and the country, refreshed by the rain, was by no means uninteresting, he sank back into his corner, and over-powered by weariness fell fast asleep. When he awoke it was quite dark, and as he raised himself slowly from his slumbers the conductor called out, 'Halt! Who is booked for Aschaffen-burg? Who gets out here?'

Some passenger from the inside of the coach spoke, and Hamilton asked, 'Is there a good hotel here?'

'Very good.'

'Then let me out. My legs are cramped, and my head and shoulders battered and bruised. I say, Hans, you can go on to Frankfort, and bespeak rooms for me at the Hôtel d'Angle-terre. Give me my carpet-bag and dressing-case as fast as you can;' and Hamilton was stamping his feet on the ground with a feeling of relief amounting to pleasure, when a man with a lantern came up to him, and demanded his passport.

'My passport? Directly. I shall be in Frankfort about twelve o'clock to-morrow, Hans,' cried Hamilton, as the coach drove off; and having delivered up his passport, he watched the man with the lantern enter an adjacent house, saw the light pass from one window to the other, until it finally dis-appeared, and all was dark.

'This is pleasant,' he said, looking round him, 'and I don't know the way to the hotel, or even the name of it!'

'I'm here, sir, with a wheelbarrow for the luggage,' said a voice near him, and Hamilton's eyes now becoming accustomed to the darkness, he perceived a man standing close to him, and a dark figure at a little distance sitting among some trunks and boxes.

'Can you show me the way to the best hotel?' asked Hamilton.

'To be sure I can; for what else am I here every night, wet or dry?' answered the man, good-humouredly, as he placed Hamilton's luggage in the wheelbarrow. 'If you have no objection, sir, I'll take the lady's things, too.'

'By all means,' said Hamilton, looking towards the dark

figure, which now rose and endeavoured to assist the man to move a rather large trunk.

'Allow me,' said Hamilton, instantly taking her place; and everything was soon arranged.

Thank you a thousand times,' whispered the lady, placing her arm within his almost familiarly; and Hamilton, half surprised, half amused, looked somewhat curiously at his companion as she afterwards unreservedly drew closer to him, and at last clasped her small well-gloved hands over his arm. They followed for some minutes in silence the man with the wheelbarrow, who trudged on before them whistling; but as they drew near one of the miserable street lamps, Hamilton leant forward and endeavoured, rather unceremoniously, to peer under his companion's bonnet. A thick black veil rendered the effort fruitless.

'You wish to see my face,' she said, in a voice that made him stop suddenly, with an exclamation of astonishment; and when she pushed aside her veil the flickering light played dimly over the well-known features of Hildegarde.

And where were Hamilton's doubts and fears at that moment? Removed?—dispersed? No; but they were dormant —sleeping as soundly, perhaps as uneasily, as he had been doing about an hour before. He scarcely understood Hildegarde, as, with repeated assurances that she was very, very glad to see him again, she incoherently related that she had travelled to Wurtzburg with some friends of Mademoiselle Hortense's; they had been very kind, and had insisted on her remaining with them a couple of days, to recover from the fatigues of her night journey; that they had accompanied her to the coach, and advised her to sleep at Aschaffenburg; that she had recognised Hamilton's voice when speaking to Hans, had seen his face when the man demanded his passport; 'And then,' she added, 'I knew that all my difficulties about travelling were at an end; so I sat down quietly on my trunk, and waited to see when you would recognise me.'

'How could I recognise your voice when you whispered, or your face, when covered with that impervious veil? Indeed it is impossible to see anything at a few feet distance from these lamps, which seem but intended to make the " darkness visible." The moment you spoke I knew you.'

'That I expected,' said Hildegarde; 'otherwise I should have been tempted to preserve my incognito a little longer.'

'I am very glad you did not. But where is the man with our bags and boxes?' he cried, looking round. He was no longer visible, though they could still indistinctly hear the sound of the jogging of the wheelbarrow over the rough paving-stones in the distance. With a merry laugh they ran together down the street, and overtook him just as he rolled his clumsy little vehicle under an archway, lighted by two handsome lamps, and where their arrival was immediately announced by the ringing of a large bell.

They reached Frankfort the next day, just in time to dine at the table d'hôte; but Hildegarde's appearance caused so many inquiries, that Hamilton followed her to her room to advise her not dining there in future.

'I shall scarcely be here to-morrow,' she said, pushing back her bonnet, while she rummaged a little writing-desk for some paper. 'Oh! here it is,' she added, 'Hortense's letter of introduction. I am sure you will be so kind as to go with me to find out the house of this lady—this Baroness Waldorf!'

'Who?' cried Hamilton.

'Baroness Waldorf.'

'Why did you not tell me it was to her you were going?'

'Because I did not think it could interest you in any way. I never heard you speak of her. Have you seen her? Do you know anything about her?'

'I met her at Edelhof—Zedwitz is guardian to her daughter, and I think she would have no objection to make him step-father also.'

'Oh, tell me something about her!' cried Hildegarde, eagerly, to Hamilton's surprise quite indifferent to the latter part of his speech. 'Tell me all you know about her. Is she a person to whom I am likely to become attached?'

'I don't know—I rather think not. Oh, Hildegarde, let me advise you, as a friend, to give up this plan altogether, and go back to your stepmother.—If you would only listen to me patiently for ten minutes—'

'I cannot listen to you,' said Hildegarde, interrupting him, 'for I have made an engagement—a promise to remain a whole year under all circumstances with the Baroness Waldorf. She would not make any other sort of agreement, as she is going to Florence for the winter. She alone can release me from this promise—but I cannot say I wish it, as I rather enjoy the idea of going to Italy.'

'Under other circumstances I could easily imagine it.'

'And under what other circumstances am I likely to see Italy—or, even the Rhine, near as it now is to me?'

Hamilton was silent.

'Let us go,' said Hildegarde, taking up her gloves. 'You will not, I am sure, try to dissuade me any longer, when I tell you that I cannot endure the life I should have to lead at the Iron Works; my habits and education have unfortunately made me totally unfit for it. I have made the trial, and must now with regret confess that the details of domestic life are not only tiresome, but absolutely disgusting to me!'

'So then,' said Hamilton, 'you have discovered that riches are necessary to your happiness?'

'Not exactly riches,' replied Hildegarde, little aware of the importance attached to her answer, 'but something beyond the actual means of subsistence—enough at least to insure me from the vulgar cares of life, and enable me to associate with people whose habits and manners are similar to mine.'

'And how much would be necessary for this?' asked Hamilton, gravely.

'Oh, indeed I do n't know,' she answered carelessly, laughing, 'nor is it necessary to calculate. That I have it not, is certain; and in being a governess I see the only means of satisfying my wishes at present, and securing a competence hereafter. If I remain ten years with the Baroness Waldorf, I shall receive a pension for the rest of my life.'

'And do you think you could not endure these vulgar cares of life, as you call them, even with a person you loved?' asked Hamilton, still more earnestly.

'I shall never be tried in that way,' answered Hildegarde, firmly; and while she walked on, wholly occupied with her immediate concerns, Hamilton, altogether misunderstanding the meaning of her words, concluded she referred to a marriage with Zedwitz at some future period. Thus unconsciously tormenting each other, they reached the Baroness Waldorf's house, and, finding a burly porter lounging outside the door, they asked if she were at home.

'No—she was not—she had gone to Mayence.'

'And when is she expected to return?' asked Hildegarde, anxiously.

'We do not in the least know, mademoiselle; she left very suddenly, in consequence of a letter which she received. She is sometimes not more than a few days absent, and most of the carriages and horses are still here. Who shall I say—?'

'It is of no consequence,' said Hamilton; 'we merely wished to know if a young lady from Munich was not expected about this time?'

The man said he would inquire, entered the house, but returned almost directly, saying that no one was expected, excepting perhaps Count Zedwitz on his way home.

Hamilton and Hildegarde walked on together for some minutes in silence; at length the latter observed, half inquiringly, 'I suppose I have no right to be offended with this Baroness Waldorf? It must have been urgent business which could make her leave Frankfort just when she appointed me to be here?'

'I should think so,' said Hamilton; 'but she might have made some arrangement for your reception during her absence. This thoughtlessness about you will scarcely prepossess you in her favour.'

'Rich people are seldom considerate,' began Hildegarde, as if she intended to moralise: but suddenly stopping, she added, 'You are right—she has placed me in a very unpleasant position—if she do not return in a day or two I shall neither have the means of remaining here, or going home!'

'Our fortunate meeting at Aschaffenburg,' said Hamilton, 'will save you from all annoyances of that description, as you know I can arrange everything with your mother. At all events, I shall not leave you now until you are either at home again, or residing with this—to say the least—very thoughtless person.'

'But will not delay inconvenience you?' asked Hildegarde.

'Not in the least. As far as I am concerned, I should be glad that the Baroness would not return for six weeks! All places are alike to me where you are; and much as we were together at the Iron Works, you have more time to bestow on me here, and therefore I am proportionably happier.'

This kind of speech she never answered; and after a short pause, Hamilton proposed showing her the gardens which surrounded the town, and in their shady walks they wandered until evening.

CHAPTER XLV.

WHAT OCCURRED AT THE HÔTEL D'ANGLETERRE, IN FRANKFORT.

THE next day after dinner, while Hamilton went to his banker's, Hildegarde looked out of her window, and watched, with a sort of quiet indifference, the arrival of two travelling carriages at the hotel. Out of the first sprang a tall, large man, who, merely raising two fingers to his travelling cap by way of salutation, instantly disappeared—and even while the heated and tired horses were still being led up and down the yard, others were brought out, and the servant, after great bustling and hurrying, followed his master into the hotel. Again the cracking of whips and ringing of bells became audible, and another and larger carriage arrived—decidedly English. The well-built vehicle swung easily with all its weight of imperials and servants' seats behind, and out of it stepped a tall, thin gentleman, with a gray hat, a gray coat, gray trousers, gray gaiters, and gray whiskers! An elderly lady followed, her face half concealed by her pendent lace veil, and two young and pretty girls stopped for a moment to inspect the building they were about to enter. Hildegarde looked at her watch; it was the hour that Hamilton told her he would return; so she locked her door, and began slowly to walk along the corridor and descend the stairs. The English family were just turning into a large suite of rooms on the first floor as she passed—the gentleman in gray had stopped at the door, his hat fast on his head; he turned to his wife, who was entering, and observed, quite loudly enough for Hildegarde to hear, 'By Jove, that's the handsomest girl I have seen for a long time!' The lady turned round and deliberately raised her *lorgnette* to her eye; while their two daughters, after a hasty glance, exclaimed, 'Oh, papa! I really do think she understood you.' Hildegarde walked quickly on; but met so many servants and strangers that she took refuge at last in the large dining-room, which at that hour was generally quite unoccupied.

One solitary individual sat at the enormous table; he seemed to have been dining, and Hildegarde walked to one of the windows without looking at him. Soon after, she heard him striding up and down the room, and as a waiter entered with some fruit and *confitures*, he asked, rather impatiently, 'Has my servant not yet dined ? Tell him to make haste—he knows we have no time to lose !'

The voice was familiar to Hildegarde; she unconsciously turned round to look at the speaker, and was instantly recognised by Count Zedwitz, who, with a look of astonishment, hurried towards her, exclaiming, 'Mademoiselle Rosenberg! what on earth has brought you to Frankfort?'

'I came here intending to go to a Baroness Waldorf, as governess to her daughter. She has gone to Mayence, I hear, and—'

'And you are here alone, unprotected, and I cannot offer to stay with you. I do not know if you have heard that my father is dying—no hope whatever of his recovery; I only received the intelligence yesterday, and am now travelling night and day to reach home in time to see him once more !'

At this moment the servant entered to say that the carriage was ready.

'Very well—you may go—and—shut the door—Hildegarde —I mean Mademoiselle Rosenberg—do not remain here. Give up this idea of going to Ida Waldorf—it will never answer— believe me, you will be most unhappy !'

'It must answer,' said Hildegarde, 'and I shall not be unhappy, for the idea of being a governess is familiar to me from my infancy, and has therefore lost all its terrors.'

'Excuse my questioning you,' cried Zedwitz, quickly, ' but may I ask how you happened to become acquainted with the Baroness Waldorf?'

'I do not know her at all—I never saw her—it was all arranged by Mademoiselle Hortense, one of the governesses of our school.'

'Did the Baroness Waldorf know your name?' asked Zedwitz, eagerly.

'At first, perhaps not,' answered Hildegarde, with a look of surprise, 'but in the letter which told her that I had left Munich, Mademoiselle Hortense must have mentioned it—I should think my name a matter of very little importance !'

'In this instance you are mistaken—I—I fear the Baroness is not likely to return for some time—I—'

'Her servant said she would not be long absent—that her leaving was quite a sudden thing,' observed Hildegarde.

'Her leaving when she expected you was unpardonable, cruel, ungenerous,' exclaimed Zedwitz, vehemently.

'I was rather shocked at first myself, but I afterwards thought she had not perhaps received the letter in time—'

'She did receive it; I am sure she did—it was the letter which—Oh, Mademoiselle Rosenberg, do not remain here any longer—return to your relations—return with me now—at once.'

Hildegarde blushed intensely.

'I shall send my servant with the carriage,' he added, quickly, 'and we can travel in the diligence, or in any way you please.'

'You are very kind,' said Hildegarde, 'but I consider myself engaged to this Baroness Waldorf, and until I hear from her—'

'You will not hear from her; you will never hear from her!' he cried, impatiently; 'and I must leave you—I cannot, dare not delay my return home now!'

Again Hildegarde blushed; she endeavoured to name Hamilton, but the words died on her lips, and her confusion increased every moment. Some people began to stray into the room, and Zedwitz added, in an agitated whisper, 'God forgive me, for thinking of anything but my father when he is lying on his death-bed—the peculiarity of our position must be my excuse for telling you, at such a time, that my feelings towards you are unchanged, unchangeable. Return to your family, and let me hope that time may so far overcome your dislike, or indifference, whichever it be—'

'Oh, Count Zedwitz, it is neither,' said Hildegarde, with evident effort. 'I should be unworthy of such regard as you feel for me, were I not now to tell you that—I have—long— loved—'

'Hamilton, of course—I always feared it.'

Hildegarde was silent.

'If you are engaged to him, tell me so—it is the only means of effectually crushing all my hopes at once!'

'We have no engagement—he cannot enter into any—he does not even know that I regard him otherwise than as a friend!'

'Then listen to me, Hildegarde. Notwithstanding all the admiration, all the love which he undoubtedly feels for you now—when he has been some time at home among the friends and companions of his youth—he will—forget you!'

'I think he will,' said Hildegarde, with a deep sigh.

'And you too will forget this youthful fancy,' continued Zedwitz.

'Youthful fancy!' she repeated, slowly; 'I fear I have neither youthful fancies nor youthful feelings—I have had no youth!'

'It will come like a late spring, and bestow on you at once those blessings which others receive so gradually that they are insensible to them.'

Hildegarde shook her head, and turned to the window. Zedwitz seemed to wish to say something which embarrassed him. 'In case you should find this hotel more expensive than you expected,' he began, in a hesitating manner.

'Oh, not at all expensive,' said Hildegarde. 'I had no idea one could live so cheaply at such a place!'

Zedwitz looked surprised; he would have been more so if he had seen the bill which she had paid Hamilton with such childish satisfaction a couple of hours before. It is needless to say that it had been written by him, as soon as he had discovered that she had not the most remote idea of the expenses of travelling—that he had taken advantage of her ignorance, to prevent her feeling any annoyance or uneasiness.

'I cannot tell you how unwilling I am to leave you,' said Zedwitz, after a pause: 'but go I must. Until we meet again, let me indulge the hope that a time may come—'

Just at that moment the hotel-keeper entered the room, and approached the window where they were standing. Zedwitz turned round, and Hildegarde, in her anxiety to undeceive him, and fearing he was leaving her under a false impression, stretched out her hand to detain him. The action was misunderstood; he caught it between both his, and while she endeavoured in vain to stammer a few words of explanation, he whispered, 'Thank you a thousand times! You do not know how even this faint ray of hope will lighten the gloominess of my present journey!'

He then took the inn-keeper aside, and spoke long and earnestly to him about her; said he knew her family; requested him to let her know every opportunity that might offer for a return to Munich in respectable society; gave him his address, the name of his banker, and unlimited credit on her account; and just as the inn-keeper, with an only half-suppressed smile of amusement, was about to explain to him that he need not be so uneasy about the lady, as she was already under the

protection of a young Englishman, Zedwitz, reproaching himself for the delay which had occurred, sprang into the carriage;
and a moment after, it rolled from under the archway past the
window where Hildegarde still stood, a prey to the most
distressing and contending emotions.

After waiting more than half an hour longer, and Hamilton not appearing, she retired to her room, supposing some
unexpected business had detained him; but when several
hours elapsed, and he was still absent, she became uneasy. A
feeling of delicacy prevented her from making any inquiries;
and she sat at her window, long after dusk, trying to discover
him in every tall, dark figure she saw moving near the
entrance or in the court below. A sensation of utter loneliness
came over her, thoughts of the most melancholy description
chased each other through her mind; when, from a reverie of
this kind, she recognised the well-known quick step, and a
low knock at her door made her conscious that Hamilton was
near. All her painful reminiscences—uncertainties—Zedwitz
—everything was in a moment forgotten; and she rose quickly
and joyously from her chair to meet him. It was too dark for
Hamilton to see the tears which still lingered in her long
eyelashes, and too dark for her to observe the flushed and
irritated expression of his whole countenance.

'Shall I light the candles?' she asked, cheerfully.

'If you wish it; but I prefer the room as it is.'

She sat down near him, and after a pause observed, 'You
were long absent; was there any difficulty at the banker's?'

'None whatever.' Another pause. Then, suddenly turning
towards her, he said, quickly, 'I have been thinking that, as
the Baroness Waldorf has a house at Mayence, she may be
longer absent than her servants supposed. A few hours
would take you to Mayence!'

'Do you think it necessary for me to follow her there?'

'Not exactly necessary; but why not? You have often
wished to see the Rhine.'

'Oh, it would be too delightful!' exclaimed Hildegarde.

'If you think so,' said Hamilton, every trace of annoyance
disappearing from his face, 'why, the sooner we go, the better.'

'But the expense—' said Hildegarde, hesitatingly.

'Will not be greater than remaining here. Do not let that
weigh with you for a moment.'

'Perhaps I ought to write to my mother, or Hortense?'

G G

'You cannot have an answer for several days, and it is better to wait until you have seen the Baroness Waldorf. I should think, whether you were here or at Mayence must be a matter of indifference to them; and I am sure your mother would be quite satisfied if she knew that you were under my care.'

'That I think too,' said Hildegarde; 'and I should like to put an end to my present state of uncertainty as soon as possible. I do not,' she continued, half laughing, 'I do not feel any sort of scruples about travelling with you, I suppose because we have lived so long in the same house, and I know you so well; but when Count Zedwitz to-day proposed my returning home with him—'

'Zedwitz! To-day!' repeated Hamilton, amazed.

'Yes. In passing through Frankfort to-day, he dined and changed horses here. I saw him for a few minutes when I was waiting for your return. He strongly advised me not to go to the Baroness Waldorf, and seemed, oddly enough, to think she had gone away on purpose.'

'Not impossible—not improbable. Did he explain in any way the cause of his suspicions?'

'No; he had not time. His father is dying, and he is, of course, most anxious to get home. He – he went away just as I was going to tell him that you were here—' She stopped, embarrassed.

'Hildegarde, let us go to Mayence,' cried Hamilton, abruptly.

'As early as you please to-morrow morning,' she answered, cheerfully.

'Not to-morrow morning—this evening—in an hour—in half an hour!'

'But—but it is night—almost dark already.'

'Well, what difference does that make?'

'They told me never to travel at night. It was to avoid doing so that I stopped at Aschaffenburg.'

'That was when you were alone, and travelling in a public carriage.'

'I do not, however, see any necessity for such haste,' she said, quietly; 'and therefore, if you have no objection, I should greatly prefer waiting until morning.'

'But I have an objection; and you will greatly oblige me by leaving to-night.'

'I suppose you have some very good reason for what appears to me a most unnecessary exercise of the power which chance has given you over me.'

'I *have* a reason,' began Hamilton, and there he stopped How could he tell her that he had recognised his own coat of arms on a carriage in the yard—that he had questioned the courier who was unpacking it, and discovered that the same uncle who had been in Salzburg the year before, was now on his way to Baden-Baden with his wife and daughters ; that he dreaded their discovering Hildegarde's being with him; feared the ungenerous conclusions they might draw from her present position ; and that, to avoid a chance meeting, he had wandered about the least frequented streets until the shades of evening, and the certainty of their being engaged at the tea-table, had enabled him to pass their apartments with the hope of not being discovered?   To attempt an explanation with Hildegarde would be sufficient to make her insist on his leaving her instantly ; his only chance was to use his personal influence and try to persuade her to leave Frankfort that night, before they had seen——before the 'strangers' book' had given rise to any inquiries about them.

'Well,' said Hildegarde, 'I have surely a right to hear your reason?'

'Right! Oh, if we talk of rights, it is you alone who should name the day and hour of departure—you alone who have a right to dictate ; but I was asking a favour—I wish most particularly to be in Mayence at a very early hour to-morrow.'

'And if we leave at three or four o'clock in the morning, will not that be early enough ?'

Hamilton only looked half satisfied.

'I do not like the appearance of going off at night in so sudden and mysterious a manner—not even—with you,' said Hildegarde, candidly.

'Perhaps you are right—but at three o'clock in the morning, if the exertion be not too great—'

'Oh,' said Hildegarde, laughing, 'you will find it more difficult to be ready than I shall.'

'Not to-morrow,' said Hamilton.   'I shall be at your door waiting for you, even before the clock strikes.'

And in the morning, when she opened her door, there he stood.   He unconsciously stepped lighter as he passed the rooms containing his sleeping relations. Hildegarde pointed to them, and said they were occupied by English people ; she had seen them arrive the day before, had passed them on her way downstairs ; and, while still talking of the gray man and the veiled lady, Hamilton hurried her into the carriage, and they drove off.

CHAPTER XLVI.

HALT !

It was still early when Hildegarde and Hamilton reached Mayence ; so early that, after lingering over their breakfast an unusually long time, the latter said he would make some inquiries about the Baroness Waldorf, and Hildegarde could go to her at a later hour. After a very short absence he returned, and, throwing himself into a chair, exclaimed, ' Well, certainly, this is the most unaccountable conduct ! '

' What is the matter ? ' asked Hildegarde, turning very pale. ' Has she left Mayence too ? '

' Yes—gone again ; and without leaving any message for you ! '

' There must be some extraordinary mistake or confusion, either on her part or Hortense's ! I could almost agree with Count Zedwitz, and think she was purposely avoiding me, if I had not read the letters which she wrote—her hopes that we should be long together—her regrets that I was not a few years older—her entreaties that Hortense would not let me leave Munich until she had found some person to take charge of me; and now to leave me to wander about after her in this way! So apparently to forget my existence ! It is quite incomprehensible ! '

' She has gone to Waldorf,' said Hamilton, and a—Waldorf is not far from Coblentz.'

' You surely would not advise me to pursue her farther!' cried Hildegarde, indignantly.

' Oh, no ; I have advised, and still advise you to go home.'

' And yet I shall make one effort more, though most unwillingly,' said Hildegarde. ' I should be ashamed to go home after a wild-goose chase of this kind ; I must know at least what to say to my relations. Suppose I were to write to the Baroness, and await her answer here ? That will—that must explain everything.'

' Write,' said Hamilton, 'and we can take it to the post ourselves, when we go out with a *valet de place*, who must show
us everything worth seeing. I dare say we can spend two or
three days very pleasantly here.'

'I shall be dreadfully in your debt!' observed Hildegarde,
blushing.

'Not at all,' said Hamilton, with the most serious face
imaginable. 'You have more than enough money for all
your expenses here, though perhaps not quite enough to take
you home.'

The letter was written, and they sallied forth, preceded by
a loquacious *valet de place*, to whose remarks, after the first
five minutes, they did not pay the slightest attention.

When they were returning to the hotel, by a newly-made
walk along the banks of the Rhine, Hildegarde stopped to look
at a new and beautifully built steamboat, on which there was a
placard hung up to say that she would sail the next morning
for Cologne.

Should you like to see the interior, Hildegarde?'

' Oh, of all things!' And the steamboat was examined with
a degree of curiosity, interest, and admiration, of which those
accustomed to the sight from infancy can form no idea. The
captain of the ship, who happened to be on board, attracted
probably by her appearance, had every drawer and cupboard
opened for her inspection, and Hamilton was beginning to find
his explanations rather long and tiresome, when he suddenly
concluded them by hoping that she was to be one of his pas-
sengers the next day.

' We have not yet quite decided,' said Hamilton, laughing at
her embarrassment; 'though I do not,' he added, turning to
her, ' I do not in fact see what there is to prevent us.'

' We shall have fine weather,' observed the captain, 'and
shall be in Cologne in good time in the evening.'

' I don't think we could do better, Hildegarde,' said Hamilton, in a low voice in English.

' I am afraid it would be improper—wrong, without any object but amusement! Just consider for a moment.'

' I cannot,' said Hamilton, ' see any greater impropriety in
your passing a day or two in a crowded steamboat, than at au
hotel alone with me—rather less, perhaps—but I deny the impropriety altogether when I take into consideration that I
have been one of your family for the last year, and that you

have learned so completely to consider me a friend—almost a relation.'

'That is true,' said Hildegarde; 'but still—'

'Then,' continued Hamilton, 'you cannot have an answer to your letter for three days at least; we shall be back just in time to receive it. Whether we pass to-morrow night at Cologne or Mayence, is quite unimportant, and I should like to show you the Rhine scenery. Let it be hereafter associated in your mind with your recollections of me!'

This last sentence was pronounced half pathetically, half beseechingly, and—Hildegarde made no further opposition to a plan which accorded but too well with her own inclinations.

We will spare our reader the description of the impression made on her by the Rheingau, Johannisberg, the Lùrlei, Coblentz, Rolandseck, the Drachenfels, &c. &c. &c.

'What a pretty room!' said Hildegarde to Hamilton, who had followed her up the stairs of the Hôtel Bellevue at Deutz. 'What a pretty room! We have a complete view of the Rhine, and quite overlook the garden. I really should like to stay here a week—if I dared.'

'I have no objection,' said Hamilton, laughing; 'though I have just heard there are so many princes and serene highnesses in the house, that I must sleep on the sofa in this room, if you have no objection; for only this and the bedroom adjoining are to be had.'

The waiter entered the room just at this moment to inquire if M. and Madame would sup there, or at the table d'hôte.

'Here,' said Hamilton; and he blushed deeply, as he turned to Hildegarde, who was sitting on the window-stool, but no longer looking at the Rhine, or into the garden; she had fixed her eyes on the door as the waiter closed it, and with parted lips, and slightly contracted brow, seemed expecting to hear more.

'You look quite shocked at that man's stupid mistake,' said Hamilton, with affected carelessness.

'It was not a stupid mistake; it was a very natural conclusion.'

'You mean on account of the rooms, perhaps? Don't let that annoy you, for you shall have undisturbed possession of both—I dare say I can get a bed at one of the inns at the other side of the river ; indeed, I should have proposed it at once, only I did not like to leave you here alone.'

'I am afraid you will think me very selfish,' said Hildegarde.

'Not at all.'

'Unnecessarily prudish, then?'

'Rather.'

'You are right,' she said with a sigh. 'After having gone off with you in this—this very—thoughtless manner, any attempt at prudery is preposterous—ridiculous! There is, in fact, nothing to prevent your sleeping in this room, if you do not fear the sofa being too uncomfortable.'

'There *is* something to prevent me,' said Hamilton, 'and that is, you do not wish it. I will go at once across the bridge, and if there be any room to be had, not quite at the other end of the town, I shall not return until morning.'

'But had you not better wait until after supper?'

'It is scarcely advisable, for at this time of the year there are so many travellers, that nothing in the neighbourhood may be to be had ; and you know, we start early.' While he spoke, however, the waiter appeared with the tray containing their supper, and half-blushing, half-laughing, they sat down together, and between talking and eating, in the course of a few minutes, forgot all about the matter.

It was the waiter, the 'stupid man,' who was again to remind them of the impropriety of their conduct. He had returned to say that the band of one of the regiments at Cologne would play in the garden—perhaps Madame would like a table and chair to be kept for her?

Hamilton did not venture to look at his companion, as he refused the offered civility, but, snatching up his hat, hurried away as fast as he could.

But he returned, and very soon too, and great was his annoyance to find Hildegarde already in her room, and the door closed; he walked backwards and forwards, not very patiently or quietly, for about ten minutes, and then knocked.

'Good night,' said Hildegarde.

'I am sorry to tell you that I have not been able to find a room, excepting in a very out-of-the-way place. As the packet leaves so early, and I am so apt to be late, I thought it better to ask you what I should do?'

'I am very sorry,' began Hildegarde.

'So am I,' said Hamilton; 'but, as it cannot be helped, I think you might just as well come out here for an hour, and talk over our journey back.'

'I am going to bed ; I am tired.'

'Have you any objection to my smoking a cigar, if I open the window ?'

'None whatever; you may smoke a dozen if you like.'

He opened the window, and leaned out to watch the gay scene which was passing below him. The garden was crowded with guests, and well lit with candles, protected from the wind by glass globes ; the murmuring of voices and gay laughter reached him, and, had he not still entertained a faint hope of seeing Hildegarde again, he would have joined the revellers, not in the hope of actual enjoyment, but to banish thoughts which were crowding thick upon him, and producing a state of nervous irritation most unusual to him. He felt so provoked at Hildegarde's tranquil friendly manner, it contrasted so painfully with his own state of feverish uncertainty, that the jealous vision of Zedwitz, unrepulsed, rose more and more distinctly before him. Would not the situation of governess be intolerable to one of her proud nature, and, after having tried it, would she not joyfully accept the hand of Zedwitz, who she said 'loved her better than anyone ever did—better than she deserved ?' These thoughts at length became intolerable, and with one bound he was again at her door.

'Hildegarde, the band is beginning to play in the garden. Will you not come to listen to it ?'

'No, thank you.'

'But you have not gone to bed, I hope?'

There was no answer audible.

'You have not yet gone to bed ? I want to speak to you— open the door, I beg—I entreat.'

'Whatever you have to say can be said to-morrow, just as well as now.'

'I should rather say it now.'

'And I should rather hear it to-morrow.'

Hamilton knew her too well to persevere, and returned again to his window, where he remained for more than an hour, unconscious of everything passing beneath him, and merely hearing a confused sound of instruments, which had the effect of producing an almost painful feeling of fatigue. He closed the window, and, looking rather despondingly round the room, which, as a dormitory, promised but few comforts, he extinguished the candles, and then threw himself at full length on the sofa: he had been thinking intensely, and as he lay there in the darkened chamber, he resolved that another night should not find him in his present state of uncertainty; and why should he endure it now? Why not know his fate at once! He would insist on Hildegarde's listening to him, and answering him too! Starting up, his eyes were instantly riveted on a line of bright light visible under her door; she was still awake—up perhaps. He knocked, and observed in a low voice, as he leaned against the door, 'Hildegarde, I cannot sleep!'

'I am so sorry!' she answered; 'the sofa, I suppose—'

'Yes; the sofa,' said Hamilton.

'I wish,' she said, coming towards the door, 'I wish I could resign this room to you; but—'

'There is no necessity; give me some of the pillows which you do not want, and I shall be quite comfortable.'

'How stupid of me not to have thought of that before!' she exclaimed, opening the door.

'When you were absent, I could have arranged everything; but the fact is, I have been for the last two hours *thinking*— really thinking, more than I have ever done in my life!'

'So have I,' said Hamilton, quite overlooking the pillows she was collecting for him. 'Suppose we compare thoughts!'

'Not now—to-morrow.'

'Now, now; this very instant,' he said, seating himself on the sofa, and motioning to her to take the place beside him.

She shook her head, and continued standing.

'What on earth do you mean by this reserve—this unusual prudery?' he continued, moving towards the side against which she was leaning.

'Nothing,' she said, drawing back. 'I only think it would be better to defer anything you wish to speak about until to-morrow—it is so late—so very late.'

'This is not the first time we have been together at midnight,' said Hamilton, laughing; but as he spoke, she blushed so deeply, that he added seriously, 'When there was any impropriety in it, I told you; you may believe me now, when I tell you there is none!'

'You are not quite infallible, I fear,' she said, sorrowfully, 'for you did not see any impropriety in my travelling alone with you here, and I now both see and feel it, and shall regret it all my life!'

'Good heavens!' exclaimed Hamilton. 'Have I ever said or done anything—'

'Oh, no, never — never!' cried Hildegarde, interrupting him.

'Then why withdraw your confidence from me, if I have not done anything to forfeit it?'

'I have the same confidence in you I ever had,' she answered with a sigh, 'but I—have unfortunately lost all confidence in myself.'

'How do you mean?'

'I have discovered that it was not a wish to see the Rhine or to be in a steamboat which made me leave Mayence with you.'

'And what was it, then?' cried Hamilton, eagerly.

'It was the desire to be with you — to enjoy your society undisturbed for a few days before we parted for ever!'

'Not for ever,' said Hamilton.

'I am ashamed to think how easily I allowed myself to imagine that I ought to follow this Baroness Waldorf to Mayence, still more so to think how soon I stifled my scruples about coming here—and so effectually, too, that the whole obvious impropriety never struck me until this evening, when the waiter—'

'Was guilty of the horrible supposition that you were my wife! Would that be so dreadful?' asked Hamilton.

'The waiter showed me by his simple remark,' she continued, without noticing his interruption, 'that I ought never to have been with you as I have been, under any other circumstances, and I felt condemned at once. I must return home to my stepmother.'

'Perhaps, for a couple of years, it would be the best thing you could do,' said Hamilton.

'To my stepmother, or—to Mademoiselle Hortense?' she said, musingly, as she seated herself on a chair, and unconsciously moved it towards him. 'Of course I have given up all idea of going to the Baroness Waldorf.'

'I am glad to hear it. I never liked the plan.'

'And I am so sorry to be obliged to give it up!'

'Do not regret it—it would not have answered. I never saw anyone for whom the situation of governess was less

eligible, notwithstanding your excellent education and extraordinary talent for languages.'

'Eligible!' repeated Hildegarde. 'You are right. I am
no longer eligible. I am no longer fit to direct the education
of—of any girl.'

'I hope you will never speak to anyone else in this manner,'
said Hamilton, gravely. 'You would make people suppose
you had been guilty of some serious misdemeanor.'

'I have been guilty of a misdemeanor,' said Hildegarde,
despondingly, 'and one which I should think it necessary to
confess to the Baroness Waldorf before I entered her house ;
having done so, I conclude she would refuse to resign her
daughter to my care. To avoid the merited mortification, I
shall go home, tell everything to Hortense, and be guided by
her advice for the next year or two. And now,' she added, 'I
have only one thing more to observe, and that is, that we
ought to repair our thoughtlessness as well as we can, or,
rather, avoid a continuation of it by separating at once. I
shall return to Mayence to-morrow, and you must go on to
England.'

'I will go to—Scotland, if you will go with me, Hildegarde,'
said Hamilton. 'Don't be angry; I am not joking. I have
listened to the subject of your two hours' meditation, and now
I expect you to listen to mine.' And he entered into a long,
and, all things considered, not very prejudiced exposition of the
state of his affairs ; informed her of the five thousand pounds
which he should inherit in two years, and, after hoping that
they could contrive to buy something and live somewhere with
that sum, ended, as he had begun, by proposing her going with
him to Scotland, and then returning to her mother until he
could claim her altogether.

She listened in silence, the expression of deep attention
changing by degrees into surprise and perplexity. It was the
first time that the idea of a marriage with him had entered
her mind ; she had taught herself to consider it so completely
an impossibility that his occasional outbursts of passion or
tenderness had ceased to make any impression on her. Ashamed
of the confession which she had herself so ingenuously made
to him just before, and not prepared for the sudden change of
feelings which his words produced, she turned away, and,
when he paused for an answer, did not even make an attempt
to speak.

As Hamilton waited in vain for an answer, his former doubts became certainties—she liked, but did not love him. With a difficulty in utterance, in strong contrast to his former fluency, he now stammered out his hopes that he had not deceived himself as to the nature of her feelings towards him.

'No—oh, no!' answered Hildegarde, but without turning round.

'And you do or will try to love me sufficiently to—'

'Why force me to make unnecessary confessions?' she said, with a deep blush; 'rather let me ask you when you heard that you would inherit this fortune which makes you independent. In Frankfort, perhaps?'

'No,' replied Hamilton; 'l knew it when I was a child, and considered it then, though not quite a fortune, certainly a very large sum of money.'

'And is it not a very large sum of money?'

'For a boy to buy playthings and ponies, yes; but for a man to live upon—' He paused; there was too much intelligence in her eager glance.

'For a man,' she said, 'brought up as you have been, it is probably too little—nothing!'

'Not so,' cried Hamilton, quickly. 'With my present ideas and feelings it is a competence—it is all I require—all I wish.'

'You could, then, have married Crescenz if you had desired it?' she said, slowly

'I could never have loved her well enough to induce me to make the sacrifice—'

'The sacrifice! And it is great—very great, perhaps?'

'It ceases to be one when made for you.'

'And you have only lately—only very lately, perhaps—been able to resolve on this sacrifice?'

'Let me use your own words, Hildegarde. Do not force me to make unnecessary confessions,' said Hamilton, blushing more deeply than she herself had done.

She leaned on the table, and bent her head over her hands. Hamilton felt very uncomfortable. 'I expected,' he said at length, with some irritation, 'I expected that this explanation would have been differently received.'

'I wish,' she answered, 'it had never been made. I would rather have remembered you as I thought you—dependent on your father's will—having no option.'

'This is too much!' cried Hamilton, starting from the sofa

and striding up and down the room. 'I have fallen in your esteem when—but you do not understand.'

'Probably not quite; but this is evident to me, the sacrifice must be something enormous—beyond what I can imagine— or you would not have hesitated so long, for—I think—yes— I am sure you—love me.'

Hamilton stopped opposite to her, and exclaimed, 'Oh Hildegarde! how can you torture me in this manner?'

'I would rather torture myself,' she said; 'but'—and she looked at him steadily—'but I must nevertheless tell you that I cannot, will not, accept your sacrifice.'

'Then, Hildegarde, you do not love me!' he cried, impetuously.

'Do I not? Can you not see that I am giving the greatest proof of it of which I am capable? Can you not believe that I too can make a sacrifice?'

'I understand and appreciate your motives better than you have done mine,' he answered. 'Wounded pride is assisting your magnanimity. You are mortified at my having hesitated —deliberated; it was prudent perhaps, but I am heartily sorry for it now. I see it has made you so control your thoughts and inclinations that friendship, and not love, is all I have obtained for an affection deserving something more—if you knew but all—— ;' he paused, but, as Hildegarde made no attempt to speak, he continued, 'I thought when we met at Aschaffenburg, I hoped, from what you said just now—that— Hildegarde!' he cried, vehemently, 'you require too much from me; spoiled by adulation, you expect me, without a struggle, to change my nature, my habits, and my manners! I cannot rave like your cousin—'

Hildegarde became deadly pale; she tried to speak, and moved her lips. but no sound issued from them.

'Nor,' he continued, still more vehemently, 'nor can I bear repulses like Zedwitz!'

Hamilton heard her murmur the words 'ungenerous'— 'unjust.'

'Forgive me, Hildegarde. I spoke in anger, and am sorry for it — I ought not to have named your cousin—can you forgive me?'

She held out her hand in silence.

'Now,' he said, seating himself beside her, 'do n' let us ask each other any more questions, or talk any more of sacrifices:

but, like a dear love, you will promise to go to England with me to-morrow!—won't you?'

She remained silent, her eyes cast down, while she slowly shook her head.

'You will not?'

'I dare not,' she answered, gently; but observing him again about to start up, she laid her hand on his arm, and continued —'Do not ask me to do what may cause us both unhappiness hereafter. I will enter into an engagement with you on reasonable terms.'

'Oh, on reasonable terms!' he repeated, ironically.

'I cannot go on—you are too unkind,' she said, while the tears started to her eyes.

A long and painful pause ensued. Hamilton broke it by saying, 'Well, what are your terms? Anything is better than nothing—name them—I agree to everything, provided I may claim you in two years.'

'Even if you do not,' said Hildegarde, 'I promise to forgive you.'

'And forget me too, perhaps,' said Hamilton, with a forced smile.

'That I—cannot promise: but it is of little consequence what concerns me. You must return home for these two years. Weigh well this sacrifice which you must make: it will not be altogether a pecuniary one, for I suppose there is not the slightest chance of obtaining the consent of your family to our marriage; and as you spoke of residing in Germany, I conclude you must give up all your relations and your country too!'

'Go on,' said Hamilton, without moving, or looking at her.

'I shall consider myself bound by a promise, which I now freely make, to await your decision. You are free.'

'Go on,' he again repeated, as he had done before.

'What can you desire more?'

'Why, nothing, though I almost expected you to propose committing to paper, in due form, this most rational "engagement on reasonable terms."' And he drew some paper towards him as he spoke, and took up a pen; directly, however, throwing it down, he exclaimed, passionately, 'Oh, Hildegarde, this will never do! Much as I admire your decision of character, and freedom from the usual weaknesses of your sex, I—I did hope—I do wish that for once you would be like a girl of your age. I am ready, without regret, to leave all my relations and friends, give up all my hopes of fame or success in life—expatriate myself for ever—'

'I see—I understand now,' cried Hildegarde, interrupting him. 'A man has hopes of fame, expectations of success in life. We have nothing of that kind; and, therefore, our love is perfectly exclusive, all-absorbing.'

'Not yours,' said Hamilton, 'though I confess I expected something of the kind from you, some little enthusiasm, at least. However, our contract is made irrevocably, even though I see and feel that your love is of the very coldest description, in fact scarcely deserving the name.'

'Oh! why,' cried Hildegarde, with all her natural vehemence of manner, 'why is there no sacrifice that I can make to convince you that you are mistaken! There is none I would not make, provided it were not injurious to *you* !'

Hamilton shook his head, and turned away.

'You do not believe me? Try me—ask any proof—anything !'

He started from his seat, walked to the window, threw it wide open, and leaned as far out as he could in the night air.

All this was too much for Hildegarde; her efforts had been great to conceal her feelings, and she perceived she had been misunderstood; her sincere desire to act magnanimously had been treated with contempt. Hamilton, whom she had learned to trust without reserve or examination, was displeased, angry with her, perhaps! Perplexed, worried, and wearied, she did, at length, what it would have been better had she done half an hour before; she covered her face with her handkerchief, and burst into tears.

The moment Hamilton turned round and perceived that she was crying as heartily as could be desired of any girl of her age, he forgot his anger at her unexpected opposition to his wishes, and, rushing towards her, commenced an incoherent succession of excuses, entreaties, and explanations. It would have been difficult for a third person to have known what he meant. Hildegarde, however, seemed to understand him perfectly. In a short time she began to look up and smile again, and in about a quarter of an hour they were discussing their future plans in the most amicable manner imaginable. Once more Hamilton had recourse to the pen and paper; but this time it was to make a sketch of the peasant's house -near

Hohenfels, which was to be their home two years hence. He would write to the Z——s about it directly, or go to them—that would be better still!

No; Hildegarde thought it would be wiser to wait until he could purchase.

'We shall have cows and calves, and all those sort of things, I suppose?' said Hamilton.

'I should think so,' replied Hildegarde, very gravely.

'I wonder shall we be able to keep a pair of horses?' said Hamilton.

'Cart horses? Perhaps we may,' answered Hildegarde, merrily.

'No; but seriously, Hildegarde, I should like to know how many servants we shall have?'

'Very few, I suspect,' said Hildegarde; 'and therefore, directly I return to my mother, I shall endeavour to learn to be really useful.'

'But,' said Hamilton, 'but these domestic details, which were so disgusting to you—these vulgar cares—'

'All, all will now be full of interest,' said Hildegarde, laughing. 'I really feel as if I could even learn to cook!'

'No, no; I do not wish that—we shall certainly have a cook. A. Z. seemed to think we could get on quite comfortably if we lived in the country. I shall not at all mind going out with the plough, if it be necessary, and you—you can spin, you know; nothing I admire so much as a graceful figure at a spinning wheel. You shall have one made of ebony, and—but can you spin?'

'Not yet; but I can easily learn, and in time, I dare say, we shall have a whole press full of linen.'

'Oh, I am sure we shall get on famously. The Z——s are not at all rich—rather poor, I believe; and they are so happy, and really live so respectably; they will be our neighbours, and I am sure you would like them.'

'I remember, I rather liked her at Seon, because she lent me books,' observed Hildegarde.

'They will be society for us—that is, if we ever want any. Baron Z—— is very cheerful, and his wife is really a very sensible woman. She understands housekeeping and soapmaking, and all that sort of thing, and will be of great use to you, I am sure. Then I shall rent half their alp, and send up our cows there in summer, and then we shall go to look after them, and make little parties with the Z——s. I must tell you all about that.'

And he did tell her all about that, and so many other things too, that the night wore away, the candles burnt down, and as at length the flame extinguished itself in the melted wax, they looked at each other in the gray, cold light of breaking day!

The two days which Hamilton and Hildegarde passed in the Rhine steamboat, on their return to Mayence, were perhaps the happiest of their still so youthful lives. As they sat together, watching the beautiful windings of the river, or glancing up the sides of the wooded mountains, the most perfect confidence was established between them. The events of the last year were discussed with a minuteness which proved either that their memories were exceedingly retentive, or that the most trifling circumstances of that period had been full of unusual interest to both. Their confessions and explanations were not ended even when they reached Mayence, where Hildegarde found a letter from the Baroness Waldorf; as she gave it to Hamilton, she observed, 'After what you told me this morning, I can pardon, though I cannot approve of, her conduct. She says, however, that she wrote to Hortense to prevent my leaving Munich; and I am glad of it, as it will save me from all explanations, and I can show both my mother and Hortense this letter too—so everything has ended just as we could have wished.'

'Yes,' said Hamilton; 'and we will endeavour to believe all the Baroness's excuses. I dare say she has changed all her plans, and perhaps she may *not* engage a governess for her daughter for a year or two; we will also consent to her marriage with Zedwitz, to whom she is as attached as such a person can be, though she is not likely to rise in his estimation by the proof which she has given of her jealousy. But what do you mean to do with this order on her banker at Frankfort—this peace-offering which she so diffidently calls her debt?'

'I should like very much to return it,' said Hildegarde, hesitatingly.

'I thought so,' said Hamilton; 'and in the mean while I can write to A. Z., to let her know that if we are all alive in two years, we shall be together, and to request Baron Z—— to enter into negotiations with that Felsenbauer—the peasant on the rocks, as he is called. I shall tell A. Z. to send you my journal; it may amuse you to read it; and in the margin you

H H

must write whatever is necessary in explanation, or, in short, whatever you think likely to interest us when we look it over at the end of ten or twelve years. A journal, you know, like vine, is marvellously improved by age!'

*   *   *   *   *

Hamilton accompanied Hildegarde on her way home as far as she would allow him. The last day's journey she chose to be alone, and at Ingolstadt they parted. For two years? Or for ever?

CHAPTER XLVII.

CONCLUSION.

THERE may be some, there may be many of my readers, who would think that Hamilton had been ' a confounded fool,' were they to hear that at the appointed time he braved the threats, resisted all the bribes of his uncle, remitted his five thousand pounds to Munich, and returned to Bavaria, with the intention there to live and die, ' the world (viz. London) forgetting, by the world forgot.' We do not wish him to fall in the opinion of anyone, and therefore request all persons disposed to entertain such an opinion of him, under such circumstances, to close this book, and imagine he acted as they would have done in his place. Often have vows as solemn as his been broken, and for the same mercenary motives which might have tempted him; and if the world have not applauded, it has at least not censured such derelictions in a manner to deter others from practising them.

Suppose him, then, reader, (not gentle reader, for such would never consent to the supposition,) suppose him at the end of two years a man of the world, or a worldly man, whichever you please, Hildegarde not exactly forgotten, but remembered only as a 'beautiful girl with whom he had been at one time so much in love as to have entertained the absurd idea of rusticating with her on a couple of hundred pounds per annum in the Bavarian Highlands!' Suppose him attached to some embassy, young, handsome, and rich, the chosen partner of all still dancing princesses! Or suppose we put an end to Uncle Jack at once, and allow Hamilton, without further delay, to inherit a fortune which would give him a position in the London and Yorkshire world; if you wish it, we can double his income too; in books, fifty or sixty thousand a year is quite a common thing, and as to old uncles, they are only mentioned in order that they may die just when their fortune is necessary to the happiness or comfort of younger and more interesting persons. Suppose—suppose—suppose you close the book, as before recommended; for nothing of this kind occurred. Uncle Jack (who in his youth had taken a trip to Gretna Green) might have pardoned his nephew's 'loving not wisely but too well,' but he neither would do so, nor would he die; and so Hamilton, after having listened to his father's reproaches and expostulations, endured his brother's sneers, and steadily set at defiance his uncle's anger, returned to Munich and claimed his bride, of whose coldness or want of enthusiasm he was never after heard to complain.

Felsenbauer's little property was purchased, and Hans, after having officiated as Hamilton's 'gentleman' for two years in England, returned to his primitive occupation of directing the plough—not quite, indeed, with the satisfaction of a Cincinnatus, for years elapsed before he ceased to regret his fallen greatness or to expatiate to his few ignorant fellow-servants on the splendours of his master's home.

Hamilton resigned himself more cheerfully than his servant to his change of fortune; he never spoke of home, with which his communication became very indirect and uncertain from the time his sister had married and gone to reside in the north of Scotland. His brother John seldom wrote, his father and uncle never; he made no effort to conciliate the latter, not even taking advantage of the occasions which presented themselves at a later period of requesting him to become a godfather to a little Jack or a little Joan. He became a good farmer, a keen sportsman, and so celebrated a rifle shot, that he was feared as competitor at all the *Scheiben-schiessen* in the neighbourhood. He generally wore a mountaineer's dress—perhaps because it was comfortable, perhaps, also, because it was becoming; and in the course of a few years, his family would scarcely have recognised him in the vigorous sunburnt man, whose very features were changed in expression by his altered mode of life—energy and strength had taken the place of ease and gracefulness. A. Z. pronounced the change advantageous, and often said it would have been difficult to have found a more picturesquely bandit-looking figure than his when, on a return from a hunt, he sprang along the rocky path leading to his mountain home, his slouched hat shading the upper, as much as his long moustache the lower part of his face.

As to Hildegarde, the calm, contented tenor of her life preserved her beauty in so remarkable a manner that Hamilton seriously believed she grew handsomer every year; they and the Z——s almost lived together; no summer heat or winter storm kept them asunder; their Alpine parties and sledging expeditions to the neighbouring balls were made together, and many a little adventure is still remembered by both families, with a mixture of amusement and regret—regret that those times are past—gone—never to return again.

At the end of eight years, Uncle Jack, unsolicited, relented, and Hamilton was recalled. Can it be believed that for some days he hesitated to obey the mandate?—that Hildegarde wept bitterly for the first time since her marriage? But so it was. The offers which ten years before would have filled their hearts with gratitude and joy, were now accepted as a sacrifice made to the future prospects of their children. A. Z. to the last insisted that she would be the greatest sufferer of all. 'In you,' she said, turning to Hildegarde, 'I lose the most patient and intelligent of listeners; in your husband, the most attentive of friends. Eight years' intimate intercourse, such as ours has been, has made you both so completely a part of our family, that knowing how much we shall miss you, Herrmann and I have at length come to the long-protracted desperate resolution of leaving Hohenfels; we ought to have done so long ago, on account of the education of our children.'

'Oh, no! Don't leave Hohenfels; we shall be sure to return here next year—every summer!' cried Hamilton and Hildegarde, almost together.

But they have not returned, nor are they likely to do so. Changes of a political and social nature have taken place in Germany, the end of which it is impossible to foresee. This much is, however, certain, that Bavaria is not likely to be soon again, if ever, as tranquil and happy as when these pages were first written; *then* the most intelligent peasant would have refused to leave his waltz, his pot of beer, or his joyous *jodel*, for the sake of any newspaper that ever was printed, or even to hear a political discussion between the schoolmaster and the parish priest! Newspapers now circulate in all directions, and the peasant reads, thinks, and talks more of politics than of his crops, and naturally feels inclined to adopt opinions calculated to elevate him in his own estimation, and draw those down to his level whom he had formerly considered far above him.

Hohenfels is sold. Baron Z—— found the brewery more expensive than profitable, when his visits of inspection were limited to an occasional week or ten days. He is half inclined to purchase Hamilton's house, which still remains shut up and uninhabited; presenting, as A. Z. observed in her last letter, the perfect picture of a deserted house, with all its 'garden flowers growing wild.'

*　　　*　　　*　　　*　　　*

'After all, Hildegarde,' said Hamilton, one morning, as they looked out of the breakfast-room window into his uncle's handsome domain, 'after all, if we could conjure a few of your mountains, with some chamois upon them, here, I believe I could again prefer England to Germany — that is, in my present position. A poor man really may enjoy life in Germany—it is only a rich one who can do so in England!'

G. C. & Co.

PRINTED BY
SPOTTISWOODE AND CO., NEW-STREET SQUARE
LONDON

www.ingramcontent.com/pod-product-compliance
Lightning Source LLC
Chambersburg PA
CBHW052346110726
47901CB00005B/1379